The Guesthouse on the Green Books 4, 5 & 6

Michelle Vernal

Copyright © 2022 by Michelle Vernal

All rights reserved.

No portion of this book, The Guesthouse on the Green Box Set, Books 4, 5 and 6 may be reproduced in any form without written permission from the publisher or author, except as permitted by U.S. copyright law.

Rosi's Regrets

Prologue

The black nose poked through the gap under the bricks, twitching as it sniffed the frosty night air. A bristly red head popped through the hole, eyes sweeping the courtyard to check the coast was clear. A strip of light illuminated the familiar path to the rubbish bin; his bin. The beam was shining through the gap, where the curtains hadn't quite been closed in the room directly over this outdoor area. It might only be a short distance across the concreted ground to his destination but it was one fraught with potential landmines. One big one in particular who waved a rolling pin and screamed louder than he could! Satisfied the cook who had it in for him was long gone for the day, the little red fox squeezed his body through the hole. It was harder work than usual; he'd been eating well of late. But he was nothing if not determined and after one good push, out he popped.

He padded across to the bin, a sniper with his target in sight, a bin where a myriad of treats added a splash of variety to a fox's diet and a layer of padding around his middle. A noise broke the silence and he froze, statue-like, ears pricked on high alert. He didn't move, prepared to wait it out until he knew what had made the sound. An acrid smoky smell danced over the high walls surrounding the courtyard. It would be the man next door; he would be puffing on that smelly stick he so loved while the woman in the house shrieked it was high time he gave the things away. She would tell the man he'd catch his death standing around in the cold and the man would reply, 'If a man who'd worked hard all his life could partake of the one pleasure he had left inside, then he wouldn't catch his death.' She'd shout back that he could 'Fecking well freeze.'

The little red fox didn't like their backyard, it wasn't worth visiting. There was never anything worthwhile in their bin. Not like here; this was the piece de resistance of rubbish bins. His tongue poked out as he carried on his stealthy path to where, if he was lucky, he might find a sliver of black pudding, or even better white pudding, bacon rind, and soda bread. If there was an award for rubbish bins this one would get the Oscar. He reached it and began to salivate as he stretched up to nose the lid off with well-practised ease, and as it clattered to the ground he worked fast. His luck was in, white pudding! It was a night to celebrate, indeed! He nose-dived gleefully into the bin and retrieved it, snaffling it down. There was bacon rind too, oh yes he was fine dining tonight. He was about to go in for seconds when the window above the courtyard squeaked open. A man, with a mean thin face which looked angrier than the rolling pin woman's, peered out.

The fox didn't like the look of him. He meant business and although it broke his heart to leave, he scarpered across that courtyard to the safety of the gap under the wall. A splash of icy water hit his tail as he pushed his way back through from where he'd come, the midnight garden beyond the wall.

The man with the thin, pinched face shook his head and wrenched the window back down. Vermin, no better than rats those things. He put the empty glass down on the bedside table and got back into bed. He'd have words with the manager in the morning. The girl with the mane of red-gold hair and silly shoes. Oh yes, he'd be telling her: for the ridiculous sums of money he was being charged for the dubious privilege of staying in this establishment, O'Mara's needed to up its standards.

Chapter 1

♥

London, 1999

Roisin twisted the plain gold band on her finger and stared at the statement lying open in front of her. There were two sharp creases across the piece of paper where it had been folded inside the envelope and she smoothed them hoping that the action might magically erase the information neatly set out before her. It didn't of course and she blinked trying to convince herself she hadn't read what was laid out in neat, black font but when she re-focused the words were the same as they'd been a split-second ago.

The table at which she was sitting still wore the debris from breakfast—from normal day to day life. A puddle of milk left behind by Noah who'd been craning his neck trying to catch sight of the cartoon he'd left blaring in the living room as he shovelled in cornflakes. Dirty dishes waited to be cleared and toast crumbs kept the puddle company as they waited to be wiped up. The postcards Noah had received from Mammy and Moira sent from their Vietnam holiday were resting against the salt and pepper shakers.

Speaking of Noah, he'd left the television on and it was almost but not quite drowned out by the kitchen radio which Roisin had tuned to BBC 1. It was her routine to change the station over from the newsy BBC World Colin preferred of a morning the moment he shut the front door behind him.

She was dimly aware of an annoyingly preppy pop hit, currently storming the charts, playing. It seemed at odds with what she'd just discovered. Beethoven's classic da-da-da-du-uum from *Symphony No. 5* would have been more appropriate.

She stopped twisting her ring, only to find it felt like the precious metal was branding her. The sensation, she knew was in her head but it felt real and unable to stand it she wrested the band from her finger before dropping it on the table. She watched as it rocked and rolled like a penny piece before finally giving up its dance. Her finger looked naked without its gold adornment. She'd stopped wearing her engagement ring eons ago. The marquise cut diamond had been a stunning choice but it had proven to be an impractical one. She'd constantly snagged her tights, pulled sweaters, and in the end, when Noah had been born, terrified she'd scratch him with it she'd put it back in its box and tucked it away down the back of her knicker drawer. If Colin had noticed she'd stopped wearing it he'd never commented.

Roisin didn't know where the impractical gene she'd been bestowed with had come from but making fanciful decisions was the story of her life. Not once in her thirty-six years had anyone said, 'Gosh that Roisin O'Mara is a practical girl,' or 'Sure, Rosi O'Mara's full of sensible ideas, so she is.' She'd never been the girl people turned to for sage advice or the person you'd rely on to hold you steady through one of life's storms. It wasn't that she was unreliable as such, and she was fiercely loyal when it came to family and friends, it was just she was what Mammy liked to call a little bit airy-fairy.

If you were to ask Maureen O'Mara to sum up her three daughters, Rosi knew exactly what she'd say. Moira, her baby, was a prima donna who thought she'd been born with a silver spoon in her mouth. She hadn't, although in Roisin's opinion

CHAPTER 17

she was spoilt and got away with a lot more than her three siblings ever had. Aisling, the changeling with her red-gold hair was one of life's peacemakers and she spent far too much time sorting out other people's problems while ignoring her own. A bit of an ostrich was Aisling. As for Rosi, her eldest daughter, well, Mammy would say, she'd been a pain in the arse teenager—all attitude and such but, one thing was for sure, she'd been born with her head in the clouds. Anyone would think the milkman had had a hand in things when it came to her girls, she'd lament laughingly to anyone listening, if it weren't for the fact Aisling took after her father's side of the family, God rest his soul. Rosi and Moira were the dark haired, olive skinned spits of their dear mammy.

Annoyingly, and a little unfairly in Roisin's opinion, Mammy never included her only son and eldest child, Patrick in this equation because to her mind, she could sum him up on one word, 'perfect'. It irked all three of the sisters because he was far from it but she of all people knew love was blind. She also knew, since becoming a mammy herself, that you'd forgive your children anything, even for being an arsey, vain, eejit like her brother was.

Roisin thought she'd made a proper, practical, grown-up choice when she'd said yes to Colin's proposal. It had come about after a very impractical decision—forgetting to use a condom. He'd been very old-fashioned about the whole business, quietly ringing her dad to ask if he'd give his daughter's hand in marriage before popping the question. Seeing as Roisin was over thirty and pregnant, Brian would have bitten his hand off had he done this in person, or at the very least thrown a dowry at him, but it had been done over the telephone and so far as she knew no money had exchanged hands. So, with her father's permission and unbeknown to her, the rest of the O'Mara clan were eagerly awaiting a further telephone call to confirm her engagement; Colin had taken her out for a meal in a posh London eatery.

It was somewhere in between the main and dessert he'd gotten down on bended knee. At first she'd been unsure what he was up to. He'd leaped out of his seat, crouched down and looked very red in the face. She'd wondered if he'd been seized by cramp and contemplated getting down beside him and rubbing his leg to try and ease it but then dessert had arrived as he simultaneously asked if she'd like to marry him.

In hindsight Roisin didn't know if she'd been so quick to say yes because she wanted to get stuck into her crème brûlée. She was four months pregnant and dessert really, really mattered to her. She'd managed to hold back long enough for Colin to open a red velvet box and found herself blinking at the sparkle. Inside the box nestled a diamond ring. It was exactly like the one she'd pointed out in the window of the jewellers as being the sort of thing she'd like *were* they ever to get engaged. She didn't trust Colin's taste and had a feeling if she wasn't clear about what she wanted she could very well wind up being offered his great granny's hideous heirloom opal if he decided to make an honest woman of her.

The thing was though, she'd thought, torn between the glittering stone and the golden sugary crust of her brûlée, saying yes wasn't just about her. There was little bean too. This was not the time to be flighty and act on the spur of the moment, nor, she told herself sternly was it the moment to crack that gorgeous crust so she could tuck in. Oh no, this was the time to behave like a sensible, pregnant women. Accordingly, she'd paused and taken a moment to run through a mental marriage checklist.

Would Colin be a good husband and father? *Yes, she thought he probably would.*

Would he make a good provider? (Yes, okay it was old-fashioned, but Rosi fully intended to stay at home throughout little bean's formative years and make lots of wholesome, whole foods) *Yes, he was a hard worker and liked to think of himself as one of life's movers and shakers.*

CHAPTER 19

Was he trustworthy? *Well, if he'd lied to her, she didn't know about it.*

Did he love her? *He must do, mustn't he? Just look at the enormous blingy ring he was offering her.*

Did she love him? *Yes, she thought she did, not that she had much experience of being in love but he made her feel safe and while it wasn't the grand passion she'd seen in films, he was steady and reliable and there was a lot to be said for that when you had a little bean on the way.*

Accordingly, as Colin began to grimace from spending so long balancing on one knee, Roisin had accepted the ring and beamed that yes she'd love to marry him. All the while she'd been eyeing the crème brûlée and thinking to herself *righty-ho, let's get this show on the road.* The custard dessert had been delicious too, when much to her relief he'd finally slid the ring on her finger and she'd been able to thwack that toasted sugar with the back of her spoon.

That had been nearly six years ago. She hadn't eaten crème brûlée since, she realised wondering how she'd gotten it so wrong? She picked up the bank statement that had thrown her morning into a complete tizz. Without thinking she screwed it up into a ball and threw it at the wall.

Chapter 2

♥

'Mummy.' There was the sound of little feet pattering down the stairs. 'I've brushed my teeth and been to the toilet. I'm ready.'

Roisin pushed her chair back and got up from her seat. 'And washed your hands?' The question burst forth automatically. Her world might have just crashed down around her but she would have to pick her way through the rubble and take Noah to school. Life had to go on. There would be time to think about what she was going to do when she got home. She looked at his face and reading his expression sighed. 'Noah, how many times do I have to tell you? We go through this same routine every morning.'

His little face looked petulant and she could see him weighing up the odds as to whether he should make a fuss for fuss's sake or whether he should do as he was told. He'd been making a fuss lots lately. For his sake, she was hoping he would choose the latter, she didn't trust herself not to lose patience with him this morning. She never thought she had it in her to be a fisherwoman until she'd had a small child whom she loved more than life itself but who also had an amazing ability to bring out her inner fishwife. Mind you she'd thought she'd put homemade vegetable purees in his baby bird mouth when he went on solids and handwash all his nappies too. Look how that had gone!

There must have been something about her expression because Noah turned and ran back up the stairs. Roisin stood rooted to the spot and without thinking embarked on a round of the breathing exercises she'd been shown. She took a long slow breath in through her nose feeling the air fill her lower lungs and then her upper lungs. She held it there for a count of three before exhaling through pursed lips, trying to relax her facial muscles, jaw, shoulders and stomach, as her yoga teacher Harriet had demonstrated. She'd have liked to have practiced her forward bend because sitting on the floor with head resting on her knees while she held onto her toes had a surprisingly calming effect on her but there was no time for that. Nor could she meditate herself off into another zone. Instead she picked up her house keys, shrugged into her coat and, as Noah raced backed down the stairs, she wrapped a scarf around her neck.

She grabbed hold of her son. 'Coat!' She picked it up off the back of the chair where it had been slung yesterday afternoon and held it open for him. He shoved his arms inside it before picking up his school bag and heading for the front door, urging his mummy on, 'I can't be late. I don't want to miss show and tell. Charlie Wentworth-Islington-Greene is bringing her pet gerbil, Beyoncé in today.'

Chapter 3

Roisin was only half listening to Noah's steady stream of chatter as they crunched through the last of the leaves under an arbour of stripped trees toward Clover Hill Primary. Her heart had returned to its normal rate of beats per minute after the awful barky Alsatian had reared up at them. It did the same thing every morning and it never ceased to startle her when it appeared, paws resting on the top of the front gate, saliva dripping from its mouth, ruffing furiously at them. The dog always managed to startle her but this morning she'd had enough. She would not allow herself to be intimidated anymore. So, instead of hurrying past, she stood her ground glaring back at the dog, daring him to do his worst. He'd carried on for a second or two longer and then jumped back down, tail wagging as he wandered off around the garden to his cock his leg or whatever party trick he had planned next.

Noah high-fived her, and she felt proud like she'd just given him one of those really important life lessons. Her son had really blossomed in confidence these last months, ever since he'd started attending the exclusive primary, or so his teacher had told her at the Meet the Teacher evening. It seemed to her he was a different boy when he was at school.

Children did not come with an instruction manual, that was for sure, and Mammy had said to her not long after Noah was born that raising a child was one big phase after another and that probably the best bit came around the middle years, eleven and twelve. It was a reprieve before the horrible teenage bit. She'd given Roisin the hairy eyeball as she said that, before adding, 'and then when they grow out of that all you can hope for is that somehow you've managed to raise a good person who can stand on their own two feet.' Her mammy's words echoed in her head because that was what frightened Roisin now—could she stand on her own two feet? It felt like ever such a long time since she'd had to and frankly she hadn't been all that good at it when she had.

Noah's behaviour had deteriorated at home lately and she suspected the atmosphere between her and Colin was the catalyst. There were lots of barbed comments in lowered voices and if she were being honest she would say it was because they just didn't like each other very much these days. Things couldn't go on the way they had been. It wasn't fair on Noah. *Oh, what a great big, fecking mess.* If it were just her she'd have packed her bags a long time ago but it wasn't just her and Noah was Colin's son too.

If anyone were to ask, Roisin would say he loved his son but he expected a lot of his little boy, too much in her opinion. She flashed back to the toddler football matches where her husband would stand on the side lines shouting—he was a man who liked to win. The tips and tricks he'd bombard his son with at half time had seen him start refusing to go of a Saturday morning. She'd tried to talk to Colin about it but he'd said it was down to Noah, and that he needed to toughen up.

A car raced past them farting out exhaust fumes and Roisin scowled and muttered, 'Slow down you, eejit.' She wished Noah would let her hold his hand but he insisted he was too big for that now he was at school. She still wasn't used to the hole his not being home between nine and three had left in her days. The idea of having all that glorious time to herself used to seem so tantalising on those days when she was up to her ears in Lego and Play-Doh, the reality however was quite different. Their Victorian semi seemed overly large and full of echoes when it was just her rattling around in it. She hadn't realised until he'd started school how reliant she'd become on her son for company. Colin was rarely home before eight these days and when he was home they weren't very nice to each other. She missed her sisters and her mammy and the noisy, coming and goings of the O'Mara's household growing up.

She, Colin and Noah lived in a house chosen for its smart postcode, something that had been very important to her husband even if it had stretched them financially, just as Noah's school fees were doing. Appearances mattered to her husband. It was the world in which he moved. Sometimes she wondered what it was he'd seen in her apart from that initial physical attraction because they were opposites in so many aspects of their personalities. 'Things' had never really mattered to Roisin or at least they hadn't. Now, the thought of having nothing terrified her. She knew it was becoming a mum that had wrought that change in her, that and the years spent with Colin listening to his big talk.

Roisin caught the word, 'gerbil' as Noah tugged at her coat sleeve. 'Mum, you're not listening to me.' His little face looked hurt and she felt a pang of guilt.

'Sorry, sweetheart. Tell me again.'

He did that thing with his mouth that Colin did when he was annoyed before replying. 'I *said*, do you think gerbils eat toast?'

Roisin was almost afraid to ask. 'Why, darling?'

'Because I've got a piece in my pocket I saved from breakfast.' Noah said this as though it should be obvious and make perfect sense for him to have stashed a piece of toast in his pocket.

Roisin chewed her lip, biting back a sigh because, knowing her luck, it would be a piece slathered in sticky marmalade.

Mrs Flaherty, the O'Mara's guesthouse, cook always weighed his mammy down with jars of her homemade jam when she came to visit. She knew how partial Roisin was to her jam having caught her more than once as a child with her finger in the pot. Indeed, Roisin had been like Pooh Bear was to honey with Mrs Flaherty's sweet marmalade. Now, she tried not to envisage her son's gooey shorts pocket as she replied, 'Hmm, well I'm no expert when it comes to gerbils, Noah, but I think they eat leafy lettuce sort-a things. It might pay to check with Charlie before you feed, er Beyoncé.' An image of a gerbil lying flat on its back with its little legs stiff in the air sprang to mind and she shook it away. Her son being responsible for the offing of Charlie Wentworth-Islington-Greene's gerbil she did not need, not on top of what she'd discovered this morning.

They rounded the corner and spied the usual swarm of parents ahead, along with the shiny cars that were far too big for the narrow road they were vying for space on. Noah picked up his pace and despite everything, the sight of his little legs pumping along made her smile; she was lucky he loved going to school. There were some children who clung sobbing to their mummies of a morning and Roisin always felt so sad for them both, knowing how hard she'd find it if Noah were to do the same.

'Morning, Roisin,' an attractive woman, clad in exercise gear with her hair pulled back in a ponytail called out. 'Are you going to Harriet's this morning?'

'Hi, Nessa.' She managed a wan smile in her direction. "No, not this morning. I'm feeling a bit under the weather will you pass on my apologies to her.'

'Oh dear. Well I hope you feel better soon.' She took a step back as though frightened she might catch whatever lurgy Roisin was incubating.

Yoga with Harriet would have done her good this morning, Roisin mused, following Noah's lead to the gates. It would have calmed her down and helped her think about what she was going to do in a rational manner. She couldn't go though, she needed to head home and face up to what Colin had done and, if she were honest, it was easier to stay angry than to try and make sense of it all. 'Bye, bye, love.' She kissed the top of Noah's head. 'Have a good day, I'll see you at home time.' He had no idea how much his little world was about to change and the thought made her feel physically sick.

It was a relief to be distracted by his excited squeal as he caught sight of Charlotte standing lopsided with her pet cage in hand. She was looking impatient as her mother, Stephanie, tightened the band on one of her pigtails before giving her a kiss goodbye. 'Noah, remember to ask Charlie before you try and feed Beyoncé.' Her words fell on deaf ears as he propelled himself through the huddle of mums toward the little girl.

Roisin's gaze settled on the group of women she called the SLOB gang clustered outside the entrance as though guarding it. They were smiling and chatting in voices designed to carry. Tiff Cooper-Jones caught her eye and mouthed. 'Coffee?'

Roisin shook her head and shouted over, 'No, not today, Tiff, I'm feeling a bit sick.'

The other woman's pert nose curled. 'Oh, well best keep your distance, you don't want to spread it whatever it is.' She turned back to her cronies.

Roisin mentally poked her tongue out at her. She'd rather be afflicted with multiple cold sores than join her and her pals for coffee. SLOB stood for Soy Latte, Obnoxious Bitches. To her shame it was a group that she hovered on the periphery of, occasionally joining them for a cup after they'd waved their offspring goodbye instead of heading for her usual destination, Harriet's yoga studio. She was only invited on the basis of Colin having a working connection with Tiff's husband and didn't know why she bothered going because she always came away from their gatherings feeling annoyed and out of sorts. The only thing she could put her inability to ignore them completely down to was her mammy having told her years ago that it was better to keep your enemies close.

Over to one side and definitely on the outer fringe was Lily—she was not the norm here at Clover Hill. A top fashion model, she was very beautiful but a little rough around the edges having grown up on a council estate. Lily had a smouldering cigarette permanently attached to her hand as part of her Weight Watchers plan. Roisin didn't exactly approve of her smoking at the school gates, it wasn't a good look but so long as she didn't blow the smoke in her and Noah's direction she couldn't see how it affected her. She wasn't the judgmental sort, live and let live had always been her motto. There was a part of her that secretly admired Lily for not caring what the other mothers thought of her. She knew the SLOB gang called her Fag Ash Lil behind her back and were all in silent awe of her jutting hipbones.

Roisin wished she could adopt the same kind of aloofness but she was too sensitive for that. She'd even found herself espousing on Noah's burgeoning musical gift—he'd recently undertaken recorder lessons—in direct competition with Tiff who was convinced her daughter was the next Charlotte Church. She hadn't liked herself for it much and had wondered why she'd felt the need to enter the arena with Tiff. The odds were never going to be in her favour. Besides, she was proud of Noah for just being Noah and truth be told every time he announced he was going to practice that fecking instrument, Roisin flinched. She never used to be like that. Easy-osi Rosi, her sisters used to call her.

Her gaze flicked from one SLOB member to another. Their husbands wouldn't have kissed them goodbye that morning with guilty consciences. Well that wasn't strictly true, Claire Stanford's husband might have been feeling guilty. The word had gone round the last time she'd sat sipping her frothy brew, that the reason Claire hadn't shown her face at school all week was because she'd found out he was having it off with his secretary. There'd been lots of tutting about what a cliché he was in between mouthfuls of scones or muffins.

Oh Jaysus! Roisin shuddered despite the warmth of her coat. Would she be the subject of their tittle-tattle when it got out what Colin had done? And it would get out, it was inevitable. Gossip was like water. It found its way through everything eventually. She could imagine the juicy story would have them salivating for days. 'And Roisin had no idea, imagine that?' It wasn't fecking well fair! Their days were panning out so normally whereas hers, since she'd found the bundle of letters shoved in the glove box of their Merc, the Merc she hardly ever drove, had imploded.

Chapter 4

Roisin had been looking for her earrings, delicate dangling silver stars. She wasn't a jewellery girl but she did like her earrings and this set was her favourite, a twenty-first present from her mammy and dad. They were her lucky earrings and whether it had been a premonition of sorts she didn't know, but that morning as she peered in the mirror after her shower, she'd felt she might need a bit of luck today. It had perturbed her when she couldn't find them and she'd set off on a mission to locate the missing earrings. Perhaps she'd taken them off in the car on the way home from that awful kiss-arsey dinner Colin had insisted she attend? She'd stopped looking when she found the envelopes, the bold red URGENT stamped on the front catching her eye.

She'd only needed to open one, she knew the others would all contain the same information and since she'd scanned the crisp and clearly laid out page it had been like sitting on a seesaw. One minute she bounced toward disbelief, the next fury. Angry tears threatened at the injustice of it all and she blinked rapidly. Tears at the school gate would definitely get the tongues wagging.

Her vision cleared in time for her to realise Stephanie was waving over at her. *That was all she needed.* Roisin waved back cursing the fact she hadn't made her escape while she'd had the chance instead of having a mental slanging match with the SLOBs. She recognised the determined look on Charlie's mother's face as she marched toward her. When Stephanie Wentworth-Islington-Greene had you in her sights it only meant one thing. She was looking for recruits for the school fete. Stephanie was a fundraising extraordinaire the likes of which Clover Hill had never known before.

It was ridiculous really given the fees they all paid to have their children at Clover Hill but the fete was Stephanie's baby and she was impossible to say no to. Mind, the mood Roisin was in today, she might just go a step further than saying no if she wasn't careful. Today was not the day for Stephanie to ask her whether she'd prefer to be in charge of the craft stall or manning the apple bobbing stand. The very idea of a fete seemed at odds with the urban London landscape around them. The word 'fete' made Roisin think of village greens and rolling hills, a quaint church in the background and a plethora of members of the Women's Institute. Oh, and Morris dancers, there had to be Morris dancers somewhere in the mix.

'Roisin, I'm so glad I caught you! Have you heard about the fete I am planning on organising for this spring?' Stephanie's plummy tones sang out.

Of course, she bloody had, the flyers were stuck to every lamppost from here to Knightsbridge. She managed a watery smile and put her hand up as though warding Stephanie off. Indeed, if she'd had garlic to hand she would have waved that about or better still a large wooden cross. The upset of the morning was making her nasty, Stephanie wasn't that bad, although she did have really pointy incisors. 'Now's not a good time, I'm sorry Stephanie. I'm not feeling well. I need to get home.'

'Oh dear. Poor you. Plenty of chicken soup and a day spent under a warm blanket will be just the ticket. Can I give you a lift? My car's just over there.' She pointed to one of the shiny petrol guzzlers parked across the way.

There was genuine kindness in her voice and to her horror Roisin felt a golf ball sized lump form in her throat and there was no blinking back the tears this time.

Stephanie's eyes widened. 'Oh dear. Look the children have gone in. Come on. I'll take you home.' Brooking no argument, she took Roisin's elbow and steered her away from prying eyes over to her car.

Roisin clambered in sniffing loudly. Stephanie got behind the wheel and leant over to open the glove box. It instantly made Roisin flash back to what she'd found in the glovebox of their car and she sniffed even louder. There was nothing incriminating in Stephanie's glovebox only a packet of tissues which she passed to Roisin. 'Thank you,' Roisin said, blowing her nose. She buckled in as Stephanie indicated and pulled away from the kerb. 'You're on Edmond Street, right?'

'Yes,' Roisin mumbled, feeling foolish. She only lived a block away, an easy walk. 'Stephanie, I'm sorry about this. I don't know what got into me.'

'Don't be silly. It's no bother and you know I find a good strong cup of tea and something sweet goes a long way to fixing most things. So, it's up to you. Home, or shall we go to a café where I happen to know the Chelsea buns are to die for?'

Roisin thought about the SLOBs and, as though reading her mind, Stephanie tapped the side of her nose. 'It's a well-kept secret this café, I don't want them putting the prices up on me if word gets out.'

Roisin's mouth twitched despite everything. 'I think I could do with a cup of tea and a something sweet.'

'Right then, Chelsea buns here we come.'

Chapter 5

Roisin was impressed by Stephanie's parking manoeuvres as, against the odds, she managed to squeeze them into a tiny space opposite the aptly named Chelsea Bun Café.

'Here we are,' Stephanie said, switching off the ignition and smiling over at Roisin. 'This is my treat. No arguing,' she bossed seeing Roisin open her mouth to protest.

Roisin followed Stephanie through the break in the traffic in quiet disbelief at how her morning was turning out. The absolute last thing she'd expected when the alarm had shrilled earlier that morning was to be going out for tea and sympathy with Stephanie Wentworth-Islington-Greene. Yet, here she was. The door to the tearoom was painted a cheery red and the windows looking out onto the street were shielded by net curtains—the frost on the outside panes looked like a dusting of icing sugar. She watched as Stephanie ducked down in order to enter, and knew she wouldn't have to follow suit. The building had obviously been built in a time when people were the same size as the O'Mara women.

The moment they stepped inside they were wrapped in a warm and snuggly aroma of fresh baking mingling with fried bacon, toast and brewing coffee. It reminded Roisin of O'Mara's or more to the point, Mrs Flaherty's kitchen and she inhaled greedily, a feeling of homesickness washing over her as she did so. It was a scent that should be bottled she thought as Stephanie gestured she should sit down while she ordered. The aroma was one that told the senses everything would be alright no matter how dire things might seem. It was the smell of home.

A quick sweep of the place saw her sum it up as quaint and chintzy and she chose a table near the window. Floral curtains were pulled back with matching ties and the table was covered in a lace cloth. A small white vase stood to attention next to the salt and pepper shakers with a sprig of lavender adding a splash of colour to the plain condiments. The lighting, given the gloomy day outside, was cosy and the floor was carpeted in well-worn Axminster. It made a nice change from the trendy, noisy, chair scraping cafés housed inside repurposed industrial warehouses the SLOBs frequented.

A man in a suit was seated across the room tucking into a fry-up and an elderly woman was sipping from a china teacup, a newspaper open, in front of her. A teenaged schoolgirl who should have been sitting at her desk and not in a tearoom picking up crumbs from whatever she'd ordered with her index finger looked up and met Roisin's eye challengingly. She swivelled her eyes downward, if the girl wanted to skive off school it was none of her business. She had problems of her own thank you very much. Other than them, the place was quiet being too far for the post-school drop off, mums rush, and it being too late in the morning for the 'latte to go' office brigade.

Roisin watched Stephanie ordering and again pinched herself to see if she was really here. She tried not to think about it being testament to the fact she didn't have many friends here in London despite having lived here for nearly ten years. She'd had a core group of gal pals in Dublin but they'd drifted away in the years since she'd been with Colin. She missed the belly laughs she used to have them but knew she was as much to blame for the lack of contact as they were. She could have telephoned her old friends more, or invited them to London.

She'd tried touching base when she'd gone home for visits but they'd all seemed so busy getting on with their own lives. She knew they felt they'd been forgotten about once she'd set up home with Colin. It was just that he wasn't big on having people to stay. Come to that, he wasn't big on her having a social circle that didn't involve him. He struggled enough when his mam-in-law arrived with her suitcase in hand and truth be told, Roisin found his prickly behaviour toward those that mattered to her embarrassing. It was easier to distance herself.

There was Rowena from yoga who she occasionally met for lunch and Suzy her neighbour who she popped in on from time to time, but they weren't the sort of women you'd want to confide in. Rowena would pack her off for holistic healing which would not help her cause and Suzy would tell her to have a nice glass of wine, which, while delicious wouldn't fix anything either. She could have phoned Aisling, but she wasn't ready to share what she'd discovered with any of her family, not yet. None of them were fond of Colin, she knew they thought he was controlling and she wasn't ready to listen to any *I told you so*'s not until she'd made her mind up as to what she was going to do next. So, here she was instead, about to share her woes with Stephanie Wentworth-Islington-Greene.

Stephanie put a plate with a plump Chelsea bun drizzled in white icing down in front of her before sitting down. 'The tea won't be long. English Breakfast alright?'

'Mm, lovely.'

'What do you think of the place? It reminds me of a tea shop my granny used to take me to as a treat at Christmas time.'

Roisin nodded. 'It's very cosy and that bun looks wonderful.'

'Dig in,' Stephanie urged, breaking hers apart and popping a piece in her mouth.

CHAPTER 25

Roisin didn't think she'd be able to eat a bite but she didn't want to disappoint Stephanie and so she did the same. To her surprise it went down well and she broke off another piece. There was a silence between them and Roisin hoped it wouldn't stretch out awkwardly. She knew by coming here she'd be expected to explain why she'd burst into tears outside school but she didn't know where to start. Stephanie saved her the trouble.

'Do you know, Roisin, I realised we've seen each other outside school every day for three months and we know nothing about one another.' She shook her head and her stylishly cut blonde hair swayed momentarily before settling back into place. Roisin felt a pang; she'd always wanted swishy hair that sat where it was supposed to. Her dark mop had a natural kink, prone to misbehaving in damp weather. She'd often mused that she'd have great hair if she lived somewhere like LA instead of London.

'I grew up in a town that wasn't much bigger than a village. It was one of those places where everybody knew everybody. Big cities can be awfully impersonal places, I think. Where do you come from in Ireland, Roisin?'

Roisin swallowed her mouthful. 'Dublin. I grew up on the top floor of a guesthouse opposite St Stephen's Green, called O'Mara's.'

'Oh, now that would have been interesting.'

'It was, do you know Dublin?'

'I've done the sights, and fed the ducks in the Green.'

'Well the Green was our garden, it was wonderful.'

'Is the guesthouse still in your family?'

'Yes, it is, although it nearly wasn't.' She thought back to how, after her dad had died Mammy had decided there were too many memories in the old Georgian manor house and she needed a fresh start. She'd announced she was going to sell if one of the family didn't decide to take over the managing role. Her brother Patrick had been chomping at the bit to put the place on the market knowing in the current climate with the Celtic Tiger roaring it would have fetched a very pretty penny indeed. He wanted his share of his inheritance freed up so he could invest in whatever pie he currently had his finger in over in America.

Colin had been behind him. At the time it had annoyed her—more than annoyed her. It wasn't his family home they were talking about. It wasn't him that used to ride the dumbwaiter all the way from the kitchen to the family's apartment on the top floor, or play hide and seek throughout the vast rooms of the guesthouse. They weren't his memories secreted in the very fabric of the place and so far as she was concerned O'Mara's was nothing to do with him. She'd not let on to the others how she felt. Roisin was well aware what her sisters thought of her husband and she didn't want to add fuel to the fire so to speak. She'd saved it until later when they were on their own. They'd had many a cross word on the subject. Of course, now she knew why he'd been so keen for O'Mara's to be sold. He'd wanted, no *needed*, the capital.

If she were asked to name the exact moment she'd fallen out of love with her husband, she wouldn't have been able to. She did know she'd seen Colin through fresh eyes after he'd sided so vigorously with her brother on selling their family home. She'd realised he didn't care what she thought, or how she felt. It wasn't a nice phrase and she didn't know if it had always been that way but somewhere along the way she'd become nothing more than arm candy for Colin. She scrubbed up well when she dressed up and he liked to parade her in front of his colleagues at the mind-numbing networking dinner parties he was forever attending. She was Julia Roberts to his Richard Gere only she'd never been a prostitute. The realisation had made her feel sick; not the Julia Roberts bit, she'd have loved to have been tall and willowy like her instead of short and Irish, and thinking about that analogy now, Colin looked nothing like Richard Gere. It was a stupid comparison.

CHAPTER 52

It had been Aisling who'd saved the day and the guesthouse, giving up her job in resort management to return from where she'd been based in Crete to take over from Mammy. She wouldn't see the place sold she'd announced. It was called O'Mara's and as such it would stay in the O'Mara family. Roisin had cheered her sister silently, thanking her when they got a moment on their own. And so, Mammy had bought an apartment in Howth, Aisling had moved home, and Moira had stayed right where she was, in her bedroom at the guesthouse. Patrick had sulked off back to Los Angeles and Colin had huffed and puffed for weeks after over the whole business.

It had all worked out rather well for Aisling in the end because she had a lovely fella on the go now and was well and truly settled in her life in Dublin. She and Moira rubbed along well enough, although Moira of late had been struggling a bit with losing her dad. They'd all struggled terribly with that. She relayed a shortened version of all of this to Stephanie then took the opportunity when the tea arrived to finish her bun, savouring the sweetness. This was just the ticket, there was something to be said for a sugar hit, no matter what Rowena and Harriet had to say on the subject. Stephanie played mother pouring the tea. 'Milk?'

'Yes, please, and one sugar.' She might as well go the full hog, she decided.

'So did you meet your husband in Dublin?' Stephanie slid the pretty china cup and saucer across the table.

'No here in London. I moved here ten years ago although I've only been with Colin for six of those. I was chomping at the bit to see something of the world other than Dublin. Colin and I met through my old job, at NatWest.' Roisin had enjoyed working at the bank even if she hadn't been particularly adept at her job as a teller. She couldn't tell you what it was exactly she'd liked about the work but suspected it might have had something to do with the sense of order in the otherwise disorderly world she moved in.

She remembered the day she'd telephoned Mammy to tell her where her latest temp job was. For once, Mammy had been lost for words but it didn't last long. 'But, Rosi, you're the most un-banky sort-a person there is. How on earth did that happen?' Roisin supposed she couldn't blame her mammy for being surprised. Maths had not been a strong subject for her when she'd been at school but that was mostly down to Sister Agnes. The nun had a face on her like a paper bag that had been popped and her lessons had been so dry it had been hard to stay awake. Actually, school in general had been rather dry, rather square. The boxlike shape was one Roisin had never fitted into and she'd been eager to escape its stifling confines and try her hand at different things until she found a good fit. That was why the temping life in London suited her. She wasn't boxed in.

She'd left school all those years ago and embarked on a rather varied career initially securing an apprenticeship hairdressing. She'd been given the heave-ho a year into it when she left a colour on a client's hair too long. Her only excuse was she'd been so busy thinking about ways to patch things up with Ewan, her then boyfriend, she'd completely forgotten about Mrs Geraghty. The poor woman had asked to be a soft blonde but she'd left the salon a geriatric Pamela Anderson.

She'd found work in promotions after that. Mammy told her friends somewhat enigmatically that Roisin was working in the Entertainment industry and she was... sort of. Dressing up in hot pants and a singlet to promote the latest alcopops around the city's nightclubs certainly entertained a good portion of the patrons. Personally though, Roisin felt her career low point had come when she'd found herself employed as a receptionist in a car sales yard. The job itself was perfectly fine but she was certain sweaty Mr 'call me Ron' Pike with his comb-over hadn't employed her for her clerical skills. She and Ewan never did get back together and the day Mr Pike's hand slipped from the small of her back to her bottom, giving it a good squeeze, was the day she decided it might be time for a change of scene.

It was then she realised Stephanie was asking her a question as she looked across the table at her expectantly. 'Sorry, Stephanie, I was lost in thought then, what were you saying?'

'I was asking if your husband worked in banking too.'

'Yes, he did, only he was upstairs in management and I was on the front line. He's branched out into investing these days and I haven't worked...' she paused, that wasn't true. Just because she hadn't drawn an income didn't mean she hadn't worked bloody hard these last few years. '...outside of home at any rate, since I had Noah. To tell you the truth I'm finding it a bit strange being home without him. I'm not quite sure what to do with myself.'

'I know what you mean. You do rather find yourself at a loose end after running around after a little person for so many years. It's why I've thrown myself into planning the fete. It was that or go mad. Now I'm just driving everybody else mad.'

The two women smiled at each other in complicit understanding. 'What about you?' Roisin asked. 'You said you were from the country?'

'Mm,' Stephanie patted her mouth with a napkin. 'Chipping Norton in the Cotswolds. Pretty as a picture it is too.' She sounded wistful.

'You miss it?'

'Aspects, yes. The thing with living in a small town is that it is all tickety-boo until things go wrong and then there's no getting away from it. Jeffrey, is Charlie's father for all extents and purposes but my first husband, Damien is her biological father. He wasn't a very nice man. He had a bit of a problem with hitting the bottle and he wasn't a pleasant drunk. He could be a bit fisty. Charlie was two when I left, and it was a hard decision to make. I knew I couldn't rely on my family for help. They're very stiff upper lip and soldier on because you made your bed. My lot and Damien controlled all aspects of our life including the finances. I had no money of my own to fall back on. It was Charlie who gave me the strength to leave.' She gave an ironic little laugh. 'He still lives in the same house, the house I furnished and decorated, only he's a new wife ensconced there now.' She shook her head. 'Poor woman. I did try to warn her but she just thought I was the bitter ex-wife and wouldn't listen. He won't have changed you know. A leopard doesn't change his spots.'

Roisin sat with her teacup frozen in mid-air. 'I'm so sorry, Stephanie.' She was unsure what else to say and felt ashamed of herself for having prejudged this woman, who'd kindly taken her for tea, as one of the moneyed horsey set who, as such, would have led a privileged life. She never used to be a judgemental sort of person; she'd seen everybody as an open book waiting for her to get to know them. It was being married to Colin that had done that to her.

Stephanie waved her hand airily. 'Oh, it feels a lifetime ago now, even if it's only been three years and leaving him was the making of me.' She tapped the side of her cup with a peachy-pink nail and looked thoughtful for a moment. 'He never wanted children, Charlie took up too much of my time and attention and he's never tried to contact us since we left.'

'But where did you go? It must have been very hard if you didn't have any money behind you.'

She nodded, 'I came here, to London. I landed on an old school chum of mine here and she was marvellous. Top up?' She indicated the teapot.

Roisin shook her head. 'No thank you.'

'I might.' As she poured she carried on talking. "It was embarrassing how clueless I was about...' she pursed her lips searching for the words she wanted and put the teapot down. '...well, life really, but Ronnie helped set me up so I could stand on my own two feet with Charlie. As it happened I didn't have to for very long. I wound up working in PR and that's how I met Jeffrey, he was a client. I knew straight away he was the one even if I did insist on us just being friends initially. Friendship makes a good basis for a relationship. He was so very different to Damien and we've never looked back. Life's too short to be unhappy, Roisin.'

Roisin made a 'hmming' noise of agreement as she mulled over what she'd just heard. She'd never been friends with Colin. He'd sidled up to her at work drinks and knowing she was new to the city had offered to show her around. He'd showed her a lot more than London on their third date and when she'd told him she was pregnant he'd asked her to move in with him. She'd be lying if she didn't say she was glad to see the back of the room she was renting in a shared house. It was damp and cheerless and all she could afford. She often wondered now if Colin had seen her as one of his projects. Something worth putting a bit of time and effort into to get the required end result.

Perhaps she'd have felt their relationship was on more of an equal footing if they had been friends first. Perhaps she'd never have married him if she'd gotten to know him properly first. Maybe she should have looked at going back to work when Noah started school. She'd definitely taken her foot off the accelerator once they'd said 'I do'. She'd allowed Colin to take charge because her focus, her sole focus had been Noah. Her pregnancy had been such a source of wonder to her and she'd gotten so caught up in the idea of becoming a mother that she'd lost sight of who she was somewhere along the way. If she thought about it like that then the only person to blame for the mess she was in was herself. It wasn't a thought that held much appeal but it was one she couldn't ignore any longer. She'd been a pushover for most of her marriage. Well, no longer. She opened her mouth to tell Stephanie what had gotten her in a state.

Chapter 6

'This morning I discovered my husband re-mortgaged our home six months ago without telling me. I'm guessing he did so to free up capital to invest in his latest dalliance because we were over extended on the house as it is.' Roisin sighed all the way from the tips of her trainers. 'Colin's a firm believer in keeping up with the Joneses and then some. He is what my mammy would call, a flash Harry.' She picked up the teaspoon on the side of her cup and toyed with it. 'He's never been any different but it didn't use to bother me. When we first met I put his need to look the part down to insecurity and I think, initially anyway, it was one of the things that made me love him just that little bit more. The thought he might be vulnerable under that smooth, confident exterior.' She glanced up trying to read Stephanie's expression. Was this too much? Because they hardly knew each other and she really was pouring her heart out.

The thing with Colin was that he was a man who was always on the cusp of making it big. He yearned to be in with the movers and shakers of the business world, but somehow his ventures never panned out not like they did for his clients. To Roisin's mind there was no such thing as getting rich quick. Sure, look at her mam and dad. You got there through hard work, determination and by being guided by those who'd been there and done that. Colin worked hard and he was determined, but where he let himself down, she'd come to realise, was that he knew it all. He couldn't stomach taking advice from anyone not even those who'd been successful. It was his downfall.

It hadn't mattered to her so far. He was who he was and they'd been managing well enough. They were warm, well fed, had a roof over their head, even had nice holidays in Spain. They didn't go without. She spied Stephanie's sympathetic face and it egged her on. 'He's not made any repayment on the loan for the last three months and the bank's threatening foreclosure.' She shrugged. 'He obviously hasn't got the money or it wouldn't have got to this point. We're going to lose the house.'

'Oh, Roisin, I'm so sorry. And you had no idea things were dire?'

'None whatsoever.' Roisin could almost hear her thinking and logically too, 'But surely you signed the loan application?' She'd told Stephanie this much, she figured she might as well tell her the rest. 'I feel stupid saying this out loud. In fact; I can't believe how stupid I've been. I should never have agreed to it but the house is in the name of one of Colin's company's and I'm not a director.' She felt her face heat up. It was embarrassing to admit her naivety and it was a ridiculous state of affairs given the era they lived in. She should have insisted on being listed as a director and ensuring her name had gone on the deeds. She'd trusted him when it came to making their financial decisions though, had taken her eye off the ball and look where it had gotten her. Soon to be homeless.

Stephanie reached across the table and patted Roisin's. 'I'm not judging you, Roisin, believe me I'm in no position to judge anyone with my past choices in men. We love who we love and if they take that love and wring it out then it's not us who's to blame.'

Roisin looked at Stephanie for a moment mulling over her words. It was true, she realised that was how she felt, as though he'd taken that love and wrung it out. She'd realised when the contents of the letter had begun to sink in earlier that morning that there was nothing left. It had frightened her more than the thought of losing the house. Her emotional well where her husband was concerned had run dry. Stephanie sat back in her chair and she looked like a CEO chairing a meeting as she steepled her fingers together and said, 'I find when we hit life's low points that it pays to have a plan.'

Roisin didn't think she'd ever had a plan, she'd always just winged it, but she knew she could do with one now. She looked at Stephanie hopefully, waiting to hear what her plan should be but the other woman eyed her back expectantly. Roisin realised she was waiting for her to speak up. 'I'm not very good at making plans. I tend to go with the flow,' she said.

'And that is a perfectly fine way to be when the flow is good but when it hits a dam and turns into a shit heap, it doesn't tend to work too well. So, ask yourself what do you want to do about what's happened?'

Roisin was startled, Stephanie with her plummy tones did not look like the sort of woman to use bad language. It had a galvanising effect though, which she suspected was what Stephanie had intended. 'Okay, well if we're running with gut instinct then what I really want to do is pack mine and Noah's bags and go back to Dublin. I want some breathing space between me and Colin while I figure out what to do next.' All Roisin wanted right at that moment was her mammy. She wanted to hear her tell her she'd find a way through this mess and that it would all be alright.

'Then that's what you should do, Roisin. Go, take a break and put some distance between yourself and what's happened. It will help give you, perspective to deal with the situation more calmly.'

Roisin flashed back to the answerphone message yesterday afternoon. Aisling had informed her she'd returned from the airport with Mammy and Moira in tow. Mammy was after breaking her ankle in some back of beyond hill tribe place in Northern Vietnam but apart from that the pair of them were grand and full of their trip. Mammy was going to stay at O'Mara's with Aisling and Moira until she got the hang of her crutches. Sure, it would be like the old days if she were to land on them too.

She knew too if she were to confront Colin when he got home tonight he would talk at her not to her. He'd bamboozle her with how this deal was about to pay off or that one was only days off from being cashed in and then they'd be in the clear. It was a storm but they'd weather it. They just had to hold on tight. It wasn't about any of that though. It was about Colin having gone behind her back. He hadn't had enough respect for her to talk to her about what his plans were even though they had a direct impact on her and Noah. She felt cheated.

As though reading her mind Stephanie said, 'It's a thing you know, financial infidelity. It is a form of cheating.'

Roisin nodded. Yes, Colin had cheated on her; he'd shattered the trust she'd had in him only he'd done it not with another woman but with their finances. 'I wonder if I can get me and Noah on a flight later today.'

'Well, there's only one way to find out. Shall we?'

'You'll come with me?' Roisin felt a surge of gratitude toward Stephanie. The thought of trying to organise it all herself was too much with the scrambled way her head was feeling.

'Of course, I will.' Stephanie got to her feet. 'Come on let's go book you and Noah a ticket to Dublin.'

Chapter 7

♥

'But, Mummy, why are we going to Ireland?' The little voice from the back of the car had a decidedly whiney tone, the tiredness from a day at school evident in it.

Roisin chewed her bottom lip, and her hand went to her left ear to toy with the plain silver studs she wore. It was a nervous habit. She didn't turn around as she replied, 'We're going to see your nana and your aunties, Noah, and it's really kind of Mrs Wentworth-Islington-Greene to take us to the train station.'

'Noah, you can call me Mrs Stephanie, that's what Charlie's friends call me,' Stephanie interjected, her gaze not wavering from the slow-moving traffic ahead of her.

'But Nana and Auntie Moira are on their holidays. I got postcards.'

Roisin didn't have to look behind her, she instinctively knew his arms would be crossed over his small chest and his bottom lip would be protruding. Noah didn't like changes in his routine, most kids didn't.

'They got home yesterday, Noah, remember I told you. Poor Nana's got her foot in a plaster cast and she's staying at O'Mara's so Aunty Aisling and Aunty Moira can look after her. I think a visit from us will cheer her up, don't you?' It would probably stop Mammy driving her sisters demented too, she thought as a motorbike zipped past them, weaving its way through the congested road.

'But what about Daddy?' The whine was revving up. "Who will cook his dinner? And I didn't get to say goodbye.'

Roisin inhaled slowly and exhaled with the same speed. It would do no good to snap at Noah and it wouldn't be fair, besides, she'd heard the quiver in his voice. Snapping would set off a deluge and she didn't need that. Not now when she was close to tears herself. She couldn't believe it had actually come to this. She swivelled around in her seat and looked to where her son was sitting strapped in the back. His eyes looked large in his little face as he tried to process what was happening. A pet cage separated him and Charlotte who was looking at her with curiosity waiting to hear what she would say. They might only be five years old but they were smart these kids. Not much got by them.

'Ah, Noah love, don't be worrying about your daddy. Sure, he's a grown-up and he can manage on his own for a few days. If he wants to he can go and see his mammy, now can't he? She'll feed him up so she will.'

Noah nodded slowly; he hadn't thought of that. Satisfied that would be the end of the questions, Roisin turned her attention back to the road ahead. She was certain once Colin read the note she'd left at Stephanie's insistence—she didn't want him having her and Noah listed as missing persons after all—he would skulk home to his mam's, for a few days. She pictured him turning up with the armful of shirts she'd planned on ironing that day on her mam-in-law's polished doorstep hoping for a hot meal and plenty of TLC. Elsa Quealey had never been a big fan of Roisin's she'd realised this the Christmas Elsa had splashed out on underwear for her daughter-in-law a good two sizes larger than what Roisin actually wore. She suspected Elsa wouldn't be a big fan of any woman who took her son's time and attention away from her. What was it with mammies and their sons? Her own mammy was as blind as a bat when it came to Patrick's foibles. She resolved there and then that she would not put Noah on a pedestal because it wouldn't do him any good, not in the long run.

Whenever Colin's mam came calling, she was always quick to cast her gaze to the skirting boards and Roisin was certain that when she left the room she'd run a finger along them inspecting for dust. 'My Colin can't abide dust you know, Roisin? It sets his sinuses off,' she'd informed Roisin more than once. She'd also overheard her asking Colin if he was eating properly when she thought her daughter-in-law was out of earshot. Well she could fuss over her son all she fecking well liked now.

She stole another glance back at Noah and saw his eyes looked heavy. She hoped he wouldn't nod off; he'd never been good when woken up and she'd have to wake him when they got to Paddington. He'd put his thumb in his mouth too, a sure sign he was moments away from falling asleep. It was a habit Colin was insistent they break but Colin wasn't here and if sucking his thumb made the poor love feel secure so what? Then again the thought of dragging an ill-tempered five-year-old through the rush hour Paddington Station crowds was not inspiring. 'Noah, why don't you check on Beyoncé?' she shouted over the back seat causing Stephanie to jump.

'Beyoncé's on the naughty step,' Charlotte piped up. 'That means she's not allowed to talk to anybody until she's had a chance to think about why she's sitting there.'

The gerbil, from what Roisin could see, was actually scuffling around on the bits of shredded newspaper not contemplating her behaviour. She looked at Stephanie and saw her mouth was twitching. It was obviously her go-to punishment, because out of the mouths of babes and all that.

'Oh dear, what did Beyoncé do then, Charlie?' Stephanie asked, her eyes flitting up to meet her daughter's in the rear-view mirror.

'She got out of her cage—'

'You mean you got her out of her cage after I told you not to.' Stephanie's mouth tightened.

'It was Jemima's fault, she wanted to hold her.'

Stephanie gave a weighty sigh. 'Charlie, we've talked about this. You don't make friends by trying to impress them and certainly not by letting her hold your pet when you were told specifically not to take her out of the cage. What happened?'

Charlotte's voice was very small. 'Beyoncé didn't like Jemima because she did a wee-wee on her and she only does that when she doesn't like someone. Jemima squealed and dropped her and poor Beyoncé ran away frightened.'

Roisin tried to picture the small brown gerbil jubilantly making a bid for freedom.

'Well you obviously found her, that's something I suppose.'

'Not really. It was Mrs Harris who found her. She screamed the whole school down, didn't she, Noah?'

Noah agreed that yes the headmistress had indeed screamed very loudly. 'It hurt my ears,' he said. He removed his thumb to demonstrate by covering both his ears.

Stephanie shook her head and her fingers tapped at the steering wheel, in anticipation of a chastising call from the head once she got home, no doubt, Roisin surmised.

'Where did Mrs Harris find her then, Charlie?' Out of the corner of her mouth she added for Roisin's benefit, 'I'm almost scared to ask.'

'She was hiding behind the toilet.'

Roisin couldn't help it, she snorted and a giggle escaped her lips. She was assailed by the image of prim Mrs Harris entering the toilet cubicle and spying a pair of beady black eyes peering up at her from behind the pan. Stephanie shot her a look telling her it wasn't funny but the twinkle in her eye told her otherwise.

'Well all I can say is that if I was Mrs Harris I would have screamed very loudly if I came across a gerbil in the toilets. You were lucky you got her back, young lady, and that is the last time she will be going on a school visit, do you hear me?'

Charlotte's 'yes' was barely audible over the frantic scrabbling from the cage. Roisin took it to mean Beyoncé was in agreement with Stephanie.

The station came into sight a few minutes later. 'This was really good of you, Stephanie,' she lowered her voice, not wanting big ears in the backseat to overhear. 'I don't know what I would have done without your help today.'

'It's been my pleasure and a welcome break from sorting the finer points of the fete out. You will let me know how you're getting on over in Dublin won't you? And I mean that, Roisin, if you need anything or if just want an ear to bend, just call.'

'Of course.' She'd jotted down Stephanie's number earlier and stuffed it safely inside her bag. She really had been marvellous taking her under her wing to help her sort the tickets for the flight before taking her home to pack a bag for her and Noah and then, finally, dropping them here at Paddington to get the train to Heathrow. It was funny how things worked out. This had quite possibly been the shittiest day of Roisin's life but there was always a silver lining no matter how bleak things might seem because she'd made a new friend today.

Chapter 8

Roisin pushed open the door to the guesthouse and Noah ducked under her arm eager to get inside. She hauled their bags in and let the door close on the darkened, cold night with its steady drizzle outside. The taxi had cost a small fortune, one, given the current state of her finances, she could ill afford. She couldn't face explaining herself to her mammy or her sisters though and she'd have been put through a grilling if she'd telephoned out of the blue to ask if she and Noah could be picked up from the airport. Her family just weren't the no questions asked type.

She dropped the bags at her feet and rubbed her hands together to try and warm them up. The reception area was lit with a welcoming cosy glow from the lamp by the sofa and a dark head bobbed up from where it had been bent over the computer behind the front desk. The fax whirred into life against the far wall as a pair of enormous brown eyes met Roisin's. She could see the bewilderment on Nina's, the young Spanish girl who took over on reception when Bronagh went home, face.

For Nina's part she was trying to put the pieces of the puzzle together. She knew nobody was due to check in and a walk-in, especially with a small child in tow at this time of the evening was unusual. Not to mention there was something very familiar about the woman smiling over at her, something very familiar indeed. She looked very much like—

'Hi Nina, I'm Roisin O'Mara, well it's Quealey now.' Or was it? Roisin hesitated as the implication of having left Colin sank in. Would she revert to O'Mara? Noah was a Quealey, she couldn't very well change his surname and she didn't want to go by a different last name to her son. Had she even left Colin or was she just taking time out? She felt like she was going mad as the questions bombarded her. The letter she'd left him had laid her feelings out clearly and she'd signed off by asking him to give her some room and not contact her. She'd be in touch in the next day or so, when she'd had time to think.

She blinked realising Nina was looking expectantly at her. 'Sorry, it's been a long day. We met a while back.' She didn't want to add, 'at my dad's funeral' because the way she was feeling at the moment she was likely to collapse in a big sobbing heap. Thankfully she was spared from having to do so as Nina's face broke into a wide smile as she tapped her forehead.

'Ah yes, Roisin, sorry I should have realised. It was the surprise of you being here that's why I didn't place you right away. You look so much like your mama and Moira. It's just the hair that's different. Especially with your mama's new look.'

It was true, Roisin conceded, Moira's mane was long and sleek thanks to rigorous hair straightening and Mammy's was a swishy, shiny bob thanks to regular salon appointments, while hers was an unruly curly mass best worn up. She put a hand to it knowing it would have gone into spriggy overdrive given the damp weather outside.

Nina came around from the desk and she crouched down in front of Noah. 'I remember you too but you were smaller last time we met. It's Noah isn't it?'

Noah nodded. 'I'm a schoolboy now.'

Nina could see that; he was still in his grey wool-blend uniform. 'Well, you've certainly got very big.' Her smile was warm, she loved children. If she'd had the opportunity she would have liked to have been a teacher but it wasn't to be. 'I bet your mama is very proud of her big schoolboy, yes?'

'I am.' Roisin smiled and watched her son. Normally a comment like this would see him stand a little straighter. He was like that boy in the old Tom Hanks' film, *Big*—in a hurry to grow up. To have someone refer to him as such was a compliment indeed. Now though, he just stared back at the receptionist and looked like he might cry. He was worn out, Roisin realised. It had been an unusual day for him too, what with escaped gerbils and being whisked away from school only to find himself in Dublin a few hours later, minus his daddy. 'He's exhausted, Nina,' she explained apologetically. 'Are they in?' She raised her eyes to the ceiling.

'Yes, they are all home. It is a surprise you're coming?' Her English was good but her accent was heavy. 'I like surprises.'

'Yes, deciding to come here was spur of the moment.' Roisin's gaze shifted to her son and Nina picked up on an underlying tension behind her words, but it was none of her business and unlike young Evie who worked the weekend night shift, she was not a gossip. She came from a small Spanish hill town, more a village really and she knew first-hand what it was to be the subject of tittle-tattle. She stood up, smoothing the creases that had formed in her trousers.

'I think you are both very tired. I will help you carry these upstairs.' She picked up the larger of Roisin's bags and hefted the strap over her shoulder.

'Oh, thanks, Nina, that would be grand.' Roisin flashed a grateful smile as she was hit by a wave of fatigue now her destination was in sight. All she wanted to do was collapse in a heap on the sofa and have her family run around after her. She took the last of her luggage and with Noah in the lead, sturdy legs on a mission to find his aunties and nana, she followed Nina up the winding staircase to the family's top floor apartment.

Chapter 9

Light flooded the dimly lit landing outside the family's apartment as the door swung open to reveal Moira. Roisin took in her sloppy sweater, pyjama bottoms and woolly socks, surmising she was clearly in for the evening. Her sister looked a little like someone had just tapped her on the shoulder and told her that her skirt was tucked into the back of her knickers as she stared from Nina to Roisin and finally down at Noah. She repeated the process before opening her mouth to holler, 'Mammy, you'll never guess, it's Roisin and Noah!'

'What are you on about, Moira?' Maureen bellowed back from deeper inside the apartment.

'It's me and Noah, Mam.' Roisin yelled. 'Stop staring, Moira, and let us in. We're knackered, so we are. Thanks so much for bringing my bag up, Nina, you're a star.'

Moira managed to galvanise herself enough to take the bag from Nina who said goodnight to them before taking herself back down the stairs. For a moment Roisin's eyes followed her wondering if she should make a break for it. It wasn't too late; she'd forgotten how loud her family was. As if to reinforce this, Maureen's voice shouted once more. 'Is it really you, Rosi, or is Moira being an eejit?'

Aisling appeared, peering over Moira's shoulder at her oldest sister and nephew who'd managed to get as far as the hallway. Her face was covered in thick pink goo and her copper hair was held back by an Alice band. 'It's them, Mammy, Moira's after telling the truth,' she called.

'For fecks sake,' Roisin muttered. 'I've arrived at the circus. What have you got on your face, Ash?'

'It's a girls' night in since Mammy and Moira are only just back from their holiday so I thought I'd try my new rose petal infused masque. It's supposed to do wonders for open pores.'

Noah stared at the apparition. It sounded like his aunty Aisling but why would she have pink marshmallow all over her face? He didn't like the pink ones only the white ones. His day was getting stranger by the minute.

'Moira, put that bag in my room,' Aisling bossed, pushing her sister aside in order to hug Roisin. Aisling's room was in fact the room she'd shared with Roisin and Moira for many years but the days of three twin beds had long since passed. Moira had commandeered Patrick's old room as soon as he moved out and Mammy was taking up space back in her old master suite for the time being. 'It's not like you not to tell us you're coming, Rosi. I can't believe you're here.'

'Well, I am.' Rosi untangled herself from her sister and took a step back trying to keep the defensive note from her voice. Her world was decidedly off-kilter. Moira meanwhile dropped the bags where she was standing, ignoring Aisling's instructions to take it to her bedroom. She shut the door and turned her attention to Noah. 'Look at you, you're still in your uniform and it's after seven. You look exhausted wee man.'

Aisling too honed in on Noah and the two sisters elbowed one in another in order to get to him first. To his relief Moira won, he was very unsure about Aunty Aisling with her pink sticky face. Moira hauled him up, groaning with the effort to get him airborne. 'Ooh you've gotten a big boy, Noah.'

'What are you all doing out there?' Maureen's frustration at not being privy to what was going on out in the hall was evident.

'Can she not walk at all then?' Roisin asked.

Moira shook her head. 'It was a right fecking—'

'Moira!' Aisling admonished casting her eyes meaningfully at Noah.

'Sorry, Noah, close your ears. It was a performance getting her up here I can tell you. Poor Quinn and Tom—you haven't met him yet, he's a friend of mine, were like hunchbacks hauling her up the stairs. We picked up crutches for her today and she's had a few practice runs around the living room, but she's a slow learner.' Moira jiggled her hip. 'Honestly, Rosi, Mammy's doing my f—,' she stopped herself in the nick of time, 'head in, so she is. She's not a good patient.'

'Moira, I know you're talking about me!'

Noah, overwhelmed by all the shouting, had begun to sniff.

'Don't you worry about your nana, Noah, her ears are bigger than her bum.' Moira gave him a squeeze and kissed him on his chubby cheek before staggering forth, hip jutting out at an awkward angle as her nephew held on for dear life. 'C'mon, Rosi, you'd best go through and see her Royal Highness.'

Aisling pulled Roisin aside. 'A word of warning. Mammy's after doing something with her hair.'

Roisin eyed her sister, 'What's she had done? Ah Jaysus, she's not after getting a perm again, is she? Remember when we were kids and she came home from the hairdressers looking like yer man, Brian wotsit from Queen but she was adamant the look she was going for was Cher. Moira cried when she saw her.'

'Brian May and yes I do. I wouldn't let her pick me up from school until the fecking thing had dropped.' She lowered her voice, 'Listen, Rosi, I don't want to frighten you but I think this is actually worse. Best you go see for yourself.'

Roisin steeled herself as she followed Moira and Noah through to the living room. The television she noted was on but the sound had been turned down. Her eyes swept the room. All was as it should be in the living room with its high

CHAPTER 9

Georgian ceilings apart from the person sitting on the couch. One leg was stretched out with a foot in thick plaster resting on the coffee table. A cup and saucer next to it and an empty Jacob's bar wrapper. Roisin's eyes travelled slowly upwards and she gave a sharp intake of breath as her gaze settled on the familiar face of her mammy.

Moira had put Noah down so he could sit next to his nana. She was busily patting the space on the sofa next to her for him to come and sit next to her but he took one look at her and burst into tears. 'You're not my nana,' he shouted turning away and, spying his mum he ran to her so he could bury his head between her legs. Roisin reached down and stroked his hair.

'Jaysus, Mammy, you can't blame the poor love! What are you after doing to yourself?'

'Oh, keep your knickers on, Rosi, you're as bad as your sisters. I had it braided in Vietnam. Nha Trang to be exact and it's very low maintenance so it is.' She swung her head and all the beads on the hundreds of braids decorating her head clacked.

'Well you're in Dublin, Ireland now Mammy. Most people don't get out about in bikinis and sarongs with their headful of plaits.'

'I've told her that but she won't let me near them,' Moira stated.

'And who's she, the cat's mother? I want a hairdresser to take them out. I'm not letting you all cack-handed near them.'

'You should have seen her,' Aisling lamented, ignoring her mammy. 'I was waiting ages at the arrival gates yesterday, beginning to think the worst, when they appeared. You know things like Mammy had offered to carry some man's teddy bear through customs and been arrested for drugs or the like but then I saw Moira and this woman in a wheelchair. I didn't recognise her at first not with her hair like that. That's not the worst of it though. She had this enormous wooden willy rearing up from her lap.'

Roisin swung toward her sister, her own problems forgotten as she wondered what in the name of Mary, her mammy and Moira had gotten up to on their Vietnam hols.'

'Aisling O'Mara, I did not!' Maureen wailed. 'It's a canoe, so it is, Roisin, and I carved it myself when we were in the village of Mui Ha, they're very big on woodwork there, and I made a good job of it.' Seeing Roisin's incredulous expression, she kept digging her hole. 'I wanted to carve a junk but I couldn't do the sails, they were too complicated. I keep telling her,' she pointed at Aisling, 'and Moira that but they've dirty minds the pair of them. Look, it's over there, see for yourself.' She flung her arm toward the fire's mantelpiece.

Roisin followed her directive and found herself looking upon a majestic wooden fertility symbol. Canoe my arse, she thought shaking her head. Out of the frying pan and into the fire, because she'd arrived home to a mad house.

'And you can get your mind out of the gutter too, my girl. I know what you're thinking and all I can say is you girls must have had some peculiar experiences in your time because it looks nothing like what you think it looks like.' Maureen's eyes narrowed as she took stock of her eldest daughter. 'And anyway, you haven't come all the way from London to talk about my canoe. What's going on, Rosi? What are you doing turning up unannounced when Fair City's on the television?'

'We can go if you like.' Roisin's lip trembled.

'Don't be silly, this is your home. Now sort Noah out, the poor dote looks dead on his feet. Has he had his tea?' Maureen smiled at her grandson who stared back at her mutinously. He was not liking the look of this woman with the funny hair. It was like with Aunty Aisling. It looked like his nana and sounded like his nana but his nana did not have silly hair. 'Moira go and heat him up a bowl of what's left over from our dinner—you like shepherd's pie, don't you, lovie? It's a posh

CHAPTER 49

one, Marks & Spencer's no less, heating and eating is Moira's idea of cooking, so it is. It was her turn tonight.'

'Does it have peas in it?' Noah's voice was barely audible.

Moira sighed. 'I like the Marks and Spencer's pie and after a month of noodley food I fancied it. I am perfectly able to cook a meal from scratch thank you very much, Mammy.'

Aisling raised an eyebrow, 'Well I wish you'd prove it some time.'

Moira poked her tongue out at her sister seeing her mammy open her mouth yet again.

'Oh, made of money are you? And you after jacking your job in too.'

Roisin's head swivelled between her mammy and sisters. It was beginning to hurt with trying to keep up. *Moira had jacked her job in?* Why hadn't anyone told her?

Suddenly Noah found his voice. 'I hate peas!' He burst into tears as both aunties and his nana stared at him.

Maureen spoke first, 'How can you not like peas, Noah? There, there it's not worth getting all upset about a tiny, round green thing now is it? Come on and sit with your nana while Aunty Moira gets you something to eat.'

'You're not my nana and I don't like them.' The tone was getting decidedly belligerent as he dug his heels in.

Roisin, recognising the warning signs of a full-blown cyclonic tantrum gaining momentum, tried to smooth things over. 'Ah sure, Mammy, he's grand, don't fuss over him, he had something to eat at the airport, what he really needs is to get to bed.'

'I want to go home and I want my daddy!'

That was when Moira, Aisling and Maureen all paused and took stock.

'Where *is* Colin, Rosi? I think you'd better tell us what's going on,' Mammy said.

Chapter 10

♥

'Cup of coffee?' Aisling, looking extremely perky given the early hour, gestured to the kettle which was on the cusp of boiling. 'I don't think we'll be seeing Mammy or Moira for a good while yet.'

'Jet lag's a sod. It will take them a few days to come right I expect and I'd love a peppermint tea if there's any?' Roisin replied before yawning.

'Jaysus, I saw your tonsils then. We don't have any of that herbal shite as Moira calls it. I can do you an English Breakfast though,' Aisling grinned. She was ready to face the day ahead dressed in a sweater, and black trousers. Her make-up was on and her hair fell in glossy waves. Roisin felt short and washed out as she stood next to her sister, rubbing bleary eyes before tightening the cord of her dressing gown. It was only after she yawned again that she realised she hadn't shrunk overnight; Aisling had her customary heels on hence the height difference. Roisin was not yet awake enough to name which designer brand the black mules belonged to but she was just enough awake to say yes to a brew.

'English Breakfast will be grand.' She left her sister to it and, noticing the curtains were still drawn, Roisin moved through the darkened living room keen to see what sort of day it was outside. She pulled back the heavy drapes, hooking them away from the window with the tiebacks. The panes of glass hiding behind them were frosty. She peered through a clear patch, to the familiar Green across the busy road below. How spindly the trees looked dotted around the park, stripped bare like they were for winter. She wondered if the duck pond had frozen over and if so what would the ducks do? She'd take Noah across for a blast of fresh air later. She made a mental note to herself to see if Mrs Flaherty had any stale bread she could spare so they could feed the ducks.

It would be freezing out but they could rug up. She loved winter days like this one was promising to be. To her mind they felt hopeful. The sort of day that would break through winter's damp gloom to wash the sky blue. The air outside, she knew, would be sharp and crisp like a tart apple and although she didn't know what today would bring, she did know it couldn't be worse than what yesterday morning had brought. Roisin turned away from the window in order to commandeer her favourite chair. It was an old-fashioned wingback beside the large picture window she'd just been peering through. She curled up in it before pulling the throw blanket draped over its arm across her lap to wait for her cuppa.

The pipes were gurgling as the central heating worked its magic and the sound was oddly comforting, until her mind drifted back over the conversation she'd had with her mammy before taking herself off to bed.

***

Roisin wasn't one for swearing, unlike Moira, but Jaysus, feck what a nightmare last night had been. It replayed before her like an appalling episode of a family sitcom. 'There you are, Rosi, I thought you'd got the plane back to London you were gone so long,' Maureen said spying her pale faced eldest daughter dallying in the doorway. 'Holy God above tonight, Roisin, will you stop your fidgeting, and sit down and tell me what's going on?'

Roisin sat down at the table before clearing her throat and blurting, 'I've left Colin.' *Had she really just said the words out loud? Yes, judging by Mammy's, Moira's and Aisling's bulging eyes, she had.*

The only sound in the ensuing seconds was that of the old grandfather clock as the pendulum swung back and forth. It was a noise Roisin had always liked. A ticking clock for some was irritating but for her she found the steady rhythm soothing. Now, it sounded ominous like a bomb about to go off. She smoothed the ruck in the tablecloth for want of something to do with her hands.

'I think I'm after mishearing you.'

Roisin looked up and found herself pinned by Mammy's buggy eyes while her sisters sat statue-still trying not to be noticed. Aisling had a biscuit half raised to her mouth and Moira who'd been about to trim a toenail had a pair of open nail scissors in her hand. They'd all done the same thing as kids when they thought they might be asked to leave the room because 'this was an adult conversation'.

'No, Mammy, I think you heard me. I said I've left Colin.'

'Sweet and merciful Jesus, I heard you the first time.' Maureen shook her head, her beads a-clacking as she spied Moira. 'God Almighty how many times do I have to tell you not to cut your toenails in here? That's a job best done in the privacy of the bathroom, so it is.' She flapped her hand, her agitation obvious in the excessive references to God and his son. 'Ah go on with yer and fetch your sister a cup of tea, and Aisling put that biscuit down it's the last one, give it to Rosi, she needs it more than you do.' Maureen paused for breath, she felt better when she was handing out instructions—like she was in control.

Aisling, who'd gotten up to do as she was told, would have scowled at handing over the last custard cream were it not for the pink goop on her face and the gravity of the situation. Roisin nibbled away at it fascinated by the way Mammy's lips were working feverishly as she batted, back and forth with herself over what she wanted to say next.

'Rosi, to announce you're after leaving your husband like that, well it's not good for a woman of my years. There's my heart to be thinking of you know.'

'There's nothing wrong with your heart, Mammy, it's your foot that's the problem,' Moira called overtop of the boiling kettle before mouthing at Roisin, 'dramatic.'

Maureen ignored her. 'Could you not word things a little more softly? You're all floaty and vague normally, why'd you pick now to get all hard? It doesn't suit you.'

'Because I can't dress it up, Mammy, there's no other way of saying it and you asked me what was going on.'

'Sure, use your imagination. What about 'me and Colin we're after having a bit of time apart?' There now doesn't that sound better? Much less final.' She looked to her other two daughters, seeking confirmation that this did indeed work much better. Moira was busy stirring the tea but Aisling nodded her agreement. Roisin shot her a look that said she was a brown-noser. She was feeling very much on the back foot and as such her defences were up. It was ridiculous how Mammy could make her, a grown woman, feel like a teenager. Sure, hadn't she found her first white hair just the other day.

'Is it the...' all their eyes followed their mammy's gaze to the sideboard where the wooden fertility canoe stood proudly erect, '...rumpy-pumpy?'

Roisin made a strangled sound as she mentally screamed, 'nooo, I'm not having this conversation.' But she was.

'Because, Rosi,' Maureen looked from one to the other, 'sure we're all adults here, all girls together.' Aisling and Moira had both paled at the turn the conversation had taken. 'Your father and I, we went through a dry patch so we did. Oh yes, there wasn't any rooty-toot-tootin going on, and I thought that was it for us. Now, granted I was a little bit older than you and having the hot flushes at the time but I reached out for help and my friend Kate, you know Kate Finnegan, Ita's mammy, got me onto a herbal supplement. She said it had worked wonders for her and Ned. And girls, I don't mind telling you, whatever it was in those vitamin thing-a-me bobs, it was rocket fuel. It gave my libido a new lease of life.' She looked pleased with herself as she continued, 'And, if you're not keen on taking something, there's always counselling. There's, people who specialise in that area you know, Rosi. It's not just left to the family priest to offer advice like it was in my day. Sure, it's nothing to be ashamed of. Although, talking to a stranger about what you do or don't get up to in the marital chamber wouldn't be any easy thing to do and, from my experience, men are very defensive when it comes that sort-a thing. Still and all it's your marriage that's on the line, Rosi, and you've that little boy to be thinking of.'

'Mammy!' Roisin leapt in seeing Maureen had finally paused for breath. 'Sex isn't the problem.'

'Softly, Rosi, I said softly!' She sat forward and the inquisition began, rapid fire drilling until finally Roisin blurted.

'It's money that's the fecking problem. Colin's after borrowing on the house to finance some deal he was involved in and it's all fallen through. We're going to lose everything.'

'Roisin O'Mara, I raised you to be a better woman than to quit when the going gets tough.'

If she were to launch into *Stand by Your Man*, Roisin knew she would not be responsible for her actions. 'He didn't tell me about any of it, Mammy. He re-mortgaged the house behind my back and the only reason I know the bank's foreclosing on us is because I found the letters with the big red ink all over them that he's been hiding.'

'Oh.' Maureen was silent but only briefly. 'Granted, that's not good. No, for a woman to lose the roof over her head, that's not good at all, but sure if you love him, Rosi, you can find a way through. I won't see my family homeless. I've a bit put by.'

'That's just it, Mammy, I don't love him anymore. I'd been pretending to myself that everything was alright but it made me realise I'd stopped loving him quite a while ago. So, you see, I don't think there's any way through.'

'I always knew that chinless feck was an arse,' Moira said, putting Rosi's tea down on the table in front of her.

'Moira, that's not helpful,' Mammy said.

'No, but it's true.' Aisling backed her sister up.

'Ah, Rosi, what are you going to do?' Maureen bemoaned.

'I don't know, Mammy. I need some time to sort myself out and to figure out what my next step is going to be. How we're going to manage. I've got to work out what's best for Noah too, whether we stay here or go back to London.' She shrugged, 'I just don't know and my head's buzzing, so it is.'

'I'm not surprised. Well, this is yours and Noah's home, you know that.'

'I know, thanks.' She looked at her mammy and sisters and raised a small smile.

Maureen patted the seat beside her, much like she'd done to her grandson earlier. 'C'mere.'

Roisin made her way over and flopped down in between her mammy and Aisling finding herself enveloped in a bosomy maternal hug. She smelled the familiar scent of Arpège and snuggled in.

'It'll be alright, Rosi,' Aisling said. 'You're made of strong stuff. You're an O'Mara so you are. I didn't think I'd ever be happy again after Marcus left but things happen for a reason. Old doors shut and new doors with much better things behind them open.'

Moira perched down on the arm of the sofa. 'Can I ring him and call him a chinless feck?'

'No!' The three women chimed.

Chapter 11

Roisin blinked coming back to the here and now as she realised Aisling was standing in front of her clutching a mug. She was looking at her expectantly. 'Sorry, I was miles away. Thanks.' She took the tea.

'Did you sleep alright?' Aisling asked, settling herself on the sofa.

Roisin blew on the steaming brew and took a tentative sip before answering, 'No, not really my mind was whirring and Noah turned into a kick-boxing champ in his sleep. I feel like I'm black and blue.' She told her sister how he'd been restless all night but then she was grateful for small blessings like the fact he'd actually slept. His meltdown the night before had been of epic proportions and as he revved up, Moira had announced she was off downstairs to pinch a packet of custard creams from Bronagh's stash. 'It's Mammy's fault,' she'd said shooting Maureen a look, 'she ate the last of the Jacob's Clubs.' Roisin had passed her sister returning with the biscuits as she hauled a kicking and screaming five-year-old off to her old room.

She'd had to lie in bed with him, listening to his sniffling and snuffling as he sobbed that he wanted his daddy to come and tuck him in. Children always expected you to be able to perform the impossible, she'd mused, stroking his soft, sweet smelling hair and contemplating whether she should ring Colin so he could say goodnight to his son. She couldn't face it though; it was too soon. He'd demand to know what she was playing at; he'd twist things around so that, somehow, she'd begin to feel as though it was her who was behaving unreasonably. It would only serve to make matters worse. So, she'd left well alone and finally Noah's breathing had slowed and evened out as he slipped into a deep slumber.

She'd waited until she was certain he was asleep before doing a commando roll off the bed and crawling out of the room on her hands and knees, not willing to risk waking him up. It was going to be bad enough facing the Irish Inquisition—Mammy and her sisters. Once safely in the hallway she stood up and knowing she couldn't lurk about out there all night she took a deep breath and, hoping they'd left her a biscuit, went to tell them why she'd left Colin.

'Just like top and tailing with Moira then. I had her big, smelly foot in my face most of the night.' Aisling said when Roisin had finished.

'Sorry,' Roisin said shooting her a small apologetic grin. Aisling had given up her bed for Roisin and Noah.

'Ah well, it was better than having Mammy's big casty foot under my nose.' The alternative had been to share with Maureen.

Roisin couldn't help herself; the tea was waking her up. 'We should start calling her Bigfoot.'

'Or Sasquatch,' Aisling giggled.

'There's been an unconfirmed sighting of that elusive creature, the Yeti in a Dublin guesthouse.'

The sisters both snorted. 'Seriously, though,' Aisling said putting her mug down on the coffee table, 'she could have come away from their holiday in a lot worse state. Moira did well, keeping it together and finding help. Rather her than me. They were in the middle of nowhere when Mammy fell by all accounts.'

'Hmm. Why she needed to go trekking around in some mountain village area is beyond me. I mean Vietnam, it's not your usual week in Spain is it?'

'No, but she says she's ticked sailing on a junk off her bucket list now.'

'I'd hate to think what's next on the list. Roisin frowned. 'Moira seems different.'

'She does, doesn't she? I think the trip changed her. You know she's decided to quit her job and go to art college. She says she had an epiphany while she was travelling.'

Roisin raised an eyebrow; so that was what Mammy had been on about last night. 'Really? Good for her. She always did have a real talent when it came to painting. Remember Foxy Loxy?' Roisin glanced around the room and saw the mark on the wall where the painting her sister had done of the little red fox who was prone to visiting the bins out the back of the guesthouse had always hung. It had won Moira first place in a prestigious children's art competition. 'Where's it gone?'

'Mammy took it with her.'

'Ah,' Roisin nodded. That made sense. It always had been a source of pride to Mammy and her favourite conversational piece. 'I'll find out more about this epiphany of Moira's today. I didn't get a chance to talk to her last night, not properly at any rate. Wasn't it the worst?'

Aisling nodded.

'I nearly died when Mammy asked me if Colin and I were having problems in the rumpy-pumpy department. God, she missed her calling. She'd have done well in the gards. She's like your Mirren woman in the *Prime Suspect* only not sexy and with ridiculous braids the way she manages to get stuff out of you. I can just see her sitting across a table grilling some poor sod until he caves. She was the same when we were teenagers and we asked if we could go to a party remember?'

Aisling nodded. 'I soon copped on to that and I'd always go and ask Dad first. He was a yes-man when it came to that sort of thing. Anything for a bit of peace.' She smiled and Roisin smiled back both drifting off for a moment in their own memories of their dad.

'I miss him,' Aisling spoke up first.

'Me too.'

'I thought I'd get used to him not being here anymore but it still feels like there's a hole where he used to be.'

'I don't think grief works like that, Ash. I think it's more of a gradual acceptance that they're not going to walk through the door ever again but I don't know if you ever stop missing them. It just shifts so it doesn't hurt so badly. How's Mammy doing? I always ask how she's getting on and she always says she's grand and launches into whoever is getting up her nose that week at golf, or something like.'

'Well, apart from doing mad things like heading off to Vietnam and dragging Moira along for the ride, I think she's doing okay. She's making noises about getting a dog. The company will be good for her and,' Aisling tapped the side of her nose, 'Moira told me they went and saw this fortune teller lady who predicts your love life while they were away. She said Mammy was behaving most enigmatically after she'd seen her. So,' she shrugged, 'who knows.'

'Really?' Roisin was thrown. She simply couldn't imagine her mammy with anyone else other than her dad but she was only in her sixties and she didn't like the thought of her being on her own for the rest of her days either. A thought jabbed her. Oh Jaysus, who was to say she wouldn't wind up living her days out with Mammy in her Howth apartment? The only bright spot in that scenario was Mammy was talking dogs not cats, that way she wouldn't turn into a mad old cat lady. At least Aisling was in a good place with Quinn. She'd known her sister's other half since he and Aisling had been students. He was a lovely fella and she'd always wondered why the pair of them had never hooked up. They'd seemed like the perfect match to everyone but each other.

CHAPTER 1161

'I'm pleased you and Quinn have finally got your act together.' Roisin had been as shocked as the rest of them when Aisling's fiancé, Marcus, had walked out on her in the weeks before their planned wedding but sometimes things happened for a reason. It might not seem like there was any rhyme or reason at the time but sure, look at how it had all worked out. That was something she very much needed to hold onto right now.

'Me too,' Aisling got a daft look on her face. 'You haven't been to his bistro have you?'

'No, but from what you've said it's a popular spot.'

'It is. Why don't we go there for dinner tonight? You'll love it, the craic's great with the traditional music and the food is fantastic. Quinn's is always a hit with our guests.'

'And you're not biased at all.'

'Not a bit.'

Dad would have been really happy to see you two together, you know.'

'You think?'

'I know.'

Roisin could recall the conversation where he'd shaken his head in bewilderment over Aisling and Quinn, saying it was plain as day they were meant for each other. He'd bewailed that short of banging their heads together and giving their current boyfriend and girlfriend the auld heave-ho, it wasn't happening.

Aisling looked pleased and they sat in silence lost in their own thoughts until Aisling spoke up, 'So you're really not going back to him then?'

Roisin shook her head slowly, 'I'm really not.'

'I don't blame you not after what you told us. He's broken your trust.'

'I know you, Moira and Mammy never liked him. As for Daddy, well he was just grateful I wasn't going to be an unmarried mother.' She pondered her brother. 'Him and Pat were always thick as thieves, a shared mutual passion for money.'

Aisling squirmed in her seat. 'It's not that we didn't like him exactly, Rosi, it was more you seemed such an odd match.'

Roisin raised an eyebrow. 'Moira calls him Colin the Arse and I know she thinks he's got no chin.'

'Yes but that's Moira, she calls most people arses and to be fair he actually doesn't have a chin.'

The two sisters looked at each other and snickered. Aisling said, 'At least Noah didn't get the chinless gene.'

'I think you were right about us being an odd match,' Roisin said when she'd stopped giggling. 'As the years have rolled over we seem to have had less and less in common. If I'm honest, Ash, I married him because I was trying to be sensible for the first time in my life, and I suppose I thought I loved him.'

'Ah, Rosi, sure, that's not who you are. You've never been sensible.'

'Thanks very much.'

Aisling wasn't contrite in the least. 'It's true. But you know it's a big thing to leave him and start afresh what with Noah and everything.'

'Other women do it.' Roisin thought about the conversation she'd had in the café yesterday with Stephanie. 'It's not sudden my leaving, not really. Like I said the money thing was just the straw that broke the camel's back and it gave me the push I needed to take action. If I'm honest though, Ash, the thought of standing on my own two feet after all this time terrifies me. I never thought I'd be the type to sit back and let someone else take charge of my life but that's exactly what I let happen.'

'Well, we're here for you. You know that and it'll be a good craic having you and Noah stay.'

Roisin smiled at her sister. 'Thanks, Ash.'

Aisling got up and stretched before carting her mug over to the sink. 'I'm not looking forward to going downstairs.

There's the wrath of Bronagh for one thing. She'll know we pinched her custards creams by now and the most awful grump checked in yesterday. Mr Donovan, he's staying in room one, he's done nothing but complain since he got here. The world's against him so it is.'

'Ah sure, blame Moira for stealing the biscuits. Bronagh's a soft spot for Moira and yer man in room one will be putty in your hands. Just turn on the old Aisling charm. You've always had a way with people.'

'Not with him, I haven't. He's a very rude man, so he is, but you're right about Moira. I'll tell Bronagh it was all down to her. She smiled at her sister. 'What have you planned this morning?'

'I think I shall sit here a little longer and then if nobody's up, do some yoga. It makes me feel more centred.'

'I never got yoga, all that stretching and breathing but each to their own, like.'

Roisin grinned. Aisling didn't exercise full stop, although she had taken up the salsa dancing. That would get her heart rate going. She remembered Moira ringing her to tell her Quinn and Aisling had done a demonstration of the moves they'd learned at their salsa classes and she'd said it was obscene, so it was, all the hip gyrating the pair of them were after doing. 'I'd like to take Noah over to the Green later to feed the ducks too. And, I suppose I shall have to telephone Colin and tell him we arrived alright and that this is where we're staying for the time being.'

She hadn't switched her phone back on when they'd gotten off the plane and checking it before bed last night she'd seen she had half a dozen calls from Colin. She'd been clear in the note she left about him giving her space to think but in typical Colin style, he was having none of it. She'd texted him to tell him she was serious about not wanting to speak to him and that he was NOT to try and ring her at O'Mara's or try her mobile again. Her fingers had worked furiously as she let him know she'd ring him soon.

'I don't envy you that. Good luck and don't let him bully you, Rosi.'

'I won't.' It was easy to be strong over the phone and with over three hundred miles between them.

Aisling disappeared down the hall and Roisin sat in the ensuing silence, bathed in a pool of wintery sunlight which had begun puddling over her. She'd take Noah down to see Bronagh and Mrs Flaherty once he was awake properly. Mrs Flaherty might make him his favourite, a rasher sandwich that was sure to get his day off to a good start. Whatever she did, she mustn't let him pick up on how she was feeling.

She'd have to put a cheery face on things even if she did feel sick at the thought of what she was supposed to do now. It wouldn't do him any good to pick up on his mam's inner turmoil and if he was miserable then Colin was sure to insist she bring him home. Roisin sighed and picked at a thread on the blanket. Noah couldn't stay off school forever, at best she might get away with a week or two before the school began making noises and she didn't want to give Colin any ammunition. She shivered as a thought occurred to her; what would she do if Colin decided Noah should live with him? She pushed it aside. Colin loved his son but he couldn't cope with him on his own. Mind you, could she?

'This is no good, Rosi,' she muttered to the empty room. She needed to be proactive. It wouldn't do her any good to dwell on 'what ifs'. She pushed the blanket aside; first things first. She got up and padded over to the kitchen and opened the cupboard doors. Mammy had always kept the treats hidden behind the mushy pea tins and the like; she pulled the cans out and yes! Her luck was in, there it was a solitary Jacob's Mint Club bar. How long it had lain there undetected she didn't know. What she did know was that her usual whole grain, high energy breakfast would not cut it today. She ate the biscuit in two bites and then at the realisation it had probably sat there since 1990, felt a little sick. Served her right she thought, regretting her breakfast choice as she put the cans back and closed the cupboard doors.

The apartment was still silent so she moved back through to the living room undoing her dressing gown and taking it off, she threw it on the chair. She hadn't brought her yoga mat, the rug in front of the television would have to do this morning. She didn't want to go into the bedroom to retrieve her workout gear either because if she woke Noah, she'd have no show of clearing her buzzing brain with a few meditational stretches. Nope, her jailbreak striped pyjamas would suffice.

Roisin placed her hands over her heart before swinging them wide and lifting them skyward to stand in a raised arm, mountain pose. She breathed in and then out, slow and steady, feeling her heart rate slow as she slipped into her well-honed routine. She arched her back in cat-cow pose then sat in pigeon pose; she was a proud warrior and her round of sun salutations balanced her equilibrium and warmed her body before she eased her body up into downward facing dog. She was in the zone and feeling tranquil as she rested briefly in this position only to collapse in a heap as a voice sounded behind her.

'For fecks sake, Rosi, you'll rip the arse out of your bottoms waving it in the air like that. Put it away would yer? Jaysus nobody needs to be greeted with that first thing in the morning.' Moira's hair was mussed and her eyes were still heavy with sleep. She looked, Roisin thought, like a wild woman. She'd forgotten what her little sister was like before she'd had her morning cup of tea.

'And good morning to you too, Moira.'

Chapter 12

Reggie Donovan had been in a foul mood as he exited his room that morning. He'd overslept thanks to his broken night. It had him out of sorts because Reggie was a man of routine, even when he was away from home. Not that he left his home in the small village of Castlebeg, where he'd lived for most of his days, very often for the simple reason of, where would he go? His befuddled head was all down to that blasted fox who'd raided the rubbish bin under his window last night. It had taken him an age to slip back off to sleep after the ruckus it had made and when he had, he'd slept heavily.

It wasn't good enough given the exorbitant amount he was paying for his room. Daylight robbery was what it was and that was another thing, he'd griped, closing his door behind him, breakfast should be included in the room rate. He'd paused, with his hand resting on the rail at the top of the stairs leading down to the dining room, his nose twitching not unlike the fox's had last night at the whiff of bacon tickling his nostrils. The aroma was wafting up from what once would have been the basement servant quarters. He'd been of two minds, should he tell the woman on reception about his interrupted night or head down those stairs where the promise of a cup of tea and a pile of rashers waited. It was the smell of bacon that won out in the end. He didn't eat much these days, he'd no appetite for food, but the smell of that bacon had him peckish for the first time in a long while.

Now, as he dipped his toast into his egg yolk he spied the girl with the copper hair who was in charge of the place. She was making her rounds of the dining room, smiling and chatting with her guests as they told her of their plans for the day. It occurred to him that he could bypass yer one who seemed to permanently have a biscuit raised halfway to her mouth on reception and go straight to the top brass with his complaint about last night's unwelcome visitor. To his surprise though, he realised he was no longer of a mind to. He would rather enjoy his breakfast. It was a treat to find the food wasn't sticking in his gullet.

Aisling had seen Mr Donovan as soon as she'd left the kitchen and ventured into the dining room. He was sitting as far away from the other guests as he could. She'd noticed he was tucking in to his breakfast with gusto which she hoped meant he wouldn't find fault with it. His suit hung on him like a sack and his face was gaunt with shadows. He was in need of a good breakfast, she thought, and besides she didn't need him complaining. Mrs Flaherty, the cook, would go into orbit were he to make noises about their being anything not quite right with what she'd presented him with.

Mrs Flaherty's mood was not as sunny as it could it be this morning thanks to Mr Fox having paid a call last night. She shook her head. How that woman managed to string so many fecks alongside the word fox was beyond her but she'd finally pacified her by telling her Noah and Roisin had come to stay. The thought of a little lad to fuss over improved both her language and her mood instantaneously.

She chatted to Mr and Mrs Bunting as to their plans for the day while they enjoyed a pot of tea and waited for their eggs on toast. The couple were over on a city break from Portsmouth. Mrs Bunting chatted away about their planned tour of Kilmainham Gaol where the Easter Rising Rebels had been held. 'Do you know the quickest route to Church Street from here, Aisling?' Mr Bunting interrupted his wife. 'We'd like to pop in on the mummies at St Michan's Crypt on Church Street after breakfast.' He was seemingly oblivious to how his question sounded and Aisling did her best to keep a straight face as she gave him directions. Mrs Flaherty appeared a tick later balancing two plates boasting thick buttery slabs of soda bread each topped with plump poached eggs. She left them to tuck in, moving on to the family from South Africa who were touring the country with their two daughters under ten in tow.

There were no guests left to converse with by the time she'd exchanged pleasantries with Ciara Brady who was in the city for a conference and the Reillys from Cork. Their son and his wife had just had a baby—their first grandchild. The couple lived in a flat you couldn't swing a cat in so the Reillys had opted for O'Mara's which happened to be where they'd honeymooned many years earlier. Back then it had been run by a young Maureen O'Mara and her husband.

Aisling had told them that her daddy had passed away but that her mammy was still very much with them. She told them she was certain Maureen would dearly love for them to pop up and remember themselves to her as she was incapacitated at present on account of a broken foot which was a long story for another morning given they were keen for the off. She could see they were itching to have a hold of their new granddaughter. So it was, she found herself having worked her way around the room to the far corner where Reggie Donovan was sitting. Above his head was the sepia print of turn of the century O'Connell Street.

She made sure her smile was firmly in place as she said, 'Good morning, Mr Donovan, and how are you today? I trust everything's to your satisfaction.' She crossed her fingers behind her back and to her amazement he paused in his toast dipping to tell her he was thoroughly enjoying his choice of a full Irish, thank you very much. She'd been braced for another round of complaints and it took her a moment to reply. 'That's grand so it is, I shall pass on your compliments to our cook, Mrs Flaherty, she'll be delighted. Now then what have you planned for the day ahead?'

Reggie had no intention of telling her or any other nosy so and so what he was going to be getting up to. 'This and that,' he replied, returning to the task at hand.

Common sense told Aisling she should leave while the going was good and so she wished him a good day and left him to finish his meal in peace. She ducked back into the kitchen on her way out to pass on his praise. Two rosy red spots of pleasure appeared on the cook's dumpling cheeks and Aisling left her humming as she set about washing dishes. It was time she went and faced the wrath of Bronagh who would be waiting for an explanation as to the whereabouts of her custard creams.

Reggie watched Aisling go and then, satisfied he wouldn't be further interrupted, he polished off what was left on his plate. It wasn't often he dined out, nor in these latter months did he often manage a full meal. This morning though he'd decided to throw caution to the wind and have the full monty so to speak. He had nothing to lose after all. He hadn't been disappointed either because the white pudding had been cooked exactly the way he liked it, crispy on the outside, smooth and creamy on the inside. There'd been a mound of bacon too and the rounds of toast had been generous. If it was his last meal, he'd die happy. There was no doubt about it, that Mrs Flaherty woman knew her way around a kitchen.

Yes, it was hands down the best breakfast he'd had in a long time he mused placing his knife and fork down on the plate and settling back in his seat. His Deirdre used to make him a good breakfast. She'd spouted many times during their marriage that a man needed a full belly of a morning to see him through his day. Reggie had been grateful for it too, especially on those cold winter's mornings when he'd set off down the icy laneway to the woollen mill. It was on the edge of the village where he'd worked his way up through the ranks since leaving the high school. Back then he'd been in charge of overseeing the operation of the looms and his days had been long, but the thought of a hot meal and the company of his Deirdre at the end of the day always spurred him on.

He'd never been a man for pints at The Mill like some of the lads he'd worked with over the years, well not often anyway. If he were to close his eyes he could still see ruddy faced Jimmy O'Leary on one of those rare occasions when he had wet his lips after his shift. The long-suffering Mrs O'Leary had burst through the door of the pub, a face on her that would curdle the freshest of milk and a bowl of stew in hand which she'd banged down in front of her man. 'Well now, since you spend more time here than you do at home you might as well have your dinner here too,' the woman had sneered before turning on her heel and banging back out from whence she came.

Reggie had worked at that woollen mill his entire life until the day he'd been given a gold watch and a bottle of Bushmills finest. He'd lived through the industry's lean times when it was thought the Castlebeg mill might close and the rumours on the floor were rife, to the boom time when Irish knits became fashionable. There'd come a time when it hadn't just been Deirdre he'd been coming home to see at the end of the day either. Ah, his Jodie had been a bonny baby—how Deirdre had doted on that child. Mind she'd been a miracle they'd never thought the good Lord would see fit to bless them with.

A smile at the thought of his late wife twitched his lips as he topped up his cup of tea and wondered over the restorative properties of a good breakfast. Not even the thought of what lay ahead today could dent his good humour. It was as he raised his teacup to his lips that he saw the cook herself bustling toward him. She was wiping her hands on her apron as she bore down on him. It was most disconcerting especially given the blue language he'd heard coming from the kitchen along with the sizzle of bacon hitting the fat earlier.

For Mrs Flaherty's part there was nothing she liked more than a clean plate. It was, to her mind, the highest compliment a cook could be given. It ranked above being told as Aisling had just done, that a guest had enjoyed their meal because it was, so to speak, the proof of the pudding. The plate she had in her line of sight now looked as though it had been licked clean and it warmed her heart to see the beatific if slightly startled expression on Mr Donovan's face. For a man who was no taller than she was and whose scrawny build was dwarfed by her thick padding, he'd done himself proud. She could see the curmudgeonly mood he'd been in when he'd sat down at the table and proceeded to hold his knife and fork up to the light for inspection had been quashed by her full Irish. *Ah, it warmed her heart, so it did.*

She wasn't a silly woman. Her time spent working as a cook at O'Mara's had fine-tuned her ability to read the guests who'd frequented her dining room over the years. She'd had Reggie Donovan pegged from the moment he sat down. It was in the hunch of his shoulders and the pleats of discontent on his forehead. He wasn't a well man, she could tell. He was also a man who'd reached his twilight years and found himself disappointed by the journey undertaken to get there. He'd make no bones about this disappointment and his waspish manner would only serve to push people away. Beneath his bearish coat, the man was no doubt lonely and Mrs Flaherty was a firm believer that a good meal and a kind word could slough away even the prickliest of exteriors. She came to a halt beside his table, her cheeks dimpling into soft doughy mounds as she asked, seeing how he was clearly finished, whether she could take his plate and might he be tempted to sample her homemade marmalade with an extra round of toast—on the house of course.

Reggie was flustered by the woman's jovial manner and beaming face. People didn't often send a smile his way these days and when they did, he usually gave them short shrift. There was something about her though that told him he'd do well to mind his p's and q's. Perhaps it was her no-nonsense demeanour or the expletives he'd heard her uttering before, or maybe it was as simple as the way she'd just wiped her floury hands on the apron she wore over her clothes in order to take his plate. Whatever it was, there was something about her that reminded him of Deirdre. 'That would be grand, thank you,' he managed to reply as he put his plate in her outstretched hands. She gave him a nod and as he watched her waddling frame retreat to the kitchen a wave of sadness washed over him.

He'd once lived in a cottage that smelt of slow cooking mutton and soda bread. You could have yer fancy French lotions and potions because to his mind the smell of a meal to be served alongside a fresh loaf was the scent of true love. His throat tightened with memories. He missed his Deirdre as keenly now as he had the day she'd died! It had all gone so terribly wrong after that. He'd made such a mess of things. He'd been a better man when she was in the world that was for sure. It was as if a part of him, the part that had been warm and kind, had withered inside after she passed. They'd had a grand life together. It was just an altogether too short life.

Reggie had become bitter at his loss. Why was it his wife who'd gotten the cancer so young? Deirdre, who'd never had a cross word with anyone, who'd do anything for anyone and who was good through to her very bones. He'd never understand the workings of Him upstairs.

He'd been left to raise Jodie at a time when he hadn't been fit to look after himself let alone his daughter. He recalled the concerned face of Deirdre's auld mam as she suggested that perhaps the best thing all around would be for Jodie to come and live with her and Bill but he wouldn't have it. Selfish eejit that he was. He'd lost Deirdre, he wouldn't lose Jodie too. He'd seen their good intentions as interference, taken their offers of help as a slight on his fathering abilities, and as such had cross words. Ugly words. Words that couldn't be unsaid once uttered and then years later when she needed him most he'd done the unthinkable.

Reggie glanced at the large clock on the wall by the entrance to the dining room, its hands tick, tick, ticking around. If by getting up and pushing those hands backward he could turn back time, then he'd do it in a heartbeat. He'd let Deirdre down with his disservice to Jodie but pride ran through the Donovan family's veins thicker than blood itself and it had brought many a meeker man down than him.

Today he'd see his girl again, only she'd stopped being a girl a long time ago. He'd summon the courage to say sorry before it was too late. The cancer that had taken his Deirdre was taking him now and he knew that when his time came he wouldn't be able to look his Deirdre in the eyes if he hadn't made his peace with Jodie.

Chapter 13

♥

1971 - Jodie

Jodie placed the bottle of Collis Browne liquid, Mr Hogan the pharmacist had just made up, in the bag. 'There you are, Mrs Buckley. I hope Mr Buckley feels better soon,' she said to the woman standing on the other side of the counter as she ripped a piece of Sellotape from the dispenser. Mrs Buckley had a scarf knotted tightly under her chin and a floral housecoat on, which suggested she'd just nipped out to collect her husband's fortnightly supply of cough mixture before the chemist shop closed for the evening.

Mr Buckley's was a cough Jodie was dubious about as, given the length of time Mrs Buckley had been calling in for a top up of the Collis Browne tincture meant he'd had it for the best part of six months. He sent his wife to Hogan's Pharmacy on the main street of Castlebeg Village to pick him up a bottle of the linctus every Friday. 'See if Mr Hogan would be kind enough to make me up a drop of that marvellous mixture, young Jodie,' Mrs Buckley would say. 'It's the only thing that eases my poor Donald's chest.' Now the woman added, 'Oh and I'll take a packet of Bonnington's while you're at it.'

Jodie dutifully retrieved the packet of Irish moss from the shelf behind the counter. She'd weighed and bagged them earlier in the day. She popped them in the bag alongside the cough syrup knowing the woman ate the Irish moss like sweets. The thought of the black, sugar coated jubes mild laxative effect meant she always had to choke back a wee giggle. As for Mr Buckley, well she was sure he used the opium tincture it contained it to help him sleep of a night. Sure, hadn't he stopped to say hello as he headed out of The Mill on his way home a few evenings ago and him with a sprightly spring in his step and not so much as a frog in this throat! He probably needed to knock himself out what with all that Irish moss his wife was after eating! she'd sniggered to herself.

Her employer, Mr Hogan, was one for letting sleeping dogs lie when it came to his customers and if a drop of tincture helped a man through a long night, then so be it. Who was he to make a fuss? She could hear the familiar sound of tablets being spilled into the tray behind her before he began counting them out for Mr Kiley's prescription. She glanced over to where Jim Kiley was eyeing a hair tonic for baldness. Sometimes Mr Hogan got her to help him out the back as it was a busy dispensary given the small village they lived in. The day would fly on those occasions and it beat the dusting of the shelves hands down.

Jodie remembered herself. 'Sorry, I was miles away then Mrs Buckley— is it on account?'

'Yes, thank you, dear.' The older woman took the paper bag. 'Enjoy the weekend, won't you, and remember me to your da. We're in for sunshine, I think. Have a nice weekend, Mr Hogan.'

Mr Hogan looked up and gave her a wave.

'I will do, you too, Mrs Buckley,' Jodie said, stopping herself from adding, see you next week. There's was a routine but it was a routine not to be acknowledged and with her package in hand the woman bustled out of the shop.

'Jodie,' Mr Hogan summoned her and she stepped up into the dispensary and took the prescription he was holding out to her. 'Be sure to tell Mr Kiley to take two, three times a day with food or a glass of milk at the very least and he's not to mix them with alcohol.'

She nodded and returned to the shop floor. 'Mr Kiley, I have your prescription.' The little man jumped at the sound of her voice and looked sheepish at having been caught looking at the tonic. Jodie thought it would take more than tonic to sort him out as she bagged his pills up and he made a show of fishing his wallet out of his back pocket. He might be small of stature but just because he was eye level with her boobs didn't mean he had to direct his conversation at them. What did he expect them to say? She recited Mr Hogan's instructions and when she got to the part about not imbibing she heard him snort behind her. She took that to mean he didn't fancy Jim Kiley's chances of leaving the bottle alone long enough for the antibiotics to clear up his infection.

Jim was often seen staggering out of The Mill at closing time, singing at the top of his lungs, determined to carry on even if the party was only for one. 'Ah, you can put your wallet away. There's no charge for that, Mr Kiley,' she added brightly taking a perverse pleasure in speaking to his bald spot as she remembered Mr Hogan telling her on her first day, fresh out of school, that the customer was king. She received a leering smile for her troubles. King or not she still pulled a face at the auld perve's back as she followed him to the door, seeing him out before flipping the sign from open to closed. There was only the nightly routine of settling up the till left to do and then she could be on her way.

Jodie was itching to leave tonight. Not because she was in a rush to get home. She was never in a rush to get home but because the sooner she did, the sooner she could sort Da's dinner and be off down the road to Bridie's. It was the first Friday of the month and they were grabbing a ride over to Tubberclair with Bridie's big sister Edie and her fella to the parish hall disco. It had been the longest four weeks of her life.

She'd bitten her nails down to the quick, which more than one customer had remarked upon with a tut, waiting for tonight's monthly disco to roll around.

She had her eye on a lad she'd spotted under the flickering lights, just before she and Bridie had gotten the look from Edie to say they were leaving, the last time they'd gone. She'd not seen him at the dance before and she'd not stopped thinking about the slow, easy smile he'd shot her way since. Her tummy would do the strangest flip every time she conjured him up and she wondered if he'd look as much like David Cassidy as she remembered—she loved David Cassidy. She'd even dipped into her savings to buy a new dress for tonight, her and Bridie giggling over its indecent length.

'You'd better wear your best knickers come Friday,' Bridie had laughed, 'you'll be flashing them right enough every time you bend over.' A note of wistfulness had crept into her friend's voice. 'Still and all, if anyone can get away with it, it's you. You look gorgeous so you do. He won't be able to keep his hands off you.'

'Ah sure,' Jodie batted the comment away, 'you'd look grand in it too.'

'No, I would not! These could be mistaken for pins and I'd be likely to get a bowling ball rolled across the dancefloor at them,' she'd mourned, lifting one of her lily-white legs making Jodie laugh again. One thing was sure Jodie thought, counting out the coins she'd scooped from the till onto the counter into the palm of her hand as she added up the float, she would not be getting ready to go out at home. If Da caught sight of her in the dress she could forget about ever going to any disco ever again! No, she'd get ready at Bridie's.

'G'night then, Mr Hogan, see you Monday,' she said now, handing him the tallied receipt and takings. They would be deposited when he drove over to Tubberclair to do the banking Monday lunchtime.

'Goodnight, Jodie. Enjoy your weekend,' he replied, taking off his white coat and hanging it on the back door. He wasn't the conversational type, wasn't Mr Hogan but he was a fair boss and the lack of chat during the day gave Jodie plenty of time to daydream of bigger, brighter things than sleepy Castlebeg as she flipped her duster about the place.

Jodie didn't hang about; she closed the chemist's shop door behind her and nearly ran the short distance to where the cottage she'd lived all her life sat lopsidedly down the laneway leading away from the main road. She'd put the stew on to simmer when she'd raced home at lunchtime and as she banged through the front door she could smell the aroma of mutton, onion, carrots, parsnip and potato she'd tossed in the pot along with the stock. After her mammy had died, she'd learned to cook by shadowing Bridie's mammy about her kitchen, her da proving himself to be worse than useless when it came to that sort of thing.

He'd been useless when it came to all sorts of things. If it weren't for Bridie's older sisters, who'd been only too eager to fill the two girls in on the pains and the blood, she'd have thought she was dying the day she got her period. It was Bridie who'd made sure she was kitted out with pads and the like, pinching a few from her sisters so she wouldn't be caught short when the time came. That morning when she'd woken with stabbing cramps in her tummy and blood in her knickers, she'd missed her mammy more than ever. She'd taken herself off to the lavvy at the bottom of the garden and cried.

Sure, there wasn't much she couldn't turn her hand to these days in the kitchen though, she thought turning her thoughts back to the simmering pot. Not that Da ever showed much in the way of appreciation for her efforts. It irked her given how hard she'd tried over the years to fill the hole her mammy had left. She'd always made sure a hot meal wasn't far off when he walked through the door at the end of the day and the laundry and housework was always done. It was what her mammy would have wanted and she hoped that she at least would look down from above and be proud of her efforts.

She lifted the lid from the pot and sniffed appreciatively before dipping a spoon in for a taste. It scalded her tongue but she was satisfied she hadn't over salted it. Her tummy was in knots, it had been doing very strange things ever since she'd seen David, as she'd decided to call the lad from the disco. It would send all sorts of sensations shooting through her when she imagined him cupping her face in his hands as he tilted her mouth toward his. So real would this seem, she even fancied she could hear the strains of the slow number you'd want to make sure you'd paired off with the fella you fancied for—Donny Osmond's *Go Away Little Girl*.

Jodie had only ever been kissed twice, on separate occasions by two different lads, as the slow song played at the end of the night. Neither experience was one she wished to lock away for a rainy day. Wet and sloppy, and fast and fumbling were the adjectives that sprang to mind. She was certain it would be altogether different were David to kiss her. She dropped the spoon into the sink and put the lid back on the pot, she wouldn't be able to eat a bite. Still, Da wouldn't complain at the extra serving of meat. Last time they'd gone to the disco, Edie's boyfriend had a hipflask of whisky which they'd passed around when prying eyes were looking the other way. It had made her gag but sure it had been a great craic. She hoped he'd have managed to sneak some more this week, a few nips of that would bolster her confidence.

Her da, she knew, would not long be in himself but she'd wager—if one in the family fond of the gee-gees wasn't enough—he'd already be studying the odds for the Saturday races over in Kilbeggan. He might not be a drinking man but he was a betting man, something Jodie doubted Mammy would have approved of. She was right, she saw, sticking her head around the door of the front room. He was in his chair by the fire, which was raked out and ready for when the cooler weather set in. A pen was tucked behind his ear and the paper open like a shield in front of him.

'How're ye, Da, was it a good day?'

'Right enough,' he said, not looking up and not bouncing the question back at her.

She sighed; he hadn't always been like this. She could remember a time when he'd tickle her until she'd be crying with laughter as Mammy told him to 'leave the poor girl alone.' Or, how he'd let her sit on his knee while he told her a story. He used to tell such good stories. That Da had died along with her mammy. It made her angry sometimes that he'd let himself become bitter because he wasn't the only one who'd loved Mam and Mam would not have liked the man he'd become. Jodie had resolved a long time ago that she wouldn't turn out like him. She'd do her duty by him until she was eighteen and by then she'd have saved enough to move to Dublin. She and Bridie planned on finding lodgings up there. Both girls agreed life was passing them by in Castlebeg, she at the chemist, Bridie at the woollen mill. By leaving their crooked cottage down the laneway she'd step out from under that giant rain cloud Mammy had left hovering over them and begin living a life full of rainbows. It was what Mammy would have wanted; she knew it was.

'You haven't forgotten I'm off round to Bridie's soon have you, Da? We're heading to the disco in Tubberclair.'

He grunted, 'Home no later than ten thirty.'

'Alright,' Jodie said knowing he'd be fast asleep by then and unaware when she crept through the front door whether it was ten thirty or one in the morning. 'Dinner won't be long, stew tonight. I'll do you up a bowl and then I'll be on my way.' She took the rustling of the paper to mean 'grand' and left him to it.

CHAPTER 13

***

'What's wrong with Edie? Sure, she has a face on her that would turn a funeral up a side street.' Jodie whispered out the corner of her mouth to Bridie as they clambered out the back of Ronan's Cortina. On cue Edie shot a black look over at her younger sister and her friend. Bridie linked her arm through Jodie's. 'Ah, don't mind her, she's got a touch of the green eye that's all. Ronan kept looking in his mirror all the way here trying to see up your dress.'

'He did not!' Jodie elbowed her friend.

'He did too,' she laughed, 'I was in fear of my life. Thought he'd drive off the road and we'd spend our night in a field with the sheep so busy was he trying to cop a look. Thanks for the ride, Ronan, Jodie and I really appreciate it,' she called back, just to annoy her sister that little bit more. Jodie didn't dare look over. The two girls tagged on the end of the queue snaking out the door and Bridie rummaged around in her shoulder bag for the coins they'd need to get in before peeling the wrapper off a packet of peppermints and popping one in her mouth. She passed them over to Jodie who did the same, casting about the place to see if David was in the line but there was no sign of him out here. Doors opened at seven and it was nearly half past now so, she hoped he might already be inside.

He was. Jodie's pulse jittered as she spotted him on the far side of the hall. He was leaning up against the wall, a bottle of Coke in his hand, flanked either side by his pals as they all watched the dance floor. The lights dappled the hall's old wooden boards and Jodie shouted in Bridie's ear, 'He's here,' as her friend dragged her into the mix of sweaty teenage bodies bopping to the beat.

'Fella's like girls who look like they're having a grand time, so they do. I read it in *Tiger Beat* so laugh and look like you're having the time of your life, alright?' Bridie instructed.

Jodie grinned before swallowing the peppermint she'd been sucking on so as not to breathe boozy fumes all over the goody-two-shoes taking their money at the door. There was no drink allowed at the disco but everybody smuggled it in anyway to surreptitiously tip into their bottles of fizz; that or they'd knock it back before they arrived, sure it was all part of the craic. Ronan hadn't let them down on the drive over and they'd all slugged back the bottle he passed around of his father's finest malt. It had been disgusting and it burned all the way down to her belly, but now Jodie felt a little like she was floating on air as she swayed to the sounds of *Me and You and a Dog Named Boo*. She could feel David's eyes on her as she smiled inanely at Bridie and tossed her hair this way and that. The liquor made her feel beautiful, vibrant and confident like a girl on a shampoo advert and she was sure she and Bridie had the best moves in the place, hands down!

The song wound down and the crowd went mad and as the DJ announced he was going to play a number one hit from Ike and Tina Turner she saw David push off from against the wall. 'Jaysus, he's after coming over,' she squealed at Bridie trying to remember she was beautiful and confident like yer woman on the Agree advert.

'Act cool, Jodie. Don't be too keen.' Bridie was suddenly the expert on boys as she looked about to see who she could hook up with for the rest of the dance seeing how she was obviously about to lose her friend for the evening.

'How're ye?' He sidled up to her, his fingers hooked through the belt loops of his jeans. He smelt of Tabac—she recognised the aftershave from the chemist—cigarettes, and she caught a whiff of alcohol. It wasn't just Coke in his bottle, then.

She smiled shyly despite her best efforts at confidence. 'I'm grand.'

'Do you fancy a dance, like?'

Jodie nodded and pushed her hair back over her shoulders as he began to move to the fast tempo of *Proud Mary*. He was a good dancer she thought, looking up at him through her lashes.

'I'm Davey, what's your name?' He leaned down and his breath tickled her ear.

'Jodie,' She couldn't believe it, his name was Davey! It was fate she thought as Tina began to wail.

Chapter 14

♥

Present

'Moira, Rosi! I'm after dropping my crutches,' Maureen hollered from deep inside the apartment.

Moira and Roisin locked eyes across the table where Moira was sitting with a coffee and a bowl of cereal in front of her. The sisters had been catching up on one another's lives, or more to the point Moira's, and what she planned on doing with hers now she was back from her holiday. Noah was sprawled out on the mat in front of the television. There was a plate of toast on the floor next to him which he was ignoring. He was too engrossed in the bright and bouncy children's show flickering in front of him to eat and seemingly oblivious to his nana's cry for help, too.

'You go,' Moira said through her mouthful pointing her spoon at Roisin. 'I'm eating my Shredded Wheat, and I've just had nearly a whole month of being at her beck and call. It's your turn now.'

Roisin scowled at her before glancing at Noah. She debated sending him to rescue his nana but didn't fancy her chances of dragging him away from those eejits wearing what looked like Star Trek outfits dancing about to some song about potatoes on the screen in front of him.

'Hurry up, would yer! I don't want to sit here all day. Jaysus, girls, are your legs painted on or what?'

Roisin sighed. She had a sinking feeling that she knew where her mammy was and that this was not going to be pretty. Shooting one last squinty-eyed look at her sister, she pushed her chair back and got up before venturing out into the hallway.

'Mammy?'

'I'm in here, indisposed so I am, Roisin.'

Feck it, as she'd suspected Maureen's voice was emanating from the er, bowels of the throne room. She knocked tentatively.

'Roisin O'Mara, stop messing, I've just told you I'm in here, open the door and help me.'

Roisin turned the handle and pushed open the door not sure what she would find. Her mammy stared up at her with a piqued expression at having been kept waiting. She was sat on the toilet with the sweatpants she'd cut the elasticated bottoms out of in order to accommodate her casty foot down around her knees. The crutches were lying just out of reach on the linoleum floor.

'Well don't stand there gawping like an eejit. Help me up. I'm not getting on with those feckity things.' She kicked at the nearest crutch with her good foot. 'I think they're faulty. And you can wipe that look off your face, sure you'd never make a nurse. And me the woman who birthed you an' all.'

Roisin swung into action having no wish to listen to any further ear bashing. 'Right then, first things first.' She picked up the crutches, faffing around arranging them under her mammy's arms. 'There now, have you got hold of them properly?'

Maureen was gripping the sticks so tightly she was white knuckled. 'I do.'

'Okay then, on the count of three I'll pull you up.'

'And pull me pants up because I won't be laughing if you leave them round my ankles thinking it's all a great joke.'

Roisin rolled her eyes. 'I'm not ten, Mammy. Believe me there's nothing funny about this, whatsoever.'

'Okay then,' Maureen gave her the nod, satisfied, 'count of three it is.'

'One, two, three and up.' Roisin heaved and a moment later had restored her mammy's dignity. 'There you go, alright now?'

'Grand. Now then, if you can just help me wash my hands, I'll be all set. Oh and, Rosi, flush the toilet, I didn't do it while I was waiting for you to come because I didn't want water splashing—'

Roisin flushed not wanting to hear the end of the sentence. She followed her hopping mammy through to the bathroom and went through the motions with her hanging up the hand towel as Maureen announced she was starving after all that performance. 'I've weeks of this, Rosi, not being able to do anything for myself. I don't know how I'm going to cope.' The beads clacked as she sadly shook her head before making her way awkwardly through into the living room.

Roisin swallowed back that she didn't think she'd cope either. She'd only been in her mammy's company a short while and she was already driving her potty. Hats off to Moira for sticking at it for nearly month, and in a foreign country too. Sure, she'd have tossed her over the side of that fecking junk she'd been so determined to sail on, if it had been her. Still and all, from what Moira had been telling her, the two of them had had a grand time right up until Mammy tripped over and broke her ankle in the hiking wilderness of some far away Vietnamese town.

Maureen sat down with a heavy sigh at the table, leaning her crutches alongside her. Moira looked up from her cereal.

'Ah, it takes it out of me having to hop about the place. Moira, I'm knackered so I am, be a love would you and get me a bowl of whatever it is you're having. I can't manage it the way I am.'

Moira didn't reply. Instead she picked her bowl up and drank down the dregs of milk.

'Moira O'Mara, I taught you better than that. It's like visiting Dublin zoo sitting at the table with you, so it is.'

Moira looked over at Roisin, who was waving the untouched toast under her son's nose, hope in her eyes but Roisin was having none of it. She shook her head before giving up on Noah eating. 'I just got her off the toilet, the least you can do is the Shredded Wheat,' she said taking the plate through to the kitchen.

Moira knew when she was beat.

'Good morning, Noah.' Maureen twisted around in her seat to see her grandson. 'You'll get square eyes sitting that close to the television, so you will. Why don't you come and sit up here with your nana?' She patted her knee invitingly and squinted hard at the screen. 'What are grown men doing dressed like that and singing about fruit?' There was lots of bead clacking.

'It was potatoes a few minutes ago,' Roisin said, 'and you used to say the same thing to us about sitting too close to the tele and we've all got perfectly normal eyes.' She thought for a moment. 'Except for Patrick, he's most definitely got a roving one. Noah, Nana's speaking to you.'

The sharpness in his mammy's tone saw the little boy pull his eyes away and look over his shoulder. He gave his imposter nana with the funny hair a look that said he'd no intention of sitting by her.

'It's the braids, Mammy,' Roisin said apologetically, not liking this belligerent streak her son had been demonstrating, 'he doesn't like change.'

Maureen's lips tightened, 'It's more than my hair that has him in a mood, Rosi. Children sense things.'

Roisin felt guilt pierce her. Had she done the right thing by leaving the way she had? But what else could she have done? She couldn't have stayed in the house waiting for Colin to come home and browbeat her as to how it wasn't his fault the deal had gone sour. She knew he wouldn't understand that it wasn't about that. She eyed the telephone nervously as though by thinking about Colin she'd make it ring, but thankfully it remained silent. Noah would want to speak to him today though, she wouldn't be able to hold off ringing Colin because he might be only five but the O'Mara stubborn streak ran through him and she knew Noah wouldn't be fobbed off.

With that uncanny ability to read her mind, Maureen looked at her daughter. 'You'll have to speak to him sometime, Rosi, and the longer you leave it the harder it will get. Strike while the iron's hot. Besides,' she inclined her head toward Noah, 'he'll want to say hello to his daddy, and you can't blame him. Whatever's gone on between the two of you is nothing to do with him and you don't want another performance like last night come bedtime now do you?'

Roisin shook her head, she most certainly did not.

'I wouldn't be worried about being fair where the chinless eejit is concerned.' Moira banged a bowl of Shredded Wheat down on the table and Roisin shushed her with her finger to her lips.

'Oh, I think it might need just a smidgen of sugar, Moira, love.'

Roisin couldn't help but grin at the look on her sister's face as she marched back into the kitchen to retrieve the sugar bowl.

'And what have the pair of you planned for today then?' Maureen asked, giving up on Noah joining her.

Roisin inclined her head toward her son. 'Well as soon as his programme's finished he can get dressed and then we'll pop downstairs to say hello to Bronagh and Mrs Flaherty. I'm hoping Mrs Flaherty will be able to tempt him with one of her rasher sandwiches; he hasn't eaten anything yet. Then, I thought we might take some old bread over the road and feed the ducks.'

'That sounds a grand plan and, Rosi...'

'Hmm?'

'Think hard about what you're doing my girl. Don't make rash decisions.'

Roisin studied the ring her mug had left on the coaster. 'I will.' She decided to change the subject, not wanting to think about anything other than getting through the day. 'I might give Jenny a ring too.' The thought of her pal brightened her.

'Jenny as in Jenny Fitzpatrick?'

'Yes, it's been ages since we caught up,' Roisin's voice trailed off. It would be nice to catch up with some of the old crowd. The last time they'd all been together was at Jenny's wedding and that was nearly three years ago. Where had the time gone?

'I saw her at Quinn's a while back,' Moira said. 'I think I told you. She's after cutting all her hair off.'

Roisin nodded; she recalled the conversation. It was hard to imagine her old workmate from her stint at the hairdressers with short hair.

'No! All that long, shiny blonde hair gone. Has she gone and done a Sinead O'Connor or does she look like yer wan from that band you girls went mad for, the Arithmetics?'

Moira snorted, 'Eurythmics, Mammy, and it was Rosi and Ash who were into them, they were before my time. But yes, she has a look of Annie Lennox about her.'

'What was she thinking? She's not a rock singer, she's not even in the hairdressing anymore, sure, she's a mammy?'

'What were you thinking?' Moira muttered.

'I heard that.'

Roisin and Moira grinned at each other, jumping a second later as Maureen banged her hand down on the table, rattling the spoon in her bowl. 'That's it, I've had enough! My own grandson won't come near me and my daughters won't give me a moment's peace on the matter, and me an invalid and all. I'll ring Rosemary Farrell so I shall and ask her to come and un-braid me. She worked in the hairdressing.'

'So did I, Mammy.'

'Yes but it wasn't your forte now was it, Rosi. No, best leave it to Rosemary besides it will kill two birds with one stone because I can tell her all about our holiday too. Oh, and that reminds me, I've a present for you and Aisling, Rosi. Would you like it now or do you want to wait for your sister?'

Roisin didn't like the smirk that had appeared on Moira's face at the mention of these mystery gifts; she'd wait because there was strength in numbers. 'I'll wait for Aisling, thanks, Mammy.'

'Fair play. I hope you'll be delighted with them.' The inflection in her voice suggested that they'd better be, or else.

'I'm sure we will be.' So long as Mammy had only done the one wood carving while she was away, she'd be grand, Roisin thought to herself.

'I might ring the DSPCA this morning too, and see if they have any little dogs needing a home. Did you hear that, Noah, my love, I'm thinking about getting a dog?'

'I like dogs but not big, mean ones like the one on the way to school,' Noah said, turning away from the television.

The credits were rolling down the screen and Roisin said, 'Turn that off now, you've watched your show. It's an Alsatian he's on about,' she explained to her mammy and Moira. 'I call him Cujo. He lies in wait in the front garden and then when we draw near he jumps up at the gate barking and carrying on. He looks like he'd enjoy us for breakfast, but I'm sure his bark's worse than his bite.'

'Ah, Mammy, don't be after getting one of those horrible little ankle biters,' Moira said, holding her arms out for Noah to come and sit on her knee. 'Or one of those funny bug-eyed one's you stick in your handbag.'

Noah ran over and clambered up on Moira's lap. Maureen looked put out.

'Rosi, fetch me the phone, I'll give Rosemary a call now and see how she's placed.' She sat mumbling about her own grandson having disowned her while Roisin got up to retrieve the telephone. 'I've my day sorted and Rosi and Noah are off to feed the ducks shortly. What have you planned, Moira? Because if you think you're going to lie about being a lady of leisure, then you're sorely mistaken. The holiday's over my girl.'

'Humph! Chance would be a fine thing what with all the running around after you.' Moira jiggled Noah on her lap making him giggle. 'I'm going to see Grainne, the HR manager at Mason Price first and hand in my resignation. I've an appointment for ten thirty.' Moira had worked at the law firm as a receptionist for years now and it would be strange not being part of the front desk machinations each day.

'You've made your mind up then?'

'I have. I'm hoping Grainne might see her way to giving me a bit of evening work in the word processing department to help tide me over until I can get organised with my student loan. I'm due at the NCAD after that. I want to be enrolled in time for the new term, it's only a few weeks away.'

'Listen to you, *the NCAD*.' She wasn't letting the grass grow under her feet, Roisin thought feeling proud of her little sister, the National College of Art and Design was where she should have gone at the end of her schooling but it was never too late to go back and realise your dreams. Moira might have only been home five minutes but she was cracking on with all her new plans. *Good for her.* Roisin put the phone down in front of her mammy, looking on bemused as her sister's pretty features softened.

'And I'm meeting Tom for a late lunch.'

'Well now, I hope he's planning on treating you because you'll have to watch your pennies if you're going to be a student so you are,' Maureen said.

Roisin had a feeling Mammy would be giving her a helping hand here and there. She wouldn't see Moira go short for all her bluster.

'He's a student too, Mammy, you know that.'

She answered Roisin's questioning stare at the mention of Tom—it was the second time she'd heard the name now and she had no idea who he was. 'Tom's studying to be a doctor. He waits tables at Quinn's of an evening. That's how I met him.' She wasn't going to tell the whole story of how she'd drunkenly dragged him home then asked him to leave before anything happened, not with elephant ears, Mammy, at the table.

'A doctor! You've got to be happy about that, Mammy.'

Maureen wasn't listening; she'd drifted off into a fantasy scenario whereby Moira was after having a private exhibition at the City Gallery and Maureen was introducing Rosemary Farrell to her son-in-law, *Doctor* Tom. She had to finish it there because she couldn't remember the lad's surname.

'A student doctor, and we've not known each other long. I met him just before Mammy and I went to Vietnam.' She shrugged. 'I like him, he's nice. And he has the best bum,' she added feeling a frisson of delight at the thought of it. The word 'bum' set Noah off giggling.

'Get your mind out of the gutter, Moira, there's a child present, but he does have rather a shapely bottom, Rosi. You know, put him in a pair of blue jeans and a cowboy hat looking back over his shoulder and he could be on the cover of one of those romance novels your granny used to devour.'

'Mammy! You better not have been looking.'

'I'm not blind, Moira.' She whispered conspiratorially to Roisin, 'He's a better match than that other fella we don't mention any more, so he is.'

Moira pulled a face but didn't say a word. Roisin had heard the story of how her sister had gotten entangled with a married man. She was still grieving Daddy, as they all were in their own ways, but she'd been drinking too much and needed to get away from the messy situation she'd gotten herself into, hence the mammy, daughter trip to Vietnam.

'Aisling's keen for me to check out the delights of Quinn's tonight, if you come too, Moira, then you can introduce me to Tom.' Roisin was pleased Moira was obviously moving on. How strange to think for years it had been her who'd been the settled one and now just as her marriage imploded her sisters both had fine fellows on the scene.

'Sure, that sounds a grand plan.' She shot a look at Maureen. 'Sorry, Mammy, you won't be able to come, you'll have to look after this young man here.' She gave an extra jiggle and Noah squealed delightedly. 'Sure, we'd never get you down the stairs anyway let alone back up them and we can't be asking the lads to fetch and carry you every five minutes.'

Maureen looked unimpressed.

Rosi looked at the time, it was just after nine. 'C'mon, Noah, time to get dressed and when you're sorted, we're going to pop downstairs to say hello to Bronagh. If you're lucky, Mrs Flaherty might fry you up some bacon for a rasher sandwich and give us a bag of bread for the ducks.

That got him moving.

'Noah, tuck your vest into your knickers,' Maureen called after him. 'It'll be cold out.'

'Underpants, Mammy, boys wear undies not knickers.'

Chapter 15

'Don't be thundering down the stairs, Noah! Think of the guests. You're a little boy not an elephant,' Roisin admonished, just as her mammy used to do to her and her sisters. He ignored her just as they used to and carried on his merry way. He'd be sliding down the bannisters next, that had been Patrick's party trick she thought, shaking her head as she tailed him. A figure appeared in the hallway of the first floor and Roisin paused with her hand on the rail about to apologise for her son's ruckus when she realised it was Ita doing her rounds. 'Morning, Ita! How're you doing?'

Ita looked furtive and Roisin realised she'd been on her mobile as she dropped it into the pocket of her apron smock. She could see, even in the dim lighting of the hallway, that her face was a similar hue to the red runner that ran the length of the hall at having been caught out. She couldn't resist adding, 'Busy morning, is it?' She'd heard Aisling bemoan the housekeeper's lack of get up and go when it came to her daily routine and Moira had nicknamed her Idle Ita. She was only kept on because their mammies were old friends.

'How're ye, Roisin, I'm grand, thank you. When did you arrive?' She made a show of rattling the cleaning trolley she'd been pulling from the room a second earlier as her hand had busily worked the digits on the phone in her other.

'Noah and I arrived last night.' She didn't elaborate further and Ita must have assumed she'd come to help look after her mammy because she asked, 'Your poor mammy will be pleased to see you. It must be frustrating having to sit around all day.'

You'd know, Roisin choked back the snort. 'Actually, she seems to have taken to it like a duck to water.'

'Ah well, the less she does the sooner she'll be up on her feet again.' This was said as if she were in the know when it came to broken ankles. 'Well now, I'd best push on. I'm flat out, so I am.' She tilted her head toward the room she'd just left. 'It's taken me an age to clean the shower in there. I think yer man must have been a werewolf or something the amount of hair he shed. I'll be having a word with Aisling about employment boundaries so I will.' And with a sanctimonious air, she rattled off to make up the next room on her list.

Roisin grimaced at the retreating figure. Rather her than me, she thought, hoping she'd donned her Marigolds for that job. It sounded like poor old Ash was in for some earache too. 'Well, I'll be seeing you,' she called after her, before carrying on downstairs to the kitchen. She found Mrs Flaherty with her back to her, up to her arms in soapy water—she insisted the dishwasher didn't do a proper job, not like she could. Noah was waiting outside the doorway to the dining room, too shy to go in on his own. She held her fingers to her lips and beckoned for him to follow her through into the kitchen.

'Boo!' It was her childhood trick.

'Feck! My poor heart.' There was a clattering as the cook dropped whatever utensils had been in her hand. 'Roisin O'Mara, I'm an old woman these days. Sure, don't you be sneaking up on me like that!' She reached for the hand towel and dried her hands off, her smiling face belying her sharp tone.

'There's nothing old about you, Mrs Flaherty,' Roisin said, her voice muffled as she found herself embedded in the cook's chest. It was true Mrs Flaherty had looked exactly the same thirty odd years ago when she'd started work at the guesthouse.

'It's been too long since we last saw you, Rosi, my girl. And what a good girl you are coming back to help look after your mammy, so. Mind you always were a good girl, for the most part.'

Roisin was relieved she too had jumped to that conclusion as Mrs Flaherty gave her one final squeeze before releasing her. She set about buttering a piece of soda bread, slathering it in her homemade marmalade and passing it to Roisin. 'You always liked my marmalade. It's much better than that foreign rubbish Mrs Baicu makes when she's in of a weekend.'

Roisin wasn't hungry but she could never resist marmalade on soda bread and she chomped away.

'And where's that young fella of yours? Would that be him hiding behind his mammy's legs?'

Noah peeped around.

'My goodness, I wouldn't have recognised you. When did you get so big?'

'When I started school.'

'Well now, you're not too big to sit on my bench while I make you a rasher sandwich, are you?'

Noah grinned, revealing a missing baby tooth that he thought made him look like a pirate, and nodded.

'And where did those teeth of yours go?'

'To the tooth fairy.'

'Ah well now, you must've been a good boy because the tooth fairy only comes to children who do what their mammy and da say.'

Noah nodded cherubically and Roisin raised an eyebrow.

'Rosi, can I tempt you? You were always partial.'

It was true she used to help clear the tables in exchange for the slices of thickly buttered bread with a crispy rasher or two squashed between them when she was a child. 'No thank you, Mrs Flaherty, I've had breakfast.'

Mrs Flaherty frowned. 'I don't remember parliament passing a law to say you couldn't have one of my sandwiches, because you've had your breakfast. Have I missed something?'

Roisin grinned, she didn't dare tell the cook she was vegetarian and had been for quite some time. 'Honestly, I couldn't eat a thing. I had Mammy feeding me up, upstairs.' The white lie appeased the older woman as she dried off her fry pan and banging it down on the stove top said, 'Noah, tell me all about what you've been doing at that school of yours.'

Roisin smiled to herself as he began to chirrup away about how Beyoncé, the gerbil, had made the headmistress scream, Mrs Flaherty making appropriate tutting noises in the right places. She left them to it, slipping back into her childhood routine of clearing the tables and, carrying the dishes back through to the kitchen, saw the cook and her son were in deep conversation. The bacon was sizzling and spitting in the pan. It smelled good and her mouth watered but she wouldn't be tempted. 'I'll just pop upstairs and say hello to Bronagh,' she said, not receiving a reply as Noah was now regaling Mrs Flaherty with the unfairness of his friend Ben Brown getting hundreds and thousands sandwiches every Friday.

She skipped up the stairs and ducked around the corner, past Room 1 to the entrance area to be assailed by a pungent whiff of Lily of the Valley. The fragrant blooms set her nose tingling and her eyes watering. She screwed them up as a loud sneeze erupted, three more followed in rapid-fire succession. It was gorgeous but the bouquet on the front desk had already managed to set her off.

'Don't expect a 'Bless you' after the fifth one,' Aisling said, grinning as she looked up from the fax machine which was making the high-pitched whine that signalled something was on its way through. 'I'm waiting for confirmation of a group booking for December,' she explained, leaving it to do its thing as she reached over to retrieve the box of tissues from the desk, and passing them to her sister.

Roisin blew her nose. 'That's better.' She pulled a funny face, her nose still itching, and tossed the balled-up tissue in the rubbish bin under Bronagh's desk. The receptionist, a dab hand at multitasking, was beaming madly at her as she cradled the phone in the crook of her shoulder and scribbled down a reservation in the open diary in front of her. Her bowl of half-finished Special K cereal was beside the computer keyboard. Some things never changed, Roisin thought, smiling to herself. For as long as she could recall, Bronagh had been on her own version of a Special K, custard cream biscuit diet.

'I'll pop these in the guest lounge for now.' Aisling picked up the heavy crystal vase. 'I'd forgotten how bad your hay fever gets around flowers and we don't want you wetting yourself now, do we.'

'Excuse me,' Roisin said, taking umbrage, glad no guests were within earshot. 'It's not me who's prone to little accidents.' She pointed to the ceiling above her head. 'It's her, Bo Derek upstairs. Remember the incident at my wedding reception when Colin's best man was giving his speech and she laughed really loudly to be polite because nobody else was. Jaysus, talk about a knock-kneed mammy of the bride.'

Aisling laughed at the memory of her mammy waddling from the dinner table on a mission to get to the powder room as she carried the vase through to the adjacent lounge.

'Grand, that's all booked for you, Mrs Saunders. We look forward to seeing you and Mr Saunders on the tenth and we'll be sure to have the champagne on ice. Fifty years is not to be sniffed at. Alright then. Take care. Bye for now.' Bronagh put the phone back in its cradle and wiping the biscuit crumbs off her lap she got up from her seat, arms outstretched. 'Rosi, c'mere you and give me a hug.'

Roisin hugged her hard before taking a step back to appraise her. 'It's good to see you, Bronagh. You're looking well.'

'Ah, sure, I need to get my roots seen to.' She pointed to the zebra line down the middle of her black hair, 'but I couldn't get an appointment with my lady until next week. And,' she huffed tugging at her skirt which was bunching up around her middle, 'I'd be looking better if the Irish fashion industry could get its act together.'

'What do you mean?' Roisin took in the blouse and cardigan worn over the fitted charcoal skirt. Bronagh had worn the same sort of get up for as long as she could remember. She herself had gone through all sorts of teen phases, Goth girl and hippy to name a couple and all the while Bronagh had steadfastly turned up for work in her cardigan, blouse and pencil skirt.

The receptionist glanced around the empty foyer before holding her hand to her mouth in a conspiratorial manner. 'The menopause wasn't kind to me, Rosi. Sure, I've cut back on all of life's pleasures, and can I lose a pound? No, I cannot. I'm wearing a size sixteen. A sixteen! The label on the skirt says so, plain as day.' She twisted about as though trying to retrieve it to prove her point. Aisling had appeared behind her and was half listening, a bemused expression on her face at the oft heard lamentation as she pulled the fax from the machine.

'It's alright, I'll take your word for it.' Roisin wondered where she was going with this.

'Size sixteen my arse. It's a fourteen if it's a day. Why else would it keep riding up on me? I'm telling you, the sizing in this country is jiggered. And,' she eyed Roisin up and down slowly, 'you're too thin. Are you still doing all that bendy yoga?'

'I am. I love it.' She did, it was part of her daily routine, part of her life now.

Bronagh's lips pressed together tightly. 'Each to their own, I say, but you need feeding up now you're here. Here,' she opened her drawer and retrieved a half-eaten packet of bourbon creams. 'That one there,' she inclined her head toward an indignant Aisling, 'and Moira ate the custard creams, a bourbon one will have to do.'

'It was Rosi and Mammy too,' Aisling butted in. 'I'll pick you up some more on my way back from Quinn's, Bronagh.'

Roisin helped herself.

'Is Noah upstairs with Mammy and Moira?' Aisling asked.

'No, I left him chatting to Mrs Flaherty who was making him a rasher sandwich. He'll be up to say hello shortly, Bronagh.'

'Aisling said he's after getting big.'

'Well,' Roisin smiled, 'it tends to happen when you feed and water them.'

They were interrupted by the phone and Roisin spotted the brochures over in the rack. 'Is that Quinn's place?' she asked, pulling one from the stack and looking at the glossy picture of a quaint bistro boasting local food and music.

'It is.' Aisling puffed up proudly.

'It looks great.'

'You'll get to see it for yourself tonight, I've told him we're coming. He's looking forward to seeing you.'

'And me him. It's been ages.' Bronagh, she saw had hung the phone up. 'How's your mammy doing, Bronagh?'

'She has her good days and her bad days. I'll tell her you were asking after her.'

'Do.' Roisin smiled. Bronagh had looked after her invalid mammy for years.

'I'll give you what for if I catch you! First that blasted fox and now this.' The angry shout was coming from around the corner.

Aisling looked at Bronagh and mouthed, 'That's Mr Donovan.'

Bronagh nodded.

Roisin's stomach plummeted; she had a bad feeling as to what was going on. An elderly gent leaning on his walking stick rounded the corner, his face an ugly contortion as he came to a halt. He raised his stick and pointed it at Aisling so it was only inches from jabbing her in the chest. 'Just what sort of an establishment are you running here, young lady?'

'Mr Donovan, please put the stick down. What seems to be the problem, sir?'

Looking like he would combust, Reggie Donovan lowered his walking stick. 'There's nothing *seems to be* about it. Some scallywag keeps knocking on my door and when, at great pains with my bad leg, I get up and open it there's nobody there. Four times it's happened. So, unless you're going to tell me the place is haunted, to which I would say poppycock, you've a young trouble maker in your midst. And don't get me started on that rodent raiding the bins keeping me up half the night.'

Mr Fox, Aisling had already received an earful from Mrs Flaherty on the subject.

Roisin shifted uncomfortably; certain she knew exactly who the young scallywag was. She flashed back to Noah and their next-door neighbour on the other side to Suzy's eight-year-old son, Jordan, doing the same to Colin when he was sat on the loo. Colin had been apoplectic but the two lads had thought their game of knock on the door and runaway hilarious. He was a bad influence, that Jordan. She felt her face grow hot as Aisling shot her a look.

'I'm er, very sorry, sir, but I think my son, Noah might be the culprit. He's only five,' she added hoping for leniency, 'but he should know better.'

'Yes, he should.'

Roisin didn't catch what was muttered next but she was certain it was a slur on her parenting skills. He was quite clear however as he stated. 'I shan't be moving from this spot until I've had an apology.' He did move but only as far as the sofa as his leg was clearly paining him.

'Now, now, Mr Donovan, it was very annoying I'm sure but it's just a youngster getting up to hi-jinks, we were all young once, weren't we?' Bronagh soothed. 'How's about I make you a nice cup of tea, and you can have one of my bourbon creams.

Roisin could tell by the look on his face it was going to take more than a bourbon cream to appease Mr Donovan and with an apologetic smile she marched off in search of Noah. Where would she have hidden when she was little? Easy. Back down the stairs she went and into the kitchen where she opened the door to the cupboard and there, sitting in the dumbwaiter looking like butter wouldn't melt, was her son.

Chapter 16

♥

'Right, young man, out you come and get yourself up those stairs this minute. There's an elderly gentleman sitting in reception with a very sore leg who's waiting for you to come and explain what you found so funny about making him get up and down to open his door.'

Noah looked long and hard at his mammy and then he poked his tongue out, shunting himself as far back as he could into the dumbwaiter.

Mrs Flaherty bustled over. 'Noah Quealey that's not the way we behave towards our mammy now is it?'

Noah didn't dare answer Mrs Flaherty back and Roisin who was seeing red was not waiting around to see if he agreed with her or not. She hauled him out and stood him upright before herding him up the stairs. She was issuing all manner of threats and had a firm grip on the little boy's shoulder as she nudged him through to reception.

Noah stood by the desk wide eyed and looked from Bronagh to Aisling to see if there was any chance of getting them onside. They were doing their best to look stern. If that was the scariest face Aisling could muster, there was no hope for her on the parenting front should she and Quinn go down that road, Roisin thought. 'Mr Donovan. This is my son, Noah, he's got something he'd like to say to you.'

Tears welled up in Noah's eyes as he looked at the wizened old man who reminded him of the evil wizard, Gargamel from the Smurfs. He felt like Scaredy Smurf as he said, 'I'm sorry for being naughty and hurting your sore leg, Mr Donovan. Please don't turn me into gold.' He broke into noisy tears and Roisin felt a tug on her heart strings. *Please just accept his apology and be done with it.* The old man had no idea what was going on in their life at the moment and yelling and bawling at her son would not help matters.

'What does he mean not turn him into gold?' Reggie asked looking at the boy's mam.

'He's a vivid imagination. I dare say he thinks you might be a wizard or something,' Roisin replied.

'Gargamel,' Noah said, his voice thick with tears.

Roisin knelt down and whispered in his ear. 'That's not helping, shush now. It's not the end of the world.'

For all his blustering indignation the old man looked lost as to what he should say next. Roisin looked at him questioningly.

'I won't turn him into gold. Just don't be doing it again.'

'Noah. What do you say?'

'I won't, I promise.'

'Well now that's an end to all of that,' Aisling said, her voice drawing a line under the episode. 'You mentioned you were going to be heading out shortly, Mr Donovan, would you like me to order you a taxi?'

Roisin and Noah beat a hasty retreat up the stairs. They'd get their coats on and go visit the ducks, get away from the scene of the crime for an hour or so.

***

Roisin sat on the bench, her hands thrust deep into her pockets for warmth as she huddled inside her coat, breathing puffs of white into the frigid air. The lake in front of her was patchy with an icy crust and the trees dotted through the park wore their birthday suits and nothing more. There were still plenty of hardy tourists keen to explore the Green, she noticed watching them trickle in through Fusiliers' Arch before turning her attention back to Noah. He was wrapped up in his jacket; she'd zipped it right up to his chin before pulling his bobble hat down low over his ears. He had two red splotches on his cheeks from the chill air and a big grin on his face. It made her smile to see him dancing about delightedly at the lake's edge. 'Not too close, Noah, I don't want you falling in now.' He'd forgotten all about Mr Donovan and was enjoying playing the bountiful benefactor tossing the crusts Mrs Flaherty—who'd forgiven him his earlier tongue poking out transgression—had collected for him to the pudgy ducks.

They were clearly not underfed, Roisin thought, watching one waddle leisurely toward her son. It cheered her somewhat to see him look so carefree. The shiny spot on his chin was evidence of a rasher sandwich enjoyed a short while ago, before he'd gotten himself into bother. Her mouth curved into a smile as she heard him telling the persistent drake, that he was being greedy and that he should let the others have some. A tour group wandered past, a woman with a red umbrella held aloft at the helm as she marched her charges along. Roisin watched them scurrying behind trying to keep up.

Her eyes caught sight of a couple meandering along the path hand in hand. There was a look of contentment about them and sadness stabbed her. When was the last time she and Colin had walked anywhere holding hands, in no particular hurry to get to wherever it was they were going? She couldn't remember. Their life seemed to have turned into one giant treadmill and she'd had enough. It was time to get off.

Now would be a good time to call him. She knew how she felt and that wasn't going to change no matter how many days she put between them. Her feelings were not something a couple's counsellor or a few romantic date nights could fix. You couldn't turn love on and off like a switch. It was only fair to tell him where she was at and were she to do so in the apartment she knew Mammy wouldn't be able to stop her ears flapping. This was a call she needed to make in private. *Roisin O'Mara, there's no point procrastinating, just do it.* She fished her phone out of her pocket. She was pleased to see Colin hadn't tried to phone her again. Her stomach began to churn as she went through the motions of placing the call and she half hoped he wouldn't pick up, but of course he did.

'Roisin, what the fuck are you playing at just taking off like that?'

She didn't know what she'd expected but the angry venom in his voice made her sit up straight on the seat and clutch the phone a little harder. *How dare he?!* 'You lied to me, Colin. Jaysus you didn't bother to tell me you'd re-mortgaged our home for one of your fly-by-night ventures. What were you planning on doing? Wait until the bailiffs came around and served us with an eviction notice before you told me? You've lost our home so don't ask me what I'm playing at,' Roisin hissed back at him. Her shoulders were like tightly coiled springs and her breath was like a steam train hissing short angry puffs. She squeezed her eyes shut for a second and pictured Colin. She could almost see the bluster seeping from him. Sometimes you had to play bullies at their own game.

'Where's all this coming from, Roisin? Not once in the five years we've been married have you ever asked or shown any interest in our finances. You live in your own bubble and now, when that bubbles been popped, you decide I've been keeping secrets from you. I didn't lie to you. I just didn't tell you because I didn't feel I could. So, I really don't think you're in any position to come the high and mighty with me, do you?'

She kicked at the hard ground and looked up to see Noah was watching her uncertainly. She gave him a reassuring wave. Was he right? Was she partly to blame? She had been happy to leave the day to day running of their affairs to him but then he'd always said she didn't have a head for business. They'd assumed their roles from the day they'd said I do. They were roles they'd never talked about they'd just been slipped into like a pair of shoes that were a good fit. She'd been happy to devote her time to Noah during his pre-school years. These few months though with Noah at school she'd had time on her hands. She could have stepped up, insisted Colin involve her in things but she hadn't wanted to be involved. So long as she could zip-zap her card, sign the AMEX slip and be on her merry way she was happy. Had she let him down? Had she made a hash of things from the very start?

Colin must have sensed weakness because his tone when he next spoke was placatory. 'Now listen, Rosi, why don't you stay a few more days, spend some time with your mum and sisters and then come back to London. I'll fix things. I'll make it right. I've never let you down before now, have I?'

She stayed silent, thinking it was easier to stick to her guns when he was angry than when he was being nice. He ploughed on. 'Noah needs to be at school and in his normal routines. You said yourself his behaviour hasn't been the best of late. Yanking him from his home and taking him away from his friends won't do him any good, now will it?'

She would not be telling him what had just happened with Mr Donovan that was for sure and Colin's words had just brought home the crux of their problem. Roisin sat on that bench digging deep until she found her voice. 'The thing is, Colin, I think Noah acting out is down to us.' She repeated her mammy's sentiment. 'Children sense an atmosphere and they can't always put into words what it is upsetting them because they don't understand it themselves. You know things haven't been right between us for a good while now. We just don't seem to like each other very much these days.' Her voice caught as she uttered the last sentence and she knew she'd hit a nerve by the telling silence that followed. A sudden squawking, as two ducks squabbled over the crust Noah had tossed, startled her, galvanising her into finishing what she'd started. 'Colin, I don't want to come back to you. I want a divorce.' There now, she'd said it. Her nails dug into the palm of her hand as she clenched and unclenched her fist, there was no going back.

'What do you mean not come back, divorce? What about Noah?'

'Of course, there's Noah. I'd never stop you seeing your son and we can work that side of things out, tell him how things are going to be together. You know present a united front so he knows he's not losing his parents but they won't be living together anymore.'

'Roisin...'

She could almost feel him beginning to rev up.

'Roisin, I'm not joking around, you need to come home now. We need to sort this out properly.'

'No.' Colin was used to getting his own way. Roisin had never been one for confrontation, unless it was with her sisters or mammy. The dynamics of their relationship had always been that she'd be the one to capitulate. In the past, she'd let him have it his way if it meant an easy life but not this time and she wouldn't be spoken to like a petulant child, like Noah had been by the guest in Room 1. 'Colin. I've said my piece. I want a divorce and I'm not coming back to London until I've worked out how we move forward from here.'

'You can't do that. There's Noah to think about.'

'I am thinking about Noah. Sure, it's the school holidays next week anyway.'

Colin appeared to have run out of arguments. 'Where is he? You can't stop him from talking to me.'

'I wouldn't do that. You know I wouldn't. This is about us and whatever happens we have to put his needs over our own.'

'Now I've heard it all. If you hotfooting it over to that lunatic family of yours isn't all about you, Roisin, then I don't know what it is. You're being selfish and that's all there is to it.'

Roisin knew there was no point saying anything further, things were too raw for civility. She stood up. 'I'll get Noah. Just, please don't upset him, he thinks we're here to see his nana because she broke her ankle.'

'So, you're the one lying now.'

'How dare you!' Roisin could feel the anger boiling up in her like a pool of lava ready to explode. 'I always put Noah first.'

'If you were putting him first you'd be on your way back to London.'

'For what? So that we can live under the same roof and carry on sniping at one another day in day out? What sort of life is that for us or for Noah? Sure, we're only here once, Colin.'

'It wasn't that bad.'

'It was. We should never have got married and I think you know that deep down too. We were never suited to each other. I've never been the sort of wife you need. We move in different worlds and if I hadn't of gotten pregnant our relationship would have run its course and we'd have gone our separate ways long before now.'

'Oh, I see. I was boring old Colin you mean.' His tone was sneering. 'I'm not stupid, Roisin, I know what your mum and sisters think of me. You always saw me as a bit of a joke.'

'I didn't and they don't think that.' If she were Pinocchio her nose would have just grown. 'And that's not what I meant but be honest with yourself we are chalk and cheese.'

'Opposites attract.'

'And they did, but once you get past that, what's left?' Roisin felt hot tears threaten. She'd never envisaged this conversation five years ago when she'd stood opposite this man to exchange vows. How did it come to this? She blinked furiously not wanting Noah to see her upset. She put her hand over the receiver and in her brightest cheeriest of voices she called out, 'Noah, Daddy's on the phone wanting to say hello.' The little boy's face lit up and the sight of it was like a needle stabbing her. And as he charged toward her she wondered whether she was making a mistake, being selfish like Colin had said.

'I'm putting Noah on now. You can phone O'Mara's whenever you want to talk to him. I won't stop you having contact with your son and we will come back to London, just not yet. Please though, Colin, don't ring to talk to me. Let's give ourselves the time to digest what's happening. I don't want us to hurl hurts and horrible things back and forth.' She didn't wait to see if he agreed with her or not as Noah jumped up in front of her trying to make a grab for the phone. She handed it to him, thrusting her hands deep into her pockets for warmth and stamping the ground with her boots.

'Daddy, Daddy, guess what I've been doing.' Guess sounded like gueth with the air whistling through his missing teeth. Roisin wasn't privy to whatever Colin said but Noah's next sentence echoed around the Green loud and clear. 'I've been feeding the fucks.'

Chapter 17

Reggie

'Here we go then, number eight, Charlville Way.' The swarthy driver who looked as though he couldn't decide whether he was growing a beard or not and who'd conducted a one-way conversation on the perils of driving in the city the entire way to Santry pulled in kerbside. Reggie took in the neighbourhood. It felt affluent in the way that leafy suburbs did, only the last of the leaves were now piled in the gutter running on either side of the road waiting for the street sweeper to make short shrift of them. The driver stopped the meter and asked for a fare that made Reggie's eyes water. He retrieved his wallet from his suit jacket pocket and felt his pulse begin to race and his palms grow sweaty as he counted the notes to cover it. *He was here.*

He handed the crumpled, wad, over before snapping his wallet shut. Somehow, he managed to hold his tongue, tempting as it was to declare the fare daylight robbery. He swallowed his grievance for two reasons, one being he had bigger fish to fry and two, he'd have to ask the driver to wait around until he'd seen how the land was lying. He had no idea whether anyone would be home and if they were, what sort of reception he'd get after all these years.

'Could you wait? I didn't tell them I was coming and there might not be anyone home.'

'No problem. I'll wait right here, mate, until you give me the word.'

Reggie nodded and checked to see the driver hadn't turned the meter back on, before opening his door. A groan escaped from him as he swung his legs out of the taxi declining the driver's offer of assistance with a raise of his hand. He used his stick for leverage hauling himself upright, rather like a high jumper with his pole, onto the pavement. The driver leaned across and closed the passenger door for him. A brass number 8 was embedded on the low brick wall beside smartly stained wooden gates. The gates were open to the sweep of pebbled driveway. He took a moment to steady himself and to study the house his daughter had lived in for the last ten years.

She'd done alright for herself by all accounts, he decided, noting the double-glazed windows on the two-storey cream, semi-detached home. It was a step up from their old cottage and large—you could fit the lime washed stone cottage in the ground floor of this place and still have room left over. There was no car in the driveway he noticed with a sinking sensation, perhaps there'd be no one home. He hadn't wanted to ring ahead. He didn't want to risk her telling him over the phone not to come and had decided the best course of action was what he was about to do. Reggie spurred himself on and with an awkward lopsided gait ventured forth, past the rose bushes pruned back for the winter months, until he reached the front door. The timber was freshly stained like the gates and he didn't hesitate, there was no time left for indecision as he pushed the doorbell. His leg was paining him and he leaned heavily on his stick as he waited for the sound of approaching footsteps.

'Coming,' a voice he hadn't heard in a very long time sang out and his heart did strange things. He was beginning to wonder if he'd been forgotten about as the seconds passed

CHAPTER 173

but then, suddenly the door swung open and there she was, his Jodie.

She was wiping her floury hands on her apron. 'Sorry to keep you waiting, I just had to get a loaf out of the oven.' She smiled expectantly and the years fell away as he looked at her. She hadn't changed, not really. There were a few tell-tale signs of time having passed as was to be expected and she was wearing her hair shorter these days, the colour was different too. She was softer round the middle and he realised the coltish girl he'd known had been replaced by a woman in her middle years. He stood transfixed, drinking in the sight of her. She looked more like her mammy than ever. Although she'd be older now than Deirdre had been when she passed away. Ah, but she was a sight for sore eyes. His beautiful girl.

It took him a few seconds to find his voice. 'Hello, Jodie. You're looking well. It's been a long time, so it has.'

The unmistakable warm yeasty smell of fresh bread drifted from the house. Jodie was framed in the doorway, her hand resting on the handle, illuminated from behind by the light filled hallway and a fluffy grey cat had appeared to rub itself against her leg. The cat fixed bright blue eyes on him and meowed curiously. Reggie watched comprehension flood her still-pretty features. She looked flushed and then she paled and he was glad she was holding onto the door as he didn't want her keeling over with the shock of him having turned up the way he had.

'Da?' she rasped, her eyes widening.

Reggie nodded, aware that to her eyes he would seem withered and frail, not the hard hearted, unyielding man who'd told her to leave. He looked, he thought, like the plant struggling to hold onto life in the terracotta pot beside his feet. A random thought born from the churning ball of anxiety ravelling his innards popped into his head as he wondered if that were where she kept a spare key. It would be a silly place to do so if it were; he brought himself up short. Who was he to tell her anything? She'd clearly managed all these years without his input and some. Sure, look at the grand place she was living in. He waited to hear what she would say next. 'How did you know where I was?'

'I've always known.' It pained him to tell her this but it was the time for truths. 'I kept in touch with yer great pal Bridie's mam, Mrs Sheehan. She's a good woman. She'd let me know how you were getting on, where you were that sort-a thing.'

Jodie looked like she'd been punched as she almost bent double at the weight of his words. 'You knew where we were but you never came? You've a grandson. Did you know that? He's a grown man now and I've a husband. Jerry, he loves the bones off me.'

Reggie swallowed the rock of shame in his throat and struggled to explain something he couldn't even understand himself. 'I didn't know how to, not after what I said. I couldn't find a way to bend and I don't know why.'

'Ah, Da, you could have said you were sorry. That would have been a start...' Jodie's voice broke off in a sob.

Reggie reached out wanting to touch her, somehow convey how sorry was, because to say the word out loud would sound trite but she shrugged away from him shrinking back into the hallway. 'It's too late, Da. You've missed too much. Why'd you come? Why now?'

He wouldn't tell her about the cancer eating his body. He wouldn't put that on her. He didn't want her sympathy; he'd only wanted to tell her he was sorry and that he loved her. That he'd always loved her but he was a stubborn, stupid man who'd made mistakes.

'I'm getting old. I wanted to say I'm sorry for how I was and for not being a proper father to you. I needed to tell you that I never stopped loving you, Jodie.'

'So, you thought you'd turn up on my doorstep and I'd invite you in for a nice cosy cup of tea so we could catch up on all those lost years? Well, you're wrong, Da, there's too much water gone under the bridge for that. You can't go back. What's done is done and I've managed without you for all these years. I've my own family who love me.' She looked at him, her gaze unwavering. 'I'm not Jodie Donovan anymore. I haven't been for a long time. I'm Jodie Redmond.'

Reggie knew his time was nearly up because she was about to close the door in his face. 'Jodie, I'm staying at a guesthouse by St Stephen's Green, O'Mara's for the next few days.'

The door closed but he knew she'd caught his last words. This wasn't the Jodie he'd known. She'd been a soft-hearted lass. But he supposed, staring at the wooden door, she'd have had to become tough. How else could she have looked after her boy on her own the way she did for those first few years and her still a child herself? He deserved no less, he'd expected no less but at least he could go to his grave knowing he'd said what needed saying. He wondered if she was looking down at him from the upstairs windows as he limped back from where he'd come. She would see a pathetic old man, beaten at the last hurdle through his own foolish pride.

The driver got out of the taxi. 'Alright mate?'

No, he wasn't alright, far from it but Reggie was a proud man and accordingly he nodded his head and asked to be driven back to O'Mara's.

Chapter 18

Jodie stood with her head resting on the back of the door. She couldn't believe what had just happened. Her heart was beating so hard she felt sure it would come through her chest. She squeezed her eyes shut, why'd he, have to come? She'd had him boxed off in a part of her brain that she no longer visited for such a long time.

'Mam, are you okay? Who was that?'

Shay had appeared from the kitchen, a slice of his mam's fresh bread in his hand. Jodie gathered herself. 'I'm grand so I am and I thought I told you that loaf wasn't to be touched.'

Shay grinned and her heart melted the way it always did when she looked upon her big, handsome son. His grin faded though as he drew closer. 'Jaysus, Mam, you're awfully pale. C'mon, I think you need to sit down and tell me what's going on.'

'A cup of tea with a sugar in it will fix me,' she said as Shay led her through to their front room, which even in winter was bathed in a warm glow. He sat her down in her favourite chair, the one she'd commandeered as her own the moment the furniture van had unloaded it.

'There now, I'll go and make you that tea.'

He was such a good boy, she thought, drifting back.

Jodie - 1971

Jodie looked up from her tallying up for the day, a handful of coins in her palm and choked back a laugh. Davey was at the window and he had his nose pressed to the glass as he pulled a silly face. When he saw he had her attention he stepped back leaving smudges on the panes that would wait until Monday morning for a polish, he held up a bunch of daisies. Her heart soared as she wondered how she'd gotten so lucky. His coming to see her in Castlebeg had become a regular thing since they'd met at the disco and she knew that if she'd been smitten when she first saw him, she was now head over heels. He was all she thought about morning, noon and night. She'd even burned the colcannon the other night as she'd daydreamed about becoming Mrs Davey—, she didn't know his last name. She must ask him tonight. Da had asked her how it was possible to burn potatoes and cabbage, and she'd sheepishly murmured an apology before making up an excuse about not having slept well the night before.

Davey tapped his watch and she held up five fingers to indicate how long she'd be before checking over her shoulder to see if Mr Hogan had noticed him carrying on. He was oblivious as he finished filling the last prescription for the day and she was grateful. She didn't want word getting back to Da that she was meeting up with a lad from out of town and especially not a Traveller. He wasn't fond of the Tinkers as he called them and he'd go into orbit like yer Armstrong man if he knew.

Somehow, she managed to focus on her task and then, undoing the white jacket she wore over her clothes each day, she folded it and put it in her bag to take home for its end of week wash over the weekend. She flicked her hair back from her shoulders and caught a whiff of the sweet floral scent of L'Air du Temps, which she'd sprayed on her wrists earlier that afternoon. The tester was getting low she'd thought, putting the pretty canister back on the shelf. The three boxes behind it were gathering dust, there wasn't much call for fancy French fragrance here in Castlebeg.

She'd dressed that morning with Davey in mind, carefully choosing her denim A-line skirt, the one that buttoned all the way down to where it finished at her knees. She'd have liked to have worn her pale blue mini but hadn't dared. She'd be the talk of the village within moments of Mrs Buckley picking up Mr Buckley's Collis Browne. She'd teemed her much more sensible skirt with a green blouse; she adored the swirly paisley pattern and knew it worked well with her colouring. On her feet she had the brown leather boots that had taken almost an entire week's worth of her wages. She'd do, she thought, before swinging her bag over her shoulder. 'Have a grand weekend, Mr Hogan, I'll see you Monday.'

'Yes, thank you, Jodie, mind how you go now.'

She breezed out of the shop and spied Davey leaning nonchalantly against the wall of the newsagents two doors down, a cigarette dangling from one hand, the flowers in the other. He looked so handsome she thought, wanting to sweep that brown hair of his from his eyes. She drank in his blue jeans and white shirt worn under his denim jacket. He took one last drag of his cigarette before dropping it and grinding it out with his heel before pushing off the wall. He shot her a grin that sent the butterflies in her stomach soaring and thrust the flowers at her. 'They're not as pretty as you, mind.'

She made a show of burying her nose in the bouquet of meadow flowers which, if she were honest didn't have much of a scent, but she felt like she was in a film. Oliver and Jenny from *Love Story* only hers and Davey's version would have a happy ending. He held out his arm for her to link hers through and they set off down the main street. She'd told her da she was going straight round to Bridie's for the evening to listen to records and had left cold meat along with potatoes which he could fry if he wanted. She doubted he'd bother; he'd be more likely to slap the meat between two slices of bread and be done.

The main road was quiet, people home for their tea or in The Mill celebrating the end of the working week. She was grateful for this although she doubted most folk from around here would risk the sharp end of her da's tongue by passing it on that they'd seen her out with a lad who wasn't from round here. The door to the pub opened sending a waft of ale and cigarettes floating out onto the balmy early evening air. Mr Graughan the butcher, red nosed and red cheeked, doffed his hat at her, 'How're ye, Jodie?'

'Grand thanks, Mr Graughan, those were lovely chops I bought from you the other day.'

'Glad to hear it.' He eyed Davey speculatively for a moment and she wondered whether she was being ill mannered in not introducing him but before she could, he carried on his way up the street. His dinner would be waiting. She didn't think she'd have to worry about him telling her da anything, he never went near the butchers for one thing. It was her that did the shopping and besides, Mr Graughan wasn't a gossip although many a villager had tried and failed to engage him in the sport.

She didn't want to go to the pub for obvious reasons so she guessed they'd do what they'd done on the other occasions Davey had met her after work, stroll the country lanes until they found a quiet spot in a field to sit and talk. She'd loved listening to his stories about the travelling life and she wondered if he'd a flask with him like he'd had the last time. The whiskey had loosened her tongue and other things! They'd kissed for an age under a gnarled old oak and Jodie had felt stirrings she'd only read about in Edna O'Brien's *Country Girls*. She and Bridie had giggled their way through the well-thumbed paperback in high school imagining the look on the Sisters' faces if they were to get caught. They'd no clue as to how it had gotten into the hands of Lesley Fairclough who'd charged them for the privilege of having a gander, the fact the book was banned in Ireland making it money well spent in their opinion and all the more tantalising.

She'd confided in Bridie that Davey's hand had crept under her top the last time they'd met up and how she hadn't wanted him to stop but their passionate interlude had been interrupted by a nosy sheep. It had wandered over to see what they were up to. Bridie had fallen about laughing as Jodie painted the picture of feeling like they were being watched and opening her eyes to find one of Jim Fitzpatrick's prize black-faced ewes staring at them. Once she'd stopped laughing, she'd grown serious telling Jodie to be careful where Davey was concerned. She'd thought she meant because he was a Traveller and therefore couldn't be trusted. It had annoyed her. Davey was lovely.

'Shall we walk?' he asked now, inclining his head in the direction of the lane that would take them away from the village and into the quiet countryside.

'Sure.' There was nowhere else around here for them to go anyway and as they reached the end of the huddle of shops, they veered off down the cobbled lane. There were worse places to wander than Castlebeg in the summertime with its lush green fields laid out like squares on a patchwork quilt, Jodie thought, noting the sky was still a glorious shade of blue. She sighed happily, wishing she could box her feelings of contentment up to bring out and examine once more in winter. 'It's a gorgeous evening. I was surprised how warm it had gotten when I went on my lunch break.'

'It's good apple picking weather alright,' Davey said grinning. 'It wrecks your back though.' He'd found work this last while at an orchard and spent his days up and down ladders picking the Kerry Pippins. They'd been meandering along for five or so minutes, Davey making her laugh with his stories of life on the road. He was a good storyteller, and she was thinking she could happily listen to him forever when a shadow fell across the lane.

CHAPTER 18

'Are you cold? You can borrow my jacket if you are.'

'No, I'm grand, it's that place there.' She pointed through the iron gates that had broken the hedgerow's greenery. A stretch of pebbledash drive was visible, flanked either side by leafy oaks. If you followed the trees to the end of the drive you could just make out the three-storey Convent of St Agnes. It was almost invisible thanks to the ivy creeper wrapping itself around the stonework. Jodie thought it looked as though it were trying to strangle the building. St Agnes' had been there longer than most people in Castlebeg could recall. It was an imposing and secretive building tucked away from the hub of village life. 'It always looks full of ghosts to my mind.'

Davey pulled her close and she felt safe tucked under his arm. 'I'll protect you from the ghosties.'

She grinned up at him but still felt uneasy. She knew St Agnes' served as a mother and baby home, she also knew that when Kathleen Docherty from school went in there after getting herself in the family way, she never came out. It was common knowledge amongst the girls at school that her parents had made up the story about their middle daughter going to stay with her aunt in England so as she could help in the family's restaurant. Kathleen, through bursts of noisy tears, had told them exactly where it was she was being sent.

Now as the evening sun glinted off a window on the third floor, only just visible above the tree line, Jodie felt like eyes were looking down on them. Watching and disapproving of her and Davey. She knew she was being fanciful but still she slid her finger through his belt loop and pulled him on their way. She was glad when they approached the bend and following it around were hidden from view.

A tractor going home rumbled past them and the farmer raised his hand in a wave but apart from that and a blackbird in full song, there was no sound except for their footsteps and chatter. Davey was telling her a ribald tale about the shenanigans that had gone on after his sister's wedding when her best friend was found out the back of the pub with her tongue stuck down the groom's throat when he pulled her to a stop. 'Look, what do you reckon? Shall we see what's on the other side?' He pointed to the narrow gap in the hedgerow.

'I think we can squeeze through,' Jodie dared.

Davey's shirt snagged as he pushed his way through the prickly bushes. 'Feck! I'm caught.'

'Don't move, you'll rip your shirt. Let me help.' Jodie managed to untangle his shirt from the offending twig and then with another determined shove, Davey was through. He did his best to hold the grasping twigs back as Jodie, holding her breath, stepped through sideways. She made it through unscathed and stood for a moment brushing the leaves from her blouse. They were in a field, the late sun bathing the land in a luminous glow, and as far as her eye could see were the yellow bobbing heads of dandelions. They were standing in a field of gold.

'It's gorgeous.'

'And there's no sheep. Shall we head over there? See what's on the other side?' Davey was pointing to a verge, a cheeky look on his face and as she cocked her head, she fancied she could hear running water.

She bent down and undid the bottom three buttons of her skirt before setting off at a run. 'Bet you can't catch me!'

She'd been good at the sprints at school and she did get to the top of the verge first, though she was puffing and panting for her efforts.

'You're like the fecking wind!' Davey gasped. Catching her up and doubling over, he rested his hands on his knees panting until he caught his breath.

Jodie didn't answer. She was looking at the babbling stream running over the rocks and the tree with its drooping branches reaching for the water. She felt like they'd stumbled on a secret glen, a place just for them. She made her way down toward the tree and with the sun dappling the ground beneath her lay down to look up through the dancing leaves to the sky. She could hear the faint humming of busy insects as Davey stumbled down the bank next to her. He sat down and fished a flask bottle out of his pocket. 'Do you fancy a tot?'

She grinned and pulled herself upright, taking it from him. She took a mouthful, almost enjoying the warm burn as it hit her system. They passed it back and forth in silence and after a bit the world began to feel slow and dreamy. Jodie lay back down and Davey did the same, stretching out alongside her resting his head in the crook of his elbow as he gazed down at her, pushing her hair away from her face. She felt like the most beautiful girl in the world at that moment and when he began to kiss her, she kissed him back and this time she let his hand slide to other places.

***

That had been nearly three months ago now. Jodie had been counting down every day that passed since and with good reason. She pushed open the gate and walked up the path to the Sheehans' two-storey brick home and knocked on the front door. She shifted from foot to foot waiting for it to be opened, counting the seconds as her stomach churned. Mrs Sheehan appeared at the door seven seconds later, a Ewbank sweeper by her side. 'Hello, Jodie, love. Tis a marvellous invention the Ewbank, so it is. Saves my back from lugging that beast of a hoover we've had forever and a day. Mind, Edie was supposed to do it today but she's disappeared off with that fella of hers. Typical.' She rolled her eyes. 'You'll find that other lazy lass of mine out the back in the garden sunning herself like a great big, buttery Dublin Bay prawn ready for the pot.'

Jodie raised a smile at the description of her friend and she trailed through the Sheehans' house which smelt of lemon pledge, Clorox and love.

Chapter 19

♥

'Are you sure?' Bridie who'd been sunbathing had but a minute ago been lost in a world where she was somewhere in Spain, poolside of course, stretched out languorously on a sun-lounger. She was a foot taller in this daydream with a tan and legs that went on forever and, she was being chatted up by a handsome Spaniard who kept plying her with sangria. He bore a striking resemblance to Cat Stevens—she had a thing about Cat Stevens. He was the first man she saw of a morning and the last man she saw at night, thanks to the enormous poster of him in a white jumpsuit she'd stuck on the wall beside her bed. It was better than looking at Edie's snoring mug, any rate.

Jodie had arrived a minute earlier, her presence reminding her that she wasn't in Spain she was down the back of the garden, lying on a towel in the sunniest spot she could find with not so much as a sniff of sangria in sight and the disapproving eyes of her mam on her from the kitchen. Sure, it wasn't her fault her mam had to pick her daughter's only day off to get stuck into the housework! In her fantasy she smelt of coconut oil and her body glistened slick with the stuff. Mam had gone mad at her for pinching what was left of the butter to slather it up her arms and legs. She didn't smell like the tropical nut though she smelt greasy as though she should be put in the frying pan to sizzle, and she knew she'd go pink like a pig long before she'd tan. She'd also forgotten she was miffed with her best friend when she'd seen her stricken face.

It was a Saturday afternoon and normally she'd have been spending it with Jodie. Her friend was in her bad books though for letting her down last night. She'd turned up at the last minute saying she felt sick and couldn't go to the Tubberclair disco—she'd looked perfectly well to her. She could have gone with Edie and Ronan but being the third wheel wasn't her idea of fun so she'd stayed home and staying home with your mam and da on a Friday night was not fun. All of this was why she'd decided to spend her Saturday afternoon with Cat, in her dreams at any rate. Jodie had been acting very peculiarly of late, very secretive, and it stung because they'd always told each other everything.

It was down to that Traveller eejit Davey. Jodie was mad on him and just because he'd moved on didn't mean she had to treat her friend shabbily. It wasn't her fault. Everybody knew the Travellers came and then they went. That was why they were called Travellers for fecks sake. She should have never have gone out with him in the first place. He'd done her a favour by leaving, in her opinion. You couldn't trust a Tinker, that was what her da always said and sure, there'd be murder if it were her getting about with the likes. Mind, if Jodie's da had an inkling he wouldn't be best pleased either.

Now her friend had barely sat her arse down next to her before she'd dropped a bombshell. Bridie sat up and pushed her sunglasses up onto her head. Surely she hadn't heard her right? She searched her friend's face to see if she was being serious because if she was then this was as serious as it got.

'I'm sure. I've missed my monthlies three months in a row.' Jodie's dark eyes were enormous in her pale face. She didn't tell Bridie how she'd gone home on her lunch break with a bottle of sleeping pills she'd pinched from the dispensary, yesterday. She felt terrible stealing from Mr Hogan but she'd been desperate. Her lip trembled as she thought back to how furtive she'd felt knowing the pills were hidden down the bottom of her bag. The bag she casually hung on the back door of the dispensary alongside her jacket each day. The bag Mr Hogan never asked to see inside of before she left for the day because he trusted her.

She'd felt like a traitor calling that she was off home to put the meat on for dinner and she'd be back in a half an hour and she'd left that shop fully intending not to come back. Her legs felt wobbly and her shoulders were knotted, she half expected to feel his hand come down on her shoulder as he asked her what it was she had in her bag. How would she explain them? The pills had felt like ticking time bombs as she walked in a daze toward the cottage. She could barely feel the ground beneath her feet so disembodied did she feel and she fancied the eyes of the whole village were on her— that they were all peering out their windows whispering about her predicament behind their net curtains. Of course, she knew she was being foolish and that it was her own guilty conscience making her paranoid.

She'd closed the door of the crooked cottage behind her, and slid the bolt across before retrieving the pills and pouring herself a big glass of water. There was no point in procrastinating. She would go and lie down, that's what she'd do and that's when she felt something compelling her to go to the window and look to the street outside.

Jodie put the glass and the pills down and went into the front room, pulled the net back for a clearer view and saw Sheilagh Reynolds. She'd stopped on the lane outside, her pram in front of her and in her arms she held her baby to her chest rubbing his back to soothe him. His name was Declan and he was the dearest wee fella. Sheilagh had let Jodie have a hold when she'd brought him in the shop to show him off a few weeks back. She stood watching the scene transfixed and knew that her mam was there with her. Her mam had guided her to the window and her mam would guide her with whatever would happen next. What wouldn't happen next was that she would harm herself or her child.

Sheilagh popped Declan back in his pram and carried on her way, oblivious that she was being watched. Jodie let the curtain fall and went back into the kitchen. She tipped the water down the sink, slipped the pills back in her bag and put the meat on to simmer.

She'd barely gotten through the afternoon at work, although her conscience felt salved once the tablets had been put back from where she'd gotten them, telling Mr Hogan she thought she might be coming down with something. He'd said that he'd thought her quiet and now that he thought about it she did look peaky. 'Best get yourself home to that bed of yours then, Jodie,' he'd said, and as she'd left the chemist shop, he'd called, 'and drink plenty of fluids. It will help flush the bugs away.' Only it wouldn't because it wasn't a bug at all. It was a baby and at the thought of what was growing inside her throat constricted and she'd lost her breath for a moment or two.

Now, in that sunny back garden she realised Bridie was staring at her, her face a picture of shock, horror and sympathy. She almost felt sorry for her friend despite it being her who was the one in a terrible quandary. 'Now can you see why I couldn't go to the disco, with you? I couldn't face it.' She'd knocked on the Sheehans' door on her way home from work and asked Mrs Sheehan to tell Bridie she wasn't up to going out that night. She'd nearly cried when the woman, who at times had been like a mammy to her, clucked and fussed over her putting a hand to her forehead while Bridie who'd appeared, scowled over her shoulder.

She'd known Bridie wouldn't believe she was sick, not knowing how much she looked forward to letting off steam at the disco. The shine had gone out of it though since Davey had upped and left along with the cluster of caravans that had been

CHAPTER 19

parked in a farmer's field on the edge of Tubberclair these past few months.

She'd left Bridie to her snit and with Mrs Sheehan's 'Look after yourself, love,' ringing in her ears she'd gone home to sort her da's tea. She knew she wouldn't be able to stomach anything to eat so, feigning sickness, she put his meal in front of him and left him to eat alone. All she wanted was to be alone and taking herself off to her bed she'd pulled the covers over her head and, sobbing into her pillow until exhausted, she'd finally slept.

Bridie nodded. 'Ah, sure, don't be worrying about that. I was just miffed I had to stay home on a Friday night, that's all.' She felt foolish for her bad mood now she knew the gravity of the situation. 'I thought you said yer Davey wan knew what he was doing. That he knew a way you wouldn't get caught?'

'He did,' Jodie's voice wasn't much more than a whisper. 'He promised me it would be alright. We only did it the once.' She chewed her trembling bottom lip. Tears were no good, they weren't going to fix anything. She knew she'd been taken advantage of and now he was gone. When the queasiness in the mornings got too much to ignore she'd ventured over to the camp to see him. A glimmer of hope in her heart that perhaps everything would work out. He'd said he loved her hadn't he? Yes, she'd told herself as she'd boarded the bus, he'd make things right. She wasn't the first girl to get caught, she wouldn't be the last.

'I went to see him, before he left town.'

'You never said.' Bridie was cross at not being kept in the loop.

'I'm sorry, it's not that I've been keeping things from you on purpose. I suppose it's just that if I'd told you what was going on it would have made it real. If I could have come back and said that I was in the family way but that it was all going to be alright because Davey was going to marry me. Sure, we'd pretend the baby had come early and everything would be alright. But it didn't work out like that and I was scared, Bridie.'

Bridie would have been bleedin' terrified if it were her. She glanced toward the house and spied her mam's dipped head, busy with something at the kitchen bench. It would break her heart and as for Da, she shuddered she didn't even want to think about it. 'What happened when you went to see him?'

Jodie closed her eyes, feeling the warmth of the sunshine on her lids, fancying she could smell the peaty aroma of fires and the horses that had been grazing near the caravans that afternoon when she'd had an inkling, but not the absolute certainty she had now the third month had passed, of her condition. She'd approached the camp curiously and although she wouldn't admit it to herself, part of her was wondering what it would be like to live amongst these people. There was a freedom to their day to day life that she envied and a certain romanticism in the bright jewel colours of the caravans. It was a marvel that they fit all they needed to survive and their families under those barrel awnings.

A cluster of wild tousle-haired children, who were of school age but only just, were jeering and clapping as two small lads, their chests bare and faces smeared with dirt paused in their tussling to watch her. 'What are you after, miss?' One of the boys who'd been making fists at the other asked. His hair was a wiry shock of ginger and his face a cheeky mass of freckles.

'I'm looking for Davey.' She didn't even know his surname.

'Davey O'Driscoll?'

'I think so,' she gave a brief description.

'That's him and he's working in the orchard today,' the boy answered. 'That's his wagon over there. What do you want with him anyway?' Jodie looked in the direction he was pointing and spied a bow wagon painted red. The open entrance offered a glimpse of a secret darkened interior but it wasn't curiosity as to what lay inside that her gaze locked on. Nor, was it the flamboyant embellishments flanking either side of the chequered red and white curtains blowing on the morning breeze. It was the dark-haired girl with the big belly, one hand resting below the mound of her stomach as she bent to stir the pot over the smouldering fire out front of the caravan. She must have felt Jodie's stare because she looked up and fixed black eyes on her. Jodie looked away and asked the boy who she was?

'Sure, you're a nosy one, aren't you?' the lad said. 'It's Muirne, Davey's wife of course. I'll tell her you're after Davey.' He winked in a manner far too wise for his years and raised his hand to wave but before he could call out Jodie stopped him.

'Forget I came. It wasn't important.' She walked away from the camp as briskly as she could, her face burning. She could feel Muirne's eyes boring into her back and she didn't slow her pace until she was well away from the place.

He'd lied to her. He was married. Jodie felt such a fool. She wanted to forget Davey bloody O'Driscoll had ever existed only she couldn't because her tender breasts and sickly stomach were a constant reminder.

She'd heard Mrs Buckley tutting with Mrs Gerraghty in the shop a week or so later over the mess those Tinkers had left behind when they'd moved on. 'Are you alright, young Jodie, you're looking pale?' she'd said, noticing the young girl's pallor.

'I'm grand thanks, Mrs Buckley.'

'Are you getting enough iron? Young women need their iron don't they, Mrs Gerraghty?'

'They do indeed, Mrs Buckley, but then I'm sure Jodie knows that, working in a chemist and all.'

Jodie smiled politely but the only thing she knew for certain was that she'd still not come on her monthlies.

She finished her story and Bridie reached over and rested her hand on top of Jodie's. She didn't know what to say. She wanted to tell her it would all be alright but the words were stuck because she knew the chance of things being alright were very slim indeed. 'You'll have to tell your da.' She hated herself for saying the words even though she knew it was true. Jodie would have to tell him but she knew how she'd feel faced with the same task.

'I can't,' Jodie was trembling. 'He'll make me go to St Agnes'. Remember Kathleen Docherty?'

Bridie nodded. There wasn't a girl in the village of Castlebeg who didn't remember poor Kathleen.

'I won't let that happen to you,' Bridie said.

Chapter 20

♥

Present

Noah skipped up the stairs with the biscuit Bronagh had given him in his hand. Roisin's pace was slower as she mulled over her conversation with Colin. It hadn't gone well but then what did she expect? At least she'd stood her ground and said her piece. She'd cringed when Noah had made his inadvertent faux pas but at the same time knew she'd laugh about it later when she told Moira and Aisling. Colin's face on the other end of the phone would have been a picture. He was a candidate for hypertension later in life that was for sure and his blood pressure would have soared at his son's description of feeding the ducks. This time her mouth did twitch a little at the memory.

She'd give Jenny a ring when she got in, see if she fancied catching up at Quinn's tonight. Her call would be a bolt from the blue—she should have made more of an effort to keep in touch, but what would she have told her old pal? That she wasn't happy, that her life wasn't working out the way she'd thought it would. Part of her was ashamed that she'd cocked things up so badly when other people managed to take the right paths. She pushed the maudlin thoughts aside. Sure, they could laugh over old times, Jenny would be the tonic she needed.

Noah had left the door wide open and she could hear voices as she climbed the last couple of stairs to the family's apartment. That's right, she remembered now, Mammy had said something about getting her friend over to sort her hair out. Anything would be an improvement on the geriatric Bo Derek look she was currently sporting, she thought, closing the door behind her.

She found Noah, still in his hat and coat, loitering near the entrance to the living room. His eyes were glued to his nana and Roisin choked back a laugh as she realised why he was holding back. Mammy, who hadn't spotted him, was sitting in the same spot she'd been earlier. Her casty foot was still resting on the coffee table but if you were to play Spot the Difference you'd find one glaring difference in the scene before them. One half of her mammy's hair was frizzed around her head giving her a look of a dark-haired Ronald McDonald. No wonder Noah was transfixed. It was a sight to behold indeed.

A woman around the same age as her mammy, dressed as if she were about to trek the Himalayas, was perched on the sofa next to her engrossed in the task of unwinding the tight plait she held in in her hand. A pile of beads was on the coffee table next to two lipstick-rimmed china cups and a plain gold band she recognised as being Mammy's wedding ring. She remembered Mammy muttering about how her knuckle had swelled and she was worried about cutting off her circulation—apparently Rosemary had managed to wrest it off her finger. She'd have to take it in and get it re-sized or perhaps she might put it on a chain and wear it around her neck. She glanced at her own ring. When was the right time to take it off? Did you ever stop feeling like you were married?

Mammy was burbling on about how Moira had gotten the pink eye on their holiday and Roisin listened in, a fly on the wall, as Rosemary interrupted her to say if she thought that was bad then just listen to this. She'd been bitten by a mosquito on the eyelid while rambling with the Howth Ramblers around Howth in Maureen's absence. Her eyelid had swollen so much she only had a little slitty eye to see through and what was worse was, it was her good eye the mosquito had targeted. The timing was terrible because Bold Brenda had been trying to tempt Niall, the new fella who'd joined their group, with her bag of fancy trail mix. Rosemary had been about to offer him one of her homemade energy bars but decided not to make her move until her eye had returned to its normal size. 'I had to take antihistamines and everything.'

'Gentler, Rosemary. I hope you didn't pull your clients' hair like that when you were hairdressing.'

Roisin looked on amused thinking if she were Rosemary she'd give that braid a bloody good tug to shut her up.

'I'm going as gently as I can, Maureen. Sure, these plaits, are tighter than Bold Brenda's tighty whiteys and that's saying something. Like a sausage stuffed into its casing, her middle is. Did you know she wears those big sucky-in knickers under her walking pants? I know because— Oh!' She didn't get to finish how she knew as she dropped the braid and her hand flew to her chest.

'Sorry. I didn't mean to give you a fright but I didn't want to interrupt your story. Your eye looks much better by the way and those knickers are the work of the devil so they are. I wore a pair once to my husband's work function not long after Noah here was born. Sure, I felt like my intestines had been shoved up to my boobs all night. I'm Roisin.' Roisin helped Noah out of his coat and pulled the hat from his head, giving his flattened hair a ruffle.

'Ah, Roisin.' She arranged her features sympathetically. 'I'm Rosemary from your mammy's rambling group. She's after telling me all about you.'

'Thanks for that, Mammy.' Roisin frowned at her but Mammy ignored her. There were never any secrets when Mammy was around.

'And, Noah, your nana's been telling me you're very artistic like your Aunty Moira.'

Maureen puffed up. 'Noah, go and get the picture you painted off the fridge to show Rosemary.'

Noah looked at his nana not sure what to make of the new look she was sporting but decided to do as he was told and when Rosi returned from having deposited their coats in her room he was holding the painting up proudly in front of the two women.

'Oh yes, it's very good. I can see you've a good eye for colour. I especially like the dog you've painted by the house, there.'

'It's a horse,' Noah lisped.

Maureen intervened. 'Did you have a nice time over at the Green?'

'Yes.' Noah nodded enthusiastically. 'I fed the fucks and spoke to Daddy.'

Rosemary looked startled and Maureen began to cough. Roisin squirmed. 'Ducks, he means ducks, it's the missing tooth,' she explained going to fetch her mammy a glass of water. She handed the water to her before fetching an old jigsaw puzzle she remembered doing when she was a kid from the bottom of the bookshelf. She put the box down on the floor noting the scene was a colourful Muppets montage, with no ducks in sight. 'Hear you go, Noah, why don't you see what you can do with this while I go and make a phone call?'

Noah crouched down and took the lid off the box before upending it and dumping all the pieces on the floor next to him. That would keep him out of trouble, Roisin thought heading over to get the phone.

'I'll just have to stand up for a minute,' Rosemary said, getting to her feet and doing a series of warm-ups like she was at the start line of an Olympic race.

'It's her hip,' Maureen explained, even though Roisin hadn't asked. 'She's after having a replacement. Who are you off to talk to then?'

'I'm going to see if Jenny's home.'

They were both distracted from pursuing the conversation further by Rosemary who, stretches finished, had begun to march around the outside of the living room, arms a-swinging. 'It seizes up on me if I sit for too long,' she said passing Roisin. 'Maureen was saying you're a fan of the yoga. That's supposed to be good for the joints isn't it?'

'It is, sure, they'd do you the world of good. I could show you some easy positions that would help keep everything supple.'

'She's very good at the bendy stuff, Rosemary. She can stand on her head too.'

'Grand.'

Roisin half expected Rosemary to give her a salute as she marched past once more. All that was missing was a tin whistle and she'd make a wonderful Girl Guide leader, Roisin thought, shaking her head and leaving them to it.

She headed for her room and picking up her bag pulled out her address book before flopping down on the bed. She flipped through it until she came to M. She wasn't Jenny Molloy the glamorous hairdresser she'd known all those years ago anymore though, she was Jenny Neeson. Her life would have changed enormously since she'd had the twins two years ago. She should have called to see how she was managing from time to time. After all, she knew as well as the next woman that having a baby was enormous and not just in the obvious respect. She found herself crossing her legs at that particular memory but that was only the start. A child was life changing, and there was Jenny having two of them at the same time!

She punched out the number and arranged the pillows behind her back, getting comfortable as it began to ring. She didn't know if her friend would be home but given she had two-year-old twins the odds were good. She heard an answering click followed by a shrieked, 'Oscar, do not put that in your mouth—Hello, the Neeson household, this is Jenny.'

'Jenny, hi it's Roisin!'

'Who sorry? Ophelia, that's the puppy's, not yours.' Her voice was fraught.

This wasn't what Roisin had expected. It had been a while, yes, but not *that* long. 'Roisin Quealey, used to be O'Mara, your old friend and partner in crime from our hairdressing days.'

'Oh, Rosi! Jeez it's been ages and ages.'

Apparently it had been that long.

'Sorry about that. My brain's, fried these days. Can you hold on just one sec, Oscar's after trying to eat the puppy's squeaky toy and Ophelia's heading for the litter tray again. They're disgusting the pair of them so they are.' Roisin heard her tell her daughter to stop right there before demanding her son hand the toy over. He obviously wasn't playing ball because her voice took on a menacing tone, 'There'll be no Teletubbies for you, young man.' In the end she must have resorted to brute force because a wail went up. Roisin frowned, maybe she'd be better ringing back later when things were less chaotic, but then Jenny came back on the line. 'I'm in the kitchen, they won't find me here,' she breathed down the phone sounding like a fugitive on the run. 'I've put the Teletubbies on so they should be good for at least fifteen minutes. They love that feckin LaLa. The yellow one always calms them down. God, Rosi, two is hard. Why doesn't anybody tell you how bloody hard it is? I never thought I'd be the sort-a mam, who'd plonk her children in front of the television just to get a moment's bloody peace.'

Roisin laughed. 'I thought I'd be a complete earth mammy, you know hand washing the nappies, pureeing the pumpkin, but I couldn't get my arse down to the Tesco's for a packet of nappies and a jar of the baby food fast enough. It does pass though, Jenny, and it does get easier.' She didn't add and then it gets hard all over again and that is what parenting is. Her breath caught in her throat, *was she mad thinking she could attempt it on her own*.

'When did you get a puppy?' she asked, wondering why on earth Jenny would want to add a puppy into the mayhem.

'It was my bright idea. You know how you have this image of how your family is going to be? I used to picture myself reclining on the sofa with a cuddly, sweet smelling baby fast asleep on my chest. That's only happened once and only because Oscar, poor love, had a bad case of constipation, and two babies at the same time was never on the cards. Not that I'd change it for the world now, obviously, but we're talking about how I imagined things would be.' She paused to draw breath.

Roisin had forgotten that Jenny was a hundred miles a minute and couldn't just get to the point she always took the long way round. As such, she settled herself down for a long chat.

'We picked Pooh up from the DSPCA a week ago but she's going to have to go back.'

Roisin had to interrupt. 'What did you just say?'

'We picked—'

'Yes, I got that bit, I meant what did you say the puppy's name is?'

'Oh, Pooh as in Pooh Bear. The twins have a picture book they love and it was the only name they could pronounce properly.'

'Ah, right.'

'Anyway, you'd think I'd learn wouldn't you, but no, I had this idea in my head, you know two kids, the mammy and the daddy and a puppy. A pet for the twins to grow up with and love, only it's like having a third fecking baby and I can't be doing with that at the moment. I mean at least I can put a nappy on the twins. This morning Eoin got up first for a change, normally I get up and put the kettle on while he has a shower, make his lunch that sort-a thing but it's been musical beds in our house, and I was knackered. We're trying the tough love—if either Oscar or Ophelia tries to get in our bed, which they do, we get up and put them back in their bed no talking, no messing like. Anyway, where was I?'

'Erm, you were saying Eoin got up first.'

'Yes, Eoin got up first and he was half asleep like because we'd been up and down like yo-yos all fecking night. He shrieked a bad word and I raced downstairs to see what the problem was because the twins are sponges at the moment and the last thing I need is them parroting their father swearing when we go to the Mum & Bubs playgroup. Turned out he'd trod on a turd.'

Roisin snorted.

'It wasn't funny, Rosi, well it is sort-a now, but he wasn't happy. The crux of it is he's given me an ultimatum, it's him or the dog.'

A remembered conversation with her mammy popped into Roisin's head. 'Are you serious about not keeping, er, Pooh?'

'Deadly.'

'What sort-a pup is he?'

'A poodle.'

A poodle would suit Mammy down to the ground, the perfect sized apartment dog. 'I might be able to help you out.' Roisin explained that her mammy was finding it lonely living on her own and was looking to get a dog for company. 'Sure, she was on about ringing the DSPCA herself only this morning.'

'Didn't your mammy move to Howth? How soon can you take him?'

CHAPTER 20

Roisin hesitated. She really should talk it over with Mammy and the others because the puppy was going to have to stay here at O'Mara's with them until Mammy was able to manage without her crutches. There was such desperation in Jenny's voice, though. 'As soon as you can drop her off. Mammy's here at the moment because she broke her ankle and can't manage on her own.'

'Oh, poor her. Eoin will drop her round first thing in the morning on his way to work.'

'Oh, er, grand.' Roisin remembered why she'd called.

'Jen...' she slipped back into the familiar abbreviation of her friend's name she'd always used. 'I'd love to catch up properly and I'm not sure how long I'm over for.'

'What has brought you over?'

Roisin didn't want to get into it over the phone. 'Like I said, Mammy's after breaking her ankle, it's a long story but she's staying here at O'Mara's so Noah and I've come over to help out. Actually, Jen, what I rang for was Aisling, Moira and I are off to Quinn's tonight. Ash's fella owns it. It's a restaurant, pub sort-a place and Ash says the craic's great. Do you fancy it?'

Jenny made an unladylike noise down the phone. 'Roisin, I haven't been out in months. Do I fancy it? Of course, I fecking do, but can I? No. Eoin can't manage the twins on his own. Things are different now. You remember what it was like, sure it wasn't that long ago Noah was two.'

Well, that told her and yes she did remember what it was like.

'Oh Christ. The puppy's after yapping which means Oscar's taken his fecking toy off him again. I've got to go. It's been great catching up so it has and thanks for taking Pooh, you're a star, Rosi, you really are. I'll catch yer.'

Rosi sat on her bed holding the phone, listening to the minutes tick by on the clock by the bed. She'd thought she could just pick up with Jen, slot back into their friendship but time didn't stand still. She felt hollow and more than a little lonely as a wave of self-pity washed over her.

'Rosi!'

It was her mammy. God, what did she want now? Could a girl not have a few minutes peace to feel sorry for herself? Roisin pushed herself up from the pillows and sat up, hoping her mammy hadn't gotten herself stuck on the toilet again. Once in any given day was more than enough. She got up and left the room to see what had her all het up this time. Mercifully she was still in the living room but the look on her face stopped Roisin dead in her tracks.

'My ring's gone!'

Chapter 21

'What do you mean it's gone; it was there on the table? I saw it. It was right there by the beads.'

'Well it's not there now is it?' Maureen's voice was erring toward hysteria. A hysterical clown now that all the braids had been removed.

Rosemary had gotten down on her hands and knees and was patting the ground around the sofa and the coffee table. 'Sure, it can't have just rolled off the table.'

All eyes drifted over to Noah who was seemingly engrossed in figuring out where a purple piece of puzzle fitted.

'Noah,' Roisin asked, 'have you seen Nana's ring? It was right there.'

He shook his head not looking up.

'Has he been there the whole time?' Roisin asked the two women.

'I don't know. We were busy talking weren't we, Rosemary?' Rosemary nodded.

'Well it has to be here then,' Roisin said, getting down on her hands and knees to join in the search. Five minutes later she sat back on her heels. 'It can't have just bloody well disappeared.' Her eyes flitted to her son once more. Perhaps it was time for a quiet word.

***

'Sit down for a moment, Noah, please.' Roisin pointed to the bed. He did so and she sat down alongside him. She'd read somewhere or other that boys responded better to a grilling if you weren't eyeballing them. 'Did you take Nana's ring?' Again, he shook his head but there was something in the way he wouldn't look at her that said he wasn't telling the truth.

'Noah, that ring is very special to Nana. Grandad gave it to her and he's with the angels now. You know that. If you have it I want you to get it for me right now.' He didn't move and Roisin felt like screaming. Why wouldn't he just own up to it? 'Please, Noah, if Nana doesn't get her ring back, she's going to be very sad. Remember how you felt when Barney died?' Barney was his class's goldfish and it wasn't quite on the same level but sure, he'd get the idea. He nodded. 'Well that's how Nana will feel if she doesn't get her ring back. Very, very sad and she will probably cry.' She could sense him weakening. 'Loads, and loads.'

He got up from the bed and went over to his case which she had yet to unpack properly. He retrieved his Bob the Builder tool kit and opened it. Roisin gasped. Her earring, the missing silver dangly stars she'd searched everywhere for was in there, along with the silver cross bracelet she'd been given for her First Communion. There was a set of cufflinks too, she could remember Colin banging on about not being able to find. Roisin got up and knelt down beside her son feeling her chest constrict as she retrieved her mammy's ring.

'Why did you take them, Noah?'

He shrugged.

'You know it was very wrong of you, don't you?' She was raising a thief; the thought that she was making such a terrible mess of things made her feel sick. She couldn't face telling Mammy that her son had been taking all manner of shiny, sparkly things. A magpie. 'Listen to me now. I am very disappointed in you for doing this, Noah. It's stealing, so it is. I want you to take this ring and go and give it to your Nana. Tell her the truth, Noah, tell her you don't know why you took it and say you're sorry and that you won't do it again.'

Noah sniffed.

'No, you can stop that because it's no good crying. What you did was wrong and now you need to go and put things right. Off you go.' She handed him the gold band and felt physically sick as she gave him a small push. She watched him walk out of the room looking like a convict off to the gallows. It was the second time in a few short hours that he'd found himself in bother and the urge to pull him back and hold him tightly to her, telling him she'd fix it all, make everything alright, was strong. It wouldn't be the right thing to do, though. He needed to understand that what he'd done was wrong. She massaged her temples, *Why did he keep doing things that got him into trouble. He knew better, he did.*

The only thing that made her feel a little better was that she knew Mammy was a soft touch when it came to her grandson. She'd tell him he'd given her an awful fright and what did he think he was playing at? Then she'd tell him not to do it again and order Rosemary to retrieve the jelly babies she kept in her handbag for moments like this. They'd never gotten the jelly babies when they'd been naughty, they'd gotten a stingy slap on the bottom. Mammy maintained it was different with a grandchild.

Roisin picked the rest of the bits and pieces out of the tool kit before closing it with a click and got up. The phone was still lying where she'd left it on the bed. She remembered how kind Stephanie had been, how understanding. She'd said for her to call to let her know how she was getting on. It had only been a day and not even a whole day and she felt like the weight of the world was on her shoulders at this moment. Was it too soon to call? Would Stephanie think her too needy?

There was no way she was going to ring Colin at this moment in time, he'd only berate her down the phone, tell her Noah's strange behaviour was her fault. She rummaged in her bag for the piece of paper she'd scribbled Stephanie's number down on. Right now, she needed to hear a friendly voice.

'Roisin, hi! I've been thinking about you.'

The kindness in Stephanie's voice set her off and sniffling down the phone she told her all about her conversation with Colin earlier and what had just transpired with Noah.

'Oh, you poor thing. You're really going through it aren't you?'

Roisin sniffled by way of reply feeling the hole in the dam burst. 'I feel lost, Stephanie, like I'm floundering in a big sea and it's threatening to pull me under. I don't know what to do next. The easy thing would be to stay here in Dublin but there's Colin to think of. He's many things but he loves his son and does his best by him. He doesn't deserve me taking him away from him and besides, Noah's happy at his school, he has friends there. If things are going to change in his living circumstances then I don't want to disrupt that side of his life too. I just don't know how we're going to do it. I mean I haven't the first clue as to how I go about finding a place for us, what we're supposed to live on. God I haven't worked outside of home in five years—' her voice broke off in a sob.

'Ah, Roisin, it will be alright. Baby steps and taking one day at a time. Believe it or not there will come a time when you'll look back on this point in your life and it'll feel like you're looking back at a different person. Look,' she hesitated, 'can I say something?'

'Mmm.'

'You've been through an awful lot in the last twenty-four hours but from what you told me the other day, things with Colin haven't been right for a long time am I right?'

'Yes, we've not been happy together for a long time now.'

'Do you remember me telling you how Charlie was two when I left my first husband?'

'Yes.'

'Well, I mentioned we went to stay in London with my friend Ronnie who was wonderful. I don't know what I'd have done without her, I really don't. The thing is Roisin, Charlie went right out of kilter when we got there. She'd always been this super easy baby and suddenly she started waking up in the night, inconsolable. It was dreadful because poor Ronnie had to be up early for work and she had no real experience of children. I felt we'd upended her life but she was lovely about it. That wasn't all Charlie did though. I think she might be responsible for Ronnie's recent declaration that she is happily single with no desire to have children.'

Roisin held the receiver closer to her ear wondering what was coming next.

'Charlie was toilet trained, had been for a while because Damien wouldn't have tolerated anything less but she began doing her number twos around the flat. She managed to pick her moments when my back was turned and poor Ronnie even found a deposit on the floor of her bedroom. I couldn't understand what was going on and then it dawned on me. She was reacting to the change in circumstances, she was protesting in the only way she knew how. It settled down fairly quickly, thank goodness, but my point is, Roisin, children can't always find ways to verbalise how they're feeling. Perhaps Noah taking things is a kneejerk reaction to you and Colin not getting along? He probably has no idea why he's doing it but he knows something isn't right in his world and that's his way of lashing out.'

Roisin thought about it. Things had deteriorated badly between her and Colin over the last few months. Now she thought about it they'd had a particularly vicious argument over her not wanting to act the part at a function he'd been invited to attend. She remembered it because Colin had won and she'd agreed to go. It was when she was getting ready, she'd noticed the earring was missing. Oh God, it was their fault Noah was acting out. She was a terrible Mammy for not realising how her and Colin's sniping was affecting him.

'I know what you're thinking,' Stephanie said. 'You're blaming yourself because that's what us mother's always do.'

'Are you psychic?'

Stephanie laughed. 'Not psychic, no, I've just been there and done that. It's time to look forward, Roisin. Don't beat yourself up about what's over and done with but you need to look at the best way to move forward for Noah's sake. For all your sakes.'

'You're right, baby steps.'

'I'd love it if you came to stay with Jeffrey, Charlie and I while you find your footing.'

'Oh, we couldn't do that but it's a really kind offer, thank you, Stephanie.'

'It's a genuine offer, Roisin. Like I said, I've been there and done that and if Ronnie hadn't offered me a lifeline, I don't know how I would've managed. Please, think about it at least.'

She really did mean it, Roisin thought. 'I will and thanks, Stephanie.'

'Good. Now how about hanging up, finding that son of yours and telling him you love him.'

Roisin realised that was exactly what she wanted to do and she said goodbye to her new friend feeling miles better than she had a few minutes earlier. She'd go and see how the land lay in the living room. She walked in upon a scene where Rosemary was telling Noah, who was curled up next to his nana with a bowlful of jelly babies resting on his lap, all about her hip surgery. He didn't look like he was listening, too busy sifting through the jelly sweets for his favourite colour, the red ones. Maureen looked over at Roisin and winked. She smiled gratefully back at her mammy and she knew at that moment, come what may, things would be okay.

Chapter 22

♥

Reggie was seated in the armchair in the corner of his room, his bad leg splayed out in front of him. He was almost grateful for the pain it was giving him because it meant he didn't have to think about the way things had turned out. Still and all, he'd said what he'd needed to say. His conscience would never be clear but at least Jodie knew he loved her even if she could never understand his actions. They were actions he could barely understand himself now he was nearly at the finish line. The thing he'd come to realise was he hadn't thought he'd die. Oh, he'd known right enough he wouldn't be here forever, didn't want to be, the sooner he got to see his Deirdre again the better. It was just he hadn't thought about when the end might come to pass. Somehow, he'd felt there'd be time to make things right with Jodie; that was until he'd been told that there was nothing to be done except make sure he was comfortable. It was to be about managing the pain from hereon in.

There were drugs to numb physical pain but there was nothing he could take for the pain lodged deep in his heart. A salty tear slid down his cheek and he wiped it away with the hanky he always carried in the breast pocket of his shirt. He had no right to tears, not when he'd brought it all upon himself. He glanced around the room, he hadn't switched the light on and it was gloomy despite the warmth from the radiators. He'd told Jodie he'd be here at O'Mara's for the next few days but he'd seen the look on her face in the split second before the door closed. She wouldn't be calling on him. There was no point in staying on. He'd go home tomorrow. He wanted to be back in the cottage where they'd all been happy together, him, Deirdre and Jodie. He could be alone with his memories there because he knew it was those happy memories that would sustain him when the time came.

The phone on the bedside table shrilled and he started in his chair feeling his heart remind him that the cancer might be doing its worst to his body but his ticker was in working order. It was no good ignoring it, yer wan who needed her roots doing on the front desk had seen him return earlier. She knew he was in here and if he didn't answer she might think something was wrong. He eased himself from the chair and wincing at the movement made his way over to answer it. 'Yes.'

'Hello there, Mr Donovan, it's Bronagh from reception here. There's a Mr Redmond here to see you. Would you like me to show him to your room or would you like to come out to reception to see him.'

Jodie's husband had come to see him. He grappled for reasons as to why he'd hotfoot it over to O'Mara's. No doubt, he'd come to warn him off. To tell him he'd let Jodie down years ago and had no right showing up on her doorstep after all this time, upsetting her.

'Mr Donovan, did you hear me?' He could hear concern in the woman's voice and found his own, telling her he'd be out to see his visitor shortly if he could just give him a minute to sort himself out. He put the phone down and spying the bottle of painkillers beside his toilet bag in the bathroom made his way through to the en suite. He shook a couple of the tablets from the bottle and washed them down with a glass of water filled from the cold tap over the basin. He ran a comb through his hair before smoothing his crumpled suit, his best and only suit, then, taking hold of his stick he made his way for the door. He opened it and shuffled forth steeling himself for listening to whatever it was Jodie's husband had come to say.

Chapter 23

♥

The man sitting amidst the plump cushions flicking through an *Ireland Today* magazine at an agitated rate of knots was not old enough to be Jodie's spouse Reggie thought, coming to a halt. He studied him as he lingered beside the front desk, noting he was in his late twenties with a thick shock of dark hair worn too long and that he was dressed in the scruffy attire of youth. He moved closer, ignoring Bronagh's greeting. The sound of the receptionist's voice saw his visitor look up, and Reggie took in his face. He was a good-looking lad but his mouth was pinched as he snapped the magazine shut and put it back on the table by the sofa. He stood up, dwarfing Reggie, but despite his height and an age Reggie was guessing to be nearing thirty there was a look of a little boy about him. He was reminded of the young-un who'd told him he looked like a wizard earlier that morning and could sense the lad's reticence as to whether he should hold his hand out in greeting or not. He kept his arms pinned to his sides as he asked, 'Are you Reginald Donovan?'

'Who's asking?'

'I'm Shay, Shay Redmond, Jodie's son.'

Reggie gripped his stick tightly as he felt the ground shift and roll beneath his feet. This was his grandson. He'd never thought he'd lay eyes on him.

'Do you want to sit down?'

Reggie shook his head and tried to focus his thoughts.

'I know this must be a shock me showing up like this but it was a shock for Mam, finding you on her doorstep this morning after all these years.'

Behind him Reggie could feel Bronagh's ears beginning to burn.

'Look, I don't want to get off on the wrong foot. I came because,' he shifted uncomfortably, 'I suppose I came because I wanted to meet you for myself. Do you fancy coming for a pint so we could, you know, have a chat?'

Reggie looked at this tall, handsome young man whom he'd never met before but whose face was familiar, nonetheless. He had the look of his mam about him around his eyes and the same dimple in the left cheek Deirdre had had. He had his nose though poor sod, he realised. 'I would like that very much. Will you wait while I get my coat? I'm afraid I can't walk very far either.'

'I've my car outside.'

Reggie nodded and made his way slowly back to his room for his coat and hat, noting Bronagh's feigned busyness as she shuffled papers around on her desk.

***

The windscreen wipers lashed back and forth and the conversation was stilted. It was the awkward, polite stuff of strangers and Reggie had struggled with polite for most of his adult life, but at last they pulled into a car park alongside a pub in the suburbs. Shay offered to help Reggie from the car and this time he swallowed that pride of his and was grateful for the strong hand offered to him. They headed for the welcoming glow beckoning through the windows and Shay stamped his feet on the mat inside the door. Reggie's eyes swept the place, pleased to see the lunchtime rush had long gone. The evening crowd wouldn't arrive for another few hours at least. Music played on the juke box but it wasn't at a level where you'd strain to hear what was being said.

'Shall we sit by the fire?' Shay asked.

Reggie nodded and followed his lead, grateful to sink into the seat pulled out for him. He leaned his stick against the table enjoying the sudden burst of heat. The smell of roast dinners and cigarettes was hovering on the air, sitting like a low hung cloud over the bar.

'What do you fancy to drink?'

'I'll get them,' Reggie said, reaching for his wallet.

'No, my treat so what'll it be?'

Reggie looked toward the bar. He hadn't a clue what was what when it came to a pint of beer these days and the black stuff would sit too heavily in his stomach. 'I don't mind so long as it's brown and wet.'

Shay nodded and weaved his way around the tables to the bar where the publican was shrouded in steam as he unloaded the dishwasher. Reggie took a moment to study the lad, still not quite believing that he was in a pub with his grandson. That confident young man leaning casually over the bar was Jodie's boy and Reggie could see he was a son you'd be proud of. Shay returned with two pints, the liquid a deep gold as he put them down on the table. 'Harper's, I hope that's alright?'

'It'll do fine, son.' Reggie watched as he shrugged out of his battered denim jacket before sitting down.

'That fire's grand, so it is.' Shay rubbed his hands together. 'So, Mam told me you worked at the woollen mill near the village where she grew up?'

Reggie closed his eyes, for a brief second hearing the clacking of those looms, a sound as familiar to him as it was to breathe. 'I did. It was an honest living. Did your mam talk much about Castlebeg?'

'A little, she told me about your cottage and how you'd an outside toilet. She was terrified of the spiders out there.' Shay grinned.

'Still do.' Reggie had never seen the point in modernising it. Why fix something that wasn't broken? 'She used to go out there with a broom like she was going into battle.' He smiled at the memory.

'I grew up hearing stories about what her and Bridie got up to and how she worked in the chemist shop when she left school. I called Bridie Aunty B until she told me I was too old to be calling her aunty and that Bridie would do fine. She's three lads, all younger than me obviously but they're like family. Annoying little brothers.' He laughed. 'Tell me about Castlebeg.'

Reggie nodded. Bridie had been a bonny lass, always laughing. He'd missed the sound of laughter in the cottage after Jodie left because Bridie had no reason to call in on him, unlike her mam. She'd been good to him—he hadn't deserved it but she'd a kind heart did Orna Sheehan. 'To tell the truth, son, there's not a lot more to be said about the place. There's a butchers, a chemist, a newsagents, a small supermarket now and a pub. Not much has changed since your mam lived there other than the tourists have decided it's a place worth taking a photo or two. Come in their droves they do and they all leave with an Aran sweater from the shop that's opened beside the mill.' He paused and took a sip of the ale before carrying on. 'It's where I was born and my da before me. I don't know anywhere else but I imagine there's worse places a man could see out his days.' He didn't want to talk about himself though, he wanted to know all there was to know about Shay Redmond. What his life had been like. 'And what about yourself, tell me what it is you do?'

Shay took a long swallow on his beer before wiping his mouth. 'I'm a Creative Producer.' He grinned at Reggie's bewildered expression. 'I coordinate music festivals. It means I travel a lot and then when I'm in Dublin, I play the fiddle in a band. We've a gig on tonight not far from where you're staying.'

Reggie didn't know much about music festivals and the like. The only clue he had was those muddy scenes that made it on the news from the big one they held over the water every year but a musician, well now that was something. Reggie stared at him in wonderment. There wasn't a musical bone in his body nor from memory, Jodie's. She used to play her records and squawk along until his ears would begin to hurt but Deirdre, she'd sung like a bird. Perhaps it was her side of the family he got his talent from. Either way he knew that if Deirdre were here with him now she'd be delighted with this fella, her grandson.

'I think it comes from the travelling blood inside me.'

Ah, his da. Reggie waited to see if he would say more. He didn't know whether Jodie had ever told the lad who his father was. He only knew what Orna Sheehan had passed on to him. The fella was part of the Travelling community who'd come to stay on the edge of Tubberclair that long ago summer and they'd moved on by the time Jodie realised she was in the family way.

'Mam's never kept secrets from me, she always said secrets come back to haunt you.' Shay shrugged. 'My da was called Davey O'Driscoll and he was married, only Mam didn't find that out until it was too late. She never told him about me.' A short silence followed as they concentrated on their beer and the dancing flames.

'Did you go looking for him?'

Shay shook his head. 'I have a da. Mam met Philip when I was still a baby and he adopted me. A father is the person who raises you, who's there to watch your hurling matches and to teach you how to drive.' He grinned, 'and to ground you good and proper for coming home drunk as a skunk when you were supposed to be studying for your exams at your pal's house.

That's not to say I'm not curious about the other side of me but for now, no I haven't tried to find him.'

Reggie felt his chest constrict and his throat close over. He pulled his hanky from his shirt pocket and began to hack into it. The spasms wracked and it took a moment before they eased.

'Are you alright? Here; have a drink.' Shay pushed his pint closer to him, concern etched on his face. Reggie took a tentative sip. He didn't want the lad's sympathy but now was not the time for skirting around truths. That fit he'd just had was a reminder that time was not a luxury he had any longer.

'No, I'm not alright. It's cancer, son and I've not long left.'

Shay stared at him, his eyes twin pools of Jodie's and Reggie felt a tug deep inside as he looked at the lad. 'So that's why you came today? You're dying.'

Reggie nodded, 'It's a hard lesson, son.' The time had come to say what had to be said, 'What I did turning your mammy out when she wasn't much more than a child herself was wrong. The times were different back then but I should have been stronger. That's what a da should do for his daughter—be strong, and I wasn't.' His voice wavered and he took a moment to steady himself. 'I let her down after her mammy died. I couldn't find my way back.'

The fog of grief had hovered over him, seeping into every crack in his armour until he'd been immobilised by it. 'There's not a day gone by since that I haven't wished I could rewind the clock. I'd do things so differently. I'd have done something to try and move forward.' He shrugged. 'I was too stubborn to say I needed help though, I didn't want people thinking I was a weak man. If I could go back I wouldn't have hurled the ugly words at her, and after all she did for me. She didn't deserve any of it.'

Oh yes, if he could go back to that day Jodie had come to him for help, he'd take her in his arms and tell they'd find a way through. He'd step right over that ridiculous Donovan pride and together they'd have weathered it. His cottage would have been filled with the sounds of life, laughter and tears but most of all it would have been filled with love. He felt Shay's hand rest on his forearm and it gave him the strength to carry on.

'Don't you be feeling sorry for me, son, I'm just telling you how it was, but I've nobody to blame for the way things turned out other than myself. I knew she was doing alright, my Jodie because Orna Sheehan, Bridie's mam, used to call in with a meal from time to time and tell me how she was getting on. She was standing on her own two feet and looking after you and then she got married and as time went by I couldn't see a need for me to be in her life. What would I contribute? What had I ever done for her? And so, I did nothing until it dawned on me that she deserved to know I never stopped loving her and I couldn't go to my grave without telling her that, and that I regret all my stupid, selfish mistakes.' Reggie slumped back in his chair, exhausted. It was a long time since he'd strung so many words together in one sitting.

Shay was quiet, absorbing what he'd heard. Reggie could see he was a lad whose thoughts would run deep and he wouldn't be the sort of lad to speak without thinking about what he wanted to say. 'It was a hard line you took with Mam but the times, they were different back then.'

'It was still wrong and I've no excuse other than I couldn't see past the end of my nose. I never stopped grieving for Jodie's mam and I let it overwhelm me.'

'There's a name for that sort of grief now. It's called depression.'

Reggie flapped his hand impatiently. 'There's fancy names for all sort-a things these days but putting a label on something doesn't change the facts. I let Deirdre and Jodie down badly.

I can't go back and change things, although I would in a flash if I could. I came to tell your mam I was sorry that's all and I wanted to thank her for all that she did for me, the cooking, the cleaning, making sure I was alright. I never said thank you to her, not once.'

Shay nodded. 'She loved you. You were her da, all she had.'

Reggie's gnarled old hand reached forward and clasped hold of Shay's as it rested on his forearm. There was urgency in his voice. 'What happened to her, son? After she left. I know she went to England and had you and that it all worked out for her. But I don't know how she managed during that time.'

Shay took a sip of his pint and fished a cigarette out of his pocket. 'Do you mind if I smoke? I only ever light up when I'm having a pint. The two go together.'

'Those things will kill you know.'

Shay raised an eyebrow. 'You don't strike me as the type of man who ever listened to what people told him to do. I must have got that from somewhere.'

Reggie raised a smile at that, he had his number alright. 'Best you light up then.'

Shay did so, inhaling deeply and relishing the act as he exhaled the smoke lazily toward the ceiling. 'It was Orna Sheehan, Bridie's mam, who helped her out. You knew that right?'

Reggie nodded, remembering how all those years ago she'd knocked on his door and when he hadn't answered she'd let herself in. She'd put the pot of stew down on the stove to heat and rolling her sleeves up she'd set about cleaning the place up. He'd let it get in a terrible state after Jodie left. She ignored his protestations and when she had the place shining, she'd told him in a voice that reminded him of his old mam that she didn't ever want to find things in a mess like that again. There was no excuse for it, she'd said. She'd left him with a hot meal and the news that she'd sent Jodie over to London to a woman she knew there who'd look after her and the baby.

'What happened to Jodie when she went to London?' It was part of her story he'd never understood. Why a stranger would take her in.

Shay took a sip of his pint and began to talk, taking him and Reggie back to another place and time.

Chapter 24

Jodie – 1971

Another month went by and Jodie's trousers were beginning to feel snug around her middle. She'd prayed and prayed for a natural intervention but just now she'd felt a fluttering in her stomach. It was as if a tiny tadpole was swimming in there, flicking its tail, and she knew it was the baby. For the first time she felt a quiver of excitement and wrapping her arms protectively around her middle she relished the sensation.

'You're away with the fairies today, Jodie,' Mrs Buckley tutted.

'Sorry?'

'I've seen that look on a young girl's face before, is there someone special you've been stepping out with? Because I said you're looking bonnie. A little more meat on your bones suits you.' The older woman intruded on Jodie's private thoughts as she plonked her handbag down on the counter to wait for Mr Hogan to make up the Collis Browne. Jodie flushed, knowing she'd be horrified if she knew the truth.

She laughed the comment off. 'I've a sweet tooth, Mrs Buckley. I need to stop eating so many cakes or I won't fit into my trousers.'

'Ah you enjoy your cakes, lass. You're looking well on it, so you are and you didn't answer my question. Is there a young man on the scene?' She smiled invitingly, leaning over the counter as she waited for the inside word.

'Oh, no, Mrs Buckley, footloose and fancy free, that's me. Now then, would you like a packet of the Irish moss today?' She knew she was looking well, too well. She was no longer feeling sickly at odd times of the day and her appetite was back with a vengeance. Her hair was shiny and full of bounce. It felt thicker somehow and the sallow skin and bluish rings under her eyes had disappeared. She might be glowing on the outside but on the inside she was terrified.

She knew she couldn't hide her condition for much longer. Bridie had urged her to tell her da and be done with it but she couldn't find the words. She'd tried, she really had, but instead of just coming out with it she'd found herself talking about how she'd seen Jim Kiley making a holy show of himself outside The Mill on her way home from work. She'd decided that tonight was the night. She had Da's favourite dinner on the stove simmering away so that the cottage would be full of the smell of onions and gravy for the sausages by the time he arrived home. It was silly to hope that a full stomach would soften her news but at least it would give him something to soak it up with.

***

'Did you enjoy that?' Jodie asked as her father put down his knife and fork and sat back in his seat. His plate was clean. She'd done her best to get hers down her but the sausages, although fat and flavourful, had lodged in her throat and she'd only managed a few slivers. She chewed her bottom lip as her da nodded before looking at her plate. He hated waste. She picked up the plates and carried them swiftly out to the kitchen leaving them on the bench. She'd clear up shortly. She took a deep breath because it was now or never and never wasn't an option.

'Da...' He hadn't moved from the table and had gone back to studying the odds.

He looked up, clearly hearing something in her tone that warned him. 'Aye?'

'Da, I'm in trouble.' Jodie began to cry, partly at the relief of having gotten the words out and partly in terror at what would happen next.

She could see her father trying to process what she'd just said. 'I'm in the family way, Da.'

His already gaunt features seemed to grow thinner as his mouth formed a hard, flat line. He slammed his racing book shut and got up from his seat, taking himself off to his room. Jodie jumped as the door slammed. She stood there numb, unsure what to do, finally realising there was nothing she could do. There was no point trying to talk to him. She would have to let him think things over himself—leave him be for the evening. It wasn't his style to rant and rave although she wished it was, it would be easier to handle anger than the disappointed silence she could feel emanating from the crack under his bedroom door. She sighed, the dishes wouldn't wash themselves and she was grateful for the mundaneness of routine as she took herself off to the kitchen and began scraping the remains of her dinner into the bin.

Jodie didn't sleep much that night as she tossed and turned mulling over what her da would do. The birds were beginning to sing when she finally slipped off and she slept through her alarm. The day was off to a bad start as she arrived to work ten minutes late and full of apologies to an unsympathetic Mr Hogan. It was the longest day of her life, not helped by the fact that nobody in Castlebeg seemed to be sick. The shop was deathly quiet, just her and Mr Hogan and his bad mood as she flicked her duster half-heartedly over the shelves. She daren't not look like she was doing something and by closing time the shelves were gleaming.

For someone who'd willed the day away, Jodie dragged her feet as she set off home and as she rounded the corner to their lane and spied the cottage ahead, she was filled with trepidation. She could still smell yesterday's dinner as she opened the door and her stomach turned over partly from the stale smell and partly from fear. She'd no clue what she'd put on the table that evening and the thought of sitting at the table across from her da made her feel even sicker. A brown leather suitcase was in the hall—she'd not seen it before because they'd never had any call to go anywhere. It was dusty and had stickers on it from a long ago trip her parents must have taken. She stared at it puzzled before calling out, 'Da?'

She heard him get up, his tread heavy as he walked the length of the front room before coming to stand in the doorway, his shadow stretching long in the patch of sunlight from the open door behind her. 'You're to pack your things and take yourself off to St Agnes'. See what they can do for you. You're not welcome under this roof. Your mam would be turning in her grave, she'd be ashamed of you, so she would.'

'Da!'

'I shan't repeat myself.'

His eyes were flinty and Jodie's throat closed over, hot tears burning their way down her cheeks as he turned away. *How could he be so hard?* She couldn't go to St Agnes', she just couldn't but she knew he'd meant every word he'd said. She picked up the case and took it to her room laying it open on her bed. The front door banged shut and she raced over to her window to see if he'd walked out but there was no one in the laneway, he'd merely been closing it.

She set about pulling open her drawers and tossing things in unthinkingly and when it was full she clipped the locks shut. She stood there for a few seconds, blinking through her tears as she looked around her room in the only home she'd ever known. The drawing pin had fallen out of the top right-hand side of her David Cassidy poster and the glossy paper curled over. His smiling face, the one she'd daydreamed over so many times seemed to mock her and she was suddenly filled with a rage as she ripped it from the wall, screwing it up and leaving it balled on the floor.

Jodie picked up the case which weighed next to nothing for something in which she'd stuffed her worldly goods. She walked from her room, sure to bang the door shut behind her because there was still time for Da to change his mind. She walked slowly down the hallway, not feeling the worn carpet beneath her feet as the world took on a dreamlike quality. Surely that's what this was, a bad dream? She'd wake up any minute and it would be Friday morning and she'd be excited because she'd be off to the disco that night with Bridie. She knew too that when Davey O'Driscoll made his way across the dance floor to ask her to dance she'd tell him no, she'd turn her back on him and dance the night away with Bridie and her life would go on much as it always had.

She knew it was no dream though as she paused outside the front room willing her da to stop her. She coughed in the hope he'd call her in and tell her he'd made a mistake and that everything would be alright—they'd muddle through. The only sound however was the rustling of his newspaper. He would not be changing his mind. She opened the front door and was met by a sky only just beginning to deepen in colour. The door of the cottage closed behind her with a final click and she stood on the front path bewildered by what had happened in such a short space of time.

Da had said she was to go to St Agnes' and not knowing what else to do she set off toward the village veering down the same cobbled lane she'd walked with Davey on the evening that had set this chain of events in motion. The case banged against her legs and her feet carried her on until she reached the convent's iron gates. She shivered and was filled with the foreboding she'd felt four months earlier. Had it been a premonition of what was to come? Her whole body began to tremble as she stood staring at the gates unable to bring herself to push them open and walk up that driveway. Jodie turned away. *She would not go there; she couldn't go there!* And she didn't look over her shoulder, not once, as she ran back to the village.

Chapter 25

Bridie took one look at Jodie's face and the tell-tale suitcase at her side before ushering her inside the house, closing the door behind her. 'Mam,' she hollered in the direction of the kitchen, 'is it alright if Jodie stays the night? We'll have to top and tail,' she said to Jodie. The television was on in the living room and Tiger, the family's inquisitive tabby cat, poked her head around the door.

'I don't know why you're asking,' Mrs Sheehan said smiling as she appeared in the hallway, wiping her hands on a tea towel. 'Jodie's one of us, so she is.'

It was the kindness in the woman's voice that did it. The floodgates opened and Jodie bent double sobbing. Mrs Sheehan hurried forward pulling her into her arms as she stroked her head and soothed her. 'There now, it can't be all that bad, surely?'

'Oh, but it is.' Jodie's voice was muffled against the other woman's chest. Edie was halfway down the stairs and she paused to watch the curious scene.

Mr Sheehan's voice floated out from the living room, 'Orna, what's going on?'

'Nothing for you to worry about, Colm,' Orna said as she spied the battered old case. She looked at Jodie's frightened face and back to Bridie and in that instance she knew. 'Bridie, go and put Jodie's case in your room and fetch a flannel for her to wipe her face with. Edie close your gormless mouth and carry on with whatever it was you were about to do. I think Jodie and I need to have a chat.' She led her through to the kitchen and shut the door behind them. 'There now, it's just us. I'll make us a cup of tea. You sit down, Jodie, love.' She did so, watching Mrs Sheehan rattle around making the tea.

'I knew your mammy well, you know that don't you, Jodie?' Orna poured boiling water over the tea leaves.

Jodie nodded.

'She'd have wanted me to keep an eye out for you and I've done my best. I know you've not had an easy time of it with your da. He's never been able to pick himself up from your mam's passing.'

Jodie nodded. She didn't know where the conversation was heading. Bridie appeared and she took the warm flannel from her gratefully. She held it to her eyes, the heat soothing.

'Bridie, why don't you leave me and Jodie for a little while? It's going to be alright, love, I promise.'

Bridie hesitated, torn between trusting her mam and staying by Jodie's side.

Jodie reached up and took her friend's hand giving it a squeeze. 'It's fine.' Bridie squeezed her hand back and left the room, closing the door behind her on her way out.

'It doesn't take a rocket scientist to figure things out. You're in the family way, aren't you?'

She nodded, not able to meet Mrs Sheehan's gaze.

'How far gone are you?' Orna asked, putting the teapot down on the table before carrying over the cups and saucers.

'Just over four months, I think.' She sniffed loudly. 'Sorry. My da, he told me to pack my bags and see if St Agnes' would take me in. I did what he said. I walked there but when I got to the gates, I was too scared to go inside. You hear things, you know?' A hiccup escaped.

'I know.' Orna poured milk into the two cups. 'I don't blame you for being frightened.' She put the strainer over the cups one at a time and poured the tea before pushing the sugar bowl toward Jodie. 'There we are. Sweeten it up, it will help settle your poor nerves.'

'Thank you.' Jodie's hand shook as she picked up the teaspoon heaping it full of sugar and dunking it in her cup. She stirred it in and tea sloshed over the rim as she raised the cup to her mouth. It was scalding hot but the sweetness did calm her.

'You know, Jodie, I wasn't always Edie and Bridie's mam. I was a young girl too once and I met a fella who told me he'd take me to America with him. Can you imagine how exciting that sounded to a girl who'd never been further than Cork?'

Jodie nodded. America was a far away, mystical place.

'He told me he loved me and that as soon as I turned eighteen we'd get married and sail to New York. I believed every single word he said and I lost myself in being in love. I got swept up and carried away with it all.' Her lips tightened. 'When I told him, I was going to have a baby, I thought he'd marry me there and then, but no. He left town and the last I heard of him, he got on that ship by himself. I went to see his family but they wouldn't give me a forwarding address. There was nothing for it but for me to go to the nuns. My mam took me to the mother and baby house on the outskirts of Cork City, Belmont House.'

If Jodie's eyes hadn't of been swollen they'd have been like organ stoppers at the turn Mrs Sheehan's story had taken.

Orna sensed her shock. 'The thing with the young, Jodie, is they think they're the first to have done everything.' She reached over and patted her hand, her smile kind. 'Do you want to hear the rest?'

'Yes, please.' Jodie's voice was barely audible. She had to know what had happened to Mrs Sheehan.

'My mam packed my case and had me wear my best coat. It was turquoise blue; funny how vivid the colour of that coat is in my mind.' She shook her head, a faraway look in her eyes. 'I can't stand the colour now, never wear it. Mam acted as though we were off on our holidays and Da never said a word from the moment the decision was made that I was to go to Belmont House. I was the oldest of six and, so far as they were concerned, I'd found work in England for the summer. We left when they were at school and I never even got to say goodbye. I can remember feeling very alone and very frightened but worse than any of that I felt so very ashamed.'

They were feelings Jodie could relate to.

'Mam jollied me along when I wouldn't walk up the driveway to that horrible place. I looked at it and I just knew that nothing good would come out of me going there. 'Well now, Orna, you've only yourself to blame, come on with you,' Ma said. And I had no choice but to follow behind her. She handed me over to the nuns without so much as a kiss or a backward glance. It took me a long time to understand how she could be so hard. I don't know that I do now but I suppose the thought of being shunned by your neighbours and friends does funny things to a person.' Orna took a sip of her tea and gave Jodie a smile that didn't reach her eyes. 'Have you heard enough?'

'Did you have an awful time there?' Jodie was hoping Mrs Sheehan would wave her hand and tell her 'sure, it wasn't too bad at all.' Perhaps the nuns were kind to her and the other girls.

'I did.'

Jodie felt her insides shrink.

'I remember those big auld doors closing behind me like prison gates and that's what it was like, Jodie, like being in a prison. Everything was taken from me and it was made clear that this was to be my home until my baby was adopted. I was given a starched dress that itched my skin and a pair of clogs to wear, and put straight to work in the kitchen. And work we did. It was penance for our sins and none of us dared complain. My knees would be red raw from being on them half the day scrubbing those ugly old tiles. All we did was sleep, work and pray. It was like our old lives had ceased to exist and there was just us 'girls' as we were called, and the nuns. We heard nothing from our homes or any news of what was happening outside those walls the whole time we were there.'

Jodie could see the distaste on Mrs Sheehan's face as she paused to wet her whistle. 'There were girls who had a harder time of it than I did. Girls who spoke up for themselves. They soon had their spirits crushed. It was my friend, Gill, who got me through my time there, and me her. Her story was similar to mine, all of us girls had similar stories but Gill and I we arrived within days of one another. We helped one another get used to the way things were and when one of us was low, the other would be strong. We had our babies within days of each other. Gill had a beautiful little girl she called Margaret after the princess and I had the loveliest baby boy.' Her lip trembled. 'He was born with a full head of hair and the brightest, knowing wee eyes. I called him James.'

Jodie hardly dared breathe as she waited for Mrs Sheehan to get to the end, instinctively knowing her story wouldn't have a happy ending.

'Gill and I used to imagine ways, as we fed our babies, we could keep them. How we could slip away with them and start a new life. We had no clue as to how we'd manage or where we'd go.' Her voice tripped over her words in a hurry to get the words out that obviously still caused pain. 'My James was adopted when he was three months old; took him from my arms they did and just like that he was gone. I don't know who adopted him or where he went to live. All the crying and screaming in the world couldn't bring him back or get them to tell me where he was.'

Jodie didn't know what to say not even realising how tightly she'd wrapped her arms around her middle. 'What about Gill's baby?'

'Gill's baby died in the home. Poor wee Margaret caught a fever and in that draughty old place it worsened quickly. By the time they finally called the doctor it was too late.'

'Oh.'

'Gill and I left Belmont House together. I went back to my parents and life carried on as though it had never happened. It was understood it wasn't to be spoken of and I never did until I met Colm. I told him the truth of it all when he asked me to marry him because I didn't want to start our life together with lies between us. He was very sorry for what I'd been through but it didn't change how he felt about me. He's a good man is Colm.'

'Do Bridie and Edie know?' Jodie couldn't imagine they did. Bridie would have shared her mam's sad story with her.

Orna shook her head. 'I could never find the right time to tell them, but now I've told you I think that time's come. I've not told you my story to frighten you. I've told you so you understand you've got two choices. You can go to the nuns, and things might have improved for the girls behind those gates, but I'm not so sure. Or you can go to Gill.'

'What do you mean?'

'Gill moved to London when she left Belmont House. She had no stomach for Ireland after what happened. She married a lovely fella but they couldn't have any children and she was widowed five years back now. He left her well provided for.' Orna leaned forward in her chair. 'Gill and I made a pact when we left that awful place that if we could ever stop another girl from going through what we went through, we would. We can't change what happened to us and our little ones but it doesn't have to be that way for you, Jodie. You're not the first girl Gill will have helped. She'll look after you while you decide what you want to do, and if you want to keep your baby she'll help you set yourself up.'

Jodie felt as though she'd been tossed a lifeline and she was going to grasp it with both hands. She would swim not sink.

Chapter 26

Present

'She was like a second mam to me, was Gill.' Shay said staring into his pint glass. 'Broke Mam's heart when she died a few years back. We stayed with her until I was three when Mam married, my dad.'

Reggie was trying to grasp what he'd just heard. Orna Sheehan's story was a sad one and it could have been Jodie's story too if it had been left up to him. He owed the woman an enormous debt of gratitude for all she'd done for his daughter, and he resolved to thank her when he returned to Castlebeg. Words would never be enough to convey how he'd felt listening to Shay talk but they were a start. 'You've had a good life, then?' He looked at the young man hopefully. He needed to hear that this was so.

Shay nodded. 'I have, a grand life, but there's always been a piece missing. It's why I came to O'Mara's to see you. I think Mam feels the same. Don't go back to Castlebeg just yet. She needs to make her peace too.' He drained his glass.

Reggie put his glass down, he'd lost the taste for his beer and knew the alcohol would not mix well with his pills. 'I'll stay.' If there was a chance that Jodie would see him, he'd stay at the place with its fox and little boys who knocked on his door and ran away until they carried him out of the guesthouse in a box.

'You two look like you've put the world to rights,' the publican said clearing the table next to where they were sitting.

'We have,' Reggie said, and Shay looked across the table and smiled.

'We have indeed.'

***

'I know you.' Aisling beamed looking up from the front desk, where she'd been in conversation with Bronagh, at the sudden arctic blast as the door opened. She'd seen the young man, who was quite the fine thing, helping Mr Donovan, who looked done in, along before. They were a most unlikely duo, indeed. 'You play the fiddle in the Sullivans, am I right?'

'I do, indeed.'

Aisling had a fan girl moment, knowing if she didn't have her lovely Quinn, she'd be making eyes at this great big hunk of a man. 'You're brilliant, so you are. You always get the crowd up on their feet. I've seen you and the rest of the fellas play at Quinn's. You've even got me up dancing in these.' She lifted her leg and showed him the pair of ridiculously high Valentino's she'd spent her day teetering around on. It had been a particularly busy day too as she'd gone to meet with a tour operator keen to see what sort of arrangement they could come to. Even she had to admit that heels when stomping around rural Wicklow looking at ancient Celtic crosses and Norman towers had not been a practical choice.

Shay grinned. 'Sure, you deserve a medal just being able to stand upright in those things let alone dance, and thanks, we do our best to please.' He recognised the pretty copper-haired woman as Quinn's girlfriend. 'I'm Shay, Shay Redmond.' He held his hand out in greeting and Aisling shook it.

'It's nice to meet you properly, Shay, Aisling O'Mara.' There was a cough behind her and she smiled to herself. 'And this is Bronagh Hanrahan our right-hand woman here at O'Mara's.'

Bronagh, who was due to knock off shortly, had paused in her tidying of her desk to peer over the top of it, curious as to the conversation playing out. Her eyes had widened at the sight of such virile manhood and she would not be missing out on an introduction even if she was old enough to be his mam and then some. Had people not heard of Joan Collins, Elizabeth Taylor, etc? Sure, if it was good enough for them it was good enough for Bronagh Hanrahan.

'Hello, Bronagh.' Shay turned his smile full wattage on Bronagh who instantly began to giggle. Aisling debated giving her a swift kick in the shins. It was ridiculous a woman her age behaving like that but it was also quite funny and she knew she'd tell Moira later. Moira found Bronagh's age indiscriminate roving eye disturbing and was adamant their receptionist should join the lawn bowls and set her sights on a fella her own age.

Shay looked a little bewildered. He didn't think he'd said anything witty; he must have missed something. 'This is your guesthouse?' he asked Aisling. O'Mara's had been part of the Dublin landscape forever and it was in a prime part of the city. She was doing well for herself if she owned the place.

'No, not mine, my family's. I manage it.' She couldn't help herself. 'If you don't mind me asking, how do you two know each other?'

Shay looked at the stooped old man next to him. 'I'm his grandson.'

In that moment, Reggie Donovan stood a little taller.

'Oh, well, it's a small world.' She was grateful for the phone ringing as it meant Bronagh would be distracted.

'I'm playing at Quinn's tonight as it happens.'

'I'll see you there then. My sister Rosi's back in town, over from London and Moira my youngest sister is quite taken with Tom who waits tables there of an evening so we're heading down for a meal. Rosi doesn't dance, not unless she's had a skinful, I bet you'll manage to get her on feet though. Nobody could stay seated when you lads do Gloria.'

'Van Morrison was made for dancing, and challenge accepted. I'll do my utmost to get Rosi on the floor.'

Reggie Donovan listened to the banter. He'd have liked to see Shay play. That would be quite something, so it would.

'Would you like to come down and listen to the band, Grandad?'

He'd called him Grandad and he would, oh he would, but the thought of going out at night on his own when he was bone achingly tired and with his leg the way it was, was overwhelming.

Aisling could see his reticence but she'd also seen the hope flare in Reggie's eyes. She really didn't want to take this cantankerous bite of a man to Quinn's but she prided herself on ensuring all O'Mara's guests were well looked after on her watch. So, ever the hostess, she opened her mouth and the words tumbled out. 'Sure, why don't you come down to Quinn's with me and my sisters, Mr Donovan, have your dinner with us. We'll look after you so we will. I can organise a taxi for you to come back in if you don't fancy staying late.'

Shay looked at Reggie. 'That could work.'

For once in his life, Reggie Donovan took a deep breath and decided to be gracious. 'I'd like that very much, thank you.' He even managed to smile.

Aisling smiled back at him, wondering what had happened to the bad-tempered man she'd encountered earlier in the day. This version was much more preferable.

The arrangements were made. They would meet here in the foyer at six thirty which gave Reggie the chance to rest for a few hours. Shay saw him to his room before leaving with a wave and a 'Catch you later.'

Aisling waved back and caught sight of Bronagh's wistful gaze. 'Why don't you come with us? A night out might do you good.' She couldn't remember the last time the receptionist had gone anywhere. She felt sad for her sometimes, knowing she must on occasion feel trapped caring for her mam the way she did, but she knew, too, Bronagh wouldn't have it any other way.

'Ah, no, sure you don't need me tagging along.' She waved her hand dismissively. 'Besides I've got Mam and I a lovely couple of chicken Kiev's in for our dinner.'

'Marks and Spencer's?'

'Only the best, Mam won't eat any other.'

'Fair play to her, enjoy.'

'We will.' Bronagh shrugged into her coat, flicking her hair out from the collar.

'Oh, Bronagh, I've been meaning to ask. You haven't heard from our lovely Mr Walsh have you?' Mr Walsh was a regular to O'Mara's each September when he'd travel from Liverpool to visit his sister here in Dublin. It wasn't long since his last visit and the way he'd asked to be remembered to Bronagh when he was checking out had gotten Aisling's matchmaking antennae quivering.

'No, and sure what would he be wanting with me?' Bronagh eyed Aisling. 'Oh, I see where you're headed with that one.'

'I think he fancies you. I told you that. He was very specific I made sure to say goodbye to you from him. I could see he was sorry he'd missed you. You know we've got his address in the Filofax, there's nothing to stop you dropping him a line, see how he's getting on.'

'Aisling O'Mara, don't you be—' Bronagh didn't get a chance to finish as the door swung open once more and Nina, pink cheeked from the cold, stepped inside, closing it quickly behind her.

'It's going to be a cold night, tonight,' she said, pulling her mittens and hat off before slipping out of her coat and draping it over the back of the chair Bronagh had not long vacated.

'I've warmed the seat for you,' Bronagh said. 'Have you had a good day?'

'Yes, thank you. The restaurant was very busy and there were good tippers in at lunchtime.'

'American?'

'Yes, they're very generous.'

Bronagh took a minute to run through what was what on the desk before singing out goodnight.

Aisling who hadn't seen her mam or sisters since earlier in the morning decided it was high time she headed upstairs to see what they'd all been up to. She wanted to hear how Moira's lunch had gone with sexy bum, Tom, and whether Rosi had spoken to Colin. She left Nina to greet the Canadian couple, Mr and Mrs Cullen, who'd just arrived back from a day exploring the city. She heard Nina asking if they'd enjoyed their day as she took to the stairs.

She pushed open the door to their apartment thinking it was a shame Leila couldn't join them tonight. It had been awhile since she'd caught up with her friend. They'd both been a bit lax in that department, each caught up in their new romance. She'd yet to meet this Bearach who had her friend so smitten. She gave a little snigger; she couldn't help it. I mean Bearach? Why not a Liam or a Connor? Perfectly good pronounceable Irish names. It was with this thought in mind she rounded the corner into the living room and let out a small scream because there sitting on the sofa with her big casty foot up on the coffee table, was Leo fecking Sayer.

Chapter 27

♥

'I'm not going to give you and Roisin your presents if you carry on laughing at me,' Maureen said to Aisling. She was feeling most put out. She'd gotten rid of the braids hadn't she? What did these girls want, blood? Of course, her hair was a little frizzy, it had been in plaits for a couple of weeks. Sure, it would sort itself out right enough once she'd given it a wash. She should have asked Rosemary to do it for her over the sink but she'd had enough of hearing about Bold Brenda. One of those three giggling eejits of hers could help her with it for their sins.

Aisling was dancing around the room singing, and if she wasn't careful she'd go over in those heels and find herself on the sofa next to her mam with her foot up on the coffee table. She wouldn't be laughing then, she thought, as her daughter jiggled past singing, *You Make Me Feel Like Dancing*. Roisin had taken it upon herself to do backup, *gonna dance the night away*, while Moira rolled around on the floor laughing. Noah was sitting at the table with his colouring-in, absolutely bewildered by what was going on, but he liked seeing his mummy laughing.

Moira came up for air long enough to snort, 'I've got it! I've got it! She's Justin Timberlake, NSYNC!' She got to her feet and joined her sisters in *Bye Bye Bye*, the three of them breaking out their moves. Noah tagged on the end. He liked this song—he remembered doing a dance to it when he played one of the shepherds in the rock 'n' roll nativity play.

'Alright, alright, you've had your fun,' Maureen clapped. The girls were all gasping for air. Aisling flopped down in the armchair and Roisin picked Noah up, twirled him around and gave him a big kiss on top of his head.

'Put me down, Mum!' he squealed, in a way that meant he wanted more. Moira sank down on the sofa next her mammy.

'I haven't laughed like that in such a long time,' Roisin said, jigging Noah up and down. It had felt good.

'You'll do your back in, Rosi, bouncing him about like that, mark my words, sure he's not a baby anymore are you, Noah?'

Noah stuck his thumb in his mouth, apparently deciding at that moment he didn't want to be a big boy. Maureen shook her head, frizz bobbing with the motion, but smiled as he buried his head in his mam's chest. 'Sure, laughter's the best medicine so it is, just not at your poor mammy's expense,' she tutted. 'Noah, be a love and go into Nana's room, there's a plastic bag on top of my suitcase. Could you fetch it for me please?'

Noah, who knew Nana still had a quarter of a bag of the jelly babies left, decided it was in his best interests to do as she asked. Roisin put him down and he raced off. He returned in record time, handing the bag over to his nana.

'Thank you, my lovely.'

He hovered, curious to see what was inside it. Maureen opened it and made a show of producing a swathe of vibrant purple silk. 'The purple's yours, Rosi.' She held it out for her to take.

It was so bright Roisin wondered whether she should put her sunglasses on. 'Erm, thanks, Mammy.' She shook it out and saw it was a dress, hearing simultaneously further rustling of the plastic bag and a strangled snorting sound from Moira.

Maureen beamed, she was enjoying playing Santa Claus, 'and this is your one, Aisling.' She passed Aisling a neatly folded bolt of peacock blue silk. 'I had them made for you especially, so I did. Aisling your dress might be a bit on the snug side, you shouldn't have eaten so many of the custard creams last night but you could always wear some of those sucky-in knickers Rosemary was on about.'

'What sucky-in knickers?' Aisling hadn't been privy to that conversation.

'Or hold your breath,' Moira added helpfully.

Aisling shot her a death stare.

'Moira said the pair of you would love them.'

Roisin joined Aisling in the death stare.

'Hold them up against you, c'mon let's have a look,' Maureen urged. 'Oh yes,' she said as her daughters obliged. 'The colours are lovely on you.'

Roisin looked at Aisling's as she draped it against her. 'The style reminds me of—'

'Yer prostitute one, China Beach,' Moira filled in the blanks. 'And you want to see Mammy in hers. You know she's on about wearing it to the Christmas yacht club dinner in Howth.'

Roisin and Aisling looked at each other, *Oh God, she was right.*

'I'm no wallflower. Well go on with you, don't just stand there, girls, try them on and give us a fashion show.'

Both sisters knew there'd be no getting out of it and so they disappeared into the bedroom Aisling had given up for Roisin and Noah.

Aisling slipped her sweater over her head. 'I almost forgot. Mr Donovan's coming with us tonight.'

Roisin paused, jeans halfway down her legs. 'What did you say?'

'I said Mr Donovan from room one, Noah's pal, is coming with us.'

CHAPTER 23

This wasn't the plan, Roisin thought. They were having a girls' night, the three musketeers out on the town not the three musketeers and a grumpy old man. 'How on earth did that come about?'

Aisling explained what had transpired downstairs. 'And to be fair, Rosi, Mr Donovan wasn't grumpy at all when he came back from his outing with his grandson. I felt sorry for him because I could see he was desperate to go and he's not a well man. And as for Shay, his grandson, you want to have seen him. If I wasn't spoken for he could come and play my fiddle any time.' She remembered Bronagh's reaction to him. 'Honestly, if Bronagh could have stopped giggling long enough I think she would have draped herself over the top of the reception desk like Jessica fecking Rabbit.'

Roisin laughed at the mental picture. 'Ah, you're a soft touch, Aisling O'Mara.'

'Seriously, though, I think Bronagh's lonely. I'm going to have to get to work there. We've a guest who comes to stay with us each September, Mr Walsh, and I'm sure he fancies the pants off her.'

'You're going to wave your matchmaking wand?' Roisin asked, kicking her jeans off before pulling her thick sweater and other numerous layers over her head.

'I might just have to.' She caught sight of her sister. 'Good God, Rosi, time for an underwear update.'

Roisin glanced down at her sensible white ensemble bought for comfort rather than sex appeal. Aisling on the other hand was all lace and string up the backside. 'We're not all in the midst of a torrid love affair,' she reminded her sister, slipping the silk dress over her head. She pulled it down, before turning her back. 'Zip me up.' She held her hair up and Aisling obliged. 'Besides the last time I wore a G-string, Noah walked in on me getting dressed and asked if I'd lost my knickers up my bottom.'

Aisling laughed as she squeezed into her matching blue number. 'Now me, and if you manage to rip it in the process, I'll be eternally grateful.'

Roisin eased the zipper up ever so carefully because if she had to parade around in her purple lady of the night dress then Aisling bloody well could too. 'That's you done.'

Aisling tugged at the fabric where it was snug around her middle, making a note to give Moira a kick when she got the chance later. They both moved in front of the mirror giving themselves the once over.

It was Aisling who spoke first. 'Do you remember at the high school when we put on that Mikado show by yer Gilbert and Sullivan fellas?'

'Yes, you were snarky for weeks because Helen Montgomery, Sally Murphy and Maggie Murdoch got to be Yum Yum, Pitti-Sing and Peep-Bo and you were one of the minions carrying an umbrella.'

Aisling nodded, she'd always fancied herself a singer, unfortunately nobody else did. 'Those three couldn't sing to save themselves and the only reason they got their parts was because they were such suck-ups to Sister Frances.'

Roisin clapped a hand to her mouth. 'I just got where you were going with that and you're so right, it's the silk. Christ on a bike, we're the Three Little Maids from School.'

Aisling raised an eyebrow, 'Only one maid's missing.'

Roisin went to the door, 'Moira get your arse down here now!'

Aisling went in search of her mammy's red version of their china silk dresses.

***

So it was Roisin, Aisling and Moira shuffled into the living room each with a folded piece of paper acting as a fan, singing, *Three little maids from school are we*. Even Mammy had to laugh when they reached the bit about being *pert as a schoolgirl well can be.*

Chapter 28

♥

'Noah, be a good boy for Nana, do you hear me?' Roisin looked at her son who was snuggled next to his nana on the sofa having decided if he couldn't beat her he might as well join her. She was reading him a story from an old picture book he'd dragged out of a box of old toys and books shoved down the back of the wardrobe in Roisin's old room. A bar of chocolate lay opened on the coffee table, a row missing and a tell-tale rim of chocolate around his face. The jelly baby bag lay empty, and abandoned next to him. When all else failed, no child could ever resist the lure of chocolate and sweets, Roisin thought, knowing that Colin would be horrified at him stuffing his face with all that sugar. But, Colin wasn't here and she was going to go out and enjoy herself tonight because it felt like forever since she'd put her glad rags on and had a good time.

She glanced down at her dress, not her choice of glad rags. There was no getting out of wearing the Chinese silk not without upsetting Mammy and she wanted her to look after Noah so she'd acquiesced. If she had to wear the dress then Aisling and Moira had to wear theirs, even if Mammy's dress did hang rather sack-like on Moira. Aisling had been adamant that it would not be happening until Roisin had gotten in her ear as to how Quinn might find the dress sexy. 'You know,' she'd whispered, 'it might er spice things up even more.' Aisling's green eyes had lit up and she'd gone to put her boldest, naughtiest red lipstick on teeming it with her red Louboutin's. Surprisingly it all worked rather well.

Moira was sulking as she loitered in the doorway waiting to go. 'Sure, I don't know Tom all that well. It will be your fault, Roisin O'Mara, if he decides I'm not the girl for him.' Roisin didn't think it was likely because only Moira could still look stunning in a dress borrowed from her mammy. Her youngest sister had turned her attention on Aisling trying to wheedle a pair of shoes from her designer collection to no avail. 'It's not fair, you're letting Rosi wear your Jimmy Choo's. That's favouritism so it is.'

'They're knock-offs.'

Roisin looked down at the purple stiletto shoes feeling cheated.

'And you don't look after things.'

'Once, Aisling! I got the teeniest scratch on the heel, once!'

'Girls that's enough. Cut it out or I'll bang your heads together.'

With that threat hanging in the air the three sisters each left a great big lipstick mark on Noah's cheeks. 'Mammy, get Noah to run downstairs and fetch Nina if you get stuck on the toilet,' Roisin tossed over her shoulder and, with Moira muttering on about them being the ugly stepsisters, and in a cloud of clashing perfumes they tottered out the door and down the stairs.

Chapter 29

♥

'Roisin O'Mara, well it's a pleasure to meet you. The missing O'Mara sister!' Alasdair kissed Roisin on both cheeks before releasing her and taking a step back. 'And what a stunning trio you ladies make tonight in your haute couture.'

'Fibber,' Aisling said grinning, waiting for where Alasdair would decide his and Rosi's paths had crossed. True to form, he picked up Roisin's hand and kissed it. She'd been forewarned about Quinn's flamboyant, maître de and his penchant for telling customers how they'd known one another in a past life. He'd even got a mention under the restaurant guide of the Irish Lonely Planet, Aisling said. It had done wonders for putting Quinn's on the map.

'Hmm...' His stare was intent. 'I'm being swept back through the sands of time and find myself standing in the shadows of the Great Pyramid of Giza. Yes, you were my Cleopatra and I, your Mark Antony.'

'Cleopatra, Queen of Egypt, I can live with that,' Roisin laughed as he gave her a final kiss on the hand.

'You said I was the love of your life last week,' Moira said, bottom lip out.

'Yes, but you left me for me another man, him over there.' He pointed over his shoulder with his thumb to where Tom was chatting to a tableful of people whose loosened ties were a giveaway they'd not long left the office. He spied Moira and winked over at her.

'Can you blame her, Alasdair, I mean look,' Aisling said as Tom turned and walked toward the kitchen with the order he'd just taken. All eyes swivelled to his bum.

Reggie was wondering what he'd let himself in for as he listened to the carry-on, sure you didn't get a greeting like that at The Mill. He craned his neck looking for Shay and saw him near the stage talking to another long-haired lad. Shay spotted him and waved over before breaking away and making his way over to the eclectic group huddled around the entrance. Aisling, he saw, was flanked by two other women, her sisters he assumed, even though they looked nothing like her. There was a striking similarity between the other two though, who were both dark haired and very pretty but it was the woman in the purple dress who caught his eye. She was gorgeous.

Roisin saw the tall guy with the messed-up hair and faded blue jeans making his way across the room. She guessed, from Aisling's effusive description earlier, he was Mr Donovan's grandson. She could quite see why he'd bring out a woman's inner Jessica Rabbit. She found herself sucking her stomach in and standing a little straighter.

'Grandad, you made it.' Shay shook the hand his grandfather held out.

'I wouldn't have missed it.'

'And, I like your style arriving with three gorgeous women.'

Reggie smiled his acknowledgement and refrained from adding that the sisters had nearly suffocated him in the taxi. There was no need to be so heavy handed with the perfume and they'd bickered all the way here. He'd been relieved to find the restaurant really was only around the corner. He couldn't have stuck much longer in a confined space with them.

Aisling introduced Moira and Roisin who were both giggly as he shook their hands in turn but not quite in Bronagh's league.

'I love your dresses. Is there a story behind them? Or do you always get around dressed identically.'

Roisin relayed the tale of how their mam had had them made for her and Aisling on a recent trip to Vietnam and given it was Moira who'd encouraged her, they'd made her wear their mammy's red version of the identical pattern. Shay tossed his head back and laughed and Roisin felt proud of herself. She couldn't remember the last time Colin had laughed at one of her stories. He usually rolled his eyes and wore a pained expression when she mentioned mammy and her sisters' carry-on.

'It's nice you're catching up with your grandad,' she said in conversation as they walked with their group to the table Alasdair was ushering them over to. Shay looked at her and not seeing any reason not to, told her above the general chatter and laugher rebounding around the room that today was the first time he'd ever met his grandad. She wanted to hear more but Alasdair was waiting patiently with her chair pulled out for her. She sat down and smiled her thanks at him, getting a kiss blown at her in return as he minced off to tend to the new arrivals who'd just burst through the doors.

Shay moved around the table to check on Reggie who assured him he was fine. 'Well I'd better get set up. I hope you enjoy your evening.' He nodded to the girls and Roisin's eyes followed him as he walked back to the stage.

'What colour are they?' Moira leaned over and asked.

'What do you mean?'

'I mean you just undressed the man, what colour are his underpants.'

'I did not. Sure, I've only been separated thirty something hours.'

'You did too.' Tom distracted Moira as he appeared and kissed her on her cheek. Roisin felt a pang as she heard him whisper, 'You look gorgeous.'

It had been a long time since a man had said that to her. Moira introduced him to Roisin and she liked him instantly. There was a genuine warmth to his smile—he would treat her baby sister well, she decided. Tom complimented the sisters on their dresses which made them all giggle and do another rendition of Three Little Maids. He shook his head as he passed around the menus, they were mad, mad as hatters the O'Mara women. 'What would you like to drink?'

Roisin looked from Moira to Aisling, 'Wine?'

'Coke for me,' Moira said.

Aisling nodded, 'White?'

'Grand.'

'A bottle of your house white please, Tom and a coke for Moira.'

Tom looked to Reggie who asked for lemonade and with a smile and a nod he set off to fill their drinks order.

'You're still off the sauce then, Moira?' Roisin asked. 'And he really does have a great bum by the way.'

'He does and I am.' She shrugged. 'I like myself better sober.'

'Good for you.'

Roisin remembered her manners as Aisling got up from her seat announcing she was going to find Quinn. She swayed off in the direction of the kitchen. 'So, Mr Donovan, where is it you come from?'

Reggie couldn't remember the last time he'd engaged in the art of polite conversation but he could do this. He wouldn't show Shay up and so, he began to tell Roisin and Moira about his home in Castlebeg and how he'd lived there most of his life. His breath snagged in his throat as he told them about his work at the woollen mill and he began to cough. It overtook him and Roisin set about pouring him a glass of water from the jug on the table. 'Here we go, Mr Donovan, have a sip of this, it should help.'

He took it from her gratefully and sipped the cool liquid, slowly feeling the tightness abate. And then he said something that both sisters were completely unprepared for. 'My daughter, Jodie, she's why I came to Dublin. I haven't seen her since I told her to leave when she was pregnant with young Shay up there. That's nearly thirty years ago. It's a long time so it is and I can hardly believe I'm sitting here in a fancy restaurant with three women I hardly know about to see my grandson perform.'

'Oh,' Roisin managed to say as she processed what he'd confided. Moira just looked at him curiously wondering whether he would elaborate.

'I don't deserve to be here tonight but I'm very glad I am. Thank you, for letting me tag along with you.'

Aisling was right, Roisin thought, this really wasn't the same man she'd encountered this morning. She reached over and put her hand on top of his, feeling the tree root veins on the back of his as she gave it a squeeze. She was lost for words and besides this was one of those occasions when anything she could have come up with would have sounded banal. Instead of speaking she kept her hand on his.

Moira piped up, 'Well I hope you enjoy your night then, Mr Donovan.'

'Call me Reggie, please.'

Shay, tuned the pegs of his fiddle and watched the exchange at the table over in the far corner, bemused.

Aisling had dragged Quinn away from his busy kitchen and Roisin got up to give him a hello hug telling Aisling to leave the poor man alone long enough for her to do so. 'You've done so well, Quinn, this place is fabulous. I hope you're proud of yourself,' she gushed, stepping back and seeing that the round-faced student she recalled had been replaced by a chiselled, successful man in his mid-thirties.

They chatted for a few minutes before Quinn excused himself. 'I've a new junior chef and I can't leave him alone with the potatoes or he'll be after mashing them when I want them roasted.'

'Oi, get a room you two!' Moira bellowed as Aisling honed in for a kiss before he left. 'Excuse them, Mr, er, Reggie, like rabbits so they are, young love and all that.' She gave him a wink.

Roisin rolled her eyes. Moira had no idea when it came to boundaries.

Reggie for his part could not believe how much the times had changed, it really was a different world these days. When Jodie had been young, sex before marriage was seen as a sin as bad as murder. He couldn't help but feel the times had changed for the better.

The waiter, Tom, reappeared and he hastily pulled his glasses from his pocket to look at the menu. He'd not much of an appetite but he'd manage a few bites of a soft fluffy mash. He looked up and ordered the Bangers n Mash. Tom scribbled down the rest of the orders and Reggie was certain he saw the youngest sister pinch the behind of the young waiter fella. Yes, she was a bold one that one, he thought.

The band's front man spoke into his microphone, introducing them as The Sullivan's and the crowd clapped, a cheer and whistle erupting from somewhere in the room. They launched straight into a toe-tapping number Reggie didn't recognise but he could see they were going to have every single person in the room in the palm of their hand before the night was through. He sat back in his chair transfixed by the way Shay's hand was expertly guiding the bow back and forth across the strings. There was a look of intense concentration and simultaneous joy on his face. He imprinted his grandson's expression to memory for when the days became dark.

Roisin too couldn't take her eyes off Shay and she got a kick under the table from Moira. 'You're gawping, shut yer gob.'

The music played through their meals which they all told Quinn when he came out to see if they were enjoying themselves, were fabulous. Reggie had managed a few forkfuls of the mash but he was still feeling the effects of having over done it with his breakfast. The day had begun to catch up with him with a vengeance and as the plates were cleared away and the O'Mara sisters' drinks were topped up, he decided he'd say goodnight when the band took a break.

~

Shay walked his grandad to the taxi rank a few doors down from the restaurant and before he settled him into the passenger seat he hugged his frail frame tightly. Reggie clung to the boy. He didn't want to let him go but the driver coughed, impatient to drop this short fare home so he could get back to the rank. 'I'll come and see you tomorrow, Grandad.'

'I'd like that, Shay, son. I'd like that more than anything.'

~

Inside Quinn's the drink flowed, Tom was run off his feet, and by the time the music cranked to the next level the three O'Mara girls took to the dance floor in all their satin glory to stamp their feet and clap their hands along to *Whiskey in the Jar*. Shay winked at Aisling, challenge met, he'd gotten Roisin up on that floor bopping with the best of them.

Chapter 30

'Ah, sure it was a gas! The best craic I've had in ages, but my feet are killing me,' Roisin muttered as Moira punched in the code to open the door. 'I'm not used to heels. How Ash gets round in them all day, is beyond me.'

It was late, Nina had long since clocked off. The reception area was lit by a warm glow from the lamp that stayed on to welcome those guests arriving back after ten pm. Roisin slipped the shoes off her feet as soon as she was in the door. She followed behind Moira, wincing at each creak of the stairs. She was worn out, bed was calling, she might even be really bad and not bother to take her make-up off she decided as they reached the third floor. Moira headed straight for the kitchen and Roisin decided she'd do well to knock back a couple of glasses of water before turning in.

'Aisling seems really happy. They make such a good couple,' Roisin said, grabbing herself a glass as Moira shovelled a few crisps in her mouth, the packet a remnant of Noah and his nana's party for two.

'Yeah, they do,' she said, wiping her mouth with the back of her hand. 'I'm not even hungry but I can never say no to cheese 'n' onion.'

'And I like Tom, he seems lovely.'

'I like him too, he is lovely.' Moira licked salt off her fingers. 'And what was with you and Mr Hot Fiddle?'

'What do you mean?' Roisin turned the tap off.

'I thought I was going to have to grab the fire extinguisher and put whatever it was going on between yer out.'

'You've a vivid imagination, that's all.' She had caught him looking her way a few times and it had sent a thrill through her. It had made her remember that she wasn't just an unhappy wife and Noah's mum, she was Roisin, a woman in her own right.

'If you say so, I'm off to bed.'

'Night, night.' Roisin stood beside the sink drinking her water slowly, thinking about Shay. He'd grabbed a beer and come and sat next to her after he'd seen his grandad out. Moira had seen an old workmate and was off chatting to her. Shay had told her about his work as a Creative Producer. His life was bright and colourful, she thought, listening with interest. He'd asked her what it was she did over in London and Roisin had hesitated. A part of her wanted to impress him and see where the evening led. She wanted to be Roisin O'Mara, the girl who'd never taken life too seriously, the girl who'd flitted about like a butterfly from job to job, and place to place, laughing along the way. She wasn't that girl anymore though and so she'd told him the truth. She was very newly separated and unsure what her next step would be but whatever happened, Noah was her priority.

Shay had taken it in his stride. He hadn't immediately vacated his seat and headed for the hills. Instead he'd talked about how it had been for his mam all those years ago when she'd found herself alone and pregnant.

'She was a brave woman,' Roisin had said when he'd finished talking.

'She was, but you are too, I can tell.' He winked. 'You'll be grand.'

In that moment, Roisin believed him. She would be grand.

With that thought in mind, she put her glass in the sink, flicked out the light and tiptoed down the hall. She was looking forward to the moment she could snuggle up next to Noah's warm little body. To her surprise though, as she opened the bedroom door, she saw her son wasn't in bed, he was up at the window. 'Hey, you, what are you doing? You should be asleep, young man.'

He hadn't heard her creep in and he looked startled but didn't move away from the window. 'Mummy, come and look, there's a fox down there.'

Mr Fox, Roisin smiled to herself. How many times had she stood where Noah was now keeping a watch out for the little fox who came to visit their courtyard? 'Don't move. I'll be back in a minute.'

She crept back to the kitchen not bothering to turn the light on as she opened the fridge and peered inside. *Ah, there it was*. She picked up the block of aged cheddar and, leaving the fridge door open so she could see, pulled a knife from the block on the bench. She sliced off a generous wedge and popped it straight in her mouth savouring the bitey flavour. Like Moira, she wasn't hungry but she could never say no to a piece of cheese. *One more for the road*, she stuffed a second generous serving in her mouth and then got round to doing what she'd come to do. She cut off a few good chunks and then covering up all evidence of her ever having been in the kitchen at midnight eating cheese, she sneaked back to their room.

Noah was where she'd left him. She gave him the cheese and then eased the window up hoping it wouldn't squeak. The fox froze, he was nearly at the bin now and his ears twitched as he looked up. 'Mum, his eyes look like they're glowing,' Noah said, his breath sending out white plumes in the night air.

'He can see in the dark, that's why. Toss a piece of the cheese down, Noah, but be careful not to hit him. He loves a bit cheddar, does Mr Fox.' Noah leaned out and dropped the cheese down, watching in wonder as the fox darted over to it, snaffling it down. Noah dropped the other two pieces one at a time, his eyes wide as the fox made short work of them both. 'I think it might be time to say goodnight to Mr Fox now, Noah. We need to get some sleep.'

'Na-night, Mr Fox.' He moved reluctantly away from the window and Roisin eased it shut, closing the curtains and sliding into her pyjamas before clambering into bed next to her son.

'Ooh, it's cold out there.' She pulled Noah close. 'Did you have a nice time with your nana?'

'I did, but she shouts at the television a lot.'

Roisin smiled in the darkness; her heart full as she pulled her boy close. Down below there was the clattering of a bin lid and she knew that come morning the air would be blue when Mrs Flaherty realised Mr Fox had been into her bin again. She kissed Noah on the back of his head and wondered if eating that cheese had been a good idea. Mammy always said eating cheese late at night would give yer strange dreams. Mind, Mammy said lots of things.

Chapter 31

♥

Roisin woke the next morning and it took her a few seconds to realise she wasn't stuck on top of a Ferris wheel, the other cars all full of red foxes, while Mrs Flaherty down on the ground waved her rolling pin at them all. She sat up and swung her legs over the bed. It would have been much nicer to have been having a sexy Shay dream. She shook off the weird feelings the dream had conjured. That was definitely the last time she hoed into the cheese before bed, she resolved. Noah was already up she saw, glancing at the dent he'd left on his side of the bed. Best she get up and see what he was up to. She stood up, knotting her dressing gown and ignored the apparition with the mascara-streaked cheeks she glimpsed in the mirror on her way out.

'Ah, there you are, Rosi. I was just about to send Noah in to get you. I think you've some explaining to do, don't you?' Mammy was tapping her foot in a way that made Roisin feel like she was twelve and had been caught with her hand in the biscuit jar, having been told specifically to leave them alone because she'd be having her dinner soon. She was also still half asleep and unsure why Jenny's husband was standing in their living room, grinning at her. *And what the feck was that in his arms?*

'You're a life saver, Roisin. Thanks so much for offering to take Pooh. You're, er, looking well.'

She wasn't awake enough to be embarrassed at looking such a state. He thrust the bundle he was holding at her. 'Sorry to drop and run but I've a meeting first thing. I've brought everything I think you'll need.' He gestured to a pile of pet paraphernalia piled up in the middle of the living room and made a run for it.

The curly haired bundle in her arms squirmed and yapped.

'Roisin?' Mammy said, 'What is going on?'

Her conversation with Jenny came flooding back. 'Well, you said you wanted a dog. Jenny and Eoin had their hands full with the twins, and they couldn't look after a puppy as well so I sort-a offered to take Pooh here on your behalf. He's a poodle and you did say you wanted a small dog, Mam. Sure, it's the perfect solution. I've saved you faffing around with the DSPCA.' Noah was jumping up and down beside her, desperate to pet the wee pup.

'Yes, Rosi, a grand plan indeed and you're right he is a poodle just not a miniature or toy one. He's a fecking standard poodle, you, eejit. A standard poodle called Pooh.'

***

Jodie stood looking out at the garden, the pile of leaves, were waiting to be bagged up and binned to mulch down for the spring. She loved her garden and she watched as a little robin danced around the stark limbs of the cherry blossom tree. She still couldn't believe her dad had turned up yesterday. The shock when she'd opened the door and seen him standing there had been like plunging into ice water. She'd been harsh, she knew she had. She could see he was sick. There'd been so many times over the years that she'd wanted to reach out but

CHAPTER 32

the finality of his words and his inaction at tracking her down had always stopped her.

She'd kept up to date as to how he was over the years thanks to Bridie, who despite all her grand plans had settled in the village, marrying a local lad she met at the dance. She was happy, though, Castlebeg was a good fit for her. She and Orna had made many trips to Dublin to stay with her, Philip and Shay over the years. They, along with Gill, had become her family. So how dare he just knock on her door and expect to pick up as though nothing ever happened?

Shay, her beautiful boy, had taken it upon himself to go and see him. He was sitting at the kitchen bench drinking his tea having raided her pantry like he always did when he called. He'd told her that her da was dying and that he had so many regrets about the way things had gone. He'd come to Dublin to tell her he loved her, had never stopped loving her. The thing was she'd never stopped loving him either.

'Mam? Are you ready?'

Jodie turned, squinting at the shards of sun framing Shay as he stood at the back door. She nodded and walked toward her son. He dropped his arm around her shoulder and, picking up his keys from where he'd dropped them on the hallway table, they headed out to his car.

***

Bronagh greeted Shay like a long-lost friend and Jodie hung back feeling the faint stirrings of nerves. 'Shall I give him a ring or did you want to go on through and give him a knock?'

'Mam?'

'We'll give him a knock.'

Jodie followed Shay past the front desk, glancing in at the empty guests' lounge before turning the corner to where

Room 1's door was shut. Shay moved aside to let her tap on the door. It took a few moments but they could hear movement and then the door opened. Reggie, who'd been about to go in search of a cup of tea, stood there blinking. He must be dreaming. *It couldn't be, could it?*

'Hello, Da, shall we start again?'

He dropped his stick and held out his arms. Jodie stepped into his embrace.

Chapter 32

♥

Two weeks later

'Rosi, God above, give me patience. Yoga?'

'Yes, Mam, yoga. It's an ancient form of mental, spiritual and physical exercise and I'm going to become an instructor.'

'I know what yoga is, Roisin. But how are you going to manage if you go back to college or wherever it is you go to learn how to teach yoga? Sweet Jaysus,' her hand flew to her chest. 'Please tell me you're not going to India.'

'I'm not going to India, Mam, and I can train under my teacher at home. It's all down to the hours I do and I can work part-time at the same time. Sure, I used to manage before I met Colin and had Noah. I'll manage again.' Roisin had made her mind up. She was going to take Stephanie up on her offer and she was going to make her way in London. Colin still didn't seem to grasp the fact she wasn't coming back but he would in time and they'd work out a routine together for Noah. It would work. Things would be fine. She might be flighty but she was also strong and she would survive this patch and come out the other side.

Shay had called in at the guesthouse the other day and Bronagh had rung upstairs with a decided tone in her voice, disgruntled that Roisin was being swept out for coffee. There was something about Shay, he was easy for her to talk to and she'd told him what her plans were. There was a connection between them, a zing when their hands accidentally met over the sugar bowl, but the timing was all out. He'd asked if, when he was next in London, he might call in and say hi, and she'd given him her number. They'd gone their separate ways from the coffee shop and she'd looked back over her shoulder watching his tall frame cutting through the crowds and felt a spark of hope that one day the timing might be right.

'Well, come on then give us a demonstration.' Maureen interrupted Roisin's thoughts. 'I want to see what's so special about this bendy business.' There'd be a great big hole in that sofa by the time Mammy got her cast off, Roisin thought, but at least she looked like Mammy again. The frizz was gone and her normal shoulder-length hair had been restored to its shiny glory thanks to Rosemary calling back around to do a shampoo and deep conditioning treatment. She kept swishing her head around because, she said, she missed hearing the clack of the beads.

Noah was rolling a ball to Pooh who was having a brilliant time chasing after it. He was going to miss the pup. Perhaps she'd see about getting a pet when they eventually got settled. Moira and Aisling were sipping their morning brews at the table.

'C'mon, you two, get off your arses and do a round of sun salutations with me,' Roisin bossed.

'Yes, go on,' Mammy urged, keen for some entertainment.

Moira and Aisling obliged, taking up their positions behind Roisin. All three sisters were still in their pyjamas as they stood statue erect. Roisin swung her arms up, raising her hands skyward and Moira and Aisling glanced at one another before following suit. They sounded like obscene phone callers as they imitated Roisin's heavy breathing. She stepped through into the next pose, her body strong in the position. Moira was muttering about it not being natural but trying to arrange herself into a similar stance to her big sister while Aisling wobbled back and forth, her thighs threatening to betray her.

'You're quite good at this, sort-a naturally authoritative,' Maureen remarked surprised as Roisin led her sisters through several more moves before sliding smoothly into downward dog.

'Sure, that's not very ladylike. The three of you with yer arses in the air like that. Move it along, Rosi.'

Roisin obliged, transitioning to the deep relaxing stretch that was child's pose. She was feeling in the zone until Moira's voice shattered the peace.

'Mammy, get that fecking dog away from my backside.'

Roisin looked back at her sister, who looked anything but tranquil, and over at her mam who'd grown very attached to Pooh despite her protestations to the contrary. Aisling was giggling at the sight of the dog. 'Sure, he's game,' she snorted. 'I wouldn't be sniffing around that for all the tea in China.'

'Oh, feck off, Aisling.'

Christmas at O'Mara's

♥

Introduction

Cliona Whelan, Clio for short, had been many things in her fifty-nine years on this earth. A daughter, a sister, an aunt, a friend, journalist and now a published and, some would say, feted novelist, but there were things she hadn't been too. Things she'd have liked to have been had fate played her a different hand. If she'd been born into these modern times, perhaps she would have had it all but in her youth, there was no such thing as, "having your cake and eating it too". She'd had to make choices, hard decisions because she couldn't have it all. She wasn't a wife, nor a mother and she would never be someone's grandmother. 'I've got you though haven't I, Bess.' It was a statement not a question and she reached down to stroke the cat's silky back as she meandered past on her way through from the kitchen where she'd finished her breakfast to bask on her favourite chair. Bess mewled but didn't pause on her well-worn path.

Clio took a sip of milky tea from her china cup. The dancing rose pattern, so delicate against the white, bone china, was beautiful and she paused briefly to admire it as she set it back down in its matching saucer. The Japanese knew the importance of things being just right when it came to drinking one's tea. They'd understand her refusal to sip her morning brew from anything other than this rose teacup. It was a habit adopted from her mam. God rest her soul. 'It tastes different when it's not in my cup,' Maeve Whelan used to say. Clio had thought her a terrible old fusspot suffering from delusions of grandeur when she was young, but now, she knew exactly what she'd meant.

She heard the familiar rattle of the cast iron letter slot being pushed open by Niall. He of the ruddy cheeks and ready grin who'd been the postman delivering to her street for forever and a day. It was followed by the soft plop of mail landing on the mat by the front door. Clio liked this time of year. Oh, she wasn't a fan of the cold. She'd have been happier banging away on her trusty old typewriter somewhere warm and sunny like Spain. Dublin could be bleak in the depth of winter. What she liked about the month of December though, was the way in which people became kinder and more engaged with one another. Those that would hurry along the streets, heads down, keen to be on their way the rest of the year, would slow a little, look one another in the eye and give a nodding smile in passing. It was as if they'd suddenly remembered what really mattered in life. She enjoyed sifting through the post of a morning too knowing there'd be a pile of cards to open—it was much more enjoyable than eyeing the electric bill while munching her toast.

Clio liked to eke out her morning routine, partly because it took longer to wind through the gears and crank into fourth these days and partly because she wasn't, and never had been, a morning person. She got up and knotted her dressing gown tie before padding through on slipper-clad feet to the kitchen. She slotted her toast into the toaster pushing the handle down before going to fetch the mail. The white envelopes lay scattered on the floor and her eyes flitted over the different handwriting as she scooped them up, but as she registered the postmark on one such envelope her breath caught and her hand fluttered to her mouth. The envelope, as her eyes drifted to the lazy, looping script she'd never expected to see again, seemed to vibrate in her hand. It was nonsensical she knew. Her heart, she realised, had begun to race in a way she should perhaps at her age find alarming but the doctor had told her just last week her ticker was strong as an ox.

'Go and sit down, Clio,' she ordered and with the envelope pulsing on top of the small pile she'd swept up, that's what she did. She pushed her glasses onto the bridge of her nose and pinched her bottom lip between her teeth as she retrieved the letter opener from the dish on the table. Then, sliding it through the crisp white paper, she retrieved the card inside. The last correspondence she'd had from him had been a letter written on a sheet of notepaper. That was forty-one years ago, although, if you were to ask her, she could tell you exactly where that letter could be found. This card, she saw inspecting it, was rather nondescript, an expensive looking nativity picture, a slightly different version of the same scenes already draped over the string she'd tied around one curtain finial stretching it across to the other as she did each year to dangle her cards from.

She wondered if he'd spent time in the newsagent's loitering for an age by the rack of Christmas cards trying to decide which to choose, in the end playing it safe and settling on something rather stock standard. Or, perhaps it had simply come from a packet of ten, selected at random from the choice of Santa Claus with his sack of presents, a Christmas tree or the nativity scene. Nerves were making her procrastinate because it wasn't the image on the front that mattered, it was what the card said inside. 'Go on, Clio, old girl. Since when you were afraid of anything? Open it.' She did so.

Chapter 1

♥

London, December 21, 1999

Roisin O'Mara was not feeling festive. In fact, she was feeling decidedly foul and full of fecks as with her free hand she closed the gate. It clanged shut with a force threatening to snap it off its hinges. The plastic bag with the presents she was carting banged against her leg as she stomped up the path to the front door. Its green colour was a beacon on a day that was threatening more snow and she sent a flurry of the sludgy stuff that had settled overnight flying as her feet skidded on the icy surface. 'Fecking, Colin,' she muttered, her breath coming in huffy, white puffs. You'd have thought he'd have swept the path for them. Mind you, she shouldn't be surprised. Considerate had never been a word that sprang to mind when she thought about her estranged husband. She was beginning to agree with her sister Moira, Arse was a much more fitting term for Colin Quealey.

Sure, a girl could fall over and do an injury on this path, she griped silently. 'Watch your step, Noah.' Her son was in a hurry to reach the house and she'd rather he made it there intact. They were late, which wasn't helping her mood because she knew their tardy arrival would be noted with a sniff.

Her soon to be ex-mother-in-law, Elsa, was the queen of the disapproving sniff. The annoying thing was it wasn't even her fault. They'd left their tiny flat in a leafy, overpriced pocket of Greenwich in plenty of time but her old banger had protested against the cold by refusing to start. Her language, muttered under her breath, had been ripe as she turned the key for the umpteenth time knowing she was in danger of flooding the engine. She'd been about to tell Noah to unbuckle because they'd have to go back inside and ring Daddy to ask him to pick them up when she'd given it one last try. She'd sent a "thank you" heavenward as the engine spluttered into life.

The traffic despite the busy time of year had been light on the drive over. Roisin was guessing most people had the sense to hunker down for the day than to venture out and about. She envied them, she'd thought, turning into Staunton Mews ten minutes later. It was the sort of Sunday that should be spent in pyjamas, snuggling under a duvet on the couch watching videos while stuffing one's face, not partaking in a farcical Christmas day with whatever you called your mother-in-law and husband once you'd pulled the pin on your marriage.

She'd managed to slide into a parking space a few doors down from number nine and even though she'd only walked from the car to the path her feet were already icicles inside her boots. This was despite her having worn socks so thick over her black tights she knew her boots would be pinching before the day was out.

Oh yes, this two Christmas days lark was a pain in the arse and she'd have rather left Colin, Elsa and Noah to the goose that was undoubtedly on the menu but Elsa had other plans. She'd been insistent she come, giving a loud sniff before remonstrating, 'It's important to present a united front you know, Roisin. That poor boy deserves a proper Christmas with both his parents given everything he's been through.'

Roisin knew she wasn't being overly sensitive—there was a definite accusatory tone in Elsa Quealey's voice. She'd been tempted to point out that her son had played a lead role in their marriage disintegrating too. Elsa seemed to have forgotten all about the bank having foreclosed on them, selling their home and assets to clear debts Colin had amassed, unbeknown to his wife, with his ill-fated, investments. This was why Roisin and Noah now lived in a flat the size of a shoebox and why she drove a temperamental car that would have been right at home cruising the streets back in nineteen seventy-one. It was also why her husband at the ripe old age of thirty-nine had slunk home to lick his wounds at his mother's house. She'd have dearly loved to have rubbed Elsa's nose in all of this as she looked down that long beak of hers waiting for her to say yes to her Christmas dinner invitation.

It rankled too the reference to 'poor Noah'. He was doing fine. Sure, the first wee while had been rough as he adjusted to all the changes their separation wrought, but of late he'd settled down and was back to his usual, happy self, pestering her constantly for a gerbil. He hadn't shut up about it, in fact. He'd forgotten all about wanting Mummy and Daddy to live together in their old house again because becoming the owner of a small, furry brown rodent was the number one priority in his life.

Roisin's friend Stephanie had warned her not to go there and she was inclined to agree, as was her landlord, who'd enunciated loudly—he was hard of hearing—that no animals were allowed. Was a gerbil an animal? Roisin wasn't sure but it was a good excuse to appease Noah, so she'd run with it. 'They look small and innocuous enough,' Stephanie had said. 'You could even say they're quite sweet looking but Rosi think about the havoc Charlie caused bringing Beyoncé to school on pet day.'

Roisin had nodded. She well remembered the story of Stephanie's daughter's gerbil escaping and terrorising the headmistress by hiding out in the toilets. Still, the look on Noah's face when he'd asked whether she thought Father

Christmas would get his letter in time because there was NOTHING he wanted more in the world than a gerbil and he'd been ever such a good boy had made her waiver. Perhaps she could get away with a soft toy version. Ah, who was she kidding?

That's what she needed to remember, she told herself looking down at her son. Today was about him, not her, and besides if she hadn't agreed to come then Colin might have put his foot down regarding her spending Christmas day proper with her family in Dublin. They'd yet to iron out all the nitty gritty finer points of custody where their son was concerned but seemed to have settled into an unspoken arrangement whereby, he spent every second weekend with his daddy and Granny Quealey.

Her son's hat was pulled down low and he was dwarfed inside the jacket Colin had bought him a few weeks ago despite his proclamations of trying to get back on his feet and that the maintenance he was currently paying out was daylight robbery. There'd been nothing wrong with Noah's old jacket but Colin was a show pony, always had been and appearances mattered to him. She could sense, despite his five-year-old body being hidden inside an expensive layer of goose down, Noah twitching with an energetic excitement at the thought of what lay in wait for him inside Granny Quealey's house. Throw in some sugary treats that were bound to be coming his way very soon and he'd be bouncing off the walls in no time.

That was another thing, she thought, a gloved finger pressing the doorbell and holding it down for longer than was necessary; those weekends spent here saw Noah get spoiled rotten. He'd burst in through the door of their small flat on a Sunday afternoon full of stories about ice creams and trips to the cinema. She felt as though she were in a competition for her son's affections, one in which not only the financial odds were stacked against her but the opportunity to simply relax and have fun with him too. What annoyed her most of all and yes, she knew it was irrational but she couldn't help how she felt was Elsa serving him up chicken nuggets and chips, his all-time favourite. Her son was very quick to point out that she didn't put anything green on his plate to ruin his dinner either. He'd say this while waving a piece of broccoli at her in an accusatory fashion. Colin would have told her off when they were still living under the same roof if she'd put an unbalanced meal like that in front of Noah. Would he say "boo" to his mother, though? No, he would not.

Their roles had changed since they'd parted ways. He it seemed, got to play at being jolly, good time daddy every second weekend, something he'd never been good at before but seemed to be hitting his stride with now, while she did the day to day parenting hard yards. It wasn't fair.

Her mood darkened as she jiggled inside her coat waiting for the door to open. She'd never breathe a word about how their new arrangement made her feel to Colin because his face would scrunch up in that annoying pinched way it did when something pained him and he'd say, 'Well, Roisin, it wasn't my decision to separate nor is it my fault Noah has to split his time between his parents.' He'd be right too; it had been her decision and not one she'd taken lightly. She and Colin had not been a good match. It was also one, despite her and Noah's flat with its moaning and groaning pipes and dodgy hot water, she didn't regret. 'Hurry up,' she muttered, her breath emitting another puff of white into the air.

'You look like you're smoking, Mummy.' Noah grinned revealing two new front teeth finally beginning to grow down. His lisp was still pronounced though. He reached over and snapped a twig from the spindly hydrangea in the front garden.

'What are you doing?'

Noah didn't get a chance to answer because the door swung open to reveal Elsa Quealey. The smile on her face drooped as she took in the sight of her beloved grandson holding a twig between his fingers and sucking on it as though his life depended on it.

Chapter 2

'What are you doing, Noah?' Elsa frowned, watching as he exhaled a white plume into the air with the kind of satisfied gusto reserved for those that had just done the deed.

'Smoking like Mummy.'

'Noah, I don't smoke.' Roisin was indignant.

'No, but it looked like you were, Mummy.'

Elsa shook her grey chin-length hair which was as inflexible as she was, thanks to the liberal misting of Elnett hairspray each morning. Roisin watched her lips purse signalling disapproval and it made her think of a cat's arse. Jaysus, she was really getting into the swing of things, Roisin thought, giving her Christmas finery the once over as they were swept in from the cold. Elsa had teemed her handknitted red reindeer sweater with a pair of fat twin Santa Clauses dangling from her ear lobes. As the front door was closed behind her, Roisin's sense of smell was assaulted simultaneously with the aroma of roasting goose and her mother-in-law's heady floral fragrance, Joy. She'd be a nightmare to get stuck in a lift with, Roisin had often thought, sure you'd suffocate from the fumes coming off her before anyone come to the rescue.

'Shoes off, Noah, please,' Roisin bossed as Elsa busied herself unwrapping him and hanging his coat up on the hooks by the door leaving her to stamp the snow off her boots and shrug out of her coat. She felt very un-Christmassy compared to her mother-in-law in her plain grey wrap dress. It had seemed simple and stylish when she'd put it on that morning, the perfect outfit for a date with her ex-husband and his mother, nothing flashy, no hint of cleavage or thigh to be disapproved over, but now it just seemed drab. She fluffed her hair up knowing the woolly hat she'd pulled on would have flattened it.

'Colin's just on a business call. He works so hard that boy, he never stops,' Elsa said, herding them into the front room. 'The fire's roaring. Go and warm yourselves up. I've just got to baste the goose and then I'll bring some light refreshments through. I'll be back in a jiffy.'

You'd think she was entertaining the landed gentry, Roisin thought. It was going to be a long day. She poked her head back out the door and called out, 'I feel terrible arriving empty handed. I would've been happy to bring a dessert or a bottle of wine.' The older woman had been insistent she not bring anything and the bag of begrudged presents she was clutching didn't count. Elsa's sprightly form didn't falter as she marched down the hall waving the comment away.

'Nonsense, Roisin, I always think homemade is so much nicer than shop bought and Colin has a good nose for wine.'

Roisin mouthed, 'Bitch,' behind her back and Colin had a fecking big conker, that's what he had, *nose for wine my arse.* She stood still for a moment and breathed in slowly through her nostrils then exhaled in a slow hiss through her mouth just as she did in her yoga sessions. She was a long way from feeling mindful but it did unknot the twisted feeling her mother-in-law was so adept at bringing out in her.

'Mummy, look at the tree!'

It was real of course, Roisin thought, turning to admire it. It was standing proudly in its bucket giving off a gorgeous scent of pine which was mingling with the woodsmoke from the crackling fire in the hearth. The house had central heating and Elsa only got the fire going on special occasions but there really was something inviting about an open fire, and she looked at the flames leap and dance for a second before turning her attention back to the tree and her son who was squealing with delight at the packages laid out around it.

The decorations dripped from the green fronds which bowed under the weight of them despite the sturdy branches. Roisin knew amongst all the tinsel and baubles were the ornaments Colin would have hung. A new one bought for each of his birthdays. It was a tradition Elsa was carrying on with Noah and five would be set aside for him to place on the tree today. She felt a pang, thinking about the measly fake excuse for a fir tree brought on a rushed trip to Argos earlier in the week. She'd poked it in the corner of their flat trying not to feel let down by its lacklustre appearance which seemed to scream, 'I couldn't be arsed!'. There'd been no point in sourcing a real tree though, not with them heading over to Dublin tomorrow.

She'd done her best to make decorating it fun, popping on the Christmas CD she always played this time of year. Christmas wasn't Christmas without a bit of Band Aid and she did so love doing the Simon le Bon bit. She'd straightened its sparse wire branches, getting Noah to unearth his favourite trimmings from the old suitcase she'd brought with them from their old house. They'd whiled away all of five minutes dressing it, and Noah had asked, as he hung the wooden gingerbread man he'd painted when he was three, if the tree was sick. 'Mummy, it really doesn't look very well you know.'

He was right and as she'd stood back to look at their handiwork she'd sighed. She could hear Mammy in her ear and knew exactly what she'd say if she was there, 'You can't make a silk purse out of a sow's ear, Roisin.' Feeling Noah's eyes on her she'd been tempted to tell him that sometimes in life you got what you paid for but he didn't need to know that, not yet anyway. So, instead she told him she thought the tree might be suffering from tinselitis. He'd whiled away a good hour after that with his little red doctor's kit. Yes, even dripping with Christmassy embellishments their Argos special came a very poor second to this majestic fir tree that had taken up residence in the Quealeys' front room. The sheer size of it rivalled Enid Blyton's Faraway tree. If only she could clamber up it and escape through the cloud at the top to the land of anywhere but here.

She remembered the bag of gifts she'd bought. There was a bar of Joy soap for Elsa—she couldn't stretch to an actual bottle this year but the Boots' girl had assured her the soap was a triple milled, French luxury that wouldn't turn to sludge as it sat beside the bath. There was the usual bottle of malt whisky for Colin and, just because she wanted her presence registered under the tree where Noah was concerned today, a box of Lego. The bloody stuff cost a fortune and should come with a health warning for parents to always wear shoes once opened she'd griped, wrapping it when her son had been brushing his teeth earlier that morning.

'Here, Noah, put these under the tree.' He was already on his hands and knees inspecting the labels on the cheerily wrapped packages leaning against the bucket and ignored the rustle of plastic she set down next to him. He picked one up and prodded at it, a frown of concentration on his face. It was mean the way Elsa always made him wait until after lunch to open his presents. She was a stickler for her traditions and Roisin knew the drill. There would be drinks and nibbles first, followed by a lunch far too big for the four of them, then it would be back here where Noah could finally rip into his presents before doling out the rest of the gifts. Then, it would be time for a game of charades followed by coffee, served in the silver plunger which, like the fire, was reserved for special occasions, and finally a film. The Quality Street would be produced with a flourish but a beady eye would be kept on those attempting to take more than one at a time. Roisin sighed at the thought of it all. She planned on making their escape by four thirty which was the earliest they could politely do so. This would give her enough time to pack for their flight in the morning.

The thought of her mammy and sisters lifted her, she was looking forward to seeing them. It had been over two months since they'd last all been together and although she spoke to one of them every other day it wasn't the same as being there amongst it all. So much had happened since she'd returned from that last trip to Dublin, a newly separated woman who had to somehow find a new life for herself in London. Her brain was still whirring with it all but she hadn't looked back, not once.

Mammy of course had been insistent on meeting them at the airport and that she and Noah come to her in Howth when they arrived. The thing was, her new apartment chosen for its seaside location wasn't O'Mara's. The apartment on the top floor of the family guesthouse was home. Roisin wanted to be back in her old room, to join in with the bickering between Moira and Aisling. Truth be told she'd have given anything to have Mammy and Daddy back under that roof too, but time didn't stand still and things had changed with Daddy's passing. She didn't blame Mammy for moving, she could understand the need for a new beginning after her life had been thrown off course.

Mammy had done the hard sell and would have given any estate agent a run for their money as she emphasised her apartment's seaside location and stunning views. To which Rosie had replied, given the time of year the water was fit for polar bears not people, come to that it was pretty much the same in summertime too. In the end it was decided they'd stay that first night at Mammy's and then play it by ear.

She wondered what the Christmas tree in the foyer of O'Mara's looked like and smiled at the thought of Aisling and Bronagh, the guesthouse's long serving receptionist, arguing over whether they should go with a silver and gold theme.

Bronagh had won, Aisling had told her, adding that fair play to her it did look gorgeous albeit enormous. It couldn't be bigger than the one she was standing here looking at though, surely? Either way she was looking forward to seeing it for herself. Yes, she thought, hugging her arms around herself, it would be nice to be back in Dublin, like putting on a pair of comfy slippers. She twiddled her toes, the fecking boots were already beginning to pinch.

To distract herself from her squished toes, Roisin did a sweep of the room, noting the tidily arranged cards on the mantle. Her eyes moved to the sideboard and she saw the Royal Doulton ballerina and the collection of porcelain Beatrix Potter figurines that normally adorned it had been put away. When Noah had been a toddler, Jemima Puddleduck and her friends had been like a magnet to him and she'd been terrified he'd break one of them. The more she'd told him not to touch the more determined he'd been to do just that. In their place was a faux gingerbread house, a red glow emanating from inside its white trimmed windows and next to it was a nativity scene, the small wooden figures, Roisin knew, having once belonged to Elsa's mother.

'Roisin, Merry Christmas. You're looking well.' Colin intruded on her inspection as he appeared in the doorway, the joviality in his tone sounding forced to her ears but she gave him ten out of ten for effort. Registering her normally staid suit-wearing ex was dressed in a navy version of his mother's reindeer sweater she choked back a giggle. Elsa had him well and truly under the thumb. He was also wearing jeans, and not very well. He was one of those men who never looked comfortable in denim. Come to that he didn't look comfortable in anything casual; it wasn't his style. An awkwardness hovered in the air as they both pondered the best way in which to greet one another. Roisin decided to run with formal which while strange felt more honest than an effusive hug and kiss hello. 'Merry Christmas, Colin.'

He homed in and gave her a peck on the cheek, his lips dry and cool as they grazed her skin. She inhaled his familiar Armani aftershave and for a moment she was tempted to grasp hold of him, to be back where everything was familiar, but she steeled herself. Just because something was familiar and easy didn't mean it was good for you, and besides, she'd done the hardest bit, the actual leaving, and look how far she'd come. No, there was no going back. Still, she acknowledged as he took a step back and ruffled Noah's hair, it was sad how it had all worked out. They'd both gone into their marriage full of hope and look where they were now.

'Thank you for coming,' he said as Noah wrapped himself around his father's legs. There was a time Colin would have been irritated by his son's playful affection but since they'd separated, he seemed to appreciate these gestures more. There was always a silver lining, Rosin mused, and she smiled back at him. He hadn't needed to say that, he was making an effort and so would she. 'The tree's a beauty.'

'Mummy wanted the biggest we could find.'

But it was going to be hard.

Chapter 3

'Noah if you shake that any more whatever is inside the wrapping paper will be in a million little pieces by the time you get to open it.'

Noah looked at his mother, the frustration evident on his face and she felt a tug on her heartstrings. 'Could he not just open one before lunch, Colin?' she whispered, watching him pick up another parcel. 'We don't need to tell Elsa.'

Colin looked at her aghast. Her ex-husband was a rule breaker in the business world where he seemed to think they didn't apply to him but when it came to the rules laid down by his mother, he might as well have been the same age as his son.

Roisin sighed and managed to inject some steel in her tone. 'Put it down, Noah.'

He did so, sitting back on his haunches and crossing his arms sulkily.

'Colin, can you get the door for me?' Elsa's voice trilled from the hallway and Colin moved toward it. She appeared with a tray, upon which three steaming goblets of mulled wine, a stick of cinnamon peeking over each of the rims, were perched along with an orange juice for Noah. It was proper juice with bits in it which for some strange reason was his favourite.

'Elsa, let me take that for you.' Roisin remembered her manners.

'I can manage, thank you.' She placed the tray down on the coffee table. 'But you could be a dear and go and get the mince pies for me. There's a plate on the worktop in the kitchen.'

'Of course. Noah, you're not to wander about with that juice, do you hear me?' His sulk over the presents was forgotten and he nodded as Elsa perched down on the sofa next to Colin. She left them to it and headed up the hallway, the walls of which were adorned with photographs of Colin at varying ages. She paused as she always did to smirk up at the last one, taken in his final year at high school. His face was spotty with adolescence and he looked like he was being strangled by his school tie. It was his hair that made her laugh though. It was hard to imagine her husband had ever idolised anybody other than himself but in that old pic he was rocking his curly mullet and had clearly been a fan of Hall & Oates. A tiny sign of rebellion because she was betting Elsa had pestered him day and night to get to the barber shop for a short back and sides. Colin's dad had passed away when he was small and she used to wonder what Colin would have been like if Elsa had had someone else to fuss over in their family dynamic.

She pulled herself away from the photograph and followed her nose into the kitchen which despite the preparations was in an orderly state with neatly stacked dishes. It was the opposite of the last Christmas spent in Dublin two years ago now when the dishes had haphazardly been piled so high, an avalanche of china was a very real threat. There'd been the usual arguing over who'd been put in charge of the roasty potatoes and who'd left the cabbage stewing. She could hear Moira proclaiming the pot of boiled greens smelt like a urinal and the memory made her grin. Mammy had thwacked her with the wooden spoon for that one.

She might not be a fan of goose but it did smell good and as she inhaled her tummy rumbled. The potatoes she saw, lifting a lid off one of the pots on the stove, were waiting to be parboiled before being tossed in the goose fat and cooked until they'd transformed into crunchy roast taties. The Brussel sprouts were ready to be put on along with the carrots and peas. Colin was terrible on the baby cabbages but it wasn't her that would have to put up with the aftermath all evening, not this year. The thought buoyed her and she picked up the mince pies, homemade of course with a dusting of icing sugar over the top of them, and carried them back through to the front room.

Noah was just hanging the last of his special decorations on the tree and as she stood in the doorway he began entertaining his granny and daddy with tales about Beyoncé the gerbil. He lived vicariously through Charlotte when it came to that gerbil of hers, she thought, wavering on her stance of not buying him a pet for Christmas. He loved that bloody gerbil and he thought of Charlie as an honorary sister ever since they'd stayed with Stephanie and Jeffrey after she and Colin had separated, lisping to her often that she was annoying, just like a real sister. She had a lot to thank the Wentworth-Islington-Greene's for. If they hadn't opened up their home to her and Noah she may well have come knocking on Elsa's door with her tail between her legs. Stephanie had helped her find her way at a time when she'd felt really, rather lost.

It was Jeffery who'd wrangled a position for her at the enormous accountancy firm in which he was a senior partner. She was now secretary for twenty-five hours of the week to Norman who really did look like a Norman with his little round glasses, small build and shiny domed head. She wasn't a very good secretary but she was trying and Norman was a very kind hearted man so, they were rubbing along nicely. Stephanie had helped her source her flat which while tiny was in the right location and meant Noah didn't have to change schools. She'd even started doing her yoga teacher training and the other night when she'd gotten up to draw the curtains and seen a star shooting across the inky sky, she'd made a wish that one day soon, she'd be in a position to open her own studio. For the first time in her life Roisin had a plan and she was determined to stick to it. Now as she stood on the periphery of the room, plate of mince pies in hand she felt disconnected from the tableau. It was a strange thought but it didn't make her sad.

'Roisin, what are doing standing there letting the cold air in?' Elsa brought her back into the room.

'Sorry.' She pushed the door shut with her foot and put the plate down on the coffee table.

'Noah,' Elsa said, 'come and sit up here now and have a mince pie.' She gestured to the low slung Ercol chair. Elsa and her late husband, Errol had bought the set of Ercol furniture not long after they were married and she was very fond of saying, 'quality lasts you know'.

Noah who knew all about being naughty or nice at this time of year decided to roll with nice. He had one more wistful glance at the shiny wrapped boxes under the tree before sitting down in the chair as his granny had asked him to do. Roisin eyed him and was reminded of an old film, Little Lord Fauntleroy. Her son knew which side his bread was buttered on, that was for sure. She sat down in the matching chair opposite him.

'Now,' Elsa said doling out dainty china side plates and red serviettes. 'Watch what I do.' Roisin had the unnerving sensation she too was being given a lesson on how to eat a mince pie as Elsa flapped the red napkin before draping it over her lap. 'That way you'll catch any stray crumbs.'

Roisin quickly did the same, eager to get the show on the road and shove a mince pie in her gob. Colin was sitting straight backed, napkin in place, looking like he was waiting for his mother to pat him on the head and tell him he was a good boy. Her finger twitched with the urge to flip him the finger. He was such a goody-two shoes where Elsa was concerned, it had always annoyed her and still did, even now when it was no longer anything to do with her. She managed to keep her finger to herself moving her eyes away from him to watch as Noah set about demonstrating a strong future as a flag bearer with his napkin before finally draping it across his trousers. Elsa nodded approvingly before passing the plate around.

'Jesus, Mary and Joseph about time,' Roisin hissed between her teeth.

'Did you say something, dear?' Elsa glanced over, questioning eyebrow raised.

'Only that you make a lovely mince pie, Elsa.'

Elsa sniffed as a spray of crumbs shot forth unbidden from Roisin's mouth. Ah well, Roisin thought, Elsa had always thought her an uncouth Irish heathen. In for a penny in for a pound, she might as well knock the mulled wine back too.

She wished she hadn't when the spices, of which there were plenty, caught in the back of her throat. She felt it begin to close over a split second before she made a holy show of herself coughing and spluttering as though she were on her last legs.

'I'll get you some water.' Colin dashed off to pour her a glass and when he reappeared, she snatched it from him gratefully taking a big gulp only to cough once again and wind up with it dribbling down her chin and onto her dress. Fat lot of good, the fecking napkin was, she thought seeing the damp stain spread over the grey fabric. Her blurred vision cleared and she saw Noah staring at her wide eyed. *Ah, poor love*, she thought, *I frightened him.* 'I'm alright now, sweetheart,' she rasped, 'It just went down the wrong way that's all.' She refrained from adding his witch of a granny had probably deliberately loaded hers with mixed spice. She really wasn't feeling her usual sunny self because when her son piped up with, 'Well, Mummy, you always tell me not to drink too fast.' It took all her strength not to tell him to cork it if he knew what was good for him. At that moment he looked very much like a little version of his father. They were a bad influence these Quealeys so they were, she decided, finally getting her breathing back under control.

'Alright now?' Elsa had watched her carry-on with alarm.

'Mm,' she nodded. 'Sorry about that.'

So, Roisin, tell us how this new job of yours is going,' Elsa said and she saw Colin's ears perk up. She opened her mouth to tell them a funny story about how Norman had caught her in Proud Warrior stance in the empty boardroom during her lunchbreak, knowing they wouldn't be amused but determined to tell the tale anyway, but Elsa cut her off. 'I'm sure the reason Noah's only just shaken that dreadful cold is because of the afterschool programme you've put him in.'

If there'd been another mulled wine sitting on the table, she'd have picked that up and gulped it down.

Chapter 4

Somehow, Roisin managed to keep her composure as the hours dragged by. Once she'd moved on from her near death, mulled wine experience she dug deep and joined in with Elsa and Colin's joviality. This was their Christmas day, their special time with Noah and even if her mother-in-law or ex-mother-in-law or whatever she flipping was, had been a horrid old bite to her in the past, she loved her grandson. It was for this reason she kept the smile plastered to her face as she sat down for lunch at the dining table in the formal dining room. Elsa had handwritten name cards and Roisin saw she'd been placed at the far end of the table. If it was intended to make her feel like an afterthought then it had worked, she thought, sitting down. She concentrated on the table which was laid beautifully with a lacy white cloth and an elaborate holly centrepiece. A gold foil-wrapped Christmas cracker was lined up next to everyone's fork, soldier straight, and Noah was already fiddling with his when Roisin next looked up. 'Hold your horses, Noah, we'll pull them in a minute. This looks lovely, Elsa.' She wouldn't show the old witch she was annoyed at being plonked in the seating equivalent of Siberia.

Elsa preened as she disappeared, returning a moment later with a tureen full of vegetables. Colin brought up the rear with more bowls of food until at last, the pièce de résistance, the goose arrived swamped by golden potatoes. 'It smells wonderful doesn't it, Noah?' Her tummy churned at the thought of the gamey meat.

'Is it like Kentucky Fried Chicken? Because I like that.'

'No, not really but it's very tasty like Kentucky Fried Chicken.' She lied.

'Where's its head gone, Mummy?'

'Well, er...'

'And doesn't a goose have feathers and a big long neck like the one in my book. And, Mummy, why's it got an orange stuck up its—'

'Righty-ho.' Roisin clapped her hands. 'Would you like me to pour the wine?'

Colin looked at her like she'd grown another head which was what she'd expected, he always did the honours but at least it had gotten David Attenborough over there, off the topic of Mrs Goose's posterior. He set about playing host.

Elsa sat down next to Noah and waved her cracker at him. 'Shall we pull it?' A fierce look of competitiveness came over her son's face and it was mirrored back at him in his granny's. Roisin watched carefully. Noah's competitive streak came from the Quealey side and knowing how much Elsa liked to win, she wouldn't put it past her to pull the little card strip. She'd done it to her last year but Noah was only five and if she cheated there'd be tears. A tug-o-war ensued, teeth were set in grim determination, and Roisin sat with teeth clenched rooting for Noah. He was flung back in his seat at the cracker popped and *Yes!* victory was his. There was no graciousness in winning where he was concerned because you'd have thought he'd just got a gold medal for cracker pulling the way he was brandishing his prized half about. Roisin watched Elsa's lips press together in a thin, tight little line and was glad it was Colin who'd have to pull with her next. It was highly likely given the long-haul flight needed to get to her end of the table she'd be pulling her own cracker.

Noah donned his party hat and put the plastic car down to unfold the piece of paper that had fallen out along with the rest of his winnings.

'Shall I read your joke out, Noah.'

He inspected the paper and decided it was beyond his 'cat, sat on the mat' capacity because he got up and gave it to his mother.

'Why does Santa's sack bulge in every picture? Because he only comes once a year.' Roisin took a moment to digest what she'd just said before looking up to see a stunned Colin and Elsa staring down the table at her.

'I don't understand, Mummy. Everybody knows Santa only comes once a year. Why is it funny?'

'Erm...'

'It's not funny, Noah, not funny at all. Colin go and get the cracker box it's in the bin outside the back door.'

Colin looked reluctant but did as he was told as Noah continued to mutter about Santa's bulging sack.

'I didn't read it before I read it,' Roisin offered lamely.

'Mummy, did you not have your glasses on when your bought these because it says Adult Only up the top there,' Colin said, returning with the offending box.

Elsa spluttered that it was a disgrace such things were even on the market and that she would be writing a letter to her local paper about it. 'Christmas,' she sniffed was about family not pornographic Christmas cracker jokes.'

Roisin sipped her wine in order to swallow down the bubble of manic laughter that was threatening to float forth.

'What's pornographic? Noah asked, his eyes swinging from one to the other.

'Something you don't need to know about,' Elsa snapped. 'Right, Colin, put that down and sort the goose.'

Colin got on with carving and dishes were passed around before the serious business of eating began. Noah forgot all about geese and pornography in his horror at finding a Brussel sprout on his plate. 'It's a baby cabbage, Noah, it won't poison you,' Roisin explained. 'They're very good for you.'

'You said baby cabbages make Daddy's blow-offs really stinky.'

Roisin stopped, fork midway to her mouth, her pinching toe itching to give her son a jolly good nudge under the table as Colin and Elsa glared down at her.

Elsa changed the subject. 'More goose, Roisin, you can manage more than a wing surely,' she asked as Roisin popped the potato she'd speared in her mouth and tried to get rid of the taste of the rich meat.

'Oh, no, I couldn't fit anything else in, thanks, Elsa. It's all so delicious.' She laid her knife and fork down and waited for the others to do the same. The lone sprout rolled around on her son's plate but she didn't have the energy to encourage him to eat it so, getting up she announced she'd clear the table, managing to spirit it away before Elsa noticed.

'You go and sit down.' Elsa appeared in the kitchen behind her. 'While I sort the brandy butter for the pudding.'

Roisin mustered up a smile and left quick smart, having no desire to be alone with the older woman. She wandered back to the dining room where Noah was playing with his plastic car and Colin, who'd set out fresh glasses, was filling them with a sweet dessert wine. The air was heavy with the memory of all the food they'd just consumed. How strange it was to feel like she was in the room with a stranger but as she looked at Colin that was exactly how she felt. She could sense his underlying animosity at the situation they were now in as he put the wine down on the table and sat back down to stare into his glass. They were both struggling with how they were supposed to be around one another. The idea of chit-chat seemed like such a lot of hard work. Divorce had not been on Colin's agenda but then neither had losing their home. She'd have felt sorry for him if he hadn't hidden the whole sorry mess from her. He'd gone behind her back re-mortgaging their home, not bothering to consult her in his arrogant certainty his business gambles would pay off.

She'd wondered more than once *when* he would have bothered informing her that he'd lost everything or whether he'd been planning to leave it up to the bailiffs to let her know. One thing she did know was she wouldn't have lasted five minutes under Elsa's roof while he toiled away at getting back on his feet. He would too, men like Colin always did. He was a mover and a shaker, he knew people, and he'd climb back up his corporate ladder. He'd get over their marriage break-up too. They weren't and never had been a well-suited couple and his shonky business deal had merely been the catalyst not the cause of their going their separate ways.

She took a sip of the wine, which was too sweet for her liking, and watched him from under her lashes. She wondered if he'd already met someone else. She examined that thought. It wasn't him moving on with another woman that bothered her, good luck to whoever filled her boots. What did bother her was whether that woman would be kind to her son. The way Colin operated he'd probably be engaged by the time she got wind of him having someone on the scene. Ah well, she'd cross that bridge when she came to it. Shay sprang to mind.

Shay with his slightly too long hair and lanky laidback demeanour. Oh, and the way he handled that fiddle of his. She'd met him on her last trip home and the timing couldn't have been worse. They'd only talked twice, the first time being at Aisling's other half's restaurant, Quinn's. He'd been playing the fiddle in the band and she'd literally locked eyes with him across the crowded room. They'd gone for a coffee too, just before she left Dublin, and aware of her messy situation he'd asked if ever he was in London, perhaps he could look her up. She'd taken his number and given him hers but she'd not heard a word since and she didn't have the nerve to call him.

There'd been an attraction between them that she'd never felt with Colin. Would she see him when she was back in

Dublin? Her insides quivered at the thought of him. And then she had the same discussion she'd had with herself every time she'd thought about Shay since she'd returned to London.

You're too old for him, Roisin. Sure, cop on to yourself, you're not in your twenties anymore you're nudging the dark side of your thirties and you're carrying cargo-sized emotional baggage. No man wants to sign on for that.

I'm not that old, thank you very much, and nobody would think twice about a man going out with a woman a few years younger than him. Why is it always different when the tables are turned?

How should I know? It just is and it's more than a few years.

Jaysus, I'm not after wanting to marry the fella, but a ride would be nice.

Yes, I'd have to agree with you on that one.

The dialogue usually closed there and a vivid scene in which she was riding Shay triumphantly toward the finish line would play out. It was the best bit but there was to be no imaginary riding today, not with the Christmas pudding having just arrived.

Elsa was carrying the dish as though it were the royal crown being brought to her Majesty. Noah's plastic car was forgotten and he was sitting up very straight in his chair staring eagerly at the steaming podgy dome as it was placed with reverence on the table. He was keen to sink his teeth into it because Granny had told him there were five-pence pieces hidden in it. Just so long as he didn't break a tooth or the like chomping into it, Roisin thought, catching a whiff of whisky and brandy butter. Jaysus, he'd be pie-eyed by the time he'd finished. Elsa doled the boozy pud out and Roisin debated whether she should suggest Noah might be better off with a bowl of ice cream. There'd be no money hidden in that though and it was only a small portion Elsa was giving him, so she decided to stay mute. Well, almost.

'Noah, chew carefully,' she warned as he tucked in. A moment later he gave an ecstatic cry and made a show of spitting the pudding out before poking his tongue out to show everyone the foil wrapped money.

'Okay, son, that's enough now.' Colin finally decided to parent as Noah did his best Gene Simmons impersonation before taking the money off his tongue and putting it down on the table.

Roisin eyed Elsa, who'd also found treasure and then Colin, who grimaced as his teeth clamped on something solid. She rifled through her pudding with her spoon but there was nothing in it other than fruit. The old bat had probably rigged it that way, she thought, stuffing the rest of it down her, knowing she was going to feel queasy later when the gamey meat and brandy butter decided to rendezvous in her stomach.

The clatter of spoons ceased and Roisin got up, keen to disappear into the kitchen for a bit of peace. Between Noah's monologue about how much he'd love a gerbil for Christmas and Elsa's chatter about how the council were letting the bin men away with murder, and Colin going on about a new deal her head was beginning to hurt. 'I'm on dishes, Elsa. It's only fair, you did all the hard work cooking.' She didn't receive any argument and she left them to retire to the front room once more to let their lunch go down and hopefully let Noah rip into a few of the packages under the tree. She set about clearing the table, carrying them through to the kitchen and stacking them on the worktop. She felt rather Cinderella-like as she rolled her sleeves up and plunged her hands into a sink full of sudsy water.

What was it Mammy used to say to them when they'd moan and groan over their chores? Roisin pondered, wiping down the worktop once she'd finally finished. 'You girls are making a mountain out of a molehill. Jaysus, Mary and Joseph if you spent as much time doing the dishes as you do moaning about being asked to get off your arses you'd have been back giving yourself the square eyes in front of that idiot box by now.' It made her smile. Well, Mammy, you'd be proud of me now, she thought casting her eyes around the sparkling kitchen. Elsa would have no cause for complaint either, it was shipshape. As she hung the tea towel over the oven door, she heard a squeal. It was a good squeal, an excited one and she was keen to see what had prompted it. In just over two hours she'd be on her way home; the thought put a spring in her step as she ventured back to the warmth of the front room.

Her son was sitting with his back to the door she saw pushing it open, and wrapping paper was strewn every which way. Noah heard her come in and swung his head around, his face lit up like the fairy lights on the tree. She'd put money on it not being a new dressing gown or bubble bath that had him grinning from ear to ear.

'Look, Mummy, look. This is the best Christmas ever!'

'What is it?' She smiled, his enthusiasm infectious as she glanced over at Elsa and Colin who were both perched on the edge of the Ercol sofa looking smug. The chinless gene had clearly been passed down from mother to son but had, mercifully, bypassed her handsome little lad. She turned her attention back to Noah who was swivelling round on his bottom dragging something along for the ride.

'Mummy,' he announced proudly, 'come and meet Mr Nibbles.'

Jaysus, feck! Roisin jumped as something made a scuttling sound. She was looking at a cage, she registered. A cage in which a chubby, brown and white gerbil was happily rifling through the torn paper scattered over the bottom of it. She blinked just to make sure she wasn't imagining things but no, the fat little mammal was showing off now doing a circuit on its wheel. Anger pricked through the surprise like a pin popping balloons. How dare Colin buy their son his first pet without checking in with her. She was going to be fun mammy, the mammy who bought her son a gerbil for Christmas. She conveniently pushed aside the little voice that said, "no you weren't". The point was she might have and now that choice had been snatched from her. Why hadn't he asked her how she felt about Noah getting a gerbil? Roisin knew the answer to that question. He hadn't asked because Colin never did. Colin did what he wanted to do. She was and always had been an irrelevant member of their family. She pivoted exorcist style to glare at him.

'It would have been nice if you'd talked to me about—'

'Mr Nibbles,' her big eared son piped up.

'Mr Nibbles.' The name came out sounding clipped and sharp.

'Well, you've been hard to get hold of now that you're working full time and he's talked about nothing else since November. I didn't think you'd mind, knowing how much he had his heart set on it.' Colin looked so pleased with himself her poor pinched toes burned with the urge to put the boot in, hard.

'You're not mad are you, Mummy?'

Roisin realised she had a choice here. She could be mean Mammy who wouldn't let her son have his heart's desire, a pet gerbil, for Christmas. Not a lot to ask for in the scheme of things, or she could embrace the fact she would be sharing her home from now on with Mr Nibbles. Colin had already pipped her at the post present wise and the thought of that saw her lips force themselves into a smile. 'Of course not, sweetheart. It's just that we're going on the aeroplane to Dublin tomorrow. I think Daddy might have forgotten about that because we won't be able to take Mr Nibbles with us. The airline won't let us, Noah.'

Noah's bottom lip jutted out and began trembling.

'Daddy didn't forget, Roisin, I rang the airline and checked and Mr Nibbles can travel as checked baggage so long as he has the proper cage, which he does. So, there's no problem.'

'There's no problem, Mummy,' Noah echoed.

'Ah, but it would be very traumatic for him.' Roisin did not want to take Mr Nibbles to Dublin. What if the little fecker had a heart attack mid-air? Noah would be beside himself and Christmas would be ruined. Besides, Mammy had a thing about small furry things ever since she'd had that encounter with a bold mouse who'd tickled her hair when she was sleeping. She'd thought their daddy was being friendly in the middle of the night and it was only when she realised he was snoring his head off that it couldn't have been him playing with her hair, and if it wasn't him then who was it? All hell had let loose, she'd charged around the apartment with the vacuum cleaner hose in the wee hours trying to get it and swearing she'd not sleep another wink ever again until she had proof he was gone. She and Aisling had thought it hilarious and tormented her something wicked by leaving a cat's toy mouse out in the most unexpected of places. No, Mammy couldn't be doing with a gerbil.

'He only has a teeny-tiny heart, Noah, and going on a big plane would be very frightening.'

'My friend, Marjorie, from the Knitters who Natter, travels with her Chihuahua, Petal, over to Ireland all the time, her daughter's over there.' Elsa joined in on the great Mr Nibbles debate waving her hand dismissively. 'Petal loves air travel.'

'Yes, but a chihuahua and a gerbil are two very different things,' Roisin pointed out, not quite believing she was having this discussion.

'Well,' Colin said, and there was something about the way in which he looked like he was playing poker and was about to lay down a royal flush that put Roisin on high alert. 'You can't expect Noah to be parted from Mr Nibbles when he's only just got him, Roisin, and if you're really not happy about him flying then Noah and the gerbil could always stay here with me and Mummy for the week.'

Arse! He had her over a barrel.

'Mummy?' Noah looked uncertain, torn between wanting to be with Mr Nibbles and the thought of not being with his mummy and seeing his other nana, and Aunty Aisling and Aunty Moira.

'Ah, well now, I'm sure he'll be fine but, Noah, he's your responsibility. That's what having a pet is all about.'

Noah nodded and began telling Mr Nibbles all about the Irish side of the family he would meet tomorrow.

'Right, that's settled. A lot of unnecessary fuss about nothing, I say.' Elsa sniffed. 'Now, who's for a game of charades?'

Chapter 5

♥

Dublin's Arrivals hall was a shifting mass of bodies. Several planes had landed and disgorged their passengers simultaneously and Roisin told Noah to stay by her side as she grabbed an empty trolley. She was sorely tempted to ram a few pushy, shovey types in the back of the legs with it as she navigated their way through their fellow travellers, most of whom didn't seem to be filled with the Christmas spirit just yet. Air travel could do that to a person, Roisin mused, looking for their carousel. 'That's us over there, come on, Noah. Here hop on.' Noah balanced on the trolley and she wheeled in close to the conveyer belt to wait for the bags and one very special gerbil to begin trundling around.

'Mummy,' Noah clambered off the trolley and tugged at her coat sleeve. 'Will Nana be back to normal or will she still have clown hair and a big cast on her foot?' He wanted to be prepared this time, Roisin realised as the carousel suddenly rumbled into life. Poor love had been disturbed by his Nana's Bo Derek braids and casty foot the last time he'd seen her. To be fair she hadn't looked much better once she'd had the braids unplaited either; she'd been left with a cloud of hair akin to Ronald McDonald's. Noah had been very standoffish with his imposter Nana and she'd had to resort to base line bribery in the form of chocolate and sweets to win him around.

'She's all back to normal,' Roisin reassured her son, leaning on the trolley, well as close to normal as Mammy was ever likely to get at any rate. The state of her hair and foot on their last visit was down to her having just arrived home from her mammy-daughter trip with Moira to Vietnam. The country was on Mammy's bucket list due to her desire to sail on a junk. They'd all thought she was mad when she announced she was going there and poor Moira had found herself roped in for the journey. As it happened the pair of them had a great time apart from an ill-fated hike which had resulted in Mammy's broken ankle, and as for the braids, well she'd had no excuse for that other than it had looked the part at the time.

Roisin shuddered at the memory of Mammy driving them all demented as she issued orders from the sofa with her big casty foot resting on the coffee table. She'd even had to help Mammy off the loo after she'd dropped her crutches. Scarred, she was, scarred she thought, shaking the visuals away. She'd only had a few weeks of it, but poor Aisling and Moira had been ready to send her back to Vietnam with a "do not return" sticker by the time she finally got the plaster off and could go home to fend for herself. The first of the cases bounced past, a welcome distraction, and Noah pushed ahead to peer around the legs of a man in a suit trying to see if there was any sign of Mr Nibbles.

'Do you think he'll be alright, Mummy?' he tossed back over his shoulder.

'Yes, bound to be.' Roisin had prayed the entire flight that he would be.

'He's coming, Mummy!' Noah jiggled up and down on the spot, knocking suit man who gave him the kind of look that was alright for a mammy and daddy to give their child but not for a stranger and Roisin resisted the urge to trolley ram once more. Self-important eejit she muttered to herself as she too spied the handle of the cage just visible above the rucksack currently doing the rounds. She eyed her son, recognising the jiggle. She'd been caught out on many occasions by it, usually when they were miles from any sort of a convenience. 'Do you need a wee-wee before we leave the airport? Because now's the time to say if you do, Noah, not when we're halfway to your nana's and there's nowhere to go.'

'No, I don't, I just want Mr Nibbles.' He pushed forward again receiving another look and she took action yanking him back. 'It's rude to push in. Let me get him off and then you can be in charge of him.'

The cage trundled closer and she readied herself sending up a quick prayer that the gerbil be alive and well before sidling in alongside the suit man, giving him an accidental shove on purpose before hoisting the cage off. She handed it to her son who took it from her reverently. 'I can see our case, wait a sec, once I've got it, we'll move out the way and you can check on Mr Nibbles,' she instructed.

How was it the case felt heavier heaving it off the conveyer than it had when she'd heaved it on the weighing scale at Heathrow? One of life's mysteries, Roisin decided, moving away from the throng still waiting to retrieve their luggage. She came to a standstill. 'Alright, Noah, let's see how he's doing.' She watched, breath held, as he set the cage down before carefully removing the cover. She exhaled as a pair of unblinking eyes stared up at them, a piece of lettuce clutched between two teeny front paws. She'd half expected to find the gerbil flat on his back, tiny legs rigid in the air and the relief of it all made her want to track down the Aer Lingus pilot and thank him for being such a good pilot and giving them a smooth flight.

Noah was inspecting the cage. 'He's done lots of poo, Mummy.'

'Ah well now, he's regular that's all. It's down to all those greens you've been feeding him. Plenty of roughage, like I'm always after telling you.'

'But I don't want to poo all the time. That's why I don't eat my broccoli.'

Ah the way a five-year-old's brain worked was a wonderous thing indeed, Roisin thought, debating whether to spiel off her broccoli is a superfood speech but then she remembered where she was and who would be doing a jiggle dance akin to Noah's if they didn't get a move on. 'C'mon with you, Nana will be waiting.' He picked up the cage once more and they trundled over to join the end of the snaking line filing through customs. It was moving swiftly which meant everybody was behaving themselves today, apart from the family of four who were now at the front of the queue. The mammy and the daddy were arguing over the organisation of their cases on the trolley which were tottering like a Jenga stack as they moved forward. They stood out, thanks to their tomato glow, and Roisin knew if Mammy were with her, she'd rush on up and tell them to get themselves a tube of the E45 cream. She wouldn't be able to help herself because just as the Bible was to the Christian, the E45 cream was to Mammy when it came to the first sign of anyone's skin erupting in anything red. She'd slathered them in the stuff if they'd caught too much sun or had any sort of a rash threating to make an appearance when they were small.

'Mummy, why's that man getting shouted at by that lady got mouse ears on? He looks silly.'

'I think they've been to Disneyland, Noah. You know where Mickey Mouse and Donald Duck live.' She didn't add and where eejits like yer man there who are old enough to know better come home with chronic sunburn and a pair of fecking mouse ears perched on his head. Impatience was making her snarky and she practised her breathing until at last the

Mouseketeer family were waved through and the line began to shorten once more. Finally, it was their turn.

'Mummy, should we have got Mr Nibbles a passport?' Noah asked as they approached the booth.

'No, son, he's grand.' She smiled at the customs man expecting him to smile back indulgently at her boy's sweet concern for his pet. He didn't. He was all business as he took the burgundy booklets from her while Noah held the cage up proudly to show him. He was too busy scrutinising Roisin's dodgy passport photo to notice Noah jiggling away desperate to get a look in. A frown Roisin fancied as one of suspicion was embedded between a pair of brows that for some reason made her think of Brooke Shields back in the day and thinking of Brooke Shields made her think of Mammy, not that there was any resemblance whatsoever but because as a teenager she'd been desperate to see *The Blue Lagoon*. Mammy had forbidden her from going even though she'd been fifteen nearly sixteen at the time. 'It's for your own good, Roisin, you'd only have to tell Father Fitzpatrick that you're after going to see a pornographic film in the confession. Kate Finnegan says there's boobies and yer man Christopher you're so keen on flashes his winky, a lot.' Roisin hadn't thought that telling her mammy that was why she wanted to see the film would sway the odds in her favour. She never had gotten to see Christopher Atkins' winky, she lamented now as Mr Customs, who she saw upon inspection was called Declan, eyed her before returning to his passport scrutiny. She could hear someone cough and imagined a great deal of impatient shuffling going on in the queue behind them.

'Is something the matter, Declan?' Yes, it was bold of her being on first name terms with a man who had the power to stop her entering her own country but sure they were all Irish, weren't they? He didn't look up and she began to feel guilty. Of what, she wasn't sure but a sweat broke out on her forehead further incriminating her, nonetheless. Okay, so she'd blinked and the half-opened eyes she was sporting in the picture he was studying along with lank hair she should have washed before getting the photo taken but had been in too much of a big, disorganised rush to do so wasn't the best. She'd hold her hand up to understanding that she had the look of someone who might have a kilo of the hard stuff strapped to their person in it but, all he had to do was look at her face to see she'd struggle to smuggle in so much as an extra carton of cigarettes, if she smoked that was. The seconds ticked by with him not answering her and just as she was about to throw herself on his mercy and shout, 'I'm innocent!' He snapped her passport shut and slid them both back to her. Noah seized his chance.

'This is Mr Nibbles, my gerbil, I only got him yesterday he's coming with me and Mum to stay with Nana and my aunties for Christmas.'

At last Declan turned his attention to the jiggling lad. 'Ah well now, I'm sure they'll be looking forward to meeting yer man there.' He leaned down from his perch and peered into the cage. 'Hello there, Mr Nibbles, did you have a good flight?'

Roisin wondered if he'd get through the rest of his shift without the two buttons stretched over his middle pinging off and Jaysus, now that she looked properly, the poor man had a nasty case of razor burn going on there, so he did. She was pleased Mammy was on the other side of the wall because if she saw the state of his neck, she'd be recommending the E45 cream to him too.

'It was his first time on an aeroplane and he's gone and done a lot of poo,' Noah explained earnestly. 'Mummy says it's because of all the greens he eats which is why I don't eat my broccoli but I think he was scared of being up in the sky.'

Declan looked a little taken aback at the turn the conversation had taken. It wasn't every day he encountered a little boy with a broccoli aversion whose mother looked like a hardened drug smuggler in her passport photo along with a gerbil that had shat himself because he was frightened of flying.

'Ah well then, best you get on your way to your nana's house so you can sort the poor fella out. A Merry Christmas to you both.' He waved them through and Roisin heard a smattering of applause behind her. She didn't look back as she said, 'And to you,' before heading for the sliding doors of freedom.

Mammy had informed Roisin over the telephone when they'd gotten home yesterday that she would wear a bright yellow sweater and black chinos so as to be easily identifiable. Her tone had been hushed as though she were a spy in the cold war. Indeed, she'd told Roisin she'd seen a very good film the night before called *From Russia with Love*. She was always very easily influenced, was Mammy.

'But, Mammy,' Roisin had said. 'It's Dublin airport, it's not exactly JFK. I'll be able to find you.'

'It's busy this time of the year, Rosi. You'll thank me for it. Yellow sweater, remember that, and you'll be grand.'

'Look for a yellow sweater, Noah.'

'There, Mum, over there.'

She followed the line of her son's finger and spotted her mammy jumping up and down waving out. She was a busy bee with swishy dark hair in a garden of weary travellers, Roisin thought poetically. Mammy was right she was grateful for her sunny colour scheme. She always felt sorry for people who walked through those doors and had no one waiting to greet them. Although, she thought waving back, she'd want to stop with the star jumps or she'd likely have an accident.

Noah rushed on ahead keen to introduce the newest member of the family. The cage was banging against his leg and Roisin called out for him to slow down even though she knew she was wasting her breath. Poor Mr Nibbles was really being put through the wringer today and once again, she cursed Colin. What had he been thinking? She slowed her pace. It was Noah who'd been adamant that Mr Nibbles was coming to Dublin so, let him explain to his nana why he had a furry friend in tow.

Dragging her heels, she witnessed fear followed by horror flashing in her mammy's eyes as she looked at the cage and shrieked, 'Jesus, Mary and Joseph, Noah, what's that?' She looked up then seeking out her daughter and pinned her down with a set of twin tasers. 'Roisin Quealey nee O'Mara, get yourself over here now.'

Charming, what happened to welcome home, darling? Her mammy's stinger was definitely out, Roisin thought, knowing there was nowhere to run to. She pulled up alongside her son.

'Did you know about this?' Maureen O'Mara, her face a mottled red, jabbed in the direction of the cage.

'Erm that Noah was bringing Mr Nibbles on holiday?'

'Don't be clever with me, young lady, it doesn't suit you. You know what I'm talking about. The rat your son has got in that cage. You do know the plague was started by rats, don't you? Dirty, filthy, vermin.' She shivered for effect.

'Nana!' Noah was aghast. 'Mr Nibbles isn't a rat, he's a gerbil and he's very nice. Look,' he held the cage up as high as he could and Maureen jumped back with a shriek.

'Get it away from me!'

'Mammy get a grip of yourself,' Roisin hissed, embarrassed by the stares they were garnering. 'It's a gerbil like Noah said. He can't hurt you.'

'It's small and furry with big teeth, what's the difference?'

'He's a mammal, not a rodent,' Roisin said. She'd looked it up knowing the information would come in handy but she hadn't expected to have to drop it in before they'd even left the airport.

'Well, I'm not going to be responsible for Pooh. He might think your gerbil rat there is a new toy.' Pooh was Maureen's poodle. It was down to Roisin she had a dog as the last time she'd been in Dublin a friend had been looking to rehome their puppy. Twins and a puppy had not been a good idea, her friend had cried down the telephone, and Roisin having heard her mammy making noises about getting a nice little doggy to keep her company had thought it a great idea for their poodle pup to come and live with Mammy. She'd heard the word "poodle" and pictured a small, yappy little dog that would prance around her mammy's ankles and sit on her lap to watch *Fair City* of an evening. Only, it transpired Pooh wasn't a toy poodle he was a standard and was now four times the size he'd been when Roisin had last seen him. She knew Mammy had made concerted efforts to change the pups name from Pooh upon adoption but he would not answer to anything else and so it had stuck.

'He'll be staying in his cage for the duration we're at yours. Won't he, Noah? Sure, it will be grand, Mammy, don't worry.'

'There she goes, Easy-osi, Rosi with her "she'll be grand" attitude.' Mammy shook her head and muttered things like dead gerbil and what was that daughter of hers thinking bringing it to Dublin, all the way out to the car.

They'd only just pulled out into the steady traffic when Noah tapped Roisin on the shoulder.

'I need a wee-wee, Mum.'

Chapter 6

Roisin was nearly knocked to the ground by a yapping blur of woolly black curls as she followed Mammy into her apartment. Noah shot off for the toilet leaving Mr Nibbles on his nana's dining table and her to fend off Pooh who had a paw resting either side of the top of her legs. She could smell his hot panting, doggy breath as he gazed up at her before trying to bury his head in her nether regions. 'Mammy, get him off me!'

'Down, boy,' Maureen said, giving him a tap.

Pooh ignored her. She looked at her daughter. 'He likes you, Rosi. He has a thing for the ladies so he does. Rosemary Farrell won't visit me at home anymore unless I promise to put him in the spare room and you want to hear the fuss he makes when he thinks he's missing out.' Maureen got him by the collar and dragged him off her. 'You're a very naughty boy, Poosy-woosy, aren't you?' She gave him a pat on the head just to really hammer her point home, and a bit of a cuddle before looking at Roisin who was sidling through the apartment with her case positioned in front of her in case he came back for round two.

'You never spoke to us like that when we were naughty, Mammy,' she shot back. 'And you certainly didn't give us a pat on the head. The wooden spoon on our backside was what we got.' She was a bit put out by the amount of attention the poodle was receiving. She wondered how Moira was coping having had her position as the baby of the family, one she revelled in, usurped.

'You only got the wooden spoon when you were bold and I've enrolled Pooh in puppy obedience school. He starts in the new year.' She looked at the poodle and then back at Roisin, lowering her voice to a barely audible whisper. 'He's getting his you know what's seen to as well in January. It's for his own good but he won't see it that way, I mean, would you? The vet's after telling me it will help with aggressive behaviour as he gets older and marking his territory that sorta thing. He won't get nasties down there either like the cancer. I'm hoping it will help with this habit of going around putting his nose in places it has no business going too because it's getting out of hand and it's embarrassing so it is. The rambling girls are beginning to talk thanks to Rosemary.'

'We can't have that now, can we?' Roisin whispered back, and Maureen shot her a look, unsure whether she was being clever or not.

She dared move her gaze from the poodle to the artwork on the wall. Moira's painting of Foxy-Loxy had won her first place in a well-respected children's art competition when she was a child. It was nice to see the familiar painting hanging on a wall in a room that otherwise felt strangely out of kilter to her. The apartment opened up into the living room, the kitchen was at the far end and to the right of the open plan space a utility room was tucked away off the kitchen. Over to Roisin's left was the door that led to the hall where two generous bedrooms were positioned opposite each other. A large picture window was the living room's focal point. On a clear day it afforded a glimpse of blue from the sea but today she could see the rain spattered glass and knew the view would be murky. She'd grown used to an urban outlook, Roisin realised, and the presence of a yipping poodle her mammy was infatuated with was only exacerbating the feeling of being somewhere new and foreign instead of in her mammy's home. She'd get used to it she supposed.

Actually, now that she was taking a moment to look around, she realised the living room had a Vietnamese village feel to it. Or, at least how she imagined a Vietnamese village would feel. Although the village houses probably didn't have sofas and big tellies in them. She smiled recalling the postcard Moira had sent to Noah that made mention of their mammy having gotten very excited over the local village's handicrafts and she'd been worried she was going to get herself a Joseph and his Technicoloured coat in the local brocade fabric. She'd contented herself with cushion covers and throw blankets instead which were now strewn artfully around the sofa and chairs. Vibrant hues of striped, pink, purple and oranges adding pops of colour to an otherwise neutral décor. Her eyes flitted about the space noting the high gloss, brilliant red, purple and blue lacquerware she'd managed to get home in one piece, on display on the built-in wall shelves. She bit back a laugh seeing the erect, wooden fertility symbol, Mammy had carved on her trip and which she was adamant was in fact a canoe. A row of Christmas cards stood to attention on the next shelf and on the top shelf was the infamous conical hat Moira had been unable to stop her from wearing during their trip. It had feet poking out from under it, she realised frowning, and she could see a tulle skirt too.

Mammy followed her gaze. That's Annabel under there. I never could stand her but I always think if I put her away, your great granny will strike me down with lightening. That, I feel, is a good compromise.'

Roisin agreed. She'd never liked the china doll heirloom either. It had always felt like she was watching them all, following them about with those icy blue eyes from wherever it was she was perched.

'Oh, you've a tree!' It was positioned in the smaller window beside the dining table, a fake one but a definite cut above Roisin's Argos special. It had twinkly fairy lights strewn around its tinsel branches and decorations she knew she'd recognise from when she was a child were she to take a closer look.

'I don't know why you sound so surprised. Just because I'm on my own, with the exception of Pooh, doesn't mean I should let my standards drop and besides it gives the neighbour across the way something to look at. Nosy old bint she is.'

Roisin peered out the window behind the tree half expecting to see a disgruntled old woman peering back at her.

'Go on and put your bag in your room. You can hang your coats up in the utility room. I'll put the kettle on. I think we'll have a nice cup of tea and a slice of Christmas cake. It's a lovely moist one this year.'

Roisin's mouth watered at the thought of a nice big slab of Mammy's fruit cake. Noah wouldn't like the cake with its boozy, fruity, spiced flavour but he'd snaffle down the marzipan icing no problem.

'Then I thought we'd wrap up and take Pooh for a stroll along the pier. It might wear him out before dinner with your sisters tonight. Moira's threatening to do the you-know-what personally if he comes near her again.'

'He's not coming, is he?' Roisin had assumed she'd have a randy puppy-free evening ahead.

'Oh, I can't leave him on his own for long, Roisin, it wouldn't be fair. You wouldn't have liked it if I'd left you home alone when you were wee, now would you?'

Roisin shook her head. Pooh was clearly part of the family these days and it would seem he was laying claim to being the favoured child despite his dirty ways. If they weren't careful, he'd be the one Mammy would leave her worldly goods to. She nearly collided with Noah who'd finished his business. 'Did you wash your hands?'

'I need to say hello to Pooh.'

'Hands! Wait a sec and give me that coat.' Roisin tugged it off him. 'Now hands.'

He stomped back to the bathroom to complete the job while she hung their coats up on the hooks on the back of the small room off the kitchen. Then she walked back through the living room seeing Mammy was busying herself in the kitchen. She picked up her bag and carried it through to the bedroom. There was no hint of her mammy's recent trip in here she saw, looking about and noting that it was tastefully done, painted in a soft cream. Curtains in a deeper green framed a window that overlooked the charming street below and a black and white photograph of a lily took centre place on the wall above the bed. The bed looked inviting with its matching cream and green linen, the pillows she noticed, with a feeling of longing, were plumped to perfection. Roisin was tempted to lie down and rest her head on one just for a few minutes but she didn't dare leave Noah alone with Mr Nibbles and Pooh for long. Mammy never scrimped when it came to bedding and she knew how to fold corners better than any nurse who'd been trained in the art by a stern matron could.

Yes, she'd be very comfortable in here. Well, as comfortable as she could expect to be with her son in the bed next to her. Noah turned into a prize kickboxer in his sleep! She opened her case and hung a few things in the wardrobe that would be a crumpled wreck if she left them folded in her bag, before opening the door once more. She peeked around it to check Pooh was otherwise engaged and wouldn't be homing in for another full-frontal assault. He was sitting on his pillow being petted by Noah, all the while watching Mammy. She was laying the tea things out on the table and the puppy had a look of total adoration on his face. She warmed to him, it was nice to know Mammy was loved and looked after, even if it was by a frisky poodle.

'Mummy?' Noah got up spying his mother skulking back into the room. 'I need to change the newspaper for Mr Nibbles.' He turned his attention to his nana who was putting a few biscuits on a plate. 'He did lots of poo on the plane because he was frightened, Nana.'

Roisin had a horrible feeling her son had developed a fixation when it came to his gerbil's motions and that everyone as well as their uncle would have heard about Mr Nibble's way of demonstrating his fear of flying by the time the day was done. 'I told Pooh that he has to be kind to him too because that's what you have to do when someone's smaller and weaker than you and I don't want poor Mr Nibbles to do any more poo.'

He'd obviously been paying attention to the Stop Bullying talk his classroom had had the other week then, Roisin deduced. It was a pity he didn't have quite the same aptitude to listening when it came to the rest of his schoolwork.

'Neither do I, thanks very much, and Noah get him off my table.' Maureen gave the cage a push nudging it precariously close to the edge 'That's my best lace cloth you've got that filthy thing on.' She looked over at Roisin with her lips pursed disapprovingly and her eyes raked over her daughter, coming to a halt when they reached her pants. 'Those are nice. They look ever so comfy, especially around your middle.' She patted her own to emphasise her point.

'They're only yoga pants, Mammy. I've tons of pairs. I live in them when I'm not working.' Roisin looked down at the soft, black stretchy synthetic material. They had a folded over waistband that sat on her hips and the leg was bootcut. They were comfortable and her go-to most days. Her days of trying to play the corporate wife, and not very successfully at that, were done. There was a glint in her mammy's eyes that made her wary of the sudden interest in her pants. She did a quick count trying to remember how many pairs she'd brought with her so she'd know if any went missing. Three, she'd brought three with her. She knew her mammy had developed a penchant for slacks because Aisling and Moira had filled her in on the fisherman pants she was so fond of, although she'd yet to see them for herself. Moira had also been horrified by the amount she spent on a pair of travel trousers for their trip. Mammy's reasoning had been that she'd needed all the pockets her whizz bang, quick dry pants afforded her. Moira reckoned she was on a mission to burn through the family inheritance.

'Yoga pants you say. Well I never. Turn around and give us a look at the back.'

Against her better judgment, Roisin did as she was told.

'Oh, Roisin, they give your bottom ever such a lovely shape. It looks like a peach so it does. Have they secret lift properties in them?'

'My bum doesn't need any secret lifting, thank you.' She craned her neck over her shoulder trying to cop a look at her peach in case things had dropped since she'd last checked.

'Well, I think they must do because I know your backside as well as I know the back of my hand and it was never that perky. Do you think they'd do the same for mine?' Maureen was fixated with Roisin's rear.

'Jaysus, Mammy, listen to you and stop staring.' She turned around.

Mammy was unapologetic she had a one-track mind at times and this was one of those times. 'They're not just for the bendy yoga stuff, then? You can wear them just because they're super soft and stretchy but look smart at the same time.'

'Yes, I wear them all the time for casual.' Roisin was wearing a white top and had a denim jacket in her suitcase she liked to team with it but today had been definite coat and scarf weather. She lived in trainers these days too, unlike her sisters who were far more likely to be found compensating for their height with ridiculously high heels. She'd given up the ghost, accepting the crick in her neck from looking up when speaking to those blessed with average height as her lot. Aisling in particular was obsessed with the stiletto and maintained she had no need of the gym because her legs got an intensive workout everyday thanks to her choice of footwear. Any chance she got she'd be flashing you her calves and saying, 'Sure just look at the muscle tone.'

'And you've tons of pairs you say?'

Roisin saw too late where this was headed.

'Then you won't mind letting your dear old mammy try a pair on, now will you?' She lifted her sweater and showed Roisin the roll of flesh spilling over the top of her black chinos. 'They're cutting me in half so they are.'

'Put it away, Mammy. You'll give Noah nightmares.'

'Nana, have you got some newspaper, please?' Noah was oblivious to his nana exposing herself.

'I'll be right with you once your mammy fetches her spare yoga pants for me.'

Roisin knew the look she was currently on the receiving end of. It was a look that said you scratch my back, I'll scratch yours. Or, in this case—you get me the pants and I won't kick up about the gerbil.

She went and got the pants.

Chapter 7

♥

'You'll find the old newspapers in the bottom cupboard of the sideboard,' Maureen said, snatching the black pants off Roisin before she changed her mind. 'I'll just go and slide these on.'

'Play tug-o-war, more likely,' Roisin muttered, going to retrieve the paper. She squatted down and pulled a few sheets of the newsprint loose; the title of a book that had been reviewed jumped out at her and falling back on to her bum she sat cross-legged scanning what the reviewer had to say about it. It was called, 'When We Were Brave' by Cliona Whelan. The author had swapped journalism for novel writing after a long career which had seen her at the forefront of women breaking into the male dominated newspaper world in Ireland back in the seventies. This was her first book, Roisin read, her attention well and truly caught. The actual review was all very high faluting and could have been summed up simply by saying *this was a great book, I recommend you read it.* They were a pretentious lot, those literary types. It *did* sound like a good story though, she thought, getting up. It would make a good Christmas present for Aisling; she was a reader. The thought of hitting the shops this time of year filled her with dread. It would be chaos but it had seemed silly to lug gifts over from London. She'd take Moira with her, she decided. Moira was good at getting people to move out of the way.

'Mummy,' Noah whined, growing ever more impatient, although she saw looking over, he had removed Mr Nibbles from the table. He'd set him down on the floor and was impatient to get on with the task at hand. For Pooh's part he seemed totally uninterested in the little creature but then, Roisin supposed that was probably because Mr Nibbles was a boy gerbil. That didn't mean she trusted him though.

'Come on then, we'll go in the bedroom to clean it all up.'

'Oh, no you don't. You can forget about cleaning that thing inside. Outside with the pair of you.' Maureen appeared in the living room doorway and gestured to her little balcony. A Parisian style table and chair looked forlorn as they were lashed by the wind and intermittent drizzle.

Roisin could almost hear the wind whistling from where she was standing. 'But, Mammy, it's freezing, the cold would kill him and what if he escapes?'

'Well you should have thought of that shouldn't you when you decided to bring that thing with you.'

'Nana, you're hurting his feelings and you're making me feel very sad.'

Another part of the Stop Bullying talk had been about how the children needed to express how they felt. Noah excelled at it and he wasn't finished yet either.

'I think you should say sorry to Mr Nibbles, Nana, or I'm going to cry. And, if he ran away or died because he was too cold, I'd be very, very, very, VERY sad.'

Maureen muttered a barely audible, 'Mr Nibbles my arse.'

'Mammy, don't be so mean.' Roisin added her pennies' worth and got straight to the point. 'And come on with you, let's see the pants.'

Maureen brightened instantly, flashing a big smile as she did her version of a model strutting down the catwalk coming to a halt in the middle of the living room, hands on hips, looking pleased with herself as she struck a pose. 'I got into them.'

'I can see that, Mammy.' Squeezed into them was more to the point. 'They don't leave much to the imagination.'

'They're grand, look...' she swung forward bending from her middle, her hair a curtain over her face as she tried to touch her toes and her voice was muffled as she said, 'I can even do the bendy yoga.'

Pooh tripped over himself in his excitement to get out of his basket.

'I'd watch out if I were you, Mammy.'

She righted herself quick smart, her face red and mottled with the exertion of it all. 'Don't you go getting any ideas.' She shook her finger at the poodle who skulked back to his basket.

'I might need to wear one of those e-strings under them you girls get about in.'

Roisin must have looked horrified at the thought because Maureen puffed up, 'Just because I'm a woman of certain years it doesn't mean I can't move with the times, Roisin.'

'To be fair, Mammy. I'm surprised you can move in them at all and I think you mean G-string.' She narrowed her eyes. She hadn't counted how many pairs of smalls she'd packed. 'You better not have—'

'As if I would.'

Noah interrupted, 'Nana, you still haven't said sorry.' He tapped his foot.

Maureen chewed her lip, her reluctance to grovel to a gerbil plain for all to see.

He raised an expectant eyebrow and Roisin choked back a laugh when he said, 'I haven't got all day you know.' He was parodying her giving him a telling off without even realising it.

Maureen saw the funny side of things and decided to go with it. 'I'm sorry I hurt your feelings, Mr Nibbles.'

'Mr Nibbles accepts your apology. There now that wasn't so bad was it. We'll say no more about it.'

'He's been here before,' Maureen said to Roisin. 'I'm sure of it.' She sighed. 'Let me keep the pants and you can use the utility room to clean his cage out.'

Roisin pulled her son in the direction of the tiny laundry space before she could change her mind. She didn't want the pants back now anyway. Not now that Mammy had stretched them.

***

The air was bracing enough to make Roisin's eyes water and a battering of stout rain drops were stinging her face. They'd enjoyed a cup of tea and a biscuit and then Mammy had made them rug up like snowmen to take Pooh for his afternoon walk. She was still in the yoga pants. 'Mammy, slow down,' she called, but her voice was lost on the salty air. She was holding Noah's hand tightly as they strode out along the pier. Maureen was grasping Pooh's leash with a grim determination, the poodle having set off down the long expanse of concrete jutting out to sea at an excitable clip. He was enjoying the briskness of his afternoon outing, his nose snuffling along smelling goodness knows what. Waves crashed either side of them and moored fishing boats bobbed in the frothing waters.

Roisin had images of her mammy getting airborne if her little legs were to pump any faster. She'd be like a red balloon floating away in that rain jacket of hers, she thought. Noah, wrapped up in his new coat, was holding the plastic bag eagerly awaiting the moment he could use the title his nana had bestowed on him of official pooper scooper. So far so good, all they'd been privy to were numerous incidents of lamppost leg cocking on the walk here. At last Pooh slowed to check out something unidentifiable and Roisin and Noah caught up to Maureen.

Maureen pointed at the yacht club and shouted over the wind. 'The Christmas dinner was last Saturday. I wore the red Vietnamese dress. You know the one Moira borrowed the night the three of you went to Quinn's for dinner in the matching dresses I had made especially for you in Hoi An. Everybody said it looked very well on me. I had a grand time. There was dancing and everything.'

How could she forget? It was the night she'd met Shay and who would have thought that the Chinese style silk dresses would have such an impact but Aisling's Quinn had barely been able to keep his hands to himself. Mind he struggled to at the best of times. As Moira was to Tom's superbly sculpted glutes, so was Quinn to Aisling's womanly rear. Tom had been rather taken with Moira in Mammy's red number even if it had hung off her in the places it would have had a stranglehold on Mammy. As for Shay, she didn't know what he'd thought about her enforced choice of evening wear but she did know there'd been a connection between them. Would she see him while she was here, or wouldn't she? Did she leave it to fate or did she call him?

'You've a daft look on your face.' Maureen peered at her daughter from under the hood of her raincoat.

'I haven't.'

'You have. Roisin, I've raised three daughters and I know that look. You've a man on your mind so you have.'

Roisin glanced guiltily at her son but he too was engaged in examining whatever the unspeakable thing Pooh was so interested in was and out of earshot. He'd adjusted to his new living arrangement but a new man on the scene was a different thing entirely, it was far too early to introduce anyone else into his life. Come to that she was getting so far ahead of herself where Shay was concerned it was ridiculous. Mammy read her mind.

'Is it yer man, Shay? You know, the grandson of the auld fella Noah was after tormenting the last time you were over.'

Noah had enjoyed a rambunctious game of knock on the door and run away with Reggie, Shay's estranged grandfather who'd been staying in Room 1 at O'Maras. The story had a happy ending, not for Noah—he'd had to apologise, but for Shay and his granddad who'd met for the first time. It was a new beginning before the end, because Reggie was terminally ill, but at least they'd had the chance to connect and get to know one another. She wondered how they were getting on, how Reggie was. He'd been a cantankerous old sod, made bitter by life but she'd seen past that and had liked him. She'd liked his grandson more but that was beside the point.

Roisin didn't say anything but Mammy looked jubilant as she prodded her in the chest. 'A-ha. It is. Moira was after telling me you were panting after him at Quinn's. I wasn't sure if it was just Moira making something out of nothing what with you and Colin only just having parted ways. But,' she jabbed at her again, 'I can tell by the way you look shifty. You had that same look on your face when you told me you'd found a job in the entertainment industry.'

'I had, though.' Roisin had lost count of how many times she'd protested this particular point.

'Roisin, wearing next to nothing and prancing your way around the city's nightspots while handing out free alcopops is not working in the entertainment industry.'

'Mammy, you make it sound seedy and it wasn't a bit like that. It was all about being entertaining as we promoted the product and the product happened to be sold in nightclubs.' Actually, it was quite a lot like that but it was a long time ago now and sure look at her these days—a mammy and a secretary in an accountancy firm. You couldn't get more respectable than that.

'Hmm, you did far too much promoting of your product in my opinion.'

They were getting off track, and what were Noah and Pooh so fascinated by? She moved closer, deciding it looked like some sort of dead mollusc. She winced as Pooh licked it and made a note not to let him near her. It was time for a subject change.

'So, you had dinner with the boatie brigade, that's nice.'

Maureen had taken sailing lessons last summer and loved to tell people she was a member of the Howth Sailing Club. Though, Roisin thought, looking at the wistful look on her face as she gazed out at the churning water, to be fair Mammy had been very brave. She'd tackled life head on after their daddy died what with moving out of O'Mara's, joining any club that would have her, trying new things and going on an Asian adventure. It was her way of finding her way without her husband at her side. The need to tell her how she felt swelled up in her like the surging waters on either side of them.

'Mammy, I'm very proud of you. I know I haven't told you that before, but I am.'

Maureen looked startled. 'Where did that come from?'

Roisin shrugged. 'I don't know. It's true though.'

'Well, I'm proud of you too, Roisin.'

Roisin's eyes inexplicably filled. 'Are you?'

'Of course, I am.' Maureen spotted the telltale glistening in Roisin's eyes. 'Ah now, don't be silly, c'mere and have a cuddle.' Mammy pulled her into a damp embrace and Roisin sniffed. So much had happened this year, so many changes, but she'd survived just as Mammy had. She looked past her mammy's shoulder and her eyes widened at the sight of Pooh frolicking around a woman in a turquoise rain jacket. A camera was in her hand and on the breeze floated what she was guessing was a Scandi version of 'feck off with you'.

'Mammy?' Roisin pulled away from her. 'You'd best sort Pooh out.'

Maureen turned just in time to see her pampered pooch joyfully snuffling around the woman's backside.

'Pooh O'Mara, you cut that out right now you dirty boy!'

Jaysus wept, thought Roisin, he really was part of the family. She'd have to tell her sisters about this.

Chapter 8

Their luck was in because Mammy had sneaked into a parking spot right outside the guesthouse and as they piled out of the car, Roisin glanced up at the red brick Georgian manor house. When she was growing up it had simply been home. Not your average family home granted, but home nonetheless. It was only once she'd moved away to London that she'd truly begun to appreciate how magical O'Mara's was and how lucky she was to have such a slice of the city's history in her family. It was part of Noah's legacy, she mused, feeling oddly poetic.

Maureen led the way, or rather Pooh did, and Roisin followed herding Noah toward the panelled, blue front door. It was topped by the small windows and white arching crown so typical of the famous Dublin doors in their pocket of the city. An enticing glow emanated through the multiple paned windows next to the door, a welcoming signal to come on in on this cold afternoon. It afforded a glimpse of the spectacular, sparkly Christmas tree inside ensuring no passers-by would be left in doubt that the festive season was upon them.

The tree was a focal point as soon as you stepped through the door. It was enormous, even bigger than Elsa's had been and Roisin hoped no tour groups were due to arrive while it stood to attention as it took up a good portion of the foyer. They'd have to line up and wait their turn outside to check in!

It was a tree that Father Christmas himself would be proud of she thought, eying it as she bundled in behind Mammy, Pooh and Noah. This seemed to be the natural order of things, that Pooh was by Mammy's side. She'd been affronted that she'd had to sit in the back of the car with Noah on the ride over while Pooh, got to sit up front. Mammy had said he thought of it as his seat and it wouldn't be fair to change his routine. She could have sworn the poodle gave her a look that said, 'You better get used to it, sister, cos it's the way it's gonna be.'

She closed the door to the guesthouse quickly before the polar blast currently whistling down the pavement outside could follow them in. It was only four o'clock but the street lights outside were already on, their glow spilling pools of light onto the damp puddles. A steady stream of homeward bound traffic trickled past the Green.

Noah's eyes were out like organ stoppers and his mouth formed a delighted 'O' as he stared up at the tree, taking in all the gold blingy decorations dripping from it. Roisin spied his little hand reaching out, unable to resist touching the shiniest of the baubles. The woman responsible for putting this, the most glorious, or ridiculously oversized depending on how you looked at it, tree together, Bronagh, peered over the front desk to see what all the commotion was about. There were two bobbing reindeer on springs attached to the Alice band on her head. They danced about as she shot up from her seat to greet them only to be stopped dead in her tracks by Pooh. He charged for the receptionist, pinning her against the fax machine. She never stood a chance, Roisin thought, as her mammy gave her triceps yet another workout trying to rein him in. A kerfuffle ensued as she tugged him off her. 'Naughty boy, Pooh. A million apologies, Bronagh. He can't help himself. The tree looks fabulous—' Her voice was lost as he dragged her up the stairs.

Bronagh smoothed her rumpled cardigan and inspected her skirt for signs of muddy paw prints. Finding none she looked at Roisin and shook her head causing a frantic bobbing of the reindeer. 'Yer mam's gone soft in the head over that dog. I never thought I'd see the day when Maureen O'Mara was at the beck and call of a poodle. How're ye, Rosi?'

She held out her arms for a hug and Roisin stepped into the embrace, smelling her familiar biscuit and hairspray smell as she squeezed her back. 'I'm grand, Bronagh.' The older woman released her and studied her face.

'You look well. Your mammy told me you're doing ever so well with your new flat and job. Good for you.'

'Thanks.' It was nice to know Mammy had been singing her praises. 'I won't lie. It hasn't been easy but it's getting easier.'

Bronagh nodded. 'It's all very brave of you.'

Roisin the Brave. She liked how that sounded. It was a much better title than Easy-osi Rosi, she decided, wondering if she could get Mammy to run with it and then, remembering herself, she asked, 'And how are you, how's your mam doing?'

'Ah, she's much the same. We're looking forward to Christmas day though, it will be a lovely treat to have our dinner with you all.'

'It's lovely you're both coming.' Bronagh and her mammy were as good as family and Bronagh deserved to enjoy Christmas, to put her feet up for the day and have a good meal served up for her in the company of those that cared about her and her mammy. Roisin knew how hard she worked looking after her ailing mammy. In between that and working at O'Mara's there wasn't much time left over for anything else in Bronagh's life. Christmas dinner was to be had in the guesthouse dining room and Aisling had said they could decorate it and give it a festive feel on Christmas Eve before they went to Midnight Mass. There would be mulled wine, she'd added temptingly. Roisin wondered idly if Pooh was invited. Odds were, he would be. The way things were looking he'd probably be at the head of the table.

Bronagh checked her watch. 'Nina should be here any minute. I want to do a shop on the way home and if I time it right it shouldn't be too busy.'

'Is she going home to Spain for Christmas?'

'No, I don't think so. She said something a while back about the airfares being too expensive at this time of year. She's a lovely girl but she doesn't give much away.'

'I'd hate to think of her on her own at Christmas.' Roisin would ask Aisling if their Spanish night receptionist had been included on the Christmas invitation list and if not, she'd be sure to include her. It would be hard to be away from family at this time of year but airfares home would be at premium so she could understand why she was staying put.

Bronagh nodded her agreement sending the reindeer dancing once more and then lowered her voice to a conspiratorial level. Her tone implied they were all girls together as she asked, 'Any word from your fella?'

Roisin knew exactly to whom she was referring but she decided to play innocent. 'What fella, Bronagh? You've lost me.'

'You know,' her eyes glazed over, 'the tall, fine looking musician whose grumpy old granddad stayed with us. The one you had,' she made inverted finger signs, 'coffee with.'

'No, sorry, Bronagh, I'm not with you.'

Bronagh pressed her lips together; she didn't believe a word of it but looking past Roisin she spied Noah turning one of the gold boxes under the tree over in his hands. 'You'll not find much in them, young man. Sure, they're just there to look pretty. A bit like me, really.' She patted her jet-black shoulder-length hair and as she chortled away, thoroughly pleased with her little joke, Roisin noticed the telltale zebra stripe down her parting was gone. She'd had her hair done in time for Christmas. It made her pat her own, and wonder whether she should try and book in for a bit of a shampoo and blow-dry. She could do with a good cut, too. Her hair and its upkeep had been at the bottom of her list this last while and she knew it could do with some TLC. Mind you, it would be murder trying to get in anywhere this time of year but you never knew, someone might make a last-minute cancellation. She could always ring Jenny, her old pal from her very short-lived hairdressing days—she hadn't been a natural. Jenny owed her. It was her who'd offloaded Pooh on Mammy. Yes, she decided that's what she'd do.

Noah put the box down and mooched over toward his mammy with a disappointed expression. What was the point in having a box all done up in bows and ribbons and gold paper with nothing inside it?

'Ah now, no need for that face. You didn't think I'd let you come all the way from London without having a little something tucked away for you, now did you?'

The gold box was forgotten as he trotted over to where Bronagh had moved behind her desk. He craned his neck trying to see what it was she was getting out of her drawer. She held whatever it was behind her back. 'You know your old Aunty Bronagh expects a hug first so I do.'

Offer him a treat, and he was anybody's, Roisin thought, looking on as Noah wrapped his padded arms around her generous middle.

He let her go and looked up at her eagerly.

'Have you been a good boy for your mam?'

'I have.' Emphatic nodding followed.

'That's good to hear. Now then don't make yourself sick on it or your mammy will have words with me.'

'Thank you!' Noah squealed taking the Terry's Chocolate Orange. His favourite chocolate in the whole world.

'And remember don't tap it, whack it,' Bronagh quoted the old advert and winked over at Roisin. 'I should tell him not to give you so much as segment of it, keeping secrets from me.'

'I'm not.'

'Oh, I've been round the block a few times and I know that look you got on your face when I mentioned his name. It's the same expression you had when you started seeing that fella with the motorbike your parents couldn't stand and you'd sneak out to meet him. I'll find out what the story is. I've got my sources you know. Your Moira's very partial to a Terry's Chocolate Orange, if my memory serves me rightly.'

'Bribery, Bronagh, that's terrible so it is!'

'Needs must,' she muttered as Noah began to tell her all about Mr Nibbles and his anxiety-driven bowel issues when it came to air travel.

'Serves you right,' Roisin whispered, leaving them to it and calling back over her shoulder, 'Send him up when he's finished, Bronagh!' She took the stairs two at a time. It was quiet in the guesthouse at this time of the day with most of the guests still out and about exploring. The landings were deserted, and Ita, the young girl in charge of housekeeping—Idle Ita as Moira called her—would be long gone for the day. This in-between time of day had always been Roisin's favourite when she was a child, she and her siblings had had the best games of hide-and-seek when they'd had the run of the old place.

The stairs creaked as she headed up the last flight to the family's apartment. Home, she thought, pushing the door open and hearing her youngest sister shrieking, 'Get that fecking dog away from me, Mammy, I mean it!' Yes, she was home.

Chapter 9

♥

Roisin walked into a scene whereby Pooh had Moira trapped up against the kitchen worktop and Aisling was bent double laughing as she said, 'Your face, I wish I had a camera.' Maureen was already ensconced on the sofa like the Queen Mother and was patting her leg trying to get Pooh to come hither. 'Mammy, if you don't get off your arse and get him off me right now, I'm not going to let you have any dessert.'

'What is it?'

'A New York cheesecake, Marks and Spencer's.'

'Ah now, Moira, that's not fair. You know the New York one is my favourite.'

'Well, sort your dog! Stop licking me you, you... and you can stop laughing.' That was aimed at Aisling.

'Rosi! How're you?' Aisling got to her sister first for a hello hug. They were elbowed aside by Maureen as she took action, taking Pooh by his collar and steering him into the living room towards a bed identical to the one at her apartment.

Roisin and Moira embraced and then Roisin stood back looking from sister to sister. 'You're both looking really well.'

'It's because we're getting some.'

'I heard that!' Maureen said sitting back down.

Roisin laughed. 'Well all the riding obviously agrees with you both.' The banter made her think of Shay but she vanquished him by staring at the red onion Moira had been slicing into for the salad before the Pooh assault. She didn't want to be caught out by her eagle-eyed sisters, one grilling from Mammy had been quite enough!

Maureen made them all jump by shrieking, 'Jaysus, Mary and Joseph, four hundred and fifty pound for the privilege of swanning about in your nightie.' She was holding up one of Aisling's glossy fashion mags and on inspection the model pouting at the camera did look like she was in her nightie, Roisin decided. A nice one, but still a nightie.

Moira muttered, 'I don't think you are in a position to comment on the world of fashion because the last time I checked, pants that could stop the blood supply to your bits were not in vogue. Where did you get them from and who told you they looked good?'

Roisin and Aisling sniggered waiting for Moira to get told off but Mammy hadn't heard—she was too busy flicking the pages of the magazine.

'They are on the snug side,' Aisling said, and Moira snorted.

'Snug? Sure, I can see what she had for breakfast. One wrong move and she'll have the arse out of them. How could you let her out of the house, Rosi? It's disgraceful so it is.'

'When did anyone ever talk Mammy out of anything?'

'True.' Her sisters nodded, each lost in their own recollections of run-ins with their headstrong mammy.

Roisin explained to them both how their mammy had come to be wearing yoga pants a couple of sizes too small for her, getting a sympathetic tut from them both at the way she'd hustled them off her. 'She pinched my new teal River Island sweater the other week. It'll be all baggy around the boobs by the time I get it back,' Moira moaned.

'Well, all I can say is watch your knickers girls, she's on about giving the thong a whirl.'

'Ewww!' The pair of them grimaced.

'What are you lot on about in there?'

'Nothing, Mammy.'

Noah burst through the door at that moment, bouncing in to give his aunties a cuddle before taking a great big gulp of air to begin another round of the gerbil chronicles.

Roisin helped herself to two glasses of the red Aisling was obviously enjoying, given the purple stain on her lips. She saw the glass of Coke fizzing on the bench by the salad the pair of them were in the throes of tossing together. Moira was still on the wagon then, she thought approvingly, hoping Noah didn't spot it. He'd be like one of those old Alvin and the Chipmunks records if he got stuck into the fizz. She carried the wine over to the sofa and handing Mammy the long-stemmed glass she plonked down next to her. 'Something smells good, doesn't it?' She took a sip, savouring the aroma as Moira opened the oven to check on the contents, sending a thick garlicky aroma wafting over.

'Moira's on dinner and she'll tell you she's after making it from scratch but don't believe a word of it. I saw the box in the bin. It's a Marks and Spencer's family sized lasagne. I hope it's not too heavy on the garlic,' Maureen sniffed. 'Garlic gives me reflux.' She patted her chest.

Roisin smiled, not about the reflux because a windy Mammy was nothing to smile about, but at Moira's lack of prowess in the kitchen despite Mammy's best efforts to teach her how to cook over the years. Ah well, so long as she got fed, she didn't care what was put in front of her. The walk along the pier had left her ravenous. She enjoyed a few more sips of wine and then, as Noah moseyed over with a piece of garlic bread in his hand, she got up to see if she could snaffle a piece.

'Oh no, you don't.' Aisling slapped her hand. 'I only gave it to Noah to stop him going on about that Mr Nibbles of his. He told me we'll get the privilege of actually meeting him when you come and stay on Christmas Eve. I can't wait.'

'It was Colin's big idea to get him a gerbil.'

'Always said he was a chinless feck,' Moira piped up.

'Shush. Big ears are always flapping.'
'Whose Noah's or Mammy's?' Aisling asked.
'Both.' Roisin leaned against the kitchen counter. 'Guess what happened when we went for a walk down the pier with Pooh this afternoon.'

As Moira began dishing out the lasagne and Aisling broke up the garlic bread, Roisin made them both laugh with her impersonation of a Scandinavian woman using bad language.

'That poodle has behavioural issues,' Moira said, then, indicating the cutlery drawer, 'You could set the table, Rosi.'

Roisin did so while Noah petted Pooh who was lying with his head resting on his paws. His doggy face in repose looked like butter wouldn't melt. 'Go and wash your hands, Noah, we'll be eating in a minute.'

Her son huffed and puffed out of the room narrowly missing his Aunty Moira who was carrying two heaped plates of food over to the table. Pooh waited until they were all seated and Maureen had said the grace before getting up and wandering over to the table. He sat at Aisling's feet having decided she was likely the softest touch and stared up at her with huge baleful eyes begging for a morsel. 'Mammy, he's making me feel ever so guilty.'

'Ignore him, Aisling, he could win an Oscar for his role in Starving Dog, so he could.' Maureen tutted, forking up the mince and pasta dish enthusiastically.

'This is delicious, Moira,' Roisin said, winking across the table at her mammy and receiving a 'Don't talk with your mouth full, Rosi,' in return.

Noah's eyes whizzed from one family member to the other, unused to so much banter at the dinner table.

Roisin caught up on her sisters' news as she tucked into her meal. Moira was immersed in her course at the National College of Art and Design and after an initial rocky start as she got used to being a student and no longer having a disposable income, she was loving it. She and Tom were getting along very well and before she could launch into exactly how well, Mammy interrupted by asking her to pass the salt. Aisling was kept busy ensuring the smooth turning of the cogs at O'Mara's during the day and was spending most of her evenings at Quinn's these days. 'Shay was asking after you last week when his band was playing. I told him you were coming home for Christmas. Meaningful and inuendo-laden glances were exchanged around the table but with Noah at the table nobody said a word on the subject. Roisin adopted her best, 'So what?' expression as her stomach did flip-flops. *He'd been asking after her. He knew she was going to be home. Perhaps she could leave it all to fate and just see what happened.* She realised Aisling was speaking. 'What did you think of the Californian Giant Redwood on display downstairs?'

'It's gorgeous but it is big, you'll have problems fitting everyone in reception if you have any large groups due to arrive.'

'It's a health and safety hazard, is what it is,' Aisling muttered, before adding she hadn't a show of getting anything smaller. There was no getting around Bronagh once she'd her heart set on something and her heart had been very firmly set on the biggest tree she could find. 'She talked one of the tour operators into putting it in their van and delivering it for her, bribed them with a custard cream and a cup of tea, so she did.'

'Now then girls.' Maureen changed the subject. 'I'd like us to visit with Father Christmas tomorrow.'

Moira sniggered and Roisin and Aisling glanced at each other, silently communicating the words, 'What the feck is she on about now?'

'I'd like to get a family photograph taken with Noah on yer man's knee and us girls can gather around them. I happen to know Father Christmas is in his grotto at the O'Connell Street, Easons.' She closed her eyes. 'I can picture it. It will be lovely to have as a keepsake.'

'I can picture it too, and I'm seeing short red dresses and Santa hats and it's not happening, Mammy.'

'Don't lower the tone, Moira, sure it's Father Christmas we're talking about here not yer man who runs all those seedy London nightclubs.'

'Peter Stringfellow,' Aisling added helpfully.

'That's him, dirty old man, so he is.'

'I want to go and see Father Christmas,' Noah chimed in.

'There we go then, that's settled. Tomorrow afternoon. Let's say two o'clock, and I don't want any excuses. You'll not spoil things for Noah here.'

Nana and grandson looked smugly complicit. He reached over the table for the last piece of garlic bread while his aunties engaged in moaning about being grown women and having to sit on Santa's knee. His nana was lobbing back that the only one sitting on his knee, thank you very much, would be Noah, when a commotion began.

Pooh woofed, startling them all silent, before getting up and stalking toward the front door, a low growl emanating from his throat. The O'Mara women looked to one another. It was peculiar behaviour. He began to bark in earnest and they all jumped as they heard the front door bang shut.

'Who's there?' Maureen called, 'State your business.'

If the sisters hadn't been feeling nervous, they would have giggled at their mammy's turn of phrase. Pooh had begun to go berserk and all the guests would be complaining about the noise, and so Maureen bravely stood up to investigate but before she could remove herself from the table a voice boomed.

'Whoever's dog this is would you tell it to get its nose the hell out of my girlfriend's crotch?'

Eyes widened and Maureen disappeared like a lightning streak in the direction of the voice.

'So,' Aisling said, looking at Roisin and Moira, 'the prodigal son's returned home for Christmas.'

Chapter 10

He looked good, in a slick American sort of way, Roisin thought, as her brother, larger than life, appeared in the living room. Mammy was hanging off his arm and gazing up at him as though the Messiah himself had wandered into the apartment. Mercifully for Patrick he'd escaped the short gene of the O'Mara women taking after their daddy. Mammy, Roisin saw, had a firm hold of Pooh's collar with her other hand. He'd always been a good-looking fella their brother and well aware of the fact too. He'd been good fun as well when they were kids. Now though it was as if his features had gotten a little more chiselled, his hair a little more groomed during his time in the States. Everything about him seemed exaggerated. As for his teeth, well they'd definitely gotten whiter. If you were to sit in a darkened cinema with him all you'd see were the whites of his eyes and those pearlies. It would be like when that awful ultraviolet light would flicker at nightclubs and show the flecks of dandruff on your shoulders. She suspected her brother's new improved smile wasn't down to flossing and twice daily use of the Colgate either.

She continued her inspection. His skin had a healthy sun-kissed glow about it, making the rest of his family look like relations of Casper the friendly Ghost, and his clothes had the casually, crumpled cool of the confident man. The man who didn't have to prove anything to anyone, he was his own boss. *For fecks sake, Rosi, you're not doing an aftershave commercial.* She knew though, if he wasn't her brother and if he wasn't such a selfish arse at times, she would say he cut a fine figure of a man. All her and Aisling's friends had thought so back in the day. It had been very annoying.

A woman materialised from behind Mammy and son. She was wearing a fitted, short pink dress not fit for the Irish winter. It hugged every inch of her upper torso and could rival the snugness of Mammy's yoga pants. Roisin's eyes were mesmerised by the twin peaks jutting forth, like two watermelons, disproportionate to the woman's slender figure. Aisling and Moira were staring too, jaws agape. The woman was keeping a wary distance from the excitable poodle who kept twisting his head trying to catch another glimpse of his paramour. Roisin managed to raise her eyes to stare at the tanned, golden blonde apparition's face. No wonder Pooh had gone to town; he'd found his dream girl. Patrick's girlfriend, Cindy, was in fact, Barbie. Come to think of it her brother did have a look of that Ken doll he'd been so fond of talking to when he was small. They were a good match.

'Look who's here, girls,' Maureen stated the obvious, 'your brother. He's home for Christmas. Sure, it's the best present any mammy could have and he's brought his girlfriend, Cindy, with him.'

Patrick looked down at his mammy and Mammy gazed up at her son and Roisin knew Aisling was choking back gagging noises. Mammy had a short-term memory when it came to her son. They'd barely heard a word since he'd flounced off back to Los Angeles, a sulky, spoiled child after not getting his way over O'Mara's being sold. Roisin had always sat on the fence where her brother was concerned. Yes, he looked out for number one but she only had one brother and she loved him. He'd pushed her over into Aisling's school of thought though, with his behaviour this last year. Had he contacted any of them to see how they were getting on? No, he had not, and there was poor Moira who'd been on the sauce making a mess of things. Aisling, too had been heartbroken when that eejit fiancé of hers left her high and dry. Not to mention herself with a marriage break-up and Mammy laid up for weeks with a broken ankle. Now here he was standing there with that irritating smug look she knew so well, waiting to be made a fuss of. Well, he could feck off, she thought.

Moira, who'd always thought the sun rose and set over her brother, forgot she was annoyed at feeling like he'd abandoned her and she was the first up, throwing her arms around him. The Coca-Cola had gone to her head, Roisin thought, suddenly remembering her manners where his poor girlfriend was concerned. 'Hello there, Cindy. Welcome to O'Mara's. I'm Roisin and this is my son, Noah.' She got up from the table and stepped forward to kiss her brother's girlfriend on the cheek, receiving a grateful, boob squishy, embrace in return. She smelled like fruity chewing gum, and vanilla and if she hadn't been full it would have made her hungry. Aisling followed suit while Moira joined in with Patrick and Mammy's mutual admiration society. Poor Cindy would have a hard time getting a look-in with these two on the scene, Roisin thought, giving Noah a nudge to say hello. She looked down at him, seeing he was starstruck with a very silly look on his face not dissimilar to Pooh's, as he whispered a shy greeting.

'Hey there, honey, aren't you just the cutest wee man.'

Roisin watched on amused as her son flushed at the praise.

'It was Patrick's idea to surprise you.' She addressed the sisters. Her drawl was more southern than LA and Roisin instantly thought of fried chicken and had to squash the urge to say, Y'all c'mon back now, y'hear.

'Well, you did that. Here, come and sit down, make yourself at home. No, don't worry about him. I'll make sure Mammy keeps an eye on him.' Roisin gave Pooh the death stare as she led Cindy over to the sofa. Aisling offered her a drink but she didn't want anything. She looked the type that would keep a watchful eye on her waistline, Roisin decided, a sparkling water and egg white omelette sort of a girl. She couldn't afford not to be if the dress she was poured into was an indicator as to the rest of her wardrobe. Ha! Just wait until Mrs Flaherty got hold of her! O'Mara's breakfast cook, believed diet to be a dirty word and you did not mess with Mrs Flaherty.

Patrick extricated himself from his mammy and Moira long enough to give his other two sisters a hello kiss and hug. 'Aisling, you're looking very well on it.'

Aisling eyed him suspiciously. She was never sure whether you're looking very well on it meant she looked like she'd been eating all the pies or not.

'And I was sorry to hear about you and Colin, Rosi. I hope you're doing okay?'

'Ah, sure.' Roisin waved the comment away. 'We're grand.'

Patrick turned to Noah who was looking at him uncertainly. 'Now then, young fella, have you a hug for your Uncle Patrick who's flown all the way from America?'

'I've got a gerbil,' Noah said, testing the water. 'His name's Mr Nibbles.'

'That's a fine sounding name for a gerbil,' Patrick said, receiving a hug. He was easily bought her son, Roisin thought, not for the first time as her brother pulled a tube of M&M's from his pocket and gave them to Noah.

'Come on and sit down,' Maureen urged, patting the space between her and Moira they had left for him to squeeze into. He did so.

'Rosi, Aisling, go and see that your brother's room's made up and put his and Cindy's bags in there while you're at it. We're all very modern here,' she added.

Roisin resisted the urge to tell Mammy nobody had chopped Patrick's legs off. She supposed he had just flown in from LA though. Just this once, she thought, and she begrudgingly followed her equally begrudging sister from the room.

Noah seized the opportunity to sit next to Cindy, delighted to secure a position next to her and certain she would be the type of girl who would love gerbils and not the type to try and pinch the M&M's off him.

***

'Why do you think he's back?' Roisin said, tucking in her corner of the bed and smoothing the sheet.

Aisling did the same. 'I don't know but if he's any plans of putting the squeeze on Mammy about selling O'Mara's again, I'll personally stick him in a box and send him back to Los Angeles with a do not return sticker.'

'Ah, Ash, maybe we should give him the benefit of the doubt. You know maybe he just misses us and thought it would be nice to spend Christmas with his family. Or, maybe things are getting serious between him and Cindy and he thought he should introduce her to us all.'

Aisling sighed. 'Rosi, it's Patrick you're talking about. The only person Patrick's ever had a deep and meaningful relationship with is himself. No, he'll have one of his deals on the go, it'll be business that's brought him back, not us.'

'You're too cynical,' Roisin said, although her sister's description of their brother was bang on. 'What did you make of Cindy?' she asked, pausing in her stuffing of the pillow into the case. 'I think she seems sweet, but I can't stop staring at her breasts.'

'Me neither, they're enormous, but sure, she must be used to it. There's no way they're natural. I reckon she went along to yer plastic surgeon one and said, 'I'll have the Pam Anderson special please, and speaking of unnatural. Who am I?' Aisling cracked a cheesy grin and said, 'Ah, Mammy, you're the best mammy in the whole world and I'm a fecky big brown noser, so I am.'

Roisin giggled. 'Pat. The state of those teeth. Honest to God any whiter you'd want to wear sunglasses around him.'

Aisling plumped her pillow and put it on the bed. 'It will be strange having him back in his old room.'

'I wonder if you'll hear the old headboard banging.' Roisin pointed to it.

'That's disgusting, so it is. Besides I'm off round to Quinn's later and Moira's going to Tom's so Pat and Ms Pneumatic Breasts can bang away to their hearts delight, but I won't be changing the sheets at the end of the week.' She paused in her smoothing of the eiderdown. 'How does Mammy seem to you?'

'Oh, you know, Mammy's Mammy.'

'You don't think she seems a little,' Aisling cast about for the word she was looking for. 'Preoccupied?'

'I hadn't noticed. Why?'

'I don't know. She had dinner at the yacht club a weekend or so back. She got her hair done and everything for it because it was quite a posh do she reckons, and she's been wandering around with her head in the clouds since. Moira reckons she's after meeting a fella.'

'No!' The thought of Mammy with anyone other than their daddy was a bizarre one, but it was over two years since he'd passed now and while their mammy was their mammy, she was also a woman in her own right. That was a bizarre thought too! 'Although she did say there was dancing and that she'd had a grand time.'

'Well, something's up and she's not saying whatever it is but when I quizzed as to how her night was, she was very cagey. She had that look on her face, you know, the one where she's after borrowing something like your lipstick, or—'

'Yoga pants and I know the look well.'

'Yeah,' Aisling smiled.

'How would you feel about it if she did meet someone?' Roisin probed.

'Weird at first, I guess, but she has every right to be happy and it wouldn't mean she loved Daddy any less.'

'No, you're right. I hadn't thought about it like that but it wouldn't.'

'Moira surprised me because you know how much of a daddy's girl she was. I always thought she'd struggle if Mammy did meet anyone else but she was kind of nonchalant about it all. That trip to Vietnam changed her. For the better too.'

'Who'd have thought?'

'I know, and I suppose I'm getting ahead of myself. We don't know she *has* met anyone but with all the clubs she belongs to she's bound to hook up with a merry widower at some point.'

'Yes, I suppose she is.'

They finished their task in silence and then Roisin remembered the dessert. 'Do you reckon, Moira's cut into the cheesecake yet?' Seeing as she was the only sibling who would not be doing any riding tonight, she planned to compensate with a big helping.

'I hope not, I want to make sure she doesn't give Patrick a bigger slice than me.'

On that note they took themselves off back to the living room.

***

What a strange turn the evening had taken, Roisin thought, wiping the last of the dishes dry as Aisling, the washing up done, began making everybody coffee. Patrick was regaling them with stories about life in the LA fast lane while Mammy sat on one side of him on the sofa, Moira on the other, hanging off his every word. Poor Cindy was squished down the end next to Mammy and hadn't taken her eyes off Pooh; her legs were tightly crossed. Neither Pooh nor Noah who was sprawled on the carpet, elbows resting on the floor, chin cupped in his hands, had taken their eyes off Cindy.

It was then that her phone began to vibrate in her pocket and pulling it out she expected it to be Colin wanting to know they'd arrived safe and sound. It wasn't Colin though. It was Shay.

Chapter 11

♥

Clio

Clio stared down at the card, open on the table in front of her, almost afraid to read the words squeezed around the bog-standard Christmas greeting. The phone ringing in the hallway jolted her from her trance. 'You're being silly, Clio, old girl. It was over four decades ago. And you can sod off.' She directed the latter at the telephone. It was probably Mags, her agent, and she could wait. Sure, if it was that important, she'd call back she decided, waiting for it to ring off. She'd always thought the literary agent's role was to support their author but Clio felt as though she were the one keeping Mags on an even keel since the book had hit the shelves. When her house was once more bathed in silence apart from him next door's motorcycle engine revving off into the distance she began to read.

Dear Clio,

I realise this card will be a bolt from the blue but when I read the review of your book in the Irish Times I had to write and congratulate you. You always said you'd write a novel that would be a bestseller and now you've only gone and done it! Congratulations, what an achievement. Of course, I rushed straight out and bought a copy which I devoured *over three days. It's wonderful, but Harry and Lyssa's story raised a lot of questions because I can't help but wonder if you wrote it about us. Or am I being arrogant? That's something I've been accused of before. I still live in Boston in case you were wondering but I've always liked to keep my finger on the pulse of what was happening in Dublin. I've subscribed to the Times for over forty years. I followed your reporting and well-written pieces with interest over the years too. I miss stumbling across them. I always felt inordinately proud when I'd see your name in the byline. I'd want to nudge the person on the train next to me and tell them that I knew you when you were a girl. And that you were the most feisty, determined woman I ever met. I'm going to run out of room and there's so much more I'd like to say. The thing is, Clio, I'm writing to you because I'm coming back. Your story made me nostalgic for all my old haunts from that wonderful year and now that I have finally hung my hat up and retired, the time is ripe. I arrive on the afternoon of the 24th and I would like to invite you to share Christmas dinner with me. I have made a booking for two at the Merrion Hotel in the Garden Room at one o'clock and will be waiting in the Drawing Room at 12.45pm. Please don't think me presumptuous, merely hopeful.*

Yours, hopefully,

Gerry.

Clio's tea had gone cold and her toast, although filling the air with its malty aroma, was long since popped and had been forgotten about. The almost milky scent of fresh toast usually filled her with a sense that all was well in her world just as cigarettes once had. Oh, how she used to eat the things when she was working! She'd given up before it had a chance to catch up with her though. Right now though, feeling as though her world had been upended, she'd kill for one. Gerry had always had that effect on her but she'd been too young to know better then. At eighteen her defences had been down and she'd had a trusting openness to seize all the possibilities life had to offer her. Now she was a fifty-nine-year-old woman who should know better than to allow her breath to quicken and pulse to race at the memory of the man she'd once loved with her whole being. A man whose heart she'd had to break.

A thought struck her then, rather like the stinging slap her mother wielded to the back of her legs when she'd been cheeky as a child. 'He won't look like you remember him, Clio. He's been forever frozen in your mind as he was but time hasn't stood still. He's a pensioner, old girl.' It was swiftly followed by the realisation that she no longer had the dewy skin of a girl on the cusp of womanhood. She too was rapidly approaching her pensionable years, unless of course the government pushed back the age for hanging one's hat up as they'd been making noises of doing. Of course, it made no bones to her. She was a long way from putting her hat anywhere other than firmly on her head. Still, fifty-nine, how on earth did that happen?

How did one go from being a girl who thought she had the right to have it all to being a woman who now thought nothing of holding a discussion with herself?

She remembered how bereft she'd been when Gerry left. He'd never lied to her. He'd never made promises he couldn't keep, but she'd been swept along by the heady tide of first love and had believed that somehow it would all work out. It hadn't and it had been her fault. She'd decided to throw herself into her work at the paper, dragging herself up the rungs of the ladder in a male dominated era. It hadn't been easy. It had taken her fifteen years to smash through that glass ceiling. She'd known when she'd had to make her choice that it was sink or swim time for her career and she'd chosen to swim. Gerry Byrne and his family obligations would not sink her.

It *was* presumptuous on his part to assume she would drop everything and have her Christmas dinner with him. How did he know she didn't have a family who were desperate for her to be a part of their festivities? Sure, there was Fidelma and her lot expecting her. She'd spent every Christmas with her sister's brood since Mam passed. Fidelma's children, although now adults with children of their own, would surely miss their aunt if she weren't there? She'd spoiled them enough over the years to warrant the title of 'favourite aunty'.

Clio's neatly trimmed nails, a must when one spent the majority of one's time on a typewriter, drummed the table. She wouldn't think about it anymore. She would tuck the card away in the top drawer of her sideboard over there and she would bin the cold toast and make some more. She'd have her breakfast and begin her day. 'You've a novel you're supposed to be writing, Clio. You've a deadline to make and you do not have time for Gerry Byrne to come-a-calling. You're going to pretend you never received his card. It went missing in the post, so it did, like hundreds of letters and cards do at this time of the year. There, problem solved.' As she pushed her seat back and stood up, she didn't believe a word she'd just said.

Chapter 12

♥

'I better not see anybody I know,' Moira grumbled, flicking her hair back over her shoulder as they elbowed their way into Easons. 'I feel like a complete eejit next to you lot.'

'Odds are you will then. That's what always happens. It's like when you nip out to Tesco's with no make-up on and your rattiest Sunday sloth clothes and there's your arch nemesis from the high school looking like they're off clubbing.' Aisling was embittered by personal experience. She pointed through the sea of faces. 'Oh look, speaking of high school, isn't that your old school pal, Emma, over there? You know the one who fancied herself as Ginger Spice getting around in that Union Jack T-shirt.'

'Where?!' Moira looked panicked as she stared around at the sea of faces.

'I'm joking with you.'

'Oh, feck off, Ash.'

'You feel like an eejit, Moira, because you look like one. We all do,' Roisin stated, keeping a tight hold of Noah's hand. It was a mosh pit of mammies and their offspring in here. She glanced down at her son; even he looked eejitty in his crew neck, red sweater. He reminded her a little of Charlie, from their favourite Christmas film Charlie and the Chocolate Factory. His nana had presented the sweater to him this morning and combed his hair into a smooth side parting rather than leave it to stand on end like Roisin did. She'd had one of her golfing ladies, a prolific knitter, whip the cable patterned red, sweater up specially for him.

'It itches, Mummy, do I have to wear it?' he'd whispered in her ear.

'What do you think?' she replied, gesturing at his nana who was singing her heart out to Mariah Carey's *All I Want for Christmas* on the radio as she waited for her toast to pop. He'd slunk off miserably to play with Mr Nibbles. Poor love looked like it was choking him, she thought now. Mammy had insisted, in a way that brooked no argument, on them all wearing red tops and blue jeans for this, their family Christmas photo.

Red, she'd declared last night over coffee and the after dinner mints Patrick had picked up in duty free, was festive and the blue jeans added the perfect casual accompaniment. She didn't want the photograph to look contrived. All three sisters had said, 'Bollocks,' in reply to this and Roisin could tell Cindy would have liked to have joined in with the sentiment but was too intimidated by Mammy to do so. Patrick had said a family photo sounded just the ticket and Roisin had heard Aisling mumble her favourite phrase where her brother was concerned, 'brown nosey fecker,' under her breath as she helped herself to two of the chocolate mints before stuffing them both in her mouth. Aisling always ate when she was feeling stressed.

'We look like we're a family band, you know like the Corrs except we're not cool,' Aisling said, now nibbling on the chocolate chip muesli bar she'd stashed in her handbag for emergency situations. Being forced out in public wearing matching outfits with her mammy, nephew, siblings and her brother's girlfriend counted as such.

'Or like we've stepped out of the television screen from some cheesy family sitcom,' Roisin said. 'We're the Keatons from *Family Ties*, remember that show?'

'Bags be Mallory,' Aisling said through her mouthful.

Roisin ignored her. 'Mammy always used to say, why couldn't we be more like the Keaton family and sort our problems out without all the bickering, remember?' She rolled her eyes at the memory.

'I do. It was very annoying.' Aisling sniggered as she pointed at Patrick's back ahead of her. 'And there's ole Michael J. Fox over there.' He'd had to shoot off down to Grafton Street earlier that morning with Cindy to get something suitably red for them both to wear—there was no chance of Cindy getting that chest of hers inside anything the O'Mara women owned. Although suitable was a term that could be used loosely when it came to Cindy's choice of plunging red mesh top and jeans that had Mammy whispering in the sisters' ears, would need to be surgically removed at the after hours later on.

Aisling glanced down at her filmy blouse; it was chiffon, the sort of thing she wouldn't normally be seen dead in. It reeked of Arpège, Mammy's signature fragrance. She'd thrust it at her earlier that morning when she'd arrived at O'Mara's with Roisin and Noah meekly following behind announcing she'd come early to ensure her wardrobe instructions were obeyed. 'It's alright for you three, red suits you with your colouring but it makes me look like I've picked up some sort of chronic disease.' She'd not been happy, telling Moira to shut up when she smirked at the state of her in the blouse. Mammy had told her she'd better be careful or the wind would change and she'd be stuck with a face on her like a gin-soaked prune forever. Roisin had got off lightly, borrowing a turtle neck from Moira that looked very well on her and Moira looked the part in her preppy red jacket.

'We're the fecking Addams family,' Moira added her pennies' worth. 'And there's Morticia,' she pointed at Mammy, who had—thank the Lord—opted for chinos with her red shirt.

'The Bundys, and Mammy's Peg Bundy.' Aisling giggled getting into it now, and Moira and Roisin joined in.

'No, I've got it.' Roisin jiggled on the spot. 'The Waltons.' This time there was proper giggling as Aisling and Roisin chimed, 'John Boy' as they pointed at their brother. Roisin began humming the theme tune.

Mammy looked back over her shoulder. 'What are you three on about.'

'Nothing, Mammy.' Moira smiled sweetly. 'Just saying what a grand idea of yours this was.'

Maureen narrowed her eyes, unsure if she was picking up on sarcasm in her youngest daughter's tone or not.

'I suppose we should be grateful she didn't try and bring Pooh along in a little red doggy coat for the occasion,' Roisin said, once Mammy had returned to her chat with Patrick. She'd had to have words with Noah who'd been desperate to introduce Father Christmas to Mr Nibbles. She'd only managed to dissuade him by saying that if Mr Nibbles got frightened and had an accident, Father Christmas might not be too happy about it and it could possibly have a roll-on effect as to what appeared in Noah's Christmas stocking.

'Oi, you.' Moira nudged Roisin as she recalled her sister's flushed face and coy expression upon answering her phone last night. 'Who was that you were speaking to last night. I know it wasn't Colin because you always get this screwed up expression on your face like you've got the piles when you talk to him, and I know it wasn't a friend because your voice went all sort of low and Macy Gray like. My money's on Mr Hot Fiddle.'

Roisin hesitated; she didn't want to share her phone call with her sisters. She wanted to keep her exchange with Shay tucked away to bring out in private to mull over. Not that privacy was a big feature on her trips home! Every time she recalled the melodic timbre of his voice, heat shunted through her core and the feeling that evoked was not one she wanted her family privy to for obvious reasons. It had taken her by surprise, him calling so soon after she'd arrived back in Dublin, his obvious interest only adding to the thrill of listening to him ask how life in London was treating her. She'd seen her sisters' curious glances as she told him she'd found work, and a new flat for her and Noah. She'd glared over at them before turning her back on her all-seeing, all-hearing family.

They hadn't talked for long; he was due to go on stage in a few minutes having left the rest of the band warming up and it was the first chance he'd had all day to give her a call. The way he'd said 'stage' conjured an image of his rangy body clothed in a blue plaid shirt, the sleeves of which were rolled up, the buttons undone to reveal a smooth muscular chest, and his faded Levi's battered and worn with a brown leather belt. The cowboy hat was dipped low over one eye and his thumbs were hooked through his belt loops. She realised she'd seen a book cover not dissimilar to the scenario she was envisaging at Mammy's and quickly banished it. He played Irish folk music and rock not country and western and he was not the type of man to walk around Dublin with a cowboy hat on.

Standing there in the kitchen she'd suddenly wanted to see him performing more than anything. To sit down the back of the crowded pub he was gigging at and just watch him. A door had banged then and she'd heard music and shouts of laughter in the background. He'd said he had to go but before he hung up he asked her if she'd like to catch up for a drink or dinner before Christmas, whatever she could squeeze in because he knew it was short notice and she'd be busy given the time of the year. She could manage dinner tomorrow evening she said, hoping she hadn't sounded too eager.

She was already imagining the feel of his knee as she accidentally on purpose grazed hers against his under the table.

They'd said their goodbyes with him arranging to pick her up from O'Mara's at seven. She was certain Mammy or one of her siblings would have Noah although she didn't relish telling them where she was going. She'd held the phone to her ear for a few more seconds after the call had disconnected, putting the parts of herself that had disassembled at the sound of his voice back together before joining the others in the living room once more.

Now, standing in the heaving book shop, Moira nudged her again. 'Well, was it, Shay?'

'Ow, don't do that.'

Aisling moved closer to hear what Roisin had to say.

'Who's Shay, Mummy?'

She shot Moira a look. 'He's an old friend of Mummy's.'

Noah was nonplussed but Moira took the hint for the time being and dropped the subject.

***

Twenty minutes later, tensions outside Santa's grotto were running high and even Patrick was beginning to make noises of dissent. 'Could we not just gather outside on the street and ask someone to take a photograph, Mammy?' he asked.

Maureen was aghast. 'With no Father Christmas?'

'We could get one of those random Santas that stand on the street corners.'

The withering look Patrick received saw him back down. He winced and rubbed his temples as a toddler somewhere in the midden began to screech, 'No, Santa. No like! NOOOOO!' A baby, fed up with the waiting and startled by the sudden outburst, began to shriek and the mammies, all determined to get a photograph of their precious offspring with Father Christmas, were beginning to look in need of gin.

The line they'd found themselves in shuffled forward every now and then and Roisin watched enviously as a victorious mammy herded her four immaculately dressed children past. Each was sucking a lollypop and clutching a balloon. She didn't have to turn around to know the victorious expression would have been wiped clean from her face when a loud pop made them all jump. It was followed by a howl that suggested the ended of the world was nigh. 'My balloon! I want another one. Mammy, I want another one. It's not fair! Eva, Connor and Mary have all got theirs.'

Oh yes, she thought, Christmas was a precious time for families.

Mammy swung around and jabbed at Moira, 'I remember you putting on a holy show like that when your balloon popped the year I took you to meet Father Christmas at Brown Thomas. Mortifying it was.'

Moira was unrepentant. 'Well, I'd say you're getting payback now, Mammy, wouldn't you?'

'Mummy,' Noah tugged on Roisin's sleeve. 'I can smell poo.'

Ah Jaysus, Roisin thought, her son was to the number two what David Attenborough was to the animal kingdom. He was getting obsessed and it was all down to Colin trying to get one up on her with the gerbil. She sniffed the air cautiously and at first all she could smell was too many women wearing too many clashing perfumes which mingled cloyingly together. Hang on, she thought, sniffing again and this time hit with the unmistakable smell of filled nappy. *Oh, dear God, could this afternoon get any worse!*

'Can you smell that,' Moira nudged her. 'Sure, it's worse than Mammy when she's been at the Brussels.' She deliberately said this loud enough to turn heads.

'I heard that,' Maureen said. 'Don't believe a word of it, Cindy. She's a one for making things up.'

This was a living nightmare, Roisin thought, shaking her head and wondering when she'd wake up.

At last, after forty-five or so minutes of unspeakable noise and smells, Santa's helper, who was keeping guard at the entrance to the grotto, came into their line of sight. She was a fierce looking girl with a frizz of red hair who looked as happy with her short red dress with white fur trim and matching hat as Aisling did with her blouse. Her arms were crossed over her chest, and stout, black-booted legs assumed the stance of a nightclub bouncer as she stood squarely in the entrance to the glittering cave where the end to their torment lay. Mechanical reindeer were positioned on either side of the grotto, heads bobbing slowly to the incessant Christmas carols being piped through the building.

'Would you look at the face on her,' Mammy hissed over her shoulder. 'Sure, she'd put the fear of God into you so she would.'

'Shush, Mammy, she'll hear you and send us to the back of the queue,' Aisling hissed back.

Roisin looked at her brother and Cindy, who were almost catatonic with the jet leg and the ordeal they were suffering through. Poor, poor Cindy, she'd put money on Patrick not having warned her what she was in for by coming to visit his family.

And then at last, like the parting of the red sea, the fierce one stepped aside and gestured for them to enter Father Christmas's inner sanctum.

Chapter 13

♥

'Ho-ho-ho and who've we got here,' boomed Father Christmas from his gilt throne. A feeling of calm descended over the O'Mara group as they ducked through the glittery entrance and emerged into a peaceful Christmas bubble. The air felt fresh, thanks to the little fan blowing gently in the corner of the grotto. Faux presents were stacked up on either side of the big man's chair and a Christmas tree laden with red baubles dominated the small space. Roisin peered closely at him wanting to see if he was a nice, plump, jolly Santa or one of those skinny ones who looked nothing like your man. This one obviously liked his food, she thought, spying the crumbs stuck in his beard. It bode well; they were off to a good start after the nightmare of the shop floor outside. A young woman stepped out from behind a camera tripod. She was dressed identically to the fearsome helper on the door but looked much nicer insomuch that she at least mustered a weary smile even if it didn't quite reach her eyes.

Mammy was the family's self-appointed spokesperson. 'Ho-ho-ho yourself, Father Christmas, we're the O'Mara family.'

'The Waltons,' whispered Aisling, and Roisin choked out, 'G'night John-boy.' They erupted in giggles and Maureen shot them both a death stare.

'My son, Patrick here, has just returned home from Los Angeles with his girlfriend, Cindy.'

'Just for the week, Mammy,' Patrick was quick to interject lest she get any ideas and Cindy waved at the snowy-bearded man enthusiastically announcing in a breathy voice, 'I love Christmas.'

Father Christmas's eyes nearly popped out of his head as her bosom bounced along with her hand.

'It's the best present a mammy could have, so it is, having all her children around her and I want to capture the moment for prosterior.'

'Posterity, Mammy,' Patrick corrected her.

'And what a fine-looking family you are too in your matching tops and trousers.' Father Christmas's twinkly currant eyes were still firmly fastened on Cindy's chest.

'Aul perv, I'm not sitting on his knee,' Moira whispered.

Maureen carried on, 'Now then, I've a picture in my mind as to how I want my photograph to look.' She hustled Santa's helper out the way as she pulled Noah over to sit up on Father Christmas's knee. 'Upsy daisy, there you go, you perch yourself up there, Noah.'

Desperate to get home and get out of his sweater, Noah clambered up onto the solid red knee and began reeling off a list of things he'd like to find in his stocking on Christmas morning. Father Christmas's eyes never budged from where they'd lodged on Cindy's bosom as he nodded and muttered, 'Well now, you must have been a good boy.'

'Patrick, Cindy,' Maureen ordered, 'I want you two to stand behind Mr Claus on either side with your hands resting on his shoulder, like he's an old pal. Off you go.'

Maureen kept an eagle eye on her son and his girlfriend as they arranged themselves, before huffing, 'No, Cindy, stand up straight, shoulders back, you're not doing a Marilyn Monroe. Cop on to yourself.'

CHAPTER 12

Fair play, Roisin thought. Cindy had leaned over Father Christmas's shoulder, pouting, and while Father Christmas was all for the Marilyn pose, it wasn't the stuff of the family portrait. Noah was supposed to be Father Christmas's focal point and the poor love was trying to tell him about Mr Nibbles but Cindy's cleavage was getting in the way.

Satisfied she now had Cindy in a suitably chaste pose, Maureen pointed to Roisin, Aisling and Moira, 'Right you three, you're on.'

'It's like being in a stage musical, so it is. She'll be telling us to break a leg next,' Aisling muttered as she was instructed to kneel beside the chair, hands clasped and resting on her lap, Roisin was next to her.

'Moira, you're on the other side, same pose please.'

Moira rolled her eyes but did as she was told, while Roisin looked at her mammy wondering where she was going to sit. A thought occurred to her, ah Jaysus, she wasn't going to perch herself on his other knee, was she?

'And I'm going to kneel next to Moira. Patrick I might need some help getting up again.' Maureen smiled at Santa's helper. 'I think that's us.'

Roisin half expected the girl to say, 'Thank feck for that.' She was a professional though, and assuming her position behind the tripod she said, 'On the count of three, say cheese. One, two, three...'

'Cheese!'

There was a satisfying click and the family was herded from the grotto by the helper lass. They stood blinking in the bright light of the store. The photograph wouldn't be ready to collect for another ten minutes or so, and Patrick and Cindy announced they were off to tackle the crowds and finish their Christmas shopping. Moira, Aisling and Roisin planned on doing the same, once they'd seen the photograph, and Noah was to go home with his nana, who'd another bracing pier walk with Pooh planned.

'I'm going to have a look around while we wait,' Roisin said, ensuring her son's hand was held firmly by his nana before moving away from the milling mammies and children waiting to meet Father Christmas, in order to browse the book aisles. She could see a small gathering by a stand at the other end of the store and, curious, she moseyed closer as she realised a book signing was underway. A poster behind the table at which the author sat revealed it to be for the book she'd read the review of in the paper yesterday, When We Were Brave.

The author Cliona Whelan had silvered hair, pulled back in a loose bun. Stray tendrils escaped to frame her face, which was animated as she chatted to a woman around the same age as her. She had the face of a storyteller, Roisin decided, and she was what Mammy would describe as a handsome woman with inquisitive grey eyes framed by tortoiseshell glasses. She was dressed in a crisp white dress shirt with a jauntily-tied scarf in the same shade of grey as her eyes. Roisin couldn't see what she was wearing on her bottom half as she was hidden by the table she sat at, but she was guessing it would be tailored pants. The type with little pleated nips and tucks around the waistband. Her style gave her the manner of someone direct, someone you didn't pussyfoot around, someone used to moving in a male dominated world. She had been a journalist after all. Her pen was poised, ready to sign the book the woman she was talking to had thrust in front of her.

The queue was nothing like the one she'd just endured and it was a grand opportunity to get the gift she planned on buying for Aisling personalised, Roisin decided. She sidled up to the stand of books next to the table and took one from it, handing it to the girl who was working the till at the end of the table before joining the line.

'Hello.' Cliona greeted Roisin with a smile that must have been getting tired around the edges. 'Have you a special message in mind?' Her pen was poised over the book.

'Hello,' Roisin was suddenly shy. It wasn't every day she was face to face with an author whose book was storming the charts. 'Erm could you say, Dear Aisling—' she went blank.

'How about, "Dear Aisling, I hope you enjoy this book?"'

'Grand.'

Cliona signed her sentiment with flourish and Roisin remembered her manners, thanking her and wishing her a Merry Christmas before sliding the book back in the paper bag. She put it in her bag and looking around for the others, decided the photo should be ready by now.

She found them at the main counter. The picture was being placed inside a festive red, cardboard wallet which Maureen took from the young girl with her Santa hat who was in charge of the developing. 'C'mon, Mammy, let's go outside to look at it. I'm desperate for some fresh air,' Moira said linking her arm through her mammy's and herding her toward the exit. Aisling, Roisin and Noah pushed their way out after them.

They all took grateful gulps of the carbon monoxide filled air on O'Connell Street and clustered around Maureen under the awning of a nearby shop. Noah clung to his nana's leg, tired and fed up, as she eked out the drama by pretending to be interested in the Christmas message on the cardboard wallet.

'Get on with it, Mammy. Put us out of our misery,' Roisin urged, mindful of her son who'd obviously had enough.

Maureen opened it and inspected the glossy print. Her face was unreadable as the sisters craned to see for themselves but Maureen snapped it shut before they could get a look, muttering, 'Sweet Mother of Divine.'

'Let me see,' Moira snatched at it but Maureen held it out of reach, shaking her head so her dark hair swished back and forth, her face a picture of misery.

'No.' She played the guilt card. 'All I wanted was a family photograph. A memento to pull out on those long afternoons when you've all gone back to your busy lives. Something to proudly show off to my friends. Was that so much to ask?'

Roisin draped her arm around her mammy's shoulder and gave it a squeeze. 'No, of course it wasn't, Mammy, and it can't be that bad.'

'It's going in the bin as soon as we get home, so it is.'

'Ah no, not after what we went through to get it taken. C'mon now, Mammy, let us have a look,' Aisling said. They were burning with curiosity but Maureen was not going to be swayed easily and she unzipped her handbag making to put it away, sniffing all the while.

'We'll treat you to tea at Bewley's.' Aisling knew she'd hit on a winner by bribing her mammy with a cuppa at her favourite tearooms, when she zipped her handbag up.

'Well don't expect me to pitch in,' Moira said. 'I'm a student.'

'A sticky bun, too?' Mammy eyed Aisling.

'Alright, a sticky bun too, now hand it over.' She took the wallet from Maureen, and her sisters leaned in expectantly.

She opened it and stared, in horror, at the sight of them all immortalised in their red tops and blue jeans.

'Jaysus wept, it's the fecking Addams family alright.' Moira was the first to speak, her two sisters rendered speechless as they soaked up the scene. Cindy had blatantly disobeyed Mammy's instructions and her heaving chest was resting on Father Christmas's shoulder. Patrick was staring at her assets with an expression of lust and consternation on his face. Father Christmas had obviously jumped, startled by the bosoms that had landed on his shoulder, and poor Noah was holding on to his leg for grim death like he was on a horse just off the starter blocks. Roisin's hair, thanks to the damp Dublin day, was a bushy frizz about her face—give her a top hat and she'd look like yer Slash man from Guns n Roses. Moira had her eyes shut and looked like she'd been doing the drugs while Aisling appeared to have grown a black mole on the side of her mouth. 'Why didn't any of you tell me I had a chocolate chip stuck there?'

The sisters shrugged. 'Because it was funny.'

The only one smiling beatifically at the camera was Mammy.

'And it's such a nice one of me,' Maureen lamented sadly.

Chapter 14

♥

1957

Eighteen-year-old Cliona Whelan had never been in love before and, falling in love was the last thing on her mind as she sat on a warm, sunny patch of grass near Trinity College. A bee buzzed lazily past and the air had an autumnal tang to it she fancied she could taste. It was a curious mix of grass and damp fallen leaves. She was people watching, her favourite way in which to while away her lunch break and today was a grand day for it, given the burst of unseasonal October sunshine. On her lap was an open notebook, her scrawled shorthand filling the page as she wrote down the different characteristics of the people milling about her.

She'd been particularly fascinated by the nervous looking girl she'd seen scurry across the park, a tote bag weighed down with text books hanging from her shoulder. There'd been something about the stoop in her shoulders and the way she wouldn't meet any of her fellow students' smiles. She'd been dressed plainly in a non-descript cardigan and skirt. It was the sort of outfit that would fade from your memory moments after she faded from your line of sight. Her hair had been scraped back in a ponytail and she'd kept pushing her glasses back onto the bridge of her nose. She'd not had so much as a slick of lipstick on her face which made her look younger than she was, given she was obviously a student. There was an air of vulnerability about her as she made her way toward the college buildings, a frown firmly embedded on her forehead.

Cliona scribbled away *nervous disposition due to stress over impending exam results, probably from a small village and finding it hard to make friends in the big smoke.* She paused, pen hovering over her notebook. She needed to eat. It was lunchtime after all and if she didn't put something in her stomach, she could be sure it would make embarrassing rumblings at inopportune moments that afternoon. Accordingly, she tucked the pen behind her ear and retrieved the grease paper-wrapped sandwiches Mammy had thrust at her on her way out the door that morning.

It was a conundrum of sorts the whole falling in love thing, she mused, biting into the corned beef sandwich. She needed to experience it first-hand if she was going to write her novel, which she'd already decided would be a love story. She didn't want to use her imagination to reshape others' words. That would have felt like cheating, somehow. The thing was, most boys were scared of her. It wasn't just her height. They wanted girls in pretty frocks who agreed with everything they said. Cliona sighed.

There had been one boy brave enough to ask her out, Niall Fitzsimmons. A lanky lad who stood a whole half inch taller than her, it was enough to be respectable. He caught the same bus to Westmoreland Street as her of a morning. Niall had spent weeks positioning himself opposite her and the first time she'd caught him staring shyly at her with those dark brown eyes peering out from under his cap, she'd wondered if she had a spot or, even worse, a telltale sign she'd had egg for breakfast on her face. Then, one day he'd taken her by surprise and as she'd looked up to find him staring at her he'd asked her out in a red-faced blurt he'd clearly practised. She hadn't the heart to say no.

So, you see, it wasn't as if she was completely inexperienced when it came to romance. She'd kissed Niall at the end of their evening together too but if she were to tell the truth she'd only done so out of obligation and curiosity. He'd forked out for a fine fish supper and film. It was the least she could do. Besides, he was a nice enough lad even if he did smell of menthol and eucalyptus. That was down to the Brylcreem he styled his duck's arse with. He must go through tubs and tubs of the stuff, she'd thought, trying not to inhale as he leaned in toward her with his wet, nervous lips puckered. The feel of them as they locked on to hers like a sucker fish made her think of two things. Her father with his slicked back hair, he was a Brylcreem man, and her heavy-handed mammy wielding the Vicks VapoRub. A girl did not want to be thinking about her mammy and da, or cold remedies, when she was being kissed, thank you very much. There'd been nothing in the least poetic about it all and she hadn't gone out with him again. She suspected he caught the bus that came twenty minutes earlier as she hadn't seen him since either. She didn't have time for fellas right now, anyhow.

Cliona had decided the day the letter arrived confirming her employment at the Times that she was too practical to fall in love. Sure, what was the point? Love led to marriage and it was written right there in front of her in bold black typeface that her employment would be terminated when she married. She didn't know much about the ways of the world but she did know that it would take time to work her way up through the hierarchy to where she wanted to be. What was the point in all that steady, hard graft if just as the finish line came into sight it was all whipped away from her because she'd said, "I, do."? There was no point was the simple answer and that's why she had a plan.

She would learn the trade from the ground floor up. She would be smarter, and work harder and faster than all those other reporters with their air of self-importance as they tapped out their stories, cigarettes smouldering in the ashtrays beside their typewriters. They were always at the ready with a wise-arse answer and keen to make the girls from the typing pool blush. She would prove she was up to the job. Cliona Whelan would make sure of that. She'd become indispensable.

She thought of her mammy and her brothers and sisters. Her tribe of younger siblings were always demanding something and never very grateful for having got it. She had no desire to find herself shackled to the kitchen sink with runny-nosed little ones tugging at her apron strings crying for attention in years to come. No, she wanted to write. Writing was something she'd always done. The proof was in her diary, hidden away under her mattress, safe from her nosy, spying sisters' eyes. It was something she needed to do because it stilled the restlessness in her. How else were you supposed to get all those feelings out? Sure, Father Sheridan didn't have time to sit in his confessional box and hear her outpourings. Cliona wrote because, well because she had such a lot to say about what she saw all around her and how it made her feel.

The, world was changing, she liked to tell Mammy, and she was too modern for marriage. Sure, hadn't she got Honours in her English Leaving Certificate. She was going to be a career woman, so she was. She'd even told Mammy to stop shortening her name to Clio and under no circumstances was she to call her Clio-Cat in the presence of others. The nickname had stuck since she was in nappies and had had a fascination with pulling poor Mittens', God rest her grumpy old soul, tail. The thing was she'd said, hands on hips, as Mammy stood at the sink with her Marigolds plunged into the hot, soapy water, when she finally got to do some proper reporting—not just the rewrites and advertising editorial mind, her byline would read Cliona Whelan. Not Clio-Cat, thanks very much. It was hard enough to be taken seriously but if anyone got wind of that nickname, sure it'd be the end of her. Mammy had huffed and made an awful clattering with the plates in the sink upon hearing this and said, she was getting ideas above her station since joining the newspaper and it would be a lonely washing that had no man's shirt in it, if she continued along the way she seemed determined to go.

Clio absently pulled a piece of crust from her sandwich and tossed it onto the grass. A squalling seagull instantly swooped from where he'd been circling keeping a watchful eye on her and the other students enjoying their lunch. She didn't like crusts. something she blamed her mammy for. It was the disappointment you see. All those years of dutifully eating them and her hair still hung straight as a curtain to her shoulders. There was not so much as a kink in it, let alone a curl. Most days she pulled it back into a ponytail but once in a while, like when she'd gone out with Niall, she'd dig deep for her inner girl and coax it along with the mesh rollers, lots of backcombing and lashings of setting spray. She frowned. She'd be having words with Fidelma when she got home, so she would. She was sure she'd been helping herself to the spray. It had been three quarters full the last time she'd used it and now there was only a third left.

She watched the bird as it pranced about, sending the smaller sparrows hoping for a crumb scattering as it asserted its bullyish presence. She liked bullies even less than she liked crusts. She'd always been one to stand up for the underdog. Sure, look at the trouble she'd gotten into with Sister Evangeline when she'd told her she was being very unfair to poor Patricia Murphy. She only stuttered all the more when she was shouted at and how was the sting of the ruler being brought down on her hand supposed to help her speech? It was why she dreamed of becoming a fully-fledged journalist. She wanted to report on the injustices she saw around her. Put those bullies to rights. And then, one day, she'd publish a novel. A great sweeping, epic of a thing. Oh yes, Cliona thought, she had a plan alright.

CHAPTER 13

She finished what was left of her sandwich, sweeping the crumbs from the lap of her ink-blue cigarette pants. Mammy was aghast at her insistence on wearing trousers to work, telling her it wasn't right and what would the neighbours think seeing her prance down the street bold as brass in them. Clio told her, if it was good enough for Katherine Hepburn in her heyday then it was good enough for Cliona Whelan thanks very much. How could she expect to ever have a serious assignment passed her way if she looked like a cake decoration? Besides, she'd reminded Mammy, she'd bought the pants with her own money.

Indeed, the small brown envelope she'd been handed at the end of her first week's work had been her wages. They'd burned a hole in her pocket and she'd felt ever so grown up shopping on her own. She'd come back down to earth with a bump when Mammy had greeted her at the door, eyeing her shopping bags before holding her hand out. 'You're earning now, Cliona, it's time you paid for your keep.'

A gentle breeze whipped over the green and Clio felt it tickle the downy hair on her arms. She'd rolled the sleeves of her white shirt up in order to feel the sun's kiss. The seagull was still there stalking about and so she flung the remainder of her crust in the opposite direction, kicking her foot out at the greedy bird and telling him to shoo and give the others a chance. He squawked and flapped at her indignantly.

'What did the poor guy ever do to you?' a crisply cut American accent asked.

Clio looked up startled, her hand shielding her eyes from the sun, to see the rangy outline of a student, with a pile of text books tucked under his arms, grinning down at her. He looked to be around twenty or so and had a quiet confidence about himself as he waited for her reply. She automatically noted he was taller than she was.

'The seagull?'

He nodded and she could tell by the way his sandy-blond hair blew into his eyes, moved by the sudden gust of wind, that he didn't use Brylcreem.

'I wanted to make sure the sparrows got fed,' Cliona said, her usual bravado slipping under his gaze. His blue eyes were the colour of the marbles her little brother played with and she tried not to stare but there was something about him that made her want to keep looking.

He held out his free hand, 'I'm Gerald Byrne, but everybody calls me Gerry.'

'I'm Cliona Whelan, but everybody calls me Clio.' She was rather pleased with her comeback, even more so when she received an approving grin. She liked the way the dimples in his cheeks softened his face when he smiled and she liked the trail of freckles across the bridge of his nose, too.

'And what are you studying…?'

She filled in the gap, 'Clio, you can call me Clio.' She conveniently pushed her outburst to her mammy regarding the shortening of her name aside. Cliona suddenly seemed far too much of a mouthful, too serious all of a sudden, which was fine when it came to work but no good when you were talking to a handsome American. She half wished she'd listened to Mammy now and worn her fitted jacket and pencil skirt. She'd held it out hopefully to Clio that morning, telling her it looked a picture on her. Remembering his assumption, she replied, 'Oh, and I'm not a student.'

'What do you do then, Clio?' He eyed her notebook curiously and she snapped it shut, pinching her bottom lip between her teeth as she debated how she should describe herself. Journalist or reporter was a stretch given she spent the best part of her day typing other people's work and making tea. In the end she went with, 'I work for the Times.'

'I'm a Times man myself. I was reading this morning about that Soviet satellite, Sputnik. It's been seen over the city a second time. It's like something from a science fiction novel.'

Cliona nodded. Every newspaper in the city would have been hustling to get their story to print on time for that morning's run. 'The space race has begun.' She quoted the headline.

'Do you write for the paper?'

My, but he had a lot of questions given they were complete strangers. Cliona was unnerved. It was usually her who had all the questions. Perhaps it was just the American way of things. She liked his assumption that it was a possibility she was a journalist though, perhaps the trousers had been the right choice after all and, flattered, she told him, 'I'm a junior typist but I want to be a reporter. You have to work your way up.'

'Do you enjoy it?'

'I love it,' she replied simply. 'There's always something happening.' The clacking of typewriter keys, the shuffling of papers, telephones ringing, reporters anxiously pacing, and best of all the buzz of a big story about to break. It filled her days with excitement and anticipation. It was a long way from the typing pool to being out in the field breaking your teeth on a meaty story though. 'You're at Trinity?' She gestured to the books he was carrying.

'Yup. Third year law student on exchange from Boston Law College. My great-grandparents were both from Dublin.' He shrugged. 'Most of Boston's from somewhere in Ireland. My folks thought it was high time I came back to the motherland and saw the place for myself.' He hesitated and then asked, 'Do you mind if I join you?'

She looked him over, this confident, good-looking boy from Boston and found herself telling him she didn't mind, she'd have to go in ten minutes or so anyway. Sure, what was the harm? He sat down, his legs stretched out in front of him as he leaned his head back, raising his face to the sun and closing his eyes for a fleeting moment. 'Those rays are good. I think the whole city is outside enjoying the weather.' He gestured around him at the busy slip of green. 'Or at least the entire college.'

'That's the Irish for you. We turn into basking African meerkats at the slightest hint of sunshine.'

He laughed. 'Wow, that's some analogy.'

'I saw a photograph of them in a book once, all of them with their heads pointing up at the sun. I've never forgotten it.'

'What were you writing in there? If you don't mind me asking?' He pointed to her notebook.

'I collect character descriptions.'

He looked puzzled.

'I write down things about people that stand out or catch my eye.'

'Uh-huh, but why?'

'Because I want to write a novel one day and I figured that it would be good to have something to call on when I describe my characters.'

'So, it's a reference book?'

'Yes, I suppose it is.'

'You've a pen behind your ear, did you know that?' There was a cheeky glint in the blue irises.

She pulled it down and opened her notebook making an entry.

'Is that shorthand?'

Cliona nodded.

'What does it say?'

'A Bostonian law student with intelligent, deep-set blue eyes and twin dimples. Hair a curious mix somewhere between blond and brown. A looming, athletic build. Wearing brown trousers and a green sweater and carrying a clutch of text books. An air of insatiable curiosity about him.'

Gerry looked taken aback momentarily and this time when he threw his head back it was to laugh. Clio grinned and snapped her book shut.

'Look over there,' he said once he'd sobered. She followed the direction of where he'd pointed and saw a young woman with the most unusual shade of red hair. She stood out from the crowd, not just because she was pretty, but because of the confidence with which she moved and Cliona felt something stir. A kernel of something unpleasant knotted in her stomach, an unfamiliar feeling and she didn't like it. Nor did she understand why, his pointing out a good-looking girl, should make her react that way. Why did she suddenly want to be pretty and feminine like that girl? Her looks had never mattered all that much to her. You were given what you were given and there wasn't much you could do about it, so you might as well make the most of it and get on with things. She was glad for the most part that she wasn't a great beauty. To be beautiful would be a distraction from what she had to say.

She wasn't unattractive. According to Mammy's women's magazine she had a heart-shaped face and she'd been blessed with clear skin, bright inquisitive grey eyes and a nose that could have been a little smaller but one that was passable. Her nan had sighed over her waist just the other day, saying she could remember when she'd had a waist you could fit her hands around like Clio's. It was hard to imagine Nan ever being small, she'd always had a middle like a sack of spuds, but eight children would do that to you, and there was another good reason not to fall in love, and get married.

'Hair the colour of autumn fire, skin like milk,' Gerry began.

Clio snapped her notebook shut and got up, annoyance pricking. So much for him being different. 'I've got to go.' She really did have to go, she only had five minutes to get back behind her typewriter. She remembered her manners. 'It was nice talking to you, Gerry.' And then, without looking back, she strode off unaware of his admiring gaze as he watched her wind her way through the various basking bodies to the street.

Chapter 15

♥

Roisin drove down the unfamiliar treelined street Jenny now lived on, keeping an eye out for the numbers. It was a far cry from the one-bedroomed apartment on the Quays she'd once swanned about in, where Roisin had dossed down on her lumpy old sofa many times after a night on the lash. Her hands tapped the steering wheel enjoying the poppy beat of the music playing. It was a treat being out and about on her own. No Noah chattering incessantly about Mr Nibbles or Mammy pointing out what every other driver on the road was doing wrong. The first thing she'd done after adjusting the rear view and side mirrors had been to change the radio station. Mammy liked a talky-talky one because she enjoyed arguing with the host even though he couldn't hear her. She slowed a little and peered over to the left looking for a house number. 'Twenty-three,' she said out loud, 'twenty-five. Nearly there.'

She'd been sitting in Bewley's with Mammy and her sisters yesterday afternoon with a well-earned cup of tea and sticky bun in front of her—they'd all opted for sticky buns needing the sugar hit after the Christmas photo debacle. She needed sustenance too for braving the shops if she was going to finish her shopping. The air in the popular café was thick with the scent of brewing coffee and that peculiar easy-going joviality that the winding down into the festive season brought. Mammy kept opening the cardboard wallet for another look at the photo, saying that it was growing on her. Roisin suspected that was only because it was ever such a nice one of herself. She'd reached across the table to brave another glance, then wished she hadn't. The state of her. The state of them all. She couldn't be meeting Shay with a head of hair on her like that. Moira kept humming *November Rain* and she was going to put the boot in under the table if she wasn't careful. There was nothing else for it, she'd have to see if Jenny could tidy her up before tomorrow night and, rummaging around in her handbag to retrieve her mobile, she looked up her old hairdressing pal's number.

Her friend's harried voice answered a few rings later. 'It's nice to hear from you Roisin and I'm sorry your split-ends have gotten so bad, but I'm very busy, so I am. There's the twins and we've Eoin's mam and da arriving the day after tomorrow and the house is in a state, and you know what that witch of a woman is like when it comes to inspecting my skirting boards for dust,' Jenny had garbled upon hearing Roisin's request.

Roisin held her mobile away from her ear grimacing as an ear-piercing and ongoing squealing sounded in the background. She'd forgotten what the terrible twos were like and Jenny had a double dose going on.

'Don't be playing fire engines when Mammy's on the phone,' Jenny chided. 'Oscar loves making the siren noise so he does, and it's doing my head in. Jaysus now Ophelia is after being an ambulance coming to the scene. Hang on a sec would ya and I'll go in the toilet. It's the only room with a lock where I can get some peace.'

Roisin busied herself with her bun waiting for Jenny to come back on the line and when she did her voice was echoey. She hoped she wouldn't hear any other sounds while they chatted. 'As I was saying, Rosi, I'm very busy. How long are you back for because I might be able to fit you in come the new year? How does that sound, we could have a good catch up then too?'

Roisin picked up a clump of hair and eyed the ends. She wouldn't be fobbed off, not when it was imperative she look her best. She inspected her nails. Would she have time to get them done? No probably not. She'd ask Moira, she was good at manicures and Aisling would let her borrow a pair of her heels and give her some wardrobe advice. All of that was a waste of time though if her crowning glory made her look like she should be playing bass in a hard rock band. She really didn't like to do a Mammy and waltz on down the guilt-tripping road but sometimes needs must. 'Pooh's gotten very big so he has.' She aimed her dart hoping to hit the bull's eye.

Jenny cleared her throat in what Roisin decided was a nervous manner. 'I was just about to ask you how your mammy and him were getting on? It was ever so good of you to take him off our hands, like. The twins missed him for about five minutes and then forgot we ever had a puppy. Thank God.'

'Well, I was glad to help because that's what friends do and he's settled in well with Mammy. Although, it's looking like she'll be leaving her worldly goods to him, he's the apple of her eye, so he is. I have to say it was a shock to her, to all of us to realise he wasn't going to be one of your tiny lap doggy poodles like I thought, though. Sure, I wouldn't have offered to take him off your hands if it had been made clear.' She waited and when she heard Jenny's heavy sigh, she knew she'd won.

She gave Aisling who was eavesdropping across the table the thumbs up as Jenny said, 'Alright then, seeing as it's you. I can sort you out at ten but, Roisin, don't be late, I mean it. I've to get to the shops in the afternoon or I'll have no food in for the Christmas dinner and shopping with the twins is harder than coordinating the Queen's fecking daily planner.'

Roisin smiled at the analogy. She was looking forward to seeing the gruesome twosome as their mammy called them.

CHAPTER 13

She slowed and indicated before turning into the driveway of 109. A tricycle lay abandoned in the front garden of the two-storey brick semi, and the flowerbeds either side of the front door could have done with a winter prune back, she noticed, getting out of her car and making her way up the front steps.

She hardly recognised Jenny when she opened the door. Where was the glamorous girl who'd had a penchant for silver jewellery and very cool clothes, more often than not in black? She'd always said black showcased whatever colour she'd put through her hair that month. The woman in front of her, whose hair was a bleached crop, looked tired as she glanced down at the jammy hand print on her oversized sweat top. She was wearing leggings and fluffy slippers that reminded Roisin of a pair she recalled her nana living in during her later years. In her hand was a mascara wand which she waved liked a traffic baton ushering Roisin in. Once the door was shut, she was wrapped in a hello hug, although she didn't squeeze back too tightly not wanting the jam to rub off on her. She knew wearing cream to visit her friend had been a bad idea but she'd wanted to go neutral after all that red yesterday.

'You're looking well on it, Jenny,' she lied. She wanted a decent haircut after all and she'd her fingers crossed for a freebie. 'Motherhood obviously agrees with you.'

'Liar.' She rustled up a wan smile. 'And I can see why you were desperate for a trim. I'm a mess but if you watch Ophelia and Oscar for ten minutes, I could tidy myself up and then make you beautiful.'

'Sounds like a good plan.' Roisin remembered her friend saying she was heading out shopping. She could recall going to get the groceries being an outing when Noah was small, *any* chance to get out of the house was an outing. 'I've nowhere I need to be, take your time. Now, where are they. They were babies last time I saw them.'

***

Famous, fecking last words! Roisin thought, lying on the living room floor as a scarf was wound around her leg. She already had a series of plasters decorating any exposed bits of her face and body. Ophelia was bandaging her leg for her. Her little face, almost hidden by the cloud of gorgeous, golden curls, was a picture of seriousness in her dress-up nurse's uniform. Oscar, her double apart from the short haircut, did an even more impressive version than the one she'd heard yesterday of a siren. *What was Jenny doing, having a nice soak in the bath and reading a good book? Had she sneaked out to do her shopping?*

A good half hour after she'd disappeared faster than a piece of chocolate cake at a Slimmer's World meeting, Jenny reappeared. It could have been a different woman. Roisin sat up and took stock of the transformation and the twins were rendered silent for all of ten seconds as they checked out this new version of their mammy. This was the Jenny she remembered. 'You look gorgeous.' She beamed.

'I feel amazing. Thanks a million for watching them, Rosi. It was such a treat to put my face on without giving a blow by blow account of everything I was doing.'

'It was no bother. We've had fun haven't we, you two?' Roisin said unpeeling the plaster from her eyebrow and hoping she didn't take half of it with it.

The twins nodded cherubically as their mammy flicked the television on for them and some eejits, dancing about in colours so bright they'd make your eyes bleed, filled the screen. She told them to be good while she gave Roisin a haircut and dragging a dining room chair behind her, beckoned for Roisin to follow her into the kitchen. 'I can't do a dry cut so I'll give you a shampoo and condition over the sink,' she said depositing the chair in the middle of the kitchen.

CHAPTER 13

The smell of fish hung faintly in the air; last night's dinner Roisin guessed as Jenny gestured at the sink. The bottles to the side were salon products, Roisin thought, recognising the labels. It would make a nice change from her supermarket duo. She picked up the folded towel, also on the worktop, and draped it around her shoulders before dutifully bending over and angling her head under the taps.

'How's the temperature?' Jenny asked, running the water.

Near scalding water trickled over Roisin's scalp and she yelped, 'Ouch, too hot.'

'What about now?'

'Jaysus, too cold.'

'Sorry, the tap's very temperamental. How's this?'

'Just right.'

She sounded like Goldilocks, Roisin thought, wincing as shampoo was rubbed into her scalp. Jenny had lost her touch because it wasn't a relaxing head massage she was after receiving and her back was killing her already from the stooping. There were a few moments of drama when shampoo got in her eye and she had to hold the towel to her eye to stem the stinging but aside from that she was smelling sweet and sitting in the chair ready to be pruned in no time.

A lot had happened since the last time she'd been in Dublin and she chattered about her life as a newly single woman, learning to stand on her own two feet and her hopes for eventually running yoga classes, as Jenny snipped away.

'I'd love to do yoga but there's never any time.'

'I could teach you a few basic moves. I managed to get Mammy doing some with me this morning.' She shuddered at the memory of her mammy in her yoga pants attempting the triangle pose. 'You could do them when the kids are napping or watching television.'

'I'd like that.'

'It really helped keep me sane when Noah was small.'

'And how is the young fella?'

'He's grand. He's after bringing his pet gerbil with him from London which didn't go down well with Mammy at first but she seems to be warming to the little chap. He is rather sweet.'

'I'm done with pets for the foreseeable future. Although we might stretch to a goldfish or something, you know, just so as they've got something to cart along to pet day when they start in the infants. Now shall I add some soft layers?'

'Soft layers it is.'

'So,' Jenny's voice took on an almost sly quality, 'is this desperate need for a haircut down to a certain fella?'

'I've only been separated a few months.'

'Don't come all holier than thou. It's me, Roisin, I know you of old. What's his name?'

'Shay. And it's only a drink we're going for.' She explained how they'd come to meet.

'Do you think you'll do the wild thing?'

'No! Sure, I hardly know the fella. And it's not a date or anything it's just a...' *What was it?*

'Don't move!' Jenny chided. 'It's a date, and hardly knowing a fella never stopped you in the past.'

'I was young and wild then.'

'Tell me about it, and I'm only asking because I live vicariously through other people's sex lives these days. Eoin and I were at it like rabbits when we first got married, we even did it on the kitchen worktop once.'

Roisin's eyes slid to the worktop and she decided that if, per chance, a cuppa and biscuit were offered after the haircut she'd decline.

'The last time we got jiggy, Oscar waltzed in right in the middle of it and Eoin had to pretend he was doing press-ups. By the time he'd finished explaining why he was doing them over Mammy neither of us were in the mood anymore. It's not funny!' she protested as Roisin laughed. 'Now with his mammy and daddy coming to stay there'll be no show of him practising his press-ups, not while they're in the room next door. He said it makes him feel peculiar knowing they're under the same roof.'

'Catholic guilt,' Roisin said knowingly. They all had it.

'It's that alright. What are you going to wear?'

Roisin shrugged, getting told off again for the sudden movement. 'I haven't a clue. Not that I have a lot of choice, just what I stuffed in my suitcase.'

'So, you'll try on everything you have with you, make a big mess, and then wear the first thing you tossed on.'

'Probably,' Roisin laughed.

'Have you done all your Christmas shopping?'

'I finished the last of it yesterday afternoon. Moira, Aisling and I tackled the shops. I was dead on my feet by the end of it.' Roisin closed her eyes for a moment recalling the elbow room only of most of the stores they'd visited. Unlike when the sales were on though and it was every man for himself, people were good natured and smiley. She'd enjoyed the atmosphere as they'd made their way down Grafton Street, pausing to listen to a group of young children singing carols. Seeing the Euros piling up in the upside-down hat in front of them she'd been tempted to go and fetch Noah back from his nana's and get him joining in on the Jingle Bells.

'Yes, thank God for catalogues. I did most of mine months ago from the comfort of my sofa. I've only the food to sort out now.'

'Aisling put her hand up to do our shop because with Quinn being in the restaurant business, he knows where all the best deals are to be found.'

'Lucky you lot. Now then, we're nearly done. Sit up straight.' She came and stood in front of Roisin pulling two bits of hair down either side of her face and comparing them. 'That's going to feel a lot better. I haven't taken much off just half an inch or so but it will get rid of those chewed up ends and the layers have gotten rid of all that bulk. Did you want a little bit taken off your fringe?'

'Just a teensy bit, please, Jenny.' She held up her thumb and index finger to demonstrate the quarter centimetre she wanted nipping off.

Snip, snip, snippity snip, 'Feck, Roisin, why did you jump!'

Roisin's eyes were bulbous with horror and Jenny who was looking horrified at what had just happened to Roisin's fringe spun around. She let out a scream that made Oscar's siren seem like a whispered sentiment. Standing in the kitchen doorway, not sure what all the fuss was about, was Ophelia. Her halo of curls, the curls Roisin had been admiring under half an hour ago were a memory. She looked like a little orphan girl whose head had been dealt with for the lice. 'Oscar and me played hairdressers,' she lisped.

Chapter 16

♥

'I can't go out, not like this,' Roisin cried from the bathroom. 'I'm not coming out.'

'Rosi, sweetheart, it suits you. It shows off your pretty face,' Maureen shouted through the door but despite the fact she was shouting she still had that slightly high-pitched tone that told Roisin she was fibbing. 'Sure, it's the shock of a change that's all. Remember me with my braids? The way you all carried on? Well, that was just because you weren't used to it. A fringe like yours is what we would have called the gamin look in my day. You know like your woman, Audrey Hepburn.' Maureen paused waiting for a reply and when none was forthcoming, she urged, 'Come on out now, your sisters have just arrived. They'll sort you out. Aisling's bought cake.' She added. 'It's chocolate with a cream filling.'

Roisin was not in the least bit comforted by Mammy bringing up the Bo Derek braids she'd sported during and post her Vietnam trip. It hadn't been the change they'd all struggled with. It had been the fact that their mammy was getting about looking like an aging one-hit wonder movie star who belonged on a beach, and Howth harbour did not count. As for gamin she might as well have said gamey. She heard frantic whispering on the other side of the door as her sisters and Mammy compared notes. It seemed Mammy had brought out the big guns, insisting Moira and Aisling drop everything to come around and try and bribe Roisin from the bathroom with cake. Well, she was definitely not coming out now.

Roisin stared in the mirror. She'd tried wetting the bangs and smoothing them straight to try and add length but like a tennis ball they bounced right on up again to sit smack back in the middle of her forehead. She looked, what did she look like? She bit her bottom lip as it came to her. She looked not quite right for want of a different turn of phrase. Bloody, Jenny! She'd had to keep snipping at it until it was even after she'd slipped with the scissors. As for the twins, they'd found the discarded pair of nail scissors Oscar had used for his haircutting debut having pilfered them from the bathroom drawer, under the sofa. It had taken Roisin ages to calm Jenny down over Ophelia's new look. 'It'll grow back in no time,' she'd soothed. 'And at least it's winter and you can put a hat on her when you go out.'

They'd had to swap roles once Roisin caught sight of her crowning glory with Jenny tossing her own words back at her. 'But I'm meeting Shay tonight, I don't have time to wait for it to fecking well grow back! And I don't suit bloody hats,' she'd wailed. Jenny had followed her to the front door apologising the whole way and wringing her hands over what Eoin would say when he got home and saw Ophelia.

Roisin had driven home feeling sure every time she stopped at the lights that the person in the car next to hers was shaking their heads and thinking 'Jaysus, would you look at the state of that, God love her.' It was ridiculous but she was bordering on hysteria, and it wasn't all down to the fringe she knew. The fringe had merely exacerbated the tension building over meeting Shay tonight. When they'd gone for coffee the last time she'd seen him it had felt relaxed, and natural, but going out for a dinner well, that fell into the formal bracket of a date didn't it? She'd make an eejit of herself; she was sure of it. Well, one thing was certain she'd thought, bursting through the door of Mammy's apartment, she'd fecking well look like one.

If she'd been looking for words of comfort from her nearest and dearest, 'Mummy! You look like Mr Nibbles,' wasn't what she was after. Mr Nibbles might be cute but she had no wish to take after him whatsoever and she did not have buck teeth and chubby cheeks. As for Mammy she hadn't had to say a word. The way she'd clapped her hand to her mouth said it all. Of course, being Mammy, she'd had to say something and when she'd finally found her voice it had come out in a squeak. 'Jenny's done you proud so she has.' The only one who failed to spot the difference or simply didn't care was Pooh, who let her know he thought she was looking just fine. She shoved him away and not trusting herself to speak took herself off to the bathroom, locking the door behind her. That had been well over an hour ago.

'Ah c'mon now, Rosi. I've bought my bag of tricks. I'll have you looking gorgeous in no time,' Moira cajoled. 'Sure, it can't be that bad.'

'It is!'

'And I've bought my black Valentino's. You know, the ones with the silver diamantes on the strap that you love,' Aisling called.

'You never let me wear those,' Moira griped.

'This isn't about you, Moira. And besides, this is a crisis, so it is. The poor girl's been butchered.'

Noah was next, 'And, Mummy, I will give you the biggest and best cuddle even though I'm getting to be a big boy.' There was a pause followed by. 'Is that what you wanted me to say, Nana? Can I have a biscuit now?'

'Shush, Noah.'

Roisin looked at her reflection, trying to be objective. Jenny had done a lovely cut on the whole, her hair was shiny and had a shampoo advertisement bounce to it now the scraggly ends were gone. Maybe she *was* being silly. Maybe it was just that she wasn't used to having such a short fringe. A new look was always a shock, that much of what Mammy had said was true. Perhaps she was looking for an excuse not to meet Shay tonight. Self-sabotaging. 'Sometimes you have to step out of your comfort zone, Roisin,' she said, a misty patch forming on the mirror. 'Roisin the Brave, remember?' If Shay was worth a pinch of salt, he wouldn't care what she looked like, he'd be interested in what she had to say tonight. She reminded herself that that was exactly what she'd found so attractive about him in the first place, good looks and sexy bod aside. It had been the way his head tilted slightly to the left when she was talking, as though he was trying to listen harder. He'd found her interesting and he'd laughed when she said something funny. He genuinely seemed to like her just for her being her.

She took a deep breath and knowing her mammy and sisters were likely pressed up against the door listening, she called, 'Back away from the door, I'm coming out.'

She heard Moira mutter something about 'Who does she think she is, a cornered criminal?'

Roisin turned the lock and flung the door open. Her sisters stared at her, eyes wide, and she saw Moira clamp her mouth shut and press her lips together tightly so as not to let the laugh bubbling in her throat escape. Aisling was digging her nails into her palms in an effort to distract herself.

'What?' Roisin demanded. 'C'mon, say your piece, the pair of you. Let's get it over with.'

'No, it's nothing,' Moira's voice cracked on the word nothing.

'Moira, behave yourself,' Maureen warned.

'Oh, Mammy, I think I have to say it or I might burst. It just keeps going around in my head.'

'No. Keep your gob shut. We've had enough drama as it is. You'll not get a piece of cake if you stir up more trouble.'

'Say what?' Roisin asked, not sure if she wanted to know but wanting to know in that way you did.

Moira moved out of Mammy's reach. 'It's that old nursery rhyme, it popped in my head as soon as I saw you. *Simple Simon met a pieman,*' she broke off in peals of laughter

'Ah, God, yes. *Going to the fair,*' Aisling snorted, 'I'm sorry, Rosi,' she choked out as her giggles erupted.

'*Says simple Simon to the pieman let me taste your ware,*' Maureen finished.

'Mammy, you're supposed to be on my side.'

'I am, but it is sort of funny, Rosi.'

Roisin looked from one to the other and felt her own mouth twitch. Ah feck it, she couldn't beat them so she might as well join them.

Chapter 17

The phone rang and Moira held up her hand, 'Don't move, your nails are only just after drying. I'll get it.'

Roisin stayed where she was on the sofa and admired the natural pink shiny hue of her nails. It was an effort to sit still though when she was such a jangly bag of nerves. She made an O shape with her mouth, her face felt strange. She wasn't used to wearing so much make-up. Moira had somehow achieved that holy grail of make-up looks. The one that said I'm not wearing hardly any make-up, I'm naturally gorgeous with dewy skin and rosy pink cheeks. A-ha fooled you! Really, I've truckloads of the stuff plastered on.

'Hello.'

She heard her sister's voice from the kitchen. *Was it Nina to say Shay had arrived?* Roisin wanted to bite her lip but she didn't want to ruin the lipstick Moira had carefully applied with a brush. 'It's a long lasting one so it won't come off when you eat and drink. It might come off if you go in for a full-on snog though,' she'd warned.

'Oh, hi-ya, Nina.'

Ah Jaysus, it was Nina, he was here!

'I will do. Tell him she'll be down in a sec and she's looking hot to trot. She's one foxy mama!'

'Moira, shut up! Do not tell him that, Nina,' Roisin shouted.

'No, I was only joking with you. Just say she'll be down in a tick. Thanks, Nina.' Moira put the phone down and reappeared in the living room. 'Prince Charming is downstairs and your carriage is waiting.'

'So, I gathered.' Roisin got up and smoothed the skirt of the little black dress she'd borrowed from Aisling. 'Sure, I couldn't get my arse in it if I tried these days,' her sister had lamented, pulling it from her wardrobe and handing it to Roisin. 'It'll be looking smashing on you though.' She'd kept her word too, loaning her the much-coveted Valentino's telling her she expected everything to be returned to her in the same condition as it had been loaned.'

She'd shot Moira a look and Moira had been indignant. 'For the millionth time, I did not scratch your Louboutin's, Aisling.' Aisling raised an eyebrow and Moira looked shifty. 'It was microscopic.' She turned to Roisin, 'She can't let it go.'

Aisling had stuck around to see the end result of Roisin's makeover and had declared her beautiful before spraying a cloud of the bottle of Oscar de la Renta perfume Quinn had bought her and ordering her to walk through it. Roisin felt the tiny droplets of perfume land on her as Aisling proclaimed she was officially hot-date ready. The fringe, she said, gave her the look of one of those pin-up girls of old. It was in the artful pencilling in of her eyebrows and the choice of bold red lipstick. Moira had done a fine job, she'd said, before picking up her overnight bag and heading for the door. 'Have a good time, Rosi, and don't do anything I wouldn't do.'

'I certainly won't be,' Roisin had replied.

Aisling was staying the night at Quinn's and Roisin planned on sleeping in her old room. Patrick and Cindy were having dinner with Noah and Mammy in Howth and would stay the night there. She was glad Noah was with his nana because he'd have a lovely time with her and it would give him the chance to get to know his uncle and Cindy a little better. Mostly though it was because whatever tonight with Shay was, Noah didn't need to be privy to any of it.

'Right then,' she said, picking up her purse. She was keen to rid herself of the nervous anticipation that was making her body tingle. 'I'll be off. Thanks, Moira, for everything.'

'My pleasure, but before you go, one quick question. Are you all erm, you know? Spruced up.'

Roisin looked up from where she was checking her purse for her phone and key to the apartment for the tenth time since she'd finished getting ready. 'No, I don't know, what do you mean? This is as spruced as it gets. And I thought you and Ash said I looked good.'

'You do, I did a grand job, if I do say so myself but it's your bits I'm talking about. Are they in shipshape, presentable order?' Moira cast a meaningful downward glance.

'Moira! For fecks sake.'

'Ah, don't be such a prude. It's your best interests I've got at heart. It's just I know it's been a while and I'm checking it's not the Amazon rainforest down there. You know in case you lose control of yourself and jump his bones. I could stall him if you need to go and have a quick sort out.'

'Thank you for your concern, Moira, but I'm perfectly respectable down yonder, not that it matters because last time I checked you don't drop your knickers and flash your bits when you're out for dinner. Because, that's all it is, dinner!' Her voice went up a notch and Moira held up a placatory hand.

'Alright, if you say so. Don't get your knickers in a knot. Now come on let's get you downstairs.'

'You're not coming.'

'I didn't give you an hour of my life not to watch your man's reaction when he sees you.'

'Stay right where you are,' Roisin ordered, her eyes narrowed.

Moira hesitated.

'I mean it.'

Moira looked at her oldest sister's face and knew she meant business. Reluctantly she picked up the television remote and flopped down on the sofa.

Satisfied she wasn't going to be followed, Roisin closed the apartment door behind her and, taking hold of the rail, made her way down the stairs. It was a while since she'd stepped out in heels this high and she didn't want to greet Shay by tumbling down the stairs and rolling into the reception area! She reached the first-floor landing and heard a squeak on the floorboards on the landing above her. 'Moira, I know you're there, feck off with yer!'

She waited a beat and heard the footsteps backtracking, shaking her head before carrying on down. The light from the foyer was a welcoming glow as she safely descended the last flight, blinking as she emerged into it. Her stomach flipped and flopped like a thrashing fish on a hook at the sight of him. She wondered if dinner was going to be a waste of time because she wasn't going to be able to eat a thing the way she felt at that moment. It had crossed her mind as she'd waited for the minutes to tick by upstairs that perhaps she'd built Shay up into this demi-God and that when she saw him, she'd be disappointed to find he was only human and a fairly average one at that. It wasn't the case.

He was leaning against the reception desk chatting to Nina. His dark but not quite black hair was long enough to curl at the collar of his jacket. It was brown leather and she felt the urge to rest her face against it and inhale its battered smell. He had a white T-shirt on and blue jeans worn with boots. They were cowboy boots and she was reminded of her romance book cover fantasy. It was a look he wore well. He registered her presence and she remembered to close her mouth. Appreciation flickered in his eyes and she lost herself in those dark pools. He grinned, breaking the spell and she blinked as he produced a posy of vibrant blooms from behind his back. 'These are for you. You look lovely by the way.'

Roisin smiled shyly. She wanted to pinch herself, this beautiful man had brought her flowers! 'Thank you, they're gorgeous,' she managed to say, holding out her hand and hoping he wouldn't notice her faint tremor as she took the flowers and hid her face for a moment. She inhaled their sweet aroma, grateful for the chance to compose herself.

'I can put them in water for you, Roisin,' Nina offered.

'Thanks, Nina, that would be grand.'

'Have a lovely evening.' Her face was wistful.

'We will do.'

'It was nice talking to you, Nina,' Shay said, before turning his attention to Roisin. 'I've booked a table at La Bamba. I hope you like Mexican food.'

She'd eat a bowl of tripe if it meant sitting opposite him and gazing upon his gorgeousness for an entire evening.

'I love Mexican.'

Chapter 18

The Mariachi band were playing in the corner of the restaurant and Roisin sipped her beer, enjoying the traditional sounds that would make the stoniest of faces crack a smile. It was happy music, she thought, admiring their sombreros and charro outfits. A waft of cigarette smoke tickled her nose as the door opened to the balcony and a man went out to join the couple who were braving the cold in order to puff away. The restaurant was buzzing with bonhomie and shouts of laughter sounded sporadically from the group seated near her and Shay. They looked like they'd come straight from the office for a spontaneous pre-Christmas dinner. Roisin glanced over and wondered if any of them would wake up tomorrow red-faced, having gotten too friendly with a colleague after one too many slammers!

She hadn't been sure what to order to drink but Shay had said the only thing that would cool down the jalapenos and chilis in the bowl of chili she'd ordered was a Steinlager and so she'd ordered a bottle of the beer. The fluttering anxiety she'd felt earlier had dissipated, helped by the pre-dinner tequila shots at the bar and she forgot she was exceedingly out of practice when it came to having dinner with men she barely knew. He was easy to talk to. There was an openness to him that invited her to tell him about herself and over their shared entrée of corn chips and guacamole, she had. He'd done that thing, tilting his head just enough to let her know he wanted to hear what she had to say. He made her feel witty and interesting and when the waiter arrived with two bowls of steaming chili con carne he'd been in stitches over her description of Noah's informative chat with the Customs man about Mr Nibbles.

She inhaled the warm, spiced aroma and stirred the puddle of sour cream in as Shay told her what his plans were for Christmas.

'Mam, Philip and I are going down to Castlebeg on Christmas Eve. It will be strange to wake up on Christmas morning in the cottage where Mam grew up but special, too.'

Roisin nodded. She knew the story of how his granddad and mammy had not spoken after he'd told her to leave his house as a pregnant teenager. It was only when Shay acted as the olive branch between them that they'd made a fresh start.

'How's Reggie, doing?'

'It will be his last Christmas.' A shadow crossed his face and Roisin reached across the table without thinking to place her hand on top of his.

'I'm sorry to hear that.'

He shrugged, and she moved her hand away hoping she'd not been forward. 'It would have been nice if we could have had him for longer but, you know, at least I've had the chance to get to know him and Mam and him have put things right between themselves. He told me he can go to his grave happy, knowing everything turned out well for her.'

'It's never too late for second chances,' Roisin murmured with a sad smile, thinking of her own dad's passing. It had been hard to see someone you love wither until there was no light left inside him, but he'd known he was loved and there had to be something to be said for that—a comfort to be found in having those that loved you best in the world there with you when your time came.

'Exactly.'

They smiled at each other in mutual understanding and a current flickered between them. It unsettled Roisin and she looked away, scooping up a mouthful of her chili.

'Jaysus!' She flapped her hand in front of her mouth and Shay slid the water across the table. She gulped at it gratefully, hoping her face hadn't turned the colour of the chili she'd just been assaulted by. She could feel the beads of sweat popping on her forehead and wished with all her might she'd asked for flipping nachos and not chili. *She must look like such a prize.* Her eyes were streaming.

'Are you okay?'

'I will be,' she rasped, wondering how she'd get the rest of her meal down her without looking like she'd just emerged from a Swedish sauna.

Somehow, she managed it. The key, Roisin told herself, was little mouthfuls washed down with plenty of beer. Shay who wasn't bothered in the slightest by the heat was telling her about the festival he'd organised in Cancun on Mexico's Yucatan peninsula a few years back. It had cemented his love of the food. The hotter and spicier the better! His life, she thought, listening to his funny stories about some of the prima donna musos he'd encountered through his work as a creative producer, was fun. How many people got to do what they loved for a living? She watched his animated expression, feeling inspired.

'I want to open a yoga school, and one day I'd like to visit India,' she blurted, not knowing if the sudden revelation of her hopes and dreams was down to the beer, or whether hearing him speak with so much enthusiasm about what he did for a crust, made her want to inform him that she didn't plan on being a not very good secretary forever.

'Really?'

She nodded. 'I'm doing my training for my teaching certificate but I'll need a bit behind me before I can set up on my own. I'll get there though. I love it. Yoga makes me feel whole and I want to help other people feel like that too. When life gets tough, it's an outlet for the soul.' She might be waxing a bit too lyrically with that last bit, she thought, but it was too late to take it back and she thought she saw a spark of amusement in his eyes.

'I've never tried it but I'd like to. Things can sail close to the wind in my business and it would be good to have a stress outlet other than the pub.'

'I could show you some of the basic positions and some simple breathing exercises. They really do help to calm and focus the mind.' *Oh lordy, she had some positions she'd like to show him alright*.

'Yeah, I'd like that, thanks, and you know I don't know you all that well, Roisin, but you strike me as the sorta woman who, once she sets her mind to something, can achieve anything. I think you'll have that school of yours up and running sooner than you think.'

Oh, how she wished Mammy and her sisters were here right now to hear him say that. Actually she didn't but nobody had ever seen her as a kind of warrior woman before and she liked it. She liked it a lot.

'Another beer?'

'Yes, please.' She felt like living a little dangerously.

She decided against dessert, opting instead for a tequila sunrise from the cocktail menu. Shay went for a margarita. It had been a long time since she'd had a night out. There wasn't much in the way of spare cash for hitting the nightspots in her London life and, truth be told she didn't want to. Shay made her feel carefree, like the girl she used to be. She tossed her head back and laughed at the tale of a well-known heavy metal performer's toddler-like meltdown upon finding the wrong brand of Earl Grey teabags had been put in his dressing room.

CHAPTER 18

'You've ruined him for me forever now. What happened to hard living?'

Shay wasn't apologetic.

Nature called and Roisin excused herself, getting up and making her way over to the ladies. She fanned her face, it was hot in here and her legs felt a little unsteady, but then that's what you got when you wore strappy six-inch heels. It was as she was washing her hands that she looked in the mirror and gave a small yelp at the reflection staring back at her. Christ on a bike, she'd forgotten all about the fringe. She didn't think she'd ever get used to it, or by the time she had it would have grown back to a respectable length. Still, she thought, drying her hands, Shay hadn't done that thing where he kept glancing up at it and then, realising he was staring, made himself look away. Colin had been a right gem for doing that. She never needed to look in the mirror to know she had a spot, not when Colin was on the scene.

She'd have liked to have splashed cold water on her face but didn't want to ruin Moira's efforts, besides she thought, with one last glance in the mirror, it'd be her luck the mascara she'd used wouldn't be waterproof and she'd re-emerge looking like Alice Cooper. The buzz of the restaurant washed over her as she opened the door to the Ladies and weaving her way back to their table, she saw a woman was crouching down at their table chatting animatedly with Shay. She immediately took in the fact she looked to be in her early twenties, a lithely-framed model type, all cheekbones and peachy skin. The sort of woman whose hair did what it was supposed to effortlessly, and whose fringe would never be too short.

Looking at her, Roisin suddenly felt all wrong. She was nearly thirty-seven, a mother and a soon-to-be divorcee. Who was she kidding? What was she doing here? Shay was in his late twenties and lived the kind of drifting lifestyle that didn't loan itself to fitting in with her regimented life in London. So, what was this? Why was she here? Deep breaths,

Roisin, she told herself, practising the exercises she'd been telling Shay about a few minutes earlier. She approached the table with a smile firmly attached to her face.

'Roisin, this is Estelle,' Shay said as she sat back down.

She would be called Estelle. It had been too much to hope for a good old Geraldine or the likes, Roisin took the girl's soft, dainty hand and managed to refrain from giving it a hard squeeze. 'Hi, lovely to meet you,' she said in a breathy voice and Roisin instantly felt mean. Her face was open and honest as she smiled at her. Even so, Roisin was pleased to note that she had lipstick on her teeth.

'You, too.'

'Estelle and I go way back,' Shay explained. 'We met when I was just starting out.'

'At a gig in Galway.' Estelle filled in the blanks.

God, what was she then, twelve? Stop it, Roisin.

'I was dating Lex from Bad Noise,' Estelle grimaced. 'God, he was a nightmare. It took him longer to do his hair than me and he was forever pinching my smoothing serum.'

Roisin smiled despite herself at the mental picture invoked and the girl beamed back straightening up. Roisin was glad she was sitting down. Her head would have only come up to the girl's chest and as for her legs, well, they'd finish at Estelle's kneecaps.

'Well, Roisin, it was lovely to meet you and Shay.' She leaned in and kissed him on the cheek. 'Always fabulous to see you but I'll have to love you and leave you, Maxim is like a spoiled baby when he's not getting attention.' She giggled and pointed to her date who looked like a Calvin Klein advertisement as he pouted around the restaurant, a moody vision in denim.

'Yeah, you too, say hi to Bella, Sebastian and the gang for me when you catch up next. It's been way too long.'

Roisin looked at him and back at Estelle and felt like the square peg who'd never fit into the round hole world, they moved in. She knocked back her sunrise and ordered another.

Chapter 19

1957

'Nice flowers kid,' Dermot Muldoon said, gum snapping as he passed by her desk. She'd put the bouquet in an emptied-out pencil holder and was almost hidden behind the colourful blooms as she attacked her typewriter in an effort to catch up on the pile of rewrites dumped in her in-tray. The gum chewing usually annoyed Clio, they weren't Americans and Dermot loved to play the hardened, New York reporter type, modelled no doubt after films he'd seen. Today however, the thought of America and anything to do with the country made her feel like singing. In fact, she'd just had a tap on the shoulder from Ciara, who sat at the desk behind her, asking her to stop humming *Loving You*. She hadn't known she was but Ciara said she'd inadvertently typed Elvis Presley into the editorial she was working on.

Nobody had ever given her flowers before and this posy had been brought to her desk by a young delivery boy who'd winked at her and said, 'Somebody must be sweet on you.'. It had made her feel all warm inside and she knew her face had coloured. She'd been centre of attention as the other girls in the typing pool had speculated as to who her admirer was. Clio had been coy, although she'd enjoyed all the fuss. She'd ignored the whispered remark bitchy Brigid, who wore her skirts just a little too tight, had made about there being no accounting for taste. She was only jealous, she told herself. All that mincing around the office she did was getting her nowhere.

The note she'd pulled from the envelope attached to the blooms was from Gerry. There was no one else they could have been from and her pulse beat a little quicker at the thought of him thinking enough of her to splurge on a bouquet. She'd held the message close as she read it, well away from the others' prying eyes.

Dear Clio, I hope I didn't offend you the other day and if I did well, this is my way of apologizing for being a brash and insensitive American. I thoroughly enjoyed our conversation and would like to invite you to afternoon tea at that most Irish of establishments, the Merrion Hotel this Saturday at 3.30pm. I shall wait for you in the drawing room where I believe the people watching is excellent and I hope I'll see you there.

Clio gazed at the flowers, once more losing herself in the intricate patterns of the petals. Nature was a wonderous thing she thought dreamily, jumping a moment later as the chief's booming growl sounded from his office. 'Clio where are those damned rewrites? They should have been on my desk half an hour ago.' Her fingers began to fly over the keys once more. Nature was all well and good but she had a job to do, she told herself sternly.

***

Clio's week was mercifully busy although her mind kept drifting to Saturday and what she would wear. She'd seen a dress in the window of Brown Thomas on her way to get the bus and had stopped to stare. It was lemon coloured with a nipped-in waist and full skirt and the slogan next to it said 'Be a Ray of

CHAPTER 1941

Sunshine on an Autumn Day. Yellow looked well on her, she knew that. The dress was far prettier than anything she had hanging in her half of the wardrobe at home. She mentally poured herself into the dress and imagined the admiration in Gerry's eyes as she swept in through the hotel's doors, white gloves on and cardigan draped over her shoulders. The doorman would fall over himself to greet her and Gerry would think himself a fortunate fellow indeed. She'd blinked, aware of the people hurrying past her and feeling rather foolish standing gawping at a shop window. She reminded herself that she wasn't really a ray of sunshine on an autumn day sort of a girl. No, she'd resolved, come Saturday afternoon she would be herself because that's exactly the sort of girl she was and if he didn't like it then he wasn't the fella she hoped he might be.

Even so, she'd taken an age to get ready come Saturday. She'd fussed with the rollers and had been pleased with the way her hair curled under at the ends. As for her bouffant, for once it didn't look like a sponge pudding sat on top of her head. All in all, someone was on her side she thought, giving it a final dousing with the setting spray. She'd compromised inasmuch as she ever did by teeming her checked pants with a lemon sweater. She didn't normally bother with make-up; she was always in too much of a hurry to head out the door and find out what was happening in the world. Today however, she applied a peachy, pink lipstick before standing back from the dressing table mirror to admire her handiwork. A giggling sounded from the doorway and she spun around to see Fidelma peering around it. She made kissing noises and, as Clio lunged at her, she tore off down the hallway, her feet thundering down the stairs to the safety of her mam's skirts in the kitchen. Clio followed at a pace befitting a young woman about to go for afternoon tea at the Merrion.

'Leave your sister alone, Fidelma,' she heard Mammy admonish over the cacophonous noise coming from the kitchen.

She poked her head around the door in time to see her sister's cheeky face peer around her mam to see how the land lay. A pot was bubbling on the stove, its lid rattling, and the savoury smell of stew clung to the air. The twins Tom and Neasa were banging spoons on upside down pots playing the drums and looking pleased with their musical ability. Tom was clutching a piece of cheese in his spare hand and Tabitha; Mittens' predecessor was cowering in the corner ever hopeful of a tasty titbit being sent her way.

It was a madhouse, she thought calling over top of the ruckus, 'I'll be off then, Mammy.'

'Ah now, hang on just one moment, young lady. Tom, Neasa, give that a rest, you're giving me an awful headache so you are. And Tom give me that cheese if you're not going to eat it.' Tom pressed the cheese into his mouth defiantly and Mammy sighed, turning her attention back to Clio.

'Now who is he this fellow of yours? And what is it he does?'

'Mammy!' Clio rolled her eyes. She'd already told her more than once. 'We've been through all of this.'

'Don't you Mammy me, not when you're after stepping out with a fella we've not met.'

Clio decided to tread a little more carefully. She was lucky it was just Mammy she was having to deal with, Da thanks be to God had gone to watch the match. 'His name's Gerald Byrne and he's an Irish American from Boston. He's in Dublin for the year studying at Trinity—a third-year law student.'

'A law student, and from Boston, you say.' Mammy's eyes were alight and slightly glazed. Clio knew she'd just transported herself from her kitchen in Phibsborough to a swanky Boston society wedding where she, as mother of the bride, was clad in the very latest haute couture. She'd have a hat on too, Clio mused, a great big one with feathers like one of the three musketeers knowing Mammy. She read far too many magazines for her own good.

CHAPTER 1943

***

Clio felt like she'd stepped into another world as she was ushered through the doors of the elegant Georgian hotel. She paused for a moment in the foyer and fancied she could smell the stories imprinted on the Merrion's walls. The air was fragrant with extravagant floral arrangements and, to Clio's mind, there was a hushed, almost reverent atmosphere rather like being in church. The foyer was quiet this time of the day and a well-groomed young man with a pencil-thin moustache looked up from the concierge desk to ask if he could help her. 'I'm meeting a friend in the drawing room,' she explained a hand automatically going to her hair to check it was still sitting where it was supposed to be and hadn't morphed into a bird's nest on the journey here.

'Certainly, madam.' He gave a tight smile, his moustache curving upwards, and gestured to a porter asking if he would 'Show madam to the drawing room.' She hurried behind the liveried boy who didn't look much older than herself and found herself in the entrance of an understated, refined room full of intimate tables and comfortable armchairs in which several guests lounged with the casual air of people well used to the finer things life had to offer. A colossal chandelier dominated the space sending shafts of rainbow lights darting about the room. Flames spluttered and coughed from the open log fire and there, sitting in the middle of it all and looking every bit as handsome as she remembered, was Gerry.

His face lit up as he saw her, and Clio thanked the porter. She tried to stop the big goofy grin from spreading over her face as he got up to greet her. 'I wasn't sure you'd come. You look wonderful by the way.' He kissed her on the cheek and she inhaled his scent closing her eyes for the briefest of moments trying to pinpoint the familiar, fresh smells. It was

Pears soap and green apple shampoo she deduced, accepting his invitation to sit down in the chair opposite him.

'Shall I order us tea and scones?'

'Grand.'

He did so and then produced a packet of Player's from his shirt pocket. He opened it and giving it a tap offered the protruding cigarette to her.

'Oh, no I don't, thanks.' She'd had a puff on the cigarette her friend, Deirdre, pinched from her mammy's apron pocket when they were thirteen. She'd thought she was going to cough up a lung and when she'd finished wheezing, she'd felt violently ill. It had put her off for good.

'Do you mind if I do?'

'No, of course not.'

She watched him from under her lashes as he lit the cigarette with a gold Zippo. It was engraved but she couldn't read what with. He saw her looking at it.

'A twenty-first present from my folks. I've a matching hip flask.'

'So, you're twenty-one.' She'd wondered.

'Closer to twenty-two and what about you, Clio, how old are you?'

'Eighteen. I'll be nineteen in June.' She watched him lift his head and exhale a plume of smoke. There was something elegant about the process and she almost wished she did smoke.

'So,' he said lazily. 'Tell me more about yourself. What makes you tick, Clio Whelan.'

'Well,' Clio thought about his question, 'I suppose what drives me is my need to break the mould.'

'What do you mean?'

'I mean, I don't want to wind up being an Agony Aunt for the paper or writing a women's lifestyle column. That isn't what I want to read when I pick up the paper. I want to read about what's going on in the city and that's what I want to report on. There aren't any women doing that and I think it will be a while before there are, but I intend to be right there with my pen and pad at the ready when things change. And I want to write my book of course.'

Gerry could see the passion in her eyes as she spoke. 'And, I think you'll do both.'

Clio checked his smile but there was no hint of condensation or indication that he might be humouring her, as was apt to happen when she put voice to her dreams. The only thing she could read in his expression was admiration.

'There's more to you than your ambition, though. What about family, you know brothers and sisters?'

'Oh,' she waved her hand dismissively, 'I've too many of both.'

Something, her words or her expression, Clio wasn't sure, made him laugh and encouraged she told him all about the Whelan madhouse.

'It sounds like fun.'

'Chaos more like. They drive me mad all of them but I love them dearly. What about yourself?' She looked at him sitting back in his chair, legs crossed, relaxed, and was struck by how at ease he was here in the hotel. Taking tea in upmarket establishments was clearly something he was used to unlike herself who was perched on the edge of her seat half expecting a tap on the shoulder from the concierge asking exactly what she, Cliona Whelan from Phibsborough was doing there. She could sense from his quiet confidence how different their lives were and the seed of an idea was planted.

'What do you want to know?'

'Everything and do you mind if I take notes?' Her hand was already closing around the notebook she never left home without.

'For your character profile?' He looked amused as he took a long drag on his cigarette.

Clio watched the tip glow brightly and the ash begin to bend. He flicked it in the ashtray and looked at her expectantly.

'No, I've an article I'd like to write.'

'About me? I can assure you, your far more interesting than me Clio.'

She shook her head. 'I disagree. Your life's so different to mine and the average Dubliner, Gerry therefore it's automatically of interest especially as so many Irish have family in Boston. I want to know about what your life there's like. Why you feel connected to Ireland even though your third generation. The, things you did growing up that sort of thing. What it means to you and your family for you to spend a year at Trinity and how it differs from college life in Boston. I'm sure others would too.'

'I think you're quite mad, Clio.' He shook his head and ground his cigarette out.

'A little maybe, but most of us Irish are.' He smiled at that and encouraged, she clicked her pen testing it on the blank page she'd opened her notebook to. 'Well, what do you say?'

'Will you let me read it when you've written it?'

'Of course.'

He studied her intently for a moment. 'I don't think you are the sort of girl who takes no for an answer are you, Clio?'

'I'm most certainly not,' she said, mock-sternly.

He grinned. 'Well then, I've no choice. Where should I start?'

'Tell me about your family and what it was like growing up in Boston.'

Clio listened intently, her hand flying across the page, not wanting to miss a word of what he was saying. She was right, his life was as different to hers as could be and reading between the lines, she sensed his family was wealthy. What they called in America, old money wealthy. Gerry was one of three boys who'd had a pretty sheltered childhood. He'd gone to good Catholic schools, summered in Cape Cod, that sort of thing. She watched his face grow illuminated as he described the wide sky and endless stretches of sand and the sense of freedom he'd always felt arriving at the Cape, knowing the whole summer was his to lie on the warm sand, to run down the beach as the waves caught his feet, and to swim. As a teenager he'd been good at track and he'd have liked to have studied medicine. Medicine was a noble profession, he said, but as the oldest son, a career in politics was predetermined. His father moved in those circles and it was an assumption Gerry had grown up with that he would follow in his father's weighty footsteps. She detected a slight bitterness in his tone and tried to imagine having no choice over what direction you pointed your life in.

He only stopped talking when the pot of tea and a plate of scones with fresh cream and a bowl of strawberry jam arrived and were put down on the table in front of them. They dived into them and when he leaned across the table to wipe off the blob of cream she'd somehow managed to get on the tip of her nose, Clio knew she was falling in love with the good-looking American with the candid smile opposite her.

Chapter 20

♥

Present

Clio's fingers hovered over the keys. She was in her writing room, the room that doubled as a guest room when she'd had Fidelma's children stay over through the years. Her desk overlooked the back garden, which was an unruly display of cottage garden flowers in the summertime. Clio liked the disorderly and riotous colour that ran rampant through the warmer months in her otherwise orderly world. She liked to get amongst her flowerbeds and hear the humming bees as she pulled weeds and trimmed edges. She'd found over the years that, when she was in her garden getting her hands dirty, her mind was free to roam and the scene that had been tied in knots would become untangled so that when she sat back down behind her typewriter the words flowed.

Today the lawn was covered in a blanket of snow and she watched her little friend the robin redbreast, who visited her apple tree most days. It came to nibble on the bird feeder she hung from the branch of the tree. She'd placed it safely out of reach of Bess whose arthritic old bones meant her climbing days were over. The bird's shiny black eyes fixed on something only it could see as it perched on the spindly branch. She admired its stillness and the vibrant orange, red feathers of its breast. There was a lot of folk lore associated with the bird; Clio knew the stories. To kill the robin, the tale went, would result in a tremor in the hand of the perpetrator for the rest of their days. They were messengers from the spirit world, that signalled the death of a loved one. She didn't go in for all of that, she just liked to watch the little bird's graceful, darting movements and enjoyed the splash of colour its visit brought on an otherwise dull day.

She was also glad of the distraction because since she'd received Gerry's card, the words refused to come. She'd sat down in front of her typewriter, a cup of coffee you could stand a spoon up in alongside it because she liked the mellowed rich smell. It reminded her of her days working in a newsroom and she liked to think it was the scent of industriousness. There'd been nothing industrious about her sitting at her desk staring at the window these past days though, as she found herself lost in the past. It didn't pay to look backwards when you got to her age, Clio thought. There was no point in questioning the decisions you made when you were young. What was done was done.

She sighed and got up, knowing she was going to read through the box of letters she'd tucked away in the attic years ago, and which from time to time she'd revisited over the years. There was one for every week Gerry was away from her for those three months until she'd broken things off. Love letters full of hope for the future. Mostly, Clio scanned through them, her eyes misting as she wondered how her life might have been had she gone to Boston as they'd planned. She knew he'd married from grainy newspaper copies of the Boston Globe thumbed through at the library. She knew too he was a widower and had been for some time. The knowledge he'd married had caused a bittersweet pain, especially when she'd read he'd had children too. Sons, three handsome mini versions of their father, and she wondered if the eldest would be expected to rise high in politics like his father and grandfather had before him. The shoebox was where she'd left it, downstairs on the side table next to her sofa. She'd been going through the letters again last night, enjoying the warmth from the fire as she'd travelled back in time.

Chapter 21

♥

1958

Clio huddled inside her coat as she waited on the corner of Grafton and Dame Street for Gerry. The weather had been brutal these last few days. Winter seemed to be intent on not letting spring get so much as a look in, despite it nearly being April. She was wishing they'd arranged to meet inside a cosy pub instead of on this street corner where the wind whipped around. She watched a pile of leaves in the gutter dance about in a private whirlpool and then, looking up, spied Gerry's familiar loping gait as he strode toward her. The smile, the one she could never contain when she saw him, broke out on her face despite the fact she was on the verge of hypothermia.

'Hello, darling, you look frozen. You weren't waiting long, were you?' He kissed her with a passion that received a disapproving look from a woman marching past, whose headscarf was knotted so tightly against the wind it had given her an extra chin. He took her hands in his and tried to warm them.

'That wind cuts you in half, c'mon let's go somewhere warm,' Clio said through chattering teeth once he'd released her.

'Kehoes?' he suggested, and she nodded, not really caring where they went so long as there was a fire. She tucked in under his arm enjoying the way she fitted just right and they made their way up Grafton Street. They veered into Anne Street where they burst in through the saloon style, stained glass doors of the pub with the same gusto as the cowboys of old. Clio loved the old place. It was to the Irish literary world what Sloppy Joe's bar in Key West had been to Hemingway. Clio adored Hemingway although she admired Virginia Woolf more.

The pub, with its dark wood panels and booths, smoky atmosphere, and aroma of whiskey that somehow permeated it all, felt like a space in which a great novel would have been plotted out. Since she'd turned eighteen and had finally been old enough to frequent the city's pubs, Kehoes had become a firm favourite for its most excellent people watching. Although, she was happier sipping on a glass of lemonade than a pint of the black stuff Gerry had been so determined to enjoy. 'I can't be considered a proper Irishman if I don't drink Guinness, Clio,' he'd said.

She'd replied, 'But you're Irish American.'

'Same difference where I come from,' he'd said grinning, and she'd pointed to his foam moustache with a smile.

Now, she slid into a booth. The pub was toasty warm thanks to the fire, and a group of men who looked like they'd had a hard day's labouring were clustered at the bar, putting the world to rights over their pints. There were a few younger people, students who fancied themselves intellectual types with little round glasses perched on their noses, hair a little too long, and wearing cool, black polo necks. They wore earnest expressions as they sat deep in debate, smoking languorously with their half-finished drinks in front of them.

There were only two other women in the pub, Clio noticed. The girlfriends of the intellectuals, but it pleased her to see they were taking part in the heated debate with just as much passion as their male counterparts. She glanced at her watch. It was five o'clock. She had time for one drink and then she'd have to get off home. Not that her parents would make too much fuss were she to run a little late for dinner. They thought Gerry was the best thing since sliced bread and had high hopes of her forgetting about her career and concentrating on more important things like marrying well. Marrying into Boston society to be precise. Clio planned on having both.

She watched him ordering their drinks. It was hard to believe they'd been courting since September. Time had passed so quickly and in the last six months Gerry had become so much a part of her life she could no longer imagine herself without him beside her. A shiver passed through her. In a few weeks he would be leaving. His passage was booked across the pond to America. Him not being here in Dublin would be like… well, it would be like losing a limb, or an integral part of herself at the very least. It was a pain she didn't want to think about. All her spare time was spent with him, so much so that her mammy had warned her not to neglect her friends or she'd have none to choose from as bridesmaids. Fidelma and Neasa had been most indignant because, they'd told Mammy, it was they who should be bridesmaids. At that point Clio had held up her hand and told them that she had no idea where all this talk of bridesmaids had come from because she wasn't even engaged.

'Ah, but you keep playing your cards right, Clio, and you might just find a lovely, sparkly ring on your finger.'

'It's Cliona, Mammy,' was all Clio had dignified her mammy with by way of response.

Gerry returned with their drinks and slid into the seat opposite her. He'd no sooner settled himself and raised his pint glass to his lips when she launched into the breaking news from America. It was a story she'd typed for their World News reporter, Ed, that afternoon and one she was itching to share. The United States had launched its Vanguard 1 Satellite. 'Isn't it incredible to think of it orbiting up there?' She pointed skyward. 'They say it will be up there for two thousand years, imagine that?'

Gerry nodded his agreement but, as she opened her mouth to fill him in on the finer points of the US's latest space mission he held a hand up to silence her. 'Clio, honey, let me get a word in would you.'

'Oh, sorry.' She was contrite, and looking at Gerry's serious expression a little worried as to what it was he wanted to say. She clutched her glass a little tighter, her knuckles suddenly white. To her relief his face softened.

'Don't look so worried. It's just I think we need to talk about the future, don't you?'

Clio studied him and her mouth suddenly felt dry. She took a sip of the sweet syrupy drink in order to stall the tête-a-tête she wasn't sure she wanted to have. She didn't want to *think* about him leaving, let alone put voice to it. His steady blue-eyed gaze didn't falter from hers and finally she replied with a weighty sigh, 'Yes, I suppose we do.'

'I want you to come to Boston.'

Her eyes widened and he hurried on. 'Hear me out. I'll go back as planned and then in a month or so, when I've had a chance to talk things through with my folks and to put the arrangements in place, I want you to come over.'

Clio couldn't make sense of what he was saying and her face must have reflected this because Gerry took her hand in his and said, 'I'm not making a good job of this and I have a ring. It's my grandmother's actually but it's not here.' He stopped, his usual confidence having deserted him, his words sounding jumbled to his own ears, and took a deep, steadying breath. 'What I'm trying to say, Clio, in my ham-fisted way is, I want you to be my wife.'

Clio gave a tiny gasp as his grip on her tightened ever so slightly.

'Marry me, Clio Whelan. I've never met anyone like you before and I can't imagine my world without you in it.'

'Oh.' She blinked. She hadn't been expecting that but suddenly her mouth twitched and that big goofy grin, the one she could never contain for long when she looked at Gerry, spread across her face. 'I would love nothing more than to marry you.'

***

Present

Clio gazed at the letter she had clutched in her hand. It was the last correspondence she'd ever received from Gerry until the Christmas card that had arrived the other day had sent her into such a spin. Old memories seemed so fresh when they were brought out and examined like this, she mused, eying the words in that oh so familiar handwriting in front of her. Words she could almost recite by heart. The letter was dated the eighth of July 1958. Gerry had been home for three long months when she'd received it. She'd run up to her bedroom, ripping it open eagerly, as she did every Friday when his letters arrived like clockwork, and the ticket for her passage had fallen out along with a note from his mother.

It was real, it was really going to happen, she was going to Boston, she'd thought, picking the ticket up and staring at it with both fear and excitement. The note, she saw, was neatly written on embossed personalised stationery and it was intended to welcome Clio to the family. Mrs Byrne wrote how excited she and Mr Byrne were over her and Gerry's engagement. How lovely it was going to be to welcome a daughter into the family, and that they were so looking forward to meeting her. She'd expressed sympathy, understanding the idea of setting sail for a new country must be daunting both for herself and her family, but that she, and her parents were not to worry. She'd be well looked after. Arrangements had been made for the sake of propriety for her to stay with a Mrs Geraghty who was used to lodging homesick young women and would look after her well. She ran a clean and respectable establishment where Clio would stay until the wedding. After which she and Gerry would be gifted a townhouse in which to start their married life. Cliona had skimmed over the rest of the note.

We've a lot to organize, my dear, with your engagement party and the wedding. John pulled some strings and the Holy Cross Cathedral is booked for the 9th of November. It's quite the coup given the short notice. Wait until you see inside it, Cliona, my dear, it is breathtaking and the acoustics have to be heard to be believed. I get goosebumps just thinking about it all. You and Gerald will be the toast of the town! Now, given it's to be a winter wedding I'm thinking Balmain for the gown. Audrey Hepburn wore a Balmain on her wedding day and the sleeves were magnificent and perhaps, Balenciaga for your engagement? Oh, we're going to have such fun, you and I, Cliona. As for the invitations plain black ink on cream paper is simple but stylish don't you think?

The rest of the words had blurred. It was like trying to read a foreign language. She'd put the note to one side and scanned Gerry's letter, wanting to find comfort in hearing his voice through his words. It hadn't helped quell her anxiety though, as he'd written his mother was driving him nuts because all she could talk about was the engagement party and the wedding. The engagement party was intended to formally introduce Clio to Boston society and Mrs Byrne was hopeful of the Kennedys attending both. She was getting herself very agitated over the arrangements and was impatient for Clio to arrive so they could finalise the details. There was a lot to be done, or so his mother said. He'd be just as happy for them to elope but he'd never be forgiven if they did. Don't worry, my darling, he'd written. Once we're married our life will begin.

The letter and its enclosures had arrived seven days before she was due to sail, plenty of time for Clio to begin to feel apprehensive about the idea of crossing the Atlantic on her own. She wanted Mammy to come with her but she couldn't leave the littlies and 'Besides,' she'd said, 'wasn't it better they saved their pennies for the wedding? Sure, you'll be grand, Clio, aren't you a capable young woman, who's going to be welcomed into her new family. There's nothing to be anxious about.' But Clio was anxious.

Mammy and Daddy were in raptures the more they learned of what she could expect on her arrival. 'You'll never have to work again, Clio. Sure, it's a life of fine clothes and a fine home for you, my girl. You'll be living in the lap of luxury,' Mammy had trilled. She'd caught her telling Mrs Fitzpatrick two doors down that she and Gerry were being given a townhouse in Boston as a wedding present. 'Imagine that?' she'd said to the hard-faced old woman who used to tell Clio and her friends off for being boisterous when she was younger. Mrs Fitzpatrick had turned pea green. Mrs Byrne had said she and Gerry would be the toast of the town. Well, she was definitely the talk of the street, Clio had humphed to herself, because she'd also overheard Mrs Fitzpatrick telling Mrs Murphy in a voice designed to carry, that young Cliona Whelan had gotten ideas above her station.

When Mammy wasn't telling anyone who cared to listen about Clio's new life in Boston she was fretting over the Whelans showing her up. Worried they'd arrive in Boston looking like country hicks from over the sea. She'd been making cutbacks when it came to the food bill so as to deck them all out in clothes befitting a society wedding. This was to the disgruntlement of Clio's brothers and sisters who were sick to the back teeth of being told they'd have to behave themselves when they were in Boston. 'Why couldn't you marry someone normal?' Fidelma had whined, upon finding the strawberry jam had not been replenished.

Clio recalled her mammy asking her, on the Thursday before she was due to sail, what they'd said when she'd told them she was getting married at work. She'd carried on eating her toast even though, like everything else she tried to eat of late, it tasted like cardboard. Her mammy, who had her back to her at the worktop as she strained the tea, hadn't waited for an answer. 'I'd have thought they might want to run a story on you. You know local girl makes good, that sort of thing. Did you tell them there's a possibility Mr and Mrs Kennedy might be at your wedding?' She turned around then and Clio had just smiled and nodded vaguely which was enough to appease her. She'd picked up her plate and rinsed it in the sink before kissing her mam goodbye on the cheek and heading out to catch the bus. She'd tried not to think about it being the second to last time she'd ride this bus through the streets she knew like the back of her hand but her eyes had burned with threatened tears, nonetheless.

She hadn't said a word to anyone at the newspaper, not a word and she didn't know why. Oh, she'd tried. She'd hovered outside her boss's office and when he'd shouted at her to stop loitering and get on with her work, she'd scurried off instead of saying what needed to be said. That long-ago Thursday as she clacked away at her typewriter she'd found it hard to believe that come Monday she wouldn't be there. Her chair would be empty and all she'd be remembered for was the girl who'd skulked off to America to get married without so much as a word. Nobody would ever say, 'Cliona Whelan, she was one of the finest reporters we ever had.' So it was, she left the building at 4.30pm on the Friday afternoon as though it were just any other day. She waved to the girls from the typing pool and called back to them to enjoy the weekend before getting on her bus and going home.

The next few days had passed in a strange twilight-like fugue for her. She went through the motions of packing her case—she planned to travel lightly—and on Saturday night there'd been a farewell supper held in her honour. As her friends and family laughed, chatted and clinked glasses she'd felt as if she were standing outside herself, a stranger listening in to people talking about some girl she didn't know. Nobody noticed anything amiss with her and Clio had wished more than anything that she could sit down with Gerry, face to face, and tell him how she was feeling, but he was literally an ocean away from her.

The day itself rolled around as big occasions always do and in this new dreamlike state that had overtaken her, she'd found herself being jostled by the crowds gathering at Dublin Port, waiting to board or wave off loved ones on the Orion. The huge liner loomed over them all with its steady stream of passengers walking up the gangplank. The day was cold but it didn't touch Clio; she was unaware of the sorrow, anticipation and excitement that filled the crowded dockside. She was oblivious to the scent of the sea, salty and fishy, which made Neasa's nose curl and Tom declare the port, "stinky" which saw him get a cuff around the ear.

She was hugged and kissed and aware of Fidelma urging her to look out for her orange scarf when she stood on the deck to wave down at them; she'd worn it in order to stand out. Mammy was crying, and Daddy was stoic as he nudged her into the throng filing up the gangplank. Her case banged against her leg as she was swallowed up in the crowd, all eager to board the ship and begin their journey. She showed her ticket and passport and then followed the sea of coats and hats to the upper deck where she squeezed in between two families to scan the dock for a last glimpse at her own family's familiar faces.

An orange slash of colour split the grey day and her gaze settled on Fidelma waving frantically with her scarf. A wave of love for her sister crashed over her and she waved back, hoping she could see her. Her arm began to ache with the effort, and the stupor Clio had been in began to lift. The calls of the men working on the wharf below mingled with the excited chatter all around her became overly loud. She could smell the salt air and everything sharpened and cleared like the lens of a camera being twisted into focus. Her arm dropped to her side as it hit her what had been niggling at her since she'd received that last letter from Gerry.

If she were to marry him, she would cease to be. That girl who'd stood outside Brown Thomas admiring the yellow dress, the dress that suggested she be a ray of sunshine on an autumn day, the girl who'd been strong enough to know her own mind, would be swallowed up. Because just as she wasn't a ray of sunshine on an autumn day sort of a girl, nor was she cut out for Balenciaga or Balmain. Her life she realised, were she to travel to Boston would be immersed in Gerry's. Her job from the moment she said "I do" would be to support him, and his family's political aspirations.

She loved Gerry. She loved him with all her heart, but she knew right then that she couldn't marry him. She began to elbow her way back through from where she'd come, moving against the tide as she pushed her way back down the gangplank toward the orange scarf. She was Cliona Whelan, she told herself. The girl who would not quit until she was reporting newsworthy stories for the Times. The girl who would write a bestseller. She'd gotten sidetracked, but she'd found her way back to herself.

***

Clio folded the letter and put it back in the box before placing the lid down firmly. She hoped by doing so she was shutting those memories in so she could get back to work. To her surprise she found her cheeks were wet and she wiped the tears away angrily. She had a book to be getting on with. She didn't have time for dwelling on ancient history. Why had Gerry decided to come back now? What could he possibly hope to have happen at their time of life? She was only a year away from getting her bus pass for God's sake.

Chapter 22

♥

Roisin made her way down the stairs, her nose quivering like the little red fox at the smell of bacon frying. The aroma was curling its way up the stairwell from the kitchen in the basement. She clutched the bannister, feeling unsteady on her feet despite her sensible footwear. Her head was pounding and she vowed for the tenth time since she'd opened one eye earlier that morning, only to be assailed by a needle like pain in her head, she'd never touch tequila again. She hadn't had all that much to drink but she was out of practice given she hardly led the life of a party girl these days and it had gone straight to her head. The apartment was silent when she dragged herself out of bed, for which she was grateful.

She could vaguely recall Aisling having said something yesterday about taking the opportunity to head off early do a spot of Christmas shopping. There was a tour party returning from their travels later this afternoon and she'd have to be back by then. Moira, she'd deduced, was probably out with Tom making the most of the college break. She didn't want to deal with her sisters quizzing her about her night out with Shay. Come to that she didn't want to think about her night out. All she wanted was a new head. That wasn't too much to ask was it? Failing a new head then a visit see what Mrs Flaherty had on offer in the kitchen would suffice. 'A rasher sandwich will fix me up.'

'What was that, Roisin?'

Roisin started, she hadn't seen Ita, O'Mara's director of housekeeping as she insisted on being called, loitering in the doorway of Room 7, the trolley of cleaning products nowhere to be seen. Ita's phone made a telltale ding from her pocket and the younger woman looked sheepish.

'Oh, hello, Ita. I didn't see you there. I was just saying I fancy one of Mrs Flaherty's rasher sandwiches.'

'Talking to yourself is the first sign of madness, so it is.' Ita moved closer and peered at her. 'You don't look very well, Roisin.'

Roisin knew she was an unbecoming shade of green and she should have brushed her hair. She had managed to brush her teeth and get dressed, that was something at least.

The younger woman looked sly. 'Big night on the lash, was it then? Has your mammy got your lad?'

Roisin saw the gum in her mouth and felt irritated. There was just something about Ita that was annoying. It wasn't just her insufferable air of superiority, evident in the fact she seemed to think her work or more aptly lack of work at O'Maras was beneath her. Or the way she lurked about the hallways of the guesthouse not doing much of anything other than earwigging and playing on her phone. Roisin knew she drove Aisling, who was obligated to employ her through Ita's mammy and their mammy's longstanding friendship, mad. 'Not at all, Ita, I'm grand so I am, and yes, Noah stayed overnight at his nana's along with Pat and his girlfriend Cindy.'

'Patrick's home?' Ita breathed, her pinched features taking on a moony quality. Roisin mentally rolled her eyes; she was obviously another one of her brother's many admirers.

'Yes, he's home for Christmas. Mammy's made up, so she is.' She answered as brightly as she could then, keen to get downstairs, added, 'Oh, Aisling asked me to mention if I saw you that she'd shortly be checking on the rooms that needed to be made up for the guests returning from their tour this afternoon.' She felt better watching Ita pale and scurry off. It was a little white lie but it was satisfying watching her get moving. It was about time she earned her wages!

Roisin carried on her way, reaching the ground floor without bumping into any guests, and with the smell of a good old Irish fry-up getting stronger, her mouth began to salivate. *Salvation was nigh!* She spied the back of Bronagh's head, dipped slightly as she huffed over entering the pile of faxed bookings into the computer and was relieved she was busy. She'd creep past and say hello once she had some good old greasy, soaky-uppy, sustenance inside her. She'd only got one foot on the last flight of stairs leading down to the basement when Bronagh's voice rang out.

'Roisin, don't try and sneak past without telling me how your night went with the handsome Shay. I've eyes in the back of my head so I have and I've been waiting for you to make an appearance. Show yourself.'

Roisin froze. There was nothing for it. She mooched forth. 'Morning, Bronagh.'

'Jaysus wept, look at the state of you! You're the poster girl for the evils of alcohol at Christmastime so you are. Your eyes are like road maps. I could find my way all the way down to Kerry just looking in those.' She put down the papers she was holding in her hand.

'Not so loud, Bronagh. My head hurts.' Roisin tried squinting her eyes to see if that helped ease the throbbing. It didn't.

'Am I to take it, it was a good night then?'

Roisin nodded.

'Then why do you look like someone just stole the last piece of your pie?'

'I made an eejit of myself, that's why.'

'Really, I'd never believe that?'

Roisin wasn't sure whether Bronagh was taking the mickey or not. 'Well, I did.'

Bronagh studied her face and raised a sympathetic smile as she made a clucking sound. 'Ah, c'mon now, it can't be that bad. Tell your aunty Bronagh all about it.'

Roisin felt a little like she was standing in front of a schoolteacher as she bowed her head, her hands clasped in front of her while she confided in the receptionist how her evening had been going really well until she'd had a reality check as to her situation. 'He's only in his twenties, Bronagh. Sure, what would he want with me. Anyway,' she shrugged. 'I began knocking back the tequila sunrises and the rest is history.'

'That's not so bad. You won't be the only one to get a little too merry this time of year.'

'I tripped over leaving the restaurant and fell in a heap near the entrance.' Her face flamed because even in her inebriated state she'd felt the curious stares of the other diners on her. Shay had helped her up, checking she hadn't hurt herself, before taking a firm grip of her and hustling her out of the restaurant and into a taxi.

'Oh.'

'He was a gentleman, saw me all the way to the sofa upstairs. He fetched me a big glass of water and listened to me ramble on. I think I told him we weren't a good match due to him being footloose and fancy free and me having enough baggage to sink the Titanic, but that's not to say I didn't find him highly rideable. Ah Jaysus, Bronagh I can't believe I said that. Anyway I must have fallen asleep at some point, and that's when he made his escape because I woke up alone on the sofa with a terrible crick in my neck as the sun was coming up.' Roisin rubbed her temples. She was old enough to know better. *Never, ever again.*

Bronagh opened her drawer. 'Here,' she held out the packet of biscuits. 'I think you need one of these.'

Roisin took the custard cream and nibbled it, relishing the sweetness.

'Don't be too hard on yourself, Roisin. You've had an awful lot of changes this year and you were bound to let off steam some time. As for having luggage—'

'It's baggage, Bronagh.' Roisin managed a weak smile.

'Whatever, you know what I mean. There's not many of us who get through life without picking up a few heavy bags along the way. I don't know why you're making a fuss about being a few years older than your man, either.'

'Nearly ten years older, a whole decade, Bronagh.'

Bronagh flapped her hand. 'Age is just a number. Do you like him?'

'I do, he's a very nice man.'

'And he obviously likes you, suitcases and all so, there you go. I've seen that beautiful bouquet in the guests' lounge. Cut yourself some slack, Roisin. You're not after marrying him, you went out for dinner and a few drinks that's all.'

'Too many drinks, and I couldn't marry him because then I'd be a bigamist.'

'You're as bad as your sisters with an answer for everything.'

'Sorry, I know you're trying to help.' Roisin licked the crumbs off her bottom lip which felt dry and cracked from sleeping with her mouth open all night.

Bronagh was mollified. 'Roisin, I've been around the block a few times.'

She was fond of that saying, Roisin thought, finding it very hard to imagine Bronagh doing any such thing, but she'd obviously had a life outside of O'Mara's. It was just one they'd not been privy to.

'And if there's one thing I know it's this.' Bronagh's expression was sage. 'We women tend to spoil things for ourselves by spinning things round and round in our heads. Things we have no control over. We weave our own version of events. Save your energy, Rosi, I'd put money on him phoning to check how you're feeling today.'

'Do you think?' Roisin wasn't sure she wanted him to. The part of her that wanted to throw caution to the wind and be damned, desperately wanted to hear his voice. To know she hadn't blown things. The other part, the sensible mother part, thought it best if they just left things alone. She wasn't right for him; he wasn't right for her so why pursue it? She squinted again; her head hurt too much for all this analysis.

'I think. Now why don't you get yourself down those stairs and see what Mrs Flaherty can whip up to sort you out and next time I see you make sure you've brushed that hair of yours. Is it a new look you were after with the you know?' She pointed at Roisin's fringe..

'No, it's a long story and one I definitely don't want to talk about.' Roisin leaned in and gave the receptionist a quick hug, 'Thanks, Bronagh.' Straightening up, she tried to smooth her fringe down with her hands.

Bronagh patted her hand. 'Go on. Away with you now.'

Before she headed off down the stairs, she poked her head around the door to the guests' lounge and there on the coffee table was the beautiful bunch of flowers Shay had presented her with last night. She recalled the boyishly shy look on his face as he handed them to her and her heart ached. Why did life have to be so hard sometimes?

***

'Where's my boy?' Mrs Flaherty demanded, releasing Roisin from a bearlike embrace and giving her the once over.

'He'll be in to see you later, Mrs Flaherty. He stayed at Mammy's last night,' Roisin explained.

'So as you could have a night out, by the looks of things.' The dumpling cheeked cook, whose apron straining around her middle bore the hallmarks of a busy morning at the stove, made a tutting sound.

Roisin mumbled, 'I wish I hadn't now.'

'Ah well, good sense is as important as good food and since you obviously had no sense last night it'll have to be the good food. A rasher sandwich do you?'

'Oh, yes please, Mrs Flaherty, nobody makes a rasher sandwich as good as yours and do you think there's a chance of a fried egg going in there too?' Roisin tried her luck and, watching Mrs Flaherty puff up proudly at the compliment, she knew her luck was in because there was nothing Mrs Flaherty liked more than her food being enjoyed.

'Sit yourself down and tell me what's been happening since I last saw you,' she said, wielding the fry pan with expertise as Roisin brought her up to date with how she and Noah were getting on in London. Roisin felt better already. She was at home in the kitchen with its delicious smells that always transported her back to her childhood. Mrs Flaherty's kitchen, as they all thought of it, had always been a place of sanctuary where something tasty usually got passed their way. By the time she'd brought the cook up to speed, the rashers were being placed between two thick slabs of buttered, real butter mind, soda bread. The finishing touch was an egg cooked on both sides. She plopped it on a plate and Roisin took it from her reverently.

'Thank you. Food of the Gods this is, Mrs Flaherty.'

Mrs Flaherty wiped her hands on her apron. 'You can earn your keep by helping clear the tables when you're finished.'

Roisin nodded; her mouth too full to speak. She ate in silence, greedily gobbling the sandwich down and already beginning to feel like there was a real possibility she may be able to rejoin the human race after all.

'That was wonderful, thank you.' She made herself a milky, sugary cup of tea, which she gulped at before stacking her dishes in the dishwasher, while Mrs Flaherty began to tackle the frying pan and other pots in the sudsy sink water. She hadn't forgotten her promise and she felt capable of nattering politely with the guests now she was fed and watered, so she ventured into the dining room. The tables were laid with white cloths and the walls of what once would have been servants' quarters were adorned with black and white prints of the Dublin of old. A handful of guests were still enjoying the remains of breakfast, mopping up the last of their yolk with a slice of bread or enjoying a leisurely cup of tea. She smiled and introduced herself before asking an older couple if they were enjoying their stay.

'We are thank you, dear,' the woman, who looked a little older than Mammy in her sensible cardigan and blouse, replied. She would not be the sort to come home from a holiday in Asia with her hair braided, Roisin decided, smiling back at her. Nor would she be likely to get about in trousers three sizes too small!

'We go home tomorrow, in time for Christmas.'

'And where would home be?'

'We're from Sligo,' the woman added, beaming proudly.

'Oh lovely.' Roisin had never been there. The only thing she knew about Sligo was Westlife came from there.

Her husband put his teacup down. 'The wife here, wanted to do her Christmas shopping in Dublin. We'll have to hire our own bus to get home with the amount of parcels she's been after buying. Spoils the grandchildren rotten. In my day it was an orange in the stocking if you were lucky.'

'Don't believe a word of it, he's worse than me when it comes to the grandchildren and it wasn't just an orange. I remember your dear old mam telling me you got a peashooter when you were ten and menaced the village with the thing.'

They smiled across the table at each other with the warmth of a life lived well together.

'My son's five and he's the only grandson and nephew so I expect his stocking will have more than an orange and peashooter in it too.' She smiled from one to the other. 'A Merry Christmas to you both and safe journey home.' Roisin moved on. The table at the far end of the room was ready to be cleared but as she made her way toward it, she spied a dapper gentleman who seemed lost in his thoughts as he sat with a plate of toast in front of him. He had sandy colouring, the sort that didn't show the grey hairs, and she guessed he would have had freckles in his youth. Either way this wouldn't do, Roisin thought. Mrs Flaherty would have conniptions if the toast were returned to the kitchen with her homemade marmalade jam untouched.

'A penny for them?'

The man blinked. He had bright, intelligent blue eyes, framed by neatly trimmed eyebrows. He looked surprised and mustn't have seen her approach the table, Roisin thought. It was then she spotted the book on the table. When We Were Brave, by Cliona Whelan, the book she'd had signed by the author just the other day for Aisling. She gestured toward the book and told the man she'd met Cliona Whelan, the author, at a signing. At the mention of her name his face seemed to transform as he looked at her keenly. 'You met Clio you say?' He was American with a clipped, cool accent.

Roisin nodded; her curiosity piqued. 'I did, well insomuch as she signed the copy of the book I bought for my sister as a Christmas present at Easons.' No need to tell him about the Christmas photo debacle.

'Have you read it?'

'No, although I read a review of it in the paper and it sounds very good.'

He nodded. "It is. It's brilliant but Clio always was brilliant.'

'Oh, you know her?'

'I do, yes, from a long time ago.'

'Is that why you've come to Dublin? To catch up with her again?'

'I'm hoping to, my dear. I've invited her to Christmas dinner at the Merrion but whether she'll come.' He shrugged. 'Well, a lot of water's gone under the bridge. I can only hope. My name's Gerald. Gerald Byrne, I'm from Boston but you can call me Gerry.'

'Roisin Quealey but I used to be Roisin O'Mara.' She explained her connection to the guesthouse and he invited her to sit down.

She did so and he placed a hand on the book. 'It's our story you know. Mine and Clio's. Only the ending is different. The story in this book has a happier ending than ours did. I'd like to make mine and Clio's ending different too.'

Roisin forgot all about everything as she sat transfixed by the story he told her.

Chapter 23

'It's lovely being ladies who lunch,' Mammy said, her arms linked firmly through Moira and Roisin's. All three of their faces were only visible in the gaps between the hats and scarves they'd donned as they stamped their feet against the cold, waiting for the lights to change so as to cross over to Baggot Street. An impromptu lunch had been Mammy's bright idea and they'd opted to walk to Quinn's bistro, aware of the amount of overeating they would be doing from hereon in until the New Year. Aisling, who'd had a successful morning shopping, had checked to make sure Quinn saved them a table.

She'd said to Roisin it would be a chance to get to know Cindy a little better. 'I've to be back at O'Mara's for three to meet the American group off the bus, they're back from their tour of the south and I want to make sure all their Christmas Day dinner reservations are confirmed,' she'd said shrugging into her coat before they left.

Baggot Street's foot traffic was busy, Roisin noticed, as the lights changed at last and they made their way across the road, merging in with the Christmas shoppers. Aisling and Cindy, their heads bent as they talked and tottered in impractical shoes, were slightly ahead of them. Cindy, not used to the cold, looked like a well-endowed Russian Cossack with her faux fur hat, Roisin thought, smirking as a middle-aged man who should know better had an incident with a lamppost. Served him right for being so fixated on the blonde apparition mincing down Baggot.

'It was good of your brother to offer to take Noah to the cinema,' Maureen said. 'It will be nice for the two men of the family to get to know one another better.'

'It was,' Roisin agreed. Patrick had surprised her with how much attention he'd given Noah and she'd been pleased when he suggested he and Noah go and see the Disney Christmas flick showing at the IMAX. Noah had been jumping up and down at the prospect of a boys' outing. 'I hope Pat doesn't let him have the extra-large popcorn. If I know Noah, he'll plump for it but he'll make himself sick, stuffing all that down on top of the rasher sandwich Mrs Flaherty made him.' Mind you, she wasn't in a position to talk the way she'd snaffled hers down and now here she was off for a slap-up lunch! Thank goodness for yoga pants.

'They'll be grand. Don't worry so, Roisin,' Maureen said. 'So, are you going to tell us how your evening went with your man? I hope you changed the sheets in your room.'

'Mammy, nothing happened!'

'I should hope not on a first date!' Maureen was indignant. 'You girls' minds dwell in the gutter so they do. What I meant was your room smelt like a brewery when I poked my head around the door and as it's a full house tonight, I'd hope you'd have at least put clean linen on the bed. I'm looking forward to us all being together under one roof again. And it's been far too long since the O'Mara family attended Midnight Mass together.'

'So, there was no riding,' Moira lamented, looking disappointed.

'No.'

'Moira O'Mara!'

'Did you kiss?' Moira ignored her mammy.

CHAPTER 23

'Moira, mind your own business.' Roisin peered around their mammy and eyeballed her sister.

'Ah, Rosi, that's not fair, especially after all the hard work I did sorting you and your fringe out,' Moira moaned.

'Will you be seeing him again do you think?' Maureen asked.

'I don't know,' Rosi said. Her head was beginning to hurt again.

'Jaysus, it's harder getting information out of you than a cold war spy,' Moira muttered.

'She always did play her cards close to her chest,' Maureen added, nearly tripping as Moira pulled them to a stop in order to admire the vibrant new Revlon display in the window of Boots.

'That's your woman who looks like a man one, isn't it? I danced to that at the yacht club dinner.'

'Shania Twain, Man I feel Like a Woman. Read the slogan, Mammy!' Moira rolled her eyes. 'I like that shade of purple.'

'It's lavender,' Maureen said.

'It's not lavender, that sounds old ladyish,' Moira bounced back.

'She looks well on it, your Shania one, doesn't she?' Maureen said wistfully.

'She does,' Roisin agreed, though she was unsure why they were all stood staring at her poster. It was tempting fate in her opinion because she wouldn't put it past Mammy to break into a line dancing routine. She kept a firm grip of her arm just in case.

'Do you think she uses the magic skin plumpy thing-a-me-bobs that are all the go at the moment?' Maureen asked.

'Serum do you mean, Mammy?' Roisin said.

Maureen nodded, 'Yes, semen.'

'SERUM! And yes, for sure.' Moira nodded knowledgably as though she was privy to Shania's night time beauty routine.

'Do you think I could do with a bit of plumping?'

Both sisters peered at their mammy's face.

'Your face has plenty of plump, so it does,' Moira said.

Roisin recalled her exchange with Aisling where her sister had told her their mammy had been acting a little strangely since the yacht club dinner. 'Why do you need plumping all of a sudden?' Her eyes narrowed as she studied her mammy's face.

'A woman of certain years is bound to wonder from time to time whether she might need plumping.' Maureen looked shifty.

'Well you don't. You're fine the way you are,' Roisin snapped, pulling her and Moira away from the window. 'Come on, Cindy and Ash will be on dessert by the time we get there.'

***

The familiar and quintessential, whitewashed building, with its brass nameplate, that was Quinn's, came into their line of sight and Roisin found herself anticipating the cosy and warm atmosphere she knew they'd find inside. They bustled in through the door in time to witness Alasdair fawning all over Cindy.

'I never thought I'd see you again, my darling!'

Cindy looked bewildered, 'I'm sorry but I don't think we've met before. This is my first time visiting Dublin.'

'Ah non!' The flamboyant maître de clapped a hand to his chest. 'You must remember! It is me, the Fellini to your Ekberg. La Dolce Vita, my darling.' He blew her a kiss and Cindy looked at Aisling slightly alarmed by his carry-on. Aisling didn't appear fazed; in fact she was smiling.

She leaned in towards her getting a strong whiff of her sugary sweet perfume and stage whispered, 'Alasdair has had more past lives than I've had hot dinners. He's famous for them. He even gets a mention in the Lonely Planet. He's what you'd call a Dublin icon and he's very good for business. My guess is he's decided you were Anita Ekberg when he was Frederico Fellini.' Aisling, copping an eyeful of cleavage as Cindy undid the buttons on her coat, could see where he'd gotten the idea from.

Cindy's mouth formed an 'O' as though she got it. She didn't; they were all a bit mad in Ireland from what she'd seen, but she let Alasdair help her out of her coat, nonetheless.

Maureen pushed forward, more than happy to be on the receiving end of one of Alasdair's effusive greetings. He didn't disappoint her, exclaiming over how divine she was looking – how divine they were all looking as he took their coats and whisked away the pile of hats and scarves so they disappeared like magic. Paula, the waitress working the lunchtime Christmas Eve shift, saw them to their table which was in a prime spot in the middle of the heaving restaurant. They sat themselves down and Roisin looked on enviously as Cindy fluffed her hair and it formed a becoming halo around her face despite her Cossack hat. She fluffed her own hair knowing it would have moulded itself into the shape of the woollen hat she'd pulled down low enough to keep her ears warm on the walk over.

Aisling looked pleased as Cindy oohed and aahed over how "Irish" the restaurant was. The chatter filling the inviting space around them was convivial and interspersed with the sounds of glasses clinking, the chink of knives and forks on plates, and bursts of laughter. The aroma of hearty food, the sort that would stick to your ribs, clung to the air, and Roisin's tummy grumbled despite her hearty breakfast.

'I love the wooden beams and the fire, it's so cute,' Cindy gushed, and Aisling puffed up proudly although she deflated slightly when Cindy followed this up with a giggling, 'It reminds me of the cottage out of Snow White and the Seven Dwarfs or Goldilocks.' Aisling excused herself eager to find Quinn so she could introduce him to her brother's new girlfriend, hoping she'd keep her fairy-tale comparisons to herself.

'Will we have wine?' Maureen asked, looking from one to the other and shaking her head as her eyes settled on Moira. 'Well not for you, Moira, obviously.' She turned to Roisin. 'And given your mushy peas complexion I think you'd do better on the Coca-Cola like your sister.' She smiled at Cindy, 'There's no reason Aisling, Cindy and myself shouldn't enjoy a tipple though.'

'I'll stick with the mineral water, thanks, Maureen,' Cindy dimpled. 'I have to keep an eye on my calorie intake.'

Maureen looked down at her own middle.

Aisling returned with Quinn, who was looking handsome and incredibly immaculate in his chef's whites. It always amazed Roisin, given his profession, how he kept them so clean. If it were her let loose in the kitchen, she'd have more sauce down her front than simmering in the pots! 'How're you all,' he grinned. 'It's an honour having all the beautiful O'Mara women here together. And, Cindy, it's grand to have you here all the way from Los Angeles. Welcome.'

'Get away with you,' Maureen said, preening. She loved being made a fuss of. It had been a highlight in her social calendar year when she'd treated Rosemary Farrell from her rambling group to a birthday lunch at Quinn's. He'd made them feel like proper VIP guests and Rosemary had been very impressed, especially when the chef gave them his personal lunch recommendations. 'Now then what would you recommend we order today, Quinn?' she asked as Paula passed around the menus.

'Well now, Maureen, I know you're partial to coddle and it's particularly tasty today. The sausages are specialty free range pork and I used new potatoes.'

'What's coddle?' Cindy simpered over the top of her menu. Aisling frowned. Was she flirting with Quinn? She was one of those women who flirted not even knowing she was flirting.

CHAPTER 2377

She looked at Quinn who was oblivious to her charms as he replied theatrically, 'Only the finest meal in Ireland.'

'It's sausage and potato boiled up in one pot,' Moira stated.

'Oh, sounds, um, wonderful.'

'That's settled then,' Mammy said. 'Cindy and I will have the coddle. Aisling will you share a carafe of the house red with me?'

Aisling nodded, yes, she would, and Quinn kissed her on the cheek. It wasn't all he did.

'I saw that pat on the bottom,' Maureen tutted, and he gave her a grin that made him look like a naughty schoolboy, before leaving Paula to take care of them.

She scribbled down their orders. Two coddles and three Dublin Bay prawns. 'Easy,' she said with a smile before taking their order through to the kitchen.

Maureen rummaged in her bag which was hanging on the side of her chair and retrieved a pen and notepad. 'There's no such thing as a free lunch, ladies,' she announced looking very businesslike. 'To save squabbling in the kitchen over who's doing what tomorrow I thought we'd write a list allocating all the jobs to be done.'

Moira interrupted, 'Bags not stuff the turkey. I can't stand sticking my hand up its arse.'

'Moira!'

'I'll do the turkey, Mammy, and once I've got it in the oven, I'll set the table, oh and don't forget Quinn's made the plum pudding. It's curing as we speak.' Aisling smiled, knowing if she put her hand up for this then she wouldn't get the job of scrubbing potatoes or prepping the Brussels.

Maureen scribbled earnestly before looking at Cindy. 'Now then, Cindy, how about we put you on carrots, parsnips and the Brussels. Hmm, and,' she chewed the end of the pen for a moment, 'Moira you're on potatoes and you can help your sister decorate the dining room. Roisin, you can be in charge of the smoked salmon starters and mulled wine.'

'What are you doing, Mammy?'

'I'm on the roast ham and bread sauce.'

'I don't suppose there's any point asking what Pat's going to be doing,' Aisling said.

'Sitting on his arse, that's what,' Moira said.

'Leave your brother alone, girls. Sure, he works hard all year, he deserves to put his feet up.'

All three sisters looked from one to another in mutual outrage. 'It's nearly the Millennium, Mammy, that kind of thinking went out with the dark ages,' Aisling said, but Mammy pretended she couldn't hear her as she stowed her pen and pad back in her bag. She decided to let it go, knowing she'd be wasting her breath and turned her attention to Moira and Cindy who were chatting.

Roisin glanced around the restaurant. There were no empty tables, she saw, as her eyes settled on the empty stage upon which two littlies were playing a game of chase. She pictured Shay standing there and remembered how their eyes had literally met over a crowded bar. Mammy talking in her ear brought her back to the here and now and her chat with their American guest, Gerry sprang to mind. 'Mammy,' she said her voice lowered so Aisling wouldn't overhear and have her Christmas surprise ruined, 'have you heard of Cliona Whelan?'

'Sure, of course I have, she's a fine journalist, and she was a role model in my day, so she was, for women in the workforce. She's written a book hasn't she?'

'She has, and, Mammy, you won't believe it, listen to this...' Roisin filled her in on the story Gerry, the guest she'd encountered over breakfast, had told her about his and Cliona's ill-fated romance back in the late nineteen-fifties. 'He told me she changed the names and the story's been fictionalised but at the core it's their story only in Cliona's book, instead of her staying in Dublin she goes to Boston and marries him. He claws his way up to the top echelon of American politics and she manages, against the odds, to carve a career for herself as a journalist. He said Cliona was always a woman before her time.'

'That's a big word, Roisin.'

'Echelon? I know, Gerry used it.'

'Well, it's quite the story. I'll have to read the book now and would you credit it, him staying at O'Mara's?'

'Yes, I couldn't believe it, especially with me having bought the book the day before for Aisling. She broke his heart he said. Although he came to understand her reasons for doing so.'

'And did he marry?'

'Eventually. He told me he followed the path laid out for him and when his parents steered him toward a woman from what they called "good stock" he went along with it. He married her but it didn't last. They had two children, boys who are grown up with children of their own now.'

'Did she, Cliona, I mean ever marry?'

'No, her work always came first. I read in the foreword of the book that she said it had to in the times she moved in, if she wanted to succeed.'

'She smashed through the glass ceiling alright, and it wouldn't have been easy.'

'It came at a cost, too. Do you think she'll meet him at the Merrion, Mammy?' Roisin had seen the look in Gerry's eyes when he spoke about Cliona and knew his heart would be broken if they didn't get a second chance at love.

'You're a softy you are.' Maureen patted her daughter's hand and looked pensive. 'I like to think we all deserve a second chance when it comes to love, Rosi, because life's too short to spend it sad.'

Again, there was something unsettling about the expression that passed over her mammy's face and Roisin squirmed in her seat, grateful when Paula appeared at the table and set about distributing the drinks. She was glad when the glass of red wine that was put in front of Mammy broke the strange spell that had settled over her.

Chapter 24

Roisin watched Cindy out of the corner of her eye. She had a ritualistic style of eating that was fascinating to observe. Her brother's girlfriend forked up another piece of sausage and held it to her pert little nose, which quivered delightedly as she sniffed at it. In that instance she reminded Roisin of Mr Nibbles. A look of bliss settled over her face just like it did the gerbil's when he had hold of a lettuce leaf but instead of nibbling at it gleefully like Noah's new pet did, she put the sausage back on her plate. She then cut a tiny sliver off and popped that in her mouth, pushing what remained of it to the side of her plate to keep company with the new potatoes that had been relegated there. Roisin counted twenty chews before she swallowed. She knew all about mindfulness, and it was something she tried to practise. Mindful eating, however, was something she, Mammy, and her sisters, who were like pigs at a trough when they were hungry, could do with a lot more practise at. She added it to her mental new year's resolution list. Cindy however was taking things to the extreme.

Roisin couldn't contain herself, she had to ask, 'Erm, Cindy, if you don't mind me asking, why are you sniffing your food?'

Cindy flashed her a blinding smile. 'Of course, I don't mind. The Ciccone-Scent diet is the latest craze sweeping through

Hollywood. All the A-listers are trying it and getting great results.'

'Oh, is it a sniff your food but don't eat it diet then?' Roisin could quite see you'd get results doing that.

Cindy laughed, it sounded high pitched and girly. 'It's not quite that simple, Roisin.' She stabbed in the direction of the new potatoes with her fork. 'I don't touch potatoes in any form because they're full of carbs. Carbs are the enemy. But us girls already knew that, right?'

Roisin nodded, looking everywhere but at her own plate where she'd already wolfed down the French fries that had been served with her prawns. As for Moira, she seemed to be trying to see how many of the deep-fried potato sticks she could get in her mouth at once. Mammy's, like Roisin's, were long gone. They'd both saved the prawns for last.

'Okay, so as a devotee of the Ciccone-Scent diet, I avoid all carbs and only eat half of the protein served on my plate. Dr Ciccone's research shows that inhaling your food before you eat it tricks your stomach into thinking it's full and that way you only need to eat half your normal meal size. Makes sense, right?'

Um, no, it sounded mad, Roisin thought, as she nodded that yes it did.

'I love it because it's so easy to follow and I don't have to buy any fancy food. It really works too, I dropped five pounds before Patrick and I flew out of LA.' Her eyes drifted down to Roisin's midriff and she automatically sucked her stomach in.

'You must be very disciplined, Cindy. Sure, I couldn't be doing with sniffing and not eating.'

'Oh, you could if you lived in LA, Roisin. Everybody does it.'

Roisin was very glad she lived in London.

Cindy pushed her plate away while the rest of them carried on shovelling in their food. Roisin was feeling panicked by the idea of only being allowed to inhale her food and so she was getting her prawns from plate to mouth in record time. 'Excuse me, I'm just off to powder my nose.' Cindy got up and caused several male patrons to begin choking on their fare as she sashayed past.

Mammy elbowed Moira, pointing, 'Sure, look at your man there. He's as bad as your Hugh Hefner Playboy one.'

Mammy and Moira launched into a discussion on everything that was wrong with a man, who was clearly old enough to be Cindy's grandfather, having impure thoughts about a young woman.

'He wants to tie a knot in it at his age,' Moira said.

Once Cindy was out of earshot, Aisling leaned in close to Roisin, gesturing in Cindy's direction. 'Do you know what she's after telling me and Moira?'

'That she sniffs her food?'

'What?'

'Never mind.' Roisin couldn't be bothered explaining the whole Ciccone-Scent diet thing.

Aisling shook her head. 'You're an eejit. She told us Patrick was desperate to come home to Ireland for Christmas.'

'Really?' Roisin had always got the feeling Patrick was rather lukewarm when it came to Dublin. It wasn't fast enough or glitzy enough for him. Oh, she knew right enough he loved them all. As much as Patrick loved anyone who wasn't himself. It was just, Patrick.

He'd never been any different. Roisin could remember Mammy having to drag him away from shop windows when he'd caught sight of his reflection as a young lad. 'People will think it's the underwear on the mannequin you're after drooling over Patrick,' she'd said tugging at his arm. When they'd reached their teens, the battle of the bathroom had begun in earnest and Daddy had taken to timing them; turned out Patrick spent the longest getting ready of a morning. In the end they'd been allocated five-minute time slots apiece.

Patrick had been most put out, but then it was the eighties and hair was big.

'I know, I was surprised too, but she said he's been missing us all something terrible and that he told her Christmas is a time for family.'

'Stop it.' Roisin wasn't sure this was her brother they were talking about.

'I'm only repeating what Cindy told me.'

Roisin felt a surge of love for her brother. Beneath all that shiny polish he was still the Pat she'd grown up with.

'Apparently he's ashamed of the way he behaved after Dad died. But you know Pat, he never could say he was sorry.'

That was true. Many a time Mammy had marched him in front of his sisters and ordered him to apologise for some misdemeanour or other like giving Barbie a crew cut so as he could enlist her in his army or standing on their dolls house, which had been demolished in a surprise attack by his army. The word had seemed to get stuck in his throat as he was held firm by Mammy. In the end he'd mutter something that came out in a big whoosh and Mammy would release him having decided to interpret it as an apology.

'Cindy says he feels bad about pushing so hard for Mammy to sell O'Mara's after Daddy died. He doesn't know what got into him.'

'So, he should,' Roisin said.

Aisling nodded. It had been her who'd been the most affected by his behaviour. She was the one who'd fitted her life in around the guesthouse to ensure it stayed in the family.

'Did she say why he was so keen to offload it? Was it to back some venture over in the States?' That was what they'd all thought, after all.

'No, apparently not. Well not entirely anyway. He thinks it was a kneejerk reaction to Daddy dying. A bit like Mammy, you know, with her wanting a fresh start over in Howth. He wanted shot of it because the memories were too painful.

Everywhere he looked he saw Daddy and he didn't know how to express how he was feeling.'

'So, he came across as an arrogant, bullying, money grabbing arse instead, who dragged his sulky self back to Los Angeles.'

'Pretty much, but guess what?'

'What?'

'He's been going to therapy.'

'No!'

'Yes.'

'He's a proper American now, so he is.' Roisin tried to imagine her brother sitting on a white sofa talking about his emotions, but couldn't.

'I know. I think Cindy's good for him. She obviously brings out his softer side because he finally seems to have realised there's more to life than making money and driving flash cars.'

A leopard didn't change its spots did it? Therapy or no therapy, Roisin thought. Patrick would always have a hankering for the finer things in life and chasing after the almighty dollar. Appearances mattered a lot to her brother. She glanced at Cindy making her way back from the Ladies and rested her case. He'd never go for a wallflower type simply because she was a nice person. Still Daddy's death had obviously hit him hard, just as it had all of them. Roisin sighed into her glass of cola. Grief and the way they'd reacted to it hadn't been straightforward. They'd all acted out in different ways, his passing leaving a gaping hole in all their lives. Patrick had been the only one seemingly untouched, blustering in and pushing for O'Mara's to be sold, although apparently it had been just that, bluster. A cover for the rawness he felt from Daddy's passing.

'Anyway, I've decided Christmas is a time for forgiveness so I'm going to give Pat a second chance.' Aisling stated, and Roisin noticed her cheeks were flushed the colour of the wine.

'Good for you, Ash. We all deserve second chances.' She said as her sister announced she was going to have to forfeit dessert and make tracks back to the guesthouse. Second chances was a theme that kept popping up and her mind drifted back to Shay. She looked up and blinked, not sure whether she was hallucinating or not because there like a mirage, walking toward their table, was Shay.

Chapter 25

♥

'I called in to see you at O'Mara's. I wanted to catch up with you before I head to Castlebeg later this afternoon. See how you were feeling. Bronagh told me you were here for lunch and it's only around the corner,' he shrugged. 'So here I am. I hope you don't mind me gatecrashing like this?' He grinned apologetically at Roisin and then at the others. She blinked again several times, still not convinced she hadn't dreamed this moment into reality. She flinched as a foot connected with her ankle, Aisling's way of reassuring her she was very much in the here and now. She was reminded too that she owed this man an apology for her behaviour the previous night. The memory of her waffling on made her squirm but before she could speak Mammy leapt in.

'Oh no, she doesn't mind at all, do you, Roisin? I'm Roisin's mammy, Maureen, by the way, seeing as my daughter's forgotten her manners. We've not had the pleasure. How do you do?' Mammy beamed holding a hand out. Shay took her outstretched hand and for the briefest of seconds, Roisin thought he was going to kiss it but he didn't. He shook it, smiling at her mam in a way that made her blush. Mind, it didn't take much to make Mammy blush once she was on her second glass of the red.

'I can see where Roisin gets her good looks from.'

Maureen looked like one of those specialty Japanese fish you take your life in your hands by eating at this, and Roisin couldn't help but smile. It was cheesy but coming from Shay it didn't *seem* clichéd. It came across as genuine. She'd have words with Moira later too, she decided seeing her sister going red from the effort not to laugh at Mammy's puffer fish impersonation. They were so embarrassing the lot of them. Even Aisling and Cindy were looking eagerly at Shay as though he were going to bestow them each with a compliment like some sort of fairy godmother who'd rocked up in battle-worn denim. She couldn't blame them, she supposed, because he did look gorgeous. Not in the clean-cut coiffed way of her brother but in a rugged, earthy way, that made her think things that would definitely make Mammy tell her to get her mind out of the gutter. She couldn't understand why she kept picturing him with a Stetson on his head, though. She'd no idea she had a thing for cowboys until she met him. Cindy, clearing her throat daintily, galvanised her and she introduced the blonde bombshell to him.

As she held onto his hand longer than necessary, Roisin gave him a mental ten out of ten for keeping his eyes trained on her face the whole time. No mean feat given the heaving bosom just under his nose. She bit her bottom lip as Aisling elbowed her and whispered, 'She'll start singing Happy Birthday Mr President in a minute.'

'Bunch up, girls,' Mammy ordered, giving Cindy a look that made her drop Shay's hand like a hot potato. She scanned the room for a spare chair but Shay stopped her.

'Actually, Maureen, I wondered if I might be able to borrow Roisin for a few minutes.'

The puffer fish was back and was just about jumping up and down on her seat with the excitement of it all.

Roisin got up from her chair, feeling the hot stares of her family on her back as they excused themselves, and she followed his lead past the toilets and out the backdoor. *What had he come to say?* The door led outside to the car park which, although full of cars, didn't have a soul in sight. There was a pot on the ground near the backdoor full of cigarette butts. Hardy lot, smokers she thought, standing outside for their fix in all weather conditions. She could smell that faint greasy odour of stale fat from the extractor fan whirring overhead.

'Sorry to drag you out in the cold.'

'Not at all.' Her breath was misty in the chill air. She leaned against the cold brick wall shoving her hands deep into the pockets of her jeans for warmth. She owed him an apology and she decided she better jump in first and get it over with. 'Listen, Shay, I'm sorry about getting myself in such a state last night and the way I went on. I don't know what you must have thought of me but it's been ages since I've had a night out and I got carried away. Can you please just forget everything I said?'

His eyes twinkled, 'What, even the bit about me being highly rideable?'

'Ah Jaysus.' She freed her hands to cover her face, peeking through her fingers at him. 'Don't remind me.'

'I'm teasing.' He pulled her hands away from her face and kept hold of them. They were swallowed up by his and she marvelled that hands that size could be so quick and nimble with the fiddle. She wondered what else those hands might be good at. 'You don't need to apologise, Rosi. I had a great craic, the best I've had in ages, and you were hilarious by the way.'

'I was?' She swallowed hard. She couldn't recall having said anything particularly witty.

'Yeah, when you launched into *Who Let the Dogs Out* on the way home, I just about lost it. I loved the little paws you made with your hands and the woofing was class.'

'Please tell me I didn't?'

'Oh, you did alright.' His smile and the way it worked the dimple in his left cheek made her forget she was cold and embarrassed.

'Anyway, there's a reason I dragged you out here.'

'Oh yes?' Roisin hadn't a clue what he wanted but looking at him right then and there she'd happily throw all that nonsense about her being too old for him and their lives being too different or the timing being all wrong out the window. Life was messy, it didn't run to a timetable.

'Yeah, I wanted to tell you something before I go away.'

Roisin couldn't tear her eyes away from him and her body began to react very strangely to the proximity of his. A heat was coursing from her stomach to her chest and her limbs were tingling. How was it possible for anyone to smell as good as he did? It was a musky, spiced scent that made her nose want to twitch like Cindy's had over her sausage. She was aware of his thumbs gently stroking the back of her hands and more than anything she wanted to stand on her tippy toes so she could kiss him. It was a seize the day moment but then she remembered, *I had prawns, PRAWNS for lunch. Oh my God, what was I thinking?* Now was not the time to retrieve the tube of mints from her handbag. She couldn't surreptitiously pop one out and say, 'I'm getting ready just in case you decide to kiss me.'

'I think you're a very special lady, Roisin, and I want you to give me a chance. I promise I won't push you too fast and I'll respect what you say because I understand there's Noah to think about but please, can you give us a go?' There was a sudden vulnerability about him as a lock of his hair fell into his eyes and he looked at her almost shyly waiting for her reaction.

'Oh,' was all she could come up with. She hadn't expected that but there was no time to mull over what he'd said or to worry about Dublin Bay crustaceans or the fact her fringe was sitting two-thirds of the way up her forehead because he was leaning in towards her. Their noses bumped and she was about to giggle nervously, not quite believing what was about to happen, but it was silenced by his lips finding hers. They brushed one another's softly and then they broke apart looking into each other's eyes with surprise. Shay brushed a stray curl from her cheek.

'You have no idea how badly I have wanted to do that from the very first moment I saw you.'

'Really?'

'Really.' His mouth sought hers again and she parted her lips slightly to receive him. His fingers entwined through hers and she was glad when he pulled her close holding her steady because she was in danger of sliding down the wall if he let her go. As the heat of his mouth on hers intensified, Roisin wasn't aware of anything other than the feel of his body pressing into hers and the sweet taste of him. It was as though the world around them had ceased to exist. Nothing mattered but losing herself in this moment because, like Mammy had said, everybody deserved a second chance at love and maybe this was hers.

Chapter 26

♥

Moira, in her role as the youngest girl in the family, lit the candle and placed it well away from the curtains on the windowsill in the living room facing the street below. The Green across the road was in darkness, the bare branches of the trees' ghostly spectres, but the road was busy with cars streaming home from Midnight Mass.

'Watch your hair, Moira. Jesus, Mary and Joseph we don't need that on Christmas Eve,' Mammy called from the kitchen, where she was cutting everybody a generous chunk of seed cake. 'Nobody's going to bed without a hot chocolate and a slice of my cake. It's traditional, isn't that right Quinn?' she ordered, as they all found somewhere to flop, weary from the long, but enjoyable evening. Quinn nodded as he stirred the pot in which he was brewing the bedtime drink. The restaurant had closed early and he'd joined them for Midnight Mass. He and Aisling were taking over Room 5 which was empty for the night. Moira and Mammy were topping and tailing and Patrick and Cindy were back in his old room. Roisin and Noah were in Aisling's room. It was a case of musical beds but they'd all worked in together, apart from Moira who was muttering about Mammy being a bed hog. Tom was spending Christmas Eve with his family as his sister was home from America but he planned on joining them later in the day tomorrow.

'I hope you weren't mean with the caraway seeds like last year, Mammy,' Moira called back.

'There's more seeds than cake, I'll have you know.' Maureen was indignant. 'And they were a ridiculous price last year, so they were.'

'Why's Aunty Moira lighting a candle?' Noah asked from where he was cuddled on his mam's knee. He was playing with a lock of her hair, twisting it around his finger the way he always did when he was tired.

'It's to provide a welcome light for Mary and Joseph,' Roisin explained, enjoying the feel of his warm weight on her lap. He was dead on his feet, poor love. It had been a big day and the evening had been just as big if not bigger.

Her mind drifted back to that afternoon. She'd arranged to meet Shay the day after St Stephens Day and she could hardly wait. His kiss had gone down as her best ever Christmas present. She'd floated home from Quinn's, ignoring Cindy's smirking gaze and the one hundred and one questions from Moira and Mammy about what she'd gotten up to in the car park and why her lipstick was smudged halfway across her face. She'd been telling them to mind their own business as they barrelled in through the door of O'Mara's to find Aisling in full hostess mode. She'd been milling about chatting to the American tour party who'd not long arrived back at the guesthouse while Bronagh busied herself checking them all in.

Maureen had instantly slotted into her old role, and Roisin and Moira grabbed Cindy to make their escape. By the time they'd reached the bottom of the stairs she'd launched into a conversation about Irish Christmas traditions with a couple from Maine. Pooh's effusive greeting when she'd opened the door had brought Roisin back down to earth, not to mention flying backwards and Moira and Cindy had done a wary side-step all the way through to the lounge. They'd found Patrick and Noah sitting on the floor surrounded by coloured paper.

Patrick had explained they'd collected Pooh and Mr Nibbles after their film so as Mammy wouldn't have to drive back to Howth later that afternoon. 'That one who does the cleaning is a bit strange isn't she?' he'd added.

'Idle Ita? In what way?' Roisin had asked.

'Well every time I head down the stairs, she pops out from one of the rooms like a fecking Jack in the Box and just stands there staring at me. It's unnerving, she reminds me of your one out of that Stephen King film.'

'Carrie.' That had come from Moira.

'Yeah, that's the one.'

'I think she's sweet on you, Pat.' Roisin recalled the housekeeper's excitement at the news Patrick was home.

'You can't blame her, honey. You are one gorgeous hunk of a man.' Cindy had draped herself over him while Moira made gagging noises.

'Look, Mummy,' Noah who'd been fed up with the lack of attention had cried. He'd held up the beginnings of a paper chain. 'Uncle Pat's teaching me how to make these.'

'Can we help,' she'd asked, and the three of them had sat down cross-legged next to the two boys to begin stapling and folding in earnest, while Pooh watched with his head resting on his paws and Mr Nibbles scrabbled sporadically in his cage. It had made Roisin nostalgic for her childhood, and Mammy, when she'd run out of delights to share with the tour group, had been delighted all over again with their efforts, declaring that the colourful chains would be used to decorate the dining room.

Indeed, the paper chains had looked festive once they'd draped them around the room, digging out the box of tinsel kept in the hall cupboard to add a bit of sparkle. The dining room had looked even more festive with a mug of the mulled wine, Aisling had made, warming their insides, and they'd been pleased with their efforts as they trooped back upstairs to watch the Late Late Toy Show Moira had recorded earlier that month for them all to watch. It had whiled away the hours until Midnight Mass.

Roisin cuddled Noah closer, rocking him as she used to when he was a baby. Her heart was full. He'd nodded off on her shoulder during the mass despite the hard wooden pew on which they were all perched. It had been a lovely evening she thought as she rested her face against his soft downy head. She inhaled the faint smell of frankincense which clung to his hair from the incense that had burned inside the church. Father Fitzpatrick's service had been brief, but to the point as befitted the time of night. Roisin had always enjoyed the carol singing at Midnight Mass, it was her favourite part because that was when it felt like Christmas to her. Not even Mammy bellowing Silent Night in her ear like a cow on heat could change that.

As for Mammy, well she'd been in seventh heaven surrounded by her whole family. It was a rare event these days and even rarer to get them all under God's roof. She'd told them all, in no uncertain terms, to be on their best behaviour just as she used to when they were small only this time, thanks be to God, she didn't spit on a hanky and start wiping at their faces. She'd had to have a quiet word with Patrick before they left when Cindy bounced into the living room announcing she was good to go. She'd told him if his girlfriend were to wave those things about, she currently had on display, during the Midnight Mass, Father Patrick might do himself an injury when he was swinging the incense and could he please suggest a more sedate choice of top. Patrick had huffed off, taking Cindy by the elbow and they'd returned a few minutes later with her clad in a snug white sweater and equally snug white pants. She looked like a Christmas angel Noah had told her, starstruck. A Christmas angel for Victoria's Secret perhaps, Roisin had thought, but she'd kept it to herself. Either way it had been enough of an improvement to satisfy Maureen and for her to introduce her to friends old and new as they'd gathered inside St Teresa's for the service.

There'd been a bit of a skirmish before things got underway when the O'Reilly sisters, both spinsters for obvious reasons, tried to squeeze in alongside Patrick. There'd only been enough room for one and the older of the two sisters, Elsie, had fallen into the aisle. She'd been helped up by Mr Kelly, recently widowed, and had been appeased when he patted the seat to suggest she squish in alongside him.

Sitting in the living room now, waiting for Mammy to dole out the cake as the old grandfather clock ticked that time was marching on, Roisin could hear the odd car horn as people full of the festive spirit made their way home from the church service. The church bells that had rung out through the city earlier were silent now and she guessed all across the country children would be fighting to stay awake in order to hear Santa's reindeer on the roof. The family had walked the short distance home from St Teresa's, their breath hanging like crystals in the air. They'd filed out of the church to calls of Merry Christmas to be greeted by a magical scene. The city had been dusted in an icing sugar snow sprinkle during the service. It had seen Mammy exclaim, 'The geese are being plucked in heaven tonight, so they are.'

'Here we are, one for you and one for you. No, Pooh, back to bed, chocolate and cake isn't good for you.' Roisin didn't like to say that it wasn't good for them either. Mammy began passing out the cake and true to her word it was loaded with the pungent anise flavoured seeds. Roisin settled Noah, whose eyes, despite his valiant efforts at staying awake long enough for hot chocolate and cake, were drooping next to her. She'd get Pat to carry him to bed because he'd be sound asleep in a minute or two. Taking the mug Quinn offered her and cupping it with both hands, the serviette on her lap with her half-eaten seed cake, she looked at her brothers and sisters and smiled. It was going to be a lovely, Christmas here at home all together, so it was.

Chapter 27

Roisin woke up to feel a warm hand tapping her on the side of her face. Her eyes fluttered reluctantly open just enough to see, unsurprisingly, that Noah was the culprit. Through her sleepy fog it dawned on her it was Christmas morning and she forced her eyes open properly, blinking several times. The ability of children to be wide awake the moment they opened their eyes amazed her once more as he began performing trampoline style bounces on the bed.

'Noah, you'll break the bed.'

'I'm making sure you're awake.'

'I'm awake. Merry Christmas, sweetheart.'

'Yay for Christmas!' He fist-bumped the air and Roisin smiled at his enthusiasm before cocking an ear. The house was silent. She glanced over at the bedside clock; it was eight am. It was nothing short of a miracle that Noah had slept this late and she tossed the covers aside as she remembered last year's obscene five thirty start. It was definitely time to get up, there was a lot to be done between now and four o'clock when their guests arrived for Christmas dinner. She knotted her dressing gown and followed her son's lead to the living room, where the first thing he did was race into the kitchen to check Santa had drunk the bottle of Guinness they'd left out for him. 'It's gone, Mum.'

CHAPTER 23

'Thirsty work delivering all those presents.' She was guessing Patrick would have slept soundly after knocking that back.

At the word presents, Noah raced over to the tree to check his stocking. 'Mum, it's very heavy!' She flicked the kettle on and looked over in time to see him dragging it to the middle of the living room floor. Pooh bounced over to see what he was up to and, remembering his little friend, Noah dropped the stocking, ran to the fridge and retrieved a lettuce leaf which he gave to Mr Nibbles. 'You're doing a good job looking after him, Noah,' Roisin said, heaping a teaspoon of coffee into a mug and dropping the spoon with a clatter as she felt a snuffling where nobody should be snuffling at this time of the morning. 'Get away with you.' The dog looked thoroughly dejected and she spied the empty bowl on the newspaper near the pantry. 'Ah well, it is Christmas morning I suppose.' Holding her nose she lopped him off a slice of the meaty roll in the fridge and gave him a scoop of the dried food sitting on the corner of the bench. *There that should keep him otherwise occupied for the time being.* She made a pot of tea too, deciding it was time everyone was up because she couldn't possibly be expected to contain Noah from ripping into his stocking while they waited for everyone to rise and shine. 'Noah, go and knock on the bedroom doors and tell them all Father Christmas has been.'

***

An hour later the living room looked like a bomb had gone off with wrapping paper strewn everywhere. The air was filled with the comforting savoury and slightly salty aroma of bacon sizzling as Mammy and Quinn whipped up a full Irish large enough to feed the Irish rugby team. Roisin was making a half-hearted attempt at picking the discarded paper up and putting it all in a rubbish sack. Noah was assembling a complicated new Lego Airport Control Tower, Cindy was perched on Pat's knee in pink pyjamas whispering in his ear, and Moira was engaged in a stand-off with Pooh. Aisling was setting the table, determined that they'd all squeeze around it somehow. She'd been delighted with Roisin's gift and even more so when she'd heard the story their American guest Gerry had told Roisin about his connection with Cliona Whelan.

'Oh, Rosi, do you think she'll meet him today?'

'I hope so, I really do.'

They would have to wait until later to find out.

Roisin put the rubbish bag down. She wondered how Shay's morning was unfolding in the cottage where his mammy had grown up. Then, with a sigh, she realised Noah should call his father before they sat down to breakfast and wish him a Merry Christmas. She'd telephone him now and get it out of the way. The phone rang long enough for her to wonder how she'd feel hearing his voice after her carry-on with Shay yesterday. Would she blush bright red hearing Colin's voice? Hearing him pick up and say, 'The Quealey residence,' however, she was surprised to find she didn't feel much of anything. It seemed she really had moved on. She exchanged pleasantries and tuned out as he blathered on about it being very quiet given it was just him and his mother. She would not feel sorry for him, not after enduring the pre-Christmas, Christmas dinner with them. When he mentioned it was looking like cheese on toast for their lunch, she interrupted and called Noah over, pleased when he snatched the phone from her, eager to fill his daddy in on all the things Santa had dropped down the chimney for him. He was also bursting to tell him about the copious amount of poo Mr Nibbles had done on his journey over.

***

CHAPTER 24

When the cry went up as most of them were scraping their plates clean, Roisin was marvelling at Cindy's restraint in sniffing and only eating half the rashers on her plate. She'd never seen someone only eat the white of a fried egg before either. She was just thinking how well Patrick was doing out of it all, having seen him forking his girlfriend's discarded food onto his plate when the squeal made her drop her fork and spin around in her chair. The rest of the family followed suit.

Roisin registered two things; Noah was sitting on the floor next to Mr Nibbles cage, and the door of the cage was open.

'He's run away!' Noah wailed.

Now was not the time to ask him why the cage door was open, she decided, seeing his bottom lip was trembling and his eyes were beginning to fill up.

'Christ on a bike,' Moira said, the first to move. 'Come on, you lot, shift it.' There was a mass downing of cutlery as chairs were pushed back and the search began. Moira, who was surprisingly clear headed in emergency situations, took control ordering Cindy and Patrick to search their bedroom. 'Roisin you do yours and Noah's. Noah, see if he's hiding in the bathroom. Mammy, check ours. Quinn and Ash, you're on the living room and kitchen. And nobody is to leave the apartment. We've got a situation here that needs to be contained. Do you hear me?' Everyone nodded and nobody thought to ask Moira where she planned on searching, not when she was doing such a good job delegating. 'Right let's bring this gerbil home.' They duly headed off in the directions in which they'd been sent.

The sound of drawers slamming shut, wardrobe doors opening and closing, and audible groans as people stood back after being on their hands and knees searching under beds, emanated throughout the apartment but there was no sign of the furry fellow. Roisin was feeling sick as she checked through their cases. She'd been so sure it was going to be a perfect family Christmas and now this had happened. He was so small, so vulnerable, it didn't bear thinking about. She realised she'd gotten very fond of the little chap and would be as devastated as Noah were he to have met an unhappy end.

She appeared back in the living room in time to see Mammy waving a piece of lettuce about making kissy-kiss noises as she called, 'Here, Mr Nibbles.' The only response was the thud of Pooh's stumpy tail on the carpet. Roisin looked at Pooh and was suddenly horror-struck. Surely not? He and Mr Nibbles were related. Well, in a pet uncle, nephew way at least. She wasn't sure she wanted to go closer for fear of him licking his chops and confirming her worst fears. She was going to have to though, they needed to know what had happened, to put together the missing pieces of the puzzle.

She got down on all fours and crawled towards him. 'Have you something you want to tell me?' She didn't know what she expected the poodle to say. Should she suggest one woof for I did it, two for not guilty? As she drew nearer the tail thumping got more excited. He obviously thought she was playing some sort of game and he clambered off his bed eager to get things underway. Roisin gasped because there, curled up in the middle of the pillow, was a small brown and white furry ball. She carefully scooped up the bundle, hoping he hadn't suffocated under all that curly poodle hair but to her relief he was warm and on closer inspection she saw his eyes were closed. He was sound asleep she realised, rolling him back into his cage and closing it with a firm click before calling out that the search was over.

So it was, the O'Mara women and Cindy retreated down the stairs to the kitchen to begin their mammoth prepping session for the Christmas dinner with Mammy spouting off about Christmas miracles all the way. Aisling muttered a Christmas miracle would be if Patrick got off his arse and did the breakfast dishes while they were gone.

Chapter 28

♥

Roisin untied the apron she'd donned and stood in the kitchen doorway, admiring last night's handiwork in the dining room. It was resplendent with glitzy tinsel and lots of it, along with screeds of paper chains. It looked very Christmassy, she decided, sniffing greedily at the aroma from the roasting turkey. The smell of it was like sliding under a comforting warm blanket on a cold winter's day, she thought. She'd never have believed she'd have room for Christmas dinner after the amount of food she'd tucked away at breakfast time but there was something about coming home to Dublin that always increased her appetite and the delicious whiffs from the kitchen were making her hungry once more.

Aisling had said the bird had another half an hour in the oven and then she'd get it out to rest. Mammy had crossed turkey off her list with flourish before leaning over Quinn's shoulder to enquire about the plum pud. 'Now be sure to add a decent splash of the cognac when you bring it through, Quinn,' she bossed. She'd been walking around, Santa hat slipping down over one eye, in her yoga pants as she clutched a clipboard singing along to Frosty the Snowman. A short, bossy elf as she kept an eye on the smooth running of the kitchen, eager to get everything on her list crossed off by the time Bronagh, Mrs Hanrahan, Nina and Tom arrived. She heard her call out, 'Moira, are your roast taties crisping?'

'Yes, and could we please listen to something other than your Foster and Allen Christmas collection? Oh, and, Mammy, don't forget to get changed before everyone arrives. The only person who should be in pants that tight is Tom.'

Actually, as Tom's rear flashed to mind, Roisin had to agree with her and she didn't fancy her chances of hearing the end of Foster and Allen. Her own jobs were finished, the smoked salmon starter having gotten the nod of approval from Mammy whose cheeks were looking flushed thanks to the mulled wine she'd insisted on sampling. 'You don't need a mugful, Mammy,' Roisin had protested to no avail.

'Look, Mummy,' Noah cried, spying her in the doorway. He held up a serviette folded into the shape of... a peacock? No, Roisin realised, the fanning tail was that of a turkey. The upset of the mystery of the missing gerbil was obviously long forgotten. Mr Nibbles and Pooh were both upstairs with various Christmas treats to hand so weren't missing out, but Pooh especially couldn't be trusted down here in the kitchen. Noah was sitting at the end of the table, one of six pushed together to make a long rectangular table in the middle of the room. Aisling had done a lovely job setting it. Cindy was sitting next to Noah and it was obviously under her tutelage he was learning how to make the turkey serviettes. 'It's a Thanksgiving tradition at home,' she drawled, blinding Roisin with her teeth.

'Well, you're doing a grand job the pair of you, they look fabulous. The perfect finishing touch to the table.'

She eyed Cindy who'd dressed with her usual leave-little-to-the-imagination flair, although she hadn't escaped being mammified. On top of her head she wore a Santa hat, as did they all. It was tradition, Mammy had declared. Looking at her brother's girlfriend she felt a cloud beginning to hover. It was threatening to blanket her good humour. She wondered if

CHAPTER 24

Patrick had been entirely honest with her as to his reasons for wanting to come home this Christmas. Because he certainly hadn't been honest with his sisters. She wished she hadn't overheard the conversation she'd heard earlier but she had and she couldn't unhear it now. It was down to the table's centrepiece that she had. The burlap arrangement of gingham ribbon and pine cones had been in the family for generations and Christmas wouldn't be Christmas if it wasn't on the table, Aisling had declared. 'It must be in the box we keep the Christmas decorations in upstairs. I think I put it back in the hallway cupboard, would you mind fetching it, Rosi?'

Roisin had duly trooped up the stairs of the ghostly guesthouse; silent as its guests had all ventured out for their Christmas dinners, and as she pushed open the door to the family's apartment, she heard Patrick's voice. She was about to call out when she realised he was talking to Mammy. She'd thought she was in the kitchen with Moira and hadn't noticed her leave. There was something in her brother's tone, a wheedling, smooth sort of tone that made her ears prick up. She wasn't the type to skulk about like Ita listening to other people's conversations and this one was clearly meant to be private but she was unable to move. 'Ten thousand will do it, Mammy. That will be enough to get the project off the ground and I'll get it back to you with interest before the year's out.'

Roisin shook her head. It seemed a leopard really didn't change his spots after all. She'd made a show of banging the door shut then and shouting out she was looking for the decorations box. Mammy had appeared in the hallway looking shifty although why she should be the one who looked like she had something to hide, Roisin didn't know. She wouldn't let on, she decided, as Mammy pointed her to the cupboard and said she should find it in there. She'd not breathe a word of Patrick pressing Mammy for money to her siblings, not today anyway.

Voices at the top of the stairs saw her push the cloud away and she moved to greet Bronagh and Mrs Hanrahan knowing the frail, elderly woman would need help getting down the stairs. She had indeed grown thinner but then it had been a long time since Roisin had last seen the sweet old woman. Her bones were like spindly twigs, she thought, being careful not to snap her as she hugged her hello. Her eyes held that same naughty twinkle ever present in her daughter's though. 'It's wonderful you could come and you both look gorgeous,' she announced. Mother and daughter preened.

'Ah, Patrick,' Bronagh said as he appeared behind them. 'You're just in time to help my mammy here down the stairs.'

'It's been a long while since I've been on the arm of a handsome young man. Hello, Patrick. The last time I saw you, you were still in short pants.' It was an exaggeration but they all laughed nevertheless and Patrick played the part of gallant escort to the hilt.

Tom was the next to arrive, a bottle of wine in each hand, which left him defenceless when Moira grabbed his backside by way of greeting. She said she was checking his pockets for her Christmas present but they all knew better. It earned her a telling off by Mammy but she wasn't deterred and homed in on him for a very merry Christmas kiss. Nina followed closely behind Tom. She'd brought a plate of sweets with her. 'They are called turrón,' she told them in her accented, precise English. 'It's a traditional Spanish nougat made with almonds we always have at Christmas.'

'It looks delicious, thank you.' Roisin said taking the plate from her and hoping by the end of the afternoon Nina would have lost the sad look that always lurked in her eyes. Bronagh exclaimed over the table and the decorations. Mammy fussed around seating Mrs Hanrahan and fetching her a cup of mulled wine.

It wasn't long before they sat down to a feast and Patrick kicked the festivities off by clinking his glass with his spoon and announcing he'd like to say a few words.

'Brown nosey fecker,' Aisling mouthed at Roisin, making her smirk. She wondered what he would have to say.

'Here's to O'Mara's, not just a family legacy but a family home. To O'Mara's.'

'To O'Mara's,' everybody chimed, and Roisin kept her whirling thoughts about her brother firmly under wraps. Nothing was going to spoil today, nothing.

***

There were cries of that was delicious and oh, I'm so full as Roisin carried through the last of the dinner dishes to the kitchen and adding it to the mounting pile declared, 'I say the men do the washing up.'

'I agree,' Aisling said, soaking the oven dish, that had cooked the turkey to perfection.

'Here, here,' Moira piped up from where she was scraping leftovers into the bin.

'Ladies, away with you, I've a plum pudding to be sorting.' Quinn herded them out and sitting back down at the table Roisin looked down the length of it at the Christmas crackers that had been pulled. The lame jokes had been read out to groans and laughter and the Santa hats abandoned in favour of paper crowns. The conversations bouncing up and down and back and forth as they all awaited the arrival of pudding were full of laughter and she could feel the love in the room. She leaned back in her chair, tempted to clasp her hands over her belly. She felt for the first time in a very long while, content. This had been her year of second chances. She'd had a second chance at life, love and now today this was her second Christmas. And it had been a very good Christmas indeed.

***

'Careful you don't set fire to the paperchain!' Maureen exclaimed. 'Where's the fire extinguisher?' The plum pudding was alight with blue flames and Quinn stood back triumphantly while everybody clapped.

'He knows what he's doing, Mammy,' Aisling said, offering to help dish the dessert as the flames died and he began doling the pudding into bowls along with a healthy dollop of cream. He was quite sharp with her, Roisin thought frowning, as he told her no, he could manage passing the first of the bowls down the table.

Aisling looked a little put out too as she sat back down. Quinn never took a tone with her.

'Is there money in this, Mummy?'

'I think there might be, Noah,' Roisin replied, tucking in.

'Mammy, watch your false teeth, we don't want any accidents,' Roisin heard Bronagh say as a jubilant shriek went up from Maureen who'd found five pence. Noah too was victorious but Aisling's reaction was a bit extreme, she thought, looking across the table at her sister who, annoyed at Quinn, had tucked in with gusto. Now her mouth was opening and shutting at a rate of knots as she said, 'Oh my God, I don't believe it. I just don't believe it.'

Was she crying? Roisin looked at her incredulously. Sure, it was only five pence!

'Oh, Quinn!'

This was getting ridiculous.

'Aisling, what's gotten into you?' Maureen demanded, pointing her spoon at her. 'If you've money worries you only have to say.'

Roisin didn't look at her brother.

'Yes! Yes! Yes!'

Was that a yes to the money worries? she wondered as everybody else stared at Aisling as though she'd grown a second head. What on earth was going on?

'Look! Look what was in my pudding!' Her cheeks flushed a pretty pink and her eyes flashed with excitement as Aisling held up a sparkling solitaire diamond ring for them all to see.

Roisin didn't know who screamed the loudest out of them all, Moira, Mammy, herself or Bronagh as the penny finally dropped. She pushed back her chair and raced around the table to hug her sister.

This really was a Christmas they'd never forget.

***

The sound of a bin lid clattering to the ground startled Roisin from her sleep. It took her a moment to figure out what it was that had woken her up, but when her sleep fogged brain twigged she gently nudged Noah. He made a mumbling sort of a noise but she didn't give up, telling him to wake up because she knew he wouldn't want to miss out. 'We've got a visitor,' she whispered. 'Come on.' That stirred him and she pushed the duvet aside waiting for him to clamber out of bed first before getting up herself. They padded over to the window and Roisin pulled the curtains back, bracing herself for the polar blast as she opened the window just enough for them both to be able to peer down to the courtyard below. Just as she'd thought, illuminated by the sensor light and staring back at them was Mr Fox. The snow from Christmas Eve had melted now and the courtyard's paving stones glistened slickly.

'Mummy, should we go and get him some cheese?' Noah's whisper was loud on the silent night.

'No, no need, there's enough leftovers to feed a small army in that bin, so there is. Mr Fox is going to have himself a fine Christmas feast.' She hugged her boy close to her and they both watched as, having decided they weren't a threat, the little red fox nosedived into the bin. 'Do you think we should leave him to enjoy his dinner, Noah?'

Roisin shivered and Noah nodded, but before they closed the window he leaned out and called softly, 'Merry Christmas, Mr Fox,' before running back to their warm bed.

Epilogue

♥

Clio strode into the foyer of the Merrion. She was still very much a trouser wearing woman and had chosen a simple lemon suit today that she knew suited her well. Oh, how times changed though, she thought, remembering how out of place she'd felt in the hotel the first time she'd come to meet Gerry here. Confidence was indeed a perk of age. She nodded a greeting to the concierge and only paused in her stride to sign her name with practised flourish, wishing the guest who'd run over book in hand— her book would you believe it—a Merry Christmas. She knew the way to the drawing rooms and it was as if time had stood still as she pushed opened the door. The chandelier still shone with rainbow light, the armchairs you could sink into and forget you ever had a care in the world still invited you in, and the fire crackled and spat to ensure you forgot all about the cold outside.

He was there, just as he'd promised he would be. He looked up as soon as the door opened, holding her in his clear and beautiful blue-eyed gaze. The smile, the dimples were the same, she saw, hanging back a moment, her heart threatening to jump from her chest. This was her chance to open herself up to the possibility of them rewriting their ending just as she had in her book. They could have their happy ever after because life was full of never-ending possibility and with that

Clio stepped into the room, her face breaking into that goofy grin, the one she'd never been able to contain when she set eyes on Gerry.

A Wedding at O'Mara's

♥

Chapter 1

♥

Dublin 2000

Aisling O'Mara was feeling very grown up as she tottered down Baggot Street all tucked up inside her coat. She didn't have time to tap the young man on the shoulder who she'd spied spitting on the ground as he waited for the bus. She'd have liked to have told him spitting was a disgusting habit but had she done so, she knew she'd then fret she was morphing into her mammy. Nor did she have time to wonder why on earth that woman with the lank, greasy hair and a cigarette in one hand, a child clutching the other hadn't seen fit to put a hat on her little one. It was a day that clearly called for a hat. Never mind either the fact she was a woman in her mid-thirties about to be married at long last because Aisling was about to do the most grown up thing of her life. She was off to meet her soon-to-be husband and they had an appointment at the AIB Bank where they were going to open a joint account. It was very exciting!

Moira had called her a sad arse that morning over her enormous plate of toast which had been smothered in thick, sweet Magiun, plum jam. The jar had come courtesy of the guesthouse's weekend breakfast cook, Mrs Baiku who hailed from Romania and Aisling was extremely partial to it. Mind you she was partial to most things with copious amounts of sugar in them. Life, she often lamented would have been a lot easier if her secret fantasy wasn't to roll in a ball pit filled with coconutty, marshmallow Snowballs. At that point in time too, finding herself staring at her paltry boiled egg with NO soldiers to dip because she was frantically trying to lose a few pounds before her big day, it had taken all her strength not to try and divert her sister from her breakfast.

Diversion tactics had worked a treat when they were younger and had saved her from many a serve of the broad bean or pile of spinach. It was simple, she'd turn to Moira, being the youngest and most gullible of her siblings and exclaim, 'How did that cat get in here?' Moira's head never failed to spin searching for a non-existent cat while Aisling would dump whatever was causing her angst on her plate onto her sister's. It worked the other way too when it came to snaffling an extra fish finger or the like. She never felt a smidgen of guilt either when she was allowed to leave the table thanks to her clean plate while Moira sat staring mournfully at a mound of something green and, by that time, stone cold while Mammy prattled on about how the starving children in Africa would be grateful for a good meal like Moira's to be placed in front of them and how she ought to be grateful. Aisling would think it served her right for always helping herself to her stuff. She'd tried the diversion tactics on Patrick once, given Mammy always gave him an extra fish finger because he was the boy, but he'd caught her out and smacked her hard on her knuckles with his fork.

This morning at the breakfast table, however, Aisling had drawn on her inner willpower, of which there wasn't much, but what little there was had been enough for her to leave Moira's toast alone. She'd been tempted to pick it up and flick her in the face with it though as she sneered across the table at the fact her elder sister was about to share her finances wholeheartedly with her fiancé.

'A joint account? What's mine is yours and what's yours is mine. Feck that, what's mine is mine thanks very much,' she'd stated.

Given that Moira, a self-proclaimed poor art student these days, didn't have anything other than a collection of pricey cosmetics and some expensive and very impractical items of clothing in her wardrobe, Aisling had rolled her eyes, cracked the shell on her boiled egg and told her sister in a suitably condescending manner that one day if say Tom, for instance, was to pop the question then she'd understand.

Now, spying Quinn up ahead, waiting as he'd promised he would be, with his hands shoved in the pockets of his jacket as he stamped his feet against the cold, she grinned at him waving out. He spotted her through the bobbing heads of people ducking and diving along pavements not designed to cope with the influx their city had seen this last couple of years and strode towards her. She was pleased to note he'd listened to her and dressed in his good jeans – his going out jeans – not that they went out much. There wasn't much time for that between him running Quinn's, his busy bistro, and her managing the guesthouse with its unpredictable hours. He'd laughed when she'd told him he needed to look smart and presentable to meet Mr Cleary.

'Aisling, the days of going cap in hand to see the bank manager are long gone. Sure, they're desperate for our business,' he'd said. Quinn had plans of them putting a down payment on a house. Not for them to live in – he was going to move into O'Mara's with her and Moira after they were married – but as a rental property. 'Property prices are high, but rental property is in high demand. It's as good a time as any for us to get our feet on the property ladder,' he'd said. He'd gone so far as to get the calculator out and bang out figures based on his and her savings and had been confident that after the wedding, 'and the honeymoon,' she'd added, they could start looking around to get an idea of what was on the market.

CHAPTER 417

His nose was red from the chill air, Aisling saw as he drew nearer. The reason he'd been standing about outside his restaurant instead of waiting inside in the toasty warmth was because she'd told him she had to be back at O'Mara's for two o'clock as she had a Canadian tour party arriving. She liked to be on hand to meet their guests arriving, priding herself on the personal touch when it came to her role managing the family's guesthouse. She also knew her fiancé well enough to know if she arranged to meet him inside his bistro, he'd find something last minute that he had to do, that couldn't possibly wait. For his part he knew his intended well enough not to argue, not when she seemed to be walking a tight rope of nervous energy as their wedding drew nearer.

He reached her and wrapped her in a hello hug followed by a kiss and Aisling inhaled the familiar scent of cooking that clung to him along with the aftershave she'd bought him for his birthday. It was a warm and spicy scent that did peculiar things to her, things that were not suitable to be thinking about when one had a threesome with the bank manager planned.

'All set?' Quinn asked, releasing her and offering her his arm.

'All set,' she said, linking her arm through his and putting her best foot forward.

***

The queue, given people were on their lunch breaks, was to the door and Aisling was glad they had an appointment. She hated queuing; it seemed like such a complete waste of time, especially with her impending nuptials which meant she had one hundred and one other things she could be doing at any given time along with all her ordinary day to day tasks. They were led through to a tiny waiting room and told by a bored looking woman that Mr Cleary shouldn't be long.'

No tea or coffee was on offer then, Aisling thought, glancing around before sitting down.

Quinn perched next to her muttering, 'It's a power play thing. 'He's letting us know his time's more precious than ours.' He was working his hands, and Aisling realised he was anxious. She took hold of them and gave them a reassuring squeeze before looking about for a magazine to flick through. You never knew your luck, there might be a Bridal Today lurking or the like. There were none, only a rack of pamphlets pertaining to banking with smiley, happy people who were all saving hard on the glossy covers.

A lonely water cooler gurgled away like a hungry tummy in the corner of the closet-like space. They were a tight old lot these bankers, she thought, trying to picture Mr Cleary. 'I bet yer man in there,' she said, pointing to the closed door with its gold nameplate, 'is small and yappy like a Jack Russell.'

Her comment made Quinn smile. It was then she remembered the brochure she'd tucked in her bag. Now was as good a time to mention what she had a feeling was going to be a hard sell. It was time to talk honeymoon and given she'd worked in resort management for years; she had her heart set on something completely out of the box to the sunshine playgrounds she'd spent so much time in. She retrieved the brochure and passed it over to him asking, 'What do you think of this then?'

Quinn stared at it, frowning, before stating the obvious. 'It's a hotel made of ice.'

'I know that,' Aisling laughed. 'It's the Ice Hotel, you eejit. You know the one that's carved every year from blocks of the stuff up the top of Sweden. It's been on the tele.'

'Why?'

'Why what?'

'Why do they do it?'

'Because it's beautiful and it's unique, that's why. Every single thing right down to the glasses used in the hotel bar is carved from ice. Imagine it, Quinn.' Her smile was dreamy as she pictured the winter wonderland of Narnia. She'd lost herself in there many times as a child when she'd hidden away at the back of her wardrobe trying to find a secret doorway.

'Okay, it's erm, very creative but why are you showing me this?' Quinn had a feeling he knew where this conversation was headed.

'I think we should have our honeymoon there. That's why.'

He'd guessed right and shivered at the very thought of it. 'Won't it be a tad chilly though?'

'Well, you don't get around in your swimming trunks. You have to have the proper winter gear but sure, look,' she took the brochure from him and flicked through to a picture of a couple looking deliriously happy as they snuggled together under reindeer skins despite lying on a bed carved of ice.

'They've got hats on.' Quinn pointed out. 'And I bet they've got socks on too. I didn't picture myself wearing a hat and socks to bed on my honeymoon or freezing my arse off on a bed made of ice for that matter.'

'There's such a thing as body heat.' Aisling waggled her eyebrows at him.

'There is that.' He grinned.

Sensing weakness she warmed to her theme. 'And, it's not *just* a hotel.'

'I can see that. It's a fecking igloo too.'

She elbowed him. 'It's a living breathing ice art gallery.' She'd stolen that bit from the small print in the brochure. 'Imagine telling our children that's where we spent our honeymoon.'

'What children? My little swimmers will be frozen forever if you make me go there.'

'We could sip schnapps that would warm them back up and watch the Northern Lights.'

'Isn't it the Germans who drink schnapps?'

'The Swedes do too, I looked it up, but alright then, we'll have a hot toddy of Swedish glogg if it makes you happy.'

He looked at her blankly.

'It's like mulled wine.'

'Ah.' He liked the mulled wine and the body heat side of things but he was still having a hard time with the hats and socks.

'We could go for a sled ride through the pine forest too.'

'And will Rudolph be there, Aisling?'

'Ha ha, it's huskies that pull the sleds not reindeer.'

Quinn could see he was fighting a losing battle. It wasn't looking likely she'd agree to the B&B in Kerry he'd been going to suggest and he wanted to keep his bride happy. He played his last card even though he knew he'd lost. 'It looks expensive.'

Aisling laid down her hand and it was a blinder. 'It's not that bad when you think of what an experience it will be. What price do you put on a memory that will last us a lifetime, Quinn?'

'Feck it, Aisling, you'd better by me some thermal socks, then. And if they do a budget ice suite that's the one you're too book, alright?'

'Yay!' Aisling gave a little cheer before planting a sloppy kiss on his cheek. 'Don't you worry,' she said, giving his thigh a meaningful squeeze 'I'll make sure you have a good time, big boy. You won't feel the cold on my bedtime watch.'

Quinn coughed, 'Er, Ash.'

She looked over to see Mr Cleary, not quite a snappy Jack Russell more of a droopy eyed bloodhound, standing in the doorway of his office.

'If you'd like to come in, when you're ready,' he said, giving a little cough.

Chapter 2

Two days had passed since Quinn and Aisling's successful visit to the bank. Despite the less than auspicious start, Mr Cleary, who had insisted they call him Michael, had been quite accommodating in the end and they'd left with the promise of sizable loan when the time came and a brand spanking new account in both their names. Now though, the good mood Aisling had been floating about in at the thought of stargazing near the North Pole was dissipating. To be blunt, Aisling O'Mara was in foul humour. She could hear Mammy's voice in her head telling her, 'You always are a moody madam when you're hungry.' And, Aisling was hungry.

She eyed Bronagh's drawer, the guesthouse's receptionist had nipped to the loo and the custard creams she knew Bronagh had tucked away in there called to her. *Eat me, eat me, eat me, Aisling,* they whispered. It was like a scene from the *Little Shop of Horrors*, so it was. She glanced toward the bathroom and saw the door still closed. Her hand reached forward and grasped the knob of the drawer but the sudden glint of blue light saw her snatch it back as though burned.

A diamond solitaire engagement ring, oval cut set in white gold no less, was better than any Weight Watchers meeting or Slimmer's Club get together. The most beautiful thing she'd ever been given in her life was right there on her ring finger reminding her that in a few weeks, she, Aisling Elizabeth O'Mara would become Mrs Aisling O'Mara-Moran. *How many times had she practiced introducing herself like that these last few weeks? Yes, hello there I'm Mrs O'Mara-Moran. Mrs O'Mara-Moran is the name. Aisling, Aisling O'Mara-Moran pleased to make your acquaintance.* For some reason when she said it in her head, she sounded posh, plummy like Joanna Lumley. She thought it might be because she was going to be the proud owner of a double-barrelled surname.

Mammy had been perturbed when Aisling had said she wanted to keep the O'Mara. 'Aisling that's the sort of modern thing Moira would do to be different,' she'd said and Aisling had replied. 'It's for Daddy, Mammy. I want to carry on our surname for him.' She didn't add that her brother, Patrick was over in America so he was hardly doing his bit for carrying on the O'Mara name in Ireland. Mammy had cried hearing this and said Aisling was a wonderful daughter. Five minutes later she'd accused her of eating the last Snowball she'd been saving and had planned on savouring as she watched Ballykissangel later that evening. Aisling had said she wouldn't and hadn't but the coconut flakes on her sweater had given her away.

'What are you doing?' Bronagh's waspish voice made her jump.

'Nothing. I was about to go through the diary to see what guests we've got arriving today, that's all.'

The receptionist's dark eyes narrowed. 'I know what was on your mind. I can read you like a book so I can, and you'll not find any biscuits in there. I've hidden them. I'll not have it on my head when the zip gets stuck halfway up your back on your big day. Nobody will be able to say Bronagh Hanrahan had her own best interests at heart. Or accuse me of sabotaging your chance to lose weight for my own financial gain.'

Aisling tried to look innocent, hoping the rapid blinking and widening of her eyes would convince Bronagh she'd not been planning a custard cream biscuit heist. 'I've lost three pounds.

I'm on track, thank you very much and have no interest in sweets of any sort.' The Pope himself would be proud of how pious she sounded.

Bronagh patted her middle; the fabric of her skirt was shiny and stretched tight. 'I've lost three and a half pounds myself and I have to say I'm feeling marvellous for it. And, remember I've the menopause to do battle with too.'

Bronagh must be going through the longest running menopause on record, Aisling thought and her skirt didn't look any looser than it had done last week. She reckoned it was a tactic and Bronagh was trying to psych her out. They eyed one another. She was very competitive was Bronagh, Aisling thought. This silly competition was all down to her too because as soon as Aisling announced she wanted to lose half a stone for her wedding, Bronagh had been all for putting money on who'd reach their target weight first. She said it would keep them motivated if they were dieting for high stakes. Aisling would have been content with sticking a photo of Cindy Crawford in her swimsuit on the fridge but Moira had been lurking in the background and it was her that had egged them both on. Sure, it had been like a scene from a women's prison with her little sister's carry-on. She might as well have been yelling, 'Fight, fight, fight!'

Aisling was not one to back down from a challenge and in the end, she'd wagered a tenner that it would be her that lost her poundage first. After all, the odds were in her favour given it was her wedding she wanted to be in fine fettle for. Moira having already cleared it with Aisling that she would not be paying for her bridesmaid dress – given she was a poor student, but that in no way meant she'd wear some frothy pink ensemble and look like an eejit either – had seen a way to supplement her income instantly. She was running a book on the great weight loss race. So far, Aisling was the favourite but, Moira had stated over her toast that morning watching as Aisling lovingly caressed the honey jar, it could change, just like that. She'd clicked her fingers for effect and Aisling had shoved the pot back in the cupboard and retrieved the Marmite instead.

'Have you done the stairs this morning?' Aisling asked Bronagh.

Moira had also taken it upon herself to be both women's personal trainer. Neither had asked her to do this and as such when she'd asked for payment for services rendered, they'd both told her to feck off. She'd not given up though and had said she'd do it out of the goodness of her heart. When she'd appeared in reception in joggers with a whistle around her neck both women had told her to feck off once more, but to no avail. In the end, Bronagh had climbed the stairs on the condition Moira hand over the whistle. She'd hidden it like she had the custard creams.

'I have. Moira made me do it before she left for college. It wasn't easy in this skirt I can tell you but I made it to the top floor with no rests, that's a first for me. What about yourself?'

'She's got me booked for a session after dinner.' Aisling frowned. To avoid temptation at Quinn's she'd been eating her meals here at O'Mara's under the watchful eye of Moira. She was fed up to the back teeth with salad and lean meat or vegetables and lean meat. She wanted a great big burger with fries, lots of skinny fries. *Stop it, Aisling.*

The door to the guesthouse opened and it was a welcome distraction to watch a giant bouquet of flowers with legs walk toward them. It was their fortnightly arrangement of blooms for the reception desk from Fi's Florists and Aisling recognised young Caitlin, Fi's new apprentice's voice as she said good morning to them both.

'Here I'll take those, Caitlin, they're gorgeous. Did you arrange them?' Aisling took the flowers and inhaled the sweet aroma from the gardenias. Were they edible, she wondered, and would she have gardenias in her bridal bouquet? She filed the latter question away to bring up with Leila when they met for lunch or in her case lettuce leaves.

'I did, thanks. How're the wedding plans coming along, Aisling? It's not long to go now.' The young girl's cheeks were flushed from the cold outside and the tip of her nose bright red; she sneezed.

'Bless you.' Bronagh immediately said.

'Sorry, I've a bit of a sniffle.'

Aisling took a step back, she could not afford to get sick, not now when she had so much on her plate (a bad choice of metaphor), she decided. 'Grand, thanks, Caitlin. Everything's coming along nicely.' She liked to think the more she said this the more she'd believe it. The power of positive thinking and all that.

Bronagh put her hand up to her mouth and mouthed, 'She's a complete nightmare.' to Caitlin who grinned.

'Well I'd best be off and carry on with my rounds.'

'Thanks very much,' Aisling called over her shoulder, carrying the flowers through to the kitchen. The guest's lounge room was empty and she made a note to self to replenish the tea and coffee sachets once she'd sorted the bouquet. She always found the act of placing the fresh flowers in the vase therapeutic and hopefully it would improve her mood. She didn't like being snappy and edgy; it wasn't like her and it wasn't all down to the fact she was about to start gnawing on her arm if she didn't get some sustenance in her shortly. It was her own fault. She'd set a ridiculously tight timeframe in which to organise her wedding. Everybody thought she was mad. Quinn included. They'd gotten engaged on Christmas Day and now here she was expecting to have a big, white wedding with all the trimmings on the fourteenth of February, Valentine's Day, no less.

It had given her shy of eight weeks in which to organise everything. Thank the Lord for Leila. The gods had smiled down on her the day her best friend had decided to launch her own wedding planner business. This wedding would be a rip-roaring success because Love Leila Bridal Planning services was backing her all the way. Sure, if it weren't for Leila, she'd be headed straight for the registry office dragging Quinn along behind her. Leila had the power to get them in with places that otherwise would have told them to come back in a year when they had space free in the diary. Of course, it wasn't the first time Leila had planned a wedding for her which was why Aisling had no intention of dilly-dallying for a year while all the arrangements were made. Sure, anything could happen like it had once before. She'd been let down weeks out from her wedding, which obviously was a blessing as, with the benefit of hindsight, her ex-fiancé was an eejit of the highest order. It hadn't felt like a blessing at the time though. It had been the most humiliating experience of her life.

Oh, she knew right enough Quinn wouldn't let her down but there was still the fear. The omnipresent fear she couldn't shake that unless she expedited matters something would go wrong. She sighed, and filled the vase. She should be feeling excited and full of the joys of being a bride-to-be. Instead she was an anxious, hungry wreck. She began to pen one of her imaginary letters, something she hadn't done in a long time.

Dear Aisling,

I'm getting married soon and I want to know how I can make this gnawing feeling in the pit of my stomach go away, and please don't tell me to eat a lovely, great big slice of chocolate cake with fresh cream filling and a ganache icing because that won't help.

Yours faithfully,
Me

Chapter 3

♥

'Aisling have you had any further thoughts on the reception's seating arrangements?' Maureen O'Mara asked her daughter.

'Leila and I were going to go over those again at lunchtime, why?' Aisling knew she was going to regret asking like she was already regretting having answered the phone. Mammy was driving her round the bend with her daily guestlist updates. She'd only nipped upstairs for a quick sandwich before she headed out to meet Leila. It was not on her to-do list to sit and listen to Mammy gabble on about who wouldn't be seated next to whom and who was allergic to what. She'd already been delayed by having to sort Ita out on her way upstairs.

She'd spotted their self-titled Director of Housekeeping on the first-floor landing. She'd been pretending to look for supplies in the cupboard at the end of the hall where all the cleaning products were kept. Aisling had tiptoed toward her, guessing she was engrossed in a game on her phone. 'Ita, could you make up room six please. The Fenchurch family are arriving within the hour and they need the cot as well,' she'd said, in a voice designed to let her know she knew exactly what she'd been up to.

Ita had banged her head on the shelf above her and hastily shoved her phone back in the pocket of her smock. She'd picked up a bottle of detergent before scurrying off with a wounded look on her face. It had annoyed Aisling that she should be made to feel guilty over the way she'd spoken to her and she'd stomped up the rest of the stairs to the family's apartment on the top floor wishing she could be made of sterner stuff, like Moira.

If it had been the youngest O'Mara, she'd have told Ita to get off her idle arse and get on with the job she was being paid to do without so much as a second thought. Aisling had set about slapping two pieces of soft, white bread together, sandwiching the thick spread of honey between them as the telephone had begun to shrill. She knew who it would be before she picked up but she also knew from experience that it did no good ignoring Mammy, she'd track you down eventually.

Now, she flopped down on the armchair by the window and took a deep breath. The light doing its best to shine in through the windows was weak and wintery but at least it wasn't raining. She sniffed; it smelt a bit doggy in here. That was down to Pooh. She'd have to spray the air freshener about the place. Mammy was after buying her a can in order to stop her complaining about her bringing the poodle to visit. The downside of this was she'd bought the one that smelled like her favourite perfume, Arpège, so now the apartment either smelled of poodle or Mammy. She kept looking over her shoulder expecting to see one or both of them lurking in the shadows.

She took a bite of her honey sandwich and the sweet burst on her tongue was comforting. She chewed as Mammy informed her, 'I'm after hearing from your great aunt Noreen down in that godforsaken place she lives in again. I think they only got the electricity last year. In a right state she was. She says she won't enjoy her meal if she's put at the same table as your aunt Emer. There's bad blood between those two, not that anybody knows why. Although I'm sure Emer's mammy, Rosamunde, knows what's gone on but she's not saying. Anyway, Noreen says she'll not be held responsible for her actions if Emer winds up next to her. Your father's side of the family always were a pain in the arse except for his mammy and da, God rest their souls.' she sniffed.

Noreen wasn't technically Aisling's great aunt at all. It was all very complicated but from memory she was her dad's cousin the correct title as to what that made her to Aisling a mystery so great aunt it was. She rolled her eyes at the thought of the old biddy laying down the law to Mammy. 'The only reason your side wasn't a pain in the arse too was because you'd fallen out with them, Mammy and we never saw them.' Aisling sighed because unfortunately her mammy's brothers were making up for lost time now and had all informed their sister they were waiting for their invitations to their favourite niece's wedding. Sure, she'd only met them a handful of times. The politics of planning a wedding were all very frustrating.

'I am not a one-woman United Nations you know,' Aisling said, thinking about how Uncle Brendan had threatened to clock Uncle Frankie if he mouthed off at the reception. It was a likely scenario given Frankie's love of a drop. 'To be honest, I don't know why your brothers have to come at all, Mammy. Tom will sit there picking his nose all through the speeches like he did at Rosi's wedding and Colm couldn't keep his hands to himself with any of her friends. Disgusting he was, following the girls half his age around saying, 'Now then, how's about a kiss for the bride's uncle? As for Brendan and Frankie it will be fisticuffs at dawn mark my words.' Aisling put her hand on her chest; she could feel her heart beginning to pump a little faster at the stress of it all. 'It's not as if we ever see any of them either. And what about Cousin Jackie and her shellfish allergy, not to mention Aunt Ina who doesn't want to be seated near the band because she won't be able to hear herself think. I'm pulling my hair out here.'

'Ah now, Aisling, calm down. My brothers are heathens I'll grant you but I've no parents left in this world and family is family. Your day will be grand so it will and all this will be a storm in a teacup like the KY2 business at New Year.'

Aisling frowned, surely Mammy wasn't on about a new version of an old favourite that a girl's mammy should know nothing about in the first place – and then the penny dropped. 'Oh, you mean the Y2K bug.'

'Yes, that. Why, what did you think I meant?'

'Erm never mind.'

'Well you get my point, Aisling. We saw the millennium in with fireworks galore but despite all the merchants of doom predicting the world as we knew it was going to crash down around us, it didn't. Sure, it'll be the same with your wedding. There'll be a few crackers going off but no major catastrophes. Mark my words.'

Aisling wasn't sure she liked her impending nuptials being compared to the Millennium bug and she'd prefer it if no crackers went off thanks very much but Mammy had only paused to draw breath so she didn't get a chance to protest. 'Have you heard back from Cormac as to whether he's coming over from America to walk you down the aisle.'

Cormac was her dad's older brother. Aisling had gotten to know him when she'd visited LA on stopovers to her various resort postings. Her dad had never spoken about him much when they were growing up. There were nearly ten years between them and Cormac had left home and sailed to America in search of adventure and to make his fortune, or so Daddy had always said, when he was still a young lad. He'd done well for himself, becoming a mover and shaker in the LA fashion scene where he'd wound up making his home. From a grown-up perspective, Aisling had concluded that what had driven Uncle Cormac to America all those years ago was not the need for adventure but a need for acceptance, something his effeminate ways would have struggled to find in Ireland when he was a younger man

When the time had come, he'd had no interest in taking over the running of the family's guesthouse. So, it had fallen to his younger brother, Aisling's daddy, Brian. Her brother Patrick caught up with Cormac from time to time over there in the city of angels but apart from funerals, and weddings the rest of the family hardly saw him. It had been Mammy's bright idea to have Cormac give her away when she was supposed to walk down the aisle the first time around. A stand in for Daddy. Tears prickled and she blinked them away because more than anything she wished her dad could be the one whose arm she linked hers through as he led her down the aisle to meet Quinn. She liked to think he'd be there in spirit. Cormac was no Daddy but she was very fond of him. He was their closest male blood relative excluding her mammy's brothers and Patrick and the thought of any of them marching her up the aisle was enough to bring her out in a rash.

She'd felt sheepish when she'd telephoned Cormac a second time to ask if he would do her this favour. His relaxed drawl made her think of blond shaggy-haired surfer dudes and hum Beach Boy tunes whereas in reality Uncle Cormac was a short man whose fondness for the finer things in life saw his belly rest comfortably over the top of the flowing, loose fitting linen pants he favoured. She also suspected he wore a toupee. A very good one, granted. They made good ones in LA. Uncle Cormac, with his tendency to talk with those beringed hands of his was one of life's characters, Aisling had decided long ago and without him the world would be a little duller.

He hadn't beaten around the bush, telling her he wanted to check out travel insurance policies for their cancellation clauses this time around before saying yes, given he'd not been able to get a refund on his flights the last time she'd been going to get married.

He'd telephoned her the other day and she'd thought she'd passed the news on to Mammy that yes, he would be there and to make a room up for him at the guesthouse. It must have slipped her mind. She informed Mammy of his call.

'The reason you're forgetting things, Aisling, is because you've too much on your plate.'

Aisling thought that was an ironic thing to say, given there'd been feck all on her plate since she'd started her weight-loss journey, or nightmare, whichever way you wanted to look at it.

'And,' Maureen said, failing to see any irony in her words whatsoever. 'I understand the planning of your big day is a stressful thing but that's what the mother of the bride is for. It is my job to be a good listener, constant giver of compliments, cheerleader, and source of support to you.'

'Mammy, are you reading that out?'

'No, I am not.'

'You are too.'

'Well, according to Bridal Life magazine that's my role and as such I want you to know you can relax because I've had a grand idea. Why don't I come along for the luncheon with you and Leila? I don't mind cancelling my watercolour workshop this afternoon. I'm annoyed with Rosemary Farrell anyway and could happily give it a miss. She's after copying my idea of doing a self-portrait. You want to see hers, Aisling, she looks like yer wan with her gob wide open in that painting Moira was after putting on her wall as a teenager. Jaysus it gave us all nightmares so it did.'

Aisling knew the painting Mammy was talking about. 'Edvard Munch's, *The Scream.* He was a Norwegian expressionist.' She spieled off the explanation Moira had given them all for the disturbing print she'd hung in pride of place on her bedroom wall. It had frightened Aisling almost as much as the Bono poster her little sister used to stick to her bedroom door as payback for something or other. 'She told us we were all heathens who wouldn't know great art if it smacked us in the head.'

'So, she did. Uppity wee madam she was in her teens. Terrible phase. Anyway, what I was saying is that I could fill Leila in on all the family and who's to go where. Take a load off of it all for you.'

'No, thank you, Mammy. We'll manage.' Aisling knew her mammy was itching to take over from Leila; she'd done exactly that with Roisin's wedding and if she were to give her an inch, she'd take a mile. 'You're in charge of the RSVPs sure, and you and Bronagh are having to sort out who's staying in what room.' No guest bookings were to be taken two days prior or after the wedding. 'That's a big enough responsibility.' She'd given Mammy the task of tallying up who was coming and sorting out accommodations because she wanted her to feel part of it all, but that was a big enough part, thank you very much.

'Well it is when you only give people a few weeks' notice, Aisling.'

'Mammy, we've been through all of this. I don't see the point in dragging things out.'

'There's dragging things out and then there's your Shogun wedding. People will talk.'

'Shotgun wedding, Mammy. People don't have to get married anymore because they've a baby on the way but for the record, I'm not in the family way thanks very much. So, people can talk all they like.'

'Aisling, have you something in your mouth?'

'No, of course not.' She swallowed the bite of her sandwich.

'Aisling O'Mara, your nose grew then so it did. And don't you come crying to me when you're a tenner short and your dress won't fit.'

Aisling scowled and dropped what was left of the sandwich back on the plate. 'Look, Mammy, I've got to go.'

'Well, don't let me hold you up. I'm only your mammy after all.'

Aisling rolled her eyes; spare her the poor, hard done by Mammy act. 'Bye-bye, enjoy your watercolour painting class.' As Aisling hung up, a thought popped into her head. She hoped Mammy wasn't after doing a self-portrait as a wedding present for her and Quinn. Jaysus! Her grinning down at them as they lay in their marital bed would give her nightmares and be the end of any riding. She wrapped herself inside her coat and picked up her bag, her eyes alighting on her book, open to where she'd left it on the coffee table the night before. Roisin had given her it for Christmas and she'd managed to read two more chapters before her eyes had grown heavy. The next thing she'd known, Moira was nudging her telling her to feck off to bed because she couldn't hear the tele over her snoring. What she wouldn't give to clamber back into bed now with a nice cup of tea and a plate of hot buttered toast. Oh, to while away the afternoon with her book. Her idea of bliss. Give her that any day over an upmarket spa, she thought as she headed out the door making a mental note to self to get Moira to start giving her weekly facials and to be sure to double check her manicurist appointment and, somewhere in between her list of one hundred and one things to do, she'd have to find time to see her fiancé.

Chapter 4

♥

Noreen

Noreen Grady's knitting needles clicked and clacked to a rhythm of their own. She was knitting a jersey for the sick babies in Africa. It was a vibrant affair of yellow and orange because she thought the little baby who wore it would like the bright, cheery colour. Another twenty minutes and she'd have it done. Then she could put it in Kathleen's box along with the others waiting to be shipped off to the hospital in South Africa. Agnes, Margaret and Kathleen, with whom she met each Friday here at Alma's Tea Shop to catch up on all the week's news while they all did their bit for those less fortunate than themselves, were also clacking away. Once the jerseys were finished, they were going to start on hats for the little prem babies at the hospital in Cork.

Her three friends were in the midst of a whispered discussion over whether Alma's currant buns had been on the dry side and was she after putting yesterday's buns back in the cabinet? Noreen thought it quite likely. She was a business woman herself and Alma was as hard-nosed and sharp as they came, didn't miss a trick.

The jangle of the door opening brought in a whiff of cigarette smoke from a smouldering fag end on the pavement outside. The jangling was a sound that always took her back to her own days behind the counter. It was a familiar tinkle, signalling someone was in need of something, and had always seen her put down the tins she was restocking the shelves with or whatever she'd been busy doing to look up and say a cheery hello. Alma could do with injecting a little more of the cheer into her greeting, she thought looking at the po-faced woman as she wiped out her cabinets. Noreen missed running her little corner shop. It hadn't just been a place to get your essentials it had been a hub for hearing all about what was happening in the village of Claredoncally where she'd lived for all of her married life.

Things were changing here though, she thought, as a truck rumbled through the narrow street outside. The windows rattled and her seat juddered. Oh, they were changing alright and not for the better in her opinion. Her shop was a Spar now. A Spar! Who'd have thought. All the personality and personal service she and her late husband, Malachy, God rest his poor departed soul, prided themselves on, leached from it by a generic chain store. It had been their child that shop. They'd poured the love and energy left over from not being able to have a baby of their own into it. And it had been enough too, almost. The hole still left by the absence of children's laughter had been filled by Emer. It had broken her heart to take down the sign they'd hung over the door some fifty years earlier almost as much as it had broken her heart when Malachy passed. But passed he had and practical she had to be. She was no longer able to manage the stairs to the cosy home they'd made above the shop. The time had come to put her feet up.

The price for the premises dangled under her nose by the conglomerate was the sort that didn't come along twice and so, despite her misgivings at accepting, common sense had been the order of the day. She liked to think Malachy would have approved, or at least understood. The business and home didn't fit anymore with him gone. It had become too much to manage for a widow woman on her own.

It had been an adjustment to move into the brand new, little house she'd had built on an empty square parcel of land three streets down from the main road of Claredoncally. It was quieter for one thing, especially with the double glazing on the windows. There was something to be said for a few mod cons and creature comforts in one's old age though, and her chest at least hadn't missed the damp beginning to seep through the walls of the bathroom in the rooms above the shop.

She hoped Malachy was having a good long rest up there with the angels. He deserved it, he'd worked hard all his life. Never harder than when they were young. Fresh out of the high school they'd both gone off to earn their keep at the local fish factory, saving what pennies were left from their board to go toward their wedding and their dream of buying Mr Brosnan's corner shop when the time came. Sure, everybody had known the old man was going doolally from the way he kept handing out too much or too little change and talking about the oddest of things, yes it had been high time he sold up. And, when he did, they'd been ready and so the little corner shop in charge of servicing the village of Claredoncally had become Grady's Convenience Store.

She'd felt such pride in the place and had never tired of turning the sign hanging in the window from closed to open. There was no greater satisfaction than being one's own boss in life. She smiled to herself, recalling how she and Malachy used to laugh about how nice it was to finish their days work with him not smelling like a mackerel, her a herring. And, they never ate fish ever again except when they had to, as good Catholics, on a Friday.

'*Noreen,*' there was irritation in Kathleen's voice and Noreen looked at her blankly, coming back from her reminiscing to ask her old friend to repeat what she'd said.

'Sure, you were away with the fairies. I asked you about this big do in Dublin, Aggie's after telling me you're off to.'

'Oh yes, the wedding.' Noreen put her knitting down; she'd been trying not to think about it. She looked at the teapot on the table. Another strong cup of tea was in order if she were to relay this tale. 'Any chance of more hot water, Alma,' she called. Alma nodded, muttering something under her breath as she put her cloth down and set about filling the kettle.

'Can I interest you in another currant bun each? They'd go down a treat with your tea,' she asked, waddling over and setting the water down.

'Sure, you'd need something to wash them down. Stick in your gullet those would,' Agnes muttered.

'What did you say, Aggie?' Alma said, wincing. 'My knees aren't half giving me bother today.' Her expression was a grimace as Agnes shook her head but didn't bother to repeat her sentiment. 'It's no good for my arthritis all this standing about. I'm too old for this lark.'

'Giving the buns, away are you?' Margaret ignored her moans and groans never pausing in her purl stitch.

'You want to take a leaf out of my book, Alma, and retire,' Noreen offered up.

'Sure, and how am I supposed to afford the likes of putting my feet up when Margaret here would have me giving away my earnings. She'd have me in the poor house.'

'Ah, get away with you. I'll have a bun but heat it up would you and for the love of God put some butter on it,' Agnes said, and Alma scuttled off before she could change her mind. Noreen topped up the pot and while she waited for the tea to steep, she filled her three friends in on the invitation she'd received a few days ago.

'So, the wedding is at the family's church there in Dublin and the reception is to be held at the restaurant her fiancé owns. And you'll be accommodated at the guesthouse your grand-niece or whatever she is runs,' Kathleen clarified. None of the women had been able to come up with an appropriate title for the daughter of a cousin either so grand-niece it was.

Noreen nodded.

'Well for someone who won't have to lift a finger for a few days you don't look very happy about it all,' Agnes pointed out.

'Is it Emer?' Kathleen asked, studying Noreen's face, knowing the family history. 'Will she be there?'

Noreen's lips tightened at the mention of her sister's child, Emer, who she'd taken under her wing. Emer, who she'd treated like a daughter. Emer, who'd betrayed her.

'Yes,' she nodded. 'She will.'

Chapter 5

♥

'Aisling, eat something would you,' Leila said, watching her friend play with her food across the table. She'd have preferred to go to Quinn's for lunch but Aisling had suggested they come here to Holy Moly the self-proclaimed salad gurus of Dublin instead. The only reason Aisling wanted to steer clear of her fiancé's bistro was because she knew he'd ignore her dietary requirements and present her with a plate heaped full of her favourite, bangers 'n' mash. Quinn, Aisling had confided in Leila, did not make her efforts to lose weight before the wedding easy. Aisling, Quinn had confided in Leila, was a nightmare when she was hungry and he wished she'd buy a dress in the next size up and be done with it.

'I don't like chickpeas.' Aisling speared one viciously with her fork before eying it as though it were a cyanide pill.

'Then why did you order a Moroccan salad?'

'Because it sounded exotic but healthy. I'd have rather have had what you're having but I didn't want all the garlicy, mayonnaise stuff. Perhaps I should have asked for it without the dressing.'

Leila had chosen the chicken Caesar salad and was thoroughly enjoying it. 'Yes, but if you don't have the dressing, it doesn't *taste* like a Caesar salad which defeats the purpose.

Here have some croutons.' She flicked a couple over onto Aisling's plate.

Aisling crunched on them and then helped herself to a few more until Leila thwacked her with her fork. 'Leave some for me.'

'Sorry.' It wasn't fair Aisling lamented. Leila was a petite blue-eyed blonde who could stuff as many croutons and the like down her as she wanted and never gain a pound. Sure, all *she* had to do was sniff anything remotely tasty and it took up residence on her hips. She debated briefly as to whether she should risk one more, crispy piece of the dried bread but then decided no, she'd crack on with what they'd come here to talk about. It would take her mind off eating, for the interim at any rate. 'I don't want anything to be the same, Leila. Not one single thing. You know that don't you?'

'As when you were planning to marry Marcus the Fecker McDonagh? Yes, Aisling, you've mentioned it more than once.'

'Exactly.' She waved her fork at her friend and the chickpea fell back into the bowl. 'I'm not shopping at Ivory Bridal Couture this time around either because I think it jinxed me the last time.'

'The only thing jinxing you was that ex-fecker of a fiancé of yours and good riddance to him.'

Aisling agreed with the latter sentiment. 'I know, if Marcus hadn't jilted me then I wouldn't have gotten together with Quinn but I'm not taking any chances, Leila. I've booked us an appointment at Bridal Emporium on Friday afternoon, which, as you know is a one-stop shop for the bride, the bridesmaid, and the mother of the bride, then on the Saturday we've an appointment at Hair She Goes to figure out how we're all going to be wearing our hair. I texted you the times, did you get it? It's going to be a busy weekend.'

Leila held a hand up. 'You're speaking way too fast, Aisling. Slow down and take a deep breath.'

Aisling knew she was beginning to sound like one of the Chipmunks whenever she talked about her wedding but she couldn't help it. She inhaled slowly through her nose and out through her mouth like Roisin had showed her. It helped a little.

Leila carried on. 'It is going to be busy, but sure, it's great Rosi's coming over to be part of it all.'

'Yes, she can help me keep Mammy in line. I think Mammy's feeling a little left out of things but one of the reasons I chose Bridal Emporium was so she'll be occupied choosing her mammy of the bride outfit instead of focussing on my dress. Do you remember, Roisin's?'

'I do.' Leila said sobering at the memory of the white crochet toilet dolly dress, Roisin had been lumbered with in order to keep her mammy happy. Then, thinking of Maureen O'Mara sitting all alone in her apartment in Howth when she could be joining them for lunch added, 'Poor Maureen. You should have brought her along with you today, Aisling. She could have been brought up to speed with all the plans.'

'There's not shutting her out and being a complete roll-over, Leila.'

'True.'

They giggled. 'Anyway, enough about Mammy. I want a completely different style of dress this time and need you there to be honest with me but in a nice way, okay?' She pinned her gaze on her friend, already hearing Moira in her head, *'It makes you look like a milk bottle with a red top and freckles, Ash, get it off.'*

Leila raised two fingers to her temple, 'I promise to do my best, Brownie's honour.' Her smile however drooped at the realisation Aisling's insistence everything be different this time around meant she could say goodbye to the beautiful bridesmaids' dresses previously picked out.

Aisling registered the disappointed look on her friend's face. 'I'm sorry, Leila, I know you look gorgeous in soft blue but we're going for a whole new look for all of us. I don't want any reminders, okay?'

'Fair play to you, although they were divine. You don't have to pay for mine either. You're spending enough as it is and, speaking of money…'

Were they? Aisling thought finding the topic distasteful.

'I am keeping a running total of your expenditure, here.' Leila produced a notebook in which was a handwritten tally of columns with deposits put down and a note as to the balance and when it was due. She pushed it toward Aisling who gazed at it blankly before sliding it back to Leila.

'It's a good idea to check-in with this regularly, Ash. So you don't get any nasty surprises.' She snapped the book shut. 'It's amazing how costs for a wedding can escalate and these days bridesmaids don't expect the bride to cover their dresses.'

Aisling had no choice but to spring for Moira's dress and as such it was only fair she did the same for Roisin, who wasn't cashed up either. As for Leila, she was grateful to her for coming to the rescue with the organising of her day on such short notice. The dress was her way of saying thank you to her friend. 'I want to.'

'Well, I appreciate it, Ash, but promise me you won't go overboard alright? You're the star of the show. And we don't want anything short either, alright? Or, we'll all have fecking goosebumps in the photographs, and can we have a cape or jacket of some description so we don't freeze our arses off? I saw some horrendous photos of a winter wedding the other day where the bridal party was all lined up with the bridesmaids' headlights on full beam. Imagine passing it around the family?' She shuddered.

Aisling grimaced. 'Uncle Colm would love it! He'd probably ask if he could have the negatives.'

Leila laughed. She'd been targeted for a kiss from Uncle Colm on the dance floor at Roisin's wedding reception. 'And, are we still on for next Saturday night, too?'

Aisling nodded although she could do without it, to be honest. A hen night was at the bottom of her list of priorities but Moira had insisted on organising it and with Roisin coming to stay for the weekend, there was no getting out of it. 'Yes, and I've told Moira I will not be wearing an Alice band with glittery purple willies bobbing about on it, or carrying a blow-up doll called Seamus around town like she was planning last time around. I said we're all older, and wiser and I'd wear a veil at a push.'

'I don't blame you.' Leila smiled, knowing Aisling could say what she liked to Moira. It would make no difference and she'd organise exactly what she wanted regardless of her sister's wishes. She was glad because to be frank, Aisling was so tightly wound she could do with letting her hair down and having a little fun.

'How's Bazzer? He's definitely on board to do the photographs isn't he?' Aisling grinned across the table. He was in demand for his photography skills but thanks to Leila he'd fitted their date in and offered a discount. Leila had told her Bearach didn't come cheap, even with the discount, and she shouldn't feel obligated to use him because she was dating him. He didn't expect them to. Aisling had barely listened to her. She was focussed only on the fact he was one of the best in the city. Her justification for using a top gun at his game was the discount he was going to give them.

Leila scowled at her. '*Bearach* thank you, is grand. And don't you dare call him Bazzer on the day or he'll take loads of unflattering pics and still charge an astronomical fee. Repeat after me Bearach.'

'Bearach.' She followed it up with a whispered, 'Bazzer.' And got a kick under the table.

'Sorry, I can't seem to help myself. I don't know why because he doesn't look like a Barry.'

'Because he's Bearach.'

'Yes, but he might as well be seeing as it means Barry.'

'What's wrong with Barry anyhow?' Leila frowned popping a piece of chicken in her mouth.

'Do you Leila take the Bazzer?'

Leila couldn't help herself, she laughed. 'Don't make me laugh when I'm eating. I could choke and, alright, I get your point but we're hardly about to march down the aisle. And he's grand, thank you. Although I did want to ask your advice about something.' She noticed Aisling's gaze was fixated on the remainder of her croutons once more and she quickly forked them up along with the rest of her salad.

Aisling waited patiently for her to swallow, lamenting the loss of the croutons as she watched Leila chew.

'Bearach's asked me to go down to Connemara to meet his parents and I don't think it's a good idea.'

'Why not? Connemara's one of my favourite places in Ireland. It's beautiful.'

'I know that but, Aisling,' Leila voice had the intonation of an exasperated parent trying to explain something to a small child. 'Meeting your boyfriend's parents is akin to announcing your serious about their son and I'm not sure I am.'

This was news to Aisling, but then she had been self-absorbed of late.

'But you said everything was grand.'

'No, I said *he's* grand.'

Aisling studied her friend. She knew the signs well. As soon as the fellow she was stepping out with began to make noises about moving things along in their relationship, Leila got cold feet. 'I think you should go.'

'You do?'

'Yes. You need to take his invitation at face value and not analyse it. What do I always say to you?'

'Analysis is paralysis.' Leila recited; a good student.

'Go and enjoy the opportunity to sample the delights of Connemara. Spend some time with his family who are probably very nice people keen to get know the woman who's been spending time with their son. The only person reading more into the invitation, is you.'

Leila smoothed the serviette she'd unwittingly been folding. 'You're right. Thanks, Ash. You know if you ever get tired of running O'Mara's you'd make a grand counsellor.'

Aisling smiled. She was good at helping other people see things clearly. Unfortunately, it was a life skill which didn't extend itself to her own life. She didn't dwell on this though as Leila retrieved the wedding file from her bag and, pushing her plate to one side put it on the table. She was all business now, flicking through the various pages of notes and pictures clipped inside until she came to what she was looking for.

'I wanted to know what you thought of these themes for the table settings.' Leila slid the folder toward her friend and Aisling began to flick through the various cuttings of different ideas filed and clipped inside it.

'They're all gorgeous. You know me so well,' she sighed, pausing over one particularly lovely idea with pinecones, lots of flickering tealight candles and white hydrangeas 'This one's lovely, simple but elegant. Perfect for a winter wedding. What do you think?' Her expression darkened, 'Do you think the hydrangeas would set Rosi's hay fever off? And what if one of Mammy's eejity brothers gets drunk and knocks the candles over?' She began to chew at her thumbnail as she was assailed with a high drama, action packed vision, whereby Roisin was bent double with the sneezes and her uncles were running about the place brandishing fire extinguishers like they were trained assassins. 'Do you think the candles might be a recipe for disaster?'

'Ash, calm down. Remember your mantra, breathe. It's your day and Quinn's. You should have exactly what you want and not be worrying about anyone else. Get your thumb out of your mouth, would you. If you start biting your nails now, you'll have to have falsies put on.'

Aisling dropped her hand. 'You're right.' She took a calming breath as instructed. 'It's my wedding and I can have what I want.'

'And Quinn's,' Leila corrected.

'Yes, yes, his too. Can I take this with me to show him?'

'Of course you can.'

Aisling unclipped the picture and folded it in half before sliding it into her bag. 'Where are you at with securing the carriage?' She wanted to sit inside a horse drawn carriage and wave to the commoners like the Princess Diana and even yer Fergie one had. She'd been practising her wave in the bathroom mirror.

'I'm in talks with Fergus Muldoon. I've put a lot of work his way in the past so he should come to the party despite the short notice and give us a good price.'

'Grand, thanks, Leila. Can you ask him to make sure the carriage looks as much like a pumpkin as possible? Oh, and I don't want any mangy horses off the estate either.'

'I will. Sure, you'll have a fine pumpkin carriage drawn by dancing white horses. You'll be Cinderella on the way to meet her prince.'

Aisling smiled liking the analogy. Quinn was her Prince Charming and she would live happily ever after – she'd make damned sure of it even if it was the death of her.

Chapter 6

♥

'Aisling O'Mara, the woman who has not only broken my heart but shattered it into a million tiny pieces!' Alasdair flounced forth as Aisling burst in through the door of Quinn's eager to escape the cold.

It was no good her being cold when she was trying to lose weight because it made her want to stuff things down like stodgy, rib-sticking dinners followed by creamy rice pudding, with a dollop of Mrs Baicu's jam to sweeten it. Ah Jaysus, her mouth was already watering.

'The Cathy to my Heathcliff. Are we destined to always be kept apart?' Alasdair began to hum Kate Bush's *Wuthering Heights* his hands fluttering to his heart.

Aisling laughed as she unwound her scarf, 'Get away with you. It's freezing out.'

His voice returned to its normal cadence as he held his hand out, 'Here let me take your coat.'

She unbelted it and divested herself of it, passing the coat to him along with her scarf. He draped them over his arm. 'Thanks. The fire looks lovely.' Her expression was wistful as her eyes drifted across the restaurant to the fireplace aglow with dancing orange flames. Several patrons were basking in its warmth, enjoying the ambience it created as they savoured their desserts.

'Well, why don't you pull up a chair and put your feet up for a while, Aisling – I have no idea how your careen about town the way you do in those shoes.' He looked pointedly at her black Miu Miu's with their impossible high heels which meant she came up to Alasdair's chin. Without them she'd be navel gazing. 'Although, I have to say they are gorgeous.'

'Thank you, they are my favourites.' It was a half-truth. She loved all her designer shoes and had spent a small fortune collecting them over the years. They were all her favourites. 'And I'd love to curl up over there.'

'With a glass of vino,' Alasdair said enticingly. 'A cheeky little red perhaps?'

'Oh, you're tempting me.'

'That's the idea. You know you're my favourite redhead.'

'Ah now, there's a fib if ever I heard one. The fella you were seeing last month, what was his name?'

'Jamie.'

'Yes, Jamie. I heard you telling him he was your favourite redhead.'

'Ah but the fellas come and go, you, Aisling, my one true love, you are a constant.'

'Flatterer.' She grinned. 'And I can't sit and drink wine not when I've a wedding to be organising. Speaking of which, is he back from the suppliers?' She inclined her head toward the kitchen.

'He is, you'll find him out the back prepping for tonight's service.'

She smiled her thanks and passed through the restaurant saying hello to Paula whose ponytail was flicking about the place as she cleared tables. A smattering of diners were dotted about the space lingering over their lunches even though they probably should have been back at the office long since. Her stomach rumbled at the lingering hearty smells and spying a man tucking into a bowl of Irish stew she fought the good fight not to pick up a piece of the crusty bread on the plate next to it. Oh, how she'd love to dunk it into his stew! *Think of your dress, Aisling. No pain, no gain. Cindy Crawford, Cindy Crawford,* she added for good measure. She pushed through the doors into the kitchen and narrowly missed being hit by a flying piece of carrot. 'Hey, watch it!'

'Sorry, Aisling,' the sous-chef, Tony said. 'I was aiming for him.' He pointed to Quinn who was laughing.

'What are you to up to?' she asked taking in the scene.

Quinn put down the piece of potato he'd been about to fire and held his hands up. 'Truce?'

'Truce, so long as I don't have to sweep it up.' Tony pointed at the handful of chopped vegetables on the floor.

Aisling could see she wasn't going to get an answer, besides it was obvious the pair had been having some sort of food fight and irritation pricked at her. Here she was run off her feet organising their wedding and yet Quinn had time to arse about in the kitchen. 'You need a shave, Quinn Moran,' she said, a little snappier than she'd intended as she noticed his blond whiskers glinting in the light.

He didn't notice her pique and homed in for a kiss causing her to squeal.

'You're all prickly!'

Quinn grinned wolfishly before rubbing his chin on her cheek.

'Get off, you'll give me a rash,' she said, pushing him away.

He admitted defeat and headed to the sink to wash his hands. 'You're a hard woman so you are, Aisling O'Mara. Now then, is this a social visit or an official wedding visit?' He didn't know why he was asking given he knew the answer already. Aisling lived and breathed the wedding – it was all she'd talked about since they'd gotten engaged on Christmas Day. Truth be told she was driving him a little mad because you'd think they were Posh and Becks the way she was carrying on. He understood her insecurity where the wedding was concerned although it rankled she couldn't shake the anxiety her eejit-ex

Marcus had left her with. She should be able to move past what had happened because she knew he'd never do anything to let her down. For whatever reason though, she couldn't and had insisted on a ridiculously tight window of time in which to organise their day. It wouldn't have been so bad if she was happy to have a low-key affair but she wasn't, she wanted the works. He turned the tap off and picked up the towel, drying his hands off as she answered.

'I'm here on official wedding business,' Aisling said, rummaging in her bag and pulling out a piece of paper. She didn't ask whether he had time to take a look at the photograph because if he had time for horsing around with Tony, he had time to help her make an important decision. 'Here, have a look at this. I've come from lunch with Leila and she showed me some fabulous ideas for table settings but this was the one I liked the best. What do you think?'

She waited, eager for his response, while he looked at the picture.

'A wise man agrees to everything,' Tony said going back to dicing his carrots.

It was a sentiment Aisling had to agree with.

However, it would seem Quinn wasn't feeling wise because instead of the expected, 'It looks great, Ash, go for it,' she was waiting to hear he pulled a face and said, 'It's a bit, you know?'

'What?'

'I don't know,' he shrugged, already sensing this was not going to go down well, but it was too late now. 'A little over the top, I guess.'

Aisling snatched the paper back inspecting it. She couldn't see what was over the top about it. It was beautiful was what it was.

'Sorry, Ash, but you wanted my opinion.'

She hadn't. She'd wanted his agreement. 'Well what did you have in mind then?' She couldn't help the belligerent air creeping into her voice.

'Something laid back, simple I suppose.'

'Yes, that's all well and good, Quinn, but you're not giving me any examples, are you? I mean do we even bother having a head table or are you talking a picnic blanket on the fecking floor.' Her pitch had amped up several notches. 'Or, you know we could go the full hog and do a Pam Anderson, Tommy Lee job and wear our swimsuits and head off to the beach.'

'Bit cold, don't you think?' Quinn tried to make light of it. He didn't get where she was coming from. He was sure if she had longer to organise their nuptials, they'd be saying 'I do' in a castle and she'd have him in a purple suit like the one your man Becks wore on his big day. He'd seen the shiny photos thanks to his mammy having shoved the *Hello* magazine under his nose. She'd laughed and said if he wasn't careful his bride-to-be would have him decked out in similar gear and had he any thoughts on getting the highlights done because they looked ever so well in the photographs? No, he had not, he'd replied, failing to see the humour because it was all a bit too close to home. He risked a look at Aisling, she hadn't cracked a smile. 'Ash, don't you think you're getting a little carried away.'

Tony's chop, chop, chopping picked up pace and he kept his head down. Aisling wished he'd disappear and as the door burst open and Paula walked through her arms laden with dirty dishes, she wished she could click her fingers and make both her and Tony disappear. She didn't want the staff gossiping about her and Quinn. She took a deep breath.

'I'll get back to Leila and see if we can find something plainer.'

Quinn backtracked. 'No, don't do that. I want you to be happy with everything. It's grand so it is and sure, I'm a fella, what do we know about table settings and the like?'

The tightening in Aisling's chest eased as he offered her the olive branch. She took it.

'We'll find something in between,' she said, finally smiling. Quinn grinned back, pleased to have sidestepped an argument. Aisling made her excuses to leave saying she was needed back at the guesthouse and as she kissed him goodbye, she penned one of her letters to self.

Dear Aisling,

I'd like some advice please on the best way to tell my fiancé that the pumpkin shaped carriage I've my heart set on to take me to the church on our wedding day looks likely to be in the bag. I'm asking because he seems to have his heart set on a low-key day and there's nothing low key about a horse and carriage.

Yours faithfully,
Me

Chapter 7

♥

Noreen

Noreen looked in the mirror of the fitting room. Shopping had been much more enjoyable when she was young. Mind there wasn't much money for shopping back then. Her mammy had made most of her clothes when she was a youngster and Noreen had been a dab hand with the sewing machine too. She'd even made her own wedding dress, repurposing the fabric from her mammy's gown into a modern style with a bolero jacket. Everybody had said she looked a picture. The old singer machine their dear mammy had sat hunched over until her eyes were no longer up to the task had gone to her. Rosamunde her younger sister had not objected but then she'd had a hard time putting so much as a pillow case together the year they'd done home economics! She conjured up an image of herself on her wedding day. The memory of how she'd nearly skipped up the aisle to stand next to her Malachy, so tall and handsome in his suit never failed to make her smile. How full of hopes and dreams for their future they'd been!

Life's not worth living if you don't have dreams when you're young Noreen often thought. She'd been heard to remark on occasion too that this was what was wrong with the youth of today. They had no oomph, no spark, worst of all no ambition.

She'd seen spark in Rosamunde's daughter Emer's eyes from a young age and she'd found a kindred spirit in her niece. She'd felt back then, Emer would grow up to do great things and she closed her eyes for a moment remembering.

***

1961

'Here she is then.' Rosamunde pushed open the door to the shop, her oldest daughter Emer carrying her overnight bag by her side. 'Sure, you're a saint, Noreen.'

'Not at all.' Noreen straightened, her hand automatically going to the small of her back to ease the ache always lodged there from bending over. She'd been tidying the morning papers and the counter display while it was still quiet. 'Sure, I'm in need of someone to help me in the shop today what with Uncle Malachy away off to Galway for the races.' Malachy wasn't much of a betting man and she counted her blessing he wasn't a drinker like poor Bridie McAuley's husband, Tom, but he did like a flutter at the summer gee-gees and who was she to begrudge him that? 'Are you up to the job, Emer?'

'I am, Aunty Nono.' The little girl beamed at her. Emer had called her Aunty Nono when she was a tot and it had stuck. The two smiled at each other complicit in their understanding that no money would exchange hands but that Emer would be allowed to choose from an assortment of sweets to take upstairs later to munch on while her aunty carried on where they'd left off reading *The Water-Babies* the last time she'd stayed.

'Well, one less gives me a break, fives an odd number so it is. It's always four against one. Mammy told me to have another, even the number up or otherwise they'd be at each other day and night. She was right too.' She realised who she was babbling on to. 'Sorry, Noreen, that was thoughtless.'

'Ah, you're grand.' Noreen brushed the comment away although the casualness with which her younger sister spoke of having children stung. How many tears had she shed month after month since she got married? Rosamunde could be a tactless mare. Sure, she'd have been happy with one baby to bounce on her knee let alone five. Children though were a blessing the good Lord hadn't seen fit to bless her and Malachy with. It was something she'd grappled with and it had tested her faith but she was a good Catholic and, in the end, she'd listened to Father Michael who said God always had his reasons for doing what he did. He'd simply chosen a different path for her and Malachy, and it was up to her to steer them down it. She'd looked at things differently after that because her life was full of blessings. She had Malachy, they had their shop, and she made her mind up that God had bequeathed them the role of watching out for young Emer. It was a role she took seriously, very seriously indeed.

'Well,' Rosamunde said. 'I'd best be getting off home, I've a million and one done things to do and you know how useless Terry is. The last time I left him in charge on a Saturday, I got home and he'd tossed a sheet over the kitchen table and made it into a tent for the children. But, had he washed a dish or made a bed? No, he had not.'

Again, Noreen warded off the sting of her sister's words. Rosamunde didn't mean anything by it, she adored Terry as she adored her Malachy. He would have been the sort of dad who'd make a tent with a sheet over the kitchen table, too. She watched the way he was with Emer and it was bittersweet at times knowing he'd have made a grand daddy. She remembered herself. 'Here, Rosamunde, before you go, take one of these for the others.' She held out the jar with the lollipops and her sister smiled, 'You spoil them, Noreen, but I won't say no. One of them stuck in each of their gobs will give me some peace so it will.'

Her sister left and Noreen and Emer looked at each smiling. 'Now then, I've a box of tinned food needs putting away, do you think you can manage that, Emer?'

'I do, Aunty NoNo.'

'And then we'll have a bowl of soup and toast for lunch. How does that sound?'

'Grand, Aunty NoNo.'

Noreen's heart filled as she set the little girl her task and when Mrs Bunting bustled in wanting her order of bread and milk, she fussed over Emer exclaiming she was certain she'd grown this last while and wasn't she a good girl helping her aunt so.

Noreen had puffed up proud as she would have if Emer had been hers.

***

The knock on the fitting room door, startled her back to the present and it took her a moment to reconcile the reflection in the mirror with the same woman who used to cherish those times with Emer forty years ago, now.

'How are you getting on, madam?' There was an edge of concern in the woman's voice and Noreen realised she'd been lost in her thoughts far longer than it should take to say yay or nay to a dress.

'I'm grand.'

'Is the size right, madam?'

'It is.'

'And does the jacket go well with it?'

'It does.'

'I'll leave you to it then, shall I?'

'Yes, please.'

Noreen smoothed the shiny royal blue fabric and sighed. She'd had a slim waist once, a girlish waist but look at her now.

'Put silk on a goat and it's still a goat,' she muttered deciding she might like the dress better in green. She wondered if the jacket the sales assistant had picked out came in green, too.

Chapter 8

Roisin followed her mammy through the car park, the sting of raindrops hitting her face despite her having pulled the hood of her coat up. The flight had been bumpy and she was feeling a little green around the gills.

'You'll be grand now you're back on solid ground, Rosi,' Maureen said, slowing her pace, 'So then, was your boss man alright about you having a Friday off?'

'He was, Mammy.'

'Will you be seeing Shay while you're here.'

'I hope so. It's not going to be easy finding time around everything Aisling's got planned.'

'Ah well, I'm sure you'll manage. And what's on Noah's agenda for the weekend?'

Roisin pulled a face. 'Colin will be taking him out and showing him the high life in London like he always does and Granny Quealey will be after filling him full of all his favourite foods. He'll have a grand time, so he will.'

'I'm still his number one nana though.' Maureen came to a screeching halt as she made a mental note to load Rosi up with her grandson's favourite sweets to take home with her. 'His Granny Quealey doesn't have a dog and Noah loves Pooh. Sure, he thought he was the best thing since sliced bread when

I put him in charge of picking up his doings on our walks last time he was over.'

'He did, Mammy.' Roisin was pleased her son's fascination with the number two had waned. His latest predilection seemed to be trying to talk to Mr Nibbles like Doctor Doolittle could. She'd overheard him holding a conversation with him the other day that went along the lines of, 'Mr Nibbles, do you like lettuce or spinach better?' 'Lettuce. I don't blame you. Spinach makes me want to sick-up too.' She reassured her mammy, 'And of course, you're his number one.'

Satisfied, Maureen carried on toward the grey-storied car parking building. 'And do we ask how the gerbil is?'

'Mr Nibbles is thriving, Mammy. Apparently, he prefers the lettuce leaf to spinach and sure, this will make you laugh.' She relayed the tale of how Noah's beloved gerbil had performed another of his Houdini acts when he'd been staying overnight at the Quealey house. Colin's sour-faced mother had hit the roof when she found him nestled in the cup of her bra.

'What!' Maureen shrieked, envisaging all sorts of scenarios.

Roisin laughed, 'She wasn't wearing it at the time. It was on her bed and he decided her left cup made a lovely nest to hunker down in.

'Poor little thing, he lived to tell the tale obviously.'

'He did, but Colin wasn't popular with his mother. She said she felt violated and that the bra was her best Marks and Spencer's one and she'd had to bin it. She blames him for getting Noah Mr Nibbles in the first place. You know how I felt about him having a pet initially too, but I'm used to having him about the place now and I'd miss the sound of his mad scrabbling if he wasn't there.'

They reached the car and Roisin spied the eager poodle strapped into the front seat.

'You're in the back, Rosi.'

'But I feel sick and you know sitting in the back will only make it worse.'

'Rosi, don't be awkward. I can't drive with a howling dog in the back, now can I?' Maureen unlocked the car as Roisin opened the boot, lifting her case into it. She slammed it down mumbling something about a fecking dog coming before her eldest daughter as she ducked into the backseat. The poodle looked over the seat at her and she swore if she could talk to the animals like your man Doolittle, he'd have made a na-nana-naa-nah noise and stuck his paw to his nose to taunt her. She poked her tongue out at him.

'Have you said hello to Pooh, Rosi?' Maureen swivelled in her seat and Roisin knew they wouldn't be going anywhere until she'd given the dog a fuss. She sighed and petted the top of his head; he lapped up the attention.

'It's lovely to see our Rosi isn't it, Pooh? He's been ever such a good boy after the you know what.'

Roisin assumed she was talking about his having been neutered. Hopefully that meant the end of his amorous nose diving.

'Yes,' Maureen carried on, turning the key in the ignition. 'Rosemary Farrell's taken to calling in with a packet of doggy treats for him when she pops by. They're getting on great guns the pair of them these days, so they are.'

'Pleased to hear it,' Roisin said, folding her arms across her chest as her mammy reversed out of the parking space. Mammy's hair had kinked as Roisin's was prone to doing with the wet weather and she looked from Pooh and then back to her mammy. 'Did you know, Mammy, it is a scientific fact that people begin to resemble their dogs.'

Maureen swung around in her seat. 'I do not have facial hair, Roisin, thank you very much! If that's what you're getting at. It's the women on your father's side who all have the moustaches. It's very hard to hold a conversation with your great aunty Noreen because you wind up staring at it and the more you tell yourself not to the more you find yourself doing so. You'd want to watch out because it is a scientific fact, young lady, that the facial hair gene follows the father's side of the family.'

'You made that up, Mammy, and would you watch where you're going! We nearly hit that concrete bollard.'

Chapter 9

♥

'What on earth is going on?' Roisin walked in through the door of O'Mara's dropping her suitcase down beside her as she surveyed the scene. She was still feeling nauseous from sitting in the back of the car and had spent the journey trying to focus on her breathing. She'd been tempted to get in Mammy's ear when they'd stopped at the lights and chant her childhood mantra of 'are we there yet' but as it happened she hadn't been able to get a word in which was annoying because she'd hoped she might be able, while they were on their own, to pump her for information about this mysterious man-friend of hers. She'd not said a word more since her New Year's Eve announcement and refused to be drawn on the topic. She was the proverbial closed book. Moira and Aisling had tried and now it was Roisin's turn. There'd been no chance though, Mammy had been full of the chat about the wedding and who the latest family member to announce they were coming was. Before she knew it, they were pulling up in front of the guesthouse.

Now Maureen, with a tight hold on the prancing Pooh, shut the door behind them as Roisin checked out Aisling. Her sister was red in the face and looked sweaty which was an anomaly for the time of year. Come to that so was Bronagh. She frowned, noticing they were both dressed in their normal work attire yet Moira who didn't have so much as a bead of sweat on her forehead was posed at the foot of the stairs looking like she could possibly be the niece of Jane Fonda and was about to follow in her footsteps by making her own fitness video.

'How're ye, Rosi.' Aisling made to embrace her sister.

'Get off, wait until you've had a shower. What are you three up to?' She shot a look that conveyed the same sentiment to Bronagh.

'You've heard about our friendly little competition?' Moira asked, knowing full well she had because she'd written down Rosi's bet in her trusty notebook.

'I have.' Roisin wasn't owning up to who she was backing though. Bronagh could be fierce when she wanted to be. She surreptitiously looked from the two slimming competitors to see if either of them was looking a little less full in the face. Neither woman looked much different in her opinion.

'It's ridiculous. Two grown women competing to see who can lose weight the fastest,' Maureen tutted. She was backing Bronagh all the way despite her custard cream affliction or should that be addiction? Either way she knew Aisling inside and out. Her daughter took after her Nanna Dee and not just with her colouring. When she was under pressure, you'd be sure to find her with a gob full of something she'd helped herself to from the pantry. Nanna Dee had been exactly the same. 'I suggested they come along to line-dancing with myself and Rosemary Farrell. It's exercise that doesn't feel like exercise, Rosemary says. She loves it, so she does, although between us she's not very coordinated, always turning the wrong way and sticking the wrong leg out.' Maureen gave a demonstration of her new found line-dancing skills. 'I can do it better when I've got my boots on,' she said with a final clap of her hands.

'Since when did you like Country and Western, Mammy?' Roisin asked.

CHAPTER 46

'I love Country and Western,' Maureen said. 'It always gets the toes a-tapping.'

'News to me.' Roisin shook her head. 'And what exactly are you doing, Moira?'

'Well,' Moira said, her hand resting on the bannister at the bottom of the stairs, a study of casualness in her active wear. 'Like I was saying before Mammy interrupted and gave us all her best Billy Ray Cyrus impersonation. I've decided to take on the role of personal trainer.'

'Good of you,' Roisin muttered, glancing at Bronagh and Aisling sympathetically.

It was Bronagh that piped up, 'She tried to make us pay her. Can you believe that?'

Roisin could quite believe it of her youngest sister. She took the opportunity to look at Bronagh's skirt. It was still straining across her middle but there was a possibility there weren't quite so many creases there as there'd been a month ago. She wondered if Moira might let her change her bet.

'And we told her to feck off,' Aisling added.

'Excuse me, ladies.' Moira tossed her ponytail indignantly, reminding Roisin of Black Beauty and she half expected her to whinny. She didn't but her voice did take on a braying timbre. 'This is my time.' She tapped her watch for effect. 'I could be in bed with a cup of tea and a plate of toast but I decided to get down these stairs and help you two along the road to weight loss success and do I get so much as thank you?' She looked to Roisin and her mammy expecting them to agree it was terribly ungrateful behaviour on Aisling and Bronagh's part. Roisin had already decided she wasn't getting caught in the middle and as for Maureen she gave Aisling a stingy flick on the backside as she caught sight of her giving her sister a rude finger sign.

'Don't you be doing things like that down here, Aisling. You know better than that. Sure, what would our guests think if they were to walk in and see their hostess giving them the finger.'

'I wasn't doing it at any of our guests, Mammy, and that hurt.'

'Yes, but they wouldn't know that would they?'

Roisin sighed she was home alright.

'Well, tell her to stop going on, Mammy,' Aisling whined.

'I'll bang both your heads together in a minute, so I will.'

'How's Pooh getting on, since his,' Bronagh mouthed the word, 'snip?'

'He's doing ever so well. Top of the class at puppy school. They all looked to where the puppy had a leg cocked threateningly over by the sofa.

'Pooh!' Maureen herded him out the door reappearing a moment later. It's alright,' she said. 'It was a number one, that's all. He's going through a phase of marking his territory. I think it's the trauma after the, you know what. He's feeling insecure.'

'Well you can't blame him now, can you?' Bronagh petted the dog. She was feeling a lot more affection for the fellow now he wasn't constantly trying to assault her. It was the wrong thing to do – there was life in the old dog (so to speak) yet it would seem. 'Get down, you naughty boy,' she shrieked.

'Right,' Roisin interjected. 'I want to get this case upstairs because as lovely as it is standing about in reception listening to you lot carrying on, I've a phone call to make before we head off to the bridal shop.'

'Lover boy?' Moira asked, blocking the stairs.

'If you mean Shay, then yes. He knows this weekend is all about Aisling and the wedding but I'm sure we can manage to squeeze in a catch-up. Maybe tonight; there's not much planned this evening is there, Ash?'

Aisling shook her head.

'It's not a catch-up you're after, it's a ride,' Moira said. 'A gallop around the track with your stallion,' she added lewdly.

'Moira O'Mara, have you forgotten your mammy is standing right here.'

Silence fell as a thought occurred to all three sisters simultaneously. Their eyes swung to their mammy. Could she be...? *Nooo!* they silently screamed. That would be wrong on so many counts. Moira decided to change the subject, still not allowing Roisin to pass.

'Mammy, you're not wearing those out, are you? Sure, you've worn the material across the arse so thin I can tell you what colour your knickers are. Wedding boutiques are posh places not geriatric strip joints.'

Maureen glanced down at the yoga pants she'd commandeered off Roisin the last time she'd come to stay. They were her favourites, her trusty go-tos for comfort and ability to bend, stride and lunge. Her eyes darted toward Roisin's case and she wondered if she'd packed any more. She'd try her luck later. Now though, she had a mouthy daughter to contend with. 'It's called common sense, Moira. They're very easy to whip on and off for trying outfits on, thank you, and your posh wedding shop woman won't giving a flying fig what any of us are wearing so long as we splash the cash.'

Aisling thought Mammy had a point there. The bridal shop woman, she'd gleaned from her dealings with her over the telephone, was a bit of a fecky brown noser type, she'd get on well with Patrick.

'And for your information, madam, you couldn't possibly know what colour my underpants are, because I am wearing the thing.'

Aisling frowned her mind beginning to boggle. 'What thing?'

'You know, the thing. The thing you girls all get about with.'

Her three daughters shook their heads with no clue as to what she was on about.

'The thing, the string thing that goes up your—'

'Jaysus wept, Mammy, the thong,' Moira cringed. 'Too much information!'

Roisin went pale, wondering if there was a reason her mammy had stopped wearing the underpants that came up to her chin.

Aisling, aghast, said, 'No, Mammy, it's my day and I don't want to see your arse every time I step into the changing room. You're to put some sensible knickers on before we go.'

The bickering carried on all the way up the stairs to the family apartment.

Chapter 10

♥

Madame Mullan with her gleaming blonde chignon and exquisitely cut yellow silk wrap dress was like a golden vision and Aisling had whispered this sentiment to Moira moments after they'd arrived at the Bridal Emporium. They'd received the sort of welcome reserved for royalty or Westlife as they piled boisterously in the door of the boutique but as their feet sank into the luxuriously thick pile carpet and they'd taken in their surrounds, they'd quietened down. The Bridal Emporium was the type of establishment where it felt appropriate to whisper reverently, a bit like being in church. Moira had whispered back that Madame Mullan reminded her of a giant dandelion but in a good way. Aisling wasn't sure what to make of that comment but she'd begun to feel a tad nervous at Madame's effusiveness. She was, after all, a shopkeeper, albeit a golden one, and shopkeepers were only ever *that* nice to people they thought were going to spend loads of money.

Mammy was giving her and Quinn a very generous contribution toward the wedding but even so, this place reeked of the green stuff in a way that was making her tummy jump about. Especially with Quinn making noises about house buying and the like. And was that a runway? There was a raised platform with curtains leading into the fitting rooms from which, she presumed she'd emerge. A cluster of seats were arranged in front of the stage for the bridal party to pass verdict. Aisling sniffed, detecting the hint of a floral fragrance floating on the air. Chanel No. 5 perhaps? She shook the nerves aside; she'd come this far, now was not the time to worry about her finances. She sniffed again, wondering what the odds were of Madame Mullan using the same air freshener Mammy had been doing the hard sell on lately. Anyone would think she was getting a backhander from the company the way she went on about it. Moira elbowed her. 'Don't do that.'

'What?'

'That sniffy thing you're after doing, it makes you look like a gingery seal coming up for air.'

She ignored Moira as she pondered whether she'd made a mistake coming here. She caught sight of her face, pale and slightly drawn, in the reflection of one of the freestanding gilt framed mirrors that seemed to be dotted about the place. They were all set to a flattering angle but still, she wished she hadn't. Maybe she should have gotten over herself and gone back to Ivory Bridal Couture; at least she knew what to expect there. It didn't feel right though not after last time. It would be a bit like rendezvousing with her ex. She glanced nervously at Leila who smiled back at her reassuringly and she felt a little better until Moira broke rank and made a beeline for a rack of shimmering sheaths.

'Oh, Aisling, this is gorgeous, so it is, look,' she held the wisps of soft lilac fabric up against her and had a delirious look on her face that said she was imagining herself on the red carpet, about to give her Oscars' night speech, or something like.

It was also microscopic, Aisling noted with alarm. Well not quite, but in Aisling's experience the less fabric the more expensive it was likely to be. An internal tug-o-war ensued. She wanted to march over and inspect the price tag but at the same time she didn't want Madame Mullan over there to think she was a penniless hick. She was still wrestling with herself as Moira whipped the same dress in pink and baby blue off the rack and trotted off toward the dressing room. Happy as a pig in muck.

Leila whispered in her ear, 'Discourage her, no matter how gorgeous she looks. You need to keep three things in mind. Price tag, headlights and Uncle Colm. Alright? Remember this is a winter wedding not a Maldives getaway.'

Aisling nodded obediently.

'Come on, let's check out the wedding gowns.' Leila pulled her toward the headless mannequins posed in a group of three, all draped in sumptuous silks. 'Oh, these are stunning, Ash,' she said, pausing in front of a sophisticated ivory dress that had Aisling sighing wistfully. She'd never get away with that, not with her thighs. Leila however put it more tactfully. 'Ivory's not your colour. We need diamond white or champagne would be lovely. Have you a particular style in mind?'

They both looked at the row of dresses spanning the length of the emporium. The opposite wall was devoted to the bridesmaids and the back wall catered to the mother of the bride. Aisling hadn't a clue where to start and was grateful she had her friend here to help her. 'I suppose I'd like a mermaid trumpet-style dress with lace, lots of lace.' She wondered why Leila was staring at her sympathetically and then it dawned on her. She'd described the dress she'd chosen the last time. She pressed her lips together in a grim line. 'What I should have said was I want the exact opposite of a lacy mermaid trumpet dress.'

Before they could even begin their search however, Moira poked her head through the curtains, about to be the first to strut the catwalk as she demanded everybody stop what they were doing. When she was certain she had everyone's attention she flung the curtains open and struck a hands on hip pose, one shapely leg thrust out of a split between the lilac wisps as though she had indeed stopped for a photo call on the red carpet.

Madame Mullan was a bee to honey as she took the two steps to the platform and homed in on Moira to begin adjusting the straps and pinching the dress in at the waist before looking toward Aisling expectantly.

'It's lovely, and you look a picture, Moira. But don't you think you might be a little cold on the day and that material is awfully sheer. It's going to be February after all. Madame Mullan do you have anything with long sleeves you could show Moira? In a more, erm, substantial fabric perhaps.'

Moira scowled at her sister, 'Should we wear our flannelette nighties and be done with it,' she muttered, stomping back into the fitting room while Madame Mullan fluttered off, a golden butterfly gone in search of bridesmaids' dresses in a more appropriate style.

Leila patted Aisling on the back. 'Well done you.'

Aisling mustered up a smile and began to sift through the heavy dresses on the rack. They were beautiful, all of them, but some were too fussy, some too simple. The perfect dress had yet to put in an appearance.

'Ash, what do you think of this one?' Leila asked, breaking her price tag first rule.

Aisling's breath caught at the sight of the dress her friend was holding up with some difficulty for her to see. 'It's like something from a fairy tale.'

'Fabulous isn't it? It makes me wish I was getting married so I could wear it. Look at the way it ties at the back here. Oh, I can so see you in this, Aisling.' The note of excitement in Leila's voice was catching and Aisling reached out to touch the neckline above the bodice gently.

'Are those crystals do you think?' she asked, admiring the way the light was catching them.

'They're Swarovski crystals, all hand sewn on. A divine gown. I can see you're both women of exquisite taste.' Madame Mullan had floated over to catch the tail end of their conversation. 'Shall I put it in the dressing room for you to try.'

Yes, she was a definite fecky brown noser, Aisling thought, looking at Leila who was nodding emphatically.

'You definitely want to try.'

Aisling didn't want to ruin the moment by asking how much it cost so she trailed behind Madame Mullan, nearly bumping into Moira who was dressed in her civvies once more as she exited the fitting room. 'I've several dresses for you to look at, as soon as I've hung this in the dressing room for our bride-to-be, here,' Madam Mullan directed at her and Moira nodded, more interested in the gown she had over her arm. 'Wow! That's gorgeous. What colour do you call that?'

'It's champagne,' Madame Mullan said. 'The perfect choice for madam's delicate colouring.'

'Can't wait to see you in it, Aisling.'

Aisling felt a spark of excitement at her younger sister's unusually generous words. It was a gorgeous, fabulous fairy tale dress and she couldn't wait to step into it. A little voice spoke up. She suspected it belonged to her conscience because it was telling her if she were going to be buying a house in the foreseeable future then she should check out the price before going any further. There was no point falling in love with the gown and then not being able to justify the price. She hesitated but only briefly before telling her conscience to feck off away with itself as she traipsed on into the fitting room.

A moment later Aisling found herself alone with the dress which Madame Mullan had hung up telling her she'd be back to assist her with the grand reveal in ten minutes. She fluffed off to show Moira, Roisin and Leila her suggestions in the bridesmaid department. Aisling gazed around the spacious fitting room, breathing in the subtle fragrance of flowers clinging to the air thanks to the aromatherapy diffuser on the occasional table. A pile of wedding magazines and a box of tissues were artfully arranged next to it and in the corner was a white Queen Anne styled chair with a plush red velvet seat. She clambered out of her trousers and was pleased the lighting was subtle. Otherwise she'd have been gasping at the sight of her flesh in all its bare, fluorescent glory reflected back at her, thanks to the floor to ceiling mirrors. Her sweater was halfway over her head when Mammy's voice echoed around the room.

'Holy God above tonight, Aisling, could you not have put underwear on!'

Aisling pulled the sweater off feeling her hair frizz out from the static. 'Mammy, don't shout and what are you on about? I have a bra and knickers on. Sensible, suitable ones too.'

Maureen's hand rested on her chest and her expression was one of relief as she got nearer. 'Jesus, Mary and Joseph thank God you do. It's the colour. I couldn't see it when I walked in. You gave me a terrible fright, so you did. You girls don't normally wear beige undergarments.'

'They're not beige thank you very much, Mammy, the colour is nude.' Jaysus, Mammy could be an ignoramus; as if she'd ever wear beige anything, Aisling was outraged at the very thought. 'And I chose it so my bra straps wouldn't be glaringly obvious when I tried the dresses on.'

'Yes, well nude is exactly what I thought you were.'

Aisling shook her head and mumbled, 'Give me strength,' before moving toward the dress.

'I've come to help you get into that. Moira's got your Madame one running around like a headless chicken.' She looked to where the dress was shimmering under the lights and her gasp was audible.

'Aisling, oh my word.' The hand went to the chest once more. 'It's beautiful, so it is.'

'It is, isn't it? Leila spotted it.'

'I can't wait to see you in it,' She echoed Moira's sentiment. 'Come on.' Maureen was pleased to feel useful as she carefully removed the dress from the hanger and helped her daughter into it. 'Alright now then, let's zip you up. Raise your arms.'

'Go slowly, don't pinch me.' Aisling said as her mammy began to inch the zipper up.

'That only happened the once, Aisling.'

Once was more than enough, Aisling thought wincing at the memory of the formal dress she'd insisted on squeezing into for her high school leavers dance.

'Alright so. We're a quarter of the way there, on the count of three it's time to breathe in. Alright?'

Aisling nodded assent.

'One, two, three.'

She sucked everything in with all her might but still Maureen could only get the zip halfway up. 'I don't want to force it, Aisling, and breathe out or you'll be after fainting. I'm sure it can be let out a little.'

'It won't need to be. I'm on track to have lost five pounds by D-Day.'

Maureen stepped away from her daughter in order to give her a head to toe once over. Her hands formed a steeple which she held to her mouth and she began blinking rapidly.

'Mammy, you're not going to cry, are you?'

'Not at all.' Her voice wavered in a manner that said that's exactly what she was about to do.

Aisling looked at her reflection and a smile began to form on her lips as she felt her anxiety unknot itself and float away. How could anything go wrong on her wedding day if she looked like this? Sure, she felt like a princess.

'Mammy, I love it' Her voice was quiet as she took in the sheer long sleeves and high neckline iridescent with crystals. The bodice beneath was corset styled and she held her hair up and looked in the mirror behind her so she could see the pearl beading which began at the top of the corset ribbons and finished at her neck. The heavy sateen fabric of the skirt had a lace overlay and it flowed from the waist without being full. She turned this way and that, not quite believing it was her looking back at her in the mirror.

'Aisling O'Mara, you are perfect.' Maureen sniffled, reaching for a tissue from the box on the occasional table and giving her nose an almighty blow.

Madame Mullan announced her presence, her eyes lighting up at the sight of Aisling as she made all the right noises before titivating with the fabric. Maureen was sniffling away and Madame Mullan passed her the box of tissues, well used to tearful mammies. 'Why don't you go and join the rest of the bridal party and ask them to take a seat?

Maureen gave a final sniff before doing as she was asked.

'Are you ready?'

Aisling's stomach fluttered at the thought of showing her sisters and Leila her dress and she nodded as Madame Mullan arranged her in front of the curtains before pulling the cord and opening them.

She was suddenly vulnerable as she stood under the lights. Would her sisters and best friend see what she and Mammy had seen or would they think the dress ostentatious? She knew she could count on Moira for an honest opinion. She smiled tremulously looking from one to the other. Delight and admiration was mirrored back at her and her worries settled as she enjoyed her moment in the sun. Roisin joined her mammy with the sniffling, Leila clapped her hands together and Moira got up and jumped on stage throwing her arms around her sister as she said, 'You look amazing, Ash.' It was all the confirmation she needed.

Chapter 11

Aisling sipped her champagne enjoying the sparkly, seductive flavour that was making her feel even more giddy than she already did. It was a lovely touch on Leila's part, the cracking open of a bottle of Moet to celebrate her having chosen her dress. She'd arranged the glasses to be on hand prior to the appointment with Madame Mullan who'd declined a glass even though she should be celebrating given how much Aisling was going to be spending this afternoon. Leila had even thought to bring a bottle of bubbly grape juice for Moira, a gesture which made her want to hug her, so she did. 'You're the best wedding planner in the world,' she'd gushed as Moira popped the cork on her fizz.

Now her gaze flitted to where her dress was hanging on the rack beside the counter awaiting the equivalent of a down payment on a house before she'd be allowed to take it home where it belonged. The sensible part of her brain, the part that told her nobody needed to spend that much on a dress decided to put in an appearance. But then she recalled how the dress had made her feel. It truly was a Cinderella dress and what sum did you put on a gown that made you feel like you were the star of your very own fairy story?

Would Quinn buy into her fairy tale dream or would he see pound signs when he saw her in the dress. Perhaps when she told him they were saving on the shoes he'd come around to what it cost. He could be quite thrifty when he wanted to be could Quinn. To appease him she'd wear the Prada satin pumps she'd tucked away from her first attempt at getting married. They would go perfectly and she held no fear of being jinxed where shoes were concerned, besides which, she knew she'd be hard pressed to find another pair she loved as much. So, it wasn't much of a compromise at all on her part to roll with the shoes she already had but Quinn didn't need to know that. Come to that there was no need for him to know how much this dress and the bridesmaids' dresses, once decided upon, were setting her back. Men hadn't a clue when it came to things like that anyway. Again, she ignored the niggle that given they were about to share the rest of their life together he should be privy to how much the wedding was costing them but, it wasn't as if he'd asked. When she had tried to broach things with him his eyes had glazed over as if she were doing a long and involved maths equation.

She'd been reluctant to climb out of the dress; she'd have liked to have stayed in it forever and if she'd had her way, she'd have worn it home. She'd pictured herself riding on the top of the double decker bus as it rumbled through the streets of Dublin, waving to all and sundry. But then she'd seen it was still raining outside and had changed the fantasy to her sitting in the back of a taxi with tinted windows. The windows had to be tinted because people always wondered who was behind them. She could roll them down when they were stopped at the lights and give the peasants, whoops, pedestrians, going about their normal working day a wave. Gosh, the champers was going to her head, she thought, eyeing the flute glass, knowing her cheeks had flushed pink.

That the dress was meant for her was a given. Madame Mullan had seized the sales opportunity gushing about how rare it was to find the perfect gown so quickly. Aisling fancied she could see the dollar signs in her eyes and hear her brain making a *ker-ching* sound. She'd only been brave enough to look at the price tag once she'd taken the precious dress off and had nearly fallen over at all the zeros. There was no going back though and a song had sprung to mind, Sinead O'Connor's *Nothing Compares to You*. It was now stuck in her head.

She downed what was left in her glass and dragged her eyes away from the dress. She might be sorted but nobody else was and time was a-ticking. 'Right, ladies,' she said, 'what have you found?' It was directed at her bridesmaids.

Moira was the first to hold a dress up. It was midnight blue with ruching around the waist and bell sleeves. 'I love this.'

'It's gorgeous, but does it come in a different colour. Midnight blue's not Leila's colour.' It would wash her out Aisling thought.

They all looked expectantly at Madame Mullan who shook her head with an expression that could have been about to convey the most tragic of news. 'No, it is a one-off and as such only in the blue.'

'A one-off,' Moira said, clearly liking the idea as she stroked the silky fabric. 'And I look very well in blue, so I do.'

'Moira you'd look grand in a sack and remember who's paying,' Aisling said.

Moira put the dress back.

'What about this?' Roisin pulled a gown from the rack and showed them it. She'd checked the price and it wasn't exorbitant although she hadn't worked out the times three. It was very generous of Aisling to fork out for her, Leila and Moira's dresses and she was grateful given her current financial situation. Thanks to her feckless ex-husband there wouldn't be much of a financial settlement once the divorce was finalised and with the cost of living in London, she had to watch every penny. Unlike Moira, however, she didn't want to send her sister to the poor house.

'Oh, I like that!' Leila exclaimed. Moira mooched over and gave a grunt that signalled she thought it was alright but wasn't ready to relinquish her blue dress yet.

'Mammy? What do you think?' Aisling asked. She was feeling magnanimous toward her mammy after her effusive gushing over the dress, that and the champers.

Maureen came over and stroked the maroon silk fabric. 'It's a wrap style which is very flattering so it is and none of you'd have to worry about the sucky-in knickers but I'm not sure about the colour. It would be grand on Moira and Rosi but it's on the dark side for Leila.'

'What about this, ladies.' Madame Mullan produced, seemingly from thin air, a blush velvet drop waist dress. 'And I happen to have it in each of your sizes.'

'Oh, I like that,' Maureen gushed. 'You won't catch your death in it either. Sure, you could almost get away with a spencer underneath it.'

Leila bit back her smile at the look of horror on Moira's face the mention of a spencer had invoked. 'Maureen's spoken, ladies, looks like we're trying the velvet number on,' she said.

'This one is perfect for you, mademoiselle.' Madame handed the dress to Leila. 'I shall fetch the other two from out the back,' Madame Mullan said, gliding off with the sort of speed that had Aisling checking to see if it were roller skates and not shoes on her feet. Roisin, Leila and Moira took themselves off to the fitting room to wait, leaving Maureen and Aisling alone.

'Mammy, have you seen anything you like?'

'I haven't had a chance to look yet, Aisling. I was keeping an eye on Moira for you. She's not got an ounce of common sense in that head of hers at times. It's a winter wedding but she'd be following you down the aisle in a floaty sundress if it was up to her.'

Aisling agreed with her. It was hard trying to keep everyone happy but she had her fingers crossed for the blush pink numbers. Officially, Roisin was supposed to be helping Mammy with her outfit. Aisling had put her in charge of supervising her. She'd told her big sister in no uncertain terms that Mammy wasn't to be so much as sniffing in the direction of anything silky and red. There'd be no China Beach, prostitute style dresses at her wedding, she'd declared out of earshot of Mammy while they'd sheltered from the rain under a shop awning, waiting for the bus to bring them here to the Bridal Emporium.

It wasn't working out like that though and it looked like she was going to be the one overseeing what she picked out. Maybe it wasn't such a bad thing. Roisin could have been looking for payback for the crochet toilet dolly wedding dress Mammy had talked her into wearing on her big day. 'Shall we see if anything jumps out at you then?' she asked, steering her over to the mother of the bride section. 'It would be grand if we all went home with our dresses today. I could cross that off my list then.' The handwritten list of things to organise between now and February 14 seemed never ending, even with Leila's services, because it was still up to her, to yay or nay everything and Quinn wasn't much cop.

'Would you like any assistance?' Madame Mullan simpered, with two more of the velvet dresses draped over her arm. 'I won't be a moment.'

'No, thank you, but if you could keep an eye on them in there, that would be grand.' Aisling inclined her head toward the fitting room from where fits of giggles were emanating.

'Certainly, madam.' She disappeared off in that direction and Aisling and Maureen began to mill around the mother of the bride section. The outfits on the mannequins didn't grab either of them.

'Dowdy, so they are,' Maureen declared. 'Have you seen Quinn's mam's outfit?'

'I don't think Mrs Moran's bought anything yet.'

Maureen frowned, she'd have liked a heads-up as to what the competition was wearing.

'How's she doing these days?'

'Grand, she's doing grand.' Quinn's mam had suffered a stroke the previous year but had battled her way through to recovery, although she got tired very quickly these days. Aisling explained this to her mammy. 'It's why she didn't come with us today. She didn't want to slow us down. I wouldn't have minded though.'

'It's a shame she didn't come. I'd have liked the opportunity to get to know her better. I must invite her to lunch now that we're going to be family. What will you call her?'

'What do you mean?' Aisling asked.

'Well you can hardly call her Mrs Moran after you're married, now can you? And you already have a mammy.' She pointed to her chest. 'Me.'

'I know that, thank you, and one mammy is plenty.'

'Well then, what's it going to be?'

'I'll probably call her Maeve. She keeps asking me to.' It didn't roll easily off Aisling's tongue, she'd always been Mrs Moran to her.

'That's very forward, Aisling. I didn't raise you to call your elders by their first names. Sure, do you not remember that precocious little madam from your playgroup who called her mammy, Dervla? It was all Dervla this and Dervla that. It didn't sound right coming from a child and if she'd tried it on me, I'd have sorted her out.'

'No, I don't remember, Mammy, but then I'd have only been three at the time. And I don't see the point of your story anyway, given the difference between a little girl calling her mammy by her first name and a woman in her mid-thirties addressing her mammy-in-law by her first name.'

Maureen made the face she always made when she didn't want to admit she could be wrong, but she was saved from having to say anything by the sudden sound of Madame Mullan's excited voice.

'Oh, éclatant!' she exclaimed from the fitting room.

Mammy and Aisling looked at one another although neither had a clue as to what she'd said.

'She's not French you know. I think she's from Tipperary. Listen closely, it's in the way she rolls her r's and McBride is about as French as—'

'My arse,' Aisling finished for her and Maureen nodded her agreement. They giggled, co-conspirators.

'It might be nice for your outfit to coordinate with the bridesmaids' dresses.' Aisling said moving toward the more subtle colours on the rack.

Maureen nodded thoughtfully but said, 'I like the bold colours more myself.' She homed in on a red two-piece suit. Aisling grimaced behind her back, the warm champagne fuzz wearing off at the sight of it. She knew her mammy well enough though to be tactful or she'd dig her heels in and the red outfit would be the one going home with them, purely because she didn't like being told what to do. Where Mammy was concerned, she considered it her job to be telling everyone else what *they* should be doing.

'Ah but, Mammy,' Aisling cast about quickly and whipped the first item off the rack that came to hand. Distraction was key. 'Look at this.' She waved it under her nose. 'Sure, you'd look like a million dollars in this. Oh yes, you'd look like you'd stepped out of the pages of *Hello*.' She knew Mammy scoured the magazine's shiny pages each time she went to the hairdressers.

Maureen paused and took stock of the dress Aisling was shaking about. 'Hold still for a minute would you so I can get a better look. It was simple and elegant which a woman of her height and bust size needed in order not to look fussy. She stopped stroking the red suit and moved toward the champagne coloured, fitted dress. She liked the lacy sleeves. 'Sure, it's the same colour as your wedding gown.'

Aisling looked at it properly and liked what she saw. It was elegant and classy. Not words that sprang to mind when she thought of her mammy but there was a first time for everything. She sensed she could be on to a winner if she played her cards right. 'Mammy,' she encouraged. 'The photographs would look ever so stylish with us all coordinated like and you could go big with your hat. It's a dress that needs a big hat.'

'A big hat, you say?' Maureen envisaged herself in all her champagne-matching-dress glory peeping out from under the brim of a large hat which was dipping down over one eye to give her an air of the mysterious mammy of the bride. She was sold. 'I'll try it on.'

Aisling did a mental happy dance. The icing on the cake came a moment later when Moira appeared from between the fitting room curtains, 'Are you watching.'

'Yes,' Aisling and Maureen turned their attention to the platform. The curtains opened and Moira danced her way out in front of them looking pretty in pink. She was seemingly happy with her dress as she began to sing, *Girl's Just Want to Have Fun*. Leila and Roisin were on backing.

Chapter 12

♥

Noreen

Noreen's feet were aching from the day's shopping and it was a relief to board the bus that would take her home to Claredoncally. She was always glad to see the back of the city and return to her village where people were civilised and still managed to say good morning and good afternoon to one another. Manners cost nothing but they'd been in short supply on the town's streets today. Sure, look at the driver, he'd barely acknowledged her as she'd presented her senior's card to him. Still, at least it had been a successful day's shopping and she wasn't going home empty handed, she thought, bustling her way down the aisle. She had to be careful not to knock the bag containing her new hat or the bubble wrapped and boxed Waterford crystal vase she'd chosen as a wedding gift for Aisling and whatever his name was. Her lips curved at the bargain she'd gotten.

She picked a seat halfway down the bus then immediately wished she hadn't as the woman in front of her reeked of perfume. Noreen wouldn't have been surprised if she'd been in Boots having free squirts of whatever was on offer because the smell was an eyewatering and confusing mix of flowers and spices. She shuffled across her seat so she was next to the window and placed her bags down on the aisle seat. It was done in the hope of warding anyone off who was of a mind to sit down next to her and while away the hour-long journey by chattering because she was too weary for small talk.

She glanced at the Debenham's bag on the seat beside her. Noreen missed Roches Stores where the service had been second to none but she'd done alright in its replacement department store. The sales assistant had carefully folded and wrapped her dress, with the matching jacket she'd managed to find, in tissue paper which she hoped would be enough to prevent it taking on the scent of whatever that woman in front of her had tipped all over herself. She'd gone for the green in the end because Malachy had always liked her in green.

Of course, once she'd solved the problem of what she was going to wear to Aisling's wedding, she'd had to think about shoes, handbag and a hat. There was no point letting the dress down with mismatched accessories. Speaking of shoes, her ankles felt like they were spilling over the top of hers. Fluid retention Doctor Finnegan had said when she'd been to see him about it. It happened when she'd been on her feet too long. She'd soak them in Epsom salts tonight.

A young lad slouched past her and she tsked silently. No oomph in him, no get up and go, and he could do with pulling his trousers up, too. A slovenly appearance made for a slovenly mind in her opinion. Not that she'd tell him this; she'd probably get a mouthful for her efforts because these young ones had no respect for their elders. She was wishing they could get on their way when the bus rumbled into life, slowly pulling out into the afternoon traffic. It was nearly time for the children to be getting out of school and their mammies would all be roaring off to pick them up. When did children stop walking to school? she wondered. It was no wonder this generation were a pack of lazy so-and-sos, not willing to work hard to get to where they wanted to be in life. Emer had tried to take shortcuts too and look where it had gotten her.

CHAPTER 14

The urban scenery gave way to the rocky, rugged landscape of her beloved County Cork. As she spied a rainbow stretching boldly over the fields, Noreen began to breathe easier now there was distance between herself and the city. She was in two minds about her upcoming visit to Dublin. The pace of the place terrified her but it would be nice to have a weekend of being waited on at O'Mara's and to see the family. Maureen had told her when she'd rung to confirm she was coming that it looked likely Cormac would be over from America. He'd be giving Aisling away in place of her daddy. Sad business that was, Brian getting the cancer she thought. It would be good to see Cormac again though. It had been far too long between visits. She'd always had a soft spot for him although she'd never understood why he'd upped and left and gone all that way to boot. He'd never married either which was a shame because he had a lovely nature as a young lad, very gentle. He'd have made some lucky lass a grand husband. It was a waste was what it was.

Her mind flitted back to Emer as the bus stopped to let the scraggly bunch of sheep, who'd decided they had the right of way, mosey across to the opposite field. What would she look like now? She didn't like to think about the last time she'd laid eyes on her. Words had been said that had sliced like a knife through the bond between them. Emer had been eighteen years old. She'd be in her late forties now or was she fifty? Noreen was too tired to do the sums. Rosamunde had telephoned not long after Aisling's wedding invitation had arrived. She'd said it was an opportunity to mend bridges as Emer had accepted the invite and would Noreen see her way to patching things up with her? Sure, Rosamunde had said, it was years ago and it did no one any good to hold onto grudges. What Rosamunde didn't understand, Noreen thought listening to her, was that it wasn't a grudge she held. No, not at all. It was a wound she carried with her. A wound that, even now, hurt when it was being prodded like it was being prodded by this wedding.

The bus juddered forth and the fields outside, as the rainbow had done moments earlier, faded into the background her mind spinning backwards.

***

1966

'Oh, Aunty Nono, Uncle Malachy! It's gorgeous, so it is.' Emer with a party hat perched precariously on top of her dark head held the sterling silver cross pendant up to the light. Her dark brown eyes were shining. The jeweller's box along with the birthday card they'd chosen for her were open on the table in front of the place they all thought of as hers at the table.

Noreen and Malachy exchanged pleased glances with one another. They'd made a special trip into town to Longford's the Jewellers last Friday having got young Seamus, who helped out after school with the deliveries, to man the fort for them. Off they'd tootled in their little white van that Malachy used to collect the fresh produce from the markets over in Culdoon. Noreen never had learned to drive. She'd sat enjoying the ride with her handbag perched on her knee, feeling very smart in her new green, boiled wool coat and matching hat.

Longford's was the same jewellery shop from where they'd bought their wedding bands all those years ago and Noreen had been nostalgic as she stepped over the threshold, the memories of their younger selves washing over her. Mr Longford Senior had retired but his son had taken over the family business. He was the spit of his father which was rather unnerving because it had made Noreen feel as though time had stood still inside the doors of store until she'd caught sight of her and Malachy in the reflection of the glass cabinet. Mr

Longford Junior had been happy to show them his range of necklaces, in particular those suitable for a young lady.

It had been Malachy's idea to get Emer a pendant. He wanted her to have something she could keep. Sixteen was an awkward age from memory, he'd said, turning the open sign to closed on the door of their convenience store a fortnight before. It would be nice to get her something that made her feel like a young lady and what did Noreen think to a necklace of some sort. Noreen had been proud of her husband. He was such a wonderfully, thoughtful man.

They'd spent an age pouring over the tray in Longford's wanting to get it right because sixteen was an awkward age in more ways than one, and girls these days knew what they liked.

Malachy had something in mind that wouldn't snap if Emer forgot to take it off when she was sleeping; she tended on the forgetful side he explained to Mr Longford, who told them he knew exactly the sort of thing they were after. He was the father of three girls himself he'd informed them, steering them toward a chain that while strong was not chunky. The cross they decided on was small and delicate. Emer would wear it not the other way around which was as it should be, Noreen thought. She didn't like ostentatious jewellery. Malachy had looked to her and she'd nodded that yes, the chain and the cross were just right. The pendant was placed with satisfying finesse into a pale lavender box with a silk lining and Noreen was sure Mr Longford's ears had twitched as she turned to Malachy and said, 'You know we'll have to do the same for the others when they turn sixteen don't you. We can't be seen to have favourites.' Malachy had agreed with her. It didn't need to be said that while they couldn't be *seen* to have a favourite niece or nephew it didn't mean they didn't have one.

There was a spring in both their steps as Mr Longford saw them to the door. It was at the thought of young Emer's face when she opened this special gift safely tucked inside Noreen's handbag.

'Shall we have a fish and chip supper?' Malachy had suggested as Noreen linked her arm through his and, even though it wasn't Friday and they never ate fish on any day except Friday, Noreen said that was a grand idea indeed and very nice it had been too.

Emer, Noreen saw now, was undoing the clasp. She got up from her seat. 'Here I'll help you with that. Pass me my glasses, Malachy.' He did so and she slid them on to the end of her nose instructing her niece. 'Hold your hair up, Emer.' She placed the chain around her neck and, peering through the bottom of her lens, secured it. 'There we are. Now then, let's have a look at you.'

Emer's thick waves fell back down around her shoulders and she swivelled in her seat to show her aunty the necklace.

'Sure, you look a picture, Emer,' Noreen said, feeling the smarting of tears in her eyes as she gazed at her nearly grown-up niece. Her heart swelled at what a beautiful young woman she was becoming. Malachy too, made an approving noise and Emer got up, eager to see her gift for herself. 'I'm going to have a look in the bathroom mirror.'

Noreen waited for her niece to disappear and then, winking at Malachy, she went into the kitchen to retrieve the Victoria sponge she'd laboured over. How pleased she'd been to see a deep cake emerge from the oven which sprang back when pressed as it should do. The airy sponge was filled with fresh cream and she shook the icing sugar on top, the finishing touch. She wouldn't bother with candles. They'd already had a birthday celebration at Rosamunde and Terry's with the younger children all squealing with delight over the chocolate cake their mammy had made. It wasn't long before their faces were covered in buttercream and the floor littered with crumbs as with mouths stuffed full of cake, they begged their sister to open her presents.

Emer had been keen to come back with her aunty and uncle to stay the night because she was going to catch the bus to town to go to the cinema with her friends as a birthday treat in the morning. The shop was only five-minute's walk from where the bus stopped. Noreen had been unable to resist making the sponge even though none of them needed any more cake. As she carried it out to the table, Malachy, with his sweet tooth, sat up a little straighter in his chair at the prospect of two slices of cake in one day and Emer who'd re-joined her uncle at the table clapped her hands.

'You spoil me, Aunty Nono!' She beamed up at her, her cheeks rosy with pleasure at all the attention. Noreen put the cake down and sliced a fat wedge for the birthday girl. She knew she spoiled her but she was worth the spoiling and sure, it wasn't like they had anyone else to fuss around.

Chapter 13

Aisling looked in the mirror as Tara, whose own hair was cut in a symmetrical jet-black bob a la Uma Thurman, *Pulp Fiction*, pulled her hair back from her shoulders. 'Did you bring in any pictures of what you had in mind, Aisling?' Her gravelly voice suggested she spent a lot of time standing around out the back of the salon on cigarette breaks. She had an incredible number of piercings too, which were making Aisling wince just looking at them. She glanced down the row of mirrors where she, Moira, Leila, Roisin and Mammy were lined up. 'We're like sitting ducks,' she'd heard Moira mumble as she flopped down into the chair and began to flick through a magazine for hairstyle ideas.

'I did, yes' Aisling was prepared and she retrieved her bag from beside the chair where she'd put her carefully chosen cuttings from one of the bridal magazines, Leila had given her. The first picture she held up to show Tara was of a pretty blonde woman whose hair was slicked back and piled on her head in a loose top knot, flowers entwined in her hair, and Aisling thought the effect was ethereal.

'Nope.' Tara tapped her black booted toes on the floor. 'Won't work. Your face is too round.'

CHAPTER 14

'I told her she'd look like Moonface with some sort of deposit on top of his head, you know yer funny little man from the *Faraway Tree* books, with that style,' Moira said to Tara.

Much to Aisling's satisfaction, Tara looked at Moira as though she'd flown in from Mars. She would have liked to kick her sister but she wasn't close enough and she wished she'd been quicker off the mark when they arrived at the salon; she'd have made sure Leila was sitting next to her.

'Let's see what else you've got there,' Tara said.

Aisling showed her the next one which was a half up, half down do of cascading waves.

'That's more like it.'

'Can I see.' Maureen poked her head forward trying to see past Roisin, Leila and Moira to where Aisling was sitting. She reminded Aisling of a turtle.

'Don't show her,' she hissed, but Maureen asked again only louder and Tara wasn't ready for a stand-off with the bolshie little woman down the end. Accordingly, the picture got passed down the line.

'No,' Maureen said shaking her head. 'Not with those ends of hers. Tara could you not give her a little snip.' She demonstrated with her thumb and index finger exactly how much she'd like her to take off Aisling's ends.

Tara looked at Aisling with an eyebrow raised questioningly and Aisling shook her head emphatically. 'Mammy,' she peered past her bridesmaids. 'I don't want my hair trimmed. I want it as long as possible on the day. I've been growing it, so I have.'

'But, Aisling, that's not a style.' She showed the picture to the stylist who'd drawn the short straw with Mammy on account of her being the youngest. 'Look, Polly, you can't call that a hairstyle, now can you?' Poor Polly looked like a rabbit caught in headlights. She was a girl who'd been raised not to argue with her mammy.

'Aisling, your woman there looks like she's been rolling around in the haystack prior to saying her nuptials with her intended.'

Aisling had had enough. 'Mammy, give that picture back right now. It's my wedding and my hair.'

Maureen reluctantly passed the picture to Roisin who handed it on. She turned to Polly and said, 'It's a sad day when your own daughter won't let you have a say in her wedding, so it is.'

Polly made a sympathetic sound and refused to look in Aisling's direction as she began to titivate Maureen's hair. Mercifully, Aisling saw she was distracted by Polly who was asking her what she had in mind.

'I was thinking curls, pin curls perhaps. I quite fancy the idea of looking like an olde worlde Hollywood starlet.'

'Bit long in the tooth for starlet, Mammy,' Moira said. 'Think *Golden Girls*, Polly.'

Roisin snorted. 'Curls? I told you, Mammy. It's a fact, people do begin to resemble their pets.'

'Not much hope for you then,' Moira bounced back with. 'Come to think of it, I can see the resemblance between you and Mr Nibbles. It's in the cheeks.'

It was the second time Moira missed receiving a kick on account of her sister not being able to reach.

Leila spoke up before the stylists could begin in earnest. 'We need to all have the same style obviously. Aisling what were you thinking?' She took charge.

'An updo of some description since I'm wearing mine half up and half down.'

'I'm mammy-of-the-bride,' Maureen piped up. 'I can have whatever style I want. Curls it is, Polly and don't you say another word on the subject.' She eyeballed Roisin.

Moira told Tegan, who was sensing her client might be trouble, that she didn't want anything severe. 'I was thinking more Andrea Corr so if we're to have it up think relaxed, bedhead that sort of thing,' she informed the stylist bossily.

'There'll be none of the bedhead, thank you very much, Tegan. I'll not have bedhead bridesmaids at a child of mine's wedding,' Maureen interrupted.

Tegan, Sten and Ciara, the stylists assigned to the bridesmaids, all froze and looked to Leila. She seemed the most sensible person here.

'Perhaps not bed hair but we don't have to go all out ballerina bun either.'

The three stylists all nodded and put their heads together murmuring in a hushed manner as they conferred. It was Sten who addressed them.

'I have suggested the latest updo that is storming Amsterdam.' His dark goatee quivered with excitement as he made his announcement. It looked at odds with the bleached crop of hair on his head and he was also clad head to toe in black.

Moira perked up. 'Amsterdam, well it's bound to be cool then. Go for it, Tegan.'

Leila agreed it sounded grand. Only Roisin was dubious but the Dutchman was somewhat intimidating so she wasn't about to argue. She watched as he began sorting through his trayful of hairstyling accessories with a studious expression on his face. She tried to relax in the seat but her shoulders, everything come to that, were tense and she realised her hands were in tight fists. The last time she'd let anyone near her hair it had been a disaster. Her fringe had wound up closer to her hairline than her eyebrows. It was not a look she wore well, although mercifully Shay hadn't seemed to notice. By the time it had finally grown back to a respectable length though she'd been sick to the back teeth of people talking to the expanse of forehead between her brows and fringe.

Think about Shay, she told herself and her fists unfurled; her shoulders too loosened at the memory of the night she'd spent with him. They'd met up once she'd gotten back from their successful outing to the Bridal Emporium. It had been so lovely to see him again and they'd gone for a quick bite to eat although neither of them could concentrate on the food placed in front of them as they stared into each other's eyes. A game of footsie under the table had ensued which had caused their breathing to quicken and pupils to dilate so they'd decided to skip dessert and had hotfooted it straight back to Shay's place for an entirely different and not so quick after dinner digestif.

Roisin's mouth curved into a smile she couldn't control as she recalled the way he'd propped himself up in bed on one elbow afterward, looking down at her with a softness in his eyes that made her feel like she was the most beautiful creature to ever walk the earth. It was one of those moments she wished she could bottle so she could uncork it and relive the memory on those lonely nights in London when Noah was at his father's and she found herself home alone. It was hard being in separate countries, even if they were only a hop, skip and a jump from each other. On the bright side of things though she'd be back in Dublin for the wedding in a fortnight. It wasn't too long to wait.

She realised Sten thought she was smiling at him and she noticed he'd sucked his stomach in because the slight paunch under his shirt had vanished. He was also pulling a moody pout in the mirror and looking at her in what he obviously thought was a flirtatious manner but which in Roisin's opinion gave him an unhinged look. Jaysus wept, just her luck she thought as her phone rang. The timing was perfect and she was grateful for the intrusion. She shot the Dutchman an apologetic glance. 'Sorry, Sten, I'll have to get this it could be my son or my boyfriend.' She wasn't missing the opportunity to say hello to either, even if it did make Sten's goatee quiver once more. He snorted huffily through his nostrils and began digging out bobby pins from his tray.

CHAPTER 14

Roisin retrieved her phone from her bag and upon answering it was greeted by her son's sing-song voice. He was all excited to talk to her even though she'd only been away for a night and he spent every second weekend with his dad, anyway. It was lovely, Roisin thought feeling all warm inside and refusing to meet Sten's eyes in the mirror as he began tapping the comb he was holding in the palm of his hand as if to say, time is money. She listened to Noah fill her in on how much fun he was having. He'd been to see a film with his daddy and had been allowed an enormous bucket of popcorn. He didn't stop to draw breath as he informed her Granny Quealey was cooking him chicken nuggets with no vegetables not even a carrot for his dinner. Roisin rolled her eyes, that woman and her double standards.

'Where are you, Mummy?'

'I'm at the hairdressers with Aunty Aisling, Aunty Moira, your nana and Aisling's friend Leila. We're having a practise session to see how we're going to wear our hair on the day of the wedding.'

'Mummy?'

'Yes, Noah.'

'Can you please tell Nana she needs to look like Nana for the wedding.'

The poor child was still traumatised by his nana's post-Vietnam holiday braids, Roisin thought. 'I will.'

'Mummy, can you please do it now.'

'Alright, I'll hold the phone out so you can hear me tell her.' Roisin turned to Mammy whose hair was being clipped into a round coil. 'Noah's on the telephone, Mammy, and he says you're to look like you at Aisling's wedding.' She heard a tinny voice say, 'Tell Nana I used my manners, I said please.' 'He said please, Mammy.'

'Who else does he think I'm going to look like?' Maureen held out her hand. 'Here give that to me, I'll talk to him.'

Roisin passed it over and Sten took the opportunity to tug and twist Roisin's hair into the beginnings of a bun. He told her off for tilting her head, all business now he knew there was no chance of any post-hairdo shenanigans. She was straining to listen to what her mammy was saying to her son and managed to catch. 'Alright, Noah, Nana promises there'll be no teeny-tiny plaits and no Ronald McDonald fuzzy hair either. I can't wait to see you. Mammy's after telling me she's got your suit all sorted. Sure, you'll be the grandest pageboy who ever walked up the aisle, so you will. Oh, and before I go, be sure to tell Mr Nibbles, Nana loves him too. Yes, with all her heart. I'll pass you back to your mammy now.'

Roisin took the phone back and said her goodbyes to her son. She put her mobile back in her bag and decided she'd best sit statue still from here on in. She wasn't risking annoying Sten further. She'd learned the hard way, hairdressers wielded a lot of power. Her eyes swivelled to her right but her head didn't move as she looked at Mammy in the mirror. To use Aisling's favourite turn of phrase, she was such a fecky brown noser. All that business about being sure to tell Mr Nibbles I love him. She was only saying it to get one up on Noah's Granny Quealey. If the gerbil found his way into her undergarments, he'd be history. She returned her gaze to the mirror in front of her to see what was happening to her hair. Oh, dear God, what was Sten doing? She was beginning to resemble a praying mantis. What were those pieces of hair he'd pulled loose doing? They looked like tentacles for feck's sake.

'You like it?' he asked, catching her eye in the mirror. 'Like I said, this look is hot, hot, hot in Holland.'

Well it could fecking well stay in Holland, Roisin thought, looking to her sister and Leila who were looking back at her, eyes wide with alarm.

Um, perhaps we could have something a little more traditional?' Aisling asked upon seeing her bridesmaids. 'Something a little more...' she tried to find the word she was looking for but Moira jumped in for her.

'Something more human and less insect-like would be good.'

Chapter 14

♥

Maureen was the first out of the doors of Hair She Goes and she announced to Aisling, Roisin, Moira and Leila who followed that she would head home from there. 'I've a dog who'll be desperate to see me and he'll need a walk before we paint the town red.'

'But your curls will drop in the damp sea air, Mammy,' Aisling pointed out.

'I thought of that, Aisling, I'll wear a headscarf.'

'And will you show everyone you pass on your walk your wartime ration card, Mammy.' Moira said.

'Don't be clever with me, young lady. And if you'd paid attention in your history classes at school, you'd know Ireland was neutral in the war. Besides, it wasn't me who was after looking like she belonged on a twig in the Amazonian rain forest.'

Moira couldn't think of a comeback because Mammy was right. At least middle ground had been reached and the antennae were no more. They were all relatively happy with the outcome, especially Aisling, which was the main thing, Leila had pointed out once the stylists had stepped back to admire their handiwork.

Roisin rubbed her scalp, Sten had been unnecessarily firm with the pulling of her hair and placement of bobby pins once he'd learned she had a boyfriend and there would be no riding happening once the salon closed. She, for one, was glad to be out of there.

Arrangements were made for Mammy and Leila to be back at O'Mara's later that evening for drinks, hen party games and, what Moira promised would be plenty of craic, before the limousine came to pick them up and take them out on the town. With that, the bride and her two sisters made their way back to the guesthouse.

The trio piled in through the door, giggling, a short while later. 'What's so funny?' James asked looking wary. The student manned the front desk on a weekend during the day while Evie, a fellow student, did the evening shift. She'd be on board in forty minutes at four pm. He wished it was four o'clock now. Giggling groups of women like this made him nervous.

'What do you think of our hair, James?' Moira asked, patting hers.

'You all look the same.' He'd yet to grasp that women preferred more flowery nuances.

'That's the idea,' Roisin said. 'We've been for a trial run at the hairdressers for Aisling's wedding.'

'Oh right.' James looked down at the fax he'd taken off the machine, studying it as though it might explain the workings of the female mind. He got the feeling a compliment of some sort was in order so he dug deep and came up with. 'Well, you all look grand.'

'Thank you, James,' Moira said, sensing it was as good as they were going to get. She led the way toward the stairs but before she got there, she spied the guests from room eight sitting in the guest lounge. Mr and Mrs Dunbar had arrived for a long weekend in the fair city yesterday morning for no reason other than they'd always fancied exploring Dublin. They were a chatty couple with broad Scottish accents who said things like dinnae and laddie and lassie a lot. They hailed from a village near Edinburgh and Moira had whiled away a good half hour talking with them while she herded Aisling and Bronagh up and down the stairs yesterday morning. They'd said their goodbyes when Bronagh, red in the face, had threatened Moira with bodily harm if she made her do it again. 'Hello again, Mr and Mrs Dunbar.' She paused to smile at the older couple although Mr Dunbar was oblivious given he'd nodded off in the wingback chair. The hairs of his bushy moustache were blowing with each little snore she noticed as Mrs Dunbar waved over, a cup of tea in her hand.

'Hullo, Moira. We're not long back from doing the hop-on hop-off bus tour and now we're enjoying a well-earned cup of tea, or at least I am. We've been on the go all day and we're dead on our feet.' She gestured toward her husband. 'As you can see.' The sweet-faced woman with faded red hair that curled at her chin smiled at the small group gathered in the doorway. 'Did I overhear you lassies telling the wee laddie on the front desk you'd been having your hair done as a trial run for a wedding?'

'Yes, it's my wedding, Mrs Dunbar,' Aisling said, pushing past Moira into the lounge. She wanted to go and see Quinn but she always had time to chat with their guests.

'Call me Maggie, dearie.'

Aisling smiled.

'Well, don't you look a bonnie lassie with those flowers in your hair. Now, what is it my grandson says when something's good?' She looked to her husband who gave a rumbling snore followed by a whistling sound. 'Fat lot of good you are. It'll come to me.' She screwed her bright blue eyes up trying to find the words and then her face brightened. 'Pure barry, that's it. Your hair looks pure barry, Aisling. Mine used to be that colour when I was younger believe it or not. And you two bonnie lassies are the bridesmaids I take it?'

Roisin and Moira nodded.

'Come in and have a blether about these wedding plans of yours,' she invited.

They weren't in any rush and so Roisin played mother making the tea while Aisling sat down on the sofa with Moira chatting away to the friendly Scots woman. She told her all about the latest look in Holland that had her bridesmaids resembling praying mantises. Mrs Dunbar was chuckling away at the picture Aisling was painting when Roisin, dunking a teabag into a cup, interrupted and told them all about Sten misinterpreting her expression and how he'd not had the lightest of touches after she'd made it clear she was spoken for. They all laughed as she relayed how his goatee quivered when he got excited or annoyed.

'Oh, and what about Mammy,' Moira snorted, mimicking her informing her poor stylist, Polly that she was the mammy of the bride and as such could wear her hair, however which way she wanted.

'Mother of the bride is a lovely thing to be indeed. My hair was on my shoulders when my daughter got married, I had it blow waved and set for her big day and wore a magenta hat with my dress. Navy it was with a magenta rose pattern. What did your mammy decide to do with her hair?'

'Curls, Maggie.' Aisling said. 'And for some reason when I think of Mammy's curls I want to start singing and doing a spot of the tap-dancing,' Aisling said.

All eyes turned toward her, unsure what she was on about.

She got up from the sofa beginning to jig about as she burst into song. *On the Good Ship Lollipop*, she tapped away.

'Shirley Temple!' Maggie clapped delightedly. 'She went for ringlets then.'

'They were supposed to be pin curls but they were very tight. The drizzle out there should sort them out though, even if she does wear a headscarf over them.' Aisling gestured to the large windows facing the street from where they could see a glimpse of the glistening, slick pavement outside before sitting back down again.

Roisin carried two cups of tea over and as she started laughing, they rattled ominously on the saucers.

'What's so funny?' Moira asked.

She managed to set the tea down in front of her sisters without spilling it and took centre stage in the room before launching into her heartfelt take on *Tomorrow*.

'Little Orphan Annie!' Mrs Dunbar chortled, thoroughly enjoying this impromptu version of charades.

The giggles were getting loud and James poked his head around the door to see what was going on. He shook his head on seeing a room full of women and a snoring man. It reminded him of when his mammy got together with her sisters, and his da always nodded off thanks to the extra glass of whisky he'd have knocked back in order to cope with his sisters-in-law.

Moira wasn't going to be left out. 'My turn.' She stood up and began to perform some fancy footwork while singing Michael Jackson's *ABC*. The others were in fits and when poor Mr Dunbar woke himself up with a particularly violent snore he had to blink rapidly because he'd found himself in a room full of giggling women. And what he'd like to know was why was the bonnie lassie he'd been speaking to yesterday dancing around singing a song he hadn't heard since the seventies? They were a mad lot these Irish, he thought, reaching for his cup of tea.

Chapter 15

Aisling swept into the house in Blanchardstown that Quinn shared with his mam and dad, glad to be in out of the cold. She'd felt like your character from the Narnia book the half human, half horse one that got frozen as she waited for the bus. Now, the homely smell of fabric softener and fresh baking washed over her. She greeted her soon-to-be mammy-in-law with a big fecky brown noser smile and received a warm one in return. She'd known Mrs Moran since her student days and was very fond of her but lately she'd found herself feeling irritated by her fiancé's mam's incessant fussing over Quinn. He wasn't a baby, he was a grown man and it was ridiculous the way she ran after him.

Quinn's siblings had all long since left home, as had he until he decided to open his bistro. It was a decision that saw him leave behind his career in London to move back to Dublin. He hadn't intended to move home but given the soaring accommodation costs in the city and the uncertainty of trying to get a new business off the ground, it had been the sensible thing to do. Sometimes, Aisling thought he'd gotten a little too used to being back in the family fold. She expected them to be a partnership when they finally moved in together at O'Mara's, the sensible option given Aisling needed to be on site and Quinn's bistro was a hop, skip and a jump away, and began their married life. You would not find her waiting on her new husband hand and foot the way Mrs Moran was prone to doing with her husband and sons.

Of course, it wasn't all down to her. Quinn seemed perfectly happy to let his mammy do so. She'd broached the subject with him a few weeks back but he'd shrugged in that laid-back way of his that was at times endearing and at times frustrating and said, 'I think she feels she has to prove herself after her stroke, you know. She likes to feel needed.'

Aisling had blustered back, 'But that's silly.'

'Aisling,' Quinn had said in a way that suggested she was very naïve when it came to the stuff of life. 'Sometimes it's easier to go with the flow than to upset someone over things that don't matter in the big picture.' She'd had the feeling he was talking about her and hadn't pressed it further, not wanting to hear something she might not like.

'How're you, Mrs Moran,' Aisling asked now, noting she had her customary shamrock apron tied around her waist.

'Aisling dear, I've told you a million times you're family. It's Maeve and I'm very well although I'm having problems getting the stains out of Quinn's chef whites. I'm after trying vinegar and baking soda.'

Aisling wished her mammy could hear this conversation. Not the part about slaving over Quinn's whites, the other part, because it was her fault she struggled with being on a first name basis with her soon to be in-laws. It had indeed been ingrained in her to address her elders with a Mr, Mrs or Aunty this or that. Perhaps she should go for the middle ground and call Mrs Moran, Mrs Maeve. 'Have you been baking? It smells wonderful in here.' She was only being polite because Mrs Maeve was always after whipping something up in that kitchen of hers. This house was a dieting woman's worst nightmare.

'I have and you're in luck. There's a batch of biscuit brownies fresh out of the oven, that's if Quinn's not eaten them all.'

Aisling groaned inwardly. Mrs Maeve's biscuit brownies were the best.

'They're his favourites as you know,' the little woman continued. She reached out and rested a hand on Aisling's forearm to waylay her a moment longer. Her voice dropped almost conspiratorially. 'When you've a moment, Aisling I'll show you how to bake them, I've been making notes of all his favourite foods for you because you know how the saying goes. The way to a man's heart—'

'Is through his stomach,' Aisling finished for her. Mr Moran had told her the other day he was on the fence about his son finally leaving home because he was sure the baked goods on offer would go downhill.

'You'll find Quinn in the kitchen going over his books. Oh, I nearly forgot. How did you get on with your hair appointment?' She looked at Aisling's hair which was flowing loose as per her usual style. She'd taken all the bobby pins and woven flowers out once back at the guesthouse. She didn't want to ruin the surprise on her wedding day. She patted her hair self-consciously and told Mrs Maeve this.

'And your dress, did you find what you wanted?'

The thought of her beautiful dress made Aisling smile. 'I did and I love it, it's perfect.' She quickly added. 'You know you were welcome to come along with us. My mammy was saying she'd like to get to know you better, now we're all going to be family. Are you sure I can't tempt you to join us tonight too?'

'I must organise a lunch for us all and it was thoughtful of you to include me, Aisling, but sure you know how tired I can get when I'm out and about too long and you didn't need me huffing and puffing about the place. As for a hen night, I've not got the stamina.' Maeve felt guilty seeing the earnest expression on Aisling's face. She was telling the truth about not having the stamina for this evening's festivities but the truth of why she hadn't gone along to help Aisling choose her dress was because her future daughter-in-law was so frazzled of late. She'd only met Maureen a handful of times too and she'd been worried about treading on toes, or saying the wrong thing to Aisling. Not that she'd told Quinn that of course.

'I wouldn't have minded.' She didn't want her future mammy-in-law to feel pushed out of things because this wedding was as much about her son as it was about Aisling and her side of the family.

'Well I'm sure you're going to be the most beautiful bride, Dublin's ever seen, dear. And sure, you'll have a grand time tonight. It will do you good to let your hair down. You'll find Cathal on his chair in the front room if you want to pop your head in and say hello. I'd best get back to the whites.'

Mrs Maeve scuttled off and Aisling ventured into the front room where Mr Moran was reclining in his La-Z-Boy chair with a newspaper held open in front of him.

'Hello there,' she called, stooping down to pet Tabatha the cat who'd gotten up from her corner of the sofa in order to greet her. The cat rubbed against her legs purring loudly as Mr Moran lowered his paper and peered over top of it. 'Hello there, yourself, Aisling. How're you doing?'

'Grand thanks, yourself?'

'Oh, I can't complain.'

Aisling noticed the cup of tea with a piece of the brownie tucked in alongside it on the saucer on the side table next to where he was sitting, and picturing his wife buzzing around making sure he was comfortable thought, no you can't. It's the life of Riley you're after living. He was a lovely man but he was also a solid, lazy, lump of a man and woe betide Quinn if he made noises about purchasing a La-Z-Boy chair when he moved into O'Mara's.

'All set for tonight, then?' she asked, referencing Quinn's stag do. Hugh, the oldest of the Moran boys, was to be his baby brother's best man and it was in this role that he'd organised the stag do. Aisling was pleased about this because Hugh at forty, married with four sons of his own, was a sensible family man unlike the two middle Morans, Ivo and Rowan, neither of whom was married and both of whom who had long-suffering girlfriends. Aisling would never say it to Quinn but she'd mentally given the two eejity brothers the nicknames of Lloyd and Harry from the Jim Carey film, *Dumb and Dumber*.

'I'm conserving my energy, Aisling, in order to keep up with the young ones.'

'Fair play to you, Mr Moran.'

'Call me Cathal, for goodness sake, Aisling.'

'Sorry.'

'You're too polite for your own good, so you are.' He grinned to soften his words before vanishing behind his paper once more. She took her cue to leave him to it and with a final tickle behind Tabitha's ear ventured off to the kitchen to find Quinn.

He was sitting at the big family-sized pine table about to stuff a piece of the biscuit brownie in his gob. Spread out in front of him were the books from the bistro and he looked up with a sheepish grin when he saw Aisling in the doorway.

'Caught me.'

'I'm betting it's not your first piece either.' Her eyes flitted to where the tray was on top of the oven. The slab of the chocolate treat was missing quite a few pieces.

'No comment. Can I tempt you?' He gestured toward the oven and she frowned as her mouth watered at the thought of it. Quinn did not make her efforts to lose a few pounds before the fourteenth of February, easy.

She focussed on her dress and the need to be able to slide that zipper up and down with ease. 'No, thanks. I won't.

Quinn shovelled the brownie down as though frightened it might be taken off him. He wouldn't it put it past her, she'd been kind of crazy lately in the build-up to this bloody wedding of theirs. He'd seen her checking out his middle the other day and did not want to find himself being ordered to do a crash course of the Weight Watchers. He pushed his chair back and patted his knee. She went and sat down slipping her arms around his neck.

'I wanted to see you before tonight.'

'Why do you look so worried?'

'I don't, do I?'

'Yeah, you do and you know you don't need to be. We're going for a meal and a few drinks that's it. There won't be any strippers or that sort of carry on, you know that, not with Hugh having organised it. Ivo and Rowan were all for it but I put my foot down. It's my stag night and that isn't my bag. Besides, Dad would be mortified if anyone waggled any naked bits under his nose.'

The two middle brothers went up a notch in the eejit stakes. They were elevated from mere eejits to super eejits. Hugh however was allocated a halo.

'I'm not worried, I trust you. I feel edgy, I suppose.' Aisling paused, unsure how far she should go. Quinn had told her often enough that she had nothing to worry about where he was concerned, he loved her. She knew all this in the logical part of her brain but still there was this feeling she couldn't shake that somehow things would go wrong. She decided not to put her fears into words. She didn't want to put a dampener on his evening. She wanted him to enjoy himself tonight and not be worrying about his overly sensitive wife-to-be.

'Do you know what I think your problem is,' he said, nuzzling her neck.

'Don't do that, your mammy might walk in.'

He paused in his nuzzling. 'You're hungry, Ash. Have a piece of that brownie, it'll sort you out so it will.' He was teasing her.

'Ah, ignore me and my moaning, I'm grand and I do not, read my lips, do not need the brownie.'

He looked sceptical but didn't push matters. 'And what about you, what's Leila got planned for you? Is it the Chippendales you'll be going to see or have those Riverdance fellows ventured into the murky waters of Irish dancing with nothing but a bow tie on to keep them warm?'

Aisling screwed her face up. 'God Almighty, Quinn. That would give me nightmares so it would. All those high kicks, it doesn't bear thinking about.'

He laughed.

'So far as I know, Leila's organised a few drinks at O'Mara's with party games then we've a limousine picking us up to take us for a meal and onto a few pubs.'

'Does the unsuspecting Dublin public know your mammy and Bronagh are being let loose on the town?'

Aisling elbowed him playfully, her mood lifting. It was one of the things she loved most about him, his ability to make her laugh. She kissed him full on the lips, suddenly uncaring if his mammy were to walk in on them. 'I love you very much, Quinn Moran.'

'And I love you, Aisling O'Mara.'

Chapter 16

♥

Maureen could hear the phone ringing as she turned the key in her lock and she pushed the door open before stampeding over to answer it. She could murder a cup of tea but it would have to wait, she thought as Pooh managed to get caught up around her legs in his haste to get to the laundry. He was desperate to see what was on offer in his food bowl. Cursing, she let go of his leash and righted herself before she hit the deck. Thoroughly flustered, she grasped hold of the receiver and answered it with a breathy, 'Hello.'

'Hello there, yourself, Maureen. How're you doing on this wet and wild afternoon?'

She smiled upon hearing the voice at the other end and forgot all about her coveted cup of tea and the high drama she'd had trying to get to the phone. She relieved herself of her rain jacket carrying it through to the laundry to hang up. 'I'm very well, Donal. Thank you for asking.' She was frozen to the bone after braving the elements on Howth Harbour but his cheery voice warmed her as much as the central heating would do. He brought out her generous side which was lucky for Pooh because she held the phone to her ear while scooping a load of dried biscuits into his bowl with her free hand. It wasn't his dinnertime for another hour, and the poodle's tail wagged at this unexpected bonus. Leaving him to enjoy his food, Maureen took herself back to the warmth of the living room and, kicking off her shoes, she settled herself down for a cosy chat.

Donal was a glass half-full man with an unfailingly positive attitude and he was exactly the sort of person she wanted to spend time with these days. Life was too short to find yourself on the arm of a crotchety old man and, thought Maureen, it was astounding the number of querulous men in their late sixties roaming the streets of Dublin at any given time. It was not something she'd noticed when her Brian was alive but once she'd been widowed a respectable length of time, they seemed to have come crawling out of the woodwork moaning and groaning all the way.

Sure, there'd they be with their walking slacks pulled up high around their armpits, their waistlines a thing of the past, as they complained at the rambling group get togethers how the price of gas was going up yet again and how was a pensioner supposed to keep warm in this godforsaken country of theirs? Or, at her painting class they'd be moaning the paperboy had tossed the newspaper onto the damp grass again and how was a man supposed to find out what was happening in the world when the front page was soggy? Oh, and she'd never come up for air again if she were to start on the curmudgeonly lot down at the bowls who were always on about how hard it was to get a decent cup of tea these days as they sipped their brew at the afternoon break.

Donal brought her back to the here and now. 'I'm ringing for no other reason than I wanted to hear your voice.'

It was rather nice to have someone want to hear the sound of her voice for a change.

'Have you had a good day?' he asked.

'I have.' She remembered her curls and would have liked him to see them. She raised a hand to fluff her hair up and realised she still had the headscarf on. 'I've not long walked in the door. I was after taking Pooh for a walk down the pier. It was very invigorating, so it was.'

'I'd say it would be. I very much enjoyed our walk the other day.'

'I did too, and I'm sorry about Pooh. He's not used to male company and he can be quite territorial where I'm concerned.' She'd been mortified when the poodle had cocked his leg and before she'd been able to stop him, peed on Donal's left trainer.

Donal laughed his big rumbly laugh. 'There's a first time for everything, Maureen, and sure he'll get used to me.'

She liked the way Donal was planning on being around enough for Pooh to get to know him. But as quickly as the warm fuzzy feeling had come it went and she felt queasy as though she'd been eating too much rich, fried food. If he was planning on winning her poodle over, it wouldn't be long before he was making noises about meeting her girls and introducing her to his girls. She wasn't sure if she was ready for that yet. It would make things official. It would open him up to judgment from her three because it would be inevitable, they'd draw comparisons between him and their father. Just as it was inevitable Donal's two daughters would compare her to their late mammy. Neither of them were looking for a replacement for their late spouses though. Through no choice of their own they'd found themselves on their own. It was a lonely thing to turn to tell someone something and find there was no one there anymore. This wasn't something she thought either of their children would understand.

Her girls, she knew, had been gobsmacked by her New Year's Eve announcement of having made a new man friend. They were itching to know more about him too but so far, every time she'd sensed they were about to pump her for information, she'd managed to head them off. She wouldn't get away with it much longer and she supposed she didn't want to either because she liked Donal. She liked him a lot; she only hoped they would too and she didn't even want to think about what Donal's girls would make of her.

She could feel Brian's eyes on her from where he gazed out of the silver frame watching over her living room. She liked to think he'd approve, not that there was anything to disapprove of. Thus far, she and Donal had met for lunch and gone for walks and spoken on the phone but there'd been no romantic encounters. She wasn't sure how she'd fare were he to make such an advance but she certainly wouldn't be averse, to him trying. Was kissing and the rest of it like riding a bike? Did it all come back to you once you got back in the saddle so to speak?

'I'm sure he will, Donal,' she said, spying Pooh licking his chops, his dinner finished as he moseyed toward her. 'What do you think about coming along with me to the puppy training class next week? It might help.'

'I'd be honoured to accompany you.'

Again, Maureen smiled, hugging the sound of his jovial voice to her before inquiring as to what he'd spent the day doing.

'I had a grand morning looking after my Gaby's little Keegan.' They whiled away a half hour chatting about the delights of being a grandparent and then, glancing at her watch, Maureen realised she needed to think about getting ready. She had a big evening ahead of her.

'I'll ring you tomorrow then, Maureen. I'm looking forward to hearing all the craic of the hen night,' Donal said.

'It will be down to me and Bronagh to keep an eye on proceedings. We'll make sure things don't get out of control,' she informed him before ringing off and floating her way over to the kitchen. She flicked the kettle on and popped a teabag in a cup before sitting down at the table to wait for the kettle to boil. Her mind flitted back to Donal and she played over, as she'd done so at least one hundred times or more, the yacht club Christmas dinner where she'd first met him.

She'd set such high store on the evening but the night was promising to be a flop and she was regretting all the effort she'd gone to having her hair and nails done. Rosemary Farrell had agreed to be her plus one for the evening, even though she didn't belong to the club, and Maureen was grateful to her for agreeing to accompany her. She'd learned since Brian had passed a lot of married women didn't take kindly to a widow joining them at their table. She imagined it would be the same for the newly divorced. Rosemary however had managed to wear her gratitude at keeping her company thin by the time they'd finished their, pre-dinner drinks with her complaining about her clicking hip.

Maureen had sat down at their allocated table for the meal and two men she'd met a handful of times while taking her sailing lessons had swooped down to sit either side of her. Rosemary and her clicking hip never stood a chance. Instead, her rambling club friend sat down across the table next to a woman who worked for the council. Rosemary, Maureen had seen glancing over, was in her apple cart at having an ear to bend about the state of some of the public walking ways. She'd gotten particularly strident as she informed the council woman how she was sure the shoddy paths had played a part in giving her a dicky hip in the first place. Maureen felt sorry for the woman, knowing she was in for a blow by blow account of Rosemary's hip replacement surgery over their entrees.

So it was, Maureen found herself sandwiched between Grady Macaleese, an aging playboy who had a penthouse overlooking the harbour here in Howth. He'd droned on and on about his boating prowess in a manner which had made her wonder whether he was talking about boating at all. He'd kept mentioning things like his big rudder and his ramrod boom. On her right was Rory Power, a wet-lipped, ruddy-cheeked man with an appalling combover who'd not been able to avert his eyes from her bosom all evening. It was a miracle how his fork had managed to find his mouth during the main course.

CHAPTER 16

Yes, she'd been wondering why she'd bothered coming and she'd been so looking forward to the evening too. She liked mingling with the boatie types, just not these two boatie eejits. As the plates were cleared away and Grady began to tell her about how he liked to manhandle his keel, she looked toward the stage and her mood brightened. The band was about to start. At least she wouldn't be able to hear him over the music. She interrupted him, past caring if he thought her rude. 'What sort of music are we in for?'

Grady looked flummoxed at having to answer a question not directly related to himself. Rory, eyes still firmly attached to Maureen's right breast, informed her it was to be a Kenny Rogers tribute band. 'The club's director of entertainment is a country and western fan, that's him prancing around in the cowboy boots, over there.' He pointed toward the stage.

Oh yes, Maureen thought, spying the gentleman in question, all he was missing was a piece of straw to chew on. She liked the sound of some Kenny Rogers though. *The Gambler* usually got everyone on their feet.

It had too, she thought now, getting to her feet as she heard the kettle begin bubbling away. She'd managed to escape the clutches of Grady and Rory by taking herself off to the bathroom and when she'd reappeared, she'd attached herself to a large group who'd taken to the dance floor. She'd felt a little like a teenager as she caught the eye of the singer who did indeed have a look of your man Kenny with his thick thatch of salt and pepper hair and matching beard. It was his twinkling eyes that won her over though and when he asked if he could fetch her a drink while the band took their break, she was very happy to accept. Rosemary's nose had been out of joint when she'd spotted Maureen in conversation with the lead singer whose name, she'd since found out, was Donal. She'd limped over to say she was calling it a night because there was no show of her being able to manage the dancing, not with her hip clicking.

Maureen poured the boiled water into her cup and waited for the tea to brew. She wondered what her children would make of Donal's retirement hobby. Sure, she decided, they'd be won over like she'd been if they got the chance to hear him sing *Lucille*. Satisfied her tea was just the right shade of tannin, she flicked the bag onto the little saucer she kept beside the kettle and then carried her drink over to the table. Pooh began to whine as she burst into the Dolly part of *Islands in the Stream*. It was something she'd been doing ever since she'd met Donal.

Chapter 17

♥

'Moira O'Mara, I can see your knickers!' Maureen said. She was perched on the edge of the sofa in the living room of the family apartment in between Bronagh and Ita. They were all awaiting the appearance of the bride-to-be. She'd opted for a slimline tonic, mixed with the gin her eyes had migrated to when she'd arrived, and it was going down a treat. Bronagh, who'd poured herself into a deep pink dress, which she told Maureen she'd had a sod of job trying to match a lipstick with, informed her she'd brought the gin along. The hidden calories in those pre-mix lolly water drinks all the young ones were so keen on knocking back would make your hair curl, she'd said, thinking herself hilarious given Maureen's curls. She was still chortling to herself as she reached forward to help herself to the cheese and crackers. It was the second time Maureen had had to slap Bronagh's hand away, telling her she'd regret her poor snack choices in the morning.

Nina had also joined them for the evening and was looking forward to a rare night out. It wasn't often she got to be a young woman with no responsibilities or cares and she intended to have fun. Mrs Flaherty had declined Aisling's invitation on the grounds of her bedtime being nine pm these days and young Evie who worked the weekend evening shift on reception, was precisely that, young.

'You can't,' Moira said, craning her neck to look back over her shoulder. She'd been standing by the dining table chatting to Aisling's old work friends when Maureen had caught sight of her skirt and nearly spilled her G&T.

'I can. They're purple and barely cover that arse of yours.'

'Well it is a hen night, Mammy. We're supposed to cause all sorts of trouble around the town. And what do you call the get-up you've on?'

'The only trouble you'll be getting, my girl, is the back of my hand on your bare legs. Now go and put something suitable on. I'll not have a daughter of mine flashing her knickers to all and sundry.' Maureen flicked her hand in the direction of the hallway, shooing her off.

Moira ignored her, knowing it would take too much energy for Mammy to get up from the sofa to smack the back of her legs. Her glory days of being fast as lightning with the wooden spoon were over. She took in her mammy's white cowboy boots and her eyes travelled upward. 'Jaysus, Mammy, please tell me those aren't rhinestones on your blouse.' She was wearing a black skirt, nothing wrong with that. It was a perfectly respectable knee length teamed with a long-sleeved silky black blouse which revealed a tad too much cleavage in Moira's opinion. One Cindy in the family was enough. It was the sparkly, swirly pattern across the chest she took umbrage with. It looked very much like rhinestones. All she needed was a big fecky off, cowboy hat, big blonde hair, enormous boobs, a smaller waist and the ability to hold a note, and she'd be like an Irish Dolly Parton.

'They're diamantes not rhinestones.'

'You're like a grandmotherly version of Madonna changing your look every fecking few minutes,' Moira muttered.

Maureen lunged forward and Moira scooted around the other side of the table, smirking as she saw Mammy was all hot air. She hadn't managed to make it out of the seat.

'Enough of the language on your sister's special night,' she said, settling back on the cushions and giving her gin and tonic, the attention it was due.

Ita looked down at her carefully chosen black dress with its white polka dots, bought specially for this evening from River Island. It had cost her nearly a week's wages and she'd teemed it with black knee-high boots as the shop assistant had suggested. She'd felt a million dollars when she'd left home earlier, her mam's voice ringing in her ears. 'Be sure to remember me to Maureen, now Ita.' She'd wanted to impress the O'Mara sisters who only ever saw her pushing a cleaning trolley about the place. She felt certain they looked down their haughty noses at her and she'd planned on showing them she scrubbed up as well as the next girl. Now though, looking at Moira in her tiny scarlet skirt she felt frumpy, as though she were off to a church social and not on a hen night. Her stomach knotted in the way it always did when she was around the O'Mara sisters.

Bronagh put in her penny's worth. 'Moira, if you prance around the city streets in that skirt, you'll be offered money in return for favours. Mark my words.'

Moira frowned, not sure what Bronagh was on about, her mammy's message had come across loud and clear though. 'What I want to know, Mammy, is why it's alright for you to swan around the city in your yoga pants showing everyone your bits but I can't wear a short skirt when I'm in the prime of my youth.'

'The yoga pants are very good for the mobility so they are. I can bend and stretch and get in and out of the car and remember, young lady, you'll still be my daughter when you're sixty and past your so-called prime. Besides, I'm after getting a new pair. It won't be me flashing my undergarments to anyone who cares to take a look.'

Roisin looked up from where she was scooping paté onto a cracker over by the kitchen worktop. 'What do you mean you've got a new pair?' Her eyes narrowed. 'Mammy, have you been nosing in my suitcase?'

Nina was sitting in the armchair near the windows and her head swivelled back and forth, like a tennis ball being thwacked across the court, between the sisters and their mother. She would never answer back to her madre the way these girls did theirs but she envied their easy relationship with her too.

Maureen had a shifty expression on her face but before Roisin could grill her further, Leila appeared looking glamorous in a silver halter neck dress.

'Leila, you look a picture, so you do,' Maureen exclaimed, grateful for the diversion.

'Thank you, Maureen, but wait until you see our bride. Aisling,' she called.

Aisling came striding out with her hands on her hips as though strutting the catwalk. Roisin whistled and Maureen and Bronagh clapped. Aisling's two girlfriends from her resort management days, Rowena call me Ro-ro and Tina-Marie like Lisa-Marie Presley only it's Tina-Marie Preston, cheered. Aisling was stunning in a sage green chiffon strappy number with impossibly high Louboutins and a fluffy white veil pinned into her hair. A drink was pressed into her hand and she took a seat alongside her old friends as Moira took charge.

'Has everyone got a drink?'

'Yes,' came the chorused reply.

'Good, because we've a few presents there on the table for Aisling to open and then I thought we could play some games before our limousine whisks us away. I thought we'd start with Bridal Bingo.'

'I love that,' Ro-ro squealed turning to Tina-Marie. 'It's great craic. I played it last month at Stephanie's hen night. Aisling you should sit at the head of the table to open your presents.'

Aisling pulled out the chair and dutifully sat down.

'Go and change that skirt, Moira,' Maureen bossed.

Seeing she was going to get no peace until she did, she told the expectant hens she'd be two ticks before racing off to the bedroom. She reappeared with a skirt that came down to the middle of her shapely thighs. 'Better, Mammy?'

'Much better.' Maureen was appeased. She was also enjoying her gin and tonic. It had been years since she'd tippled on that particular mixer. 'Bronagh, how's your drink there. Shall I top us up?'

'A grand idea, Maureen.' Bronagh said. 'Help me up would you, Ita?'

Ita took her hand and heaved the receptionist up from the sofa. They all gathered around the table, Maureen watching the proceedings from where she was sloshing tonic into a generous measure of gin.

'Open this one first, Aisling,' Roisin said, sliding a large shiny wrapped package toward her sister. 'It's from me and Moira.'

Aisling tore the paper off and stared at the wedding advent calendar inside. Little bags of varying sizes in different girly pink fabrics were pinned to the board in a two-week countdown between now and her big day. 'Did you two make this?'

The sisters nodded beaming. 'All the little bags were sewn by hand,' Roisin affirmed.

Aisling blinked back tears not wanting her mascara to run. 'It's fantastic, thank you. When did you get the time?'

'We've been making the bags for weeks and sorting the little gifts inside, but we put it all together when you shot off to see Quinn after we'd been to the Bridal Emporium yesterday.

'Well, I love it.'

'Open number fourteen,' Moira bossed, and Aisling delved into the pink gingham bag accordingly. Inside was a voucher. 'It's for a pedicure, ah thanks, Moira, Rosi.' She got up and hugged her sisters. 'That's not all we got you, open this one.' Moira picked up a small, soft package and passed it to Aisling.

She ripped off the paper, in the swing of things now, and found two pairs of knickers, one in red lace the other black.

'Jaysus wept,' she said holding them up. 'They're tiny so they are.'

'And what do you call those? There's no gusset in them. Sure, what's the point?' Bronagh said taking the gin and tonic Maureen handed to her and slurping on it.

'Crotchless panties, Bronagh. Which is exactly the point.'

Bronagh spluttered on her gin, making the others laugh.

'And I made you this.' Maureen gave her the scrapbook chronicling her daughter's life to date. She'd spent many a happy evening tripping down memory lane putting it together for Aisling, having done the same for Roisin when she got married.

'I'll treasure it, Mammy, thank you.'

Leila began to leaf through it exclaiming over Aisling in her first communion dress. 'Sure, your dress reminds me of Princess Diana's wedding dress.'

Aisling ploughed through the rest of the gifts which ranged from a bottle of Tahitian massage oil to a box of pink champagne truffles which she duly passed around.

Moira cleared the wrapping paper from the table and said, 'Aisling, can you fill this sheet out with words related to your wedding. Everybody else, did you fill in the cards I gave you earlier?'

There was a collective 'yes' and Aisling got busy writing. 'Finished,' she said, and Moira checked the group was ready with their pens before telling her to start calling out what she'd written.

'Cake,' she said, hearing the frantic clicking of ballpoint pens before carrying on with the rest of her random wedding words. It was when she called, 'Garter belt,' that Ita jumped up and shouted, 'Bingo!'

Moira handed her a decorative bottle stopper as her prize.

Maureen and Bronagh's competitive streaks put in an appearance during the ensuing game of Prosecco Pong with

Maureen demonstrating an uncanny talent for getting the ping pong ball in the cup.

'We've time for one last game,' Moira said checking her watch. 'What shall it be, ladies? The Cocktail Quiz or True or False.'

The Cocktail Quiz won.

It turned out Nina had an extensive knowledge of cocktails, thanks to her background in hospitality. She was gifted a canvas pouch which Leila told her was for keeping life's little necessities in.

'I haven't had a cocktail in a good while. The pina colada was always my go-to. I wouldn't mind one tonight.'

'Mammy, you haven't lived until you've tried a Cosmopolitan,' Moira said, glancing at her watch and announcing the limousine would be pulling up downstairs in approximately five minutes.

There was a flurry of last-minute organisation on the part of the bride-to-be and her flushed-cheeked guests in the form of lip gloss application, calls of nature, and the checking of bags for keys. Sorted, they made their way toward the door only to find Moira blocking the exit as she held up a large shopping bag. 'Before we go,' she said, 'I need you all to wear these.'

There was laughter, especially when Maureen announced if it was anything rude like willies bobbing about on a headband, you could count her out.

'Me too, I'm not wearing the pink, glittery willies on my head at my age,' Bronagh said, backing her up.

'It's traditional for the hen party to wear sashes or badges, or even crowns, not willies on headbands, Mammy and Bronagh. However, Leila, Rosi and I have gone one better. Close your eyes everybody,' Moira ordered, and they did so, wondering what on earth she was going to come up with.

'Okay, you can open them.'

'Aaggh!' Aisling screamed, 'Christ on a bike, I nearly had an accident, Moira. Anyone but him!'

Moira grinned behind her Bono face mask.

'I like U2's early music when I'm doing the housework, it's so angry and full of fire it sees me finish the hoovering in next to no time,' Ro-ro announced randomly as Moira began passing the identical masks around for the group to wear.

'Ha ha, very funny,' Aisling said, leading the charge down the stairs as she peered through the round eye holes. She had to admit though it was.

***

The chauffeur, whose name was Ned, was well used to raucous hen nights but this was a first he thought, holding the door open. A split second ago ten female Bonos, all reeking of various perfumes and booze and wearing the sort of shoes that would put holes in your lino had piled out of the guesthouse. Now they scrambled into the back of the white stretch limo one after the other. He closed the door on their squeals over having located the mini bar before getting behind the wheel. He was grateful there was a screen separating him from them lot in the back. It was relatively peaceful here in his own little bubble. A tap on the screen before he could even turn the key in the ignition put paid to that however and he pushed the button to make it slide down.

'Ned, my man, do you happen to have any U2 with you?' the Bono he'd noticed was wearing purple knickers as she clambered into the limo asked. 'We thought it would be a great craic to play *Beautiful Day* loud and when we pull up at the lights instead of mooning people, we'll Bono them.

Sweet merciful God, it was going to be a long night, Ned thought, fishing out his U2 CD.

Chapter 18

♥

The limousine slid expertly into the side of the kerb outside The Singing Bird shortly after midnight. Ned cocked an ear, no chance of the hens in the back having turned into pumpkins though, not given the amount of noise they were making. He looked at the flashing neon sign over the entrance to the bar and breathed a sigh of relief. This was his last stop on the pub crawl itinerary and he was more than ready to call it a night. He couldn't wait to hang up his chauffeur's cap and fix himself a warm milk to sup on before sliding in beside his Janice who'd be snoring her head off by now. The Bonos in the back had precisely an hour here and then he'd see them safely home. They'd all be feeling a little sorry for themselves in the morning he was guessing as he got out of the limo and adjusted his cap.

The tense situation on Wellington Quay was seemingly forgotten about with the prospect of karaoke here at The Singing Bird. The exclusive brick Clarence hotel on Wellington Quay was owned by Bono and The Edge. The nightclub tucked away downstairs in its depths was where the beautiful people of the city congregated after dark. The burly fella on the door had taken umbrage to the women impersonating the man who wasn't only his boss but also his personal hero and had refused them entry. He did say he'd let the one with the purple knickers in on account of her looking like a supermodel with a Bono mask on but she'd said it was one for all and all for one or something like that. The mammy and her friend had told him it was discrimination was what it was and threatened him with going to the papers but then they heard the next and final pub was The Singing Bird and there was a stage and proper microphones and everything and they'd all but thrown themselves back in the idling limousine.

Now Ned held the door open and stood back to let the clucking hens out thinking it was lucky for them they weren't famous with the paparazzi all lurking and waiting to snap them getting out of the back of the limo. They'd need to learn a little decorum if that were the case, especially the one in the purple knickers.

Aisling straightened her dress and fluffed up her veil before linking her arm through Moira's. 'I'm having a grand time, so I am, Moira. Thank you for organising this. It's brilliant being able to let my hair down.'

'You have been a bridezilla. It's good to see you relaxed.' Moira grinned, nudging Aisling before pointing out a group of lads wey-hey-heying as they walked down the street with chips, no doubt smothered in curry sauce, in hand. Aisling was sorely tempted to charge on over and help herself to a few soggy sorry excuses for a potato but she was also keen to get inside the bar and get hold of the microphone. She blew them a kiss and received a cheer but no offer of a chip and so, linking her other arm through Leila's, she dragged them toward the neon light.

The rest of the group staggered forth, Maureen and Bronagh bringing up the rear. Maureen nearly tripped on a cobblestone but Bronagh caught her before any damage could be done. 'Sure, it's a good thing we're here to keep an eye on the young ones,' she said steadying herself.

'It is indeed, Maureen,' said Bronagh, hiccupping.

CHAPTER 29

The group blinked as they found themselves in a darkened, smoky bar. It was hot and crowded, and the whiff of body odour was lurking in the air-conditioning ducts. They'd all pushed their Bono masks off having decided he would be too hard to emulate on stage. Roisin shouted over the top of the woman who was murdering Whitney Houston up on the stage, 'Clearly there are a lot of frustrated wannabe pop stars in Dublin.'

'Jaysus, she'll put us all to sleep. We need something lively so we do,' Aisling yelled in Leila's ear. Leila looked at her, Aisling looked at Leila and simultaneously they shrieked, 'ABBA!' Off they tottered and a coup was held on the stage where they managed to wrestle the microphone from Whitney who received no support from the audience before requesting Mamma Mia. 'I'm the blonde one,' Leila stated for obvious reasons but Aisling pulled a face, 'Yes, but I'm the bride so I should get to choose. I want to be Agnetha for once.'

The familiar opening beats sounded and Leila consented, taking her position on the left of Aisling. The pair began to sway their hips and click their fingers. The dance floor filled as the catchy tune began in earnest and Aisling and Leila gave it their all. The only glitch in the performance was when they spun around to face each other with too much gusto and narrowly missed headbutting one another. Aside from that when the song drew to a close, they received loud applause. Aisling was all set for *Super Trouper* but to her surprise Ita had gotten in with a request and was waiting to take the stage. Aisling and Leila milked the spotlight a moment longer before reluctantly handing the microphone over.

Maureen had mooched up to the bar once her middle daughter and Leila had finished their double act. 'I'll have two pina coladas please,' she shouted across the sticky bar top to the young fella who, if she half shut her left eye, had the look of the dimply one from Westlife. He gave her a cocky smirk.

'What was that love? Two penis and lagers?'

Maureen was flummoxed, her gin and tequila-addled brain thought he'd said the word penis but that couldn't be right. Surely not. 'No,' she shook her head vehemently but didn't like the way it made her head spin. 'Two pina coladas,' She gave him the fingers inadvertently before assailing him with her rendition of the chorus of the famous song by the same name. 'And, I'd like the little umbrellas in them. The ones you get when you're on your holidays.'

Jaysus, he had a right one here, he thought, setting about making the cocktails, and what was with the cowgirl look? She was taking karaoke to another level.

'Can you do the Tom Cruise thing. You know from that film, what was it called, now?'

'Cocktail and it was before my time.'

'Oh.' Maureen was disappointed, she would have liked a show, so she would.

'He's no good, Bronagh, he can't do the Tom Cruise thing,' she said as she joined her to wait for the drinks.

'Ah, never mind,' Bronagh flapped her hand. 'This place has karaoke. I love karaoke me. Moira's done Aisling proud with tonight, it's been grand so it has. The meal was very good too.'

The dimply one shook his cannister.

'Give it more elbow into it, son,' Maureen called over and turning back to Bronagh, she agreed. 'She has and it was.' They'd gone to a Mexican restaurant and had a lovely time tipping their heads back in the dentist chair for the tequila shots. Truth be told, neither woman would have been able to tell you whether they'd had nachos or a burrito to eat.

'Those two were very polished.' Bronagh pointed to the stage where Leila and Aisling were bowing deeply as though they were getting a standing ovation at the Royal Variety Show performance.

'They were. They knew all the dance moves and everything.' Maureen looked at the stage in time to see Aisling pass the microphone to Ita. 'I wonder what Ita will sing.'

CHAPTER 18

'*Sadie the Cleaning Lady*,' Bronagh said, hiccupping and giggling at the same time. 'Because singing about doing the old scrub-a-dub-dub is as close as she'll get to actually giving it what for.'

Ita or Idle Ita as Moira was fond of calling her was not the most dedicated director of housekeeping. It was a fact, but still, out of loyalty to her old friend, Ita's mammy, Maureen stuck up for her. 'Ah, she's alright Ita. She had a hard time of it after her daddy left. She deserves a break.'

Both women were rendered silent though as Ita cleared her throat before beginning to sing. She'd chosen Dusty Springfield's *Son of a Preacher Man* and her voice started off with a wobble but built in confidence until it was soaring around the bar. It was one of those rare karaoke moments when someone gets up who can actually sing and people who'd been sitting in darkened corners nursing drinks were compelled to make their way onto the dance floor to move to her sultry sound.

'Who'd have thought it?' Bronagh said.

'I wonder if her mammy knows she can sing,' Maureen said.

'Here we are ladies.' Two creamy drinks in tall glasses were placed in front of the women. Each had a cocktail umbrella swizzle stick poking out the side, much to Maureen's delight. They sipped their drinks while listening to Ita.

'Look who's after getting up next.' Bronagh nudged Maureen to where Roisin, Moira and Nina were ready to storm the stage. 'Hard act to follow,' she lamented, looking sorrowfully into the depths of her drink. 'Glad it's them not us.'

Maureen agreed, joining in with the cheers, Ita received when she'd finished. There were calls for more, more but Roisin, Moira and Nina were already up and ready. As they erupted into a poppy dance song, Maureen spluttered, sending a fine spray of pina colada forth. 'Christ on a bike! Chance would be a fine thing where those two of mine are concerned.'

They'd picked *Like a Virgin* and were earnestly singing about being touched for the very first time.

By the time Ro-ro and Tina-Marie had gyrated their way through *Black Velvet*, Bronagh could feel the urge to croon welling up in her throat.

'Come on now, we can't let the side down, Maureen. It's our turn next so it is. Let's see what there is to choose from.'

Maureen drained her drink and told Bronagh she had to spend a penny and then she'd be over to join her. 'It was a very nice pina colada,' she said to the dimply one before tottering off. True to her word she was soon back flicking through the book of songs. It was on the second page her eyes alighted on the perfect tune and she looked at Bronagh. 'What do you think?'

Bronagh gave her the thumbs up wondering if she could sing and hold her stomach in at the same time. 'And you look the part, too,' she added.

Maureen looped her thumbs through the belt hooks on her skirt like she did at the line dancing classes and began uttering a quiet 'me, me, me, me,' to warm her voice up. She wound up coughing due to the smoky atmosphere but by the time they got the signal they were up, she was recovered.

'Jaysus, Mammy, Bronagh, you're not after getting up, are you?'

'Don't you be starting with the discrimination. You're only as old as you feel and we've a fine pair of lungs on us haven't we Bronagh?'

'We have indeed, Maureen. We've been around the block a few times, so.'

Maureen cast her a 'speak for yourself' glance unsure what that was supposed to mean before wagging her finger in her youngest child's face. 'Watch and learn how it's done.'

Moira shook her head watching her mammy step up on stage. She leaned into Roisin whose hand had flown to her mouth as she swallowed a giggle. 'And she was on at me about flashing my knickers to all and sundry about town.'

CHAPTER 18

Nina's brown eyes were enormous at the sight of Mrs O'Mara with her skirt caught in the back of her knickers. 'I'll tell her.' But the song had already started and she didn't want to rain on her parade. 'Maybe she'll stay put and nobody will notice,' she added hopefully as Moira and Roisin clutched each other in fits. Staying put and doing nothing was not on Maureen's curriculum though and with due Dolly flair she began strutting around the stage to *9 To 5*. Bronagh's attempts to catch hold of her and wrest her skirt down as Maureen somehow managed to stay one step ahead of her only served to make the girls laugh harder. Even Nina had begun to giggle.

***

It was approximately one fifty-three am by the time Ned dropped the remaining hens off back at O'Mara's. He'd been very obliging in taking the other girls, Leila included, home beforehand. The mammy one in the back had not stopped going on about how she thought her drink had been spiked by your dimply one on the bar because it was not in her character to make a holy show of herself. The purple knickers one who by all accounts hadn't touched a drop all night informed her mammy there was no drink spiking involved and the holy show was down to the gins, the tequilas and the cocktails her mammy had knocked back over the course of the evening. They were still bickering over it all as they tried to open the door to the guesthouse.

'Thank you, Ned, you've been a star so you have,' the bride-to-be said, making him blush by giving him a kiss on the cheek before sorting her mammy and sisters out. She pushed the door open and herded them inside telling them to keep the noise down because it was a guesthouse not a fecking…

Whatever it was he didn't catch it, and getting back in his limousine he drove off home knowing it would be a very long time before his U2 CD saw the light of day again.

Chapter 19

♥

Noreen

Noreen tapped the side of the sieve and a sprinkle of icing sugar rained down on the Victoria sponge cake like snow. She stood back to admire her handiwork satisfied with the end result. It had become her signature cake around the village over the years. If ever there was a party, birthday or funeral and a cake was needed, she was enlisted to make one of her famous deep sponges. The baking of it never ceased to be bittersweet for the memories it evoked but memories were part of what made us who we were, Noreen always thought. You had to take the bad in order to have the good and as such there was no point in ignoring them. This sponge with its homemade jam, something she had time for now she no longer ran the shop, and fresh cream filling was intended for Father Peter. She wanted his advice as to what she should do about Emer and didn't like to appear at the rectory empty handed. She knew Father Peter, a portly man with a penchant for anything sweet, like her Malachy, could never resist her sponge cake, and as such she'd have his undivided attention. Noreen untied her apron and went to tidy herself up.

With her headscarf knotted beneath her chin to stop her hair from turning into a bird's nest in the gusty breeze, she set off. It was a short walk through the village to the church at its edge. She was carrying the cake in her trusty container. She'd bought it years ago when Rosamunde had begun dabbling in Tupperware parties, balking at the price of it but Rosamunde had convinced her it would be an investment. It had been too, she'd be lost without it now. She spied Maisie Donovan's cocker spaniel, Timmy, nosing around outside the butchers and held her container a little tighter. She didn't trust the animal one little bit and had threatened Maisie with a phone call to the powers that be more than once. Sure, she'd once watched the crafty dog leap around the legs of Mrs Sweeney outside that very butchers. The poor woman, nervy at the best of times, had dropped the sausages she'd bought for her and Mr Sweeney's dinner and the cocker spaniel had absconded with them, tail wagging all the way.

She shooed Timmy away as she passed by him and said hello to Mr Farrell, who told her he was off for a warming bowl of stew in Murphy's. Pint of ale more like, she'd thought, crossing over the stone bridge and hearing the stream babbling beneath it. The wind was cutting right through her today and she hoped Father Peter was in the rectory house and not the draughty old church.

The church, she saw, peering around the door and inhaling its familiar smell of pungent incense was deserted and she followed the path around to the house, noticing the hydrangeas had been cut back for the winter months. Father Peter, Father Jim and Father Thomas all lived here in the rectory and the pruned flowering shrubs would be down to Father Thomas. It was he who had the green fingers. Father Jim and Father Thomas would be out visiting the housebound of the parish as was their custom on a Thursday, which was why she was hoping to catch Father Peter for a quiet word. She placed her container down on the step before rapping on the door, feeling the tug in her back as she bent to retrieve it.

CHAPTER 1937

'Noreen, are you alright?' Father Peter swung the door open in time to see her grimacing as she righted herself. 'Here let me take that for you.' He relieved her of the Tupperware, his eyes lighting up as he guessed at what might be inside.

'It's age, Father Peter, nothing more.'

'Ah yes, it brings its aches and pains to be sure but how does the saying go?'

'Do not resent growing old, many are denied the privilege.'

'Truer words never spoken. Now then, come in out of the cold.'

Noreen did so and followed the priest down the shadowy hallway with its worn runner through to the kitchen where the old Aga was ticking over and keeping the room cheerful. The scent of toast hung on the air along with something else. She spied a jar with sprigs of thyme in it and realised that was the underlying smell. Beyond the back door, Noreen knew, was a well-tended garden with a raised bed of herbs and a fruitful vegetable patch. If she were to pop her head out the door, she knew she'd find parsnips, swedes, leeks and Brussel sprouts – Father Jim's penchant for the latter was well known and his reputation preceded him in the confessional box. Father Thomas kept his fellow priests well fed from his efforts in the garden. Given the priests looked after themselves, the place was kept very respectably Noreen thought, pulling out a chair and sitting down at Father Peter's bidding, noting the scrubbed table and clear worktop as she did so. They were house-proud men.

'I shall make us a cup of tea to have with what I hope I'll find in here.' He set the container down on the table at which Noreen sat.

'It's one of my Victoria sponges, Father, with fresh cream and homemade jam.'

Father Peter's eyes gleamed greedily as she'd known they would. 'Well this is a good day, a good day indeed, but to what do I owe the pleasure?'

'It's advice I'm after, Father.'

'Well now, Noreen, it has to be said I give my wisest opinions on a full stomach.' He retrieved two side plates and a knife. 'If you could do the honours while I tend to the tea that would be grand.'

'Certainly, Father.'

He nodded and set about making a pot of tea.

Noreen had placed a sliver of cake in front of herself and a large triangle for Father Jim by the time he'd set the tea things on the table. He poured them both a cup of the steaming brew before murmuring a very quick grace, smacking his lips, and tucking in.

Noreen hadn't much of an appetite but managed to fork up the best part of her cake so the priest didn't feel he was eating alone. He made short work of the sponge and in no time was pushing his chair back. He wiped his mouth with a paper napkin, missing the blob of cream on the tip of his nose. Noreen didn't like to say anything and fixed her eyes on her china cup and saucer instead.

'Now then, Noreen, let me tell you, if you were to enter that sponge of yours in a cake competition, I've no doubt it would take first place. An unexpected and most enjoyable treat on a cold winter's afternoon. Thank you.'

Noreen smiled acknowledging his praise.

'So, why don't you tell me what it is troubling you.' He clasped his hands resting them on his lap as he leaned back, satiated, in his chair.

'I've a family wedding to attend in a few weeks in Dublin and my niece who I've not spoken to after she wronged myself and my dear departed Malachy thirty years ago will be there. My sister, Rosamunde's after ringing me and telling me it's time to put old grievances aside. She wants me to find forgiveness in my heart for what her daughter did to Malachy and myself. Part of me would like very much to do this because she was like a daughter to us and I miss her, but I'm not sure I can.'

CHAPTER 15

'Why don't you start at the beginning and tell me what happened all those years ago.'

Noreen finished her tea and setting it back in the saucer took a deep breath finding, herself back in 1970.

Chapter 20

♥

1970

'This came this morning, Noreen. Read it.' Rosamunde flapped the envelope under her sister's nose. The shop was blessedly quiet because Noreen had seen from the look on her sister's face when she burst through the door she was in a state. Malachy was out and she couldn't very well close up in order to hear whatever it was in this letter that had her sister all worked up. And she certainly didn't want their customers knowing their family's private business. She glanced toward the door, willing it to stay shut for the time being, before taking the envelope from Rosamunde. She put the glasses, hanging on a chain around her neck these days, on and pulled the letter from the envelope. She recognised the handwriting instantly – it was Emer's – and her eyes scanned the page, reading quickly. As she drew near the end, her lips tightened; she could see why Rosamunde was upset.

Emer had completed a bookkeeping course in Cork after leaving school and it hadn't been long after, she'd headed for Dublin. Her new qualification had secured her a position in a furniture factory's office and she'd lodged with a group of girls she'd gotten friendly with while studying in town, all keen for a taste of capital city life. At first, she'd written regularly and had come home once a month, full of news of what life like was like in the big smoke. Noreen and Malachy had counted down the days between those visits, worrying in between times she was burning the candle at both ends, but comforting one another with the fact they knew she was happy and living life to the full. Slowly though, the letters had become fewer and the visits non-existent apart from holidays and birthdays. Independence was all part of growing up, Malachy had said, and she'd agreed with him but it didn't stop her missing Emer and was she *that* busy she couldn't write a little more often.

Noreen hadn't confided in anyone but Malachy to being a little hurt when her niece got engaged to Phelan Daly without breathing a word to her of it being on the cards. His family owned the furniture business where she worked. Emer had mentioned in passing, on a rare visit home, she'd been stepping out with the boss's son but there'd been no talk of it being serious. She hadn't even brought him home to meet the family. It had stung a little, hearing the news her precious niece was engaged to a veritable stranger via a quickly scrawled letter landing on the mat inside the front door of the shop on a Wednesday morning.

And now this. She folded the letter up and tucked it back inside the envelope before handing it back to her sister. 'Poor Emer, a broken engagement and no job as a result.' Her heart went out to her niece even as she wondered why she'd had to hear this news from Rosamunde who clearly didn't know what to do about the situation her daughter found herself in. 'She doesn't say what happened though does she? Only that her fiancé and her have parted ways which means she feels she can no longer work at the factory and she's been living off her savings this past month as finding a new job is proving a challenge.'

'Yes, but she won't be able to do that much longer. To be honest, Noreen, I'm surprised she has any savings. You know how money always burned a hole in her pocket. If she can't find work then she'll have to come home,' Rosamunde said, stuffing the envelope in the pocket of her cardigan before wringing her hands. 'But what will she do here? Sure, it's why she left in the first place. There's not much in the way of prospects for a young person in Claredoncally and around abouts.'

'There's always Cork.' Noreen had felt she should have applied for work in town when she finished her course. It was much closer to home and if it was city life she was after wanting to try, Cork was every bit as much a city as Dublin, though granted a little smaller.

'There is but I think she needs to be home with her family in order to get over all the upset with Phelan, and sure the bus to town is slower than a horse and cart. It would take her well over an hour to get in and out every day. You know how she hated it when she was studying. No, I was thinking something closer to home.'

Ah, *now* Noreen could see what had brought her sister steaming over to the shop. She'd never been very subtle. She sighed, her words coming out in an exasperated hiss, 'Rosamunde, why don't you say what it is you came to say?'

Rosamunde licked her lips and eyed her sister speculatively for a moment. 'Alright then. You always were straight to the point, Noreen. Would you see your way to giving Emer a job here at the shop, until she can get herself on her feet again?'

It was as she'd thought. 'I don't know, Rosamunde. I don't think there'd be enough work here to keep her busy.'

'Noreen, please, she needs your help.'

It was all she'd ever wanted; to be needed the way a child needs her mammy and Emer was the closest thing to a daughter she was ever going to have. Of course, she wanted to keep her close, she would like nothing more than to work alongside her but it was pointless if all they'd be doing was twiddling their thumbs. 'I'll talk it over with Malachy.'

'Bless you, Noreen, you're one in a million so you are.'

***

One month later...

'Emer, you'll rub a hole in the glass if you polish that window any harder,' Noreen said, opening the till. 'I'm going to finish up for the day. Put your rag away and get yourself off home.'

'Right-ho, Aunty Nono,' Emer called back cheerfully, finally satisfied she had the panes gleaming. She dropped the cloth back in the bucket and returned it to the cupboard under the stairs. Next, she went to take her shop coat off, but first things first, she pulled the crumpled pound note from her pocket and stuffed it into her bag hanging on the hook on the door. It separated the shop from the stairs leading to the living quarters upstairs. Then she took her coat off, glad to see the back of the ugly old thing as she hung it in place of her bag. She was off to the cinema tonight with her friend, Delia, and had been short thanks to the dress she'd treated herself to with last week's wages. Now she'd be able to wear her new dress, have dinner in the cafe Delia had suggested, *and* go to the cinema. Sure, she was only after taking what was her due anyway. She worked hard, her arm was aching from polishing the windows so it was, and received a pittance in return. Yes, it was only fair she justified, flicking her hair out from under jacket collar before wandering back into the shop to turn the sign from open to closed as had become her habit on her way out each evening.

'Goodnight, Aunty Nono, Uncle Malachy, see you tomorrow.'

Malachy grunted his goodbye from where he was sitting on a stool pricing a late delivery of tinned fruit.

'Have a good evening, Emer,' Noreen called, smiling back at her niece, pleased to note the colour was beginning to return to her cheeks now she was away from the city with all its pollution and grime. Fresh air was a tonic for most things, a broken heart included, she thought as the door banged shut behind their newest employee.

She began to tally up the day's takings counting silently as she did the arithmetic that had become second nature to her over the years. For the second time that month though it didn't add up. She prided herself on being accurate when it came to her dealings with their customers and Emer, well, Emer was a qualified bookkeeper. She knew her figures right enough. She frowned and looked down the aisle at Malachy. He needed reading glasses but refused to admit this was the case. Was he after giving out too much change? She'd have to broach the topic carefully with him, he could be a sensitive soul. She made her mind up to talk to him and nudging the till shut with her hip she put the coins and notes in the bag. They kept their money bag in the sideboard drawer with Malachy taking the week's earnings to the bank each Friday. 'I'll go and put the dinner on,' she called over to her husband. He was a pussycat on a full stomach.

***

Three months later...

'Where's our Emer?' Rosamunde asked Noreen one afternoon as she picked up a tin of baked beans and put them in her basket. 'They'll go nicely with our sausages tonight.' She put another tin in for good measure. The boys had hollow legs on them these days and she debated a third tin but decided no, they'd have to fill their boots with slices of bread on the side.

'It's Friday, she's gone into town to do the banking.'

'It was very good of Malachy to teach her to drive. Terry wouldn't have had the patience.'

CHAPTER 25

'He didn't mind. She picked it up easily by all accounts and Malachy wanted to give her a sense of responsibility by getting her to do the banking and collect the odd order. She's qualified in bookkeeping and the like so it must bore her silly stacking shelves and serving customers all day.'

'She's seems happy enough to me. It's working out well then? Having Emer here.'

'It is.' Noreen had to admit it was, they'd be lost without her now. 'I was worried we mightn't find enough for her to do but business is brisk. People always need their milk and bread and other essentials. Her being here means Malachy and I can take things a little easier, too.' They were enjoying the opportunity Emer's presence afforded them to take more breaks, she'd even found Malachy upstairs with his feet up and the paper spread out in front of him the other day! It wasn't only Malachy who was making the most of not being needed on the shop floor continuously. She'd slipped away and had her hair set the other day and found time for a cup of tea with her old friend, Kathleen, at Alma's. Mind you, she'd nearly broken a tooth on her currant bun, rock hard so they were. She'd told Alma in no uncertain terms, if she wanted to keep her customers, she needed to up her game.

Rosamunde hesitated in that way of hers which told Noreen she had something weighing on her chest.

'Come on then, Rosamunde, I can see you've not called in for the baked beans alone. Out with it.'

Her younger sister looked shifty as she dug deep for the words she was after. She cleared her throat. 'I, erm, I was wondering what you're paying Emer, that's all.'

'The going rate, why?' Noreen was put out by Rosamunde implying they were making the most of their niece being family and employing her on slave wages.

'Oh, don't get snippy, Noreen. I know you're more than fair with her. But she's forever coming home with new things that to my mind should be beyond her means.'

Noreen smoothed her ruffled feathers before speaking. 'Sure, she's young, isn't she? The young are apt to be spendthrifts.' It wasn't necessarily true. She hadn't been, she'd been a diligent saver from the moment she'd picked up her first brown envelope from the wages clerk at the fish factory but then she'd had something to save for, a shared dream with Malachy. It was neither here nor there, times were different now and Emer was entitled to enjoy herself. She worked hard and she'd obviously been through a lot with that fickle Phelan fellow in Dublin. Not that she'd ever spoken about it. She'd made it clear when Noreen had tried to broach the subject to find out what had gone wrong, it was a topic she didn't wish to talk about. Fair enough, Noreen had thought. Some things were too painful to speak of and so she'd left it, figuring Emer was healing her heart in her own way.

'Hmm,' Rosamunde mumbled, but didn't look satisfied. 'She's more clothes than she knows what to do with these days and it's not as if she needs them for work. She's gotten very offhand with me lately too because when I asked her about it, she told me it was none of my business. I told her it was my business while she was under my roof and she said something about not being under it for much longer before slamming her bedroom door. Terry was livid, said she'd have it hanging off the hinges with that sort of behaviour.'

Noreen frowned unable to picture the scene her sister had painted. 'That doesn't sound like Emer. I've never heard her say a cross word.'

Rosamunde heaved her laden basket onto the counter. 'Oh, you've always been blind to her faults, Noreen. You and Malachy both. She's a side to her at times that one. Nobody's perfect you know. She's a long way to fall from the pedestal you have her on,' Rosamunde said, before shaking her head in a manner which made Noreen feel spiky with irritation and her words niggled Noreen for a long while after she'd left.

Chapter 21

'Can I interrupt you there, Noreen?' Father Peter said. 'I can see it's distressing you talking about this and sure, everybody knows there's no trouble so great or grave that cannot be much diminished by a cup of tea.' He took the cosy off the pot and poured another strong brew for her, leaving her to help herself to the milk and sugar. She didn't normally take sugar but today she put a teaspoon in. The sugar would help calm the anxiety raking over the past had wrought.

'Another slice of your delicious cake?' Father Peter held the knife poised over the sponge hopefully.

'No thank you, Father, but sure, help yourself. I made it to be enjoyed.'

'And that it will be, Noreen, that it will be,' he muttered, slicing into it.

She sipped her tea allowing the hot, sweet liquid to settle her nerves while he slid a generous wedge onto his plate and began to wolf it down with as much gusto as he had the first piece. This time when he'd finished and wiped his mouth he managed, to Noreen's relief, to remove the cream from his nose.

'Now then, Noreen, you're looking much more composed,' Father Peter said, pushing the plate away from him, his clasped hands resting around a middle clearly straining against his shirt. 'Are you ready to carry on?'

'I am, thank you, Father.'

***

1970

It was a day of rainbows when Noreen ventured into Cork. There was a sale on in Roches Stores there on Patrick Street and as she made her way toward the building with its grand copper-covered dome, she could see the line of eager shoppers waiting for the doors to open. She and Malachy had left it to Emer to open the shop in order to pootle into the city at an ungodly hour of the morning. Malachy was going to the grocery wholesalers while she fought the crowd in the women's clothing department here at Roches. They'd arranged to meet outside the store's main door for midday in order to go and treat themselves to a spot of lunch. The thought of standing around outside the frontage like so many youngsters did on a Friday evening, waiting to meet their date made her smile. At least her stomach wouldn't be all of a flutter wondering whether he'd show up or she'd find herself stood up and sloping off home on the bus. He'd always been a reliable sort, her Malachy.

Noreen reached the store and tagged onto the end of the chattering queue. There was a sense of excitement in the air at the thought of the glorious bargains about to be found inside and she crossed her fingers in the pocket of her smart, going into town jacket hoping she'd be able to find what it was she'd come for. It wasn't herself she was after shopping for today. No, it was Emer. She'd seen the look of yearning in her niece's eye the day Mrs Darby had breezed unexpectedly into their shop.

Mrs Darby was a mythical creature who lived in the big house halfway between their village and the next town. She spoke with a plum wedged firmly in her lipsticked mouth and was hardly ever seen on the streets of Claredoncally, preferring to do her shopping in town. So, when her sleek grey, automobile pulled up on the main street, Maisie Donovan had burst through the door of Grady's Convenience Store full of this breaking news. Emer had gone to the window, pressing her nose to it as she peered down the street before declaring excitedly that the glamorous vision wrapped in a royal blue, belted wrap coat and matching hat was heading toward their shop. Noreen had fluffed her hair and straightened her shop coat before standing to attention as though she were about to greet the Queen behind the counter.

Indeed, the door had jangled a moment later and the lady herself had swept into the store bringing with her a cloud of cloying perfume. Noreen had wanted to hiss at Maisie to close her great big gawping mouth because she looked like the village idiot which was all well and good for her but there was no need to make them all look bumpkins. She was out of earshot though, lurking alongside the packets of digestive biscuits she'd been wondering whether to have with her morning tea and so Noreen had to bite her tongue. Emer had leaped to attention and was fawning all over the elegant apparition asking what she could fetch for her. She wouldn't be able to complain the service at Grady's wasn't up to speed Noreen had thought proudly as she watched her niece scurry toward her in order to fetch the newspaper which Mrs Darby was bemoaning had not arrived at Briar House that morning. It meant Mr Darby's day had not gotten off to a good start, she informed Emer tightly.

Noreen handed the correct change to Emer, observing her press it into Mrs Darby's gloved hand. She'd half thought her niece might curtsey as she received a nod by way of thank you. Then, leaving nothing but her expensive scent in her wake, Mrs Darby was gone. They all stood in reverent silence for a good few minutes until Emer, who'd resumed her position at the window, announced the car had slipped away from the main street. Their shoulders relaxed and business resumed as normal. Maisie decided she deserved a digestive with her tea and she'd push the boat out and buy a packet of the chocolate covered biscuits. It wasn't every day there was this much excitement in Claredoncally.

Noreen had been driven demented all afternoon listening to Emer drone on and on about what perfume Mrs Darby had been wearing. Did she think it was Dior or Guerlain? It was definitely French, her niece informed her. 'Did you see her coat, Aunty Nono?' It wasn't as if she could have missed it, Noreen thought, as Emer gushed further. 'I bet you it was from Paris. I heard she goes to the fashion shows there and buys her clothes direct from the designers. That's why she looks like a film star.' Her eyes were alight and her chin was resting on her cupped hands. She was leaning on the counter in a manner that would have Malachy telling her to stand up straight because the staff at Grady's Convenience Store didn't slouch, if he were to spot her. Noreen didn't ask how her niece knew all this about Mrs Darby's wardrobe but was guessing it was fodder for village gossip. She'd been unable to stop herself from rolling her eyes as Emer pondered aloud as to what the interior of Briar House was like.

'Sure, Emer,' she'd said. 'It's only a house. We've all got to live somewhere and the bigger the house the more cleaning there is to be done.'

Emer was undeterred. 'I bet it's very grand with priceless art and antiques everywhere. Imagine having someone to cook for you and someone to clean for you, Aunty Nono. Imagine if all you had to do was click your fingers and someone would come running.'

'I wouldn't like it,' Noreen stated, her niece's enthusiasm for the Darbys' ostentatious lifestyle was making her cringe. She paused in her clicking of the price gun, leaving the remaining jars of coffee she'd been unpacking in the box for a moment. 'No, it wouldn't be for me to have a stranger living in my home privy to all our private business. And sure, why does anyone need more rooms than they can ever use?'

But Emer hadn't wanted to hear about practical things; she wanted to daydream about impractical things such as big houses full of servants, French perfume, and coats the latest fashion in Paris.

'There's no point getting ideas of grandeur, Emer. It only makes you hanker for things you can't have and there's no happiness to be found in doing so,' Noreen had said, trying to snap her niece out of it. Her words were wise but still, she'd thought, there was no harm in the girl having a smart new coat and while Roches Stores might not be the Paris catwalk, she was sure she'd find a style similar to Mrs Darby's collared, wrap coat. Royal blue would look well on Emer, and she and Malachy would be lost without her these days. It would be nice to acknowledge how indispensable they found her with a thank you gift. The bottom line though, Noreen knew, was she wanted to see her face light up when she pulled the coat from the bag and it was for this reason, she was currently listening in on a most interesting tale the woman in front of her was after telling her friend as she waited for Roches to open their doors.

She was about to find out what had happened to Bridie at the dance last Friday night when she'd felt a tap on her shoulder. She swung around to see a face she recognised but couldn't quite place. The girl, around Emer's age, registered her confusion and explained. 'Hello, Mrs Grady, I'm Angela. We met a while ago when I came home with Emer for a weekend. She brought me by your shop to say hello. Emer and I shared a room in Dublin.'

Ah yes, the penny dropped, she'd been pleased to meet the girl and have a peek through the window into what Emer's life in Dublin was like. 'Angela, yes of course. It's lovely to see you again. How're you?'

'I'm grand, thanks.'

'Are you working here in town these days?' she asked, noting the girl's smart blouse and skirt. She had a name badge pinned to her chest and her hair was pulled back in a tidy ponytail.

'I am, yes. I've a job at the Bank of Ireland. I transferred from Dublin not long after Emer left.' Her expression closed a little. 'Things were a little awkward after everything that happened. I'm pleased I ran into you because I've wondered how she's doing?'

Noreen was puzzled, the girl was being very cryptic. 'Have you not been in touch with her yourself then?' Perhaps the pair had had a falling out. It couldn't have been easy sharing a poky bedroom. You'd be forever stepping on one another's toes.

Angela wouldn't meet her eye. 'No, I haven't.'

Something had definitely gone on, Noreen thought, but it wasn't any of her business. 'Well, I for one think leaving Dublin and having a fresh start has been the best thing for her. She's working for me and Mr Grady at the shop now and living back with her mammy and da for the time being.'

Angela looked startled by this news.

Noreen couldn't help herself. 'Sure, why don't you phone her. You two were thick as thieves weren't you.'

Angela blanched at Noreen's terminology and she flapped her hand dismissively, her manner telling Noreen she was keen to be on her way. 'Ah, no, tell her I was asking after her would you? I'm glad things are working out.'

'They are. She had a lucky escape when that Phelan one broke off their engagement.' Noreen could never keep the righteousness from her voice when she breathed that man's name. It raised her ire to think of him casting her beautiful niece aside the way he had and it was a good job he'd never shown his face in Claredoncally.

Angela's cheeks burned hot with two red blotches and her words tumbled out before she could stop them. 'Well, he hardly had any choice not after what Emer did. I'm sorry, Mrs Grady, but I don't think that's a fair comment.'

Noreen was taken aback by the girl's strong reaction. Her pulse quickened the way it always did when she knew things could go one of two ways. She could leave the conversation there and pretend she'd never met up with Angela. She could carry on happily about her business or, she could push further and find out something instinct was telling her she wouldn't want to hear. She and Rosamunde had assumed Phelan had gotten cold feet and Emer had never given them reason to think otherwise but here was Angela alluding to Emer being the one at fault. She couldn't help herself, the plaster had to be ripped off now. 'And what do you mean by that?'

'Nothing.' Angela wished she'd kept her mouth shut. 'I shouldn't have said anything. It's just, well it's not fair on Phelan you thinking he's faithless. I'd best be on my way or I'll be late.' She made to walk away.

Noreen put her hand on Angela's forearm, stopping her. 'Please, Angela, will you tell me what Emer did?'

Angela hesitated. There was a pleading look on Mrs Grady's face. She didn't know why she was so surprised Emer hadn't told her family the truth of what had happened with Phelan. She'd proven she wasn't to be trusted when she left Dublin in disgrace. Sure, she'd left her in the lurch having to cover her share of the rent, upping and leaving without a word of notice the way she did. Angela was a firm believer in second chances though, and she'd hoped Emer might have changed her ways. She'd hoped this because, despite her sneaky, dishonest streak, she was also brilliant fun and they'd had lots of laughs together in Dublin. She missed her old friend but not enough to pick up where they'd left off, besides which, she had a feeling Emer wouldn't thank her for visiting her in Claredoncally.

Angela hadn't a clue why she'd done what she'd done either, because if she was short of money, she'd only had to ask and Phelan would have helped her. Come to that she would have helped her. But she'd never even hinted at having money problems. She'd simply helped herself to what wasn't hers and when she got caught, she'd been tearful and apologetic, pleading with Phelan not to break things off. She'd only taken the extra she was due, she'd cried. She worked hard and deserved more than the paltry sum she was paid at the end of each week. Angela had heard all of this from where she was perched on the edge of her bed in their room. She'd stared unseeingly at the wallpaper with its faded flowers and patch of damp in the corner, biting her thumbnail in disbelief as Emer's and Phelan's voices carried up the stairs from the hallway where they stood. He'd only raised his voice the once, when Emer refused to give him back the ring he'd proposed to her with. 'It belonged to my grandmother and you're not taking that from me too!' he'd shouted, and Angela had blanched picturing the scene below. The last thing she heard him say before the door banged shut behind him was, 'You're not the girl I thought you were.'

Emer had refused to talk to her about what had transpired but Angela had seen the white band on her finger, left behind by the ring. The story of Emer thieving from her employers, her fiancé's parents no less, had filtered through their circle of friends and when she found herself ostracised, she'd packed her bags. Angela had arrived home from work to a note Emer had scrawled to say she couldn't afford to stay in Dublin and had gone back to Claredoncally to stay with family.

'Are you sure you want to know?' she asked Mrs Grady. She'd only met Emer's aunt and uncle the once but she'd seen the way they fussed over their niece and their eagerness to meet her friend. They were good people and if Emer was up to her old tricks then her poor aunt deserved to know what she was capable of, especially as she was working for her in their shop these days. She chewed her bottom lip, still uncertain she wanted to be the one to tell the sorry tale.

Noreen bobbed her head, willing the girl to spit it out whatever it was. Sure, she was beginning to wonder from the drama of it all if it was murder Emer was after committing.

'Alright then. I'm sorry, Mrs Grady, but Emer was fiddling the books at the factory. Stealing to put it plainly. She was lucky the family didn't press charges when she got caught out, but you can see why Phelan had to break their engagement off. Even if he could have found a way to get past what she'd done, his family couldn't. He was heartbroken.' Her face flashed with sympathy for Emer's ex-fiancé. Noreen stood there feeling a little other worldly and something else. It took her a moment to work out what it was. Foolish, that was how she felt. A naïve and foolish woman. She was relieved when Angela announced, 'I've got to get back to work. I thought you should know in case, well, I thought you should know.'

In case a leopard didn't change its spots, Noreen finished silently for her. She couldn't muster up any words to say to Angela and as the girl shifted from foot to foot waiting for, well, Noreen wasn't sure what exactly she was waiting for because what could she say by way of response? After a painfully eked out silence she took her cue and with an apologetic goodbye, strode off down the street. Noreen watched her, unsure if the bile that had risen in her throat was at the thought of her niece being no better than a common criminal, or whether it was because of her own stupidity in not having pressed her further. She should have kept at her until she told the truth of what had happened between her and Phelan. She should have known something wasn't right. A numbness began to creep through her limbs and she forced herself to move before it rendered her frozen to the spot.

The doors to the store had opened and the line was finally snaking inside the building but Noreen left her place in the queue and headed for the AIB Bank where she and Malachy held their account, the bewilderment Rosamunde had expressed over the money Emer seemed to be splashing about foremost in her mind. The throwaway comment, her sister had made as to Noreen and Malachy holding Emer up to be something she was not played over in her mind. They'd trusted Emer week after week with their takings. When had either of them last thought to check a bank statement? She'd do so now, she thought, pushing open the doors and joining the handful of people waiting to attend to their business. She stared at the man in front of her. He was wearing a brown suit and she didn't notice the fluffy lint stuck to it as she normally would, tutting to herself she'd never let Malachy leave the house like that. She didn't disapprove over the creased trousers either as she prayed silently she wouldn't find what the sick feeling now settled in her stomach was telling her she'd find when she looked into things.

***

'She'd been helping herself the whole time. Malachy and I were taken for gullible fools, Father.' Noreen wrung her hands as she finished her tale, her throat feeling heavy with the effort to keep the tears at bay. Even now, so many years later, the abuse of trust wounded her to her core.

'No, Noreen.' Father Peter shook his head. 'Big hearted and trusting was what you and Malachy were.'

Noreen looked at Father Peter's kindly face, drawing strength from it. 'You know it wasn't the stealing that hurt the most. It wasn't even the awful words Emer hurled at us before she left.' She shivered recalling how, when confronted, Emer had at first denied any wrongdoing. It was only when Noreen waved the statement and the book, the indisputable proof of glaring and unexplainable discrepancies, she'd begun to apologise. She'd wanted a few nice things, to treat herself, was that so bad? She was sorry, she'd pleaded. Malachy had stood by Noreen's side, his expression set in stone, and when Emer saw her apology wasn't going to be accepted with the understanding she felt was her due, she'd lashed out.

Noreen had flinched as though physically slapped when Emer threw at them she'd only taken what was her due, what she was worth, and then a nastiness had seeped in. 'You suffocated me with your neediness, did you know that?' Her eyes were as mean as her words. Malachy had spoken then, his voice hard as steel as he told her to leave the shop and not to come back. There was a look of disbelief on Emer's face and her gaze swung to Noreen, who even then wanted to take her niece in her arms and tell her all was forgiven. She stood firm by Malachy's side though, as was her duty, and Emer slammed out of the shop leaving her and Malachy to stand in hollow silence. Noreen would never forget the look on her husband's face when he at last turned to her and said, 'Well, that's that.' He never spoke of Emer again.

'What cut the deepest, Father,' Noreen said, blinking away the images from the past, 'was the way the light went out in Malachy's eyes that day.'

Chapter 21

♥

Noreen couldn't believe a week had passed since she'd been at Alma's Tea Shop. Her days didn't normally race by, they were more inclined to meander past like a lazy stream but she'd been lost in her memories and hours had disappeared at a time. Yes indeed, time had gotten away from her as she'd lingered in the past because here she was, back at the tea shop once more. She greeted Kathleen, Margaret and Agnes, who were already there knitting like the clappers. On a plate in front of each of them was a currant bun sliced in two with a miserly spread of butter, with a pot of tea in the centre of the table. Alma was clattering away behind the counter arranging the food cabinet for what she no doubt hoped would be the lunchtime rush. Noreen pulled a chair out and sat herself down next to Margaret.

'Currant bun, Noreen?' Alma called over.

'No, thank you, but a cup and saucer would be grand.' She was cutting back on extras such as currant buns between now and her trip to Dublin. It wasn't exactly a hardship when it came to Alma's offerings. The slice of cream cake visiting Father Peter the other day was eaten out of necessity to be polite but there was no risk of offending her three old friends if she didn't partake of a currant bun. Right now though, there was an acrid odour in the air hinting at a disaster in the kitchen. 'What's that awful stink, Alma?' Her nose wrinkled.

'I was after burning the scones on account of a phone call from my daughter. I forgot all about them. The smell's murder to get rid of and it's too cold to have the place airing out.' She waved the cloth she held in her hand. 'You don't notice it after a while.'

'That's true enough,' Kathleen said, looking up from her knitting. 'Although if my coat reeks of burnt scones, it's you I'll be sending the dry cleaning bill to.'

'Ah sure, hang it in on the washing line for half an hour when you get home. Give it a good airing and it'll be good as new. There's not enough money in a pot of tea and a currant bun for the likes of the drycleaners.'

Kathleen's mouth twitched, she did so enjoy getting a rise out of Alma.

'Stop baiting her, Kathleen, would you?' Agnes paused in her lightning-fast stitches.

She could knit with her eyes closed, Noreen thought, eyeing her needles, from beneath which the beginnings of a mustard sweater were emerging.

'You know what she's like. She'll refuse to top the pot up unless we pay for another brew. How're you, Noreen?' Agnes asked, turning her wily blue eyes on her friend.

Noreen would have liked to say she was grand, but she wasn't, and she'd known these three women too long to bother pretending. She felt as though she had the weight of the world on her shoulders despite her visit to Father Peter, though she'd come away clearer in her mind as to what the right thing to do as a good Catholic woman was where Emer was concerned. This was all well and good, but to take the first step towards forgiveness at the wedding was not going to be an easy thing to do. Would the proverbial olive branch withstand the amount of water that had gone under their bridge? 'I'm right enough, thank you, Aggie.' That about summed it up she thought, opening her knitting bag and setting her things down on the table. She'd a new project to be starting and she was eager to cast the cheerful red wool on. Perhaps the bright colour would lift her mood.

'Did you find an outfit for your grand niece's wedding?' Margaret asked.

Margaret had seen her waiting at the bus stop the day she'd tripped into town to go shopping. 'I did. I went to Debenhams and decided on a green dress with three quarter sleeves, given it's winter, and a matching jacket. It's very smart.'

'And you've the shoes, bag and hat too, I hope?' Agnes chirped, looking at her currant bun. 'Dust dry, so it is.' She shook her head.

'I have, indeed.'

'You'll have to give us a fashion show, Noreen,' Kathleen said.

Noreen nodded, having no intention of doing anything of the sort as she deftly looped the wool over her needles.

'And what of a present?' Margaret inquired, pausing in her clacking to sip at her tea.

'I did well there. I chose a Waterford Crystal vase, one of their lace patterns. It's lovely so it is.'

There was a low hum of 'ooh, lucky girl' along with 'that would have set you back a pretty penny.'. It was interrupted by Alma placing a cup and saucer down in front of Noreen with more of a clatter than was necessary.

'I see, so let me get this straight. There's money for Waterford Crystal vases and the like but not a penny spare for a currant bun,' Alma muttered.

'Oh, go on with you if it means you'll leave me in peace to enjoy my tea, I'll have one of your buns. No butter mind, Alma, and if I can't do the zip up on my dress on the day it'll be you who's to blame.'

Alma scuttled off to fetch the bun, thoroughly pleased with herself.

As it happened the vase had been generously discounted but nobody needed to know that. 'Sure, it's nice to receive something special when you embark on married life.'

She didn't recall Waterford Crystal or the like being received on her wedding day. From memory there'd been practical things for the kitchen. People didn't give extravagant gifts back then, there wasn't the money for it for one thing, and for another, people didn't expect so much.

'That was a sigh from the bottom of your boots.' Kathleen's keen eyes glanced over Noreen. 'What's up with you?'

Noreen pressed her lips together tightly for a second or two as her friend waited for her to speak. 'Ah, it's this business of Emer being at the wedding. Did I tell you Rosamunde's after ringing and telling me it's time to let bygones be bygones and a wedding is a time full of hope for the future. What was I supposed to say to that?'

The three women clucked in sympathy but it was Agnes who spoke. 'Not much you could say, Noreen, not without coming across as a bitter old woman. She put you on the spot there, alright.'

'Exactly, Aggie,' Noreen said, recalling how Rosamunde had gone on to say, in what she had thought a condescending manner given she was the younger sister, 'What better opportunity to put things right between the pair of you?' What Noreen didn't understand was why it had to be her who had to make the first move. It was Emer who was in the wrong and she'd vocalised this to her sister but Rosamunde had only tutted and said that was the problem where she and Emer were concerned. They were peas in a pod. Far too stubborn for their own good and someone had to reach out first. So, why shouldn't it be Noreen?

She'd left Father Peter's the other day having heard the same sentiment from him. She'd also realised, as she'd sat relaying the story of what had happened all those years ago, how much she missed Emer. Her leaving Claredoncally had left a gaping hole in her life and the plain truth of the matter was, Noreen was lonely. She'd come here to Alma's once a week and meet her friends, listening to them bat back and forth about their children and grandchildren. She liked to keep up with all the goings on in their lives but later, when she went home to her quiet, little house, she'd feel an emptiness. The sound of children's laughter would never bounce off this house's walls. She'd always thought she would take on the role of another grandmother to Emer's children just as she'd played the role of a second mother to her growing up. She'd missed out on knowing Emer's family. The children would all be grown and have no interest in spending time with their widowed great aunt.

'I think Rosamunde has a point,' Kathleen said, having clearly mulled over what Noreen had told them. Spying the expression on Noreen's face, she held up her hand. 'No, don't give me that gin-soaked-prune look of yours. Hear me out.'

Noreen's lips tightened once more and she knitted a frantic red row with her head tilted to one side. It was enough to show Kathleen she was listening.

'I've known you long enough to know it's a heavy burden you carry where Emer is concerned. What she did was wrong but Malachy dug his heels in when he could have asked her why she'd done it.'

Noreen made to protest he had asked and hadn't liked her answer but she closed her mouth knowing what Kathleen meant was, what lay at the root of what she'd done.

'You couldn't cross his decision but I think if you'd had a say in it all back then, you'd have patched things up with her. Malachy isn't here anymore, Noreen, and knowing him as I did, I'm telling you as one of your oldest friends he wouldn't want you to be alone. There are friends and there are family in this world of ours. We get to choose our friends but not our family and when it all boils down to the nitty-gritty, if we don't have family what do we have?'

'Hear, hear,' Alma said, placing the currant bun in front of Noreen. Noreen didn't have the energy to tell her not to be listening in on a private conversation, besides she knew she'd be wasting her breath. Alma was an eavesdropper of the highest order. The door jangled announcing a customer, and with a groan about her knees not being able for all this standing she waddled off back behind the counter.

'But how?' Noreen muttered to the trio, none of whom were knitting.

'How what?' Agnes asked.

'What do I say to her?' This was the part that was all a puzzle. Should she walk up to her niece at the reception with her hand held out and say, It's time we buried the hatchet. Or should she act as though nothing had happened and chat away to her as if she had no cares in the world.

'Tell her the truth. Tell her you want to put the past behind you,' Kathleen, who was full of wise advice this morning, said.

'She's right,' Agnes agreed, dabbing the crumbs up off her plate with her index finger. Despite her protestations there was nothing left of the bun. 'It's simple.' She popped her finger in her mouth.

Was it simple after all? Noreen pondered. Perhaps, she thought, a spark of hope for the future igniting, it wasn't too late to start over again after all.

Chapter 22

Aisling and Quinn shuffled about the floor trying to mimic the actions of Maria and Antonio Lozano who were gyrating toward one another in a manner that suggested they should get a room. The beat of the fast-paced salsa music Aisling had picked for their wedding dance was filling the studio above the shops on Dame Street. 'Do you not think it's a little over the top?' Quinn whispered to Aisling who had to resist the urge not to stomp on his foot.

'No, I don't. I think it's very romantic.'

'But we're Irish not South American.'

'Oh, so would you rather me wear a red ringlet wig and a short green dress and jig my way across the floor toward you?'

'Not at all, but we could do a swaying, slow dance sort of a thing, couldn't we?' Hope sparked in his eyes but it was doused as Aisling jeered back at him, 'Everybody has that. I don't want our wedding to be like everyone else's.'

Quinn gave up and tried to concentrate on emulating their instructors. He'd mastered a few steps at the lessons he and Aisling had done before they'd become a couple but he was by no means a natural.

Aisling eyed Maria and Antonio thinking Quinn had a point as the couple oozed sensuality and rhythm, unlike them. They were like two wooden puppets, Punch and Judy she thought huffily, with hip swivel problems. She flung her arms up in frustration and stepped back from him. 'This is hopeless, Maria, Antonio! I can't seem to find my rhythm.' She looked down at the swingy skirt and towering heels she'd worn thinking they'd put her in the mood to salsa about, before glaring at Quinn as though it were all his fault. The look on his face told her he'd rather be anywhere but here. She fumed silently, unsure why he kept throwing cold water over all her ideas. First the table settings were over the top and now this. Well tough, she'd asked the husband and wife salsa duo to help choreograph their wedding dance and they'd agreed, although they weren't doing it out of the goodness of their hearts. They were charging like wounded bulls, not that she'd tell Quinn. Time was money and she couldn't afford for the magic not to be happening on the dance floor tonight.

Quinn rubbed his temples, he was feeling very second-hand thanks to his uncommon night on the town. His brothers had kept it clean but had been enthusiastically sliding all manner of shooters down the bar top towards him for most of the evening. Quinn had knocked them back with equal enthusiasm. It had been a good craic at the time. He hadn't been smiling when he'd woken with a banging head on Sunday morning though. Although he'd felt a little better by the time his mam had filled him and his da, who was also suffering loudly, up with a plate of bacon, eggs and beans to soak up the remains of the night before. He'd wiped his plate clean and drunk his milky tea, thanking his mam before taking himself off to ring Aisling, eager to know how her hen night had been.

Aisling was feeling surprisingly chipper given it was the morning after her hen night. She'd put it down to the big glass of water Moira had told her she should get down her when she'd gotten home. She'd filled Quinn in on the Bono masks and the limousine that had ferried them about the city in style. He'd laughed as she told him about Maureen's karaoke faux pax. His poor mammy-in-law-to-be was, by all accounts, green around the gills today, although like him her delicate state had been helped by a full Irish. Mrs Baicu, the guesthouse's weekend cook had put a good lining on the O'Mara women's stomachs after which Maureen had announced, once she'd deposited Roisin at the airport, she was going home where she'd be receiving no calls or visitors for the rest of the day. Aisling, having finished relaying the events of her evening had reminded Quinn about this, their dance lesson, and he'd groaned into the receiver. 'Can't we give it a miss tonight, Aisling?'

She'd adopted a high-pitched timbre he was coming to recognise as one meaning she wasn't to be pushed on the subject. 'No,' she'd said, 'they could not cancel because there would be a cancellation fee. The Lozanos were busy people and, as such, they might not be able to fit them in again on short notice. And,' the pitch went up several notches, 'do I need to remind you the wedding is in less than two weeks?' Quinn had decided he was best to go with the flow and hadn't argued, which was why he was here now learning a routine to perform with Ash in front of all their friends and family. Was he happy about it? No, he was not. He felt like a complete eejit for one thing and knew his brothers would never let him live the moment down. Sure, he could imagine the names they'd be coming up with, ole swivel hips and the like. He knew why she had her heart set on salsa. It was his own fault and the knowledge of this irked him even more. He'd won her over with a salsa dance in this very studio, but it had been for her eyes only. It was no good telling her he felt ridiculous though, her mind was made up. Come February the fourteenth, they'd be performing the Latin American dance in front of an audience of family and friends. He was beginning to dread the fecking wedding.

'Aisling, Quinn,' Maria said, in a manner managing to be both sultry and smooth, which always made Aisling think of Galaxy chocolate. 'You are not feeling the music in here.'

She put her hand on her breast and Aisling elbowed Quinn. 'Remember, you're nearly a married man.'

'Salsa,' Antonio stated passionately, 'connects you with others. It is sexy and energetic. We come together to be our true selves and to be in the moment. Salsa is magic.'

'Jaysus, feck, he knows that little speech off by heart,' Quinn muttered, receiving a sharp elbow once more.

And on the count of three, away they went again. It was going to be a long night, thought Quinn as he stuck his bottom out and quickstepped toward Aisling.

Chapter 23

♥

Aisling let Moira daub the deep conditioning treatment on her head. She'd asked her sister to give her a facial but she was going the whole hog massaging the conditioner into her scalp. She closed her eyes, feeling her shoulders relax. 'You're pretty good at this.'

'Thank you,' Moira said, piling her sister's hair on top of her head before disappearing into the kitchen. 'I need the cling film.'

'Why?'

She returned with the box and pulled a length from it before ripping it off the serrated edge. 'I'm going to wrap it around your head so it keeps your scalp warm, it makes the treatment more effective.'

'Will you leave me holes to breath?' Aisling was alarmed.

'I'm not going to mummify you, you eejit.' She covered her sister's scalp in the cling film and then told her to go and knot a towel around it.

Aisling disappeared into the bathroom to do as she was told. She pulled the towel off the rail and twisted it into a turban before glancing in the mirror. Jaysus, if those circles under her eyes got any deeper, she'd look like one of those little red pandas. She'd not been sleeping properly for ages now, not since Quinn proposed. The problem was, each time she was about to nod off, she'd remember something she had to do between now and Valentine's Day and her eyes would fly open and she'd begin panicking. It was a vicious cycle and she didn't know how to calm herself down. She leaned into the mirror and whispered.

Dear Aisling,

I'm getting married in a week and a half and instead of feeling excited about what should be the most amazing day of my life, I'm terrified something's going to go wrong. Please give me some advice as to how I can shake this feeling. Oh, and any tips on how to stop Mrs O'Flaherty trying to tempt me away from my Special K and over to the dark side would be appreciated too.

Yours faithfully,

Me

Mrs Flaherty, their apple-cheeked breakfast cook who worked Monday to Friday was not impressed with the weight loss challenge Bronagh and Aisling had inadvertently undertaken thanks to Moira. She was a woman who did not believe in dieting, although apparently she was partial to the odd bet, but Moira was sworn to secrecy as to who she was backing. She'd been heard to mutter on many an occasion you couldn't trust a person who didn't wipe their plate clean with their bread. Diet was an offensive word and it did not feature in her vocabulary. As such, she was employing sabotage techniques like standing at the bottom of the stairs with a plate of freshly fried, crispy bacon long enough to ensure it didn't go cold by the time it reached the hungry guest who'd ordered it. Long enough though for the tempting aroma to fill the reception area causing the two women to pause in their morning's stair aerobics, mouths watering, resolve weakening. Moira was having none of it though and she'd taken to keeping the can of fancy air freshener Mammy was after recommending on Bronagh's desk. She'd spray it liberally and reception would smell like bacon and Arpège perfume.

Aisling turned side on to peruse her shape in the mirror. So far, she'd avoided temptation and the dance lesson the other night on top of the stairs routine seemed to be yielding results she thought, smoothing her sweater and not seeing any lumps or bumps. She'd never be a waif but aside from the cling film on her head and circles under her eyes she was looking good.

With one last flick over her reflection she went back to the living room where Moira was waiting with a tube of something in her hand. 'A face mask,' she said, waving it. 'It'll work wonders.'

'Is it your clay one?' Aisling said, sitting down.

'No, that's expensive. This one will be grand.'

'Charming, I get the bargain basement beauty treatment. Well, for your information, your whizz bang, pricey one gave me spots anyway.'

'I don't recall you asking me if you could use it,' Moira said.

'It was payback for pinching my Valentino sandals.'

'Fair play.' Moira was feeling magnanimous thanks to a very pleasant few hours whiled away with Tom that afternoon. She squeezed the gloopy green contents of the tube into the palm of her hand and told her sister to look up as she began to slather it all over her face. 'You look a little like Shrek.'

Aisling closed her eyes, not bothered with making a rebuttal. It was nice to be pampered, especially because it meant she had to stop, sit and do nothing for a while. She flexed her feet, her big toe was still tender from where Quinn had trodden on it at their dance lesson. It had brought tears to her eyes, although she didn't know if it was because of that or the fact he'd looked like he had something unpleasant in his pants as he'd minced toward her. She'd finally nailed the razzmatazz as Maria said her opening sequence of steps was called sometime after nine pm when she was nearly dead on her feet and at the same time Antonio had declared he was satisfied with Quinn's tags, taps, kicks and flicks. They were dismissed with an all the best for the wedding by the South

CHAPTER 23 371

American couple who were keen to see the back of their two left footed students and lock up the studio for the night.

'I'm done in,' Quinn had said, and Aisling had told him they'd have to practice every day if they wanted the routine down pat for the wedding. Quinn had muttered something she thought might have been for fecks sake but she couldn't be sure. She'd let it slide given his hang over.

'There we are, all done,' Moira said to her now, holding her green hands up. 'I'll go and wash these. That mask might feel a little tight and tingly but it's nothing to worry about, alright?' Aisling was about to open her mouth and reply but Moira held her green hand up once more, 'Don't speak, let it harden and do its thing.'

It was a chance to reflect on the day, Aisling thought, leaning her head back on the sofa as she mulled things over. The guesthouse had been busy with a group checking out first thing that morning in order to begin their tour around the Irish countryside. Bronagh, thankfully, was running on full throttle once more. The week had gotten off to a slow start for them after their big night out but Bronagh had been particularly pasty-faced on Monday morning. She'd told Moira she could forget it if she had any plans on making her do the stairs and also, she'd better not be thinking about getting married any time soon because she was not able for another hen night. Ita too had been very quiet and Aisling suspected from the length of time it took her to make up Room 3 she might have been having a sly forty winks in there.

She'd let it all waft over her head. It wasn't an everyday occurrence, well at least she didn't think it was. She couldn't be sure when it came to Ita and sure, they'd all had a grand night out together. The mask tightened and her skin began to feel hot beneath it and more than a little tingly. 'Moira,' she called out, feeling it crack around her mouth. 'I'm going to wash this off, it's burning.'

Moira appeared in the doorway. 'It says on the tube you're to leave it on for twenty minutes, it's only been ten.'

'Don't care.' Aisling pushed past her sister to the bathroom and splashed tepid water over her face before getting the nearest flannel and rubbing the stuff off.

'Moira!' she bellowed, looking in the mirror and seeing her face was a blotchy red mass as though she'd gotten the sunburn. 'Get in here now.'

Moira peered around the bathroom door and winced seeing her sister. 'Jaysus, Aisling, you look a fright. You don't want to be going downstairs with your face like that, you'll frighten the guests so you will.'

'Fix it. This is your fault.' Her voice was low and steely and Moira could tell she meant business.

'Listen, you rinse the conditioner out of your hair in case we have to go to the emergency doctors, you don't want to be sitting about in the waiting room with the cling film on your head.'

'Moira!'

'I'll ring Mammy, see what she says.' Moira scarpered. Aisling ran the shower and while she waited for the water to heat, she peered into the mirror. This was not good, her face felt hot and itchy. The last thing she needed was an allergic reaction. She stripped off and got in the shower rinsing off the thick conditioner.

She hoped her skin might have settled down once she got out of the shower but no, if anything the steamy water had made it worse. She got dressed and went in search of Moira.

'Well?'

'Mammy says you're to use the E45 cream.'

Moira held out a tube of their mammy's go-to fix it all cream she'd found tucked away in the first aid kit and Aisling slathered it on. It did feel better.

An hour later when her hair had dried and she was sitting in front of the tele with a greasy layer of E45 all over her face,

Moira said, 'At least your hair looks good. If you did a mammy and swished it about you could be on a shampoo commercial. So long as they only filmed you from the back.'

Aisling glared at her.

Her phone beeped a message before she could give her sister a mouthful and she saw it was from Quinn. A frown embedded itself between her eyebrows as she read the message.

'What is it?'

'It's Quinn. He's after finding a house he wants us to go and look at tomorrow.' There was an uneasy feeling in the pit of her stomach at the thought of it.

'You're not moving out of here! I promise I'll stop pinching your shoes and I'm sorry I used the cheap, green shite on your face.' Moira was aghast at the thought of having to do the housework about the place or cooking her own meals.

'You've promised me that before and you always break your word.' Aisling rubbed her temples; her head was hurting. 'But don't worry I'm not going anywhere. The house thing is an investment. He's got a bee in his bonnet that we need to get on the property ladder and rent out whatever we buy as a nest egg. Why he can't wait until after the wedding I don't know but he says here,' she waved her phone, 'it's too good not to go and take a look.' A thought occurred to her. 'What if my face hasn't settled down by tomorrow?'

'Well, it might work in your favour, Ash. The estate agent might tell the people selling about your poor, red, spotty face and they might feel so sorry for you they lower the price.' Her mouth twitched.

'That is so not funny.'

Chapter 24

♥

The house was terraced, red brick, and on the Crumlin Road. Aisling felt a surge of pride as Quinn managed with lots of turning of the steering wheel to manoeuvre his car between two others. The parallel park was not something she'd mastered. Driving was something she'd not mastered all that well for that matter. She could get from A to B so long as the vehicle was an automatic and no complicated parking issues arose but if someone else was happy to drive, then Aisling was happy to let them. If it had been down to her she thought as he pulled the handbrake up, she would have kept driving and they'd have wound up walking miles to their appointment. All thoughts of her masterful-parker fiancé dissipated as she spied the For Sale sign outside a dilapidated house with a sinking heart. She didn't know what she'd been expecting but it was identical to all the other houses on the street. The only thing setting it apart from its neighbours was its air of having been let go.

'It looks neglected,' she said, peering out the windscreen adding an, 'unloved,' for good measure. Quinn had filled her in on the way over; the reason the house was going for a song was because it was an inheritance and the family wanted a quick sale. It explained why it looked unlived in but it didn't make it any more appealing.

'The garden needs a tidy up that's all, and you haven't even seen inside yet, Ash.' He took the keys from the ignition and turned in his seat to look at her. He looked away quickly for fear she'd think he was staring at the lumps that had appeared on her face since the last time he'd seen her. Hives she'd said, due to a dodgy facial Moira had given her. He thought it as likely it was a reaction to all the stress she was heaping upon herself with the wedding. There was no point saying anything though.

Aisling could feel the heels of her shoes digging into the mat on the floor of the passenger seat and her hands were clasped tightly, resting on her black pencil skirt. She'd dressed up for the occasion in the hope of moving the focus from her face. The fact she'd power dressed though had done nothing to change her mind where this house buying business was concerned and she'd be quite happy if Quinn were to manoeuvre his way back out of the parking space. She'd give the suited-up man with the slicked back hair who was tapping his foot beside the gate, a cheery wave goodbye as they sailed past him. In fact, what she'd like, more than anything, was for them to go and get a cup of coffee and talk like they hadn't talked in ages. She wanted reassurance he was excited about their nuptials because she felt like he'd switched off.

'And he's definitely got the look of a fecky brown noser,' she muttered, turning her attention back to the waiting agent.

'What was that?' Quinn asked, opening his door.

'Nothing.'

'Come on then and keep an open mind. Remember it needs to be low maintenance and functional, that's all. It's not your dream home, it's a potential rental property.'

'Yes, yes, I will.' She was already picturing patches of damp, and mouse poo, and all manner of unsavoury things given the neglected air of the garden.

Quinn glanced back at her dubiously. 'If we can get it for the right price, the rent should cover the loan and outgoings. It comes down to the maths not emotions.'

'I know that.' Aisling was huffy. It seemed to her he'd already made his mind up about buying the place and he sounded a little condescending. She wasn't an airhead. All she wanted was her wedding to be her perfect day without major life distractions like house buying getting in the way. She didn't want them starting their married life by being saddled with a money-pit of a house they had no plans of living in either. Nevertheless, she got out of the car and waited for Quinn to lock it before walking the short distance to the estate agent, who stepped forward with his hand outstretched to greet them. He was all smiles, although Aisling fancied his full wattage beam had faltered as she got closer.

The E45 cream had helped soothe the itching but the spots were still visible and she'd made Moira run down to Boots as soon as it opened to buy a packet of antihistamines out of her own pocket. She'd taken one as soon as her sister returned and hoped the hives would soon begin to fade. For now, though, at least her hair was shining gloriously and she lurked alongside Quinn observing the vigorous handshaking and much fecky brown nosing on the agent's part. His name he revealed before opening the gate, its rusty hinge squeaking in protest, was Niall. Holding it open he ushered them in and Aisling trailed behind Quinn, her heel finding its way into a crack in the pavers which nearly sent her arse about face.

'Watch your step,' Niall said pointlessly. 'The path and front garden needs a little TLC but it's all easily fixed and the house has good bones.'

With a glance to either side she could see the poky front garden was in desperate need of a tidy up. What had once grown there, maybe even flourished, had now withered and needed to be cut back. She couldn't stop her nose curling even though she knew it made her look a spoiled brat. She also wished Quinn didn't have such a spring in his step. He looked like a child about to enter a sweet shop and his new best friend Niall's eyes were gleaming no doubt at the thought of the hefty commission soon to be coming his way if he played this the right way. He produced a bunch of keys and stepping past them unlocked the front door opening it wide.

'Come in, come in,' he welcomed with a sweep of his hand.

Aisling took a deep breath and stepped over the threshold, scanning the hallway she found herself in with a critical eye. It was narrow and dark with a threadbare red carpet adding to the gloom. You'd struggle to swing a cat in it she thought as Niall announced he'd let them have a look around on their own. It was all self-explanatory he said and when they were finished, they'd find him in the kitchen. She watched him stride down the hall, counting his steps. Four strides and he was there. It was hardly a house you'd get lost in.

Quinn was opening a cupboard in the hallway and hearing him make noises about how it was good to have extra storage space, she left him to inspect it, poking her head around the front room. Through the yellowing net curtains, she could see the outline of the garden they'd walked past and in the same red carpet as she'd seen in the hall, she could see the indents of where the furniture had been placed. The wallpaper was peeling in places and the room smelt musty. A layer of dust was visible over the fireplace mantle.

She didn't want to look around any further because she already knew the kitchen where Niall was waiting was at the end of the hall. It would have an oven with decades of food etched around the element rings. A washing line that spun around would be visible from the back window and the back garden would be bleaker than the front entrance. Upstairs there would be a bathroom with pipes that would gurgle and moan when the hot water tap was turned and the bedrooms would be boxy. It was exactly what she'd expected. Quinn had joined her in the room and must have sensed she was less than impressed as he nudged her and said, 'Use your imagination, Ash, a lick of paint, new curtains and carpet, some elbow grease and sure, it will be grand.'

They made their way to the back of the house to check out the kitchen before heading upstairs. Niall was there as he'd said he'd be. He was leaning against the sink but spying his potential purchasers sprang into action, gesturing to the cupboards and pantry. Quinn was all ears as the agent launched into a spiel. 'Retro's all the rage, although of course, for the discerning investor there's plenty of scope for improvement.' He leaned toward them conspiratorially. 'Quinn, Aisling, between me and you, this area's rapidly becoming sought after, and properties are tightly held. It's a good time to buy.'

Quinn nodded and opened a drawer. He gave it an extra tug as it got stuck halfway nearly pulling the whole thing out. Aisling eyed the oven, noticing the splashes of grease on the wall behind it. She fancied she could smell bacon fat and not in a tempting Mrs Flaherty way either. She pondered over opening the back door to get some fresh air but decided against it. The sooner they completed their tour of the house the sooner she'd be out of here. Instead she contented herself with looking out the window to where a spindly tree waved its boughs in the wind and a washing line spun round in a maniacal pirouette. The fence surrounding the nondescript garden was buckled in places. Quinn nudged her. 'Are you ready to take a look upstairs.'

She nodded and followed him from the room, refusing to look at Niall for fear of setting him off on more sales patter. Quinn skipped up the stairs and she bunny-hopped up them after him, her skirt making it impossible to do anything else, wondering if the musty smell permeating downstairs would be worse up there. Quinn wandered in and out of the first two bedrooms while she gave them a cursory glance over. The bathroom made her shudder but if she were honest, she could see all it needed was a good scrub. The shower head was over the bath and the plastic curtain had a mouldy edge to it. It was a set-up that brought to mind the verruca she'd gotten one year at the public baths. She couldn't muster up enthusiasm to match Quinn's as he turned the handle on the shower and announced the pressure was good. She let him lead her through to the smallest of the three bedrooms not listening to his prattle that it was big enough for a small double. He was already wording the advert to rent the house in his head, she realised, seeing his face was lit up with an excitement she hadn't once seen in the march toward their wedding.

'Ash,' he said, opening the wardrobe door and poking his head inside it.

'Yes.' He was taking leaving no door unopened to a new level. A wardrobe was a wardrobe for fecks sake and she played out a scenario where she pushed him inside it and shut the door.

He popped back out and the sight of his eager face sent guilt pinpricking through her. He only wanted the best for them. It wasn't very nice of her to be plotting to shove him inside a cupboard. He couldn't read her mind though and carried on excitedly, 'I think we should go for it. Subject to a building inspection obviously but I can't see how we can go wrong.'

She could see he wanted her to agree with him. To share in his enthusiasm but she couldn't. What he was saying about financial security and investments for the future all made sense but she had a bad feeling. 'I'm not trying to burst your bubble, Quinn, but I have a lot on my plate at the moment with the wedding.' She shook her head, 'I'm struggling to find room to think about anything else.'

'I know that, Ash. But if we don't act now, we'll miss out. Who knows when a buy like this will come up again?'

Quinn didn't often dig his heels in. He was the sort of fella who went with the flow but he wanted this property, she could see it in the determined set of his jaw. She wanted to react the way he wanted her to, she did. He deserved it.

Sure, look at the way he'd agreed to their honeymoon at the Ice Hotel. Marriage was about compromise and this was her moment to capitulate and agree, yes this would indeed be a good investment for them. He placed his hands on either side of the tops of her arms his blue eyes boring into hers, willing her to agree.

'It doesn't have to be hard, Ash. We can arrange to take possession after our honeymoon. It'll be one visit to the bank, there'll be a few papers to be signed with a solicitor, that's all. I'll arrange the building inspection but I think we should move on this. It's a smart move. We'll regret it if we procrastinate.' She barely heard him as he told her the figure he'd like to offer. She trusted him to have worked it all out but still the words he wanted to hear wouldn't come. She managed another nod, wanting to make him happy. There was a part of her that loved the way he was thinking ahead for them and for, hopefully, one day in the not too distant future, their children. He pulled her to him and she enjoyed the feeling of security being in his arms always gave her. 'Do I take that as a yes, let's go for it?'

'Yes.'

Her reward was a kiss and she returned it, glad he was pleased and wishing she could get rid of the sense of unease that had assailed her since she received his text the night before. He held her hand tightly as they headed back down the stairs to find Niall. He looked up from his phone as they appeared in the kitchen once more.

'Well, what did you think?'

'We can definitely see the potential,' Quinn countered.

Niall sensed he had them on the hook and in case they hadn't heard him the first time he repeated his earlier sentiment of this being a sought-after area and how he had another couple interested in viewing the property. The sense of urgency he was instilling in them made Aisling feel panicked, which was what he intended, but her head had started to hurt again, too. She was supposed to be meeting Leila in an hour and now she'd agreed to go ahead and do this, she wanted Quinn to cut to the chase and make an offer so they could find out whether or not it would be accepted and she could put some distance between herself and Niall.

Quinn squeezed her hand. 'We'd like to make an offer,' he said, before repeating the figure he'd told her he thought they should put on the table. Niall looked pleased but gave no clue as to whether they stood a chance going in with the figure, he'd just been given. He pulled his phone from his jacket pocket and tapped out a phone number his face a blank canvas as he waited for it to be answered. Despite her misgivings, now they'd come this far, Aisling wanted it all to pan out. She found herself holding her breath as Niall began to speak and Quinn's grip on her hand became vicelike. The agent was Mr Cool as he relayed their price. His end of the conversation gave nothing away and it wasn't until he'd hung up, he flashed his mega smile and said, 'If you're prepared to stretch to another two thousand then you've got yourselves a deal.'

Quinn glanced to Aisling and she mouthed go for it. What difference, given the vast sums involved with buying a house, would two thousand punt make?

There were a few hurdles to jump before they got to the finish line though. The other couple might come in with a better offer, the building inspection might throw up unseen issues, or Mr Cleary might turn down their application for a mortgage. Niall however was full of bonhomie and as they went left and he turned to the right outside the front gate. Aisling was tempted to look back over her shoulder to see if he was fist bumping the air or doing an excitable shin to shin side kick like in the old movies. She didn't though, focussing instead on steadying her breathing and wishing Rosi was there with her. She had tricks up her sleeve that would help make you feel calmer and she could have done with her sister intoning, 'in, and out' in that irritating hypnotic voice she used. It was only when she was settled in the passenger seat of Quinn's car once more, she felt able to catch her breath. Quinn was on a high and he talked all the way to Blackrock slapping the steering wheel from time to time, the adrenalin coursing through his bloodstream. She barely heard him as he yapped on about whether they should renovate the kitchen which might generate a better rental or leave it as it was until they'd paid a chunk off the house.

His grin however was infectious as he pulled up outside the charming whitewashed building from which Leila ran Love Leila Bridal Services. Her mouth twitched and stretched into a broad smile. She was pleased he was pleased and she was sure she'd come around to the idea. It did make sense. 'Right then.' Quinn slapped the steering wheel once more. 'I'll phone Michael and get the wheels in motion.'

'Who?' she frowned, her mind drawing a blank at the name.

'You know *Michael*.'

She looked at him blankly and he sighed. 'Ash, you're so old school. Mr Cleary from the AIB.'

'Oh, yeah of course. Sorry.' She'd never get her head around calling a bank manager by his first name.

'He'll probably want to check through our accounts to see everything is in order before approving the loan but he seemed fairly confident it wouldn't be a problem the other day.'

And there it was, the reason Aisling felt sick about this property. It was nothing to do with the weeds sprouting through the cracked pavers, or the ancient oven and old carpets. It was the thought of that old bloodhound, Mr Cleary, poring over her bank statements and realising not only did she not have an outstanding savings record, but she had these last couple of weeks been spending up large. Astronomically so. Bank account draining so. She was frightened as to what Quinn would have to say when he found out exactly what this wedding of theirs was costing because her gut instinct told her, he would not be happy.

She tried to brush aside the sudden panic not wanting him to pick up on anything being amiss. His lips felt papery as they grazed her flushed skin and telling him she'd speak to him later, she turned the handle and clambered out of the car. It was a relief to put some distance between them.

Chapter 25

The aroma of freshly brewed coffee assailed Aisling's nostrils as she pushed the door open and stepped into the warmth of Leila's familiar work space. There was comfort to be found, knowing that, in the small kitchenette out the back, there would be a plate with the fresh French pastries her friend picked up for her clients to enjoy on her way into work each morning. She loved the calming and neutral colours Leila had chosen to decorate the office with. They hadn't been chosen randomly she'd confided to Aisling. The pale pastels adorning the walls and soft furnishings were designed to counteract the nervous tension of her brides. The idea was that Leila's was a haven where the pressure of trying to keep both sides of the family, along with the bridal party, happy during the lead up to your wedding dissolved once you stepped over the threshold.

Leila's goal was for her brides to feel confident she had their dream day under control. She wanted them to sink down in the sofa and let her fuss around making them coffee. Then, she wanted to see their shoulders visibly unknot as they forgot their diets and tucked into a well-deserved buttery croissant while she brought them up to date with the planning of their big day. The feminine pink walls were adorned with black and white prints of famous brides through the decades. Aisling's favourite, and the one her gaze always settled upon, was

Audrey Hepburn. Inexplicably, this was because she always felt like she was gazing upon a fairy when she looked at the elegant, timeless beauty.

Now, as she stood in the entrance swivelling in her heels on the mat in case there'd been anything untoward on those threadbare carpets at the Crumlin Road property, she unclenched her jaw. It would take more than the sanctuary of Leila's to relieve her headache though, it was a constant, dull pressure above her right eye. A little like a hangover which wasn't very fair because she hadn't been drinking the night before and did not deserve this punishment. Leila glanced up from her worktable, straightening the papers she'd been poring over and placing them back in a folder. She looked especially pretty today with her hair twisted back in a loose plait which softened the look of her fitted pant suit. For Leila's part, she gave her friend a cursory once over. 'You mean business, Ash,' she said, taking in the jacket and skirt ensemble. She hesitated as she registered the lumpy blotches decorating her friend's face. 'What happened?'

For the briefest of moments, Aisling wondered if her unease about the wedding was written all over her face. Leila knew her inside and out after all, but then she remembered the hives and even though she knew it wouldn't help matters her hand touched her cheek rubbing at the itching patches self-consciously. 'Do you mean these?'

Leila nodded. 'Don't rub it. You'll only make it worse.' She was hoping it wasn't some sort of facial shingles brought on by stress. If it was, then Aisling had brought it on herself. It was exasperating insomuch as she'd offered her services as a gift to make sure her best friend relaxed and enjoyed every minute of the lead up to her big day. Despite her best efforts to convince her it was all coming together nicely, Aisling seemed intent on winding herself up into a permanent state of anxiety. She'd even seen her biting her nails the other day, a habit she'd grown out of in her early teens.

'In one word, Moira. That's what happened.'

'What did she do?' Leila was bewildered.

'She gave me a facial last night, that's what, and she used this cheap, green shite that resulted in an allergic reaction.'

Leila clamped her lips together to try to stop the giggle threatening to burst forth as she imagined the scenario post-facial in the family apartment at O'Mara's last night. She wouldn't have liked to be Moira but it would have been funny to be a fly on the wall.

'You better not laugh,' Aisling warned, wagging a finger at her. 'Because I don't feel like laughing, I feel like crying.'

'Oh, Ash, what's wrong? And I wasn't going to laugh,' Leila lied, forcing herself to swallow the giddy bubbles of mirth. 'Honestly, your face. It's not that bad. I hardly even noticed it.'

Aisling glared at her. 'When someone says 'honestly',' she made inverted fingers, 'they're always lying.'

'Okay, sorry, but they'll go right?' Have you got something for them?'

Aisling nodded. 'Mammy put us onto the E45 cream which helped a little and I made Moira go to Boots first thing too. She hadn't even done her hair and she said it was mortifying which served her right because this,' she jabbed in the direction of her face, 'is mortifying.'

Leila concentrated on keeping her face in a duly concerned expression.

'They should be gone by tomorrow,' Aisling continued. 'And if they're not then she will be demoted from her position as bridesmaid to toilet attendant duties at the reception.'

At the picture invoked of Moira handing out wads of toilet paper in exchange for penny donations, Leila did laugh.

Aisling wasn't trying to be funny though. 'It's not my face that's bothering me. Well, it is obviously, because no one wants to walk around with itchy, red lumps by choice but it's not why I feel sick.'

CHAPTER 25

Here we go, Leila thought, donning her professional hat. She was well versed with comforting her brides to be, she prided herself on her ability to do so, but on a scale of one to ten Aisling was coming in at a nine-and-a-half on the Bridezilla scale. 'You poor thing, come on, sit yourself down on the sofa and I'll get you a cup of coffee.' She hesitated, normally she'd offer a pastry but Aisling was supposed to be dieting.

Aisling solved her conundrum, 'And can I have a pastry. One of the ones with the drizzle of white icing and chocolate filling? Please.'

'Of course, you can.'

Aisling flopped down on the sofa and pulled the cushion out from behind her back hugging it to her stomach. Leila who'd been about to head to the kitchenette paused, her mouth dropping open.

'Why are you looking at me like I suddenly sprouted a second head?'

'Ash, oh my God, you're not pregnant, are you?' Leila whispered the word pregnant as though disapproving eyes were everywhere, her own were like blue gobstoppers.

'What?' Aisling glanced down at her midriff and realising she was holding the cushion over it. She tossed it down the opposite end of the two-seater before smoothing out her sweater. Not quite flat as a pancake but hardly six months gone. 'No, wash your mouth out.'

'Jaysus! You had me worried there. It was with you saying you felt sick and then asking for a pastry and the bulge of the cushion.' Leila fanned her face with her hand at the shock of it all as her voice trailed off. She had enough sense not to add that given Aisling had also been behaving like a hormonal wreck these last weeks she could hardly be blamed for jumping to conclusions. Instead, she said, 'Sorry, Ash. I'll go make that coffee and then you can tell me all about it. How does that sound?'

Aisling leaned her back against the plush fabric, placated. 'Grand. Oh, and Leila don't tell anyone about the pastry, okay? There's money involved.'

'I won't.' She tapped the side of her nose. 'It's our secret.'

Leila disappeared out the back and Aisling consciously tried to relax. She flexed her fingers and rolled her head around in slow circles. Everything would be alright. It would all be fine. She was paranoid that was all, once burned and all that. Sure, in just over a week she'd be Mrs Aisling O'Mara-Moran and the stress of the build-up would be behind her. All she'd be left with were stunning photographs and her memories. It'd be like what she'd heard about giving birth, you forgot all about the icky bits afterward. By the time Leila returned to place a pretty china mug with a curl of steam rising from it in front of her, along with a plate on which the promised pastry sat, she was feeling better. She nibbled on the sweet treat and equilibrium was restored as the sugar hit her bloodstream. Leila returned with her own coffee and once Aisling saw she was settled down the other end of the sofa, she began to talk.

Chapter 26

♥

'Did I tell you Quinn has been making noises about us buying a house as an investment?' Aisling dabbed up the pastry flakes on her plate as she waited for her friend to reply.

'No, you didn't.'

'His idea is that we'll pick up a doer upper, that doesn't need too much doing up and rent it out. We'll pay it off that way.'

'Not a silly idea,' Leila said, sipping her drink and looking over the rim at Aisling.

'It's not, I agree, and I love the way he's thinking about our future but you have to admit his timing is shite.'

'What do you mean?'

'I mean the wedding obviously. It's all I can think about and there's no room for big decisions like enormous loans and the like. It's not fair of him to add all this pressure to the mix now.'

'You shouldn't be feeling pressured. I have everything in hand. It's my job and I'm good at it.' She was wasting her breath, Leila thought as Aisling ploughed on.

'Then today he insisted we go and see a house on the Crumlin Road. He said it looked like a good buy and got himself all excited, more excited than I've seen him in weeks. I don't think he even got that worked up when I bought a suspender belt and stockings that time. Sod of a thing they were, kept pinging off.' She shook her head at the memory. 'Anyway, he was like a child exploring Disneyland and, Leila, his face has not once been as animated over our wedding as it was when he was looking around that run-down old terrace today. Not once.' It was true, Aisling thought, reliving the memories of his face closing up every time she mentioned something to do with the wedding.

'I wouldn't be reading anything into that, Aisling. You know how it goes, "Men are from Mars, women are from Venus.". Well, it's true. I have yet to see a groom who is wrapped up in the details of his wedding to the same degree as his bride. They don't understand the importance of the small details.' She shrugged. 'All they want is their stag night to be unforgettable, then to front up on the day and have it all to run smoothly. That's it. They are simple creatures.'

Aisling was almost mollified but instinct told her it was more than a lack of interest it was almost as if he wanted to bury his head in the sand over the whole thing.

'He's doing his part isn't he? Organising his and his brothers' suits and the wedding rings.'

It was Aisling's turn to shrug. 'I don't know. Every time I broach the subject, he changes it. Look what he did today. Why did we need to buy a house right now?'

Leila nearly slopped her coffee. 'You bought it?'

'We made an offer on it and it was accepted.'

'Congratulations! That's fantastic, Ash. What's it like?'

'A standard terrace house that has been let go.'

Leila frowned. She could see she wasn't going to get much more from her friend. 'Well, I think it's a fantastic start to your married life.'

'We're not married yet.'

'You will be in just over a week.'

'If Quinn doesn't call the whole thing off.'

Leila had had enough. 'For feck's sake, Aisling!' She banged her cup down on the table startling her friend who was slumping further down the couch the more she wallowed. 'Snap out of it. This has got to stop. You are a woman on the edge of a nervous breakdown.'

Aisling made to protest and defend her corner, but she'd pushed Leila too far.

'It's ridiculous. You're behaving like a complete and utter eejit over this wedding.'

Hot tears burned in Aisling's green eyes and the hives heated up. This wasn't Leila's job. Leila's job as her best friend was to listen and agree with her while simultaneously making murmuring noises of support. Moira and Mammy were the only ones in their pecking order allowed to speak to her this way.

'Why won't you accept Quinn loves you?'

Aisling sniffed and Leila passed her the tissues kept on the table for those emotional moments. Aisling pulled one from the box and dabbed her eyes.

'In ten days, Aisling, you two are going to be married but your insecurity is spoiling what should be a happy time for you both!'

Aisling blew her nose. Leila was right. It was her ruining everything but now she had good reason to be insecure. 'Leila,' she managed to get a word in before she could head off on another tangent. 'You don't understand.'

'Help me understand then because I thought you'd finally got it through that head of yours, things not working out once before doesn't mean history will repeat itself.' Leila looked at her expectantly.

Aisling took a shuddering breath and her voice wavered a little as she began to speak. 'There's been this fear from the moment I accepted Quinn's proposal something would go wrong before we could head down the aisle.' Aisling twisted the edge of her sweater. 'And now it has.' A sob caught at the back of her throat.

Leila passed her the tissue box once more. 'Here, take one.'

She helped herself giving her nose another quick blow. 'We have to have our loan to buy the house approved by Mr Cleary at the bank. He was working out our borrowings based on the deposit we agreed to come up with for whatever we decided to buy.'

Leila nodded. 'That's standard.'

'Yes, but when Quinn first broached this with me not long after Christmas we sat down together and worked out a figure based on our joint savings. That's what he worked our offer on the Crumlin Road property around. The thing is, I've been spending since then Leila. I've been spending a lot. I don't even know how much because I haven't been keeping tabs but I do know I don't have anywhere near what I had in my account before we started putting this wedding together. I can't see how we're going to be able to go ahead with the purchase.'

Leila tilted her head to one side. She was beginning to understand what had Aisling so worked up. She had been splashing the cash what with horse-drawn pumpkin carriages, pricey photographers, a Swarovski crystal embossed dress, not to mention her insistence on splurging on all the bridesmaids' dresses and they'd been almost as eyewatering in price as the wedding gown. She'd tried to broach how much it was all costing with Aisling a couple of times but she'd been so caught up in the dream of her day she hadn't wanted any reality checks. A memory struck her. 'Your dress, Ash, that's my fault. I broke my golden rule. I showed you it before telling you what it cost. It was just so—'

Aisling held her hand up, 'Gorgeous? I know, and you hardly had to twist my arm.' And now I've gone and paid the deposit on the honeymoon too.' She winced at the memory of the smiling travel agent handing over her credit card receipt. She'd even passed her the bowl of complimentary mints. A sure sign she'd spent up large. But again, Quinn had never asked her anything more about the honeymoon. Sure, he'd made a few vague inquiries about what it cost but he'd been content to leave the arrangements up to her.

'You've kept him up to date with everything, haven't you? I mean you guys are a dream team.' Leila was struggling with the idea Aisling had gone ahead and booked what equated to the best of everything without once checking in with her future husband.

Aisling gave a small shake of her head and felt a current of anger at her fiancé's lacklustre approach to their wedding. If he'd been willing to share in it all, to contribute to the planning then she wouldn't have got herself in such a mess. The more he'd tuned out over it all, the more she'd amped things up in the bling stakes. It was very tempting to pass the blame onto Quinn. She'd like to take her anger and run with it because it was better than the sensation of impending doom she was currently saddled with. It hadn't been him wielding the credit card like he was a Saudi prince though. Oh no, the blame for that sat squarely on her shoulders and she was not a member of the Saudi royal family, she was Aisling O'Mara of O'Mara's Guesthouse on the Green.

'No, I haven't told him. He has no idea what it's all costing and I'm petrified when he finds out he's going to call the wedding off.

Chapter 27

Aisling got back to the guesthouse with Leila's advice she needed to sit down and talk things through with Quinn before they went to see their bank manager ringing in her ears. It would be far better for him to find out exactly how much this wedding had depleted their finances first-hand than through some know-it-all with a name badge at the AIB she'd warned. Aisling knew she was right. She had to come clean and she resolved to go and see Quinn as soon as she'd checked in at O'Mara's and gotten changed. The snug waistband of her skirt was a reminder of her pastry misdemeanour and besides, the conversation she was about to have with Quinn warranted comfortable trousers. There was a modicum of relief in a decision having been made as to what she needed to do but still and all, it was a confession she wasn't looking forward to having to make.

Bronagh was sliding her arms into the sleeves of her coat. Nina was yet to arrive, Aisling realised, scanning the reception area, and Bronagh had a pinched look about her as though she'd eaten an olive thinking it was a grape. She hoped everything was alright. 'Have you an appointment you've got to get to?' she inquired, fishing for information.

'Jaysus wept, Aisling, you look like you've been ravished by a mosquito. What happened to your face?'

CHAPTER 25

Aisling sighed and repeated the sorry tale of cheap skincare products and her selfish mare of a sister. Bronagh listened with half an ear, commenting if Moira passed herself as an expert in the beauty stakes and got results like the ones currently decorating Aisling's face, could she be trusted when it came to her foray into personal training? Aisling got the impression she was desperate for a legitimate excuse to get out of tomorrow morning's stair climbing. She picked her bag up but before she could leave, Aisling repeated her question. 'Do you have somewhere important you need to be?' It was asked without guile and a hint of concern.

'No, I'm in need of fresh air that's all, Aisling.' Bronagh flicked her eyes about the place and satisfied the coast was clear muttered, 'I've had it up to here today.' She saluted her forehead several times to prove her point before picking up a piece of paper and thrusting it in Aisling's direction. 'It's enough to turn a woman to drink so it is.' The crumbs on the desk in front of her suggested she hadn't turned to alcohol but had found comfort in her custard cream biscuits instead. Good, Aisling thought, quietly pleased she wasn't the only one who'd had an indiscretion this afternoon. She scanned the piece of paper, understanding dawning as to why their receptionist wasn't her usual sunny self. Her own fingers twitched with the urge to reach for one of the custard cream filled biscuits.

The Australian couple who were staying in Room 6 had complained the hot water pressure wasn't great and they'd found a hair belonging to neither of them in the bath. Not only that but the pillows were lumpy and the bed was too hard and hadn't been vacuumed under. She sighed all the way down to the tips of her patent leather, Dior stilettos. Bloody Ita! She'd be having words about her standard of cleaning. It wouldn't be the first time she'd had to rake her over the coals for her slapdash efforts and she knew from past experience their director of housekeeping was a sulker. They'd all be in for days of hoover banging on the skirtings as a result. Still, she needed to be told. As for the hot water pressure, there was nothing wrong with it. Did they want a water blaster to take the fecking skin off them? None of their other guests had ever moaned about lumpy pillows or hard beds either.

Aisling knew the couple's type. They were people for whom there would always be too much salt in the stew or not enough pepper on their steak. The kind who felt short-changed by life in general. Born complainers, and born complainers had to be handled with kid gloves to ensure they didn't make a loud noise in front of their other, perfectly happy guests. There was a saying when it came to offering a service such as their guesthouse, 'the customer was always right.' As such, it was time to don her fecky brown noser hat; Quinn would have to wait.

The door opened as Aisling screwed up the paper and tossed it in the bin and Nina, her face peeping out from the furry hood of her parker, called out an apology for being late. Bronagh, huffing, made her escape out the door and Aisling seeing Nina's face fall, explained. 'You're only a few minutes late, it's not you. Don't worry about Bronagh, she's had a day of it with the couple in Room 6. Full of moans about the place so they are.'

Nina's worried face softened. She hated upsetting people. She was a pleaser and as such she would not ask Aisling why her face was covered in red lumps. She went to hang her coat up in the small kitchen area as Aisling sat down in the seat still warm from Bronagh and placed a call to Room 6 to see if they'd like to have a chat, in the guests' lounge, about how she could improve their stay at a time that suited them.

The sniffy accented twang of Mrs Trope agreed to come down and meet with her in fifteen minutes. Aisling hung up the phone and vacated the seat for Nina before scanning their bookings and seeing, as she'd hoped, Room 8 with its

California king was free for the next few nights. An upgrade would hopefully appease them.

***

An hour later, having politely listened to a lengthy rehashing of Mr and Mrs Trope's earlier complaints, Aisling stood in her stocking feet in her bedroom, the skirt with its merciless waistband in a heap next to her feet. She was opening and closing drawers in search of her favourite pyjama bottoms. The headache that had been lurking all day had worsened to an almost migraine-like status and she needed to lie prone on the couch and let the paracetamol she'd popped work their magic. She also needed to indulge in a few snowballs which always had the exact opposite effect on her headaches, chocolate was supposed to have. Her favourite coconutty, chocolicious treat and an hour spent staring gormlessly at the television should sort her out. Then, she'd go to Quinn's.

Moira blessedly was out so the apartment was silent and she could put whatever tripe she fancied on the box and vegetate. Bliss. She deserved it after the grovelling she'd had to do where the Tropes were concerned. It had gone against the grain to place such an ungrateful pair of heathens in a larger suite, especially as she'd gotten a vibe from them upgrades were something they were well-practised at getting. She had them marked down as the kind of couple who creates a scene by saying there was a cockroach in their dinner in order to get out of paying the bill. In the long run though, it was easier to move and appease them than have the duo upset the equilibrium amongst their other guests. They were checking out the day after tomorrow. It was a small price to pay.

She'd positioned herself so she was spread the length of the sofa like an aging film star except instead of grapes she had a bowl of the snowballs within hands reach. She'd hidden them for emergency situations like this, behind the baked beans in the cupboard where Moira would not find them (she hated baked beans). A ridiculous game show was flickering on the screen in front of her with a paunchy, balding man who fancied himself a comedian hosting it. It was his blonde sidekick in the scanty evening wear who had her mesmerised though. Her facial expressions should see her in line for an Oscar. One minute she was feigning excitement akin to an orgasmic experience when a contestant won an iron and ironing board, the next great sorrow on a par with having found herself orphaned when they lost out on the toaster. The pinging of her phone distracted her. It lay abandoned on the kitchen worktop and she twisted her head to see if she could telepathically get it to float over to where she lay. She squinted her eyes and focussed but it didn't budge and she wondered whether she was strong enough to ignore it. All she wanted was another forty-five minutes or so to lie here and wallow in snowballs and gameshows.

She'd almost convinced herself it had never made a sound when a few minutes later it announced the arrival of another message. One could be ignored but not two, and with a sigh she swung her legs off the sofa and sat up. Her headache had eased which was a bonus and at least she knew it wouldn't be Mammy messaging her. She never bothered with their mobile phones which meant it might actually be something important. 'So long as it wasn't from Quinn,' she muttered, padding over to retrieve the black Nokia. She didn't bother to look at the first message knowing it would be much the same as the second one she'd just read. She wished she had ignored it because from the terse few lines telling her they needed to talk with not one single x or o at the end, Aisling knew Quinn had beaten her to it. He'd already been in touch with Mr Cleary.

Chapter 28

Aisling hadn't bothered to run a comb through her hair or put her lipstick on, having decided it was best she go and swallow whatever medicine Quinn was going to dish out. She only went so far as to swap her pyjama bottoms for jeans. She half-heartedly hoped the sight of her wan, spotty face might soften his heart a little.

Alasdair hadn't quite been his usual effusive self, greeting her as she pushed the door of the bistro open and stepped inside. She was unsure if it was out of politeness to avoid mentioning her spots or because he knew what a spendthrift she'd been. Common sense told her it was far more likely it was her guilty conscience playing paranoid tricks on her. She hadn't imagined Quinn's steely expression as he asked her to give him a few minutes before he joined her out on the floor, though. A chill akin to icy fingers had traipsed up and down her spine at his unflinching blue eyes as he paused with the pan of boiling potatoes, he'd been carrying over to the sink to drain. They were eyes that usually twinkled with unspent mirth but tonight they were stormy. His mouth too had been set like a heart monitor flatlining. She'd also caught Paula and Tony glancing at each other before putting their heads down and getting on with the business of making sure the restaurant ticked over. The boss and his fiancée might be at odds but for them it was business as usual.

Aisling had done as he'd suggested, grateful to see Tom wasn't rostered on, as she'd gone in search of a quiet table. She tucked herself into the darkened corner far enough away from the other diners to ensure they weren't privy to her and Quinn's private goings on. From where she'd positioned herself, she could see the fire with its flames, forked tongues of orange and yellow. A shadowy glow danced up the walls, illuminating the framed photographs of guests enjoying boisterous nights in the bistro. She watched a man excuse himself from the pretty woman he was dining with, and saw him dip his head to avoid the low hung ceiling beams as he made his way to the bathroom. There was no band playing tonight given it was early in the week so she and Quinn would, at least, be able to hear themselves speak. She almost wished Shay and his band were on the empty stage banging out a bit of Van Morrison so she didn't have to sit through the talking-to, she knew was coming her way.

Her hands pleated the table napkin for want of something to do with them and she turned her gaze to the salt and pepper shakers in an effort to avoid making eye contact with Paula who was clearing a nearby table. Her corneas were beginning to burn from not blinking when Quinn's voice startled her.

He loomed over the table making her feel small and inconsequential. It wasn't like him to take such a bullying stance. 'I don't understand you, Aisling.' It was said loudly enough to turn the heads of the couple at the closest table. Aisling glared at them, daring them to say anything. They went back to their meals.

'Sit down and lower your voice, Quinn,' she ordered, forgetting she'd planned on being contrite and sufficiently grovelling so he could say his piece and be done with it.

He pulled a chair out and sat down heavily across from her before pulling a folded wad of papers from his pockets which he spread on the table in front of her. The light was dim but not dim enough she couldn't see she was looking at a printout from their joint account.

'When we opened this account, we had this much to put into it.' He jabbed at a figure she couldn't quite make out at the top of the row of numbers. Nevertheless, she nodded before looking away not able to sustain eye contact with him when he was clearly furious. 'The problem is, Aisling, this much has gone out since we opened the account. He shuffled the papers and pointed to another piece of paper. 'And this is now our balance.'

He paused and she wasn't sure what he expected her to do, gasp suitably aghast at her expenditure maybe? When she remained silent, he carried on. 'The balance in our account is nothing like it was when we applied for our loan at the AIB because in the space of a few weeks you've spent it on – hmm, let me see,'

Aisling wanted to put her hands over her ears as he began to reel off a list of expenses that had, at the time, seemed so necessary in the planning of their wedding day but now, listening to the sums involved, came across as ludicrous luxuries nobody in their right mind needed. She wondered if pleading temporary insanity might help her case.

At last his voice trailed off and she looked up. 'I'm sorry,' she squeaked, hoping to see the anger leach from his face.

'Sorry isn't good enough, Aisling. We're going to lose out on the Crumlin Road property because you had to have flowers that cost enough to feed a small nation and a honeymoon in a fecking igloo.'

She opened her mouth to protest but no sound came out and Quinn jumped in once more. 'We don't have enough for the deposit anymore.' The anger had gone out of his voice, replaced by a weariness that to Aisling's mind was far more worrying.

'I'm sorry,' she repeated, not knowing what else to say.

'What's it all for?'

'I don't understand?'

'A horse drawn carriage. I mean for fecks sake, Aisling.'

She tried to summon up the words to explain all the extravagance but couldn't because she didn't understand it herself.

'I tried to involve you.' The words sounded feeble to her own ears and trying to pass the buck wasn't going to make their situation any better.

'Not hard enough obviously.'

Anger rankled. 'Hang on a minute, Quinn. That's not fair. *I did try* but every time I brought the topic up you tuned out so, I went ahead and did what I thought was best. You've not shown any interest in our wedding from the get-go.'

'Oh, so you behaving like you're Victoria fecking Beckham is all my fault, is it?'

'I didn't say that but maybe if you'd sat down with me once or twice and looked at some of my suggestions, we might have found some middle ground.'

Quinn made an unattractive snorting noise. 'There's been no middle ground where this wedding's concerned, not from the moment you accepted my proposal. You've been like a woman possessed.' He hesitated as though debating whether he should take the next step.

'Go on say it,' she taunted, unable to help herself. It was happening, as she'd known from the moment he slid the diamond ring on her finger it would.

'You're not the woman I thought you were.'

They looked at each other, blinking and catching their breath and, as what he'd said sank in, Aisling wrenched the ring from her finger and slid it across the table toward him. She pushed her seat back and weaved her way blindly across the floor. She was vaguely aware of Alasdair's voice calling after her, not Quinn's, as the tears she'd held back the whole time she'd been in the bistro poured down her cheeks. She hoped for the briefest of seconds he'd come after her, contrite and offering her a way to make everything okay but the door to the restaurant remained closed. Her heart was in a vice, being squeezed so tight she could hardly breathe, as she made her way home, penning a letter to self all the way.

Dear Aisling,

I've lost the man I loved through my own stupidity. How am I supposed to get through this?

Yours faithfully,
Me.

Chapter 29

♥

The banging on her bedroom door woke Aisling with a start. She was lying on her side in a tangle of sheets and for one blissful moment she couldn't understand why her eyes were glued together. She prised them open and it was like peering through the slats in a venetian blind. The realisation she was still in last night's clothes and the reason her eyes were so swollen was because she'd cried herself to sleep, broke over her. With a small moan she dug around in the trenches recalling how she'd swept in through reception last night, ignoring Nina to take to the stairs. She'd been desperate for the sanctity of her bedroom where she could let her tears out in peace. Poor Nina had received the rough end of the stick from Bronagh, and then later from herself. She owed her an apology.

Moira had been out and she'd locked her bedroom door before throwing herself down on her bed and sobbing into her pillow. It must have been in the small hours when she'd finally crashed out only to be woken a short while later by the familiar clatter of the rubbish bin in the courtyard below. She'd padded over to the window in time to see Mr Fox making his escape with whatever leftover treat Mrs Flaherty had tossed out. He turned, as he always did, and looked up to where she was a ghostly outline looking down at him. She waved through the frosted glass and he flicked his tail before flattening his back and disappearing under the wall.

Now the memory of what had transpired with Quinn was like a bucket of cold water being tossed over her. She was no longer engaged. She was right back where she'd been when Marcus left her. A jilted bride-to-be. The difference this time was, she only had herself to blame for the predicament she was in. It was down to her own stupidity and the realisation made her breath feel ragged as it caught in her chest. The banging started up again.

Maybe it was Quinn! The thought was a spurring jolt. He might have seen, in the cold light of day, that what she'd said last night had an element of truth to it. He had switched off when it came to their wedding. He could've come to his senses and be prepared to talk things through. It wasn't too late. They could sit down together to discuss what was frivolous and what was a necessity. Moira's voice blew out the tiny flame of hope she'd been fanning. 'Aisling, what's going on?'

'Go away, Moira.'

'Paula told Tom you gave your ring back to Quinn and walked out of the bistro last night in tears.'

She should've known it wouldn't take long for the jungle drums to begin beating. She repeated herself, 'Go away, Moira. I don't want to talk about it.'

'What was that? I can't hear you, Aisling. I need to know you're okay, open the door.'

She knew full well her sister had heard her; she was trying to trick her into opening the door.

When it didn't work, Moira changed tack. 'Aisling, if you come out, I cross my heart hope to die promise I'll waive stair-climbing today and I'll personally go downstairs to ask Mrs Flaherty to whip you up one of her specials and not say a word to Bronagh about you breaking your diet.'

Aisling didn't answer. She'd be sick if she tried to eat and what was the point in dieting and doing the stairs anyway? No point whatsoever now she was no longer getting married. She rolled over on her back and, as she stared up at the ceiling, she felt dead inside.

'I'll ring Mammy and tell her you won't come out of your room.'

'Do your worst, Moira,' Aisling threw back.

No reply was forthcoming and Aisling shut her eyes, hoping she could sleep forever like Aurora from *Sleeping Beauty*. It was an ironic thought given she was guessing she was anything but a beauty at the moment. She closed her eyes again but they flicked open of their own accord as she examined what had happened between her and Quinn. In the half light of her bedroom it was becoming clear to her she'd pushed away the person who meant the most to her in the whole world because she hadn't felt deserving of him. In a roundabout way Marcus McDonagh had reached out from her past, refusing to let her move on and accept Quinn's love wholeheartedly. She'd subconsciously been sabotaging their relationship by behaving like an extravagant eejit. There she'd been burning up her credit card as though she were some sort of cashed-up celebrity. And what did it matter, any of it? The dress, the carriage, the place settings – in the big picture they didn't mean a thing. What her wedding should have been about was standing alongside Quinn and turning to look him in the eyes. She should have been focussing on how it would feel to see her love for him reflected back at her in his face as he told God, their family and friends he wanted to spend the rest of his life with her.

***

Aisling must have dozed off again because this time when she woke, she could sense the lateness of the morning by the way chunks of filtered light broke through the curtains.

CHAPTER 27

She strained her ears listening out for Moira and caught the swish of whispering. So, Moira had made good on her threat and called Mammy. She had a more pressing problem than the fact her mammy was standing outside her bedroom door pow-wowing with her baby sister as to what they should say to lure her out. Aisling knew it wouldn't be whatever pearls of wisdom they shouted through the door that brought her out. It would be the fact she was desperate for the loo. The days of the chamber pot were long gone unfortunately and she was going to have to visit the bathroom, like it or not.

She sat up, vaguely aware her eyes were still hot and heavy. Her hand smoothed her hair but it had matted itself into a frenzy of knots, thanks to her tossing and turning. It would take more than running her fingers through it. She swung her legs over the side of the bed and stood up, surprised to feel the floor firm beneath her feet. She'd almost thought she might fall through it like Alice going down the rabbit hole because that was how she felt, as if she'd fallen through into some strange world she no longer recognised.

She moved toward the door and flung it open, stepping back as Mammy and Moira staggered forward nearly falling on top of her. 'That will teach you for pressing your ears to my door. Now, get out of my way because I need to go to the loo.' Aisling pushed past them and through to the lavatory, locking yet another door behind her. She rested her head against it for a moment and then yelled out, 'And don't stand outside the door. That always gives me stage fright. I'll talk to you when I come out.'

She heard a gratifying creak as they moved away. It was with trepidation she opened the door after flushing but the coast was clear and she slipped into the bathroom next door. A hot shower and a change of clothes was in order if she had to deal with Mammy and she knew without looking, she and Moira would have taken up camp on the sofa and neither would be leaving until they'd got to the bottom of what had gone on between her and Quinn.

***

A steaming mug of sweetened tea was placed on the table in front of her along with a plate of thickly buttered toast. Aisling stared at it, watching the golden puddles pool and melt into the toast.

'You're no good on an empty stomach, Aisling.' Maureen fussed around her. 'You've never been able to make rational decisions when you're hungry. Personally, I'm pointing the finger for all this bother at...' She flapped her hand in Moira's direction.

Moira dropped the piece of toast she'd been chewing on down on the plate and straightened from where she'd been slouched over the kitchen worktop. 'That's not fair, Mammy. I was trying to help. Aisling was the one who wanted to lose a few pounds for the wedding.'

'Don't talk with your mouth full. And did she want the spotty, red face too? Look at her, I mean look at her. People will be giving her a wide berth thinking she's contagious. What were you thinking?'

The hives were clinging on stubbornly. Aisling was blaming stress but there was no need for Mammy to point them out quite so emphatically. It wasn't the spots that had caused all this trouble.

'I didn't know she'd react to the pack I used,' Moira pouted.

'You know full well your sister has always had sensitive skin, young lady. Sure, she spent half her childhood slathered in the E45 because of some rash or other.'

Aisling didn't have the energy to protest this exaggeration. From memory she'd only had a nasty rash once. It was from eating too many strawberries. There was no point mentioning this to Mammy though. She'd twist the story around so instead of being a greedy girl with a penchant for strawberries it would morph into Aisling's first foray into stress eating. She'd blame it on the falling out she and Leila had had. The falling out part was true; they'd had a stand-off over who was the best looking member of Duran Duran. She was with John and Leila was backing Simon and ne'er the twain do meet. The point of this silent debate she was having was, the only reason she got a rash from strawberries was because she ate too many of the fecking things.

'Be quiet the pair of you.' She slapped the table to distract herself as much as Mammy and Moira. They blinked at her and then both spoke over the top of one another. 'Tom said Paula said you threw your ring back at Quinn.' 'Moira's after telling me you've called the wedding off.'

Aisling shook her head. 'Do you want to know what happened?' It was a stupid question and her answer lay in their frenetic nodding.

She took a gulp of her milky tea and then began to talk, 'Quinn wanted us to buy a house on the Crumlin Road as a rental investment. We'd been to the bank and had a verbal agreement with the manager as to what sum we could borrow based on the deposit we had.'

'Very sensible young man, your Quinn, one in a million so he is,' Mammy said.

'He's not my Quinn, Mammy. Not any more, because I'm not sensible I'm a fecking eejit.'

Maureen didn't have the heart to tell her to watch her mouth.

'I spent the best part of the deposit on the wedding without telling him.'

'So, it's your fault.'

Moira that's not helpful,' Maureen snapped. 'But Aisling what about what I offered to put towards the wedding.'

Moira's gaze whiplashed toward her mammy. 'You never said you were giving Aisling money, and me a poor student.'

Maureen gave her youngest child a look that could curdle milk straight from the cow and Moira busied herself with her toast.

Aisling shrugged. 'It's all gotten out of hand, Mammy. The dress, the bridesmaids' dresses, the photographer, the pumpkin carriage—'

'The pumpkin what?' Moira snorted. 'Who do you think you are, Cinderella?'

Aisling swung around in her seat, her temper fraying. 'And you didn't help with your poor student routine. Do you have any idea how much those dresses cost? Did you even look at the price tag?' Her voice was shrill.

'Don't blame me,' Moira shouted back. 'You offered.'

Aisling drew breath but Maureen intervened. 'Moira O'Mara, go to your room right now and don't come out until you've something helpful to say,' Maureen ordered.

'Mammy, I'm twenty-five. You can't send me to my room.'

'You're still my daughter and not too old to feel the back of my hand.' Maureen stared her daughter down – the Mammy Whisperer – Moira slunk off to her bedroom.

'I don't know where we got that one from.' She shook her head watching her go. She let Aisling drain her tea before leaning across the table and smoothing a wisp of hair stuck to her daughter's cheek. 'Well, my girl, what are we going to do to fix this? Your Uncle Cormac is somewhere over the Atlantic about now. Great Aunty Noreen telephoned to say she and Great Aunty Rosamunde are riding up together, not to mention the Brothers Grimm will be dusting off their suits about now.'

Aisling bit back the smile that came unbidden at her mammy's referencing of her brothers.

'I don't know how to fix it though, Mammy. What do I do?'

'Aisling, you are a marvel at sorting other people's lives out but when it comes to your own,' she shook her head. 'Talk to him,' she offered up simply. 'If you can't talk to each other then you shouldn't be getting married. Your daddy and I had an unspoken rule in our marriage.'

Aisling looked up meeting her mammy's dark eyes. 'What was it?'

'We'd never go to sleep on an argument.'

Aisling sparked at the blatant fib. 'Mammy, that's not true! I remember you giving Daddy the silent treatment for nearly a week when we were small.'

'Ah, well now, Aisling, that was different. Your daddy had been very bold.'

Aisling's scalp prickled. She never had found out what the week was about where Mammy had communicated through Roisin, 'Tell your daddy, I said he can cook his own tea tonight.'. Had he been unfaithful? 'What did he do, Mammy?' she half whispered, fearful of finding out.

'He spent the money I'd set aside for a new dress to wear to my friend Geraldine's birthday party on an engine overhaul for the car.'

Aisling nearly laughed with the relief of it all.

'What I was trying to say, Aisling, before you started nit-picking was, a marriage needs three simple ingredients to thrive. I like to call it the three 'c's'

'What are they?'

'Communication and compromise.'

'That's only two.'

'I can't remember the third, it might have been compassion or care for one another. I told you to stop picking holes. You get the idea.'

'Well Quinn and I aren't doing very well are we, Mammy? We haven't even gotten to the church and we can't find a way to compromise.'

'Ah, but you will, Aisling, because you and Quinn are like me and your daddy. You're meant to be together.'

A voice bellowed, 'Can I come out now?!'

Aisling and Maureen looked at one another and exchanged complicit smiles. 'No, you can't!'

Chapter 30

♥

Cormac O'Mara stood in the guesthouse lobby, larger than life for a little man, his Louis Vuitton luggage abandoned on either side of him as he waited for Maureen to bring the last case in. He'd been unable to carry it all himself because he was a man who believed in packing for all occasions, except it would seem he thought, shaking off the cold, the inclement Irish weather. He was making a statement in his trademark crumpled linen suit which was highly unsuitable for flying and for the country he found himself back in. He refused to kow-tow to the norm though, or to be sensible. He'd had far too many years doing so as a younger man in Dublin and it had nearly quashed his spirit. A quick check was in order next, to ensure the infernal wind gusting down the street outside hadn't dislodged his hair. He patted the top of his head, yes, yes, all was as it should be.

The woman who'd worked here since time began and whose name he tried to conjure, Breda or Brenda, something like that was staring over at him. He bared the perfectly aligned teeth he'd spent a small fortune on in her direction.

Bronagh blinked, feeling warmed by the glow of his neon smile. Cormac was the first of the wedding guests to arrive at O'Mara's. The guesthouse was at the sole disposal of family and friends for the next four nights. It had been no mean feat to ensure the window of time had been kept clear and it had all been for nothing. Sparks were sure to fly when he learned he'd had a wasted journey she thought, frantically swiping the telltale biscuit crumbs off her lap and getting to her feet. Her calves were sore from this morning's stair climb. She'd tried to get out of it, telling Moira all bets were off until Aisling made an appearance in reception and confirmed she was still in the running. Moira was having none of it and had warned Bronagh, given Aisling's lovesick state the odds were against her. Bronagh's competitive streak had reared and bucked and she'd taken to those stairs as though she were entering into the Olympic stair climbing race. She'd earned herself a biscuit or two, she reassured herself, turning her attention to Cormac O'Mara.

She'd only met him a handful of times and each time she'd been struck by yer man's resemblance, not to his late brother, God rest his soul, but to Elton John. She'd have loved to ask him if he could give her a few lines of *Rocketman* but had never summoned the nerve. She swept out from behind her desk, her hand extended, 'Welcome home, Mr O'Mara. It's grand to see you.' The consummate professional.

'Please, call me Cormac, Brandy.' He returned her handshake briefly.

'Bronagh,' she corrected, wondering whether all those rings on his fingers had left an indentation on her palm. He smelt very nice too, for a man who'd just come off a long-haul flight, and she tried not to sniff too obviously. The scent of pine made a pleasant change from the Arpège and fried bacon. Cormac was too busy looking about the entrance of his childhood home to acknowledge his gaffe. She marvelled over him being short and well- padded where his brother had been tall and lanky. There were similarities too though in certain expressions and she wondered if Maureen felt her loss keenly all over again when she caught sight of them.

The door opened once more and the woman herself, windswept and hobbling like Quasi Modo, appeared with the last of Cormac's designer bags. Pooh pranced in alongside her, all sugar and spice and all things nice. Bronagh eyeballed the poodle, she had the measure of him right enough. He was not to be trusted.

'Jaysus wept,' Maureen muttered, dropping the bag down next to the others. 'Are you after moving back to Dublin, Cormac?'

'Not a chance, Mo. LA is the land of sunshine. It's been good to me whereas Ireland is the land of—'

'Rainbows,' Maureen stated firmly.

Bronagh raised an eyebrow. Mo indeed.

Cormac had not been about to say the country where he'd grown up was the land of rainbows but he swallowed his words. There was nothing to be gained by allowing his acerbic tongue to get the better of him and besides he was fond of Mo, a name he'd called her from the get-go. It was for this reason he'd decided to behave himself and as such he changed the subject. 'The old place is looking good. I hope you'll be giving me the grand tour.'

'Of course I will, and this,' Maureen arced her hand in a sweeping movement, 'could have all been yours, Cormac, if you hadn't of been so desperate to get on the boat and leave us all behind.'

Bronagh's eyes widened at the thought of this flamboyant man at the helm of the guesthouse. She wondered if he knew Elton – he did live in Los Angeles after all. Sure, they were always rubbing shoulders with the rich and famous out there. Patrick was after telling her he knew yer man, Cruise. They frequented the same juice bar. She wondered if Patrick, Cindy and Cormac all went to the same dentist.

'A decision that worked out well for us all.'

'That it did.'

They smiled at each other and Pooh nuzzled up next to this new member of his family.

'He likes you.' Maureen was pleased. Cormac hadn't made a fuss like Roisin over sitting in the back of the car when she'd picked him up from the airport. He said he was used to it. Apparently, he had a driver over there in Los Angeles.

'Where's the bride-to-be? I thought she'd be here to greet me, given you've officially handed over the baton, Mo.' Cormac pouted. He was a little put out. He'd come a long way after all and the least his middle niece could do was be here when he arrived.

'Erm, Aisling's upstairs. Moira's at college and said to tell you she's looking forward to seeing you.' She pursed her lips knowing full well Moira was hoping her fashion-king uncle had brought gifts from the Land of Plenty with him. 'Patrick and Cindy are due in the day before the erm, ah, the erm wedding because Cindy had a bra commercial to film and Roisin's arriving from London with young Noah tomorrow.' She'd filled Roisin in on the unfolding drama of Aisling and Quinn but had told her she should still come because it wasn't over until the fat lady sings. Roisin had shaken her head, and told her mammy that she wasn't fat, cuddly yes, but not fat. Maureen had been put out and had huffed she hadn't been speaking literally. 'Noah's a dote so he is,' she told Cormac, her arms already itching with the urge to wrap him in a big hug. 'Now then, Cormac, let's get you settled in your room and then we'll go upstairs and have ourselves a nice cup of tea and catch up.'

'Green tea?' Cormac asked hopefully.

'Sure, tea's tan not green and anything else isn't tea, you ee-jit,' Maureen tutted before telling him she'd find their housekeeper, Ita, and get her to give them a hand with his luggage. She was eager to get Cormac away from the reception area. He was prone to dramatics and she had a feeling they were in for an explosion when he learned Aisling had announced the wedding was not going ahead despite her best efforts to talk sense into her daughter yesterday. The way things currently stood, he'd had a wasted journey.

For his part, Cormac may not have seen his sister-in-law for a good while but she had a face he could read like a book and he raised an eyebrow.

It was a lovely shape so it was, Bronagh thought, looking on and smoothing her own pencil thin ones. His skin had a glowing sheen to it too, she noticed. She could do with more glow; she'd have to ask him what products he was after using.

'Is there something I should know, Mo?'

Maureen ignored him. 'Pooh, you stay there with your uncle Cormac.' She took to the stairs calling out Ita's name.

Bronagh began whistling *Rocketman* and looking everywhere but at Cormac.

Chapter 31

♥

Maureen found Ita looking shifty in Room 3, and enlisted her to help them haul Cormac's luggage to his room. The housekeeper obliged with far more grace than she would have Aisling, but then it wasn't Aisling who was friendly with her mammy and liable to tell tales. She'd have liked to have had a few moments to admire the strange little man with the mat on top of his head's Vuitton cases because one day she'd travel the world with expensive luggage but for now she did as she was asked and followed Maureen's lead dragging the case up the stairs to Room 5.

Maureen had personally done a sweep of Cormac's room before she'd left to collect him. It was important to her that he saw first-hand what a success she and Brian had made of the guesthouse, even after all these years. Room 5 with its old-world elegance was a nod to the Georgian grandeur of the building. It afforded a grand view over the Green and as such it was one of her favourites. The pillows had been plumped by her personally, the bathroom inspected, and the bed smoothed. Her reward for her efforts came when Cormac made appreciative murmurs as he inspected his quarters. 'It's hardly recognisable from the days when Mammy and Dad ran the place.'

'It was different times and they did a grand job. We just brought it up to date,' Maureen said loyally; she'd been fond of Brian's parents. They'd been good to her and the bitter feelings between Mr and Mrs O'Mara senior and Cormac had been nothing to do with her. Like she'd said, it was different times. Cormac had been long gone when she'd come door knocking to the guesthouse seeking work, never dreaming she'd marry the handsome young man who'd opened the door to her and that one day they'd run the place. Brian hadn't spoken of his older brother often. On those few occasions when Cormac had come back to Ireland it had been clear to her why he'd gone. It was a truth the family had refused to acknowledge and in doing so had ensured he could never be at home in his own country. It saddened Maureen to think he'd shared his home with his partner Ricardo for over twenty years but even now wasn't comfortable bringing the person he'd chosen to spend his life with here to Ireland to meet them.

On the bright side her brother-in-law was a particular so and so but he was happy with the room she'd chosen for him and that was high praise. She was pleased because, once she got him away from Ita's flapping ears and up to the privacy of the family apartment to explain what was going on with her daughter, he was going to be anything but happy. A sudden movement caught her eye. 'Don't even think about it, Pooh,' she warned the poodle, who was inching toward the bed having decided it was as good a place as any for a siesta. Pooh froze and gave her what she recognised as his affronted look. The 'as if I would do something like that' expression. Ita was still loitering in the doorway. 'Thanks for your help.' She dismissed her with a smile but she wasn't quick enough to stop Cormac from whipping out his wallet.

He handed a wad of notes to Ita who looked like the cat who'd got the cream. The American guests were her favourite and thanking him, she stuffed the money in the pocket of her smock before taking herself off. She could sense Maureen's disapproval of her taking the tip from him given he was family. Well, tough, she'd interrupted her in the middle of a game of Snake and her phone was burning a hole in her pocket. It was high time she got back to it.

'Come on then, Cormac, let's get you upstairs,' Maureen said, giving him the card he'd need to access his room. She shooed Pooh out of the door ahead of her and headed up the last flight of stairs.

Cormac dawdled up behind her, muttering about elevators having been invented for over a hundred years. The apartment was, again, vastly different from his childhood memories where everything had seemed tired and worn out like the building itself. Maureen had a flair when it came to interiors. He liked the ambience she'd created. What he didn't like was the growing sensation that all was not as it should be. Maureen had begun to act skittish as she moved about the kitchen fetching cups and saucers and there was still no sign of Aisling.

'Mo, I have swapped the beautiful sunshine and palm trees of LA for winter in Dublin. Please tell me the wedding is going ahead this Saturday.'

If he'd been hoping she'd be taken aback by the intimation anything was wrong then he'd have been disappointed. He watched as her mouth performed a dance of indecision before she called out, 'Aisling O'Mara, get out here now and explain to your uncle Cormac, who's flown all the way from Los Angeles what's going on.'

It took a moment or two but Aisling mooched forth looking like she'd been sleeping rough and Cormac gave her a head to toe once over before stamping his Versace clad foot. 'No, absolutely not, Aisling. Not a second time. I'm not having it.'

Aisling stared at him dully, she'd have thought Mammy would have told everybody not to come. She was the one in charge of the guest list. She tried to catch her eye but Maureen was feigning great interest in the tea she was brewing.

CHAPTER 21

'You are not cancelling on me twice, Aisling. Now, sit yourself down and tell me what's happened.'

It was a funny thing, Aisling thought, doing as she was told, but when her uncle was mad his American accent became decidedly Irish. Cormac sat down next to her, kicking off his loafers, and she tried not to fixate on his sock clad feet as he began rotating his fat ankles in little circles. He looked at her in a way that brooked no nonsense and she caught a glimpse of her daddy in his features. It made her feel warm inside and she found herself babbling the whole sorry story out. Maureen brought his tea over, making unhelpful mmm noises at different points in Aisling's monologue.

When Aisling had run dry, Cormac looked at her. 'Is that all? You've quibbled over a few pounds?'

'It was more than a few pounds, Uncle Cormac.'

'Pfft.' He made a motion with his hand as though it were a matter too trivial to be bothered with. 'Well, you don't need to worry because your fairy godmother is here now. Once I've had my tea and my ankles have returned to their normal size, we are off to see that fiancé of yours.'

Maureen gave a strangled cough as her tea went down the wrong way.

Chapter 32

♥

Quinn and Aisling were seated opposite each other at the table in the kitchen of his mammy and daddy's house. They were both studying the rings left behind by hot drinks over the years, the marks of family life. The sweet smell of baking hung on the air but there was no cosiness to be found in the sugary smells. Aisling had her hands folded in her lap and Cormac was sitting at the head of the table like a presiding judge. She felt as if she'd been called to the headmistress's office for a playground misdemeanour. If only she could get a rap over the knuckles and be done with it but Quinn hadn't looked at her, not once, since Cormac had ordered them both to sit down. She felt sick and wasn't even the slightest bit tempted to help herself to one of Mrs Moran's brownie biscuits. There was no way she could call her Maeve, not now. Unlike her mammy who'd been all, 'Now then, Maeve, what are we going to do about these children of ours?' And whom she suspected right now had her head together with Quinn's mammy in the living room discussing their eejitty children.

If Mrs Moran had been surprised to find a washed-out Aisling, Maureen O'Mara, and a little man in a *Miami Vice* suit and a hair piece standing on her doorstep that damp Dublin afternoon, she'd hidden it well. She'd been gracious, ushering them in out of the cold before fussing about making tea. She'd even managed to retrieve a herbal teabag for Cormac. There was no need for him to know it had been lurking down the back of her cupboard since Ivo had gone out with that girl with the dippy hippy ways a few years back. If anything, Maeve was grateful that someone was taking matters in hand and she had a feeling that Cormac was the right man for the job.

Quinn had not come quietly, protesting all the way from his room, but he'd clammed up when he saw the trio of O'Maras standing around the kitchen table. He'd managed to shake Cormac's hand and mumble hellos to Maureen and Aisling. He was well mannered her boy, even if he was an eejit. He hadn't looked Aisling in the eye but she'd seen Aisling risk a glance from under her lashes at him. Her mouth had parted a little, startled by his dishevelled appearance. Maeve had tried to talk sense into her son by telling him Aisling had gotten carried away, that was all, but he was cut from the same cloth as his father and it was a stubborn one. She'd even had to remind him to shower like she'd had to when he was a teenager these last few days. She gave a surreptitious sniff hoping he'd remembered to put deodorant on.

She'd hovered on the edge of the group unsure how this would go but when Cormac asked the young couple to sit down so they could have a chat, his manner had them both doing as they were told. He was a little like a male Judge Judy she'd thought, linking her arm through Maureen's, assured things were going to be just fine. She suggested they take their tea and enjoy a slice of brownie in the front room. It would be nice to get to know Aisling's mammy a little better.

'Right then,' Cormac said, and if he'd had a gavel, Aisling suspected he would have banged it down. Instead he had to make do with placing his mug on the table. 'Aisling, I want you to explain to Quinn why you behaved like a mad woman over this wedding.'

Aisling grasped her hands a little tighter and licked her lips. She had nothing to lose by opening up. 'It doesn't make much sense, Quinn, but from the minute you put my beautiful ring on my finger I had this sinking feeling something would go wrong. I suppose I felt that because Marcus called everything off, I wasn't worthy of being married and so to compensate I overcompensated by trying to bury those thoughts in buying and booking things.'

'Bling, darling,' Cormac elaborated for her before turning to Quinn. 'You don't have to be a psychiatrist to work out that her compulsive spending was a reaction to the anxiety she was feeling. I've seen it time and time again on Rodeo Drive where my boutique is. Women throwing the cash around to try to make their problems go away.'

Quinn nodded. He got it, he did, but what he didn't get was why she hadn't trusted him. He put voice to this.

Aisling dug her nails into her palms and her voice was tinny. 'I do trust you. It's me I didn't trust.'

Quinn looked bewildered but didn't get a chance to probe further because Cormac was pointing at him. 'You're on.'

'Um,' Quinn hesitated.

'Come on, you're a chef, you should be good at expressing your feelings.'

He found the right words. 'I never wanted a big wedding, Aisling, but I didn't want to upset you because you were a force to be reckoned with. You'd ask my opinion but I could see you didn't want it, you wanted me to agree with whatever you were suggesting. All I wanted was to say our vows, me and you in front of our family and friends. Then celebrate with a party at the restaurant. Simple.' He gave a shrug as though he still couldn't believe how hard it had all gotten.

There was truth in his words. Aisling knew it had been her way or the highway. Her face felt hot and not because of the spots, they'd finally disappeared, but because she'd been so unfair. 'I'm sorry, Quinn.'

Cormac looked at Aisling and then at Quinn. They both looked to him wondering what he'd say next. 'Do you love, Aisling, Quinn?'

'Of course, I do.'

Aisling's eyes welled and a plump tear formed on her lower lashes.

Cormac nodded – this was going exactly how he'd planned. 'And, Aisling, do you love Quinn?'

'More than anything.' The tear rolled down her cheek.

'Do you remember the Beatles?' Cormac asked.

This was getting weird, Quinn thought. 'Yeah, who doesn't?'

Aisling agreed with his sentiment.

'Well as Paul sang, all you need is love.'

Aisling and Quinn locked eyes. It was Quinn who spoke first. 'Shall we start again?'

'I'd like that.'

Quinn reached over and brushed the tear from Aisling's cheek. Cormac cleared his throat and got up from his seat. Humming the classic Beatles tune, he decided his work was done. It was time to leave them to it and he wouldn't mind another slice of that brownie either.

Chapter 34

Noreen's case lay open on her bed and she folded the last of the necessities she'd need for her stay in Dublin, placing them carefully around the vase she'd bought for Aisling and Quinn. It was well padded and she'd be sure to tell Terry not to be throwing her case around when he put it in the boot. He and Rosamunde would be here shortly to pick her up. She'd hang her outfit from the handle about the window in the back of the car. She checked her watch again wishing the hands would turn faster. It was still a good twenty minutes until they were due to collect her and she was unable to settle, thanks to the nervous excitement about what lay in store these next few days. Emer, she'd gleaned from Rosamunde, was living an hour out of Dublin and planned on meeting her mammy, daddy, and the rest of her siblings, who were also spread far and wide these days, at the church. Sadly, her marriage had broken down this last year and as such she'd be attending on her own. She wasn't bringing her children either who were nearly adults now and had no interest in attending the wedding of a sort of cousin they barely knew.

The thought of Emer's children nearly grown up was a reminder of the lost years and Noreen pushed those rogue thoughts away. The past couldn't be changed; it was what lay ahead that mattered.

Chapter 33

♥

The day of the wedding

Uncle Cormac was indeed her fairy godmother, Aisling thought, admiring the way the tiny crystals on the bodice of her dress sparkled under the light. She felt like a princess. He'd insisted on footing the bill for hers and her bridesmaids' dresses. 'Aisling,' he'd said bossily, 'I have dedicated my life to fashion and a girl should have the dress of her dreams on her wedding day but a pumpkin carriage,' he'd shaken his head, 'she does not need.'

'You've got my something borrowed?' Roisin checked, and Aisling dutifully lifted the heavy fabric of her gown to display the garter belt her eldest sister had worn at her own wedding. Roisin grinned, 'I hope it brings you the sort of wedding night I had.'

Aisling wrinkled her nose at the thought of Colin and Rosi doing the deed. She knew they had to have done so at least once or they wouldn't have had Noah but still she preferred to think her nephew had been an immaculate conception.

'He was many things, my ex-husband—' Roisin continued.

'A chinless feck for one,' Moira piped up.

Roisin ignored her, 'But in those early days believe it or not, he was quite the ride.'

There was a collective gagging sound from Moira and Aisling.

'What are you on about?' Mammy bustled over. She'd been practising her mysterious mammy-of-the-bride look as she peered out from under the hat sitting heavy on her head thanks to the weight of all those feathers. If she were to venture into rural Ireland she'd be in danger of being pecked at by hens, Moira had said upon seeing it.

Feathers aside, Aisling thought, giving her mammy the once-over, she did look beautiful and she had a spring in her step of late that made Aisling wonder about this man friend of hers. When she got back from her honeymoon, she'd sit down with her and make her talk. The offer of tea and a bun at Bewley's should do the trick. Adrenalin ricocheted through her. She'd be a married woman by then, she'd be Mrs Aisling O'Mara-Moran sitting down having a very adult conversation about relationships with her mammy.

'I've given her the something blue,' Moira chirped up.

Aisling had been touched that, despite her sister's constant referencing of her student poverty, she'd splashed out what funds she had on a pearl studded, pale blue hair slide, fixing it in her sister's hair herself. She'd stood back admiring her handiwork. Aisling had decided not to ask her if she'd splurged her bookkeeping earnings to buy the barrette. The odds had been on her winning the great weight loss race and she hadn't disappointed. Moira, as such, was in the money. Bronagh's sulk had only lasted a day, by the end of which they were all sick to the back teeth of hearing how Aisling had had an unfair advantage because she wasn't suffering the ravages of the menopause.

The gift that had brought tears to her eyes along with shrieks from Moira that she was not to cry or her mascara would run, was from Maeve. It finally felt right to call Quinn's mammy by her name. She'd knocked on the door to the family apartment at the guesthouse earlier that morning having made the journey especially so she could present Aisling with a delicate gold chain with a single pearl set in a daisy filigree of white gold. 'It was my mammy's, Aisling,' she'd said. 'I wore it when I married Quinn's dad and I want you to have it now.'

Aisling knew it was her way of welcoming her into the family and she was touched. She was also relieved her hat wasn't bigger than Mammy's or there'd have been ructions.

Leila was making the rounds of the living room checking over her charges. She had been a superstar these last two days dealing with all the cancellations. With a smile of satisfaction on her face, Leila announced. 'Well, I think we have time for a glass of bubbles before Ned arrives.'

'Mummy, can I have bubbles?' Noah beseeched Roisin. He was bored of all the primping and fussing.

'No, you can't. Bubbles aren't for children.'

'Ah sure, a tiny sip won't hurt him, Roisin,' Maureen bossed. Her grandson was back in her good books after yesterday's misdemeanour. She'd been mortified when she'd introduced him to Cormac and he'd asked if he had a gerbil on top of his head. Cormac had not been amused.

Leila popped the cork and did the honours, passing out the flutes.

'Thanks for this, Leila.' Moira said, raising her sparkling grape juice.

'You're a bad influence, Mammy,' Roisin said, seeing mammy give her grandson a tiny taste.

Aisling held up her glass, clearing her throat. 'You all look so beautiful, and Noah you're very handsome. I'm so blessed to have you in my life and thanks so much for putting up with me these last few weeks.'

There was a collective murmuring and Aisling picked up on Moira saying that, yes, she had been a pain in the arse but they all loved her.

She took a sip of the golden liquid, feeling giddy with happiness as the bubbles pinged in her mouth. A few mouthfuls later, the phone rang and Roisin answered it, announcing that Ned was waiting for them downstairs. Mammy led the charge.

'Mammy, don't you be doing that that thing you're after doing with your hat, or you'll trip going down the stairs,' Roisin ordered, following behind her, a firm hold on her son's hand lest he have any thought about racing off to drag Mr Nibbles along with them. The thought of the gerbil getting loose in St Theresa's made her skin prickle.

They burst out the doors of O'Mara's to where Ned was holding the door of the limousine open for them. The blonde one had convinced him to do a cut price church run. It was a first, he thought, wondering how the mammy one was going to get in the back with that rooster on her head.

Chapter 34

'To Mr and Mrs Moran!'

Mercifully her brother-in-law had finished his long-winded speech although Aisling thought, she needed him to make a tiny correction. She tapped him on the arm before he sat down. He leaned over to listen to what she had to say before straightening and clearing his throat.

'Excuse me but that should have been to Mr Moran and Mrs O'Mara-Moran.'

'To Mr Moran and Mrs O'Mara-Moran.' Glasses were raised.

Maureen's eyes prickled at the thought of how proud Brian would have been of his middle daughter today. Cormac did you proud in more ways than one she told him silently, reaching for Cormac's hand under the table and giving it a squeeze. He returned it. She blinked those rogue tears away. Today was a happy day and as such she turned her attention instead to the bistro. There were no fancy table arrangements, although they had followed her seating plan. Dinner had been the house speciality here at Quinn's, bangers 'n' mash. Paula was doing a superb job of keeping the wine flowing she saw, watching the girl scurry from table to table. Too much of a good job given how some were imbibing – her heathen brothers for starters. She gave Frankie and Brendan a hard stare and they put their glasses down. Her other brother, Colm, was in danger of a frozen neck. He hadn't moved from his position, inches away from Cindy's cleavage, for fear of missing something, since he'd sat down. She'd have words with him later if Patrick didn't sort him out before then. Her son was glowering at his uncle. At least Roisin, Moira and Leila would be happy. Cindy's bosoms had taken the onus off them.

There was no compère. but Shay and his band were going to play shortly and were setting up on the stage now. It had all gone very well, she thought, sitting back in her chair feeling satisfied with how the day had panned out. She heard Aisling's laughter pealing across the room and she looked across at her radiant daughter. There was no doubt she was having the best day of her life. Quinn was no longer at her side and she assumed he'd gone to mingle. A finer son-in-law she couldn't have wished for and Maureen knew if she'd been given the chance to handpick the man Aisling would marry it would be him. Brian would have too.

A foreign beat flared up making her and most of the other guests jump. She saw Aisling's eyes widen, her hand fly to her mouth. Maureen swivelled her head to follow Aisling's gaze to the area in front of the stage. Holy mother of Jaysus, there was Quinn spotlighted doing some fancy footwork as he quickstepped across the floor to the cha-cha-cha rhythm his face a study of concentration. He paused to gesture for Aisling to join him and Maureen held her breath, not knowing how she'd manage to do whatever it was she was about to do on the dance floor weighted down by that dress of hers.

Aisling didn't know either but she knew she'd do her best because it didn't matter one iota if she cocked up. She had Quinn and that was all that mattered.

***

Noreen and Emer were sitting next to each other, relaxed and content in each other's company as the evening moved away from dinner and into the dancing. The table in front of them had long since been cleared, leaving a cluster of drinks – some full, some dregs. She was thin, Noreen thought, soaking up the sight of her niece in her turquoise dress as she sat engrossed in the band. She'd a pinched look about her that time and an unhappy marriage had wrought. No doubt she'd found her aunt much changed too, she mused. Despite the obvious etchings of age, she'd always see that little girl so eager to help her and Malachy in the shop when she looked at her though.

Emer felt her gaze on her and turned slightly in her chair. She smiled at her aunt and took her hand in hers giving it a squeeze. Noreen squeezed back. A burden had been lifted from her shoulders tonight. Weddings were about new beginnings and the loneliness she'd felt since Malachy's passing had eased at the knowledge their niece was back in her life.

'Shall we have a dance, Aunty Nono?'

Noreen was quite sure she'd be able to dance the night away so light did she feel. 'In a minute, Emer. I promised Cormac the first dance.'

Emer gave her another smile and turned her attention back to the band, her toes tapping to the Irish beat. She too felt light, and freer than she had in a good long while. Life hadn't been kind to her since her husband had left and as for their children, well, they were selfish mares the lot of them. All too caught up in their own lives to spare a thought for their poor mammy, left on her own struggling to make ends meet. She'd be alright now though. Aunty Nono had a tidy nest egg, and sure she was entitled to a generous helping of it, who else would she leave it to?

The End

Also, by Michelle Vernal

♥

Novels
The Cooking School on the Bay
Second-hand Jane
Staying at Eleni's
The Traveller's Daughter
Sweet Home Summer

Series
<u>Isabel's Story</u>
The Promise
The Dancer
<u>The Guesthouse on the Green</u>
O'Mara's
Moira Lisa Smile
What goes on Tour
Rosi's Regrets
Christmas at O'Mara's
A Wedding at O'Mara's
Maureen's Song
The O'Mara's in LaLa Land
Due in March

ALSO, BY MICHELLE VERNAL

A Baby at O'Mara's
The Housewarming
Rainbows over O'Maras
<u>*Liverpool Brides*</u>
The Autumn Posy
The Winter Posy
The Spring Posy
The Summer Posy

About the Author

Michelle Vernal lives in Christchurch, New Zealand with her husband, two teenage sons and attention seeking tabby cats, Humphrey and Savannah. Before she started writing novels, she had a variety of jobs:

Pharmacy shop assistant, girl who sold dried up chips and sausages at a hot food stand in a British pub, girl who sold nuts (for 2 hours) on a British market stall, receptionist, P.A...Her favourite job though is the one she has now – writing stories she hopes leave her readers with a satisfied smile on their face. If you enjoy The Winter Posy then taking the time to say so by leaving a review would be wonderful. A book review is the best present you can give an author. If you'd like to hear about Michelle's new releases, you can visit her website at www.michellevernalbooks.com